EYES WIDE
Open

BY
AMANDA G. CANNON

Eyes Wide Open

Published by Gray Water

Printed in the United States of America.
First Edition

Author photo © Julia E. Landreth 2012
Cover photo © Julia E. Landreth 2012

ISBN: 061568369X
ISBN 13: 9780615683690

Library of Congress Control Number: 2012946951
CreateSpace Independent Publishing Platform
North Charleston, South Carolina

Acknowledgements

My friends and family, thank you for listening to me ramble on and on the past three years about this book.

I owe an enormous thank-you to the few of you who read bits of it along the way and gave me your feedback. You know who you are.

Aimee and Sha, thank you so much for helping me with the editing process.

Jill and Elizabeth, thank you for editing. I could not have done it without you.

* * *

To my children, I love you so much.

Blake, you truly are an overcomer. Your dad and I are very proud of you.

Brooklyn Olivia, you make me smile every day, even though you are a smarty-pants.

Brittany Rae, my golden child, thank you for your help putting this project together and encouraging me when I wanted to give up.

The three of you were my inspiration for writing this book. I may not walk in your shoes, but I see how well you wear them. Your courage and strength that you have to feel well on a daily basis is immeasurable.

My husband, Douglas, thank you for thirty years, and for being such a great dad. I love you.

CHAPTER 1

Oh dear. I was completely and utterly overwhelmed. The day had arrived that every bone in my body should have been screaming with joy, *I did it!* But not me. Ugh, no way. I could feel all of my twenty-one years disappearing through my bare hands, but not without a fight.

This is my life! I shouted, but only in my thoughts.

My heart said, "Stop, not yet." I had so many questions about my life and not one single answer. But reality crept inside my body as I stretched and moaned with the morning sunlight navigating its way through the shutters in my old room at my parents' home. Slowly, I tried to force my eyes open, but because of my eyelash extensions, my eyes felt heavy, as if I had giant spiders resting on them. With my eyes finally open, I realized there was nothing I could do. I had to get up. It was my college graduation day!

Where had the time gone? I still didn't have a boyfriend. I'd thought that was what most of my college years were about. You know, finding *him*. Forget the whole education concept. And now this degree is supposed to assist me with my future. I don't think so. I only went to college to find him. I only wanted an "Mrs." degree. I had just wasted three years of my life.

But then again, I didn't really put myself out there. I absolutely hated going to bars without a date. I reckon that would explain my swift departure from college: I had no freaking life! What had I been thinking, graduating high school a year early? And to make things worse, I graduated college a year early, too. And for what? To either go back to school or get a job in the real world? No, thank you. Not a single friend would walk today. I knew now who the smart students were. They were the ones who had figured out how to make the most of their college years by extending them. Like an idiot, I had zoomed through college like a missile.

I was still in slow motion, and I could barely see the blue numbers on my clock. It was 6:05 a.m.—much too early to start my day. Graduation wasn't until four o'clock, so I felt no need to rush out of bed. As I slowly gained consciousness, I began searching the room for familiar things, my old things. Nothing, except some old photographs, was identifiable, and they were now encased in new frames—shiny and expensive ones, I was certain. Not the frames I had purchased and placed the pictures in myself over the past years. I couldn't find one detail that had been overlooked. My mother had put an enormous amount of time and effort into redecorating my old bedroom using neutral fabrics, new wall color, and coordinating accessories. As nice as it was, I was afraid this might become my room once again, because my parents had sold my brother's place after his graduation. Their explanation was his lack of determination to move forward with his life. And the shitty thing is he had had two part-time jobs at the time, like me. So of course, I would be expected to move back here until I had a plan—the after-college-graduation plan. There, finally, I said it. Now, what do I do?

I didn't want to budge from my cozy bed. I wanted to put the day off as long as I could. Not at all because it was a cold December 6 morning. It was simply because I just didn't want to graduate.

I could hear my family members starting to move about the house and, occasionally, voices at my door. "Is she all right?" my sister asked.

"Dunno," Noel said.

"Oh, leave Olivia Sue be," Mom scorned.

I knew they were frustrated with me because Mom called me Olivia Sue, not Livvy.

Unfortunately, the real reason my family and friends were always checking on me was so they could be assured that I had "good color" (as my mother would say in a southern and calm way). Or to make sure I wasn't clammy to the touch, in a coma, or worse, not breathing.

Oh, those words—coma and unconscious—we never used them lightly. Not in our house. My family had seen them firsthand. Mom believed in guardian angels, and she always said I was special because I had seen my angel. Three times, to be exact. I get chills, but in a peaceful kinda way, thinking about it. Not just because of her appearance, but her scent and the feeling that came over me when she was with me.

The first time I saw her, I was ten years old. I had low blood sugar and drifted into unconsciousness. It was during the night, and Mom woke up (that mama bear instinct, I suppose, or a God thing) and checked on me. My blood sugar was twenty-six. Mom gave me the big shot to counteract the low blood sugar.

"Do you see her?" I asked my parents as I began to come to.

She was still with me in my room, looking over my dad's shoulder, but moments later, she vanished.

Never had I seen anyone more beautiful. She had long, brown hair that lay in loose curls. Her face was the most exquisite I had ever seen. She looked young but mature, like she was in her late twenties. Her color was magnificent. Every feature was perfect. She was tall, dressed in all white, and smelled of the finest flowers picked for the Lord Almighty himself.

Yes, I have been in her company three times, but I have only heard her speak once. When I was fourteen, my blood sugar was sinking fast. I felt it happening, but I couldn't move. I knew I was in trouble. I tried to speak or scream out for help. I couldn't say a word, but I heard her. She simply said, "I am with you, and He will bring your mother." My angel never left my side until I was no longer struggling for my life. When I became coherent, I told my mom I wasn't afraid because she was with me again.

While fighting back her tears, Mom said she knew the angel was with me because he had softly told her. Jesus had told her.

The third and last time I saw her was similar to the first two encounters. That time, Mom and Dad felt her presence as strongly as I did. I never moved my eyes from her while I was having convulsions. She kept me focused. When the convulsions stopped, everything and everyone appeared in slow motion. Voices sounded slow and muffled. My angel disappeared, and then, all at once, like a rubber band being unleashed with a snap, everything went back to normal speed.

That was when I saw the EMTs—two of them sat on my bed with my mother, working on me, and I had sweat and vomit soaking my faded pink War Eagle T-shirt. Just horrible. Although I did have on an exceptional pair of Victoria's Secret boyshort panties. Like anyone cared.

Two police officers in the corner of my bedroom were carefully evaluating the scene. Mom had every prescription that I take daily spread out on display across my night chest. And needles—two of the fat glucagon injections—lay empty on the chest. To my surprise, I counted three firemen standing next to the bed, looking down at me. *What for*, I thought? I was sweating but not on fire. With the three of them standing there, it should have been burning up in my room.

Good God, seven complete strangers were in my room, all guys, and every one of them hot. And I looked like this. What were the chances of that ever happening again? I mean the guy thing. Well, with my crazy self, it could happen. Next time, I'll pray for no vomit and pretty pajamas.

The EMT completed his evaluation. Because I was having trouble communicating, I was transported to the hospital. My hospital stay was only two days, but we discovered I had another health crisis.

My thyroid, the dang thing, decided to stop working.

If I could only see my angel when I was really sick, I surely hoped never to see her again. On the other hand, it was comforting to know my angel was in my shadows and only a breath away.

I certainly didn't know nor did I understand why I had health issues, but God kept me here for some reason. I reached a conclusion about this. Some things weren't meant for our understanding, and this was apparently one of them.

While time was ticking away on my clock, trying desperately to rush me into my immediate future, I thought, or maybe dreamt, about my past growing up. Boy, it's a lot to think about. Some memories were gratifying, while other times I had seemed so lost, not understanding why life couldn't be a fairy tale. Couldn't our lives be full of joy and happiness? Screw sadness. That crap is painful, regardless of where the mess attacks you.

I could always remember being different from most of my friends, although Mom tried to tell me I was just simply special. I knew better. I was different.

My beautiful sister, Rae, was named after my father and looked a little like Jessica Biel: tall, blonde, a killer behind with boobs to match, and to complete her package, she was extremely smart. She had no idea how truly beautiful she was. Samantha Rae was quite unpresumptuous. If I had looked more like her and was closer to her height, what would I have done with myself?

I don't mean to sound like I was some ugly duckling. I was often asked if I was from Brazil or Hawaii. I was five feet and six inches tall, with dark, long, wavy hair. Or sometimes straight, depending on how much time I had to spend on myself. My eyes were brown, but sometimes they looked black. I had a great smile, thanks to Dr. Jones. When people told me how beautiful my skin looked, I wanted to tell them the pinkish color in my cheeks was because of the daily prednisone I took, but I didn't. And my overall skin color wasn't a fancy gene trait; it was Addison's, the chronic glandular disease that sometimes caused my skin to have a tanned appearance.

I loved Rae, and we shared everything, but there was one thing in a million years I never wanted to share with her: a diagnosis of juvenile diabetes. I was diagnosed at age eight, and Rae was diagnosed at age fourteen.

"Why?" I had asked God, crying. It didn't make sense. My family members and I went to church and Sunday school. This was not supposed to happen to good people. I prayed and begged God to take it away.

"No! No! No!" I shouted. "Don't let her be like this."

My mother had held me in her arms and cried with me, but she was quiet with her words and didn't attempt to answer my question of why God allowed this to happen. I felt, at that moment, that I would never have faith or put my trust in God again. Why should I? He wasn't faithful to my family and me.

Later that afternoon my dad took me to the hospital to visit Rae. I walked into my sister's hospital room and stood at the foot of her bed, wanting to cry. I climbed into her bed and curled up next to her, still wanting to cry. My thoughts wandered as I lay beside her. What could I do to help her? Nothing came to mind, absolutely nothing. But I managed to tell her how sorry I was that we now shared diabetes.

My big sister took my hand, kissed me right in the center of my forehead, wrapped her arms around me, and said, "It will be all right. We'll learn together."

Rae took life by the horns and never let go. She flew through high school and Auburn University with honors. I was homeschooled from the eighth grade until I graduated high school. After today, both of us would be college graduates.

Rae traveled a lot and studied abroad in Europe. As luck would have it, I got to visit. Mom went too, of course.

The sights of Rome, Italy, had been unbelievable. Imagine the history and architectural capabilities dating back before Christ. We visited every site in Rome. Didn't miss a freaking one. Even Dad surprised Rae and flew in for a visit. So Mom, Dad, and I ventured out into Florence and Pisa while Rae studied for midterms.

During our travels we stopped in small towns and visited the cutest mom-and-pop shops. The Tuscan countryside was my favorite. The rolling hills were breathtaking. The castles in the distance were positioned carefully on the property, so the surrounding territory could be seen for miles. The grapevines flowed up, over, and down the hills. Gladly, we didn't miss a single wine-tasting event in Florence.

My dad must have tried every gelato place we passed, but that was okay because we dragged him along with us to visit every site. He looked as if he would have rather watched paint dry on a wall than visit the Vatican. In all of our family photos taken that day, Dad looked exactly the same. Not one new expression, bored completely out of his mind. After he experienced a few more days of torture, Dad cleverly made up an excuse. He changed the date of his first-class ticket, and he was on the next flight back to the good ol' USA.

Someone opened my bedroom door again.

"Is she all right?" my dad asked.

I covered my face with my pillow. "Yes, Dad, I'm fine," I said in a muffled tone. *God*, I thought, *I just had a week of exams*. Stress sometimes overwhelmed me. It could take a week or longer for me to bounce back into the world of the living, mainly because of the Addison's disease.

"Can I bring your breakfast down?" *Tom, please give it up*, I thought, but sweetly answered, "I'm fine, Daddy. I'll be up shortly, but thank you."

I closed my eyes to rest. I tried not to think about the afternoon, but the thoughts crept back into my mind.

"Why am I so worried?" I asked myself. Things didn't have to change. After all, I already managed Mom's spa part-time and worked at Dad's construction business a few hours a week. I had a good life, good friends, family, and sometimes Jesus.

We were taught he can save us from our sins by grace. We only have to ask for forgiveness, but what I thought about the most was his ability to heal. But with doubt and resentment clogging up my outgoing energies, it was probably difficult for him to hear my prayers.

I wished daily Rae and I didn't have to deal with health issues. Then again, I figured everyone has daily challenges of some kind, or was it just the Hunnicutts? Don't get me wrong; we were blessed in most ways, plus we had an enormous, boisterous, and adoring extended family that I loved very much.

Feeling the need to eat and shower, I kicked the covers off and rubbed the sleepy crust and the sticky glue out of the corners of my eyes while trying desperately not to ruin my eyelash extensions. At the same time, I tried to envision what my personal shopper, Cookie, had bought for me to wear today on her last shopping adventure. Cookie's given name was Victoria. She was also my mom. She'd been married to my dad, Thomas Ray Hunnicutt, for twenty-seven years. I opened my closet door and saw the garment bag hanging there on a hook. I knew Cookie would do me proud. I loved fashion. I didn't enjoy the process of shopping, though, unless it was quick and had intent.

Not bothering to look in that black bag right now because of the deep hunger pangs in my stomach and the slight feeling of low blood sugar creeping on, I quickly showered. It was midmorning by the time I ate breakfast, but my family was happy I had sprung to life, even joining them for a rare afternoon family movie.

Following a round of family gossip, it was time to unveil the outfit in the black bag and see what Cookie had discovered for me. I opened the garment bag slowly at first, but I was overcome with excitement and ripped the zipper down. A purple Vera dress. *Perfect,* I thought. In the bottom of the bag, I found an impressive pair of shoes.

After I applied my last sweep of makeup, I pranced into my closet, carefully removed my dress from the padded hanger, and stepped into it. I gently took the Jimmy Choos out of the box and admired them, but only for a second before I slipped my feet inside. I shoved lip gloss, a tiny mirror, and my diabetic stuff into a wristlet and headed upstairs for pictures.

CHAPTER 2

J esus, *in forty-five minutes, where had they all come from?* I was
   under the impression that this somewhat-milestone event would remain small. Just us: Mom; Dad; my siblings; Andi, Noel's wife, with
the baby on the way; and Bradley, Rae's boyfriend.

Well, there they stood, all fourteen of them. Every single one of
them was staring at me and beaming like the cat that has just eaten one
of those little yellow birds. Even the Joneses were there. Although not
family by blood, they're just as precious to me.

Uncle Jack and Bradley were taking most of the pictures. That's
when I realized everyone had their important someone with them…
standing, smiling, holding hands. Everyone, that is, but me.

Dad clued in quickly. "Livvy, we got you something," he said.

He walked over to the massive chest that anchored down a corner
of the large great room, opened a drawer, and pulled out a red box.
Dad placed the small red box in my hand. I lifted the top and saw a key
inside. *They bought me a new car?* Wow! I was completely speechless. That was certainly unheard of, because I always had plenty to
say.

After a few seconds, excitement hit me. I ran to the front door,
swinging it open. Dad caught the handle before the door swung off its
hinges. I forgot about the expensive Jimmy Choos on my feet as I ran
down the front steps. There it was, a shiny black SUV.

I thanked my parents with hugs and handed them my old 4Runner keys. I left in such a hurry for the graduation ceremony I didn't take the time to fine-tune my radio.

The ten-minute drive seemed so much longer. I heard a text message beep. I ignored it until I was parked in the coliseum lot at Auburn University. As I reached for my BlackBerry, it rang. *Robert! He wasn't coming? Oh Lord! He must...he must come.* I could care less about this long, boring graduation ceremony. I answered in my usual sweet voice but with a somewhat-concerned tinge. "Hello."

"Livvy," Robert echoed, "I'm just checking to make sure we're still on for tonight."

"Yes."

"Great. See you around seven at your house, right?"

"Thank you, Robert."

"Bye, girl. Love ya."

Whew!

Jed was bringing his girlfriend. Jake—he'd bring a girl for sure, most likely one we had never met. This meant I would have been alone at yet another family event. I could not have stood that, not tonight. Even if it meant dragging some poor soul whom I barely knew and pretending for a couple of hours we were new but awesome best friends.

As I walked to the coliseum, I had butterflies. There were six hundred graduates. I was in the last group with the College of Education. I knew my family would hate it, because they'd have to stay for the whole ceremony.

The music started to play, letting all the guests know that the march was on for the Auburn University Class of December 2011. We began to make our entrance. I was resting in my seat, listening to the guest speaker make his speech, when my mind drifted back to Rae and how happy I was for her.

Rae had sat in this same coliseum almost four years before. At that time she had no idea how her life would unfold. It had been amazing to watch her grow into the wonderful young woman she had become.

Rae graduated with a degree in political science and a minor in Italian. She also learned to speak Spanish, French, and a dialect of Mandarin. Every language was self-taught but Italian. Almost as fast as Rae's diploma was placed in her hands, a large bank hired her.

She worked full-time for almost two years, traveling. That was when she met Bradley. Mr. Bradley R. Davenport. A fancy name, but not a fancy guy. Just handsome and wholesome. Bradley's business was based near Ocean Springs, Mississippi. Seeing one another was challenging for Rae and Bradley, because they both traveled so much.

On a whim, Rae decided to try something new. She had never been a stranger to the kitchen. Well, none of us kids were. Cookie and Tom had made certain of that. Somewhere in that brain of hers, Louie was reborn. Not as the family dog but as a restaurant: Louie's Tavern. With a crackerjack manager in place, she and Bradley now had more time to spend together.

The College of Education was now standing and walking slowly. I waited with butterflies. The excitement rose from my stomach to my heart. Then I heard the pounding from my heart in my ears. *Wait,* I said to myself. *Wait. It's coming.* My name, Olivia Sue Hunnicutt. I walked across the stage. My trying mission for the day was accomplished. It was official—I was a graduate. As I returned to my seat, I felt more nervous. According to this piece of paper, I was qualified to teach. *No way.* Me, walk into a classroom of high school students so close to my age? Not a good idea. Those kids would try to run all over me, and that's when Livvy would let it fly. I'll pass, thank you very much.

* * *

After graduation, I headed back to my parents' home. I walked through the front door, and suddenly I got a huge hug from behind. It was Robert. *Lord, he gives me those silly goose bumps.*

Robert was pretty easy on the eyes. He was a tad less than six feet, but he claimed it anyway. He had dark brown, almost black, hair, soft-dreamy brown eyes, and a great body. When we all went to the beach, he used suntan oil on his large muscles, and that alone just made him sparkle. And if that wasn't enough, nature had added a mixture of little sweat beads. Those little suckers ran in a perfect, narrow, straight line between his pecs. But those sweat beads didn't stop there; they continued to run in a straight line down his six-pack, and then they spread out and traveled to rest on the band of his swim trunks.

Jeez, Livvy, get a grip on your wayward daydreaming. I had to deal with the real thing—his eyes. I would get lost in them if I allowed myself to look. So I tried to stay clear of them at all times.

I visited with my family members for a few minutes. Noel was talking to Robert about hunting and who had killed what the past week. Each of them was certainly stretching his story, probably adding a point or two.

Suddenly Robert took me by the hand. "I know you said no gifts." He eased his hand inside his jacket and removed a small box from his breast pocket. "But I wanted to."

I knew he didn't choose the gift for me. He had told Katherine, his thoughtful, beautiful mother, and she had bought the gift. "Open it." He smiled widely.

There I stood, trying not to look into his eyes. But the next thing I knew, I was sucked right in. I didn't give a rat's ass about the gift I had just reached for, but those eyes of his. Crap, I knew better than to look. I opened the box.

I was looking at earrings, silver studs with a pearl in the centers. They matched the pricey bracelet he'd bought me for my birthday last year. I turned to kiss him on the cheek, the same as I had for the last three years. He turned at the same time, and right there in front of God and everyone, Robert did it. He kissed me right on the lips. Not just a peck, either. To make things worse, he did it in front of my entire family. My stomach flip-flopped. Family members gasped. I pulled away from him and gasped too.

My voice cracked a bit as I told him how beautiful the earrings were. I removed the pair I was wearing and replaced them with the new earrings. I thanked him, without another kiss.

No one mentioned a word to me about Robert's untimely kiss during dinner, but I knew when the party was over, I'd catch hell from Jake. He was the one who had held me together when Robert and I broke up after dating for two years.

I was kidding myself about being friends with Robert, because sometimes my heart still hurt. That's when I asked myself, "What if I never recover?"

After dinner, I could tell Noel was pissed at Robert. I tried to make small talk.

"Andi looks pretty tonight."

"She always does, Livvy," Noel said and cut his eyes sharply at Robert.

Noel wasn't someone to be taken lightly. He was stern and quite large but normally a big teddy bear. In his rebel days, the boy got pumped up but not naturally. No telling what he'd put into that body of his. The tattoos on his body were quite intimidating if you didn't know him. But Noel was thoughtful when decorating his body with artwork. He could dress in his Sunday best, and not one tattoo could be seen.

Andi was wearing a drop-dead little black dress and the perfect pair of black Tory Burch shoes. But she'd look beautiful wearing a brown paper bag with a Prada belt. Andi was five foot two, hair as dark as coal, and two months pregnant, thin with hips.

I looked around the table. Mom always looked great, and tonight was no exception. She loved green and wore it well. She was fair-skinned, had a great smile, hazel eyes, and brown hair with just a hint of red. She was a petite five foot four, and she worked out every day.

Rae looked just like she should look. She wore a soft, conservatively short, winter-white chiffon dress. Her silver shoes were just the right height. I could tell Bradley was proud to have her on his arm, but he would soon have her in his life forever. You see, Bradley was old-fashioned, but then again, so was Rae.

* * *

When every belly was satisfied, Bradley walked over and stood in front of the fireplace. He stared at the fire for a few moments and then said loudly, "Rae, will you join me?"

Rae happily joined him, thinking he wanted a hug or Uncle Jack to take a picture. Uncle Jack would be taking pictures all right.

But right then Bradley knelt down on one knee and took Rae's left hand with his right. "Rae, will you marry me?" he asked.

"Yes, yes, oh yes, Bradley," she said with tears streaming down her face.

He placed the ring on her finger. Rae stood up on her tiptoes, reached around Bradley's neck, and thanked him properly. Rae was five foot nine barefoot, but she was pushing six foot one with her heels on. Bradley, unlike some people who claimed to be taller, truly was six foot seven. As my Nonnie always said, "He's a tall drink of water."

Bradley looked completely relieved, like the weight of the world had just lifted off his shoulders. Poor guy, he had been worrying about that moment all day. But even if he had asked Rae the big question and popped a bracelet made of peas and pasta around her wrist, she would have still said yes. He and Rae had tears running down their faces, but so did everyone else. Mine were dripping from my chin. I couldn't find Robert for the life of me. Guess he had to go to the bathroom. He probably needed to wipe his eyes too, even though he would never admit it.

After Bradley's big question and Rae's emotional answer, Rae finally asked loudly, "Okay, who knew about this?"

Dad was quick. "Well…" Everyone stopped talking to listen, because this was a rare event. Dad never conversed unless business was involved. "Bradley called me last week and asked if he could have my blessing to marry you, Rae. I told Bradley I would be honored to have him as a son. I also told him he needed to give Cookie a heads-up. I knew your mom would want pictures."

Dad had also suggested to Bradley he needed to check with me before he proposed to Rae, because he wouldn't want to spoil my graduation excitement.

Daddy continued, "So, Livvy told him, 'Please do,' because she hated attention. But you know she has a big mouth, and she called Noel and Andi. That's it—no one else knew."

"I told Uncle Jack," Noel announced proudly.

Bradley stated the list of family members he had told.

Then Andi said, "I told Nonnie and Papa."

And Nonnie admitted, "I told everybody."

"I told you, Andi, not to tell Nonnie," Papa interrupted. "She tells everything she knows to everybody."

"No, she doesn't, Papa."

"Wanna bet?" Papa responded. "How is that little blanket you sleep with holding up?"

"How do you know about my blanket, Papa?"

"Your Nonnie told me."

We all laughed, because Papa was right about Nonnie.

Everyone had known that Bradley was planning to ask Rae except one person, and she was pissed. Aunt KK.

My great-aunt Kristine. That woman was just like Nonnie. She was always in the know about everything and everybody, but not this time. Aunt KK pouted in the kitchen.

After a few minutes, Aunt KK pulled herself back together, joined the clan in the great room, and reclaimed her chair. She took Rae's hand and kissed it. Then she looked at Bradley and said, "You did well. But make sure I know all the details from here on out."

Aunt KK was not about to let her moment escape. While all eyes were on her, she decided to ask what everyone else was thinking. "Y'all set a date? When is it going to be?"

That took Rae and Bradley by surprise. Bradley yanked his BlackBerry from his jacket pocket and pressed a few buttons. Rae looked at hers too. Bradley suggested June.

"Won't work." Rae frowned. "I have the tavern booked every weekend for weddings and other special events. What about the second week in July?"

"No, I'm booked."

"August is totally booked too," Rae said.

Leave it to Aunt KK to stay in the spotlight. "What about May, y'all?" she asked.

Bradley and Rae checked their calendars, and they both were wide open. Rae worried she wouldn't have time to properly prepare for the wedding.

That was when the three most important women in our lives all said, "Oh yes, you can." The date was set: May 19.

"Well, girls," Aunt KK said. "Meeting tomorrow at my house. Let's get things rolling."

By that time, Dad was just sitting back. He knew to keep the shut-to-the-up, because this event was going to be something else. He was already mentally calculating the costs, and no plans were even set in stone yet.

It was late, and most family members had left or disappeared. I walked Jake to the door. "Livvy, I know you love him, and we're all friends, but don't go back there."

I whispered softly, "I know."

When I returned to the great room, it was empty except for Robert. I knew we had to discuss the kiss. But I didn't know how to start the conversation. Finally I said, "Robert, you need to explain why you kissed me."

Dead silence.

"You know what?" I said. "It's been a long day."

Robert looked directly into my eyes. I quickly glanced down, because, unfortunately, I realized I was still in love with him and I couldn't let him see that. He kissed me lightly on my forehead, and he held my hand as we slowly walked to the front door.

"Robert," I murmured. "I love the earrings. Will you please thank Katherine for me?"

"I bought them for you, Livvy, not Mom."

Holy cow, I didn't see that one coming either.

"Robert," I mumbled, "I assumed, you know, from before. I'm sorry."

He took my hand. "Apology accepted."

As we stood there in silence, I thought about the three attempts he'd made to date since we'd broken up. Not one relationship had lasted for more than a month. We always spent time together, even when he was on his dating spree. Sometimes he'd drop by my house for a quick dinner, or we'd talk on the phone. But he hadn't had a girl-friend for two years, and I hadn't dated anyone or gone on a date for more than two years. Nope, not a one, sadly; however, I was asked. I just figured the dates would be a waste of my time.

I did have four guy friends, but they were only friends. There was only one word to describe that part of my life: pitiful.

"Robert," I said, "thank you for coming tonight."

"Whenever you Hunnicutts throw a party, you know I'll come." Realizing he was still holding my hand, he slowly let it go.

I could have stood at the front door for hours talking to him, but I was going to have to let my question about the kiss go. I wasn't for-getting it, though. I opened the door, and Robert turned back to face me. He grabbed my arm, paused, and asked, "Talk to you tomorrow?"

"Sure."

I wanted to swear, cry, and throw things, but getting upset only made my blood sugar run up, jumping those numbers into a state that made my glucose meter scream *high*. That's right—the word *high* ac-tually appeared in bold letters, frightening the numbers right off the small glucose meter screen.

During a high blood sugar, I would get a terrible headache, fol-lowed by a bone-dry thirst. I could drink right out of a faucet, forgoing a drinking glass. If not corrected quickly, nausea and vomiting—or worse, a coma—could follow. I slipped right into one of those once from a high blood sugar. It wasn't my fault. Well, technically, I guess none of them have been. But for that one, I could put the blame where it belonged: the negligence of a pediatrician.

My parents had taken me in to see her six times in two weeks, and the idiot had told my mom she was just looking for something that wasn't there. I had every sign of a diabetic. That bitch almost let me die, and I was only eight. Thank the Lord my mother has that mama bear instinct. I could just imagine her waking my dad up. Tom was probably in a state of snoring unconsciousness. Cookie most likely gave him a quick jab in the back, saying something like, "Tom, wake up. Something's wrong with Livvy. I'm taking her in." Meaning the ER, of course.

The ER lobby had been completely empty. We waited only a few minutes before the nurse called my name. The doctor asked my parents a lot of questions. Someone came in my room and took blood from my arm. I was so afraid and felt sick. No more than fifteen minutes had passed when the doctor snatched the curtain back, and suddenly I had the entire ER's attention.

My parents stepped back—or were pushed back—from standing next to me. I lost sight of them. Nurses were sticking me, and the doctor was shining a light into my eyes, saying, "Her heart rate is much too fast." I lost time somewhere, but I was no longer afraid for some reason. I was tired, though, and my eyes were heavy, like I was trying to wake up from a deep sleep. But the funny thing was, I don't remember going to sleep, because I could hear people and movement in the room, but I couldn't see anything.

By this time, I had a tube down my throat, a needle in my arm, and a splitting headache. My blood sugar was over nine hundred.

That pediatrician didn't manage to kill me, but Robert for sure was going to be the death of me. Damn that boy. He left only fifteen minutes ago, and now he was blowing my phone up. What on earth could he possibly want? Forget it. I was taking a shower.

CHAPTER 3

My phone was still blinking from the night before. I didn't want to listen to those messages, but I did want to ball up my fist and pop Robert right in the nose. I could never do it, though. Instead, I reluctantly picked up my phone.

"You have four new messages," my voice mail said.

"Hey, Livvy," Robert coolly said, "I thought we could go out and grab a drink. We don't have to stay out late."

Ten minutes later. "Livvy," Robert said with more urgency in his voice, "I would like to grab that drink tonight. I'll come pick you up."

Six minutes later. "Dang it, Livvy, come on." Oh, Robert was mad now. "Pick up, I...I...need to tell you something."

Closing in the gap: four minutes from his last message. "Well, Livvy." His voice was much softer. "I don't blame you for not picking up. I'm sorry, you know, about kissing you in front of everyone. I just thought...or maybe I didn't think. I guess I'll try to catch up with you tomorrow."

That's it? That's his explanation for kissing me. He didn't think.

Aunt KK sent out one massive text message: *MY HOUSE AT 11:30 SHARP!* Everyone had better get his or her butt in gear. She meant business.

I had to get the day started. It was already eight thirty, and my stomach was fussing. I needed to eat. I felt a bit shaky, I think because

I was madder than a wet cat at Robert. But I needed to check my blood sugar. I pricked and squeezed my finger. That little strip sucked my blood right in, and I waited. The number popped up: ninety-nine. I headed to the kitchen to eat breakfast.

Now I needed to respond to Robert. I decided to keep it simple. As I sipped my morning tea—Earl Grey—I sent Robert a text message: *Good morning. We have a family meeting concerning Rae's wedding plans. Okay to call when we're finished?*

My phone beeped. Robert responded quickly with one word in all capital letters: *SURE.*

Eleven fifteen. I was early but not the first to arrive. Aunt KK had already put the others to work.

She and Nonnie used to be wedding planners back in the day. According to my mom, they were in high demand. To hire them to plan a wedding, no matter how large or small, was a big deal. So this meeting was organized and moved quickly. The church and the venue for the reception were booked within minutes. We had to have a place that could handle the guest list of six hundred comfortably, so Rae's choices were somewhat hampered.

I didn't understand why I had been asked to join this meeting. Nevertheless, I willingly cleaned the kitchen following our delicious chicken salad lunch and played with the children on the floor for a few minutes until my name was called. I jumped to my feet, eager to help, and said, "Yes, ma'am." Aunt KK wanted the complete staff from the spa booked for May 18 and 19.

"You got it, KK," I said, palming down my hair, frizzy from my tickling match with the tykes.

It was almost two o'clock, and I needed to leave. I had neglected the spa for the past couple of weeks because of finals, other than my quick trip earlier this morning. I didn't feel bad speaking up, because Rae needed to leave too. It was Saturday, and Louie's Tavern would be slammed. We had permission to leave. KK said she'd have another powwow session in a few weeks to make sure things were moving along at the proper pace.

While I was reading and responding to e-mails at the spa, Danni walked past me. "Girl, I need to touch up that face and hair of yours."

I hoped she was referring to my makeup. "I played with my little cousins earlier."

Danni worked her magic on my face and hair, and I was out the door of the spa in no time.

Lordy, Mom was calling. What could she possibly need? I just spent the entire morning with her. I usually let her leave a message because Cookie sometimes reads me a novel instead of the Cliff's Notes, but I answered.

"You busy?" she asked. She had to know I wasn't busy, because I answered on the second ring. Mom wanted me to have Danni cover all the shifts at work for a few days. The days were covered completely until mid-January, but knowing Cookie, it was probably a good idea to ask why before I confirmed anything.

Her plan was for us to take a short trip. Cabo San Lucas.

Ah, Cabo. That meant a few cocktails, a lot of power naps, and a couple of good books. Add a few spa appointments, and my days would pass by fast, too fast.

Mom apologized that our trip would have to be short, since we were leaving for the ski trip soon after.

Being close to Christmas, Mom had reinforcements coming to-morrow right after church to decorate the house for Christmas: Nonnie, Aunt KK, Uncle Jack, Noel, and me. Dad and Rae would be in charge of lunch, while Papa and Andi napped. But I gave Papa and Andi passes. Andi, being in her first trimester, threw up most morn-ings, and Papa was eighty-four. Uncle Jack would help with the three large trees, making sure they could withstand the amount of orna-ments that they'd have to bear.

* * *

I dropped by my house for a while to catch up with my friends. I felt guilty, because other than Jake and Robert, I'd neglected them the past few weeks. I decided to send text messages to Bo, Patrick, Luke, and Jake. I called Abby. She is five foot one with soft blonde hair, green eyes, a pretty smile, and a cute petite figure. I will never forget the day Abby and I became best friends. I had fainted in our sixth-grade classroom. My blood pressure had dropped too low from complications due to Addison's disease. When I came to, she had been holding my hand. I left her a voice mail. Now, I was surely procrastinating on how to handle Robert. I got it over with and sent him a text: *Family meeting is over. Plans?*

Within five minutes, everyone had responded to my text messages, and Abby had returned my call. Our plans were made: dinner downtown at the café, then out to hear a local band.

Robert texted: *I'm in.*

My house was the meeting spot, and two designated drivers would be needed. I volunteered, and Patrick drew the short straw.

After everyone arrived, Robert called shotgun while running toward me to open my car door. He was trying hard to make up for last night's untimely kiss.

When we arrived, Patrick and I ordered diet sodas, while the others started with their personal favorites. Bo ordered a beer; Luke, a Goose and cranberry; Jake, Bacardi and Coke; and Abby, a pretty little mixture of some kind. Robert, after a few moments of staring off into space, said, "I'll have a beer."

The atmosphere at the café wasn't fancy. The building was old and had the work of local amateur artists hanging on the walls. Lots of dark wood made the restaurant warm and cozy. To my delight, soothing jazz music played from the overhead speakers, and the black-and-white, old-fashioned flooring was a fine touch as well.

There were absolutely no to-go boxes tonight, because the boys ate all their food and then cleaned Abby's plate and mine.

Patrick acquired a passenger on the way to the Blue Bar. Luke decided to ride with him because of Abby.

Still early—nine forty-five—we made our way into the bar and claimed a table. The band started playing around ten thirty, and the place would be packed by eleven.

Patrick arrived at the table, holding two diet sodas and one fruity something for Abby. Patrick pulled up a chair and sat by Abby. Luke sat on the opposite side of her. Luke and Abby have a little crush on one another, but neither had ever admitted it. Bo sat to my left, and Robert sat to my right. Jake pulled a chair in between Robert and Luke and plopped right down.

"Hey, Livvy, how does it feel to be done?" Bo asked.

"I don't know yet," I said. "Give me a call next week while you're working in the horticulture lab without a break for the Christmas holidays. I'll definitely fill you in on the details while I relax by a pool, soaking up the sun in Cabo."

"Bitch, not fair." He chuckled.

I shot Robert a quick glance. "Cabo? Really?" he asked.

I shrugged my shoulders and said, "With Mom."

"Still going skiing?"

I assured him we were, just as our families had done the last several years. Robert quickly asked the dates of the trip, while the band, who reminded me of The Fray, played in the background.

By now, each of my friends was leaning back in the chairs, talking and laughing a bit louder than when we had arrived.

Abby slapped Luke on the leg, grabbed his hand, and said, "Let's dance."

Luke was quick to his feet and ready to please. He spun Abby around, and they were off. Jake spotted a cute girl at the bar, and as he approached her, I was certain he was trying to think of the perfect line that would impress her. I wanted to tell that poor girl to run. Jake's a nice and good-looking guy, but he's a player, for sure.

Bo stood up, grabbing my hand. "Come on, Livvy. Show me what-cha got."

I hopped up and instructed Robert and Patrick to keep an eye on our bags. Off I went without waiting for a response from either of them.

When the song ended, Bo and I returned to the table. Before I sat down, Robert grabbed my arm and said, "My turn." He pulled me close and locked his arms low around my waist. I placed my arms around his neck while he rested the side of his face against mine. He whispered the lyrics to the song in my ear. I wanted to stay in his arms, but I knew I couldn't. I pulled away and pointed to our chairs. The song wasn't over, but our dance was.

We didn't close the bar down because of the stressful week everyone had had. A few of my friends needed some slight assistance when we left the bar, excluding Jake, who had disappeared. He must have impressed that girl, but for the life of me, I can't imagine what he could have said to woo her.

It was quiet on the drive back home. Luke was once again in my backseat, snoring lightly. Robert grunted slightly at him. I turned the music down. I hoped Robert would tell me what he was thinking, but, of course, nothing. Not a stinking word.

Patrick whipped into my driveway behind me. He helped Bo and Abby to the porch of my small three-bedroom home, and left them both propped up against post, while I dealt with Luke. I handed Robert my house key. I was thinking about firing Patrick in the morning. That fool was completely useless.

It looked like I was having a sleepover. Abby stumbled into my room and fell facedown across my bed, while Robert made sure Bo got the room with the twin beds. Robert liked Bo, but Robert thought Bo liked me, which was ridiculous. This caused a bit of tension occasionally. Robert removed Bo's shoes and gave him a little punch on the arm. He walked out and smiled at me standing in the hallway. I told him to behave as he closed the bedroom door.

"What?" He flashed a sly grin. "I am."

Luke fell across the bed in the guest room. I removed his shoes for him and looked up because I realized Robert was standing in the doorway. He laughed. "You know, this is like when most of us were freshmen."

"But now that the six of you are all grown up, being seniors and all, who takes care of you?"

"Smartass," Robert sneered.

"I have been called two big nouns tonight, and both times I only spoke the truth."

"Yeah, you have." He laughed.

"Give me a hand with Abby?"

"What do you have in mind?" he asked.

"You'll see."

I kicked my shoes off, grabbed a couple bottles of water from the refrigerator, and continued in the direction of my bedroom. He followed but stood in the doorway for a moment.

"Oh," he said. Abby had fallen facedown across the foot of the bed. I asked him to scoot her over. Robert lifted Abby and moved her over without even a groan. Abby, however, moaned like we were killing her. I removed Abby's shoes, and Robert lifted her again. I removed Luke's jacket, which she had borrowed earlier in the evening, and hung it over a chair. I whispered to Robert where the linens were. He nodded and said, "I remember."

I took a few girly minutes in the bathroom, pulled my hair up into a loopy ponytail-thing, and checked my blood sugar.

The ten minutes I was in the bathroom, Robert had turned my sofa into a queen-size bed. He had the sheets, pillows, and blanket in place and had removed his shirt and shoes, keeping his jeans on. He had chosen an On Demand movie.

Robert patted the sofa bed and said, "You're welcome to watch the movie."

I glanced down at my pj's and chewed the corner of my lower lip, thinking *this is not a good idea.* I slowly approached my sofa and eased under the covers to join him. He was lying on his back, but suddenly he shuffled to the center of the bed. After a few moments, he turned on his side to face me and wrapped his arms around me. He fell asleep. *Really?* I thought. I snuggled closer.

CHAPTER 4

"Good morning," Robert said in a sleepy voice.

I had some kickin' morning breath, so I smiled and pulled the sheet up to cover my mouth. I was trying to get my eyes to focus, but my eyelashes were a bit stuck together again because of the extensions.

"Good morning," I replied. We were still lying in the same position in which we had fallen asleep.

"We have to get up," we said at the same time.

It was eight, and church started at nine thirty.

He stood at the side of the bed, looked down at me, and said, "You are beautiful, even in the morning."

"Thank you," I said. But inwardly I sighed, *you look pretty stinking good yourself.*

Robert looked around my small den. He was trying to find the few articles of clothing he had taken off earlier that morning. He spotted his shirt. I watched him as he walked across the room with his jeans unbuttoned and his belt unbuckled, hanging in his belt loops.

"Ah," he said, "there are my shoes. Need some juice or something?"

"No, I'm fine, thanks." I offered him breakfast.

He passed on breakfast but brushed the side of my cheek gently with his fingers before leaving.

Now I had three more guests, and none of them looked like they'd be moving anytime soon. Their hangovers would haunt them the rest of the day.

I placed a bottle of Advil and three bottles of water on the kitchen counter. They'd need it.

I grabbed a gray sweater dress, leggings, and tall, black boots from my closet. Showered and dressed, I snatched my bag from the kitchen counter and dashed out the door.

* * *

During the church service, while the minister delivered his urgent message on how Christ loves us all, I felt like someone was staring a hole through the back of my head. It was Robert. I hadn't noticed his family sitting in the pew when I had dashed down the aisle to claim my seat next to my parents. Robert and his family were sitting two rows behind us. It wasn't uncommon for our families to sit so closely, but after last night, it felt different.

When the church service was over, I hugged Robert's parents, Katherine and Bob, and his brother and sister, Ducky and Ella. Bob and Katherine congratulated me on my graduation and gave their regrets for not being able to attend. I assured them both it was okay, because if my mother had not insisted that I walk, I wouldn't have attended my own graduation.

Robert draped his arm across my shoulders and asked, "Are your guests still unconscious?"

"They were when I left."

As they were leaving, I heard Robert's nineteen-year-old brother, Ducky, ask him, "What's up with Livvy?" (His given name is Redford. I still don't know why they call him Ducky after all these years.)

"Shut up," Robert told Ducky.

"You know she's hot, fool," Ducky said. "What's your problem? You're going to mess around, and someone—"

Robert shoved Ducky this time. Robert glanced back at me. I was sure he was wondering if I had overheard Ducky's comment. From my prompt dumbfounded facial expression, Robert had his answer. My dang mouth was hanging open.

* * *

Thankfully, Mom had the tree trimmings organized. All I could say was thank the Lord for three pre-lit Christmas trees. Uncle Jack and Dad took extra safety precautions with the largest tree by attaching a clear, heavy-gauge wire to the treetop and connecting it a heavy-duty hook screwed into a beam on the ceiling to hold the tree steady. It stood impressively in the middle of the foyer.

Time had flown. For lunch Dad made pecan-crusted baked chicken. But it was after six o'clock now, and Rae and I needed to eat again to prevent an insulin reaction. Dad hit the kitchen and made sandwiches for everyone: wheat hoagie buns, toasted, with everything on them.

While we ate our meal together, we discussed wedding plans. According to Aunt KK, the wedding specialist, things were on schedule. But as soon as Cookie mentioned Cabo, KK lit up like a Christmas tree, but not in a good way.

"You mean you're leaving town two times this month?" she asked. "Cookie, we have much too much to do. Please reconsider."

"You can reach me by phone anytime. Don't worry."

KK calmed down after a few moments of not getting her way. God love her.

I finished dinner and meandered to the kitchen to assist my dad with the cleanup. He gave me a hug out of the blue and asked, "Livvy, are you happy?"

"Sure, Daddy. Why wouldn't I be?"

"You seem a little down and have for a while. I love you, and if you need to talk, I'm here for you."

"I know you love me, Daddy."

It was close to seven fifteen when we finished up the fireplace mantles. They looked picture perfect, all four of them. Uncle Jack and Noel tackled the front porch and the massive front door. When my parents built their home, Mom had the door made in France. The thing stood twelve feet high, had a double swing, and weighed about five thousand pounds, so it was most definitely not a one-man job.

It was after ten o'clock at night, and the house looked like a featured home in *Southern Living* magazine. However, Mom would continue to tweak it over the next couple of days to her standards.

Everyone said good-bye, and my parents' home was once again almost quiet, aside from the Christmas music playing on the overhead speakers. I noticed Mom and Dad were holding hands beside one of the Christmas trees. Dad put his arm around Mom, and they began to dance slowly.

I hugged Rae, and she said, "You know, Livvy, that's what it's all about…dancing together after so many years."

Still watching Mom and Dad, I smiled, knowing Rae was completely right.

I decided to stay in my fancy room tonight, at my parents' home. I noticed that Rae walked in the direction of her old fancy room, as well. Regardless of how long we have lived away, this would always be home.

* * *

I was completely packed for Cabo by midweek. But I was ill as a hornet. Still no word from Robert. I didn't get it. He seemed to be all about me for a few days, and now nothing.

On Thursday I plowed through my ski clothing and cut the tags from the ugly matching duffel bags Cookie had dropped off and got a jump-start on packing for the ski trip.

After thumbing through the most recent fashion, stocks, and organic farming magazines, I texted my friends—except for Robert—and told them I'd see them New Year's Eve.

I called Robert. His phone went straight to voice mail. I left him a message: "Hey, I'm leaving early in the morning for Cabo. Thought I would say bye."

I hung up and tossed my phone on the bed. *I've got to get over him. This crap is ridiculous. If he cared about me, he would have called.*

Half asleep, I brushed my teeth and pulled my hair up in a loopy thing on top of my head, dressed casually, and slipped on a pair of flats.

I met my folks in the kitchen, they were having morning coffee. Dad popped a simple breakfast in front of me: toast, one scrambled egg, and a glass of juice.

I sat tight-lipped in the backseat on the drive to Atlanta, listening to my iPod. It seemed every song made me think of Robert. I wondered if all guys were like him. *Oh God, surely not.*

"Livvy," Dad said, over Pink's song "Glitter." I tugged one bud from my ear. "Your mom and I want you to take your time on deciding what do—I mean, applying for a job. I know you know what the 'after graduation' rules are, but you need to rest, at least for now." *Whew.* "You work enough, at the spa and for the construction business. We won't cut you off." He chuckled. "You're ambitious. We know you're not lazy. I think your goals are different from what Noel's and Rae's were, at your age. But, it's our fault you're rotten as dirt."

"Tom," Mom scolded.

"Cookie, it's the God's truth. Livvy, you can keep your house, for now. After all, you have some great folks on your street, and they look for you." *Yeah, they do.*

"Dad…Mom…thank you. I, uh, will think on it and try not to take advantage of your offer for too long." I said, totally in shock.

Mom was quiet while we waited for the boarding announcement. I knew something had her attention, because she was never at a loss for words. Finally, the person announced first class could now board for Cabo San Lucas.

Mom stood and picked up her well-used Louis Vuitton bags and asked, "All set?"

"Yes, ma'am." We were on the plane within a few minutes. Mom placed her computer bag in her seat and removed two stacks of pages held together with large black clips. Each appeared to be two inches thick. She sat down, holding the bound pages on her lap. Typed right in the center of the top page were two words: "Finding Justice."

Mom was totally quiet as she sat motionless and stared at the clipped pages. Serenely, she said, "Livvy, I brought something for you to read."

She held out one stack of the pages for me to take. Mom quickly put the buds to her iPod in her ears. She didn't allow me to ask her any questions. She moved the black clip to the left corner and flipped to the next page. So did I.

Before I read the first word, the flight attendant asked if she could get us anything to drink.

"A Bloody Mary," Mom answered quickly. I requested an orange juice.

After I read a few pages, I realized that this was the project Mom had been working on for several years. I knew because I had seen some notes on her desk a while back, but I never mentioned it. I was now submerged in the pages of *Finding Justice*, and it was just as well, because Mom hadn't spoken a word since she had handed it to me. She was reading her pages and making red marks on her copy.

A couple of hours passed before Mom looked at me and said, "Let's take a break." She didn't ask me as she stuck a little yellow sticker on the page I was reading and took the bound pages from my hands. She put both stacks back into her computer bag.

I glanced at my watch. I immediately kicked back and relaxed. We landed in Cabo an hour later, and I was a happy girl because our bags arrived at baggage claim the same time we did.

Ten minutes later our driver fetched us. In no time at all, we arrived at the resort. Mom checked us in and sent our bags to our suite. She knew I was overdue for a healthy meal.

Mom chatted while we ate in one of the resort's restaurants. She told me she had gotten the idea for the book more than four years ago.

She had made notes with the hopes that one day she could write it. Dad knew about it all along and had been supportive. She asked me to read it completely through once and then give her my opinion.

After lunch, we found our suite. Two spacious bedrooms, decorated with modern, colorful furnishings, and breathtaking ocean views from every room. After unpacking I dressed in a brown swimsuit. I quickly threw on a matching cover-up and brown wedge sandals. It was 2:45 p.m. I had time to enjoy the sun for a few hours. Before I rushed out the door, Mom placed her manuscript on the foot of my bed. I gave her a hug, and we discussed our plans for the afternoon. I put the book into my beach bag, along with my diabetic stuff and some sunblock. In a flash I headed to the pool.

I found a spot where I could read and enjoy the ocean breeze. I turned my chair to face the sun, unloaded my bag, and started to make a dash to the bar when I noticed a waiter was headed in my direction. I ordered diet soda, applied sunblock, and settled in.

It was nearly 6:30. I needed to gather up my things. I noticed a couple of cute guys had dropped towels on chairs directly on the opposite side of the pool. They had looked in my direction a couple of times. I clipped the pages of Mom's book and shoved them into my pool bag. Tomorrow I would find out who the guys were or put Cookie on it. She could talk to anyone about anything. Given fifteen minutes, she would know their names, their ages, where they were from, and who their parents were, and then she'd probably realize she'd known them for years.

I had just turned the hair dryer off when Mom called and said she was waiting downstairs in the quaint French restaurant. I slicked back my hair in a ponytail and quickly wanded on mascara. I reached in the closet and yanked a tan linen sundress from the hanger and slid on brown Tory wedges while grabbing my bag.

Mom and I were quiet while eating dinner, but we decided to extend the evening and take the long way back to the suite to give dinner time to settle. As we strolled through the pathways, I heard the waves crashing onto the beach and felt the warm, salty night breeze on my skin. It was heaven.

CHAPTER 5

I asked to be excused from the breakfast table. The sun was calling my name. I told Mom where she could find me, and she had only one request: make sure shade was available.

I made a quick run to our suite to dress for a day in the sun. I like the beach normally, but here the undertow is awful. So poolside it is.

My swimsuit needed to be an eye-catcher. After all, I had seen two cute guys by the pool yesterday. I'd had already worn my brown one. That left an ocean blue swimsuit with rhinestones, a green one with shiny little beads, which I loved, or the striped one. On second thought, I tossed the striped one. It made my butt look big. I put on the green suit and shrugged on a wispy cover-up. I slid my feet into the same brown wedge sandals I wore yesterday. I threw my sunblock in my beach bag, while not forgetting my assignment, which I planned to finish before lunch.

When I arrived at the pool, the chair I used yesterday was available, so I claimed it again and had started reading my homework when an attractive woman, I guessed in her early fifties, asked if she could sit next to me. I smiled and told her she could. I only needed one of the two adjacent lounges for my mother. The lady chose the chair to my left.

I continued reading. I noticed that the lady next to me removed some bound pages similar to mine from her bag. She appeared to only lack a few more pages before she'd finish her project. I, on the other hand, had nearly thirty to go.

The lady next to me finished whatever she was reading and picked up her BlackBerry. Behind my dark sunglasses, I could tell she looked in my direction more than a couple of times. I wasn't sure if she was curious about what I was reading or if she wanted to chat with me. I flipped to the last page and couldn't break from it. I was captivated. I had to know what happened to Ben Davis and Jan Morris.

After I finished, I sat for a few moments, just staring at the last page. *I can't believe my mother, Victoria C. Hunnicutt, wrote this.* I ran my palm over the page. I was thirsty. The waiter hadn't checked on me for more than an hour. I glanced at the lady and, pointing, I said, "Pardon me. I notice your glass is empty. I'm going to the bar. Care for a drink?"

She smiled as she stood and said, "I need to stretch. May I join you?"

"Yes." I grinned. "The company would be great, because I haven't seen my mom for hours. I bet she's in the spa."

"That's my plan tomorrow," the lady said.

While we waited on the drinks, she said, "I'm Anna Smith."

"Nice to meet you, Anna. I'm Livvy Hunnicutt." I reached to shake her hand.

She gripped my hand firmly. "It's a pleasure to meet you, Livvy."

Now that Anna and I were perched back on our loungers, enjoying our drinks, she asked, "What brings you to Cabo?"

I explained I had just graduated from college.

"What university?" she interrupted.

"Auburn. I majored in education."

She nodded. She raised her sunglasses.

"I guess my mother thought this vacation might be a good idea, because I'm undecided on what to do with my life right now. And my sister just got engaged, and my brother and sister-in-law are expecting a baby. I think my parents are afraid I'm feeling left out." As I glanced down at the book, I now realized the trip might have been as much for my mom as for me.

"What are you doing here in Cabo?" I asked Anna.

"Resting. Work has been crazy, and I haven't taken a vacation in three years. I was overdue for one."

"What do you do that keeps you from taking a vacation?"

"I was an editor, but now I own an agency, thanks to my father," she said.

I *had* to introduce her to my mother.

"I noticed you've been reading a manuscript," Anna said. "Have you written something?"

Mom would kill me for not speaking with her first, but I had to say something. I couldn't let this opportunity pass by. The words flew out my mouth.

"Anna, my mother…" I paused. "Wrote something. I read it in less than twenty-four hours, and it was good. Anna, she will shoot me for telling you." I explained about the deal I had made with Mom: I would read it first. Then, when I finished, I was supposed to report back to her.

I could tell Anna was thinking, even behind her Prada sunglasses, because of the way she nibbled at her bottom lip like I do. She finally said, "I'm always looking for new people with fresh ideas. What do you think about me taking a quick look at it? If your mom shows up, I'll take responsibility."

"You know what, Anna?" As I spoke, I handed the bound pages to her. "What are the chances that Mom could get a professional opinion so quickly anywhere else? Don't you agree?"

Anna took the book from my hand. "I'll know if we have anything in no time at all."

I'd probably be scolded for allowing it. But heck, I just had to let Anna have a quick look.

Within a few minutes, the waiter came by. Anna asked for a club soda and a lime. Not me. I needed something stronger, you know, so

I could prepare for my verbal spanking. I leaned my chair back a bit, sipping on my Goose, soda, and two limes.

* * *

I looked up and there they were, and they had brought a friend. Oooh my, those three were good-looking. Well, whatta you know? They were looking right in my direction, and I watched every step they took. I couldn't exactly tell if they were looking directly at me behind their sunglasses or just slightly over my head to the beach, but who cares? The view was fine from here.

The gorgeous guys chose three chairs directly in front of me, but across the beautiful and somewhat narrow pool. I was getting a bit warm. I glanced down at my favorite swimsuit to make sure everything was in its proper place. Minor fine-tuning was needed to the band of the bottoms, and then I stood up, determined not to look in their direction. I walked to the steps of the pool and slowly stepped in. I didn't clear two of the four steps before two of the most perfect guys were standing at the edge of the pool. They must have been warm, too. They jumped in.

"Sorry about the splash," they said simultaneously.

"No problem." I swam a few strokes in their direction. *What do you think you are doing? You do not have a plan, girl. These guys are going to think you are a total idiot.*

Winging it, I boldly said, "I'm Livvy." I was standing less than two feet from them. From the expression on each of their faces, I was certain they thought I was a complete nut.

"It's nice to meet you, Livvy," the taller guy said. "I'm Crosby."

The dark-haired and most handsome guy put his hand out for me to shake. "I'm Max Spencer."

I smiled as I shook his wet hand. With his free hand, Max pointed to the guy in the chair who was now looking at me and said, "That's Tucker, Crosby's brother."

Holy cow. I knew them.

Tucker threw his hand up and offered a lazy wave, but he never took his eyes from me as he put a cap on his head. Tucker's cap caught my attention immediately. It was khaki with blue stitching and had the letters "AU" in the center of it. Yes, I knew these guys, and I'd known them for years. But I'd changed. They didn't recognize me. I turned to Crosby with a huge smile, and, just to mess with them a little, asked, "Where are you from?"

Crosby beamed. "Birmingham."

"Alabama?" I teased.

"Yes, that's right."

I couldn't hold back any longer. "Gee, small world, Crosby Cooper. I'm from Auburn." Tucker quickly joined us in the pool, and now they were all staring. I could tell they still didn't recognize me.

"You have got to be kidding," Max said.

"No, I live there and just graduated from Auburn University a week ago."

Crosby nodded his head and probed, "Do you have an older sister?"

"Yes, I do."

Crosby smiled and asked, "Rae Hunnicutt?"

"Yes, that's right."

"Well damn, boys, this is little Livvy," Crosby said, laughing.

Each one of them had certainly filled out and looked older and even more handsome than I remembered. I didn't like being referred to as little Livvy, though. However, I took it like a big girl.

Tucker looked at me. "Only one thing—she's not so little anymore."

"That's right," Max said. "You're not little Livvy anymore." Max picked me up and tightly hugged me. I slid slowly down his perfectly built body with my arms wrapped around his neck and his arms still around my waist. *Oh my.*

Next, Crosby hugged me.

Tucker stepped up and said, "Bring it on." He kissed me on the side of my head as he released me.

I glanced back at Anna. She was reading. The boys asked me to join them on their side of the pool, but I explained Mom would be down shortly.

"No problem," Max said. "We'll join you and Cookie."

I spotted Cookie heading our way and quickly exited the pool. "Anna, I'm sorry to interrupt you, but my mom is coming. Do you mind?" I pointed carefully to the book.

Anna looked up and placed the clipped pages on my now relocated chair, because the guys took it upon themselves to move my belongings. *First things first,* I thought. *Get the guys introduced to Mom.* After all, it had been a few years since she'd seen them. Then I'd deal with Anna.

Mom walked up to me. "Well, who are your friends?"

Before I could say a word, Mom reached out her arms and said, "Oh my Lord, just look at you fellas. You have grown up, and you are so handsome." Mom hugged and kissed each of them on the cheek. "Where do you live, and what are you doing these days?"

Max spoke first. He said he lived in New York and was in banking.

Tucker lived in Birmingham and was starting a new job on Monday. He was an attorney.

Mom looked right at Crosby and said, "Spill it—what's up with you?"

He laughed and quickly gave her some details. He lived in Birmingham and worked as an engineer.

Now Anna was standing right beside me, waiting to be introduced.

"Mom," I said, "this is Anna. Anna, this is my mother, Victoria Hunnicutt."

Mom and Anna both extended their hands for a handshake. I paused, not knowing what to say next.

Anna told my mom how we had met a few hours ago. "Your daughter is delightful. And I would love to sit and chat with you a few minutes."

Anna glanced down at the clipped pages that remained open where she had left off reading. Mom followed her gaze and then looked straight at me. Anna continued, "Victoria, I am Anna Smith."

I've never known my mother to be speechless, but she was. Her mouth dropped slightly open, and she asked, "You are Anna Smith, Publishing?"

"Yes, that's right," Anna smiled. "I hope you don't mind. After Livvy finished reading it," she pointed in the direction of Mom's book, "I asked her if I could have a look. She tried to resist, but I was quite persuasive."

Mom looked at me with concern, but she began to smile. "I can't do a thing with Livvy."

I knew right at that moment things were good between Mom and me.

But the boys were still standing there. Tucker spoke up and said, "Dang it, Cookie. I thought there for a second Livvy was in trouble with that mouth of hers, like old times."

When I was younger, I had a somewhat sassy mouth. On the other hand, I still did. However, I tried to filter unless I've had a drink or two; then all bets were off.

All six of us were laughing at Tucker's comment. But after the excitement had calmed down, I was absolutely starving, and the guys were hungry too.

The guys wanted burgers. I normally eat grilled chicken or fish, but I agreed. We moved over to the snack bar near the pool.

Max asked about my degree. I smiled. "Education. Imagine me teaching high school history." He laughed.

"Can't see you teaching, little Livvy." Tucker laughed, shoving his last bite of awful red hamburger meat in his mouth.

"Nah, me either," Crosby said.

I asked them to fill me in on the past four years of their lives.

Max was working and living in New York, like he had said earlier. He worked for Global National. Even I had heard of them. I asked if he had anyone special in his life.

"No, but I recently spotted someone whom I have my eye on," he stated.

"Good luck," I shot back.

"From the looks of things, it's going to take more than luck," he said, draining his beer glass.

Tucker spoke up next. He had finished law school at Cumberland back in the spring, but didn't rush to find a job. He had just landed one he thought he'd like at an international firm.

"So, you'll write contracts for large companies when mergers occur from different countries, or international treaties-type stuff…is that right?"

He nodded. "Yeah…something like that. Actually, I'll do merging contracts, mostly." Tucker arched his brow, and then quickly added he and his girlfriend of two years had broken up a few weeks ago. I expressed my condolences.

Crosby spoke next. He said engineering school had killed him, but he finished two years ago and worked for a company in Birmingham. I asked if there was anyone special in his life. He laughed. "No, not yet."

Max asked, "What about you, Livvy? Anyone special?"

I stabbed my chicken with my fork, as if it could run away. "Not really."

"Sorry," Max said. "It seems I've upset you."

"No, Max. It's all right. Besides, it's been a while." We finished lunch and headed back in the direction of the pool.

When we got close to the pool, I felt my feet leave the ground. Crosby had picked me up, and he jumped into the pool. Crosby spun around in the water, still holding me, and said, "We are going to have a good time over the next couple of days."

Yep, we probably were. I quickly placed my hands firmly on top of his head and shoved him underwater.

His head popped up. "Oh, it is on now." He and I goofed off for a few minutes.

Mom and Anna had disappeared.

We got out of the pool to reclaim our chairs. I noticed Tucker had moved over and put Crosby's things next to me. I was cool with it.

I eavesdropped on Max and Tucker's conversation and glanced over at Crosby. Dang, he was good-looking. I guessed he was at least six foot three. He had green eyes, light brown hair, and a perfect skin tone, not too fair. His lips were full, but not as full as Tucker's or even as full as Max's. Still perfect, though. He must spend a couple of hours a day in the gym to maintain his body. He had lifted me like I was nothing more than a paperweight. Then I glanced at Max and Tucker while they were still chatting. They were just as impressive-looking.

"Excuse me. I'll be back in a few."

Crosby hopped up almost at the same time and asked if he could get me anything.

"Nope, just need to pee," I shouted.

They apparently didn't hear me as I returned. Max and Crosby were talking, and I was certain this discussion was not meant for me to hear. Max was saying there was something about me, but he could not put his finger on it.

Crosby said, "For starters, she's hot and has an awesome personality. Not bitchy like I thought she would be."

Tucker joined in. "Little brother, Livvy is what we refer to as the total package. Crosby, did you just say Livvy has an awesome personality? What the hell, boy? When did you start using the word *awesome*, anyway?"

I had heard enough. Every girl liked to be noticed but, my Lord, I was embarrassed. I began to walk more heavily. I sneezed. Snot sprayed. Dang allergies. I hurriedly wiped it away backhanded. Crosby glanced in my direction. He stood up and walked toward me. He grinned with his hands resting on his hips. Then he scooped me up in his arms and once again jumped into the pool.

When I surfaced, I noticed Max and Tucker had skedaddled. Crosby hit a couple of long stokes in my direction and said, "I can't believe some guy hasn't snatched you right up and claimed you for himself." He smiled. "I can tell you're the kind of girl that every guy wants to take home to Mama. You're kinda perfect." *Yeah, right! Bruised arms, hips, tummy, thighs, and backside, all from shots. Sore, callused fingers from checking my BG eight times a day. I have healthy, wavy hair, but it will frizz unless I use products, but not too much, or it becomes a limp, worn-out dishrag. And moments ago, I had snot on my face. Tomorrow my light pink nail polish will certainly be chipped, and that's my short list. Perfect? He thinks I'm perfect.* I wanted to laugh out loud. "I bet I need to ask you for permission to get a first kiss." I laughed, but I didn't give him an explanation. The truth is, I hadn't kissed or been kissed in more than two years, apart from that one kiss from Robert the evening of my graduation dinner. Robert certainly didn't try to kiss me when he spent the night with me, other than that stinking kiss on my forehead.

"Crosby," I asked, "have you met many of those kinds of girls?"

He nodded his head and said, "Only one. Your sister. But neither of us was looking then." Crosby Cooper just left me speechless.

I swam to the steps and paused on the top one. I swished the water around with my foot, keeping my back toward Crosby. He stepped behind me and placed his hands softly on my lower waist.

"I would like to ask permission to kiss you, Livvy."

I stood there with my back to him. He was breathing softly on my neck.

Why not? Robert hadn't given me any true hope we would ever be together. I turned around. I was standing one step higher in the pool than Crosby, and I didn't think anymore. I leaned in and kissed him. He pulled me closer. I knew when I kissed him, there was no one near us, but we must have been lip-locked longer than I realized because I heard Tucker say, "Crosby, if Cookie sees you, she will kill you."

I slowly pulled away from Crosby. "Tucker," I said, "I am all grown up, remember?"

Crosby held my hand as we walked over to reclaim our chairs. I reached for my bag. Crosby asked if he could get me anything. I told him thanks, but I had it. I removed my zipper bag that I kept my meter and supplies in. I could tell Crosby and Tucker didn't want to stare, but they were watching from behind their sunglasses. I took my meter and placed it on my leg. I shoved the strip in, waited until the meter blinked, and pricked my finger. I squeezed my finger, and a small dot of blood popped out. I picked up the meter with the strip sticking out the end of it and held it in front of the dot of blood. The strip sucked the blood right in. Five, four, three, two, one: the number popped up. One forty-two. I needed insulin. I returned my medical supplies to their proper bag, only to remove another small, insulated bag with a tiny cold pack in it. This kept my insulin cool. I pulled out the blue tube that looked similar to a large marker. I removed the cap, dialed up two units, and stuck myself in my arm.

"Hey, Livvy," Tucker said while tipping the waiter, "I read somewhere red wine is okay for diabetics." I eased back into the pool. "What about the other stuff?" He took a swig of his cold Corona. My mouth watered.

"Red wine tends to stabilize my blood sugar. But I can't speak for other diabetics. As for the good stuff—like that beer you're drinking or the fruity thing Max drank this morning—they'll shoot my BG up. I do like Bacardi and Diet Coke with lime. My favorite is club soda, Goose, and two limes."

"Shots?" he asked.

I giggled. "Yeah, I like Patron." I tightened my ponytail.

"Really?" Max said, approaching us with my purple Converse sneakers and my plaid J. Crew shorts and vintage tee. "Tucker and I ran into Cookie while I was booking us an activity for this afternoon." He glanced down at his hands. "She sent you these."

"What kind of activity?" I asked, scrambling off the chair.

"Do you have everything in your bag you need?" Tucker asked.

"Yeah. But what activity?"

"You sure?" Crosby asked, pointing at my bag, like he knew what was going on.

"We'll be gone three hours," Max added.

"Uh-huh, I have enough snacks and medical stuff," I said, pulling on my tee. "But—"

"Dune buggies," Tucker said, laughing, "on the beach and in the desert—with a guide too."

"Alrighty then," I said, lacing up my shoe. "Let's go get dirty, boys."

"Livvy," Max said, leading the way, "they had two single buggies and a double. I put you with Crosby. Is that okay?"

"As long as he doesn't kill me," I laughed.

The driver slowed down, "Hope she's our guide," Tucker said, lowering his shades. We watched the young lady spray what I hope was disinfectant inside helmets, as the driver parked.

Shh—it, I thought when I shuffled off the seat of the dusty, jacked-up SUV, *all caps* and *hyphenated.* But hey, the dark-skinned beauty in the neon green DUNE-ME-NOW T-shirt and cut-offs looked like she could handle speed, dunes—with or without a buggy—and Tucker, all at the same time. I scooted past Tucker who was chewing on the ear of his Ray-Bans and slipped the paperwork from Max's hand, who was bitching to someone in…French. *Jeez.* "I got this," I said, kickin' up dust with every step. I stared at the guide's nametag.

"Tucker, come over and meet"—a smile tickled my lips—"Hope." We shook hands. "We four are your two o'clock." I pointed and said, "Max—the guy on the phone—booked us." I motioned, "This here is Tucker and Crosby. I'm Livvy."

She thumbed over the paperwork. "Great, even the legal stuff is in order. I see you have done this before," she said in excellent English. "Choose a helmet and goggles from the board; the sizes are marked. Tucker," she said, handing him a key, "Yellow, single. Crosby and Livvy, red double. Max, where is he?" she asked.

Max strolled over, shoving his phone in his backpack. "Sorry," he said.

"Blue single." Crosby handed Max his gear, and Hope tossed him his key. "I will lead at all times. There is a compartment for your belongings in each buggy. Put the key in the ignition. Clip the kill switch to your clothing before you start the engine. Buckle up—tight. Do not unbuckle your lap or chest belt until you have shut the engine off.

No bumping or grinding—" Tucker chuckled. She gave him one evil eye. "The buggies." She glanced down at the paperwork again. "Um, this is a first," she said, and then put the paper in her compartment. "Any questions?" she said, pulling her goggles over her head. "None? Great." She strapped her helmet on. "Desert first, then the beach. The desert is rocky and curvy. Single file at all times—or whatever," she said, glancing at Max. "Do not stray from the main trail." She grinned for the first time.

"Why?" Tucker asked.

"Snakes. The two-legged kind—with guns and knives." Hope hopped in her black DUNE-ME-NOW buggy with neon green letters painted on the roll bar that spelled out GUIDE.

"Gotcha," Tucker said, belting up. "Wait. What the hell are you saying?" He hopped out of his buggy and leaned over her.

"Tucker, my brother owns this place. You and your friends are safe. We will pass three desert checkpoints. I will show them your papers and copies of your photo IDs. Once I'm cleared, we take off. Your photo will be taken as you pass, and for security purposes, the guards will match the photo, which was e-mailed to us when you signed up for DUNE-ME-NOW. So trust me when I say we have guns, too. You did read the paperwork you signed."

"None of us read shit, but Max"—who was laughing his ass off—"or signed anything either," Tucker said, whipping around.

"Need help with your helmet, Livvy?" Crosby asked, ignoring his brother and reaching for my unfastened straps.

"No, but by all means, go ahead, Mr. Cooper."

Max pulled out behind Hope, then Tucker followed. Crosby and I pulled up the rear. "Betcha Max and Tucker beat the hell out of those buggies before we get back," Crosby said, laughing.

"Hope said, 'No bumping or grinding.'"Crosby laughed, "He bought those two freaking buggies, Livvy. Tucker doesn't have clue."

"You don't say," I said, watching Max.

"Yeah."

"This will be good."

Max slowed and let Tucker go around go him. Tucker had not yet settled in behind Hope when Max gave him a 'love pat' from behind. Tucker clearly held up the universal 'eff-you" signal. Tucker dropped back and moved over, and Max cleanly took the outside, leaving Tucker hugging the canyon side, which was totally off the beaten path. "Crosby, they are going to kill one another." He sped up.

"Nah," he shouted. I gripped the handle tighter. Hope never slowed down.

Tucker took the lead from Max. Tucker's left-side panel and Max's right-side panel were beat-up and tie-dyed yellow and blue by the time we reached the first checkpoint.

"Crosby, I can ride with Hope if you want to join in."

"No. I like to go fast—most of the time." He raised his goggles and looked at me. He lowered his goggles again and shifted gears as we passed the checkpoint. "But that kind of bumping and grinding is not for me."

"Oh," I said, and my head jerked back against the seat when he shifted into third.

By the second checkpoint, I had squeezed Crosby's arms and legs more times than I could count. Had they no fear? Max and Tucker had totally banged up their right and left dune buggy panels in the rugged terrain.

I noticed that when we slowed to pass a guard with one big machine gun Tucker's back bumper was hanging. He gunned it and shot around Max to take the lead.

Moments later, without slowing down, we slid and took a sharp curve on two wheels. The buggy spun with Crosby holding the wheel tight and me his leg. The two tires that were suspended slapped the ground to join their mates on what looked like a dried-up riverbed. Max had spun around and was facing us. Tucker's buggy rolled. "Oh, Jesus," I shouted. I unfastened my belts and hopped over the side panel. I stumbled and fell on all fours but quickly got up and ran toward Tucker. His buggy was on its side. Hope had already crossed the dry riverbed but had whipped around and was heading back.

"Tucker," I shouted and fell to my knees, reaching for his bloody hand. I quickly pulled my used-to-be pale pink tee over my head. Leaving it inside-out, hoping it was cleaner, I wiped his hand. Max carefully lowered Tucker's goggles. Tucker was pale—real pale. "The blood is not from his hand," I said.

"His leg," Crosby shouted and dropped his helmet on the ground.

"Tucker, what else hurts?" I asked, wiping his leg and trying to figure out how deep the long cut was.

"I...don't...do...blood," he said and passed out.

Hope kneed down beside us with her first aid kit and phone. "His leg," Crosby said, pointing.

"Tucker, wake up buddy. C'mon," Max said.

"It's just a long scrape. Nothing is in it," Hope said.

"I'm okay," Tucker mumbled without opening his eyes.

"He really does not do blood," Crosby said.

"Tucker," Hope asked, "does your head, neck, or back hurt?"

"No. I'm okay," he said and removed his helmet. Crosby unfastened his seatbelts and helped him out of the buggy, which was still on its side.

"You don't need stiches. But I need to clean it," Hope said.

Tucker stared at her T-shirt—her boobs, really. "Do you know what you are doing?" he finally asked.

She laughed as she poured peroxide over his scrape. "Yes, I'm a third-year medical student."

Talk about whiplash. She had all of our attention now. She felt Tucker's neck area. "I work here when I can. The tips are good. It pays our rent. Look here, and follow my finger," she said, holding it up. "My father is American, mom, Mexican, and we have dual citizenship. Good," she told Tucker and lowered her hand. "I live in California with my husband, who is also in medical school. Give me your wrist. I'm checking your pulse. Are you certain nothing hurts?"

"Positive. Like I said, I don't do blood."

She smiled. "Your pulse is normal."

"Thank you, Hope," Tucker said, standing up and lending her a hand to stand.

Max and Crosby pushed the buggy, and it landed right side up.

"Okay," she said, "next checkpoint is across the riverbed. Then the beach."

Tucker rode shotgun with Crosby, and I drove the yellow-and-red tie-dyed dune buggy to the beach checkpoint. Once we cleared it, I gunned the raggedy thing and shot up next to Max. He slowed and mouthed, "Don't do it."

"Is that a dare?" I shifted the gear and floored it. I glanced in the mirror. "Whoa, bet that hurt," I shouted as the dirt storm settled around Max.

Max quickly was on my bumper. I fishedtailed around, which gave him the lead. Hope slowed down as she started up the rugged hill. She parked once at the top, and we pulled alongside her. Wow, what a view. The beach was white, and the ocean was blue. "We will park here. Bring your bags. I have towels, bottled water, and snacks, down there." She pointed at a hut.

Crosby said, "We're going swimming together, and I'm not asking for permission this time, but I'm kissing you, hard…after I wash the dirt off your face."

"Bring it on," I laughed and reached for my bag.

"Screw the dirt," he said. He slipped his arm around my bare waist and kissed me. I dropped my bag.

"Payback is going to be hell," Max chuckled when he walked by.

"Give me the damn keys," Tucker said, tapping me on the shoulder. "You could have killed your hot little self."

Crosby laughed against my lips and handed Tucker the keys.

"You kiss better than you drive," he said, gripping my hand as we walked down the rocky path, "and you drive pretty damn good."

"Thanks," I giggled. "So do you."

Tucker and Max were wet and sprawled out on DUNE-ME-NOW oversized towels. Hope was heading our way with bottled water and more towels. I checked my BG, and headed to the ocean.

The cool salty water quenched my hot skin but once I was waist-high, a wave tumbled me over and washed me back into the ankle-deep water. "Livvy," Crosby shouted, "I'm coming." My swimsuit bottoms were full of sand, and my top was hanging around my neck. I began to fish my arm around to my back for my dangling straps. The water pulled me back into deeper water—knee high—before I got the saltwater wiped from my eyes. Another wave pounded me, causing me to lose the nearly stable footing that I had and I fell again. I held on to my top—not much I could do about the crack full of sand right now.

"We're coming, Livvy," Tucker shouted.

"No. I got it," I shouted, coughing. I tried to stand with my hair covering my face, like Cousin Itt from the Addams Family. I was hoping like crazy that my backside was all the fellas were seeing. "Let me help you," Crosby said. I felt his hands touch my sides and then my back. He hooked my top. I palmed my hair from my face and turned around.

"You okay?" he asked, holding me in his arms.

"Uh-huh," I mumbled. He kissed me.

"Crosby," I whispered, "thank you for helping me, but let go of me please. My bottoms are full of sand."

* * *

A cleaner me downed the water bottle. I stretched out next between Crosby and Tucker on a towel and closed my eyes. "Hey, Livvy, almost got a peek when you lost your top," Tucker howled, never sitting up.

My eyes popped open. "No one but my doctor has seen my girls."

"Maybe so," he laughed, "but you—dirty, in a skimpy bikini top, shorts, and Converses—damn, girl."

"Shut up, Tucker," I laughed. "We need more water." I took off to find Hope.

Upon my return, the guys were talking about me—again. I could hear them a mile away. "Do you think she's a virgin?" Crosby asked.

"Probably not," Tucker said. "You know she's twenty-one."

"I don't know," Max said. "She said no one but her doctor has seen her girls."

"Well, you know what we had done by the time we were eighteen," Tucker said.

"You're right," Max popped back.

"Hey," I shouted, "need anything? They have snacks."

They turned and stared at me. No one said anything. According to their collective gaze, they were trying to decide if I had been deflowered.

Then, all at once, they replied, "No," but they were still staring at me.

I handed out the bottles of water and plopped down Indian-style. I took a bite of an apple. "Hope said we had ten minutes."

The dirt road was shorter going back, we pulled into the parking lot behind Hope with no problems at all. Max's dune buggy, stalled a few hundred yards back, was beaten to hell and smoking at both ends. With his backpack hung over one shoulder, helmet in his hand, and still wearing those goofy goggles, he jogged past Tucker and flipped him the finger. Tucker obliged him with the same gesture, wobbling into parking lot on four flat tires, two hanging bumpers, and singing "Born To Be Wild" from the top of his lungs.

"Hope," Crosby said, leaning against the dune buggy, "at least Max tips well."

"Yes, he does," she laughed, "best day I ever had."

We piled into the SUV, laughing, and got out twenty minutes later, still laughing.

"Max," I said, catching his arm, "thank you for including me today. I had a great time."

He laughed again. "We all did. But remember, I still owe you for the sand storm."

"Can I walk with you to your room?" Crosby asked.

"Absolutely. You have my bag."

He smiled. "Ladies first, Miss Livvy."

We had taken about two steps when he asked, "How long has it been?"

"Been?"

"The guy?"

"Oh, three years."

Crosby stopped and took my hand. "Three years? You were so young." He shook his head. "And you can't let go?"

My eyes dropped to my feet. I was humiliated by how ridiculous I must have sounded.

"Look at me, Livvy." I couldn't. Crosby gently put his hand under my chin and tilted my head up. "You have to let someone into that heart of yours. Love is a risk that eventually everyone takes. It works out sometimes, and sometimes it doesn't."

He kissed my forehead and then wiped a tear from my cheek that had unknowingly escaped.

"An hour and a half, okay? I would like to walk you to the restaurant."

"Uh-huh," was all I could muster.

* * *

I kicked my shoes off and tossed my bag on the bed. My cell beeped when I stepped out of the shower. Now Robert decides to text me, I thought. The text read: *Hey, be safe. Love ya.*

ESP is what he has. Back in Auburn I barely heard from him, and now he wanted to screw with me. *Really?* I tossed my phone on the bed. "What the crap does 'love ya' mean anyway?" I picked up the hair dryer, slung my head upside down, and turned the heat on. "I need to figure this out."

When I had finished my blow-out, I texted him back: *Getting lots of sun. See you soon.*

Things might be different when he graduated. But what if we never get back together? I would've wasted three years of my life, hoping, dreaming—and for what? But how do you give your heart to someone new when someone already has it? How do you love again after your heart has been broken? How long does it take for a broken heart to heal? While I asked myself these questions, I reminded myself that Robert was not totally responsible for us breaking up. We had made that difficult decision together. However, I thought we should have moved on more easily.

I stood in front of the mirror after I was dressed. I loved my purple Vera. I brought it back to life tonight, even though I had worn it only a week ago on my graduation day.

Crosby knocked on the door. I opened it immediately. His hands were in his pockets, but he removed them and caught the door as I stepped out. "Livvy, you look beautiful."

"Thank you. You clean up well yourself."

He grinned and asked, "Could I hold your hand?" I let my hand meet his.

We walked quietly for a few moments, and then Crosby said, "One more day. Have you given any thought to the conversation we had earlier?"

"I suppose you are referring to the one concerning Robert. Yes, I have."

"That's the first time you've mentioned his name."

"I know." Max and Tucker were sitting in the far corner of the restaurant. After my first glass of red wine, I told them I felt so bad for them. There were literally fewer than one hundred people at this resort, and we were the youngest. But I was having a great time while we ate dinner. I must say, Max was quite a talker, but then again, so were Crosby and Tucker. I felt like I was watching a tennis match. My head was turning back and forth as I got more reacquainted with the fellas.

It was early, so we decided to go dancing in the resort's nightclub.

Max asked me to dance, as I was about to sit. "Livvy, it's hard to believe you are Rae's little sister," he said as we moved to the small dance floor. "You know, I wish I had approached you yesterday…" He paused. "Hell, I punched Crosby on the shoulder and nodded in your direction. All I can say is that was my second mistake."

I felt myself blush as I collected my thoughts. "Max, thank you. That was one of the sweetest compliments I have ever gotten. Just so you know, I noticed you first yesterday."

He was staring directly in my eyes, and for some reason I could not break our gaze. I had to lighten our conversation up, and fast. "Of course, Max, you were standing." *Didn't work.* My eyes locked on Max's hazel ones. I felt my lips part, and when his parted in response, my insides quickened. It was time to rejoin the brothers at the table.

I was still shaken up from my dance with Max, but I looked at Tucker and said, "Your turn."

He grabbed my hand and said, smiling, "Bring it, girl."

Tucker and I danced to a more upbeat song than Max and I had. However, we talked as well. Tucker mentioned he had noticed Max struck a nerve while we were eating lunch today. *Here we go again.*

"Well," he said, "let's have it. We might have something in common."

I began to share with Tucker. "It was a long time ago—three years. For some reason I can't move on, but it seems he can't either. We're still friends—I guess that's what you could call us." I glanced up at Tucker. I knew from his expression I had elaborated too much.

"Three years? Damn, Livvy," he said. "Have you tried to date?"

"Yeah," I answered softly.

"How many times have you tried?"

"I dated someone who I really liked, but I couldn't seem to develop any feelings for him, so I knew he would never be anything more than a friend. It lasted a month. Then again a couple of months later, but…"

"Wasn't right either?"

"Not at all."

"You're kidding. At twenty-one, you've had only one boyfriend?"

"Now that you put it that way, I guess I am pretty lame."

"Livvy, we have danced through two complete songs, and I can't tell you the name of either of them, but I can tell you that that guy staring at you from our table might already have a crush on you. Don't take it lightly. He never puts himself out there."

We headed back to our table. Crosby met us, grabbed my hand, gently spun me around, and dipped me. According to Tucker, this boy was after my heart, but I truly wasn't ready to share that thing again. My heart was guarded like Fort Knox, and no one anytime soon would be allowed in.

Max and Tucker decided to head out and explore the place.

Crosby whispered in my ear, "One more slow song with you, Livvy, and I will need a dip in the cool ocean."

"Not this ocean—we would drown."

"We?"

"Yes, we."

He took my hand and asked, "How about a walk on the beach?" I took his hand.

We got closer. He asked, "Would you like to remove your shoes? They look expensive."

I sat on the last step at the entrance to the beach and reached to my buckle. Crosby stooped down in front of me. "I want to do it."

I withdrew my hand and allowed him. He unbuckled my shoe and removed it. Then he did the same with my other shoe. He moved his hand gently up my leg to my knee and paused. Then he lightly brushed the inside of my thigh, but not too high.

Oh my, no one has ever taken my shoes off for me before. I quickly stood up, and Crosby reached for my hand. In his other hand, he held my shoes while we strolled along the beach.

Crosby tightened his grip on my hand and said, "I'm not going to ask you any questions about your past. I'm more interested in your future." He stopped and kissed me.

For the first time in three years, I wanted to feel something. I kissed Crosby back, because I wanted this. I was feeling excited, but not in the way I had hoped. I wanted butterflies, sweaty palms, and a pounding heart, not tears welling up in my eyes. I gently pulled away from him and gained control of my emotions before he noticed. I wouldn't let him see me cry.

I turned in for the night, but I replayed Tucker and Crosby's conversations for hours…and the fact I haven't allowed myself or wanted to move on in years now haunted my every thought.

CHAPTER 6

I slipped on a pair of red Nike shorts and a jog bra and zipped up a black lightweight hoodie. Rainbow flip-flops would have to do. I pulled my hair up in a messy loop. I reached for my wristlet, which contained my diabetic stuff, and quickly met Mom for breakfast. She beamed as soon as I approached the table. "Anna liked my book."

"I knew she would," I laughed and plopped down on a soft dining chair.

"Livvy, darling." *Dang-it. The word darling. This is going to be serious.* "Three years ago your dad and I decided to keep our opinions to ourselves and stay out of personal choices where young men are involved," she said. "I'm not going to start speaking my mind now." She reached across the table and touched the side of my face with the back of her hand. "Livvy, it looks like Crosby has taken a liking to you."

I laughed. *Guess she changed her mind about butting in where guys are involved.*

"It was nice to see you laugh and play yesterday." She dabbed the corners of her mouth with her napkin. "Where are the guys?"

I shrugged. "Sleeping in, I guess."

I asked about Anna to change the subject. She said everything was good, but I could tell she wasn't getting her hopes up.

"Livvy, are you having a good time?" *So much for changing the subject.*

"Yes. And Mom, I'm trying, you know. I will work through all this soon. I know I've worried you and Daddy. But I'm fine."

I thought for a moment about Max. There was something about him. I almost laughed out loud. It was probably because everything about him was sexy. And then there was Tucker, who was also quite a looker and towered over me. He felt cozy, like a big teddy bear.

* * *

I wore the ocean-blue swimsuit with the same white wispy cover-up I'd worn the day before, but I added a bracelet and matching sliver rope earrings. *I do love nice shoes*, I thought as I eased my feet into a pair of Torys.

To my surprise the guys were already out, and it was early. It appeared I would sit in the same chair as yesterday, between Crosby and Max. As I approached them, I asked myself, how could a girl be so lucky?

All three stood when they spotted me, but Crosby took a few steps toward me and eased my bag from my hand.

"Good morning," I said. "Tucker, my goodness, you don't look well." He appeared to have a hangover. He sat down and lowered his shades.

Max was sitting on the edge of his chair. Crosby had remained standing.

"Tucker, what are you looking at?" Crosby asked.

"I know Livvy is going to remove that cover-up thing she has on. I don't want to miss anything, because I can tell that suit of hers is gonna be good. It's smaller than the green one she had on yesterday."

"Shut up, Tucker." Crosby threw a towel at Tucker, hitting him in the chest.

While they were fussing a bit and not paying me any attention, I shrugged off my cover-up, tossed it on the chair, and dipped my toes in the pool. "The water feels nice, y'all."

"I need a drink," Max said.

"I knew it would be a good one," Tucker shouted. His head fell back on the chair.

Crosby's hands sprang from his waist to above his head, and he shouted, "Jesus, Livvy." He waved his hands around. "That's right," he said. "Let's just say you missed your calling." He pointed at me. "The hell with being a history teacher, do *Sports Illustrated.*"

Then he reached down and pressed the button on the iPod dock. Toby Keith's "She's a Hottie" cranked up. "I swear I didn't choose that song."

Me, some sort of sex goddess? Their impression was all wrong. "Crosby," I said over Toby, "I am black and blue." I touched my sore arms. "These are all over my body, I'm puffy because of prednisone, and my stinking nose is too big." I raised my voice. "I don't see my-self, as sexy, Crosby." I spread my arms out. "I'm just me."

Tucker butted in. "Yeah, we got that. Shit, Livvy, you don't have a fu—"

"Whoa, Tucker," Max said, holding a tray of drinks. "Ever thought about not speaking what is really on your mind?" He sat the tray on a table.

Tucker never raised his head. "Not at all, buddy. But maybe you could finish my assessment of what I think about Livvy in French, or Spanish, or whatever other language you have stored in that smart-ass brain of yours and make it sound, well…more kosher."

I laughed and sat down beside Tucker. "Would you like me to put on your tattered 'Drink More Beer' T-shirt?" I said, tugging at his sleeve.

"Nah," he said with his forearm shading his face. "It's all good."

"It's early," Max said, hovering over the tray of shots, "but it's our last day. Let's have some fun."

I walked over to Max. "Step back." I fanned my hand at him. "I got this." Tucker sat up. Crosby was at my side, and Max was in front of me. I picked up two shot glasses and downed them. I placed the two empty glasses back on the tray and put both of my hands on my hips and asked Max what he was waiting for.

They tossed their shots back and chased them with beer.

"You know, we don't have to stay here today. We can charter a boat or something," I suggested.

"No, don't think we should," Tucker said. "There was trouble at the big marina last night. It's only a couple of miles from here."

"What kind of trouble?" Max asked.

"That old couple" Tucker said, pointing, "said two men from Boston were asking questions yesterday about a young businessman they thought was on vacation here. One guy was found dead last night. Shot."

Max slung his backpack over his bare shoulder and took off.

"My God," I said, shaking my head, "that's awful."

"The pool it is," Crosby said.

As soon as I was within his reach, he pulled me close. I strung my arms around his neck. I lifted my legs and locked them tightly around his waist. By now, he had his hands on my hips—well, more like my butt. Eye-to-eye, I asked, "What are you thinking about?"

"You, Livvy."

He kissed me, granting my lips no mercy. Tucker said, "You know, our room is empty."

"Better not." Max said upon his return, "if Cookie finds out, she'll kill you, Crosby." Crosby ended our kiss, but he didn't look away.

His eyes caught my gaze and said, "Tucker, you know Livvy is not that kind of a girl. You marry her first." I blushed. I never thought of myself like that either.

Food was the last thing on my mind, but the guys were hungry, and I needed to eat to prevent an insulin reaction. We ordered lunch.

While we were waiting on our order, I jumped into the pool. Crosby was right behind me, while Max returned to his book for a couple of minutes. Tucker was now sitting up and watching, and he said, "Let's go, Max."

He threw the book he had attempted to read for the past two mornings on the table and jumped into the pool right behind Tucker.

Those three hopped on rafts. I stared at mine like it was a bull. My head was swimmy. I thought I'd better tame my bull before the drinks that Tucker had ordered arrived.

I was holding the raft with one hand, but I was having difficulty trying to steady it so I could climb on. That damn thing had scooted out from under me twice, but I was determined to win with my next attempt. I carefully walked to the pool steps, pulling my raft behind me. I balanced myself by holding the handrail and tried to straddle the raft. That brainstorm didn't work worth a damn. The thing shot out from underneath me and found its resting place on top of Tucker. "Nice try," Tucker said, laughing.

Crosby fetched the raft and held it while I got on. I knew my raft was like an untamed bull, and I would not win if I were to move. I chose to lie still.

After I took a little nap, I needed to flip over. I did with no problems this time. My raft remained steady. I was feeling pretty confident now for sure. I reached back with both hands and unfastened my clasp. My straps fell to my sides.

"Watch out, Crosby, Livvy's unleashed," Tucker said. He snickered and then that idiot shouted, "Hey, Livvy, you know this is a topless resort, right? It's cool if you want to flip over."

"Only in your dreams, Tucker," I said.

Crosby had a tighter hold on the corner of my raft now, probably a good thing, because I was feeling—smart.

I decided to make a bold move to mess with the guys a bit. I looked carefully around and saw that I was close to the steps. The guys were all behind me. My raft was steady, because Crosby was still holding on. *I'm going to do it.* I quickly sat up, facing the entrance of the pool, threw my top over my left shoulder, hopped off my raft, and walked right up the steps. The boys were still behind me, and my top was hanging over my left shoulder.

Max shouted, "Tucker!"

Tucker shouted, "Crosby!"

I heard Crosby say, "I got her!"

I heard all of them splashing. I wanted to turn around, but I couldn't because I had a couple more steps before I would reach my chair, where my towel was waiting to rescue me from what now was obviously a bad decision.

I felt a hand touch my shoulder, and my top slid off. Max and Tucker had hopped out from the side of the pool. I could see them in the corner of my eye, but I didn't turn. I carefully picked my towel up from my chair, held it in front of me, turned around, and asked calmly, "Something wrong?"

I looked at Crosby holding my top and laughing.

He stepped closer. "Think you lost something." He kissed me. When his tongue swept across my tongue, I dropped my towel. *I had not planned for that to happen.*

When Crosby stopped kissing me, he didn't pull away or look down, but he pulled me closer to him and held me tighter so I couldn't move. No one moved until Crosby said, "Hey, Max, how about grabbing Livvy a towel."

I felt Max wrap a towel around me. Tucker groaned, "Today isn't over yet, Livvy."

Max chuckled and said, "Almost, Livvy."

Crosby was still holding my top and me. He released me slowly but pulled the towel around me as he stepped away from my bare chest.

I whispered, "I didn't mean to drop my towel."

Crosby stared directly into my eyes and softly said, "I'm glad you did."

Moments later, my top was back in place, and everyone said they couldn't believe what I had done. "Livvy," Max shouted, "what if Cookie had seen this incident?"

I wanted to say she would be ecstatic I wasn't moping around, but I finished up with "I don't think she would bring this matter to anyone's attention."

"You know, guys," I said after a little thought, "I had a plan."

Crosby asked, "You had a plan?"

"Yes, and let me finish, please," I begged, realizing my speech was slightly slurred. "My plan was to walk right out of the pool with my top across my shoulder, pat dry, and put it back on. I had presumed, you three would in stay in the pool. Instead, you all just got stupid or something."

Tucker asked, "How long did it take you to design your plan?"

"Well, you see," I said, my words probably still a bit slurred. I was pointing my finger and trying to explain it wasn't a plan like the great General Custer might have designed for the Battle of the Little Bighorn. The guys were laughing when I said, "My plan took about five seconds and was quickly put into action."

Tucker was laughing his ass off and said, "Next time tell us so we can try to arrange to have a better view. All I got was a side view."

"Are you guys two years old?" I pointed at my girls and said, "They're just *breasts*."

Max said, "But they're your breasts, Livvy. A couple more seconds, and I could've described them to you."

"Thanks, but I already know what they look like."

I needed to make that everything was in decent order. I checked my blood sugar and gave myself insulin. I felt a nap creeping on. But they would not shut up. Those three chatted more than girls. Their conversations were mostly about business, and then I heard her name. *Nicole.* That was Tucker's ex-girlfriend's name. I listened as he spoke. He said he had loved her, but it wouldn't take three years to get over her.

All at once Max asked Crosby if I was asleep. I could feel Crosby lean over me carefully. I didn't move. "Think so."

Tucker said, "Probably more like passed out."

Max said quietly, assuming I was asleep, "I cannot figure it out."

Crosby asked, "Figure what out?"

"Whether she ever slept with what's-his-name," Max said.

Hold on, I'm right here. My temper flared. "What is it with you guys, and why does it matter? And by the way, Max, his name is Robert," I said without opening my eyes.

"Thought you were asleep, Livvy."

"Well, I'm not," I said, sitting up. I repeated myself. "Why does it matter if I have or haven't? If I *have* slept with someone, I think you all would be disappointed in me. And if I *haven't* had sex before, well, I don't even want to know what your thoughts would be." Now I was standing up at the foot of Crosby's chair, looking down at him.

He remained sitting in his chair, but he reached out and pulled me on top of him. Our sweaty bodies stuck together. "I wouldn't be disappointed in you, Livvy," he cooed.

I still didn't give them an answer about the sex thing, because it was absolutely none of their business.

My skin felt hot. Insulin made my skin sensitive, so I had to be careful.

I asked if we could meet earlier for dinner, because I needed to pack.

Crosby said he and Tucker needed to get going because of their 6 a.m. flight.

"Max, what time is your flight?" I asked.

"Not at six a.m." He laughed.

"We're leaving at seven. Our flight is at nine. You are welcome to ride with us if—"

He cut me off. "Yeah, that will work."

Crosby grabbed my beach bag for me. He said he was sorry about the have-I-or- haven't-I-had-sex thing. I told him it was all right, but I preferred not to comment. We arrived at my suite, and I invited him inside. He stepped in, placed my bag on the floor, and looked around. "Very nice," he said, as we stepped out onto the veranda and gazed out to the ocean. "Livvy," he said, easing his arm around my waist, "the past three days, I haven't been able to keep my eyes off you. And by the way," he said, tracing the rhinestone ring in the center of my top, "this blue one is my favorite. The best part of today was when you dropped your towel." I blushed crimson.

"Livvy, I didn't see a thing. But feeling you pressed against me"— he paused—"was amazing. I'd better leave." He spun around and was out the door before I could say a word.

CHAPTER 7

I needed Mom's opinion. The shoe thing wasn't working for me, but she was on the phone, and it sounded like business. After changing twice, I went with the strappy black pair and stayed out of her way.

Crosby knocked on the door. I heard Mom greet him. I grabbed my bag and stepped around the corner.

Crosby whistled.

"Guess you like my dress." I grinned.

"Maybe I like more than the dress, Livvy." Crosby raised an eyebrow. "I made reservations for all of us by the ocean tonight."

"Nice," I said and hooked my arm around his.

When we approached the table, Tucker said, "Well, little Livvy, don't you look pretty in pink." I rolled my eyes.

Max swirled his nearly empty glass around a couple of times and responded in a smart-ass kind of way. "Yeah, she wears brown, green with little beads, and even blue—oh yeah, with or without a top— pretty well too. But damn, those are some hot shoes, girl."

"Thanks," I said, quickly reaching this conclusion: these fellas were obviously bored out of their minds, since I was the only female under forty-five here at this deserted spa.

We ordered dinner. Max discussed his job more in detail while we waited. He said the bank he worked for had asked him to consider splitting his time between New York and London. He was weighing his options.

Suddenly everyone became quiet, but not me. "London! That's incredible. Which list is longer? The to-go or not-to-go?"

"Dead even," he said. "I have to make a decision by Tuesday."

"Well, good luck with that," Tucker said.

After dinner Tucker said he was going to call it a night. He popped a friendly kiss on my lips and said, "I like babysitting you. Who knew it would take a small army to take care of you? Give me your phone number."

I punched Tucker on the arm and laughed. "Shut up, you big goof. But thanks for looking out for me. I *have* acted childishly. I shouldn't have—"

"Ah, Livvy," he said, cutting me off, "you had a good time." He took his cell from his pocket. "I think we all did." I handed him my cell. I told Tucker I had a couple of guest rooms and to not be a stranger.

"Max," I said, "when you come to town to visit your mother, I expect a call from you."

He kissed my cheek and said, "See you in the morning."

My Lord, I thought. I'd been kissed more in the past two days than I had in the past three years, and I liked it.

After Max and Tucker had left, I asked Crosby, "What do you think about Max splitting living between London and New York?" I asked Crosby.

"He'll do it."

"Well, there's one positive thing about it."

"What's that?"

"London is beautiful. Hey, you'll have somewhere to take awesome vacations."

"You're right—but only if you go with me."

I smiled.

"Would you like to walk on the beach?" he asked.

I stood up but he pointed to my shoes. I sat back down. Crosby touched my left knee, and then with his fingers he feather-brushed the outside of my leg until he reached the large silver buckle on my shoe before he removed it. Once again, he slowly he teased my inner thigh with the backside of his fingers. I whimpered. He swallowed hard, but his skilled hands carried on to my right leg and repeated the process. *Okay, that was hot.* He took my hand for me to stand and held my shoes in his free hand.

As we strolled from the ocean-side restaurant directly to the beach, Crosby said, "Livvy, I'd like to visit you in Auburn and take you on a real date. I've enjoyed spending time with you. As a matter of fact, I have enjoyed spending time with you more than I've ever enjoyed being with anyone."

"Crosby," I said, "that's not possible. You're nice, funny, and, most of all, very handsome. And that body of yours…let's just say it doesn't stop."

He laughed.

"I know you've dated a lot, Crosby. You must have had lots of girlfriends along the way."

"I've dated two girls, and when I broke up with them, I wasn't upset."

"That's an awful thing to say. The girls must have been devastated."

"Nah, they moved on just fine. I don't date, but I go out."

"A lot?"

"I'm embarrassed to tell how often. But I'm tired of that mess."

"I've enjoyed spending time with you, too, Crosby." But I didn't say that I would like to see him again.

"I'm not going to ask for your number, but I would like to give you my number." I was puzzled, but he continued to explain. "If I take your number, I'll see it in my phone every day, and it'll remind me of you. I'd rather you be reminded of me. That way, when you figure out the Robert thing, maybe you'll call."

Aw…no risk of rejection. "I understand."

He asked if I was ready to call it a night. I shook my head no and pointed to a lounge chair. "You sure?" I sat on the end of the chair. He straddled it and I leaned against his chest.

I couldn't help but muse over my situation. I knew I still had feelings for Robert. *But tonight I'm in the arms of a great guy who has told me how he feels.*

I twisted slightly and looked at Crosby, then kissed him. He tugged me closer. I turned completely around and straddled his lap. He tightened his hold around me as we continued to kiss. The warmth of his mouth and body was pleasing. He gently pulled away and sweetly said, "I could hold you like this all night." *Livvy, feel something for him.* I kissed him eagerly.

He eased his hands underneath my dress, and in one swift motion, he firmly grasped my hips and yanked my lower body forward. I kept my arms around his neck and tangled my fingers in the back of his hair. I pressed down, meeting his fully clothed, upward thrust. *No butterflies, but plenty of heat.* He pulled away from my lips and removed his hands from underneath my dress. Our breathing was labored, and in the darkness he murmured, "Jesus, Livvy, I need to get you back. It's late." He wiggled from underneath me, nearly causing me to tumble off the chair. "Sorry," he said, catching me.

He snatched up my shoes from the chair next to us, took my hand, and tugged me. Lagging a few steps behind him, adjusting my thong and feeling a bit cheated for many reasons, my frazzled self hissed, "That's it?"

Not brothering to look at me or slow down, Crosby volleyed back, "For now it is." After a few long strides, he said, "I can't believe it's only been two days since we got reacquainted. Saying good-bye should be easy, but I can't find the words."

I stopped, removed my phone from my bag, and handed it to him. After he stored his number, he stepped closer to me and eased his hands around my waist. I flung my arms tightly around his neck and went for his lips. *Feel something, Livvy. Feel something for him. Why can't I feel it?* I waited, but nothing happened.

We took a few more steps until we stood directly in front of my door. He kissed my forehead and said, "Livvy, you and your mom have a safe trip home. And it's none of my business, but don't keep waiting."

He turned and walked away. I didn't call out to him as I watched his shadow disappear around the corner of the building.

* * *

I tossed and turned that night. I knew Crosby would be fine. After all, we had only flirted with each other. In a couple of days, things would be back to normal for him, but what about me?

Our annual family ski trip in a few days, and I was nervous about the trip. I had decided to take the guys' advice and talk to Robert about how I felt.

Jeez, Mom woke in a good mood. I looked and felt like I had a hangover, but that was far from the case. Just no sleep. Then again, I'd never had a hangover, so I didn't know what one would feel like.

Mom ordered us room service while I checked in with Max to see if we were still on for this morning.

"Good morning, Livvy."

"How'd you know it was me?" I asked.

He laughed. "I didn't, but I hoped it was."

"Oh." I paused. "Guess, I, uh, will—"

"Yeah," he interrupted. "See you in a few minutes."

Max and our car were already waiting when Mom and I entered the lobby. The driver loaded our luggage. Mom took shotgun, and Max and I shared the backseat. Max spoke to Mom a few minutes. But then he asked me about the holiday season. I told him we were going skiing with some other families and friends of ours.

He grabbed my leg directly above my knee and said, "Don't break anything." Then he squeezed, which tickled.

I laughed. "You're crazy, Max. I ski well. But snowboarding, I'm a klutz."

As we approached our gates, Mom darted off to purchase magazines, and I decided to sit with Max for a few minutes.

"Remember," Max said, "I saw you first, and if things don't work out with Crosby, maybe I could—"

I interrupted. "You live in New York and possibly London in a few months. You visit Auburn twice a year."

"Geography. I guess that is a slight problem," Max said with a shrewd smile. "Whatever you decide to do, cut Robert loose, Livvy."

"I don't have him on a rope."

"Yes, you do. It's just a long one. Or does he have you on one?"

"Don't know."

"Crosby is a great guy," Max said. "But you aren't going to give him a chance, are you?"

"Probably not," I admitted. "This love stuff is just too complicated. When it doesn't work out, it hurts. It's easier to flirt and move on. Don't you think?"

He shook his head. "I think at some point you have to fall in love with someone who will love you back."

I noticed out of the corner of my eye that Mom was back from her magazine quest, and boarding for Atlanta was underway. We stood up. Max gave me a hug. I kissed him on his cheek. Before I could step back, he softly kissed me on my lips, wrapping his right arm around my waist. I realized my empty arm was now around his neck, but loosely. *Jeez, he smells good. His lips are soft. He tastes pretty damn good too.* I slowly pulled away. However, he didn't immediately release his hold around me. I had to say something. Like an idiot, I reminded him I saw him first on Monday. *It's official; I am not cool.*

Max thanked me for the excitement of the last couple of days. I assured him I was lame, but it was my pleasure just the same. I walked away and thought, *Thank God Max did not French-kiss me. That would have been freaking dangerous.*

Minutes later, our plane was boarding, and Mom and I claimed our seats. I fell asleep before the plane ever took off.

Mom woke me when we were twenty minutes out of Atlanta and asked if I was okay. I nodded yes, trying to wake up from a deep comatose sleep that was not related to diabetes. I raised my seat from the reclining position, and Mom asked about the guys. I told her we exchanged phone numbers. She asked, "Well, that's it?"

"Pretty much," I replied.

We retrieved our luggage and cleared customs, all in less than an hour. Mom phoned Dad, and he said he was circling the passenger pickup line when he spotted us. Mom had been in touch with Dad several times a day. He apparently was more in the know than I had realized. Mom informed him I had a great time, and he remembered the boys.

Tom's offer of dinner was too good to pass up. Comfort food—homemade tomato soup and grilled cheese. I put my bowl in the dishwasher and headed home.

I woke when my BlackBerry beeped. Jeez, I had three unopened messages from Max, Tucker, and Abby. I opened hers first. She was packed and wanted to sleep over with me at my parents' house, because we had to leave for the airport at 4 a.m. Knowing Abby and her sleeping habits, I thought it would be a good idea.

I opened Max's text next. It was simple: *I was just thinking about you. I'm quite bored on this cold Sunday afternoon.*

After pondering over his text for a bit, I sent: *Sorry that it's cold and hate that you're bored. I'm packing for Snowmass, but I do miss you all. Hugs & kisses! I have decided to speak to Robert. Thank you, Max.*

Tucker's text message was last: *Little hot Livvy, is your guest room available New Year's Eve?*

I replied quickly: *ALWAYS!*

He responded: *See you then.*

It was dinnertime when Abby came busting through the front door of my parents' home. "Hey," she shouted. "Where is everyone?"

Dad hollered back from the kitchen, "Come on back." By now my parents' home was loud and bustling, just the way they liked it.

CHAPTER 8

At 4 a.m. sharp, in two vehicles, we pulled out of the driveway bound for the airport.

We checked twelve bags curbside and headed to the gate. Once on the plane and seated, Abby and I shoved our buds into our ears. I was hoping to sleep.

About an hour before we landed, Abby got chatty. From the start of the conversation, she wanted to talk about Luke. She liked him and asked me what she should do. Of all the people in the world, why in God's holy name would she ask me? After all, I kinda sucked at the guy thing. However, I listened like a good friend would, and I offered basic opinions but absolutely zero advice.

I asked her what kind of vibe she was getting from him when they were alone. Good Lord, I opened up a floodgate with that question. But to sum it up, she thought he had softened up while I was in Cabo. They had made out.

Colin, our driver, was waiting, and the van was quickly loaded with our duffel bags. Mom had assigned bag colors weeks ago and had everyone but me purchase their own. Dad was blue. Rae was red. Noel was black. Andi was pink. Bradley didn't get the memo—his duffels didn't match. I have no doubt that Cookie would make sure they matched next year.

Just shoot me now. My bags were a freaking-ugly burnt orange. Not a pretty orange that the sky will sometimes turn. Nor were they Auburn Tigers orange. This was a dreadful orange.

Dad had arranged for Noel, Andi, and Bradley to share a two-bedroom condo and for Mom, him, Rae, Abby, and me to share a three-bedroom. This was a fine arrangement. I didn't mind sharing a room, because my behind would be kicked after snowboarding anyway.

Abby and I unpacked. Dad asked us to join him downstairs; he wanted to know if the two young men visiting every condo looked familiar. I looked out the window, and then stepped out on the beautiful patio with an outdoor fireplace and a view to die to for. I motioned for Abby to join me. We stood there in disbelief. They were crazy. Robert and Luke were knocking on each of the condo patio doors, and the fools were also looking through the windows. Why didn't they just call? I would have given them the condo number.

After watching them for a few more minutes, I hollered out, "Hey! Looking for someone?" Both of them skied down toward us, laughing. They visited a few minutes.

The slopes would close in less than two hours, but we would join in all the fun tomorrow. I told Robert and Luke we would meet up at dinner. They stepped off the patio, hit the snow, and were out of sight in seconds.

After Abby and I had pulled ourselves together, we met everyone for dinner. Luke met Abby and hugged and kissed her. Well, after that kiss, Abby certainly shouldn't have any doubts.

I loved my friend, but I was jealous. Robert met me with a gentle hug. Dinner was served quickly. We ate with our families. Robert sat next to me, and he was chatty. He asked if I had met anyone while I was in Cabo. I lightly filled him in on Tucker, Crosby, and Max. Surprisingly, Robert remembered them.

The village was always beautiful during Christmas, but tonight it was lovelier than ever. Fresh, undisturbed snow was on the ground. The tree limbs hung heavily with more snow, and the white lights strung on the branches made them look even more enchanting. Best of all, I was with Robert, and he had his arm around me. I had those goose bumps I had wanted so badly a few days ago, but had never happened for me when I was with Crosby. I had the guy tonight that gave them to me every time he touched me.

On the short walk back to the condo, Robert asked what I was hoping could be avoided: How were the Cooper brothers and Max Spencer?

I briefly told Robert what each of them was doing and where they lived.

"Did they keep you entertained?"

"They tried," I giggled.

Abby and Luke were nowhere in sight when we arrived at the condo. I stood quietly looking out at the beautiful view before removing my coat. Robert stepped behind me and slid my coat off my shoulders. He hung it on the back of a chair with one hand and reached for my arm with his other hand. He pulled me closer to him and looked at me, as though he was desperately searching for answers. It couldn't be that difficult—he had known me for more than ten years. If he didn't have or know the answers by now, he never would. Then he looked at my lips and kissed me. Seconds later, our lips parted. I could feel his warm breath as he continued to take my lips, mouth—I could taste him for the first time in three years. I melted in his arms, wanting more, ready to give him anything he needed or wanted.

Luke and Abby ambled inside, but they quickly walked out. When Robert released me, he said softly in my ear, "I have wanted to do that for a long time."

"What took you so long?"

"Don't know."

Luke and Abby came bursting back through the door, and Luke asked if we were up for Katt Williams. "Not tonight, but knock yourself out, Luke. You will laugh your butt off." I pointed to my coat and told Robert we had an early morning.

I noticed Dad had made a fire in our patio fireplace. Robert pointed to the chairs. I nodded, and he pulled them closer to the fireplace. He sat down and then patted his leg. I got up from the chair I had just sat down in and had a seat on his lap. He put his arms around me. I kissed him this time, and he certainly didn't seem to mind. The wind was cold on my face, but I didn't care, because right now everything else was warm.

I could tell he was enjoying himself as he gently pulled away from me and said, "Hold on, Livvy." Robert was thoughtful about not letting things get out of control with us, even when we were younger, but not me. Oh no, not at all. I think it had something to do with my medications. I get excited quick. However, this time, Robert never fully released me during our short interlude.

I could tell even though we only had the stars, a half moon, and the fire as our dim lighting tonight, he was in deep thought.

"Livvy, I know you didn't spend your time alone in Cabo," he said. "I know what you look like in a swimsuit. I know I don't have a right to ask you, nor do you owe me an answer. But do I have any competition after your trip?"

Competition? What is he talking about? "Robert," I said, "no one has ever made me feel the way you do, and over the past several years, I have only tried three times."

"Three tries, huh," he said. "I see. May I ask who the third person is, or was?"

"It's not fair for you to ask. I've never asked you anything. Then again, it's easier if you don't know." However, after a couple of seconds, I said softly, "Crosby."

"I see. I thought it would have been Max. I hoped it was Max."

"Why did it matter who it was?" All I could ever seem to feel for anyone was friendship, but I had enough damn friends. "You broke me, and I can't seem to get fixed."

"We aren't broken, but it does matter who it was with." He pulled me closer to him and said, "Max is in New York and London, or will be soon. Crosby is in Birmingham."

"Oh," I said. I began to shiver a bit. He stood up but pulled me close to him once again. "Robert, are you jealous?"

"I don't have the right to answer that."

I promised myself right then I would leave this snowy mountain as part of a couple, or I would leave alone. I wouldn't waste any more time if Robert didn't make a commitment to me. However, I couldn't promise myself I wouldn't waste tears.

Robert held me close and once again said, "I don't have the right to ask, but Crosby's older…Did you spend time alone with him?"

"He never touched me like that. Crosby is older and experienced, but he is a gentleman and asked permission for a first kiss. But you were right. You don't have the right to ask me these questions."

Robert kissed me, tenderly. His warm breath was in my mouth, and I wanted more as his gloved hands moved through the ends of my hair. I could feel through the layers of clothing we were wearing that he needed a break, as he had always said.

* * *

"God, I hope I don't break anything." I chuckled as I pulled on my stylish wool hat and adjusted my pigtails. I frankly told Abby how to dress quickly, or the girl would spend two unnecessary hours getting pretty this morning. I reminded her not to forget her sunblock and ChapStick. She was a beautiful girl, but her skin was almost milky white. This was her first time skiing, so I had taken the liberty of enrolling her in ski school the day before.

After Abby was settled for the day, I was off to meet my instructor. Yesterday I had requested a male. The booking agent I spoke with laughed at first, but added she had the perfect person in mind. To her surprise, Carl had been available. She assigned the meeting spot and told me how lucky I was.

I arrived at the meeting spot, a flagpole, a few minutes early. Someone was standing there. "You Carl?" I asked.

In a perfect Australian accent, he answered, "You must be Livvy." Carl wasn't the type of guy I would consider hot, but for a snowboard instructor, he was perfect.

Carl asked for a recap on what I had retained from the past couple of years. He said we would board a blue today.

I must say, I learned a lot throughout the morning, and after lunch, Carl thought we would try a black. That made me nervous. I could ski the black slopes, but I had never snowboarded down one, because I tended to fall. He assured me he wouldn't let me out of his sight.

While we ate lunch, Carl asked, "Livvy, a pretty girl like you must have someone special in your life."

I glanced at Carl, shrugged my shoulders, and said, "Well, kinda, I think."

"Kinda—what does that mean?"

"He can't figure things out for some reason," I said.

"Well, he better not take too long trying to figure things out. Someone might just snatch you right up."

"I wish he would," I said and slurping my last bite of chicken noodle soup from the spoon.

Carl and I were about to snowboard down a black slope, whether I was ready to or not. We slowly exited off the lift chair. I dragged my board with my foot only in one boot. Once I was off to the side, out of the way of other skiers, I corrected that problem. Carl motioned. "Hit it, girl, I'm right behind you."

I took a deep breath and took off. Carl never left my side. I didn't snowboard fancy, but I went fast. We made it to the bottom of the mountain and looped down to the lift. We were going back up for my last run of the day.

I thanked Carl for his patience with me. Right there on the spot, I booked him again for the next day.

It took me an hour to fetch Abby. We discussed our experiences for the day while we walked to our condo. To my surprise, she loved skiing.

"Hey, Livvy," Abby said as we strung our scarfs around our necks, "be careful, okay? I love Robert, but I love you more."

"I don't understand why Robert doesn't want to be with me. I know he feels something for me. I understand he promised his parents that he wouldn't have a serious relationship until he graduates. But, my Lord, he only lacks three or maybe four semesters at the most. I'm not saying let's get married or anything. I only want him to love me and say he wants to be with me. After two years of dating and three years of whatever this crap is, I'm tired. I need and want more. Things have to change—I need them to change this week, or I..."

"Or what?"

"Nothing." I nodded to the guys' front door.

The four of us tiredly strolled quietly in the packed snow for nearly ten minutes to the Italian restaurant, where we bellied up to the bar at and ate dinner.

Abby and Luke disappeared as soon as we got back to the guys' condo. Robert lit a fire in the fireplace and joined me on the sofa. He pulled me into his lap, but within minutes he was lying flat on his back and I was on top of him. For the first time ever, he slid my V-neck sweater over my head and kissed right above the edges of my bra. I took a deep breath, and so did he. He whispered, "I think I need a break." I rolled over on my side, and so did he. I wanted to tell him I loved him, but I wanted him to tell me that he loved me more. My heart was aching, and I was afraid. *What if he never says the words I so desperately long to hear?*

* * *

The next morning Abby was quickly off to ski school, and I was headed to the flagpole to meet Carl. I glanced down at my black, purple, and white outfit as I exited the lift. I should be easy to spot again today.

That cute thing was waiting on me at our assigned spot. "Good morning, Livvy," he said. "We're starting with a black today."

By lunchtime, Carl had worn my butt out. We were sitting in a corner near a fireplace, having a bite, when I spotted Robert and Luke heading in our direction. As I turned, I noticed David Williams, the film star, sitting behind us, with what appeared to be a couple of buddies. He was cute, smaller than I would have guessed, though. I turned and asked, "Excuse me, may we borrow a couple of chairs?"

What do you know? Mr. Movie Star answered, "Sure—here, let me help you." He slid one of the chairs over. Robert grabbed the other one. I thanked him, but I never acknowledged I knew who he was.

After lunch Robert bent over and kissed me. Then he helped me with my jacket and my hat. He asked, "Six, my place?"

"Yeah."

I turned to Mr. Movie Star and said, "Thank you once again for—"

He interrupted me and said, "You're welcome."

I held my hand out to shake his. "I'm Livvy Hunnicutt."

He smiled and said, "David Williams. Nice to meet you."

I smiled and said, "Nice meeting you, David."

I released his hand and turned around.

"Maybe I will see you around, Livvy Hunnicutt."

By now I was ten feet away from Mr. Movie Star. I said over my shoulder, "Yeah…you never know."

As we walked out, Carl said he totally got what I had said about Robert yesterday. "None of my business or anything—it's not like I know your dude, but don't wait too long. You might let Mr. Right pass you by. I mean, you have a movie star standing at the door right behind us, and he's not looking at me."

"I'll keep that in mind," I said as I wiggled my fingers into my gloves.

Our first run was perfect. The second run, not so much. My binding snapped and caused me to take a nasty tumble, headfirst. Carl got to me quick and wouldn't let me move until he completely checked or asked about most of my body parts. Then he hiked up the mountain thirty feet or so and retrieved my board. He examined it, dropped it, and gave me two thumbs up.

"Let's go," he said. I snapped my boots back on the board and proceeded down the mountain. When we finished the run, I expressed my appreciation to Carl. He was an awesome instructor. We decided to grab coffee, and we sat and talked for a few minutes. He told me if I felt dizzy or if anything felt different to see a doctor. I assured him I would as I took his card and slipped it in my jacket pocket.

CHAPTER 9

I pranced out of the bathroom with a towel around me and a turban on my head. Abby painfully moaned. She fell across the bed and said, "Livvy, I think I'm dying. Every muscle in my body hurts." She moaned louder. "But I love it. Thank you for bringing me."

"Abby," I said, examining her lifeless body, "you're welcome. But sweetie, you really should drink some water, pop two Advil, and shower."

I wore my favorite dark straight-legged True Religion jeans and a soft blue cashmere sweater, and I polished off my outfit with couture boots, the ones with snazzy dangly jewels on the zipper pull. I scooted downstairs to give Abby some much-needed space. She appeared in forty minutes, looking pretty as ever, but still in pain.

On the short walk to the guys' condo, I mentioned to Abby that I might call it an early evening. "I am completely exhausted, and my body hurts."

"And what else?"

"Nothing, really."

"Robert just being Robert, huh." The man in question opened the door about the same time we rolled our eyes.

"What?" he asked.

"Like you don't know, asshole," she said, pulling Luke out the door.

We grabbed a quick dinner, and on the way back to the condo, a fresh layer of snow was dusting the ground. Robert's quietness was driving me nuts, so I struck up a conversation by telling him about my tumble earlier. He came to a halt, and softly brushed the side of my cold cheek. "You're okay, aren't you?"

"Yes. Carl took care of me."

Robert dropped his hand. "You're the kind of girl guys like, but the funny thing is, you could care less. That makes us like you more."

He's full of it. I changed the subject and asked if I could ski with him and Luke tomorrow.

"Giving up snowboarding so soon?"

"Yeah. It totally kicked my butt."

He winked and asked, "Do you think you can keep up?"

He knew I could. We hooked our arms together. "Shouldn't be a problem."

Robert opened the condo's front door and asked, "Where the hell are they?" I knew right then he was afraid to be alone with me. Robert grabbed a small bag and said, "I brought some movies. Choose one." He handed me the bag and disappeared for a couple of minutes. He returned wearing gym pants and a T-shirt. He said he brought me a sweatshirt to change into because I looked cold.

I laughed and said, "Robert, I will be the same person regardless of what I am wearing." He looked at my mouth, appearing to be in deep thought while placing the sweatshirt on the table. "Fine," I shouted, "I'll put it on." I crossed my arms, grabbed the bottom of my sweater, and snatched the damn thing up and over my head.

"Livvy!" he shouted, picking up the sweatshirt and holding it out for me to take. I just stood there shaking my head with one hand on my hip, holding my sweater in my other hand. By now Robert stood less than a foot from me. Something happened. He snatched the sweater from my hand and threw me on the sofa. Then he reached and grabbed me with both hands. "Oh, Robert," I moaned as he kissed me.

Suddenly the front door swung open. "Turn around, Luke," Abby immediately said, and they were gone.

Robert kissed me softly a few more times and released me. He turned and walked halfway across the room and retrieved the sweatshirt. I put it on this time.

"Guess Luke and Abby had good timing," Robert said. He sat down beside me and buried his head in his hands while his elbows rested on his knees. I didn't speak, because I wasn't sure what to say. I certainly wasn't going to apologize, because I didn't think I'd done anything wrong. But I knew Robert had just rejected me. After all, he had his own room upstairs.

Abby and Luke entered again, but with caution. They went straight to Luke's room.

"Robert, I'm tired. Pick me up in the morning, and we'll ski together." I turned around to remove his shirt.

He said, "No, keep it. It's cold out."

I kissed him softly, and he assisted me with my coat. "Hold on, Livvy. I'll walk you."

"Not tonight."

Well, that didn't go so well. What was I thinking anyway? I had never removed my shirt before, and last week was the whole swimsuit thing. Lord, I had to get my head on straight.

* * *

I didn't hear Abby come in last night, but she was sleeping soundly, even with the morning sun gleaming through the open drapes. I stretched and kicked the covers back. I needed a little family time. I joined my dad in the kitchen. He asked me if Abby and I would eat dinner with them. I smiled and said, "Yes, Daddy, we will."

I mentioned the family dinner to Abby when she came down, and she said, "Sounds good," as she ate her last bite of toast and bacon. She headed out the door for ski school and shouted, "Thanks for breakfast, Mr. Tom. See you tonight."

I did have some good news. My ski outfit for the day was a great one: red fitted ski pants and a red and black jacket trimmed in sable with a fun little hat to match. If the guys were a little faster on the slopes today, at least they would be able to spot me a mile away.

The morning passed quickly. Robert may have fancier moves, but I could ski faster. At one o'clock, the fellas were starving. "Abby and I are eating dinner with my family tonight," I said, "and I'm also hanging out with them after."

Robert tapped his fork against his plate and stared at me. I refocused on my half-eaten grilled salmon. "You and Ella are welcome to join us," I said, meeting his bewildered gaze.

"We will. Ella will be thrilled to hang out with the big girls."

"Y'all ready?" Luke asked as he stood.

"You look pretty today," Robert said as he zipped my jacket. He popped a quick kiss on my forehead.

Robert took the lead and held it for a few minutes, but when we hit the halfway mark down the mountain, I tucked and skied around him. I waited on him and Luke at the bottom of the mountain.

Well, whatta you know? I spotted Mr. Movie Star. He all but stopped right in front of me and said, "Nice moves, Livvy Hunnicutt. I thought you were a snowboarder." He flashed me his pearly whites.

"I do both, David Williams, and I see that you ski well."

He slowly skied in a small circle around me and said, "I hope to see you around," then he caught up with the group of people he was skiing with.

Robert asked who he was. "David Williams."

Luke asked, "Is he your friend yet?"

"No, you fool."

"You've been holding back," Robert said. "One more run?"

"Sure, and I'll let you win this time."

"Shut up. Gloating is not flattering."

After our family dinner, I stayed with my family for the evening, and Abby detoured to meet up with Luke.

Robert popped in with his sister, Ella, after dinner. Rae and I played board games with her until I noticed she had rubbed her eyes a few times. Robert noticed too. I helped Ella with her coat and hat while Robert put her gloves on for her. He asked, "See you tomorrow morning, right?"

"Yeah," I said, "at ten?" And then I mentioned pizza at his place tomorrow night.

He leaned close to me and said, "Only if you keep your shirt on."

"Livvy," Ella asked, "when are you and Robert going to be boyfriend and girlfriend again? I miss you."

"It's late, Ella," Robert said. "We need to go."

I hugged her bundled body and said, "I don't know, Ella."

The next morning I achingly stretched and shuffled to the bathroom. As I washed my hands, I looked at my reflection in the mirror and wondered if I would ever be truly happy. If he loved me, why not tell me? If he didn't love me, I wished he would just say it. It would hurt, but at least I would know. I shook off the heavy, dressed, and joined Dad in the kitchen.

I nibbled the entire time Dad made breakfast. I checked the time and realized I had to get a move on.

I went with lime green today—definitely not my color, but the outfit was cool.

Ten o'clock sharp, Robert and Luke came barreling through the front door. "Mr. Tom, something smells good," Luke said.

Dad pointed his finger in the direction of the kitchen and told the boys they were welcome to eat. Dad didn't have to tell those guys twice. They each grabbed a plate and quickly filled it. I poured them each a glass of juice, and they finished their last bite while walking out the door.

Luke said he liked my ski pants. He said he knew he'd be able to spot me quickly as I passed him today. Robert laughed. I apologized to Luke for being a smart-ass to him yesterday. I had sprayed him a few times, but good God, he skied like a grandpa.

Robert gave me a quick smack on my butt. I jumped, and he said, "Livvy, it's okay if you stay in front of me today. I like your view from behind as well as from the front."

"When I pass you, on my last and final run for the day, I'll remind you of what you said."

"Yeah, I know you will," he quipped back. "Hey, six tonight, right?"

"Yeah, see you then," I said as I slowly skied past him.

I wanted a power nap, but I had too much crap running through my head. I was worried about tonight. I had made myself a promise, and I was going keep it. I needed to talk to someone. I needed advice.

I thought about calling Tucker or Max. I knew Tucker would suggest something like, "Robert, look, boy, this is your last chance. Take it, or I'm outta here." Max would say something similar. Crosby thought I should have spoken up a long time ago and moved on. *Face it, Livvy. You are on your own.*

Back at the condo, I sat my iPod on the dock and listened to Jason Mraz while I applied makeup and dressed casually.

The guys were hungry as usual, so we ordered pizza and had a couple of drinks while we waited for the delivery.

Abby and Luke announced they were now a couple. Luke had asked her last night. I looked at Robert, and he looked at me. Robert said, "That's great, you two."

"Oh, Abby, that's wonderful," I said sincerely.

Thank God we had finished dinner. I needed a distraction to keep from crying. I picked up the empty pizza boxes and disappeared into the kitchen. Robert disappeared outside but returned holding my coat, gloves, hat, and a blanket. He pointed to the patio door. "I'm happy for them," I choked out, walking outside and sitting down next to the roaring fire.

Robert moved his chair closer to mine. "Yeah."

I realized my new friends were right. This was not going anywhere. I stood up but only to sit back down on his lap. I covered us with the blanket and kissed him softly on his lips, and he kissed me back. I wanted this moment to last forever. His arms were tight around me, and I was searching desperately in his deep brown eyes for some answers, but nothing was there. "Robert, do you love me?" I finally asked.

"Yes," he said, "I love you." Robert slid me off his lap. He stepped closer to the roaring fire.

I eased closer to him. "Why don't you want to be with me?" I couldn't hold the floodgate of tears any longer. I began to cry. He didn't answer.

"Is it because of my health? Is it the diabetes?" I asked.

He stopped me. "No, it's not about your health."

"What is it then? I can't take this anymore. You won't give me any answers. I don't want to be just a vacation girlfriend or a girl you take out when it's convenient. I want to be the girl you can't wait to be with, the girl that excites you in every way. I want to be the girl who you love. I only want you to love me, Robert."

"You do excite me."

"Well, what is it? Answer me, Robert. I need an answer. Then I'll know what to do with my life. I'm tired of waiting if you don't want me. I feel as though my life is at a standstill. If I knew you wanted to be with me, I would wait longer. But I'm going crazy trying to figure you out. I want you in my life, but not like this."

Robert reached out, took my hands, and held them. He looked at me and said, "I'm sorry." He kissed me on my cheek and said, "I…" He paused. "I have to…" He paused again.

"You have to what, Robert?" Louder I repeated myself. "You have to do what?"

He closed his eyes and pulled me closer to him. "Let you go," he whispered. He released me and turned to face the fire once again. I was crushed. *Maybe I misunderstood him.* But I knew after watching him for a moment I hadn't. He had really said it.

"Let me go?" I screamed. "Why? This makes no sense. You said you loved me." My heart was pounding. The tears wouldn't stop running down my cold face.

"Livvy, go. Just go—don't make this more difficult than it is."

"What?" I reached for him.

He pulled away. "Go, Livvy. I don't want you."

He doesn't want me. My palms were pressed tightly against my head. *This isn't right.* Robert turned and faced the fire again. I had to go. Leave. Get out of here. I didn't ever want to see him again. I started running, but I slipped and fell in the snow. Robert pulled at my arm to help me up.

"I don't understand," I shouted. "Get back, Robert. Go away and never touch me again." I tried three times to stand, but I continued to slip and fall. I shouted again, "Get away from me!"

He was reaching for me. "Let me help you up. Please, Livvy?"

I lowered my voice, looked right at him, and, gritting my teeth, said, "I don't want you to help me. Not ever."

Noel and Bradley were on the patio three doors down. They both ran to help me. "Back up, Robert. We got her."

"What happened?" Bradley asked when we cleared the patio door.

I was still crying, but between sniffles I managed to say, "Robert said he loved me, and I love him. But he said he had to let me go." I cried harder, if that was possible. I glanced at Abby, and her mouth dropped open. Rae unzipped my coat. Abby grabbed hers and stormed out the open patio door. Knowing Abby, she would try to get some answers, but I knew whatever Robert's problem was, he wasn't saying.

Mom and Dad were still out, thank God. At least they didn't witness my breakdown. Ducky may have been on his patio, but he thought Robert was an idiot most of the time anyway. He wouldn't tell.

I asked Bradley to find a flight tonight or earlier than noon tomorrow. I couldn't be on the same flight as Robert. Rae was packing my things for me. I knew at that moment I was locking my heart up, and no one would ever hurt me again. I had allowed this to happen. I should have known better.

Bradley stood in the doorway of the bedroom and said he found one direct flight to Birmingham at 7:25 a.m. the next morning. "Book it," Rae said.

Rae was about to stuff my jacket in the bag when I saw it was the one I had worn the last day I snowboarded with Carl. I asked her to check the pockets for a card.

I dialed the number. On the other end of the phone, a pleasant voice said, "Hello."

"Carl?" I asked. My voice was still shaking and weak from crying, and I still had tears steadily streaming down my face.

"Yes," he said. Before I could tell him my name, he asked, "Livvy, what is the matter?"

"Carl," I said, "my apologies for calling so late, but I was wondering if you…" I paused.

"Spit it out, girl."

"I need a ride to the airport."

"Now?" he asked.

"No, Carl, early in the morning," I said.

"Sure, I can do that. What time?"

"Six."

"Yeah, no worries."

"Thanks, Carl."

My sister and Andi had completely packed most of my things when I excused myself.

I had to get a handle on myself. I knew my blood sugar would get out of control if I didn't. I checked it and gave myself a correction bolus.

Now I had to make arrangements for when I landed in Birmingham. My choices were Tucker or Crosby. We also had family members there, but it was close to the holidays, and they had small children. I thought about renting a car, but I didn't know if I would feel like driving. I cried harder.

During this breakdown, I decided to text Tucker: *Hi there. I took your advice concerning Robert. It didn't turn out as I had hoped. I'm leaving Colorado in the morning. Do you think you could pick me up from the airport at 11:45? Thx, Livvy.*

I ran a tub of water. I lay back in the water and tried to relax.

My phone beeped. Tucker texted: *I'll pick you up, Livvy. I can take you to Auburn, or you can stay the night. I'm sorry.*

Seconds later Max texted: *I'm sorry, Livvy. Let me know if I can help.*

I texted Tucker: *Thank you.*

Crosby texted: *I'm sorry, Livvy. I'm here if you need me. I got your phone number in Cabo.*

I texted Max back: *I guess that rope wasn't so long after all. Thank you, Max.*

I texted Crosby: ☺

I soaked in the tub and cried. Later, I cried myself to sleep.

CHAPTER 10

I turned my alarm off before it sounded. I quickly got out of bed, dressed, and gathered up a few straggling items.

I told Abby bye and that I'd call in a couple of days. She gave me a hug and resumed her sleeping position.

I was quiet as I left the bedroom and even quieter walking down the stairs. When I turned the corner, Dad was standing at the front door where Bradley had placed my bags for me last night.

"Going somewhere?"

"Thought I'd head out before the crowd today."

"Do you have transportation to the airport?"

"Yes, sir."

"Do you have a ride home from the Atlanta airport?"

"Uh, well, you see," I said, "I'm flying into Birmingham instead. A friend is picking me up, and I might spend the night there. But I'll come home tomorrow."

"Livvy, if you need anything, call. I'm not going to ask what happened between you and Robert. But this needs to end. Understood?"

"It ended, Daddy," I said with tears pooling in my eyes. He wrapped his arms around me and told me I was still his little girl. *Yep, and always will be.* I broke his bear hold and put my sunglasses on, because face it, I looked plain awful.

Carl knocked softly on the door. I swung it open.

"Good morning, Livvy," Carl said and grabbed my large bag.

We approached the airport. I thanked Carl and attempted to pay him for his time, but he wouldn't accept anything. He unloaded my bags and helped me get checked in. I gave him a hug, and he said, "Livvy, you are a beautiful girl, inside and out."

Clear skies. That meant my plane would leave on time. Twenty minutes later I was sitting in a first-class seat.

I stuck my iPod buds in my ears and cranked up the volume. The flight attendant approached me. I removed my buds and ordered a juice.

After a three-hour nap, I checked my blood sugar and asked Dan, the flight attendant, for a sandwich and a Bloody Mary, and to go ahead and make it a double. I lowered my sunglasses into their proper position, because I knew my looks had not improved over the past four hours.

I ate my sandwich and drank my nerve pill in a glass as Dan announced we would land in twenty minutes.

While sitting on the runway waiting to taxi to the gate, I sent two text messages. First, Rae. I thanked her for the ticket. Next, Tucker. I told him the plane was taxiing, and I would meet him in baggage claim.

He texted back: *I am waiting at carousel number three. See you in a few.*

Jeez, am I weaving? "Yeah, I am," I mumbled. *Fine timing that Bloody Mary had.* I found baggage claim and carousel number three. Through my shades I saw Tucker standing there, looking straight at me from a distance. I smiled widely as I approached him. We hugged.

"Are you drunk?" he asked.

"Probably," I snapped. Tucker placed his arm around me as carousel number three began to spin.

"So what color are your bags?"

I shook my head, remembering. "Both are hideous orange duffels."

His tall, handsome self peered down at me, with his arm wrapped around me, and he grinned. Guess he thought I would fall flat on my face if he let me go. We spotted my bags. He slowly released his arm from around me. Then he reached out with both hands and lifted my bags from the spinning carousel as though they were two-liter drinks.

"Well, now, both bags at the same time," I said. He grinned and asked me once more if I was okay. "Oh yeah," I answered as we walked. I was probably talking real smart by now after my morning cocktails. "Tucker," I asked, "is that offer of yours still good? I realize tomorrow is Christmas Eve. I can go to Auburn today."

"Livvy, I don't have anything to do until tomorrow night," he said. "We'll do whatever you want, but I want to remind you Crosby and I live together."

"Oh yeah," I said. That totally had slipped my mind. "You know, Tucker, Crosby had my number."

Tucker laughed and said, "Yeah, he got it from me before we left Cabo." He stopped right at the trunk of his car.

"Niiice…Tucker. I'd never guessed you for a classy, sporty man."

He laughed while he placed my bags on the ground next to his BMW and escorted me to the passenger side. I sat down, and he not only pulled the seatbelt around me but also buckled it. I gave up and lay my head back and relaxed. The car shook when he put my ugly orange duffels in the trunk, and he was sitting at my side with his car cranked before I could lift my head up to thank him.

The radio was on, and of all the freaking songs, "Someday" was playing. I loved that song until last night. On the drive to his house—or I should say, *their* house—Tucker asked me if I wanted to talk about it.

"No," I said. But I continued, so I guess I did want to talk about it. "I decided to talk to Robert because I needed answers. I told him I refused to be his vacation girlfriend or a friend who he sometimes treated as a girlfriend." I fanned my hands around. "I wanted it all. Robert said he loved me, but within two minutes he said he had to let me go. He didn't want me. What's the deal? You love someone, but you have to let her go?"

I caught my breath and began to rant again. "After he told me he had to let me go, he turned and wouldn't look at me. He still hadn't answered me, so I asked him if it was because of my health. I'm no fool. I know that's a lot to think about and take into consideration. He said no. I asked him if he was not attracted to me—you know, if I excited him. He said I excited him, but now after thinking about it, I'm not so sure. But anyway, I started running. I fell in the snow several times. He tried to help me up, and I told him not to ever touch me again. You see, Tucker—"

Tucker interrupted me. "Back up, Livvy. Everyone is attracted to you."

"Tucker," I said with my voice louder, "I don't know so much about that. You see, a couple of nights ago, I threw myself at him. He didn't, well, you know, take me up on my…offer."

"You mean you haven't slept with him, ever?"

I shrugged my shoulders and said, "We've shared a bed." I rolled my eyes at Tucker. "It's not like I haven't wanted to."

"You mean you have not ever had sex with anyone?"

"Nope, not ever."

"That's a shocker," Tucker said, shaking his head. He glanced at me and after a slight pause, said, "Livvy, Robert must be gay."

"No, that's not it. But I know one thing: I'm done with him, and I'm considering never loving again, because I will never allow myself to get hurt again. However, I do want to have sex. I discovered that when Crosby and I had a couple of light make-out sessions. Well, heck, other than an untimely kiss from Robert earlier this month, Crosby was the first real kiss I've had in more than two years. It's been so long, I'm surprised I remembered how."

When we stepped inside their home, he pointed to the kitchen and the den. I was still tipsy, and I needed to pee. I headed in some sort of a direction and found a bathroom. When I came out of the bathroom, I needed a nap. I removed my Juicy jacket and velour pants, which I had worn for two days; however, I left my fancy T-shirt and boyshort panties on. I flung the covers back and climbed into someone's bed, but dang if it didn't spin.

A few seconds later, I heard Tucker as he brought my bags inside I didn't open my eyes, even though I could feel he was in the room with me.

Tucker's phone rang. He stepped out of the bedroom. "I think she's okay, drunk, though." *Oh great*, I thought. He was talking about me to either Crosby or Max. Then he said, "She was quite a chatterbox, and by the way, brother…" *Well, now I know he was speaking to Crosby.* "Just to give you a heads-up, she's in your bed, and her clothes are on the floor. I went out to the car to get her bags. I thought she was going to the bathroom. Guess she was tired." *All right, I'd heard enough.* I felt myself drifting off to sleep.

When I woke up, Tucker was propped up on the other side of the bed, reading. "How long did I sleep?" I yawned.

"About an hour," he said.

My weary eyes navigated to the open doorway, where Crosby was leaning.

"Didn't think I'd be seeing you so soon," he said, easing one hand into his front pocket.

Tucker scooped his scattered papers up into neat stacks. He mentioned he had more work to do and left the room.

I grinned and added a hardy yawn. The corner of Crosby's lip curled. *Dang, if he isn't just sexy-looking.*

"Well, that makes two of us." I kicked the covers off, forgetting I had no pants on.

I asked if they had a guest room I could stay in for the night. He said they used it for an office, but I could use his room.

"I'd love to shower." He nodded as I sat Indian-style on the floor and began to ransack my bags. "You know, Crosby," I said, tossing a few articles of clothing on the floor, "Rae and Andi packed for me. I have absolutely no idea where to find my clean clothes."

He sat down next to me and asked, "Need a hand?"

"Thanks, but I found what I was looking for." Clean jeans, a sweater, pajamas—I left those lying on top of my open bag, which looked like a bomb had exploded in it. Crosby hopped up. "Sorry. Let me give you some privacy."

I stood up. "No, you're good." I pointed to his bath and asked, "Okay, or do you prefer I use a different one?"

"Mine is okay, Livvy."

I picked up my toiletry bag and laid my clothing on the foot of his bed. "Thank you, Crosby."

Before I turned the shower on, I heard Tucker talking to Crosby. Tucker told him it was over with Robert, giving him a quick recap of what we'd discussed. I didn't realize I had shared so much info with Tucker.

"Do you remember what we all wondered about her?" Tucker asked. *No, oh God. Please don't say it, Tucker.*

"How could I forget?" Crosby said.

"Well, brother…"

No, Tucker, please don't."

"Livvy said it," Tucker paused. "Apparently, she offered herself to Robert, but he didn't take the bait. Watch it, Crosby. Livvy said she wants to have sex, with you."

"What?" Crosby said.

"There's more. Did you know that other than one kiss from Robert earlier this month, you are the first person she has kissed in more than two years?"

"You're kidding?" Crosby said.

I threw my hands over my face and gasped. I didn't remember telling him that. Now they all know I haven't been deflowered yet!

I felt better after I showered, but I was still enormously embarrassed. I wrapped the towel around me and gave the corner a tight tuck underneath my arm. I swooped my hair into another towel and swung open the bathroom door, not thinking. Too late. Crosby was sitting on the edge of his bed. "Have you eaten today?"

"Yes," I said, "around eleven. I should eat a simple snack, though."

Crosby said he would get me something so my blood sugar wouldn't bottom out.

I dressed quickly. Unfortunately, all I managed to get on was my bra and panties before Crosby barged in. Oh dear God, my hair was still bundled up in a towel. This, I was certain, was not a good look for me.

He quickly glanced down to the floor, handed me a yogurt and a spoon, and then backpedaled out the door faster than he'd arrived. This time, he closed the door behind him. "Thank you," I said, loud enough for him to hear.

"Welcome," he shouted back. Now that was awkward. I guess the whole virgin thing was a problem. I shook my head in disbelief and popped a spoonful of yogurt in my mouth.

Minus my socks and shoes, I put forth an effort to get completely dressed, because these fellas probably thought at this point I never wore clothing.

They closed their laptops when I walked into the room.

"You look nice," Tucker said.

Crosby nodded and lifted his brow slightly. He asked if I wanted to go out or stay in for dinner. I told him I'd rather stay in, and I'd love to cook for them. They both looked at me strangely again. Tucker said he thought they'd like to order takeout. They both had a craving for P.F. Chang's.

"That's your craving, Tucker," Crosby smarted off. "I'm afraid I won't be able to have what I'm craving." Then he looked right at me. I told Tucker Chang's sounded great.

Crosby cleared out to shower. I flopped down on the sofa. Tucker barely looked in my direction. I could tell he was thinking, because he would pinch his lips together and take deep breaths, just as he had in his car earlier. I finally told him how much I appreciated him picking me up from the airport and looking after me today. He smiled.

"You talk too much when you're drunk."

"You're right," I admitted, "but you can't keep a secret. You told Crosby everything I told you this morning."

"Yep."

I hopped up and headed back to Crosby's bedroom. I could at least make the bed. After all, it had been made neatly before I had taken a nap in it.

My back was toward the bathroom door. I didn't hear Crosby slip up behind me as I smoothed his goose down comforter, but when he wrapped his arms around my waist, I slowly tilted my neck to the side. He sweetly brushed my hair away with his hand. I felt his warm breath on my skin, and then he trailed soft kisses down my neck.

I could feel his damp, just-toweled body against me. I turned around and ran my hand through his wet hair and pulled him close as I kissed him. He gently pushed me, and we fell onto the bed. He broke our landing with his forearm as he held me tightly in his other arm.

Tucker knocked on the open door and asked to speak to Crosby.

Crosby released me, rolled over onto his back, and said, "Sorry about that." He got up and disappeared into his closet, coming out in two seconds dressed in gym pants and a T-shirt. I didn't move. I could hear them talking, even though they were in the kitchen. Tucker had a better idea of my feelings toward Crosby than Crosby did, or at least that was the impression I was under, until I heard Crosby say, "I know she's not over him, but at least I know it's over."

"Maybe, maybe not," Tucker said. "Be careful. She thinks she needs something right now. She said it herself. Don't do anything either of you would regret later." After a moment of quietness, Tucker continued. "Livvy is different. She's not like the girls you bring home from the bar at midnight, and they're lucky if you let them stay two hours. You remember what I told you, right? I don't want to see you hurt, but please don't take anything from her that she can't get back in the morning."

"You're right," Crosby said.

That was it. Those two were talking about me like I wasn't there.

I stormed into the kitchen, threw my hands up, and shouted, "My God, I heard every word you two said about me." I had their attention now. "Tucker, I'm a big girl. You're right, I haven't had sex, but I do enjoy making out. And who says you have to be in love to have sex, anyway? It seems to be working fine for Crosby, or it has up until now. Tucker, I am certain you have had your share of sex without being in love. For a minute, forget I'm a virgin, and Crosby, let's pretend," I said hotly, pointing my finger in the direction of the bedroom, "that you and I are in your room like before. I don't think any of us would be having this conversation, now would we? I'll answer that question for the both of you. No, of course not. Tucker," I said, glaring at him, "maybe you need to show me what I'm doing wrong, because you seem to know so much." I marched right up to him. "I need some more damn practice, because apparently"—my voice cracked—"I'm grossly inexperienced or hopelessly just not good enough."

He stepped back against the cabinet, and I stepped closer to him. I stood on my tiptoes and threw my arms around his neck, and I kissed him. He didn't put his arms around me. As a matter of fact, he threw his hands up like I was robbing him so he wouldn't or couldn't hold me. But I kissed him, and after a few seconds, I parted my lips, and so did he. Tucker made a sound deep in his throat, and so did I. I pulled myself closer to him, and our bodies were flat against each other. If Crosby weren't standing in the same room, I think Tucker would have enjoyed it. On second thought, he *was* enjoying it. I could feel him as he was pressed against me. *Whoa. Tucker can kiss.* I felt myself… Crosby cleared his throat.

Tucker pulled away, and I released my hold around his neck. I backed up and shouted, "So what's wrong with me?"

Tucker threw his hands back up into the air and said, "Not a damn thing. I only hate I didn't see you first. And, by the way, you are good enough."

"I guess you see what I'm talking about now, big brother," Crosby said.

Tucker picked up his cell and car keys off the counter and said he was picking up dinner. He asked, "Chicken, right, Livvy?" I nodded, and he left.

I slowly walked past Crosby. He reached for my arm. I stopped but didn't look at him. "Guess Tucker and I deserved that," he said. He pointed to the sofa.

"You sure? I mean, do you want me to leave?"

"Sit," he said, "and no, I don't want you to leave." We sat down. "Now that you've kissed Tucker, I think I'm a little jealous." He ran his hand through his hair. "Livvy, let me try to explain the way I feel. You are desirable, and I have wanted to, um, you know, since Cabo. The last night we were together on the beach when we shared the chair, it was all I could do not to ask you. But, good God, when you straddled my lap and began to kiss me…"

I smiled.

"I wanted you more than you will ever know, and I still want you. But you have waited this long. Wait for love. Let your first time be special."

"I did wait for love. I was in love."

"Livvy, wait until it's the right guy. Although I hope I'm your guy, and if I am…I won't let you go." Crosby kissed me on the side of my head and whispered, "I also promise you, if I am your guy, I will make love to you."

"Crosby," I said, a little teary, "I don't want to fall in love again, but I do want to have sex…or at least…"

"At least, what?"

"Never mind."

We sat quietly for a moment, and then I began to talk again. "Crosby, counting you and Tucker, I've kissed six people. I'm not keeping score, but come to think of it, I'm not sure if two of them even count."

"Why is that?" Crosby asked.

"No tongue."

Crosby tightened his arm around me and said, "I hope one of the two was Tucker."

"No, it was Justin and Max."

"No, you don't have to count them. Wait—you kissed Max?"

"Yeah…no. He kissed me good-bye at the airport. Crosby, since I'm telling you everything, you could help me with something."

"What's that?"

"I've never had a…" I paused and bit my bottom lip.

"Livvy, I don't understand what you're trying to ask me."

"Crosby," I said, "I've only made out with Robert and you." I closed my eyes. "I think I was close that night with you…" I opened my eyes and looked at him. "On the beach, but—"

"An orgasm?" I nodded. "Good God, Livvy. You've never? Not even if—" he started, but he didn't bother to finish his thought. He understood what I was talking about now, loud and clear. I thought he was going to jump off the sofa, carry me to his car, and take me home right then, shipping my bags to me because it would have taken too damn long to throw them into the trunk of his car.

"No, I never have."

He looked surprised. But I'm not sure if he was surprised that I asked him to help me out, or if he was more surprised that I had never. But, my Lord, it was true.

He kissed me on my lips and said, "You are perfect, Livvy Hunnicutt."

"No, I'm not."

I met Tucker at the door and helped him with the food.

I set the table for dinner while Tucker sorted out our orders. Crosby removed a couple bottles of wine from the wine rack and grabbed the Rabbit wine opener and glasses. Tucker said grace. After his "thank you, Father, for our food, family, and misbehaving friend spiel," I apologized for kissing him. "I probably owe you an apology, Crosby, because I kissed Livvy back," Tucker said. "Those are some crazy-soft lips. I'd like to kiss her again."

Crosby gave him a brotherly punch on the shoulder. "Better not. But now that you have French-kissed her…you're number four."

After dinner Crosby disappeared for a couple of minutes, and I helped Tucker clean up the kitchen. Tucker asked if eleven o'clock was okay to leave for Auburn in the morning. I told him that was great.

He kissed me on the cheek. "Good night, Livvy. Behave, would you?"

* * *

It was still early, only eight o'clock. Crosby returned to the kitchen to make sure everything was put away. He asked if I wanted to watch a movie in the den or in his room.

"Your room, but I need a girly moment first." He laughed. I scooted past him into his room. I grabbed my toothbrush and pajamas from the top of my bag and headed to the bathroom.

After I freshened up, I swung the bathroom door open. Crosby walked into the bedroom at the same time. "Lord, help me," he begged as he kicked the bedroom door closed with the back of his foot, never moving his eyes from me. I stepped closer and reached for his T-shirt, but he crossed his arms and pulled it over his head. Crosby grabbed me with such force that I lost my balance and fell against the wall. He clasped my hands, pinning them one-handed above my head. "You okay?" he murmured against my lips.

"Yes," I replied, nearly breathless. He pressed his body flat against mine. He kneed my legs apart and ran his free hand slowly down my side, pausing at my hip; then, swiftly, he firmly gripped the cheek of my butt and kissed me deeper. He released my hands and my butt. My wrists tingled where he had held them tightly. I pulled the drawstring on his black low-riding gym pants and pushed them over his hips. They hit the floor. He stepped out. He lifted me, took a few steps, and dropped me on his bed, then grinned like the devil. I grasped his shoulders and pulled him down on top of me. He covered my nearly naked body with his and took my lips so hard, I moaned, "Crosby."

We rolled, which put me on top. I broke away from kissing him and sat up, only to straddle him. Crosby grabbed my cami right in the center, ripped it from my body, and threw it. He studied my breasts for a moment and then pulled me down flat to his chest. "God, I want you, but I will not…" He paused once again, but only to kiss me, and then he whispered, "I will not touch you there. I want you to remain pure, at least for now."

I whispered, "I know."

Crosby rolled me back over. I now was on bottom, and he was lying on top of me. I parted my legs. He raised himself slightly, and with one hand, he ripped my lacy panties.

"Can I...touch you?" I murmured.

"Yes." He kissed me gently, moving from my lips to my neck, then my breasts.

"Ah," I whispered, as my body tingled to its core. For a moment he surveyed my *I want more* expression. He returned to my breasts. I touched him. My hand stilled. I knew he would be impressive, because I had gotten a glimpse of him totally naked a few moments ago, and I had felt him pressed against me a few times, but it was different to hold him. Crosby asked if I was okay. "Yes," I answered. Crosby caught my gaze. "Please, Crosby...please touch me."

He brushed the side of my face with the back of his hand and whispered, "I can't, Livvy, I wouldn't be able to stop."

We rolled and fell off the bed, but I barely noticed. His touch was soft, and he made each move carefully as he kissed my inner thighs. I ran my hands through his hair and moaned. He kneed my legs further apart and worked his way to my belly and then my breasts, which he kissed with urgency. I wrapped my arms around him and pulled him closer to my arched body. I moaned louder, but so did he. He tugged a handful of my hair at the nape of my neck, making my face spring up to his. His eyes looked different—glassy, and darker. "That's it, you're almost there," he said in a low, raspy tone. Then he kissed me and spoke against my lips. "Let go, Livvy." He tucked his knee firmly between my legs, right against me. Suddenly I felt a rush like never before surge within my body. I trembled. I could feel it happening for him as well as he pressed harder against my body, digging into my belly, with my hand tightly caged around the middle of his manhood. Crosby remained faithful to his word. But just the same, my inner princess whooped—*I did it. I had one. I want to do it again.*

Crosby released me and rolled over on his back. Moments later he stood and pulled me to my feet. He hugged me tightly. We fell back onto the bed in each other's arms.

"It appears, Livvy Hunnicutt, it is possible to finish up and not take anything from you." Crosby was right. I didn't sacrifice my virginity, but it certainly wasn't because I didn't want to.

"Are you okay?"

"Yes," I said and kneaded my hand across his meaty chest. "You know, Crosby, I've never touched a man before, nor have my breasts been touched…until tonight."

He dragged me on top of him and brushed my hair from my face. "Livvy," he said, "I hadn't pictured you to be a screamer."

"Shut up, Crosby."

"Livvy," Crosby said sweetly, "I'm sorry about not being neater…" He paused and ran his hand across my sticky stomach. "Let's shower."

CHAPTER 11

The next morning Crosby eased out of bed. Tucker had warned him to sleep on the sofa. I could feel both of them standing in the bedroom doorway staring at me.

"Shit, what happened in here?" Tucker shouted, standing next to the bed. "Livvy, wake up."

I flipped over and sat up quickly, barely holding the twisted sheet around me. "I'm fine," I shouted back.

"Crosby, did you not listen to anything I told you last night?"

"Every word. I never touched Livvy. Well…at least not like that."

"For God's sake," I shouted, "I'm still a freaking virgin, and at the rate I'm going, I'll never lose it. I never should have told you, Tucker." I fell back onto the bed and covered my face with my hands.

"Oh," he said, changing the tone of his voice. "Hope you didn't like that."

I leaned over and looked on the floor to see what he was referring to. He was staring at my ruined pajamas. "Yeah, I did."

He was still looking down at the floor. He gave my garments a kick and then hung a painting back on the wall. He laughed and punched Crosby on the arm. "I hope you know what you're doing."

"Well, it was a new experience for me, but I figured out how to make it work."

"I see. That must have been the reason for the screaming."

I buried my face in my hands. "You heard that?"

"Hell, I'm not deaf. It went on for two hours."

It was eight o'clock. I joined the guys in the kitchen, and Tucker offered to make me breakfast. Instead, I offered to make them breakfast. After last night, I hoped he'd consider it a peace offering.

I made pancakes and bacon, cut up fresh fruit, and warmed the syrup. Tucker was shocked. Not only could I cook, but I also cleaned up to boot. I wasn't as spoiled and lacking in the domestic department as he'd thought.

Afterward, I motioned for Crosby to follow me into the bathroom. After we'd brushed our teeth, he used a towel to dab some toothpaste off my chin. He tossed the towel, grabbed the hem of his white T-shirt, which I was wearing, and pulled it over my head.

It was almost a complete repeat of last night, and Crosby, unfortunately, kept his promise once again.

Crosby quickly dressed and walked out the bedroom door but then came back in. "Sorry, I forgot to do this." He kissed me. "I need to run somewhere."

Forty minutes later, I was dragging my bags to the door when he returned, from apparently, shopping.

"Hold up, I'll get those for you." When I looked up, he was holding a small wrapped gift. "Got you something. It is Christmas Eve, you know. Open it." By now Crosby had Tucker's attention as well. "It's nothing, really."

"You shouldn't have," I gigged. Pj's—identical to the ones he ruined last night.

* * *

"Girl, I'm going to miss you, but I'll see you next week," Tucker said from the backseat of Crosby's car.

I looked at Crosby. "You're coming, right?"

"Yeah, I can arrange it."

I wondered what Crosby was in deep thought about. I reached over and drew imaginary circles with my pointer finger on his thigh, thinking I sure did like his jeans, or maybe I liked the way he wore them, who knows. He lifted my hand, kissed it, and held it for a while. Tucker said, "Turn it up." Crosby released my hand and pressed the volume button on his steering wheel, and we all sang along with the band Train to "Hey, Soul Sister." When the song ended, Tucker tapped my shoulder and said he was confused about something.

Knowing Tucker, this was not going to be good. "What are you confused about?"

"Now that we've kissed, why am I ranked number four? I know I kiss better than Crosby."

"Oh, it's not about performance. It's the sequence in which they've occurred."

"You've only kissed four guys," he chuckled, "and two of us are in the same car? Damn."

"Six if I count Justin and Max. But then again, we didn't French kiss, so Crosby said I didn't have to count them."

"Yeah, Crosby's right. You don't need to count them. When did you kiss Max?"

"At the airport."

"Oh, I thought there for a minute Crosby might get jealous again."

Tucker was on a roll. He just had to ask, "How did you two knock a painting off the wall, tear clothes, destroy the bed, clear off a night table, and keep Livvy intact?"

"That's how she remained intact," Crosby laughed.

"Hey, I'm sitting right here. Stop talking about me."

We were in Auburn at a traffic light when Crosby asked, "Where to?"

"My parents' house." He took a left.

I had texted Rae earlier and told her I was bringing surprise guests and to please set two more places for our late Christmas Eve luncheon.

I had butterflies and not the good kind, but I didn't know why. I knew Robert was busy with family events over the next few days, so I wouldn't run into him. And the day after Christmas, he and his brother were going on a hunting trip up north. They wouldn't return until after New Year's.

Before I left Colorado, I had Bradley block Robert's cell number so Robert wouldn't have direct access to me. I thought it might help us both, and it would buy me some time to allow my heart to heal.

I forgot I was holding Crosby's hand when we joined my family in the kitchen. Noel noticed. I smiled at my brother, and he did that cool head nod thing guys do to Crosby and shook his hand. Well, on a positive note, there was no need for introductions, except for Bradley. But of course he had heard the lake stories about these guys and was pleased to finally meet them.

Dad shook the guys' hands. He slapped Crosby on the shoulder and told him he had always liked him. Dad turned to take the turkey out of the oven.

Mom hugged everyone. "I'm glad you brought guests, Livvy."

Rae was beside herself. She hadn't seen Tucker in four years, and it had been more than two since she had seen Crosby. Rae asked about Max, and Tucker filled her in.

I overheard Mom thanking Crosby for being there for me. He looked over at me and winked. Then I heard Cookie ask, "Is she doing all right? Tom and I are so worried."

I could tell he didn't know what to say. "I believe so. She spoke to Tucker about what had happened, not me."

Mom nodded and joined Dad, who was now carving the turkey and fussing. He usually liked the turkey to stand for a while before carving, but it had taken longer to cook than expected.

After lunch Crosby asked if there was somewhere we could talk for a few minutes. I took him by the hand, and we went downstairs to my fancy bedroom. I could tell this was about to be a serious conversation.

"Livvy, I would like to ask you to date me, but I realize you're not ready. I cannot imagine how you feel, because I think you believed that once you told Robert you loved him and wanted to be with him, he would feel the same way about you. If Robert had, obviously, we wouldn't be sitting here."

Tears streamed down my face. Crosby wiped them away and reached for my hand. I sat quietly, not knowing what to say, but he had plenty to say. "Remember when we were on the beach in Cabo? I told you your past didn't concern me, but now I think my heart is involved, and this worries me." He reminded me he had never been in love. "But I don't want to fall in love with a girl I think could be the one, if she isn't going to one day allow herself to become available."

He was staring at the floor. He said it was early in our friendship… thing, or whatever, but he wanted to come next week for New Year's Eve and see how it went. That was, of course, if the invitation I had given him earlier was still open.

I knew I needed to say something other than "certainly, your invitation is still open." *Speak, for God's sakes, Livvy!* I turned slightly to face him. "I want you to come next week. I want you to know I've never lied to anyone. So you can ask me anything. I'll be honest with you. How's that for starters?"

"I can work with it."

I explained how I handled things before I left Colorado. I mentioned Robert and I had the same friends, but I could keep our paths from crossing for a while. "Now, about us, I don't have any answers, other than I like you. But I do know I don't want to fall in love with anyone right now." I lowered my voice. "Or maybe ever."

"Never?" He wrapped his arms around me and pulled me close. "I guess we'll have to figure it out as we go." I lay my head on his shoulder. "I'm sorry you're hurting. I know I'm being selfish, but I've enjoyed being with you. Even though last night and this morning, I was physically challenged. You know that you're driving Tucker, Max, *and* me crazy, right? We've never met anyone like you."

"The three of you are crazy?" I leaned in and shoulder-bumped him. "You know I feel challenged too, and I like it, Crosby."

"Not a one of us has ever been with a virgin," he said. "If I touch you, I'm afraid God will strike me dead or something. Damn, even your lips have barely been kissed, or at least until last night. But I'm about to touch them again."

I was laughing at him, and then he started laughing while he kissed me. "When you said you had never touched a man before, I thought I was going to die right there in the bed with you. Do you realize you had virgin hands until last night? That was a complete shocker. But I must say, I was happy that I helped you with one of your requests."

"Why, yes you did, Mr. Cooper." I giggled against his lips.

Tucker and Crosby said their good-byes and thanked my parents for lunch. I walked them to the car and hugged Tucker. He smacked me right on my lips and winked. Crosby asked if he could kiss me good-bye. I nodded and threw my arms around his neck. And I kissed him.

* * *

I was nervous as I walked back inside the house. My family wanted me to be happy, but I was afraid they might ask questions. I didn't want to talk about anything. But no one mentioned anything. As a matter of fact, Mom had Christmas music playing, and she and Dad were ready to pass out gifts from beneath the tree. Noel was preparing to read the Christmas story.

We each opened one gift at a time while others watched. After everyone had finished, Mom and Dad asked me to follow them.

I hopped up and followed Dad as he led the way. Everyone followed. Dad swung open the door connecting the house to the garage, and there it sat. Oh my. It was one of the most beautiful things I had ever seen. Dad had promised me years ago when I turned twenty-one, if I was still interested, he would buy me one. I was still interested, and now I had my own black and all-chromed-out Harley Davidson Fat Boy. "Oh my God." I traced the leather seat with my hand. Not one single accessory had been overlooked, from pipes to saddlebags, and my new baby was ready to be ridden.

I was dying to ride. I changed into my boots, leather jacket, gloves, and chaps—which were still conveniently stored in my bedroom closet—and then darted out the door. I buckled my helmet, which was already on my head, as I straddled my bike and lifted the kick. Finally, I pressed the ignition. It cranked right up and sounded just as I thought it would. Man, it was music to my ears. I smiled at Dad as I pulled away.

At sunset, I pulled back into the garage. Rae was waiting. She asked how I was doing as I covered the Harley.

"I'm fine, Rae. Sorry I haven't talked to you lately." She asked about Crosby. I told her how we had met in Cabo and started hanging out. She asked if I liked him.

"He's nice, and I like the three of them very much."

"Do you want to talk about Robert?"

"No."

"I don't think you are fine, Livvy, and I think Robert—"

I interrupted. "Rae, he means absolutely nothing to me. Robert made his choice. He doesn't want me."

"I hope you haven't made a mistake," Rae said.

"Me?" I shouted. "I didn't make a mistake. He let me go. He said he didn't want me. I waited for him, Rae. I waited." I fell into her arms and cried. "Rae, Robert said he loved me. I don't understand."

"Livvy," she said, "the two of you will get through this. But it will be difficult. We all have a first love at some point, even me. Just remember, we'll always be here for you. I think you may have forgotten that."

"Rae, I love you." She handed me a tissue. "You are the best sister anyone could have."

"I am pretty great," she giggled. "Now come on," she said, threading her arm around mine, "we need to get inside."

I thanked Mom and Dad for my most wonderful gift, and I headed home.

I had just hauled in the last duffel from my trunk when my phone beeped…again.

First text message was from Abby: *I'm sorry. If you need any-thing, call. Thank you for including me on the trip. I love you.*

I texted her back: *You're welcome. Love you too.*

The second message was from Max—I thought it would be a good one because of Tucker's big mouth. *Livvy, sounds like you had a nice visit. Hate I missed all of that. Don't you forget I saw you first. I heard if I piss you off, I might get a real kiss.*

I texted that fool back: *Miss you too. You might want to check with Crosby about the kissing thing. Did Tucker tell you the only reason I kissed him is because he is so smart and I thought he could tell me what's wrong with me? But Tucker wasn't a bit of help.*

Third text was from Tucker: *Things won't be the same without you. Come to Birmingham anytime.*

Next message was from Luke: *Hey, girl, love you and I'm sorry about what happened.* Not half as sorry as I was, I thought.

My last message was from Crosby: *I had a good time today.*

I replied: *Me too. I'll call you tomorrow when I finish lunch and the Christmas Day movie with my family.*

He replied: *Looking forward to it.*

Max texted: *Yeah, Tucker briefed me on the virgin discussion, and nothing is wrong with you other than you are perfect, or at least you were until last night. Have you decided what to call your recent activities?*

I texted him back: *You three are god-awful. I have got to find you and Tucker some nice girls to date. What happened to the girl you mentioned in Cabo? Call her or send me her number, and I'll call her for you. Ask Crosby about what to call our recent activities. You will anyway.*

Max texted back: *You have her number! And I will ask Crosby.*

What was he talking about? *Oh shit, I'm her.* I didn't know how to respond to him. After a couple of seconds, I texted Max back: *Sorry! I missed that one.*

Now Luke. I kept it really simple: *Love you too.*

Max texted: *Yeah, I figured as much.*

I would let that text from Max go, I decided as I checked my blood sugar. I turned on the TV and crashed on the sofa, and that's all I remembered until I woke to a text message from Crosby: *My bed feels empty. Miss you.*

I couldn't answer him tonight. I'd call him tomorrow, like I had planned. I went to bed, but I lay there unable to sleep. I had to admit, Crosby definitely stirred my inner princess, but I wasn't feeling anything else for him. Maybe I didn't want to, or maybe I just couldn't. I thought about the conversation we had had today, and now I too was worried. Not about me, but him. His heart and how he felt. I would never hurt anyone intentionally. I would try to explore this… what we had. But I'd be careful, because the love gauge had been totally broken off my meter and was currently sporting a stamp that said *Nonrepairable.*

The longer I lay in my bed, the madder I got. I wanted to scream. I wanted to hate Robert, but I guess I hated what the situation had become, not him. Unfortunately I loved him, but I didn't want him anymore. I would get over him, and when I did, I wouldn't allow myself to get hurt again. Not ever.

* * *

My phone rang. I felt around on my night chest without opening my eyes until I found it. "Merry Christmas."

"Merry Christmas to you too." Daddy was chatting away when he realized he was having the conversation alone. He said he would see me at eleven thirty for lunch at Papa and Nonnie's. "Okay, Daddy," I mumbled.

I lay there a while, but my thoughts would not behave. Robert and Crosby were bouncing around in my brain. I finally got up.

I tidied up and dressed. It was still early, and I couldn't arrive early because my family was nosy, and I'd be asked all kind of questions about the trips to Cabo and Colorado. I could just hear Aunt KK feeling all sorry for me. Come to think of it, I felt sorry enough for myself.

I showed up for the shindig on time. I kissed everyone, and it was time to eat. But Lord help me, if Uncle Jack had prayed any longer, it could have been a Sunday morning Southern Baptist church meeting. Don't get me wrong, it was Christmas Day, and prayer was important. But man, we could have eaten a sack lunch before lunch. When Uncle Jack ended his prayer, even my papa shouted out "Hallelujah!"

Rae and Andi chose the Christmas Day movie this year. I laughed when they suggested it, and now I had the entire family's attention. I didn't want to discuss the ski trip, but I had to mention that I had met the star of the film, David Williams.

After the movie, I headed home. When I walked through the door, I kicked my shoes off, changed into comfy clothes, and stretched out on the sofa. I told Crosby I would call him, but I texted him first.

MERRY CHRISTMAS! I typed and asked if now was a good time to call.

Within a couple of seconds, my phone rang.

"Hi."

"Merry Christmas to you, too."

"Sorry your bed felt empty, but in a few days, you can sleep in my bed if you're up for it."

"Oh yeah, and I think we'll work on numbers five and six for you."

I chuckled. "While enjoying my Christmas gift, I almost took care of number five on my own."

"Excuse me?"

"My dad bought me a Harley for Christmas."

"Tom bought you a what?"

"Dad and I love to ride. It's a Fat Boy. Black and all chromed out."

"I never pictured you as an outdoorsy type, *and* you cook."

I asked him what his work schedule looked like the next few days. He said he'd taken vacation time for the rest of the week.

Crosby was hung up on the Harley thing. "So you've ridden it?"

"Yes, that's how I got excited yesterday. And I'm riding again tomorrow after lunch. Have you ever ridden a Harley before?"

"No, I haven't. I don't get it. You, on a motorcycle?"

"No, a *Harley*."

"Oh."

"Well, you see, I don't have a complete picture painted of what sex is like. But I know what the energetic end is like. Riding a Harley is small scale, compared to what I have experienced with you, but I do get a rush. Close your eyes, and imagine for a moment you're straddling a powerful machine and feeling the vibration as it rumbles underneath you. Take a deep breath, smell the leather you're sitting on, and feel the leather that tightly hugs your body. Now, combine that with the freshness of the outdoors—nothing ahead of you but the open road and the wind blowing in your face with the sun beaming down on you while you're traveling sixty-five or seventy miles per hour. There's not a single thought in your head, only music playing in your ears."

"Damn, I don't know what I should say. That was quite a picture you painted and completely…unexpected."

"My phone is beeping. Hang on." It was my cousin Piper, who lived down the street from Crosby and Tucker in Birmingham. Crosby was more than happy to let me go, because now he could be a tattle-tale, I assumed.

I spoke to Piper briefly. She wanted me to drive up in a couple of days for a visit. Piper and I are close, but due to college and my working part-time, it had been difficult to visit her and the children. Rae spoke to her at least once a week since Ryan, Piper's husband, had unfortunately died last year in an auto accident. Piper had two small children, and they were her life.

Piper's birthday was next week. I'd need to pick her up a little happy.

My phone had beeped twice while I was talking to Piper. Tucker texted: *Damn, a Harley? A Fat Boy at that! Never would have figured you to be a biker girl, but I would love to see you in a pair of those chaps.*

That was not worth responding to.

The second message was from Max: *I saw you first! And don't you ever forget it!*

I wasn't responding to him either. Those two must be downright bored to death. I called Crosby back. "You told them," I said, laughing.

"Yeah, I did. Are they giving you a hard time?"

"I'll handle them later. I need to savvy up a bit first."

"I bet you will. Is Piper okay?"

"Uh-huh. She wants me to come the day after tomorrow."

"Are you?"

"Yes."

"Spend the night with me."

"Crosby, you know where I am right now, and I don't want to do anything or say anything that might hurt you."

He was quiet for a moment. "Tell you what—you stay here with me the day after tomorrow, and I'll come to Auburn for New Year's Eve. After that, we'll see how you're feeling and go from there. After that Harley story, you owe me that much. Without our make-out sessions, you wouldn't have a thing to compare riding that damn bike to."

"You're right. I wouldn't. Can I call you tomorrow?"

"Yes! After you ride the Harley, because I want another detailed description."

"Oh no, this time I'm keeping quiet."

He laughed. "Good night, Livvy."

CHAPTER 12

The next morning, I skipped the shower and dressed quickly. I was fully determined to go to the gym this morning. I was about to walk in the door to meet my trainer when my phone rang. It was Mom. I took a deep breath and answered it. My Lord, she was stoked.

"Livvy! Anna Smith just called. My book will be published. She wants to meet with me. I have to be in New York on January second. I want you to go with me. Make arrangements for the spa."

"Mom, slow down. And yes, I will go."

She said the trip would be short, only three nights. I congratulated her.

Well, whatta you know? Victoria C. Hunnicutt did it. And she thought I was a mess. I got it from her, or at least that was what my daddy always said. But the smart thing, I got from my daddy. Honestly, I try to forget about being smart. People would expect more from me, which really stresses me, because I want to please. The dream thing, I got from my meemaw. I tend to forget about the dreams, since I rarely had them anymore. But when I was younger, I had dreams—not scary ones. They always seemed to be about the future. Meemaw said I had *it*, whatever *it* was. My mother was adopted, so for a long while, I didn't understand why I got what Meemaw had until Mom explained she was distantly blood related to her mom—my grandmother.

Dad always said I was bound for greatness, but I always laughed at him and reminded him I was the baby. And, with all my weirdness, he had to say something good about me.

Wasn't that a requirement when you had children? To find that one thing and praise your child, whether you as the parent necessarily always believed it? It's the parent's job to convince the child she can conquer the world, or at least college. Parents want us to leave the nest—or at least that's the impression I got from having two older siblings.

Or was it the parent's job to just throw you out the door and say, "There is a big, bad world out there. Go get it." No…I didn't think so. But in my case, I figured I would keep one foot in my parents' nest for as long as possible, because it was pretty darn comfortable.

I dropped by my house after the gym and changed into clothes that were better suited for my early-afternoon ride. I headed to my parents' house to get my bike. As soon as I stopped in their driveway, I texted Max: *I'm coming to New York January 2-5. Maybe we can go to dinner.*

Two seconds later, Max texted: *Dinner every night! Let me know where you are staying ASAP!*

I texted: *Not sure about every night. I will get hotel info from Mom. But I haven't told Crosby yet. I'll speak to him later today. About to ride my Fat Boy!*

He texted: *No problem. I won't mention it right now. Be careful!*

I followed up with: *Will do. Can't wait to see you.*

I touched every part of my bike. I could smell the newness. I let the garage door up and walked back over to my Fat Boy. I straddled it, put my helmet on, released the kick with my foot, and pressed the start button. My baby cranked right up. The vibration made every muscle in my body tremble.

I pulled out of the garage with absolute ease, and before long I was on I-85 with the cruise control set on seventy. I hung to the right of the center of my lane and relaxed, music streaming through tiny speakers in my helmet. I was feeling free.

I drove about twenty minutes north as the temperature plummeted. I exited I-85 only to whip around and head south back to Auburn. I parked safely in my garage next to my car, which my parents had dropped off.

I pulled off my boots and slunk out of my leather jacket as soon as I walked into my house. I checked the time and called Crosby. He answered, "Hey there. How did that Fat Boy treat you?"

"Almost as well as you."

"Touché, Miss Livvy." He laughed. "What time are you coming up tomorrow?"

"Eleven. I'll visit with Piper and the kids, and I'll see you around one. But I need to go shopping. I'd love for you to go with me. I'm going to New York with Mom. She has a meeting with Anna Smith about the book."

"Back up, Livvy. You're going to New York?"

"It's a quick trip."

"Does Max know?"

"I texted him the dates. I thought we could have dinner."

"He'll take good care of you," Crosby said. "Speaking of dinner, I want to take you on a date. What do you think?"

"Love to."

"A real date?"

"Yes, a real date. You know, there's a quote that I believe Freud said, and it has some truth to it."

"Which quote are you referring to?"

"'Being entirely honest with oneself is good exercise.'"

"Meaning what?" he asked.

"Crosby, I want to have sex with you. I know you would be completely amazing." Dead silence. "Livvy," Crosby said softly, "I won't go back on my word. I hope my actions will protect you, and now I hope my actions will prevent me from allowing myself to fall for you." I understood what he was saying.

Me and my big mouth. I just had to go on and on. "I will never ask you how many girls you have been with, but I'm guessing a lot. I want to do this, and I have to lose it at some point. I know you said you haven't slept with a virgin before. Except…I'm guessing you have. By the way, I'm not special. However, I am sorry you've been hurt, and I am also sorry I feel like I never want to love again."

After another long pause, he said, "We'll figure it out. I can't make a wrong decision with you."

"What if I had slept with Robert? Would you feel differently?"

"I'd have to think about it."

"You don't have to think about it. I know you would have already slept with me. If not on the beach that night in Cabo, it would have happened the night I slept in your bed." After a pause, I asked him if he still wanted me to come or if he only wanted to have dinner. I could sleep at Piper's.

"Livvy, I want to go shopping with you, and I want to take you on a date. But most of all, I want you to sleep in my bed with me. By the way, I can handle your misbehaving."

* * *

Gee, I thought as my alarm clock buzzed. *Where did my freaking night go?* I slapped it. It stopped buzzing when it collided with the floor.

I got up and did the usual: checked my blood sugar, showered, and dressed. But praise God, hallelujah, I could skip the hair thing. I was making a quick stop to see Danni.

Tonight I was going on a real date—the first one in more than two and a half years. What to wear? I decided I needed a second overnight bag. I hung three different outfits in the garment bag. But shoot, I still wasn't sure, because I had no idea where Crosby was taking me for dinner. So I added a couple more pairs of shoes, just in case.

Piper and the children were outside waiting for me when I arrived. Hard to believe little Katie had already had her second birthday, and Mills would be four next month. I had barely gotten out of my car before the kids were wrapped around each of my legs. I played with both of them while Piper put the finishing touches on lunch. We ate together, and then the children took a nap. Piper mentioned Rae had called her. Before she could say it, I told her not to worry about me, because Robert was in my past. I might not love again, but thanks to my new friends, I was determined to have a good time.

"Livvy, don't give up on love. It can be wonderful. Even though Ryan is gone, I know I want to love again, but having a good time under your circumstances might be okay. Just be careful, though. That too can sometimes bite you on your ass, and not in a good way." I couldn't help but laugh. Piper had always spoken her mind.

I glanced at my watch. It was almost one o'clock, and now I couldn't concentrate on a thing Piper was saying. She noticed, gave me a big hug, and told me to get outta there.

I pulled into Crosby's driveway, and before I shifted my car into park, he reached for the hatch. "Are you planning to stay longer than one night?" he asked as he gripped my bags. "I'm good with it."

I giggled and leaned against the doorframe while he put my bags in his closet. "Is Tucker around?"

"Nah, he's shopping." He walked out of the closet. "Screw it. I have to kiss you." He wrapped his arms around me, and man, if he didn't kiss me. Good God, I didn't want to go shopping then. He broke his suction from my lips, leaving them burning with desire, and then he popped me on my butt. "Let's go, Livvy, before I change my mind."

I knew exactly what I needed. I assured Crosby I would be quick. He scooped my hand into his as we passed through the door at Saks. Two pairs of jeans were on my short list. I told the salesperson my brand and size. She asked if I needed to try them on. I declined and grabbed a couple of tops and a jacket and met her at the register. "This isn't exactly what I'd call shopping," Crosby said.

"Sure it is." I struck Vanna White pose, "See exhibit A."

"Where to now?"

He reached for my bag with his free hand, as my hand was in his other. "Handbags and sunglasses."

We were about to walk past the shoe department when I paused and pointed at a pair of shoes. I asked the salesperson to get me the sexy high-heeled sandal in a size eight and a half. I would be back in a few minutes.

As the salesperson was about to ring up my new sunglasses, Crosby offered to pay for them. "Thank you, but maybe next time."

"You know, you're stubborn." He carried my bags for me once again. Back at shoes, the young salesman greeted me with a smile and asked if I would like to try the sandals on. I once again said that wasn't necessary, paid, and asked Crosby if we could stop at the perfume counter.

"It'll only take a few minutes," I assured him.

"Why not?" he said, laughing. "We've been in this store a total of twenty minutes. We have time to spare."

"What's so funny?"

"I don't have any experience tagging along with a girl who is shopping, but I thought it would take at least a couple of hours. Plus, I wanted to buy you something, but you won't let me. I thought all girls liked for guys to buy them things. But you're not like most girls, are you?"

"First of all, I do love pretty things. I just hate dragging it out. I know what I like and what I want, so I buy it and move on. And yeah, you're right. Girls do like guys to buy them things." I winked at him. "I am like most girls; you just don't see me that way."

I motioned to the candles. Crosby shook a goofy grin off his face and leaned on the counter as we waited for a Wild Blueberry Vanilla candle to be gift-wrapped.

"I'm finished. Do you need anything, Crosby? Are you okay?"

"No, no. I'm good." He ran his free hand through his soft, un-styled, wavy hair. As we walked back to the parking lot, he said, "You were in the store no longer than thirty minutes, made your purchases, and never second-guessed yourself. But for three years you waited; you had patience. I don't get it, Livvy."

Carefully I spoke. "With Robert, I thought I made a purchase, and I loved my purchase. When I love something, I never discard it unless…it no longer fits, or breaks."

As we pulled into his garage, we saw that Tucker was back from his shopping trip.

"You never throw anything away?"

"Not if I love it."

Tucker was in the kitchen, grinning from ear to ear. "Thought that was your car. Please tell me you brought your chaps."

"Nope, but I brought a lot of other stuff."

Crosby told Tucker he should have taken me shopping with him. I could have had him all fixed up in about twenty minutes. Tucker had no idea what Crosby was talking about, so while he explained, I excused myself.

I freshened up and walked out of the bathroom just as Crosby walked through the open bedroom door. He kicked the door closed with the back of his foot. He looked at me, hit the button on the iPod dock, and we never broke our stare. He unbuttoned his shirt, reached for me, and softly said, "I haven't been able to think of anything else but you riding that damn Harley."

We fell backward on the bed. My pulse quickened. The only thing I wanted was for him to fill in the details of my painting, but I knew he would never touch me, that way, unless I could love him.

Later, with his head resting on my belly, I gasped and quickly sat up, causing his head to spring from my lap.

"What's wrong?"

"I'm evaluating your room before Tucker can. I would hate to have broken something and have him find it first."

"Oh."

Everything looked fine, but the sheets were on the floor, and I couldn't find my pillow. He pulled something from underneath himself. My pink bra. The strap was dangling, and the hooks were missing. "How'd that happen?" I wondered.

"Don't know. Ugh. Suppose Saks sells them?" I laughed and told him I had thought about buying extras while we were there earlier, but I thought that ripping lingerie was a one-time thing. "Do you destroy things often?"

"Only twice. The first time was a pink-and-black sexy little thing and a pair of hot panties, and now a pink bra. You see, there is this girl that makes me crazy."

"So just my things."

"I think the destruction is because I have to focus on something to take out some aggression on."

"Is it aggression or frustration?"

"It's not frustration, but I'm practicing the discipline thing. Most guys, I'm assuming, do this a lot when they're young. I'm embarrassed to tell you, but the first person I made out with, I slept with. It was wrong. I should have never done it, and I regret most of the past ten years of decisions I've made concerning girls. I refuse to mess up now, though—I want to do things right with you."

"Crosby, I am an adult. At this point, I think it's okay if you want to paint my entire painting for me. You're not fifteen anymore, nor did we meet in a bar. I'm certain I won't go home at two in the morning." Still pleading my case, I said, "Besides, I might feel differently about my Harley if we do."

He pushed me backward, pounced on top of me, and playfully nibbled my neck. "No, we need to wait," he said. He jumped out of bed and disappeared into his closet. When he came out, we ran into each other, making me stumble over the king-size makeshift toga I was wearing. "Whoa, sorry." He grabbed my flying arm and steadied me.

Once my balance was saved, Crosby picked my bra up from the floor and read the imprinted label. He eased the sheet down slightly and took a good look at my breasts. "Umm…" He hummed and smacked me on my overworked lips. I pulled him closer and kissed him. Then I held his bottom lip hostage, between my teeth, fairly hard.

"Frustrated yet?" I asked without removing my firm clamp from his lip.

"No," he said in a raspy voice.

Without looking down, I eased his hand to my wrist. "You could, uh…tie my hands here." Crosby Cooper was panting. I released his lip, but only to take his ear hostage. "With. My. Bra," I whispered.

"Tempting." He kissed me hard, let me go, and whipped around.

"You don't have to buy me another one," I called out, feeling scarcely ashamed about teasing him.

"Sure I do, and I'm certain you'll think of some kinky shit to do with it," he said, his voice trailing off. "Won't you, Livvy?"

"Well, don't have it gift wrapped," I said louder.

When I walked out of the closet, I was met by Tucker. He asked what got broken this time. But he already knew. He was twirling my bra around and around.

"You know I love you, Tucker, but I refuse to let you and Max embarrass me. Take notes, buddy. That pink bra you're holding is the only mishap we had this time."

"You must let Max and I embarrass you. Things won't be fun anymore."

"Just be nice, Tucker," I popped back, stumbling and trying to walk properly with the huge sheet wrapped around my body.

* * *

I was standing in the kitchen drinking a glass of juice when Crosby walked in holding a large black-and-white box with a red satin bow tied on it. I shook my head. "That is an awfully big box for just one bra."

He sat the box on the counter in front of me. "Open it."

I tugged the red ribbon, and it cascaded to the floor. I lifted the lid and pulled the white tissue back. The box was full of pretty things.

"You shouldn't have done this."

"Let him," Tucker sneered. "I don't think he's ever bought a girl dinner, much less a gift."

Crosby and I gave him a blank stare, and then Crosby turned back to me and blurted, "The way I see it, you're here tonight and tomorrow. Then I'm in Auburn. I don't want to make another trip to the store." He was right, and I thanked him properly.

"Hey," Tucker said, laughing, "if I buy you a nice gift, will you thank me like that?"

We both ignored Tucker. "Sorry, I taste like orange juice," I said.

"I like orange juice." Then he kissed me again. "We have an early dinner reservation."

"Where?" I asked, because I needed to know what to wear.

"New place, down the hill."

Okay, I thought, *probably white tablecloth but not too fancy*. I looked in the mirror, feeling a bit nervous. But I was dressed. I picked up my little black bag and reached for the doorknob Crosby opened the door. "Tucker, entertain Livvy." He whirled around. "Not a good idea. Hell, Tucker, just behave." By now, Crosby had stepped into the bathroom, but he stepped back into his doorway. "Livvy, don't kiss Tucker."

Tucker walked over to a window and looked out. I followed. Out of the corner of my eye, I could tell he was looking at me. "You look pretty, Livvy." Tucker was handsome and tall, even taller than Crosby by a couple of inches. He had light brown hair that was thick but clean-cut. His lips were full, his eyes were green, and he had a great smile. Wow. At that moment, things felt awkward. But soon he refocused and was staring once again out the window.

Within a couple of minutes, Tucker seemed to get his game back and said, "Little virgin Livvy, I can tell you're not wearing one of those bras Crosby bought you."

"You're right, Tucker. I'm not. One less thing he'll have to rip off later. Besides, there wasn't anywhere to hide it."

Tucker growled under his breath and said, "You're not as fun now. You snap back too quickly."

I laughed.

I must say, over dinner, Crosby impressed me. He talked about how he loved to spend time with his parents, and once our conversation moved to his job, I realized how smart he truly was. I couldn't help but once again think about how handsome he was, and here I was, on a date with him. *Why couldn't I feel fluffy butterflies or something other than just lust?* I quickly discarded the whole butterfly and sweaty palms crap, because that was silly anyway. I had a mission. I wanted what I wanted, and I wanted my painting complete. I was tired of the missing pieces. The odds could be in my favor, because after two glasses of wine, I was feeling warm-blooded, so maybe he was too.

"Thank you for dinner, Crosby."

"Is there anything special you want to do tonight?"

The valet attendant returned Crosby's car, and Crosby opened the door for me as he always did, but I didn't get in. "I can only think of one special thing that I want to do tonight, and everything I need is standing right in front of me." I kissed him. Crosby didn't say a word as he closed my car door or on the drive home.

He pulled into the garage and insisted I sit tight so he could open my door for me. I stepped out. He pulled me close and took a deep breath, "You are more than I can handle." *This is good.* He kissed me. I was pulling at his cashmere overcoat and he was tugging at mine. We were stumbling, trying to get inside the house. He managed to get the door open, and once in the kitchen, our coats were off. I snatched his tie and got that sucker untied, but I left it hanging under his collar. I tried to unbutton his shirt. I gave up, poked my fingers in a couple of the openings between the buttons, and ripped it. Buttons flew everywhere. Crosby found the zipper to my dress and yanked it. My dress slinked down my body with his help, and I stepped out, never breaking my hold from around his neck or releasing his lips.

Suddenly I felt cool. I was now sitting on the granite kitchen countertop wearing only a blue Hanky Panky thong, Stuart Weitzman black platform shoes, and my jewelry. I pulled his belt, and he unbuttoned his pants while I unzipped them. He kicked his shoes off without looking. He assisted me with his pants, and they fell to the floor. He kicked them to the side. Crosby picked me up with my legs around his waist and carried me to his bedroom. I wasn't sure when his socks, undershirt, or boxers came off. He lowered me on his bed, and he grabbed my legs with a roughness like never before, parting them. *I liked it*. He fell forward on top of me, scooping my bare hips in his hands. I wrapped my legs tightly around him. I could feel his erection pressed against my inner thigh.

"Crosby, a condom."

He took a deep breath and buried his face between my breasts. "I got this. I'm okay now."

The bed was once again destroyed, and I possibly heard a lamp fall to the floor. Exhausted, he shared my pillow, and we fell asleep.

* * *

The next morning, I was lying on my stomach. Crosby woke me, rubbing my back. *Crap, morning breath*. I yanked the sheet, wrapped it around my body, and shuffled to the bathroom to brush my teeth. Crosby joined me. "Tucker cooked," he said around his toothbrush. "You probably need to eat." I nodded while I spat toothpaste into his sink.

In the kitchen, Tucker popped a plate down in front of me. "Eat, girl. After last night, you need nutrition."

No questions asked. I ate. Wheat toast, scrambled eggs, and baked turkey bacon.

Crosby and I were quiet, but not Tucker. "You know, you guys woke me up. Of course, I was asleep on the sofa. I did get a little show, even though the lights were dim."

I shot a quick look at Crosby and whispered, "I thought he was in his room."

"I forgot about him."

Tucker continued his bitching. "Livvy, I don't think any of your things were torn, but Crosby, that two-hundred-dollar shirt of yours has about three buttons left on it, and the rest of this shit, you two can clean up." He stepped over Crosby's pants and groused on. "And after last night, I know your breasts are better than I ever could have imagined."

"Bought and paid for, Tucker," I roared.

He finally loosened up and laughed. He even hugged me and gave Crosby a little brotherly slap on the back. He shook his head. "I hope you remember what we've talked about." He disappeared into his bedroom.

I cleared the table and insisted that Crosby do whatever he normally did when he had a day off.

"What time do you need to leave today? Or could I persuade you to stay."

"I'll stay."

"The night?"

"Yes."

He grinned and grabbed his gym bag, kissed me bye, and said he would be back in two hours.

I cleaned up our mess, including a few buttons Tucker had missed on his cleanup sweep through the kitchen. I evaluated the rest of the destruction and knew I would need to address it shortly. But first I put the sheets into the wash. I found another set of sheets and remade the bed. I picked up Crosby's ruined shirt from the kitchen counter, shoved it in my bag, and left the house on a mission. I didn't know anything about men's clothing, other than they looked good or didn't. But come to think of it, I loved a nice crisp white shirt. That's just sexy.

I walked right into Saks and went directly to the back of the store. I pulled the damaged goods out of my new oversized black bag and flung them on the counter. "May I help you?" the salesperson inquired.

Well, what did he think? I was standing there, looking desperate. Of course he could help me. "Yes," I answered. "Do you sell this brand?" As I looked down at the disabled shirt, he picked it up and sighed. I told him just to get me two of them. "We're having garment issues right now."

"Darling, I can fix you right up. Is there anything else I can help you with?"

"I need a lamp—two really, so they'll match."

"Oh sweetie," he whispered. "Go on top of the hill there," he pointed. "Pottery Barn. They have nice ones. I think you'll find what you're looking for. Tell them Ken sent you."

I bought two shirts and two lamps and was back to the house in thirty-five minutes. I threw the broken lamp in the trash and took the single one to the guys' office. I set it on a nice marble-top table that flanked the wall opposite from the desk. I stood there for a moment and studied the family photos. I moved them to the other side and plopped several books down in the center of the table, laying them flat and stacking them neatly. Then I slightly shifted the spines to the front.

I placed the two new lamps in their proper places, on the night chests next to Crosby's bed. *I like them, but what if he doesn't?* I worried.

I heard the bathroom door open as I was showering, and Crosby joined me. As he slipped his arms around me from behind, he whispered, "I like the new lamps and shirts. I appreciate the thought, but it was completely unnecessary." I giggled. His whiskers tickled my neck.

We watched a movie together for the first time, starring Peter Weston. I was surprised Crosby had chosen it—it was a total chick flick—but he said he liked the actor and usually caught his movies. "You know," he said, pointing at the TV as the credits rolled, "I didn't realize that Peter Weston was British until I saw him on the morning show a few days ago."

"British?" I had no idea either, but then again I'd seen him in only a couple of movies. "Hey, Crosby, would you like to visit Piper and the children? I want to give her the little gift I picked up for her."

Without saying a word, he put his shoes on. "Ready?"

As we strolled down the street hand in hand, I said, "Piper thinks you Cooper brothers are hot."

I filled Crosby in on Ryan. Crosby had had no idea, even though they've lived on the same street for two years. "Aw, that explains why I haven't seen him in forever," Crosby said. "I assumed they were divorced." He felt awful. Crosby said they could have at least passed their phone numbers to her in case she needed anything. I told him he should do that today as I rang the doorbell.

Piper was completely surprised. "Two visits in less than a week. You must be Crosby?"

"Yes, it's nice to meet you, Piper."

I was holding the gift box and handed it to her.

"You remembered," she exclaimed. She opened the box and unwrapped the candle from its clear cellophane paper and black ribbon. She removed the silver lid, smelled it, and promptly lit it. "My favorite candle. Thank you."

Crosby sniffed. "Smells good."

Piper and I laughed. By now the children had joined us. Katie and Mills took an immediate liking to Crosby, and when we were about to leave, Katie pulled on Crosby's pant leg. He picked her up, and she gave him the sweetest little hug, and he kissed her on the cheek. Mills asked for a hug, too, so Crosby sat Katie back on the floor and gave him a hug.

"Mills misses his daddy, but I'm not sure if Katie remembers him."

I picked up a photograph of Ryan and said, "She may not, but I know she can feel how much he loves her."

"I hope so. It feels like yesterday he walked through the back door, but it's been eleven months today."

"Piper, I'd like to give you our phone numbers. If you ever need anything, don't hesitate," Crosby said.

She picked her cell up from the kitchen counter and handed it to Crosby. He stored his and Tucker's numbers and returned it to her. "Thank you."

Tucker was MIA when we returned, so Crosby and I made dinner together. We had just discussed how I was going to try to behave while we were cuddling when he messed up by making a wrong move, and this time I said, "Lord, help me."

But as usual, he was in complete control. I wasn't, but I remained pure. As a matter of fact, the rate I was going, I would die an old maid before he ever touched me. *I gotta do something about this* was my last thought before dozing off.

Crosby was no longer beside me when I woke, but I could hear him talking to Tucker in the next room. Tucker warned Crosby to be careful. "I know she still loves him, but—"

Tucker interrupted Crosby and said, "No, don't say it. You've only known the Livvy that is in your room for a few weeks, Crosby."

"I know I've got to figure this out, and soon."

"I like Livvy," Tucker continued, "and I totally get what's going on physically with the both of you, but she's not going for the fluffy-heart stuff right now. I don't see that changing any time soon."

"I know."

I felt bad. The physical part was great with Crosby, but Tucker and Crosby were right. I knew I loved Crosby, but I was sure it was the same way I loved Tucker: only as a friend.

I was feeling shaky. I needed some juice and quick. I managed to put Crosby's T-shirt on and get to the kitchen, but I was already weak, shaking, and sweating. I was pulling on the refrigerator handle, but it wouldn't open. "I got it," Tucker calmly said.

I felt myself sliding down the side of the wall until I was sitting on the floor. Tucker handed me a glass of juice. I was holding the glass, trying to drink from it, but most of the juice ran down my chin. Crosby popped a straw into the glass and held it for me to drink. He and Tucker sat on the floor with me.

"Get her bag, Crosby. She may need the injection. Rae told me about it at lunch the other day." Tucker was sitting on the floor, holding me in his arms. Crosby dumped everything out of my bag and grabbed the red box that contained the glucagon injection.

They were reading the instructions when I said, "I feel better. I won't need it." Tucker got up and made me a grilled cheese.

Crosby wrapped his arms around me. "You need to tell me everything I need to know."

"I'll tell you both."

While I ate, I apologized to them for not explaining earlier about my health. However, I had been under the impression they already knew from hanging out with Rae, or I would have already told them. After all, I had promised my parents I would always make sure my friends were informed about what to do if an emergency occurred. I held the big shot along with the instructions and carefully explained how to administer it. I also showed them how to check my blood sugar and described the signs of a low and high blood sugar.

I asked Crosby if it would be okay if I lay back down. We both took a morning nap.

Crosby was still asleep when I woke. I needed to leave, so I showered and threw on my clothes. When I walked back in the bedroom, he was awake. Crosby reached for me and pulled me onto the bed next to him. "One more day?" he asked. I reminded him guests were coming in a few days.

He took my things to my car. "Livvy, how old is Piper?"

"Thirty."

At the same time, we said, "Tucker has got to meet her." I said I'd think about how to arrange it.

Driving home, I thought about Tucker and Piper. Tucker would turn twenty-eight in three weeks. A two-year age difference meant absolutely nothing. If Tucker was half as great with Katie and Mills as Crosby had been, the children would have him wrapped around their tiny fingers in no time.

CHAPTER 13

Danni, she loved to play matchmaker. So this morning, after I had told all, she was definitely eager to help Piper and me out for our dates tomorrow. I also quickly followed up with Mom concerning our New York plans.

I was completely bored out of my mind when Abby called. We decided to have a girls' night. We watched a movie and talked boys. I stayed clear of the topic of Robert. But I mentioned Crosby. I also told her about our New York trip and casually dropped Max's name.

I slept well for the first time in over a week, and that was a good thing, I thought as I turned off the alarm. I reached for my cell to text Max: *Good morning. Spoke to Mom. Dinner is fine. Let me know which night works best.*

Max texted back: *I plan to take you out every night. I spoke to Crosby, and he said for me to take care of you. See what Cookie says about that.*

I laughed and replied: *Very funny, Max. I will call you tomorrow. Happy New Year!*

Noel and Dad decided years ago to close the construction business for a few days around all holidays, so I didn't have a lick of paperwork. Luckily I had finished going over the spa's inventory list before noon, so my part-time work was done. I even got a kick-ass workout in with a new trainer, Gregg. He about killed me.

It was almost four o'clock when I realized Piper had sent a text an hour ago needing my address. I mentioned I had a surprise for her and she should get a move on.

I called Jake and asked him to swing by and pick Piper and me up. I told him we wouldn't need a ride back home; we were meeting friends.

I finished the grueling process of showering. The shaving-the-leg thing, I hate. If I didn't have so much pride, I'd become one of those natural chicks.

I stood in my closet, staring at a beautiful, silver, low-cut V-neck dress with a scooped back. The silver fabric appeared to have a slightly iridescent sheen, brightly illuminated by the non-glamorous florescent lighting in my closet. The bodice had narrow, thin layers of fabric that were somehow scrunched, but it was completely fitted. The length was perfect—short, but not too short. What was there not to love about this dress? It was Vera, of course.

Piper was on time. I suggested she shower immediately, because Danni was on her way. Piper asked me what I was wearing. After my description, she looked concerned. She said her outfit was a bit simpler. I took her by her hand—I could help her with that. I knew we wore the same size. I could fix her up with shoes to match, too.

I pranced in my closet and reached for a garment bag and shoes. Piper would look amazing in this strapless purple, green, and gold dress. "Go get dressed," I said, handing her the outfit.

"Livvy—"

"Hush. Now go."

Danni let herself in, and she strutted herself right into my bathroom. I showed her my outfit, and then she worked her magic on me.

After Piper finished her basic maintenance, she fetched her dress and showed it to Danni. "Okay, girl, that is one hot dress. You need smoky eyes and messy, sexy hair." Danni pointed to the stool.

It was seven thirty. I opened a bottle of wine and told Piper to chill for a while. She needed to calm her nerves, only she didn't know it. We sat on the sofa wearing robes and propped up our bare feet.

"Livvy, thank you for this," Piper said. "I feel beautiful for the first time in a long time." I hoped she would thank me later and not wring my neck.

* * *

When we arrived at the Blue Bar, there was already a long line. I spotted Logan, a bouncer I knew. "Come on," I said, and we were slipped right through a side door. I asked Logan for one more favor, describing Crosby and Tucker. He grinned. "Glad you are out tonight, Livvy. I'll look for them."

In the meantime, Jake took off, and Logan escorted us to a reserved table. I had a view of the front entrance, but it also faced the center of the dance floor and had a perfect view of the stage as well.

A bit thirsty, I told Piper to sit tight. I ordered drinks at the bar. Piper tried to repay me for her drink. I told her to put her money away, because they were free.

"Like hell," she giggled. "Who's the sponsor?"

"Like I know?" I couldn't remember the last time I paid for a drink, come to think of it. The band was warming up, and I could tell they were good. Their sound reminded me of Matt Nathanson.

I sucked that Bacardi and diet Coke down quickly through my tiny bar straw. The drink went straight to my head. *Better slow down.*

My phone beeped. Crosby said he and Tucker were in line. I told him I was sending help.

I texted Logan: *Our dates are here. Do you mind?*

He texted: *Got 'em.*

I texted Crosby: *Go to the dance floor.*

I spotted the guys as soon as Logan escorted them inside. I asked Piper if she would fetch that tall, good-looking guy wearing the black cashmere dress coat and the Burberry gray-tone scarf. I told her I had a meeting on the dance floor. Piper turned.

"Shit, Livvy, that's my hot neighbor." She was laughing but on it.

Thank goodness the band was playing a great slow song. The almost-empty dance floor made it easy to spot Crosby. He was looking around the crowded bar. I walked quietly up behind him, softly ran my hand across the back of his shoulder, and slowly danced around to his front. I locked my hands around his neck and pulled myself close to him. He placed his hands softly on my waist and met me with a kiss. I turned around so his front side was against my backside. His hands were on my hips, and he kissed me once on my neck. We were swaying, keeping rhythm with the music. I was singing the song to him, but when we turned around, he sang to me. The song ended. "Livvy Hunnicutt, what am I going to do with you?"

My palms were flat against his chest. I eased them up and draped them around his neck and took his ear with a whisper, "Crosby Cooper, you can do anything to me you want."

Crosby and I joined Piper at our table. "Where's Tucker?"

Piper pointed. "Those two guys came over and got him."

I looked, and Bo and Patrick were speaking to Tucker. Patrick shifted to the left, and I saw him.

"He was supposed to be on a hunting trip," I said under my breath. "That's Robert?"

"Yes," I said, then turned my chair slightly so I would not be in his direct view.

A moment later, Tucker returned. Crosby asked if everything was okay.

"Yeah, some of Livvy's friends wanted to meet me."

I interrupted. "Spill it, Tucker. What was that all about?"

"He wanted me to relay a message to my brother."

"What's the message?" Crosby asked.

"Be good to Livvy. She deserves the best."

"I know that."

I slapped the table. "Guess that went well."

Tucker smiled. "Livvy, you look like a sexy little Christmas ornament."

"Bullcrap," I laughed. "Guess you've met Piper. She's your neighbor."

Tucker smiled. "Yes, I've met her." Crosby asked if we wanted drinks.

"You should let Livvy go to the bar," Piper said.

"Why's that?"

"We were here less than five minutes, and she found a sponsor."

"Correction, Piper—the sponsor found me."

"My God, Livvy. Cookie is right. We can't let you go anywhere," Crosby said with a hint of sarcasm.

"Sure you can." I grabbed his hand and said, "The dance floor."

Tucker shouted, "So Piper, can you dance?"

"Who do you think taught Livvy?" She cackled.

After a couple of songs, Crosby went to the bar. I noticed Patrick, Abby, Bo, and a few others looking in my direction. I threw my hand up and gestured for them to join us. Crosby returned with our drinks, and Piper and Tucker returned from dancing. She moved her chair closer to him, and he casually threw his arm over the back of her chair.

Jake asked Piper and me for a dance. After all, he had been our taxi tonight. I grinned at Piper and said, "Come on." We turned Jake every which way but upside down.

When we returned, Tucker said, "The guy will never be the same again, but I want the both of you to dance with me like that."

Crosby and I decided to go to the bar. I ordered a bottle of water. He ordered a Jack and something—no, two Jacks and something. I told Crosby I needed to go to the bathroom. Lordy, my Prada shoes were not as stable as they were a few hours ago. Crosby said, "Hold on. I'll go with you."

About that time, Logan walked up and told me it certainly looked like I was enjoying myself tonight. I laughed, slapped him on the shoulder, and said, "You bet I am." I told Crosby that Logan could walk with me to the restroom. "I will be back." Crosby smiled and said he wouldn't move from his seat.

On our return from the restroom, Logan and I mingled our way back through the crowd until we were somewhat close to the bar where Crosby sat. I let go of Logan's arm, and that's when I physically ran into him—Robert. He knocked me two feet backward. Logan caught me by my arm before I fell. I thanked Logan for breaking my fall. "Let's go, Livvy." Logan pulled my arm. "Now!" he shouted.

As I walked past Robert, he reached for my arm, barely brushing it. He shouted, "Livvy!" I didn't turn around. Crosby met Logan and me before we reached our meeting spot. He had seen the incident. I asked for another drink. Crosby thought he needed a double.

We took the next round of cocktails to our table, and I laughed and told Crosby our little project seemed to be working out pretty well. Piper and Tucker were dancing again.

The countdown began…five, four, three, two, one, Happy New Year! Everyone was kissing their dates, and Tucker and Piper were all but making out. Tucker had drunk only one cocktail earlier in the evening and had stuck with water the remainder of the night, so obviously he was driving. He seemed to be in a hurry to leave, but come to think of it, Piper was too. Tucker asked if I could walk to the exit any faster. Crosby was holding my hand, but I guess I was walking too slowly for his liking as well, because he picked me up and threw me over his shoulder.

I swayed though the front door of my home and pointed to the sofa. "Tucker, take the pull-out. Piper, get him sheets." Crosby and I were trying to get to my room, but my damn seven-hundred-dollar shoes wouldn't work right. I heard Tucker and Crosby laughing.

We made it to the bedroom. I sat on the edge of my bed, trying to unbuckle my right shoe. Crosby's drunken self was sitting on the floor with my left foot in his lap, trying to unbuckle the other one. He asked, "Can I cut the strap? I'll buy you a new pair."

"You don't cut the straps of Prada," I said, laughing as I fell off the bed into his lap. We were both laughing and rolling on the floor. He was trying to unzip my dress, but he was having problems with that, too.

"You won't let me cut the straps on your shoes. Can I tear the dress?" he asked.

"No," I shouted. "You never tear a Vera."

I managed to get my zipper started and stood up. So did he. Crosby finished unzipping my dress. When my dress fell to the floor, I was wearing only a silver bra, matching panties, and very tall heels.

I reached for his belt and shirt at the same time. He grabbed my hips and jerked me closer to him. "You sparkled tonight," he said. "I had to remind myself you were my date. You chose to be with me, Livvy." He brushed my hair from my face. "Do you have any idea how badly I want you?" A faint smile crossed his lips. "I brought condoms…hoping…but you're not ready for a commitment are you, Livvy?"

Oh God, I could see the disappointment building in his eyes. *What do I say?* I kissed him, and he passionately kissed me. I never answered his question. I couldn't. I knew my words would hurt him more than my silence. Nonetheless, Crosby excited me, and I him. Crosby kept his promise once again.

He had almost drifted to sleep when he mumbled, "I love you, Livvy."

No, don't. Don't love me. That ruined everything. Maybe he didn't mean it. He couldn't love me. He had known me as an adult for only three weeks. No one could fall in love that soon. *Shit! Why did he say that?* I couldn't do this ever again with him. I wouldn't hurt him because I did love him, but only as a friend.

Too soon, the sun peeped through my shutters. *Just shoot me now.* I was twenty-one and had lived my life hangover-free—until now. Now I knew what one of those suckers felt like.

I glanced around my room to see if I needed to enforce damage control. Everything appeared to be in order. *But wait—what's with me?* I looked underneath the covers. I gave Crosby a playful shove on the chest and told him to wake up. He jumped and almost fell off the bed. I caught his arm and pulled him back toward me. He grabbed his head with both hands. "What's wrong? You need anything?"

"No," I said, "I'm good. Do you need Advil?" Then I demanded, "Crosby, look under the covers." He raised the tangled sheet and blanket. We both were now laughing. My thong was still completely intact and was all but glued to my body. And my shoes—I had slept in those five-inch platform heels.

Crosby sat up and looked around my room. I shoved him back down and straddled him wearing my thong and shoes. We were still laughing. I rolled off the edge of the bed and stumbled a bit when my feet hit the floor. I grabbed a robe that was lying on my dresser and put it on.

I walked in the kitchen, and there stood Tucker with my refrigerator door wide open. He looked at me and started laughing. "Livvy, did you sleep in those?" he said, pointing to my feet.

"As a matter of fact, I did. And some other stuff too." I reached around him for two bottles of water. Then I grabbed a bottle of Advil from the cabinet. As I swayed back to my bedroom, I said, "You know, Tucker, now would be a good time for you to thank me."

Crosby showered, and I tried to clean up my room, but my head was killing me. I brushed my teeth and washed my face while still wearing my shoes. I finally managed to unbuckle those suckers and throw some clothes on.

Piper and Tucker were in the kitchen. They were making breakfast together. I leaned against the counter and innocently asked them how their night was. I had already noticed the sheets for the pull-out were still folded perfectly and had not been used. Piper and Tucker looked at each other and smiled. Crosby joined us after he showered. He looked like he felt better. However, as my papa would say, I looked like I had been shot at and missed, but shit at and hit.

We ate breakfast together, and Crosby and I cleaned up. Piper started packing her things. I noticed Tucker quickly gathered up his things as well. Crosby pinned me gently against the kitchen sink. "Can I see your Harley?"

You bet," I said and led the way into the attached garage. I peeled back the black custom cover to reveal the shiny-wicked machine.

Tucker shook his head. "That's hot."

Crosby punched him on his arm. "No, you fool. It's dangerous."

Piper had to leave. Tucker said he needed to get back as well. He tossed Crosby his car keys and disappeared to get his bag. Piper hugged me and whispered, "Thank you, Livvy. He's a great guy."

"Thank Crosby, too. It was his idea to introduce you." She winked at Crosby as she got into her car.

"You did well, Livvy," Tucker said. "She reminds me of someone else I know." He smacked me on the cheek and told Crosby he would see him later.

Crosby ran his hand through his damp hair and sighed as we sat down on the sofa. "You know, we said last week we would see how things were going for you. I don't know what to do. I understand you're not ready for a boyfriend. But I'm ready for a girlfriend, and not just any girl. I want you. Before last night, I would have waited for you for as long as it took to get over him. But I saw Robert and how he looked at you—he hasn't let you go. That worries me. I don't think you'll call him or try to see him. But this is a small town. You'll run into him, because you have the same friends. I trust you when you say he is out of your life. You believe that to be true. But I need to make absolutely sure before I become more…"

He paused and took a deep breath. "Consumed with you, Livvy. You make me feel like no one else has ever made me feel. Not just the physical part, but everything. I want nothing more than to fill in the missing details of your painting for you. But for now, I'm happy for you that it's not complete."

He's breaking up with me, and we didn't even date. This sucked. But I understood. I thought about what he had said last night. Even though he had only mumbled, he had said he loved me. "Crosby, you have every right to protect your feelings. I can't speak for how Robert feels, but I can speak for myself. I will always love Robert. But I don't love him the way I once did. I hate what he said to me. I hate that I allowed myself to believe there was hope. I hate that I allowed myself to dream of what one day our lives might be like. I thought I would one day get my forever with him. But most importantly, I thought he would want his forever with me. I was hurt, and now I'm bitter, and this is not fair to you. I would never want to lead you on, because I do like you a lot."

Crosby stood up and pulled me to my feet. He painfully smiled. "When I get a handle on my feelings, can I call you?"

I nodded. "Yes."

"But, so you know, I decided after last night I would marry you first before we go all the way."

"Oh" was all I could say.

I walked him to the car. He gave me a tight hug and kissed me lightly on my lips. I waved slowly as he drove away. *How did he develop such intense feelings for me in such a short time?* I thought about Crosby the remainder of the morning and kicked myself around wondering if I shouldn't have said more. What if I could have feelings for him one day—other than feeling like he was a friend? Maybe I could try harder. But if nothing developed, that would hurt him, like Robert had hurt me. I had better just leave it be. I tidied up my house. I thought about my future and decided to apply for a teaching job. Not that I wanted to teach high school, but it was a little late for that. I already had the degree, and frankly, going back to college was not an option because of stress. That crap drove my blood sugar high, which screwed up the Addison's.

I packed my nice luggage for New York. It wasn't fancy, but it certainly was not that ugly mess I had been required to take on the ski trip.

I called Max, but it went to his voice mail.

Surprisingly, though, he returned my call immediately. I told him Mom and I should arrive in New York around three o'clock the next afternoon. After a couple of minutes of small talk, he said he had made reservations for seven thirty and asked to pick me up at seven. I was about to hang up when he said, "Hold on, Livvy. Where are you staying?"

"Sorry, Four Seasons. You know, I wasn't sure you would want to take me to dinner after what happened between Crosby and me."

"No, that's far from the case. I spoke to Crosby, he's a big boy, and you've always been completely honest about how you feel. And he probably would have been fine with everything, but he said when he saw the way Robert looked at you last night—"

"Robert didn't tell anyone he had returned from his hunting trip. If I had known he was in Auburn, I would have gone to Birmingham."

Max and I talked a while longer but not about Crosby, Tucker, or Robert. He was interested in my Harley, and I answered all of his questions. I learned more about what a banker did. And I soon got the impression he was leaving out a few details. It seemed that Max wasn't just a banker.

I did make it clear during our conversation I was certainly forgoing dating indefinitely. He had only one thing to say about that: "We'll see."

I had never talked to anyone for two hours on the phone before, and by now I was starving. He apologized for keeping me. I thought I had kept him. We both laughed and then said good night.

CHAPTER 14

Dad dropped Mom and me at curbside. We checked in and went straight to our gate where boarding was underway. I settled in my seat with my mom beside me and stuck the comfy iPod buds into my ears. I hadn't selected my playlist before the flight attendant said, "Nice to see you again, Miss Hunnicutt. May I get you a Bloody Mary?"

Mom knew he was speaking to me, but she answered for the both of us. "Make it two, Dan." She smiled weakly at me. "Livvy, are you and Crosby…okay?"

"Yes." *I hope.* "We're friends, Mom."

"Darling, he's a wonderful young man." She gave me a once-over. A knot tightened in my stomach. *There's more coming…*"Livvy, don't overthink things. You need to date. You're young and beautiful, but you're unhappy." She angel-brushed my cheek with the backs of her fingers, "Laugh again like you did a few weeks ago."

"I will, Mom," I said, trying not to sound flat. "I promise."

She reached over and patted my hand. "I'm holding you to it." Inwardly I huffed, because I knew she would.

"Livvy." *Jesus, Mom, drop it.* "Anna feels *Finding Justice* will become a film." *Whew. She changed the subject.* "We'll know more in a day or two."

I leapt at the opportunity to abandon my job search. "Congratulations, Mom. I want to work for you, not the spa. And so you know, I have decided I am not teacher material. I don't care what my diploma says."

Mom laughed. "We never thought you would be a career girl. Since you were a little girl, you've only wanted to be a wife and mother." *Well, not anymore. The heartache and disappointment of Robert not wanting me cured me of that crock of shit.*

I drank my Bloody Mary and fell right to sleep. Dan made an announcement: we would land shortly. I raised my seat to its upright position and put my things away. Mom made a phone call as we taxied to the gate. She told me Sammy would be our driver while we were in New York, and she didn't want me going anywhere alone. Mom gave me Sammy's number and said he would take me anywhere I needed or wanted to go. It seemed Anna had arranged quite a few meetings, and Mom would not have any free time.

We quickly found Sammy, a nice-looking, rather large fellow. I guessed he was in his early forties. He looked at me. "Miss Livvy Hunnicutt?" Then he looked at my mom and said, "You must be Mrs. Hunnicutt. Ladies, describe your bags."

Mom and I pointed to our bags as they spun on the luggage carousel. I reached for one of my bags, and Sammy said, "Miss Hunnicutt, I'll get that for you."

"Please call me Livvy, Sammy."

"Miss Livvy, do I need to know anything special about you?"

I tunneled deep into my large brown tote and pulled out three papers that were stapled together in the left corner. The first page listed the signs of a low blood sugar—every freaking one of them. The second sheet listed the signs of a high blood sugar, and the third contained information on Addison's. I handed the packet to him and said, "I will always have everything in my bag."

Mom looked at me and forced a smile. I could see the hurt in her eyes for both Rae and me. I've heard her beg God to let my sister and me be healthy and give her everything we were burdened with. I've also heard her ask her friends, who are medical doctors, to find a transplant doctor to take her and Dad's pancreases and give them to us, because our blood types are perfect matches. They hadn't found a taker.

Sammy had Mom and me in the car and to our hotel in no time. Mom got us checked in and handed me my room key. I went directly to the room without her, but Sammy took my bags for me. He wasn't letting me out of his sight. *Oh dear Lord*, I thought, *if dinner doesn't go well with Max, it looks like Sammy and I will be stuck together like freaking superglue.*

He took my key and opened the door. Nice. Mom always got awesome rooms. This one was a two-bedroom suite. Dad was thriftier with hotels. His theory was that you only sleep and shower in the room, so it was better to spend the money elsewhere. Boy, he would have a cow right now.

Sammy asked if I needed anything else. I said I had a friend picking me up for dinner, so I was good for today. I asked him to check with me tomorrow after he took Mom to her meeting.

While I was unpacking, I weighed my options on what to wear. I had no idea where Max and I were going for dinner. I laid out two dresses and finally decided to wear the black fitted one with the fancy shoes I had just slept in the other night.

Mom loaned me her tapered, not-quite-fitted-but-perfect sable fur for this trip.

I glanced at my basic but dependable Rolex watch and checked the time. It was 6:50 p.m. I shoved my most important items in my little black bag, took one quick look in the mirror, and draped Mom's sable over my arm. I turned the music off and heard voices in the suite.

I dashed out of the room but slowly turned the corner. There sat Mom and Anna Smith. But there were also two men I'd never seen and another who looked familiar. By now they were all standing and staring at me. I walked closer to them. Dear God, I about peed in my pretty panties. Matt Bartlett! He's a movie star. I politely smiled and offered my hand. They each shook my hand and introduced themselves, even

Matt. "Livvy," Anna said, "you have been in town only two hours, and it appears you have a date."

I threw my head back and laughed, trying not to think about the gorgeous Matt Bartlett, who now stood beside me. "Oh no, Anna," I said, "just dinner with a friend. Actually, you met him. Max."

"Yes, Max Spencer," Anna confirmed.

The shorter guy with the messy hair, Sam somebody, asked, "*The* Max Spencer?"

"Yes," Mom answered.

I announced I was meeting Max in the lobby. Everyone insisted that he come up. So with that most dazzling Matt Bartlett standing beside me—who by the way had just touched my arm—I blurted out with probably more of a Southern accent than I would have liked, "Well, of course. I'll call him."

Max was already in the lobby and said he'd be happy to come up. I neglected to mention the other people in our suite.

Matt asked how long we were in town. "Two days." Oh Lord, I thought I was going to slide right out of my Prada shoes, and they were behaving. But my legs weren't; they felt like I was trying to stand on two angel-hair noodles.

I turned when the doorbell rang. A butler, for real—wait, he wasn't not your average-looking butler. Bet he's a "lifestyle butler" or some kind of in-room concierge, I thought. I decided to stay put. I had absolutely no idea what was going on, but Cookie would be explaining herself tomorrow. I felt like I'd been ambushed, but in a good way.

Max greeted the butler and coolly headed my way. He eased one hand around my waist and softly kissed me above my temple. Max looked distinguished and professional, but most of all, handsome. He gave Mom a hug, greeted Anna, and gave Sam Somebody a firm handshake.

"Max, it's nice to finally meet you and put a face to your name," Sam said.

"You too," Max said. *What the hell is going on here?* The tall man wearing the nice suit finally spoke and said, "Max, nice to meet you." They shook hands.

"Zach Mitchell. Your name comes across my desk often."

Matt introduced himself next. As they shook hands, he said, "Sam spoke of you earlier today."

"So Victoria's book must be highly anticipated to have Sam and Zach in the same room," Max said.

Mom pleasantly smiled, but Anna answered, "Yes, we believe so."

"It's been my pleasure to meet you all," I said.

As I moved to leave, Matt touched my arm for the second time. "Livvy, I'd like to see you again before you leave town."

He would? "That would be great, Matt."

Max and I walked to the door side by side. We had not taken two steps before he placed his hand at the center of my back. I could feel him looking at me as we walked. "Livvy, you look beautiful."

"Thank you, Max."

The butler opened the door. "Thank you, Fred."

"You are welcome, Mr. Spencer," Fred squeaked.

We stepped out the door, and I glanced to make sure it shut. "Who the hell are you? As soon as I mentioned your name, everyone, including the two men I have never met before in my life, insisted you come up, because they wanted to meet the guy who was taking me on a date."

Max laughed. "Now that I know this is a date, I get to give you a real kiss, right?"

"Ugh," I growled. "Well, I didn't mean it like that. But you didn't answer my question. Why do those men know you?"

Max refused to answer my question, mumbling "a date" again.

Once in the lobby, he stopped to get his phone from his coat pocket, pressed one number, and said, "Approaching the door in thirty." He removed my coat from my arm and said, "Let me help you. It's cold out." Max held Mom's sable as I slipped my arms in.

A black Mercedes, larger than the one Sammy drove yesterday, stopped suddenly in front of the hotel. The doorman opened the door. "Nice to see you again, Mr. Spencer."

"You too, Howard." The driver of the Mercedes opened the back door for Max and me and quickly returned to the driver's seat.

I pointed to Max's driver and said, "I have one of those while I'm in New York. His name is Sammy."

"His name is Martin, and I was going to offer him to you while you're in New York, but that won't be necessary, since you already have one."

I slid across the seat. I was sitting directly behind Martin, thank goodness, because I was fidgeting and thinking. *Okay, Howard the doorman and Fred the butler know Max. Freaking crazy is what this is.* While I twirled my ring round and round, I decided not to ask Max Spencer again who he was, at least not for now.

When we arrived at the restaurant, Martin hopped out quickly, walked around the car, and opened the door for Max. I was about to reach for my door handle when Max grabbed my hand. I slid back across the seat and got out on his side. The hostess quickly approached us and said, "Nice to see you again, Mr. Spencer. Follow me." *Dear God, that girl is drooling.*

"Thank you," Max said as she placed the menus in front of us.

She smiled. "My pleasure."

"Max, the hostess is flirting with you," I said, cracking a crooked grin.

"I'd rather you flirt with me, Livvy." He coolly grinned back.

"Oh." *Well, that's not happening, buddy.*

"We'll see." *He read my mind.* Slowly he brushed his top lip with his finger to shadow his smile. I swept my eyes across the dimly lit, dark-wood-paneled, white-linen-tablecloth restaurant. It wasn't only the hostess who was drooling over Max tonight. Every female, with or without a date, drooled. *He has to realize it. So what does he see in me?* Max reached for the wine list and asked if I preferred something different.

"Wine would be great," I murmured shyly.

"Livvy, are you okay?"

"Max," I whispered, "people are staring."

"I know."

"Doesn't it bother you?"

"No."

"But you could be sitting here with one of them on a real date."

He quickly scanned the pages. "Livvy, it's not me they're staring at," he said with sureness.

"Well, it sure isn't me." I was certain.

"Duckhorn cabernet sauvignon," he suggested, "would be nice with steak or the salmon." He placed the leather-bound wine list on the table and smiled.

"Ah…a rich California wine," I said, finding my confidence again.

"Know something about wines?"

"Not really."

"I bet differently," he said.

Max remarked this was the first time he had been to an upscale restaurant in New York other than for business. My mouth dropped open. "What?"

"I've been busy, Livvy. I work long and crazy hours."

"Oh." *He's in banking,* I thought. *There's nothing crazy about those hours.*

Max said Tucker and Crosby had visited him twice, and both times he had been living at the Four Seasons while his apartment was being renovated. He started laughing and said, "Hotel living did have perks." Now I understood why Fred and Howard knew him. But that didn't explain why the other people had known him.

He wanted to know about me. We talked about the different countries I had visited and what my interests were, such as art, history, and music.

"You can skip telling me about the gym," he said. "I can tell you obviously enjoy working out." I could tell he did, too.

He did ask once more about the Harley. All I said was, "It's nice."

"What, no details?"

Max grew a bit more serious. As he stared at his wineglass, he asked me about my health. I explained everything. He listened carefully as we nibbled on an appetizer.

He wanted to know if I had plans for the rest of the week. "Shopping, maybe, one day," I said. He said he heard that if I shopped, it wouldn't take long.

He polished off his last bite of steak and asked if I would like to go back to his apartment.

Totally surprised by his invitation, I almost choked on my last bite of salmon. "Max, I…uh…"

Max changed the subject. He said he had decided to split his time between London and New York. After all, he was spending too much time flying back and forth to different countries all over Europe; it was tiring.

"Yeah, I thought you would choose to split the year. That's amazing, Max. But after the way I rambled for ten minutes, I guess you know how I feel about Europe."

We drank two bottles of wine. Before I realized what I was saying, the words just sprang out of my mouth. "I would love to see your apartment, if it's not too late." Covering my blunder, I quickly added, "Or we could do it some other time." He looked up and did a head-nod thing. Our server immediately approached.

Max asked for the check. The guy had it ready and placed it on the table. Max never looked at it as he handed his card to him. In less than two minutes, the guy was back. Max took his phone from his jacket pocket and pressed one button. "Ready," he said. The hostess held my coat for me as I slipped my arms in. Max reached for my hand. He didn't wait for the young doorman to open the door for us; he did it himself. Martin was waiting with the car door open. Martin looked so familiar, but I couldn't place him.

Seconds later Martin asked, "Where to?"

"My place, but we'll need to take Miss Hunnicutt to the Four Seasons later this evening."

I was sitting in the middle of the backseat, not on the opposite side of the car as I had before. Something happened. The right side of my body was touching the left side of his body. I glanced up at him. *He's so handsome.* I didn't think anymore, my God, I kissed him.

He didn't put his arms around me. He breathed in and allowed me to completely take his full lips. Within seconds, both of his arms were tightly around me. He parted his lips, and so did I. He pulled away from my lips just enough to whisper, "Hold on, Livvy."

Martin had stopped the car, but he was quick as he opened the back door.

Max grabbed my hand as he stepped out. The doorman greeted us as he held the door open. "Good evening, Mr. Spencer."

Max had his left arm around my waist. "You, too, Jerry." Neither of us spoke as we entered the elevator. He shoved a key in a hole on the panel, and it lit up. I stepped in front of him, and he pulled me close and whispered in my hair, "Hold on, there are cameras."

The elevator door opened, revealing one huge double door. Max unlocked the door and pushed it open with his foot, but he never released me.

My head was spinning. I tugged at his overcoat and his jacket. He shrugged out of them both and dropped them on the floor. I pulled at the knot on his tie until I snatched hard enough that it came undone. I had to kiss him again. I fumbled with the buttons on his shirt. I gave up. I clasped my fingers between two buttons and ripped the thing. I heard those buttons bouncing on the marble floor, but I had already moved on to his undershirt. He yanked it over his head. I ran my hands across Max's firm bear chest. He kicked his shoes off. I heard them hit the wall. He found the zipper to my little black dress and tugged it with such force that the strap over my left shoulder ripped. My dress puddled at my feet. He reached up and released my hair clasp. Effortlessly, my hair fell and covered my bare shoulders.

"Livvy, I know we must..." He never completed his statement, because he pulled me back into his arms and kissed me tenderly. I felt my feet leave the floor as he scooped me up into his strong arms.

"Bedroom okay?" I kissed him with confidence and was thankful he interpreted my actions as a yes.

Once my feet hit the floor, I reached for his belt, and he helped me unfasten his pants. We never removed our eyes from each other. He felt good against my almost-bare skin. I nudged him in the direction of his bed. He obliged playfully, pushing me backward. He removed my shoes with no problem and traced the insides of my legs with his fingers. With my legs apart, he trailed kisses along my inner thighs. Slowly, one and then the other.

"Oh, Max."

He whispered, "I want you, but…" He worked his way to my neck, leaving me wanting more. "We are waiting."

Woefully I uttered, "Okay." With one smooth roll, I comfortably covered the front side of his warm body. Resting my forearms on his pillow, I ran my fingers through his thick, soft, wavy hair, drinking in his looks. *Not a single flaw. Sheer perfection is what this man is.*

He tried to release my bra hook, but that didn't work out so well. He broke it. Seconds later, I was lying underneath him. His body fit dreamily between my parted legs. His eyes scanned my body once more. Suddenly, I felt shy. I tugged at the sheet. *I'm embarrassed. Crosby and now Max. This is too fast.*

"Max."

"Livvy."

What the hell is wrong with me? I let go of the sheet. I couldn't stop kissing him. *I feel so—* "Please, Max."

With one hand, Max ripped my cheeky underwear from my body. He returned to my lips. I could feel his excitement, buried against my hip. I wanted him. I softly whispered, "Touch me." I didn't ask for permission to touch him. *Holy cow*! My hand stilled.

A weak smile curved his lips. He faintly stroked the side of my cheek with the back of his hand. "I would never hurt you, Livvy." He kissed me softly and continued, "I cannot touch you, because I would want more of you." I gripped him tighter and kissed him harder.

Max pressed his body firmly against mine repeatedly. Our actions accelerated.

"Max," I pleaded.

"Livvy," he sighed, and roughly palmed me between my legs. Our emotions flared. My body trembled as it freed itself from the intense caressing of *the* Max Spencer.

Our bodies remained tangled together while we recovered for a few minutes. Max pulled his fingers through my knotted hair and asked, "Are you okay?"

"Yes, Max, I am. But I have to ask, is there something wrong with me? I threw myself at Robert. He wouldn't. I begged Crosby, and according to Tucker, Crosby makes trips to the bar and will bring home anyone with a hoo-hah." Max laughed, but I was serious when I said, "Now you."

"Livvy—"

I interrupted him. "Do not say it's because I'm special."

He smiled and said, "You are special, and I want more than just to have sex with you. It's just that simple."

"I'll never get deflowered, will I?"

"Not right now, but trust me. It's not because I don't want to deflower you." He stroked my back with his fingertips and continued, "Livvy, I've just had the most enjoyable make-out session I have ever had in my life. But not taking you was also the most difficult thing I have ever done."

I laughed. "My God, look at you, Max. You're like—I don't know—beautiful." He laughed and I said, "C'mon, Max. Don't play innocent with me. You probably date and fool around all the time."

"I don't date anymore, or have sex."

"No way."

"I mentioned it at dinner." *I thought he was joking.* I rolled over on my back, baring all. "I work long hours, and I haven't met anyone here that seems to be worth the trouble. I think I want to kiss you again." He scooted over next to me and tucked his arm underneath my back while leaning over top of me. "Can I explore?"

"Knock yourself out," I said, no longer embarrassed. He chuckled. While he was exploring my breasts and neck, I said, "I have a question, Max. And would you please consider not laughing at me?"

He was already laughing.

I asked anyway. "Just say you change your mind over the next day or two. About having sex with me. Could we?"

He kissed my stomach and didn't neglect an inch of my flesh as he worked his way up to my lips. "Livvy, if I change my mind, I can assure you we will be amazing together."

"Oh my."

"You know you're a screamer, right?" he said. But he didn't stop there. Oh no, sirree. "Livvy, did I make the list?"

"Come here." I kissed him smoothly. "Definitely."

"C'mon." He grabbed my hands, pulling me along. "Let's make out in the shower." He turned the water on and stepped out of one massive shower. Max shook his head. "Jesus, Livvy, you're even better with all the lights on."

"I'm glad I didn't see you with the lights on first. I would have run."

"And I would have run after you."

Chilled, I stepped closer to him. "Thank you for tonight." He draped me in the warmth of his arms and guided me underneath the steamy water.

With his lips against mine he said, "It's not over yet."

Max asked if I could stay the night. I told him I'd send Mom a text so she wouldn't worry if she woke before I returned in the morning. "Livvy, what are you going to say to Cookie?" he said handing me his phone.

"The truth."

"Well, PG it a little, would you?"

I giggled and read aloud as I typed: *It's late. I'm staying at Max's tonight.*

CHAPTER 15

I could feel Max was not in bed with me. When I opened my eyes, there was a note on his pillow.

Livvy,
I am sorry I left without saying good-bye this morning, but you were sleeping.
Please accept my apology for tearing your beautiful things.
There is a package for you in the foyer.
Martin's number is programmed in your phone. He is expecting your call.
Take your time this morning. I will call you later.
Thank you for calling last night a date.
Max

Why am I smiling? Furthermore, I didn't mean to call it a date, I thought as I lay in his bed. "A banker, my ass." I smiled again.

Along with the note on Max's pillow were my undergarments. My bra was missing all three hooks, and my panties…I inspected them. "How in the dickens did he do that?" The thing was shredded.

I spotted the shirt he had worn last night draped across a big tiger statue in the corner. I got out of bed, pranced myself right over to it, and grabbed the shirt, which was surely in a state of hopelessness.

From the looks of it, the shirt could never be worn on the fine body of its owner again. But dang, as I put my arms through the sleeves and pulled the shirt across the front of my body, I got a whiff of Max. It smelled good. Enough of that. I was hungry and needed to check my blood sugar.

I walked through Max's apartment in a complete state of shock. It had been dark last night, and I had been a bit preoccupied, but now I took in the details. Three balconies with incredible views of the city. The furnishings were contemporary but soft. The kitchen was a commercial style similar to my parents', but more modern and most inviting.

I walked away from the kitchen in the direction of the front door. I paused to admire his artwork. I was impressed again as I studied a few of his paintings.

I gathered the packages from the foyer and headed to his bedroom.

I opened the large box first. It contained a purple Juicy Couture outfit, which included pants, a jacket, a sparkly tee, and socks.

The medium box contained a pair of brown leather Ugg boots. The small box contained a new bra and panties. Then there was a rather large bag containing a coat. The last bag contained girly bathroom things.

Now, I knew Neiman's didn't open until ten. Who was I kidding? Max had just got my attention, loud and clear.

But for now, I had to eat. I went back to the kitchen and looked in his refrigerator. It was completely stocked. I ate a serving-size yogurt and drank a glass of juice. I was about to place the glass and spoon in the dishwasher when I heard someone close the door and scurry into the kitchen. An attractive middle-aged lady said in accented English, "You are Miss Hunnicutt?" I nodded. "I am Ester," she said. "May I make you breakfast?"

I smiled. "No, thank you. I've eaten." I became aware that I was standing there wearing Max's shirt with basically no buttons.

I closed the dishwasher and told Ester I would get out of her way shortly. I closed the bedroom door behind me. Well, no need to make the bed. I quickly showered and dressed. When I sprayed the perfume, I couldn't help but smile—one of my favorites, Trish Sexy 9.

I left the bag that contained the girly things on the bathroom counter and shoved the clothes I had worn last night into the empty boxes. I called the number Max had left me.

"I'm ready, Martin."

"I'm pulling the car around now, Miss Hunnicutt."

I glanced around the bedroom and thought about taking Max's shirt with me so I could replace it. But from the look of things, he'd never miss one shirt. I folded it and left it on his massive chest. I placed a note on top that simply said "Sorry, Max."

By the time I arrived back at our suite, I must have said good morning and thank you fifteen times, so when Fred flung open the door, I only said, "Morning." I handed him my bag and asked him to please tip the bellman. I disappeared into the bedroom and called Sammy. I changed into a nice pair of jeans, a tan ribbed sweater, and my tall, brown leather dress boots. I grabbed my Gucci tote, threw my Burberry scarf around my neck, and decided on my brown, to-the-hip J.Crew cashmere coat.

"Where to, Miss Livvy?" Sammy asked.

"How about the closest museum?" I replied.

"Sure thing, Miss Livvy."

My phone rang. It took me a couple of moments to fish it out of my tousled bag. "Thank you, Max. Everything was perfect." *Shit, Livvy, stop smiling.*

"You are welcome. I called to ask you for a second date tonight."

"Why not?" I laughed.

"Is that a yes? I hope it's a yes."

"It's a yes. But can we cook instead of going out?" He seemed surprised by my suggestion but happily agreed.

"Seven. Dress casual."

My phone rang again. I didn't recognize the number. I hesitated before I mustered up enough nerve to answer. "Hello?"

A voice from the other end said, "Livvy, Matt Bartlett."

It felt like an eternity passed before I could spit out my next word. "Yes, Matt, how are you?" He beat around the bush, and then he said he would like to see me before I left New York. Since I had plans tonight and he had plans tomorrow night, he suggested lunch tomorrow. I accepted.

After spending the entire day with my superglue sidekick, Sammy returned me safely to Fred at the Four Seasons. I stood in the closet, thinking I had to dress "casual" tonight. Let me tell you, the wardrobe thing had become a minor crisis for me, even though it was only dinner with Max. Jeans with gold sparkles on the pockets might work. And maybe my dark-purple silk blouse with a V-neck and long sleeves. Black heels tonight. I'd leave my hair down and wavy and pray for no frizz.

The doorbell rang. I didn't move. Fred was on it. I gathered my things, took a deep breath, and stepped around the corner. Max caught my gaze, met me halfway, kissed me softly, and said, "I said casual."

I forgot to filter my thoughts. "My God, Max, you know, I'm a sucker for men in white shirts and jeans."

He laughed and said, "I didn't know that, but I'll keep it in mind."

We walked to the curb outside.

"Hello, Martin."

"Nice to see you again, Miss Hunnicutt."

I sat in the middle of the backseat next to Max. He placed his left hand on my leg, and I let my right hand rest on the top of his left leg. That position lasted about five seconds. "Screw it," he said and clicked the button to my seatbelt. With one arm he pulled me almost into his lap and kissed me. I forgot we were in his car, and I totally forgot about Martin in the front seat. Within a few minutes, he parked the car in front of Max's building.

"Livvy, try to behave, okay?"

"That's not on my agenda."

He stared at my lips. "Well, hell. Can you try a little?"

I slowly licked them. "No."

As we walked through his front door, I apologized to him for not complimenting him the night before on how beautiful his home was. I told him that I took a quick look around this morning, partly because I took a wrong turn. He smiled, pressed one button on a remote control, and a fire blazed up in the fireplace. I watched him as he walked toward me and asked, "Wine okay?"

I propped myself against the kitchen counter. Max eased closer. I draped my arms loosely around his neck. Roughly he gripped my hips and yanked me forward, causing our bodies to clash, and then he deliciously kissed me.

Jesus! I gasped. *What is it with him?* My arms abandoned his neck, only for my palms to brush across his sculpted chest. Hesitantly, I pointed to the fish.

Max and I finished making dinner together. I complimented him once again, but this time on his cooking abilities. But who was the real Max Spencer? I needed answers. I placed my fork down and asked causally, "How was work today?"

He nodded. I looked around the dining room, fanned the air with a hand gesture, and raised my brow. *Dang it, do some explaining.* He got tickled at me. He knew I wanted some answers, and not the "I'm a banker" one.

I blew it. As soon as his expression changed, I laughed. He leaned toward me and said, "You know, you are a lot like Rae. She's smart and everyone knows it, but you don't want anyone to know how smart you are. Do you, Livvy?"

"Maybe."

We had ourselves a stare down, until he finally said, "I'm more in international banking."

"Yeah, I figured. What else?"

"Your turn."

"I graduated high school a year early," I offered.

"I landed a large company today," he countered.

I nodded. "Well, I didn't, but I enjoyed my day at the museum. What do you mean, *landed*?"

"Takeover. Tell me more."

"I'm not as interesting as you are, Max."

"Give me something…anything."

"I can calculate numbers pretty well."

"What else?"

"No. Your turn."

"Shot some hoops today."

"Did you play well?" I asked.

"Your turn. But yes."

I grinned. "I suck at basketball. But I enjoy mission trips. I sometimes help with medical stuff."

"Diabetes?"

"Sometimes. But mostly…do you have a weak stomach?"

"No."

"Worms. A lot of worms. But I like assisting Dr. Kurt in minor surgeries. As bad as things can be for Rae and people like us, we are so blessed, because kids that are diagnosed with diabetes at a young age in third-world countries don't make it, unless people like us go and continue to help. Wait—it was your turn."

"I can't top that, Livvy."

I stood up. One-handed, he caught me around my waist while he was sitting. When his eyes connected with mine, I kissed him softly. I got that funny feeling again. "You sit and relax." I pointed to the fireplace. "I'll clean up."

"No, we'll do it together."

I put the last dish into the dishwasher, and he turned it on. I refilled our wineglasses, and we returned to his beautiful great room. The fire was still blazing, and he lit a few candles as he gestured to the sofa. He placed his arm around me, and we stretched out with our feet propped up. I asked him about the artwork he had collected, because I recognized most of the paintings were from just a couple of different artists. He explained that he liked the artists' work and had bought almost everything in two different galleries. "But you already knew that, didn't you?"

"Yes."

Max sat his wineglass on the cocktail table, picked up a remote control, and music began to play. He took my hands and gently pulled me to my feet. "May I have this dance?" he asked.

As Max gazed at me in his arms while swaying to soft jazz music, I couldn't help but think again how handsome he was. His complexion was a tanned olive color, almost the color of mine. I had found out his skin tone was a fancy gene from his grandmother. She was from India, so his father, Dr. Spencer, had dark skin. Anne, Max's mother, had skin as fair as my mother's. Max had hazel eyes that looked more green than brown at the moment. He had full lips, and I must say they were soft. He had wavy dark hair that was clean-cut. Max's smile was literally to die for, and he was smiling right now. He was six foot one and must work out every day, because his body was gorgeous. I thought to myself, *Look out, Livvy. Don't go there. Careful; guard yourself. Keep this simple and fun.*

"I hope you know what you're doing, Max," he asked himself aloud as "I Got It Bad (and That Ain't Good)" softly played.

Max and I spent the next two hours in his bedroom. "Max, I'm sorry that you feel we need harsh restrictions. I think we need to make a decision." I paused and said, "We don't have to see each other again…like this, I mean."

He laughed deeply and pulled me back on top of him. "Hush, stop laughing at me," I said. "Let me finish. Max, please. Or we can just do it."

"No. Not yet." I huffed and tried to pretend his decision didn't bother me. *But, shit, what does a girl have to do to lose it?* I have gotten naked. I had tried being charming, sexy, and even a little kinky with Crosby. Shoot, I considered playing the smart card, but backed off. I couldn't give my stuff away.

I ran my fingers down his length. "Careful," he warned.

I firmly gripped my hand around him one last time, then nibbled at his lips. "Are you sure…Max?"

"I'm only sure about one thing. I might go to hell one day, but it won't be because I popped the cherry of Livvy Hunnicutt. She's the marrying kind."

I shoved him in the middle of his chest and said, "I'm not getting married anytime soon, and I *want* you to pop my cherry."

He was laughing, but I wasn't. "Well, when you fall in love with me, I will pop it."

"I'm not going to fall in love with you, Max Spencer, but I still want you to—"

He interrupted me. "I want to be the one." Then he told me to get up and get dressed. He couldn't take anymore.

While we were dressing, he asked if I had plans tomorrow. I told him Matt Bartlett had asked me to meet him for lunch. Max asked me if I could eat lunch as fast as Crosby told him I shopped. He didn't ask any more questions about Matt; he just picked up his cell from his bedside bachelor's chest, pressed one button, and said, "Five minutes, Martin."

On the drive back to the hotel, Max asked me out again tomorrow evening. He thought we would go to dinner and then dancing.

As we stood in the foyer of the suite, his lips softly brushed mine. Then he whispered in my ear, "You are going to kill me. And the bad thing is, I know it." He walked out.

CHAPTER 16

Fred met me in the butler's kitchen. "What can I get for you?"

"Wheat toast and hard scrambled eggs and juice." I crashed on the sofa in the living room. I had no more than closed my eyes when Magic Fred served up breakfast.

I threw on gym clothes, tightened my laces, and took off to the hotel gym. By the time I returned to our suite, that dang Fred had worked more of his magic. Hanging in the closet was my black dress that Max had torn the night before, repaired. *Fred sews? I gotta take Fred home with me.*

Almost eleven. I had to get dressed. Once again, I had no idea what to wear. Maybe I'd ask Fred. He'd give me an opinion. And then I'd have Fred make me a morning cocktail to settle my nerves. What must I have been thinking when I agreed to have lunch with Matt Bartlett anyway? He's a freaking movie star.

I was almost in a panic by the time I found Fred in the kitchen. I grabbed him by his hand and told him I needed him. He pulled back but didn't release my hand. "Miss Hunnicutt," Fred shouted, "I'm gay!"

I still had Fred by the hand. I shouted back, "I know you're gay, Fred. I need help with an outfit for a lunch date, and I also need a big fat drink."

"Miss Hunnicutt," he asked, "with whom are you having lunch?"

"Matt Bartlett!"

"Well, why didn't you speak up? I noticed you have a killer deep-orange V-neck top hanging in the closet, and it's not too much for a lunch date. You know, the one with the one long sleeve and the other shoulder bare." He stared at me and said, "Hold on, I can tell you need that drink. You relax, and I'll lay your clothes out for you."

I fell across the bed. *Thank God for Fred.*

Good Lord, if dating didn't kill me, Fred would. His drink was horrible, but I drank it anyway and showered. Fred put together an entire outfit and had it arranged on the bed.

I must have looked hopeless, staring into the bathroom mirror. Fred pulled out the vanity chair. "Girl, you're in good hands. Have a seat," he said as he picked up the hairbrush.

Sammy was waiting with the door open. I asked him to turn the music on. It sometimes calmed my nerves. But it didn't help this time; I was fidgeting.

He pulled up to the door of the restaurant. I asked Sammy what I should do. I didn't want to arrive before Matt, or what if he had decided not to come and not call? Sammy smiled and told me to sit tight. He went inside and, good Lord, returned with Matt. Matt opened my door and offered me his hand. I placed my hand in his and nervously stepped out.

"Livvy, wow." Matt kissed me on my cheek.

Oh. Dear. Lord. Where did the people come from? Cameras were clicking, and people were shouting, "Look this way!"

Matt shoved a guy. Sammy yelled, "Back up, and I'm only telling you once!" Sammy and Matt wrapped their arms around me and shuffled me inside the restaurant.

Sammy spoke to the manager of the restaurant and requested that Matt and I exit out the back door, after calling him first so he could meet us. He also told Matt he would drop him off wherever he needed to go.

Matt apologized for the paparazzi. He said he hadn't thought to warn me because things like that rarely happened to him. "Someone will publish the picture, and people will wonder who the girl is," he said. I laughed at him, thinking people could care less who I was.

Matt was nice with looks to match. He was around six feet, with clean-cut, dark-brown hair, green eyes, and fair skin, and he was buff. He was almost a pretty boy but in a hot kind of way.

He said he knew four things about me. One, I was beautiful. I blushed, an ugly shade of crimson for sure. Two, I was Victoria Hunnicutt's daughter. Three, he knew I had one friend here in New York, Max Spencer. He took a sip of water. Four, David Williams and I were friends, and he had called Matt after he met me in Colorado.

"Excuse me? I clearly remember meeting him, but I only asked to borrow a couple of empty chairs, and then I thanked him after lunch."

Matt laughed. "I received a text message from David that said 'I met a girl on top of a mountain.' He was cracking me up. I had to call him. I asked him Mountain Girl's name. He said, 'Livvy Hunnicutt.' He described your tanned skin and said you looked as if you were from a warm island somewhere in the Pacific, but that wasn't possible. I'll tell you why in a minute.

"I never gave my discussion with David another thought until Sam called. He's the director you met the other day. He said Anna called and thought she had something he needed to look at. Well, my father is an agent and friends with Sam." Matt got tickled and continued, "Dad said he had something he wanted me to read. It was from a Southern writer. She was apparently new, because he had never heard of her work before. And then he said it: Victoria Hunnicutt. It clicked. David had said in his description of the angel, Livvy Hunnicutt was unmistakably a Southern girl. This was the reason David changed his geography from the Pacific and quickly placed you in the South. I read the pages and called Anna. I asked her if Victoria had a daughter. She laughed and said no, she had two. One was engaged. Then she said the one I was referring to was Livvy."

Good God, I was just left speechless. My mouth fell open. Matt said, "I'm sorry. Apparently I said something wrong."

"Oh no, Matt. Do I sound that southern?" I asked. He assured me I didn't.

He admitted he had twisted Anna's arm to get my number. "She mentioned you have diabetes?"

"Yes, that's right."

"I would not have known, I mean, by looking at you." He wiped his forehead, seeming embarrassed. "Shit, I—"

"Matt, it's fine. Really. My sister and I get that all the time. You know, there are two types of diabetes. Some people can control it with diet and exercise. If not, medication is prescribed—"

"That's what my aunt has. She must weigh,"—he softly smiled—"a lot."

"I'm sorry she has it."

"You and your sister have the other one?"

"Yes. Type 1, or some call it juvenile; it's the same. All type 1 diabetics are insulin dependent, either by daily injections or an insulin pump. I eat right and exercise"—I looked at my empty wineglass—"I can't say I don't have a drink, though. Enough about all this."

Matt was easy to talk to. We discussed my family and his. Then he told me his best friend was also being considered for the role of Ben Davis, and he could see Peter easily getting it. I interrupted, "Peter who?"

"Peter Weston." He twirled his water glass. "Livvy, I hope I get the part*." Me too,* I thought.

"Lunch has been great," I said, "but I've accepted a dinner invitation for tonight. Do you mind if we—"

Matt got the waiter's attention, and I called Sammy. We followed the manager of the restaurant to the back door, where Sammy was waiting.

"What the hell?" Matt shouted as a photographer appeared out of nowhere. He pushed a camera out of our faces. Sammy took his jacket off and covered my head. Matt opened the back passenger door and pushed me inside. I fell into the backseat, and he landed on top of me.

"God, Livvy, I'm sorry. I didn't hurt you, did I?" He shuffled from on top of me.

I pawed my hair from my face. "No, I'm fine."

"Where to, Mr. Bartlett?" asked Sammy.

Ten minutes later, we arrived at Matt's destination. Matt and Sammy looked around before either of them allowed me to exit the car. Finally Matt opened the door and lent me his hand as I stepped out. He leaned in sweetly with his hand on my waist and kissed me on my cheek. "Livvy, it has been a pleasure, and I hope to see you this summer on the set."

I thanked him for lunch. "I too hope things work out for you, and I might be slightly disappointed if Peter Weston ends up with the role of Ben."

He kissed me once again on my cheek. "Spoken like a true southern lady."

"Ready, Miss Livvy?"

"Yes, Sammy." The two glasses of wine had gone to my head. "Sammy, I should be the happiest girl in the world, and yet because of one guy, I'm screwed up." Once again, I was crying and blabbing away to an almost complete stranger.

Sammy placed a phone call and said, "Meet me at the front entrance." After he parked, Howard opened the car door. I stepped out, and Sammy said, "Don't let go."

Fred threaded my arm through his. "Girl, you still look hot. Even with tears dripping from your chin."

Fred told me I could sleep one hour, but then I had a date, and I was going to look even hotter than I had for my lunch date. I fell across the king-size bed. I felt him remove my shoes.

I heard the bedroom door swing open. I thought, *No, it's only been five minutes*. Fred shouted, "Get up, girl. I made you an energy drink, and the coffee is brewing. Get in the shower, but do not wet the hair. You are going dancing with Mr. Spencer, and a new outfit's been sent over, thanks to your mother."

Fred was standing at the side of the bed with one hand on his hip, holding that drink, which was certainly going to taste god-awful. *Was he patting his foot? Yes, he was. Lord, this was one impatient gay man.* "I'm up."

After a shower, the god-awful drink, and a cup of coffee, I felt better. Fred came into the bathroom and threw me my undergarments. "Girl, this is all that will fit under the dress, but it is to die for." As he started on my makeup, he talked my ears off. Fred suggested a down, messy look as he proceeded with my hair.

Then he unveiled the dress. It was just the right shade of purple, and appeared to hit high on the thigh. There was a narrow strap over each shoulder, and a low V-neck. It came with a short, fitted, and tapered black leather jacket. It struck slightly above my waist. Apparently, my black Prada shoes would be needed again. Fred was standing directly in front of me, patting that foot of his again. He handed me my jewelry: one ring, large hoop earrings, and three bracelets. *Not bad*, I thought as I viewed the final result.

The doorbell rang; it had to be Max. Fred quickly returned to the bedroom and said, "Miss Livvy, you might want to follow me." Fred opened the double doors to the bedroom.

Shit. Flowers, and not just one arrangement, a buttload of them. "Fred," I said, feeling fretful, since Max was due any moment now, "will you please remove one of those cards?" He did and read it aloud: "Livvy, thank you for a most memorable lunch! Matt."

I asked Fred to remove the cards and hang on to them. I could tell his skinny little ass was dying to read them anyway. I was standing in the foyer, trying to recuperate from the flower garden. The doorbell rang again. It was Max. Mom walked in right behind him, greeted him, looked at me, and said, "Oh my, Livvy!"

Then she shook her head and walked past Max and me, but quickly popped her head back around the corner of the foyer. My eyes widened in a warning to say nothing. She shrugged her shoulders and said, "Never mind."

"Here's your clutch for the night. Oh wait, let me get your big tote, the one with all your crap in it." Fred's voice trailed off. "You really should organize it."

Max leaned close, and with his cheek against mine he whispered, "What am I going to do with you?"

Fred returned and hung the tote on my arm. He giggled. "The tote is for later," he whispered, "you know, in case Mr. Spencer keeps you late."

In the car, I scooted to the middle of the seat. Max leisurely sat down and eased his arm behind me, letting his hand rest on my hip. Swiftly he pulled me nearly in his lap and then kissed me, roughly. I shivered from the instant tingle that hijacked me, right *there*. I slowly pulled away. He coolly grinned. "I heard you had a different kind of excitement today."

How does he do that? And how did he already know about what happened at lunch? "Yes, but Sammy and Matt were great. It was over as fast as it happened."

Max's coat was open, and his scarf was loosely draped under his collar. I placed my left hand on his chest and leaned closer. "What?" he asked.

"You. The white shirt. Jeans."

"You like?" *He knows I do.*

"Very much."

Over dinner, we couldn't keep our hands to ourselves. "Let's go," he said as he signed the check. "I don't want to go out." He took my hand. "I have something else in mind."

"What, your place?"

"Not exactly," he said, giving my outfit a once-over. "Do you own ugly clothes?"

"Uh-uh," I answered, wondering what exactly "not exactly" meant.

As soon as we got into the car, he pulled me close to him. Before I realized it, I was in his lap, straddling him. His hands were up my dress and on my hips. "Oh God," I whispered.

Max was holding my hips tight. I ran my hands through his thick hair. Martin parked the car in front of Max's building. "I thought you said we weren't—"

"We're going down, not up." He grabbed my hand, opened the door, and told Martin to get my bag.

"Down?"

"The basement." He grinned as he pressed the elevator button.

"Why?"

The elevator doors opened. "What is this place?" I asked while Martin unlocked the double doors.

"My gym." Martin handed me my bag and looked at my feet.

"Smells and looks new."

"It is."

"Want to play?" He swung open the doors to a full-size basketball court. He pointed. "The gym is further back." I dropped my bag.

"I suck, remember? But yeah, I'll play." I plopped down on the floor, removed my shoes, and dug through my bag for a ponytail holder. I pulled up my hair. "Kick your loafers off, buddy." I tightened my ponytail.

Barefoot, designer jeans, and a white fitted undershirt. *That is one hot-looking man right there,* I thought as he retrieved a ball from a rack.

"What's the game?" I asked.

He dribbled a couple of times. "Game? I thought I would teach you how to shoot first."

"Well, in that case, I'm all yours."

"Come here."

I ambled closer. He stepped behind and reached around me with both arms, palming the ball. His breath was warm on my neck. "You smell good, Livvy." He lifted my arm at my wrist. "Now put this hand here. Real good, Livvy." His lips grazed my neck. "Now put this hand here." He slid my hand across the ball and kneed my legs slightly apart. "From this far away, you may need to put some leg strength into your shot, as well as arm strength."

"Is that right?" I said, wanting him to tease my neck again.

"Uh-huh." He dropped his arms and said, "Shoot, Livvy." I closed my eyes and shot the ball.

"Like that?" *Whoosh.*

"Yeah, like that."

"Want me to get the ball?" I asked. He nibbled at my ear. "I believe it's your turn."

"No." He spun me around. "Thought you sucked at basketball?"

"I do. Lucky shot, that's all."

"What about a little one-on-one?" he asked. "And to make it interesting, say, a wager?"

"What's at stake?"

"If you win, anything you want, but your virginity."

"I'm listening."

"If I win, which I will," he said, bouncing the ball, "I want to have a serious conversation. I choose the topic."

"You're on."

Twenty minutes into our one-on-one, we both were dripping wet with sweat. Twenty-three to thirty, Max on top.

We were scuffling for the ball when I felt light-headed. I reached for his arm. "My blood sugar is dropping."

"Here," he said, taking my arm, "sit down." I leaned against the wall.

He brought over my bag. "What do you need?"

"Glucose meter, juice box, and peanut butter crackers."

He turned my bag upside down. "Shit, Livvy." I laughed as he rummaged through all the crap. Peanut butter crackers, insulin pens, tampons, needles, cotton balls, lipstick, lip gloss, alcohol wipes, Capri Suns, tasty packs of Smarties, and a Granny Smith apple rolled across the floor. And that was the short list of crap on the floor. I took a meter pouch from the top of the heap.

"Fifty is low for you, right?'

"Yeah." I picked up a Capri Sun, and Max poked the straw in. "Want one? I have plenty."

"Believe I will."

I opened the crackers. "Have one," I said.

I twisted my cracker apart and licked the peanut butter out. Max laughed. "When I was little, I did that with Oreos."

"Me too, you know, before diabetes."

"Feeling better?"

"Yes. Told you I sucked at basketball. Thanks for going easy on me."

"You don't suck." He wiped a crumb from my lip and kissed me. "You said in Cabo your nose is too big. It's not. I like it."

"Oh God, please tell me my nose is not your topic of choice?"

Max chuckled as we ate the last two crackers. "No. I want to talk about us."

"Us? Come on, Max. There is no us. First of all, the geography won't work." He grinned.

"I have a jet."

"Well, that certainly beats the hell out of taking the bus, doesn't it?"

"Yeah, it does," he agreed. "Look, I won't go to London until June or July. That's five or six months. I know from the last conversation I had with Crosby, your position on dating really hasn't changed. But what you and I do and talk about stays between us, unless you tell. Understand?"

"Yes."

"Long distance might even work better for a while, since I'm hell bent on waiting for you to fall in love with me before we go all the way."

I made a noncommittal "mmm" and slurped my last bit of juice. "Livvy," he said, "I'm not asking for a commitment. I'm asking to get to know you better. I like everything about you so far. I'll answer any questions you ask, because I want you to get to know me. Think about it."

I realized I was nodding while my wheels were spinning. "I will think about it. After all, you do have a jet and a great gym."

He hopped up from the fine polished wood court and grabbed my hands. Pulling me up, he said, "I may not know you that well, Livvy Hunnicutt, but I know you well enough to know you don't give a rat's ass about the jet or the gym. Let's get you back to Fred."

In the car, I was tired and laid my head on Max's shoulder, and we both were quiet. He finally said he was flying to Paris in the morning for a couple of days and then to London. The trip would be short, and he said he'd be back in less than four days.

"Go with me."

I raised my head from his shoulder. "What? Max, I...I can't."

Max walked me to my suite, and we stood outside for a moment. I put my arms around his neck. He pulled me close. I gasped from the force of his hug. He kissed me, and he did not hold back. Fred opened the door at 1:30 a.m. *Jeez, did the man ever sleep?*

I stepped inside, saying, "Come in." Max followed.

As soon as we stepped into my temporary room, Max said, "Livvy, I'm not ready to say good-bye."

"Then don't." He kissed me again and walked out. He left me standing there with my knees feeling a tad weak.

CHAPTER 17

F red, my lifestyle butler, swayed into my room with a breakfast tray in his hand and said I needed to get up so he could get my bags packed. I certainly didn't argue with him. I hated to pack.

Fred knew how to spoil a girl. He shopped more than I did. Apparently I was wearing a classy skirt and jacket home with leather boots.

Fred put my final straggling items in my carry-on bag and placed my bags in the foyer next to Mom's things. I asked him if he would please make arrangements for the beautiful flowers Matt had sent yesterday. After all, it would be awful if no one enjoyed them.

I hugged Fred and told him I couldn't have survived the past few days without him. He totally agreed.

I called Matt and prayed for his voice mail. *Whatta you know? My lucky day.* "Hello, Matt. Livvy Hunnicutt. I apologize for calling early, but I wanted to thank you for the beautiful flowers you sent yesterday. All twenty-one bouquets. Thank you also for lunch. It was delicious, and, just as one of your cards said, memorable. Good luck! I hope to see you this summer."

The doorbell rang. No needed to move, because Fred had it. Mom and I were standing in the foyer talking, and my back was toward the door when Max came in. He asked Mom if he could speak to me for a moment. "Come to Paris and London with me, Livvy. I'll have you back in Auburn in four days."

"I…" Max stopped me before I could say anything else and kissed me. I felt my knees get weak. *No, Livvy, you can't. Good God, you barely know him. Stop! Clear your head!* But I was kissing Max back, though my arms remained at my side. I couldn't stop myself. *Why can't I stop?*

Mom cleared her throat, and Max slowly pulled away from my lips. But he didn't release me from his strong embrace or his restless stare when he spoke to Mom. "Please forgive me, Victoria. I was only hoping to spend a few more days with Livvy." He turned and walked out.

Mom took my hands and said, "Livvy, you overthought things with Crosby, and he is a wonderful young man. Now you're doing the same thing with Max. You have your passport. Go with Max. Go."

Fred was still holding the door and said, "Hurry, girl. I'm right behind you with your bags."

My legs wouldn't move. "Mom, I'm afraid. What if I make another mistake?"

She hugged me and said, "Then you will learn from it. Go, Livvy."

I ran out the door, but the elevator door completely closed just as I turned the corner. Max didn't see me. I was banging the lit-up down button on the wall shouting, "C'mon! C'mon!" The elevator felt like it took an eternity, but the door finally opened and I stepped in. When the doors reopened in the lobby, I could see Max. He was almost to the front entrance. I was running toward him, but I knew I couldn't catch up with him. I shouted, "Max!" He froze, but he didn't turn. I walked closer. When he turned, I said, "You know, Max, I've never been to Paris, and I do have my passport."

Max tried to play it cool. But he was already holding my hand when he said, "Well, that's good to know. I thought we might have to fly to Auburn first." He hugged me and whispered softly in my ear, "Thank you, Livvy."

We heard a terrible commotion from behind us. My Lord, it was Fred. Poor guy was carrying my bags, grunting and cursing. The tote was draped around his neck. My large bag, the one with shorter straps, was thrown over his arm, and he was pulling two large, wheeled bags behind him. Max chuckled and said, "Looks like Fred could use a hand." We met Fred before he hurt himself. Max reached for the two large wheeled bags, and I retrieved the tote. Fred insisted on carrying the bag that remained on his arm like a big purse.

As we approached the entrance, Martin asked us to hold up. By now, Howard the doorman and Fred were standing beside us. "It seems, due to Miss Hunnicutt, we will have some attention when we exit the building," Martin said.

I didn't understand, but Max did. He looked up and did that head thing he does. Some guy ran over. "Yes, sir, Mr. Spencer, how may I help you?"

"Take a look. Get a head count."

The gentleman walked to the door, returned, and said, "Ten." I stood quietly. It seemed I had caused some sort of trouble, and good Lord, it was only 7:20 a.m. What could I have done?

"I want everyone to walk out the door with us," Martin said. "Stay close to Mr. Spencer and Miss Hunnicutt." Max told me to put my sunglasses on as he reached in his pocket to retrieve his.

"Livvy, walk fast and don't look up. They only want a couple of pictures of you because of the lunch date you had yesterday."

"I don't understand. I'm nobody. Why?" Matt had said the pictures might show up, but I thought he was kidding. "Max, I'm sorry." I felt terrible for the trouble I had caused.

Martin was on my right side, Max on my left, and Fred stood behind us. The gentleman Max had summoned to look outside was now standing in front of us. Howard had the door. "Let's go," Max said.

Max and Martin grabbed my arms. *Okay*, I thought, *this was a bit extreme*. I only had had lunch with Matt. About that time, the door flew open, and we walked fast. I just looked at the ground. I heard cameras snapping and people asking, "Are you Olivia Hunnicutt? How long have you known Matt Bartlett?"

Martin shouted, "Back up!" Max swung open the car door, I stooped and sat, and he quickly got in, nearly sitting on top of me before pushing me across the seat. I heard the trunk pop open. My God, the entire car shook as my luggage was tossed in.

A man pressed his hands against the window and bent down as if he could see through the tinted windows, shouting, "Olivia! How long have you known Matt?"

Before Martin could get his door open, one guy shouted, "That guy with Hunnicutt is Max Spencer." The cameras were still snapping.

The photographer tried to reach around Martin and get a picture. Martin quickly sat down in his seat and attempted to close his door. The man's arm was caught and hanging inside the car. He dropped the camera. Martin threw the camera into the passenger seat. The man's arm was still caught, the door pulled tightly against it. Martin opened the door just enough for him to remove his arm and said, "Move it, or I will drag you down the street."

Martin started the car, stomped the accelerator, and sped away.

"You okay?" Max asked.

"Yes."

"Good. You do keep things exciting in more ways than one."

"Max, I only had lunch with Matt," I said, stating my case once more.

"I know."

Max asked Martin what he thought about me. Martin said he had enjoyed working the past several days more than he had for the past ten months. Max smiled. I asked Max how long Martin had worked with him. They both laughed, and Max answered, "Ten months."

Max's phone must have beeped twenty times in the past ten minutes. He reached for my hand and held it for a moment.

"I must check my e-mails, but I will devote all of the flight time to you." He kissed the back of my hand. "I promise." He placed my hand on his thigh, then removed his cell from his jacket pocket and proceeded to respond to his e-mails.

Martin glanced in the rearview mirror and grinned. I winked at him. Martin reminded me of my uncle Troy, a military man. Martin wasn't a tall man, I guessed five nine. He was broad-shouldered and firmly built. From what I could tell, he was in his fifties. I guessed that was his age only because of the soft lines around his eyes, as well as the gentle ones across his forehead. I liked his salt-and-pepper hair, more pepper than salt. Overall, "handsome" would sum up Martin. I knew I'd seen him somewhere before, but I couldn't place him. Regardless of how nice I thought he was, after today, I knew Martin had a little badass-ness running through his veins.

Martin parked ten feet from the stairs of the jet. The engines were humming. Three people stood waiting to greet us. Max introduced everyone. "Joann is our flight attendant. Phillip and Dagger are my pilots." They each shook my hand. Martin handed Phillip the car keys and asked him to move the car into the hangar. Joann and Martin loaded the luggage onto the plane. "Martin is also a pilot, so he'll join Phillip and Dagger in the cockpit." Max pointed to the stairs, and he took my hand once again.

"You know, Martin," I said, with him two steps behind me, "I fly with my dad. Unfortunately, I'm unable to be licensed, even though I've passed class." Martin asked me why I couldn't get licensed.

"I have diabetes, and I've had a few complications in the past."

"I see."

Max spoke up. "Livvy also rides a Harley, a Fat Boy."

"Is that right?"

"Yes, Martin, I do."

Joann entered the plane first. At the top of the stairs, she turned and said, "Welcome, Miss Hunnicutt." She reached for my coat.

Oh my, the plane was beautiful; smelled new, too. Max initially pointed at two large leather seats but then said, "Let's sit on the sofa instead." We buckled up. Max reached for my hand. "Thank you for coming, Livvy."

Joann asked if she could get us anything. Max told her we were
fine, but I would need to eat in an hour. She disappeared as we taxied
down the runway.

Once the plane leveled out, we unbuckled his seatbelts. He seemed
to be in deep thought. "Livvy…" Max reached for a remote control.
He pressed a button, and music began to play softly overhead. He took
my hand. "I do work for a bank. Eighteen months ago, many banks
went under. Some banks accepted bailout money from the government, but my bank was and still is strong. Four months after the major
banking crisis, the CEO walked into my office and asked me to follow him. That day was the first time I met the board members. They
said they wanted to advance someone. My degree, along with several
minors in foreign languages, impressed them. It didn't hurt that I'm
not some skinny fellow, only I didn't realize this until later." Max and
I laughed. "The board members were concerned about my age. I was
twenty-four at the time; however, they had a project for me. They explained they wanted to expand, similar to what the Weston Company
did in London. However, Weston has been building and acquiring
businesses for thirty years." He smiled and said, "Global National,
the bank I work for, has always bought small and healthy banks, but
they wanted to approach things differently. They hit a wall or two on
a project, and they were hell-bent on purchasing a specific bank. They
gave me basic, general details and told me to make it happen. I made
it happen within a month. I was hooked, and so were the board members. I can start a deal and close it fast." Max ran his hand across his
forehead and exhaled.

"Relieved?"

"Yes." *I'm surprised he admitted it.* "Livvy, I have never told anyone what I really do."

I had to ask, "Why, Max? And why do random people seem to
know you?"

Max laid his head back on the seat. *Okay, there's more.* "You see,
when I force a takeover to happen, people lose their jobs. This part
of my job, I hate." Max glanced at me. I nodded to let him know I

was listening. "After the third takeover in less than four months, I received death threats." I didn't say a word, but I swallowed hard, and my wheels were turning. "I was immediately assigned Martin after the first one. As you know, he has been with me ten months. I also look out for Global's best interests in other ways. Sometimes the bank is asked to do heavy financing for projects. I find out every detail, not only about the project, but I also investigate the people who are involved in the projects. Let's just say I haven't made many friends with that, either."

I remained quiet, and he continued. "Now Global has decided to expand—purchase businesses that are not technically for sale. This is what this Paris trip is all about, and it's been the most challenging one. But it will be completed tomorrow night."

"What are the differences between forcing a takeover and purchasing a business that is not technically for sale? It sounds the same."

"The end results are the same—Global owns it. How or why it happens makes it different." He studied me. "You need more?"

"Please."

"Takeovers vary. Say a company has ten board members. Four want to sell, six don't. I persuade two. Then the vote will go our way." *Persuade?* "Enough?"

"No."

"It's the same, just more complicated." He ran both hands through his hair.

We sat quietly for a while. I've always said what was on my mind, and I certainly was not going to stop now. "Max." I sat up straight. "Look at me, please."

He slowly turned and faced me. "You are not who I thought you were. This makes me nervous, but then again, I realized that the first night you walked into our hotel suite. You were different than the guy in Cabo. You looked, spoke, and carried yourself differently. You got my attention that evening—not to say you didn't get it a few times in Cabo." My eyes drifted to his deep hazel ones. "But you already knew that."

"Yeah, I knew."

"That was an abundant amount of information to take in. I'm not sure how I feel."

Joann appeared from her hideout. I told Max I needed a Bloody Mary with breakfast. I asked Joann to go ahead and make it a double. Max laughed and said after he saw the expression on my face when he mentioned why Martin hung around, he knew he'd need a cocktail himself. He went with a whisky straight up, over a chunk of ice.

"You're not sure how you feel about me, Livvy, or how you feel about what I do?"

I fiddled with the clasp on my Hardy bracelet.

"Both."

After Joann tidied up, she disappeared.

I had a few more questions for Max. "You said your life has been threatened. How many times?"

"Eight. We find them and take care of it."

"What the hell does that mean?"

"They're arrested. Jesus, Livvy!"

"Don't 'Jesus, Livvy' me!"

He touched my hand. "I'm sorry. I didn't mean to shout."

"Me either." I weakly smiled and cupped his cheek in my hand. *God, he's a beautiful man.* "Max, am I safe being with you?"

He held my hand against his cheek and didn't hesitate to answer. "Yes."

I slid my hand from underneath his and massaged my forehead. "I'm concerned your picture was taken this morning, and so was mine. The press knows your name. I wish you had confided in me about all this before I accepted Matt's invitation for lunch. I would have reconsidered meeting him."

"Livvy, don't worry about it. But yeah, I was jealous." He pulled me into his lap, but then he said he was afraid he was going to wrinkle my suit.

Max coolly pushed me—I slid right off his lap onto the soft leather sofa. "Don't move." He got up.

"We're on a plane, where do you think I'd go?"

"Smart ass now, are we?" he chuckled. He opened the door to Joann's hideout, said something to her, and locked the door.

He knelt in front of me and unzipped my tall leather boots. And then he removed them—one at a time. Max stood and lifted my hands from my lap and delicately pulled me to my feet. He slowly removed my jacket and hung it over the back of the leather chair. Then he released the button and unzipped my skirt. Those freaking goose bumps wildly dashed up and down my spine. My skirt fell to my hosed feet. I stepped out. Max raised my chin. "Look at me." I tried not to look into his eyes, but I was sucked right in. I stood before him wearing a few pieces of jewelry, a white blouse, designer hose, and God bless Fred for my undergarments. He stooped and picked my skirt up. While he straightened the length of his body, he brushed the outside of my leg with the back of his hand. When he reached my hip, sparks pinged throughout my entire body. *Jeez!* He shrewdly grinned and placed my skirt on the same chair as my jacket.

The butterflies and pings seemed like small problems at that moment. My breathing was screwed, and my pulse was racing. *Max Spencer is driving me mad,* I thought as he slowly unbuttoned my blouse and removed it.

My bra was lacy, a flesh nude color, with a beautiful thong and a matching garter, to which my designer hose was attached. Max stepped back and whispered, "My God, Livvy." I didn't move. I was trying to control my breathing as Max traced my bra with his fingers. *God I want him,* I thought as he let his hands slide gently down the sides of my body, caressing my curves until he reached my hose. One snap at a time, he released them from my garter and lingered there until my legs were bare.

He said, "I won't wrinkle you now." Max never offered or asked to remove my remaining undergarments. When he sat back down, I straddled his lap. As usual, I tried to complicate things, and of course he said, "Not yet."

Ice water hit my veins. I huffed in a pouty way, "Max, it's getting late. I need to eat."

He blew me off and calmly asked, "Do you have anything else to wear in your bag? I hate for you to dress, only to have me undress you again." *Might as well go with it.* I laughed and told him I had no idea what was in my bag, because Fred had packed my things. He removed his crisp, white shirt, and I put it on. He rolled the sleeves up, and I buttoned it. He laughed and said, "It kinda works as a dress." I got tickled and told him this was the second time I'd worn one of his shirts; however, this one had buttons on it. Max told me I could rip his shirts or anything else.

"Let me get Joann, but first I have to do something." He kissed me. I asked him if I could have him for dessert, or he could have me. "No," he said, "not yet, but hopefully soon."

After lunch, Max asked if I was tired. I was. He pulled his T-shirt up and over his head. My lips parted. It should be a crime for a man's chest to look like that. I ran my hands across every muscle as we cuddled on the sofa. "Am I making progress with you, Livvy?" he asked out of the blue.

"Maybe…you said five or six months. Don't rush me, Max."

"At least you're thinking about me."

Max was right. I thought about him all the time. I knew I still wasn't over Robert, or was I? Or maybe, I wasn't over what happened between us. I knew with Crosby I had possibly screwed up a friendship by allowing things to move too fast. I couldn't let the same thing happen with Max, but would it?

When I woke up, Max was completely dressed except for his tie and jacket, and he appeared to be working. He smiled at me. I apologized for taking such a long nap. Max said he didn't mind, because he enjoyed watching me sleep.

Martin called from the cockpit and said we would land in an hour. I gathered up my things to pull myself together again. Lord, when I looked into the mirror, I frightened myself. I look like I'd been hit with an ugly stick. I had a trail of what looked like bat-poop smeared down my left cheek, and four mashed fingerprints on my right. I tried to tame my hair, 'cause right now it was bigger than Dallas. I gave up and went with a ponytail poof. I touched up the makeup before rejoining Max.

Max was sitting in a large, comfortable chair. He grabbed my hand as I was about to walk past to sit on the sofa. He asked me to sit beside him so he could put away his work. "Your work looked important," I said. He grinned. "And interesting."

"What do you mean?"

"Milton Douglas, you know, he is friends with the former president." Max ran his hand through his wavy, messed-up hair that looked sexy. *Mine was just messed up*, I thought, as I ran my hand down my jacked-up ponytail, trying to look sexy. Max was staring at me. "Need more?" I asked.

"Please."

"Douglas also has oil dealings in the Middle East. I've always felt the war was as much to do with business interests as politics. Although, after 9/11, we needed to kick some butt. If Douglas is your next assignment, be careful."

Max asked what I was talking about. "Milton Douglas seems shady. Even though what you were reading had nothing to do with oil or the former president. I've heard Uncle Troy mention him." Max looked at me like he had seen a ghost. "Oh, Max," I said, "Uncle Troy also forgets to put his crap away when he visits, so maybe I've read about Douglas." He nodded and asked what else I knew. I decided to keep my mouth shut. Uncle Troy worked for some branch of the government, and I didn't think Aunt Suzanne even knew which one. "You know Paris is supposed to be the most romantic city, right? I'm counting on you," I said, changing the subject.

He kissed me and said, "Not yet, but..." *Ah...he said but. So there is hope.* "Livvy, I want to, probably more than you, but—"

"Max, God is not going to strike you dead if you sleep with me. He is much too busy for that nonsense."

Max laughed and asked, "What else do you know about Douglas?"

"Absolutely nothing."

CHAPTER 18

As soon as we landed in Paris, Martin joined us in the main cabin. Max was on the phone with someone, using short phrases such as "I understand," "Take care of it," and "No problem."

Martin opened the door of the plane and motioned for two men to board. The four of them were speaking French, and from the looks they shot in my direction, I knew there was a problem. Martin picked up my bag, removed my passport, and stepped off the plane. Max slipped his arm around my waist and said we would be riding in separate cars, but Martin would ride with me. "Max?"

"Livvy, it's okay." He kissed me on my forehead. "I'll see you in twenty minutes."

I sat down in the backseat. I looked out the window, and Max had disappeared. The driver of my car sped off. He made a sharp turn, and I slid completely across the seat to the other side of the car. Martin glanced back from the front seat.

"You all right, Miss Hunnicutt?"

I buckled up and shot back, "I'm fine, Martin, but call me Livvy." Okay, I was pissed, afraid, and wondering what I had gotten myself into. We slowed down at a traffic light but didn't stop. "The damn thing was red," I shouted. The driver took a left. Max's drivers took a right. "What the hell?"

"Everything is fine," Martin said.

"No, Martin," I hissed. "Everything is not fine." He looked over his right shoulder at me. I thought it might be best for me to shut up.

The last twenty minutes had been the longest of my life. I could feel my blood sugar spiking. I had to get a handle on it, I thought, as my car whipped in front of the beautiful hotel entrance. When the driver stopped, I was thrown forward, even with my safety belt pulled tight. Max's car turned in and parked directly behind us. I knew to sit still until someone summoned me. The two drivers, Max, and Martin were speaking in French right outside my car door. Martin went inside the hotel.

Max joined me in the backseat. "What the hell is going on?" I demanded.

He asked if we could talk about it in a few minutes.

"Do I have a choice?" I snapped.

"Livvy, please. We'll be inside in a few minutes."

I brushed back the few loose strands of hair that had escaped from my ponytail and huffed, "Whatever."

Martin returned, opened the door, and said, "Let's go." I reached for my tote, but Max told me to leave it; Martin would get it.

Max grabbed my hand, and Martin told me to put my sunglasses on. I lowered them from the top of my head. From the time Max had joined me in the backseat until Martin returned, media had gathered. They shouted Max's name repeatedly as we were escorted quickly inside the hotel and pushed onto an elevator. My heart was racing. I had tears in my eyes. I glanced down. The taller man's jacket had pulled back slightly. Dear God, he had a gun. My knees became weak, and not in a good way. I felt light-headed and dizzy, and suddenly everything around me disappeared into darkness. Max was calling my name. I could tell I was lying on a soft surface. I opened my eyes. Max was kneeling beside me, sweetly stroking my cheek and asking if I was all right. I was on a sofa. Max checked my blood sugar, and it was 120. I nodded. He kissed me on my forehead and asked if I needed a doctor.

"No." I swung my legs around and hopped up from my prone position. I pointed at the two men and shouted, "Max, for God's sake, they have guns."

"Calm down. They're like Martin. After what happened this morning in New York, I wanted extra people. That's all."

I shook my head and walked off. "Where are you going?" he asked.

I told him I needed water, and I had to pee. Some man popped around the corner and shoved a bottle of water in my face. Dang, if he didn't about make me pee in my panties. "Damn it! I get it!" I ran my hands though my tangled ponytail. "He's a ghostly version of Fred, but probably doesn't speak a freaking word of English. Now where's the fun in that?" I heard the two Frenchmen snicker. "Good to know you two speak English. How about using it, would you?"

When I returned from the bathroom, I heard Martin and Max talking about my fainting spell. Martin was concerned, and Max told him to order room service for the three of us. I noticed the henchmen had disappeared.

I was trying, but all of this was a lot for anyone to take in. I was having trouble wrapping my brain around it. Martin walked to the other side of the room and stared out across the beautiful city. He suddenly turned around and said, "Livvy, you look pale."

Max and Martin were now looking at each other—decoding one another's thoughts, I bet. Max sat down on the sofa beside me. "Livvy, if you need a doctor, I want you to be seen."

"No, I don't need a doctor. It's the Addison's. My blood pressure dropped, because those men scared the shit out of me, that's all. I can check it myself. If it's running low, I'll up my meds."

"Are you sure?"

"Yes, thank you. Did you catch me before I fell?"

He laughed and said, "Yes, I did."

"Thanks. You owed me at least that much. But I plan on losing it here in Paris, you know that, right?"

"No, we're waiting."

The French guys entered the room, pulling a cart draped in a white linen tablecloth. I guessed room service wasn't allowed to enter the suite, and the tall, skinny, white, French version of Fred was on it. He set the dining table and placed the food on our plates. It looked like a *Southern Living* photograph. I pointed to the bar. Max asked Skinny to make me a drink, and I clearly understood the word *vodka*, so I held up two fingers to go along with my translated request.

Over dinner, Max told me tomorrow he wanted me to have a good time; however, Martin, Claude, and Shawn would accompany me wherever I wanted to go. I asked only one question and added a comment: "Which one is Claude? And Shawn does not sound very French."

Max grinned. "Shawn is from New York. I've known him for several months, and he speaks excellent French. Claude is taller and a few years older."

"Oh," I deadpanned.

"The guy you called Skinny, he speaks a little English. We could opt for a more traditional butler, if you want. Their English is stellar here."

"Nah, Skinny's cool."

Max told me he would have a long workday tomorrow, but he was taking me on a date tomorrow evening. Martin shot Max a look that could have killed. "Make reservations, Martin."

Martin suggested we spend the next day visiting a museum and art gallery, and then shopping. I could tell he already knew my heart. There was only one store: Louis Vuitton. That was a must. After all, I was in Paris.

Skinny came back to check on us. I pointed to my empty glasses and held up two more fingers. Skinny returned in a jiffy, smiling, and said something to me. I looked at Max. "Need some help here."

He said something to Skinny. I asked to be excused, but as I stood there looking at Max, I didn't have a clue in which direction the bedroom was. "To the right."

"Gotcha," I mumbled and left the two of them to take care of business.

Wow, what a beautiful room. All French-looking. There was a large canopy bed and exquisite furnishings, gorgeous fabrics, and the bathroom had all the modern conveniences, such as a large bathtub. Ah... As I passed back through the bedroom, I found it even had music. I pressed a button and downed both cocktails while wondering where my bags were. I paraded across the room to a large armoire, popped the two doors open, and found my pajamas after pulling the second drawer open, right where Skinny had put them. *Now a shower, but careful, don't wet the hair.*

I propped up in the bed and checked up. My BG was 124. I was feeling quite smart, but right before I turned my thinking cap completely off for the night, I thought about what Max had said. If he wanted to make out tonight, I would make it difficult for him. I removed my purple cami and cheeky panties, then threw those suckers across the room. They landed in front of the double doors. I fell back on the pillows, flipped over on my tummy—my favorite sleeping position—and draped the covers over me, barely covering my backside. After I closed my eyes, Max entered the room. He leaned over me, swept his hand slowly down my back, and kissed my shoulder. He filled his lungs with air.

"God, you smell good, Livvy. I'm going to take a quick shower."

I managed to stay awake, but I remained in the same position. I felt Max slip under the covers. He brushed my hair to one side of my neck and kissed the other so sweetly. I turned and wrapped my arms around his damp body. He found my lips in the complete darkness.

* * *

When I woke, I noticed Max had left, but not without leaving a note on his pillow.

Dear Livvy,
You were sleeping soundly. I could not bring myself to wake you.
Tonight, I have a feeling, will be amazing.
Max

A smile sprang to my lips but quickly faded. I was trying to mentally process the information Max had shared with me yesterday. My stomach fussed. I retrieved my pj's from the floor and slipped them on.

I entered the living room. I was half naked, and there stood Martin, Claude, and Shawn. *Jeez.* I asked Martin to find Skinny. Martin said he would have him bring me breakfast. He grinned, but I didn't. I mumbled "Morning" to the two other fellas and asked them to forgive my appearance. Shawn smiled; Claude nodded. They hadn't spoken one direct word to me—in French or English—and neither started now.

I quickly showered and dressed but kept it casual. Skinny brought my breakfast in while I applied a last sweep of modest makeup. I joined my babysitters in the living room, thinking they were completely unnecessary. Pleasantly, Claude and Shawn greeted me for the first time. I smiled but never broke my stride. Skinny appeared out of nowhere and flung open one of the double doors. Shawn cut around me and took the lead, Martin fell in beside me, and Claude followed. I got the feeling right away this was how the rest of the day would play out.

We had a different car today—a Range Rover. Martin told me we would visit an art gallery first. They were expecting me. Then we would have lunch, visit a museum, and shop.

"Is the museum expecting me as well?" I asked, being a bit of a smart ass.

Martin was quick. "Yes. As well as the restaurant and Louis Vuitton."

"Oh." I didn't have a snappy comeback.

We arrived at the gallery, and my babysitters escorted me inside. A lady greeted Claude. After a couple of minutes, Martin explained I had the entire gallery for two hours. I took my iPod from my bag. I handed my large Burberry tote to Shawn and told him to make himself useful.

I put my buds in my ears and cranked up my music. I was excited, but I didn't want to show it. As I walked through the gallery, I admired each painting and every sculpture that sat stately on a pedestal. When I saw a painting that I truly loved and found a connection with, I would stand in front of it for ten minutes or so, soaking up the perfection that the artist had captured on canvas. I gazed at it until I could recall the piece from memory. I started to notice that many times after I had admired a piece, the lady would tag the piece as sold.

Martin, Claude, and Shawn kept their distance, but I was always in their sight. Martin approached me, and I pulled a bud out of one ear.

"Excuse me, but we need to wrap things up."

"Thank you." I took one last look at the piece I was admiring. I took a deep breath and looked at my babysitters as I removed the bud from my other ear and nodded. They were at least fifty feet from me, but they were spread out with twenty feet between them. Shawn, poor guy, had held my bag the entire time. I walked in his direction and handed him my iPod. In return, he handed me my sunglasses and tried to give me my bag. As I put my sunglasses on, I told him to hang on to it because Burberry was a good look for him.

When we arrived at the restaurant, Shawn and Martin walked me inside, and Claude appeared a few minutes later. They were about to sit at the table next to me when I asked if they would join me. We were the only customers. I asked Martin if all of this was really necessary. "Today it is," he said, then shoved a hefty bite of twiggy lettuce into his mouth.

"Should I be worried?" I asked after I swallowed my last bite of grilled salmon. He assured me I should not.

Martin asked if I was ready. Shawn picked up my large tote from the chair, retrieved my sunglasses, and handed them to me just as he had done when we were leaving the gallery.

The security at the museum played out exactly as the gallery did, but I told Claude it was his turn to hold my Burberry tote. Martin laughed. I told him not to laugh; we still had one more stop. Everyone laughed that time.

Back in the Range Rover, my phone rang. It was Rae.

"What is going on?" she demanded.

"What are you talking about?"

"Haven't you seen the news?"

"Course not. I'm in Paris."

"I know. You're everywhere," she shouted. "You were on *ET* and *Inside Edition* last night. And this morning, you were on local TV and every news channel, including Fox News and CNN, and all over the Internet."

"What?" I said, dumbfounded. Rae continued to say photos of Matt Bartlett kissing me on the cheek were everywhere. She said live footage ran all last night of us getting into a car together, and it appeared like he pushed me into the backseat and fell on top of me.

I knew I meant absolutely nothing to anyone; I was just caught up in all of this because of my lunch with Matt.

"Do they know my name?" I asked.

"Yeah! Not only do they know you as Livvy, but also your entire name is everywhere. They know where you're from and where you graduated college. They even reported that I was Max's college friend, when the live feed ran of the two you leaving the hotel." Martin, Claude, and Shawn were all demanding to know what was going on. I flicked up the palm of my hand. "What does Max do?" Rae asked. She didn't give me time to respond before she said, "The clip I saw of you and Max on the news looked bad. Mom and Dad are worried. Dad wants to know if you were hurt when Max shoved you into the car." I assured her I wasn't. She said the news was reporting a guy's arm had been broken when a driver closed a car door on it. Max and I weren't all that recognizable in any photographs or footage that ran, and Rae went on to say that Max was being referred to as a "handler." "Livvy, are you listening to me?"

"Yes, Rae, I hear you."

"Max does what high-powered people tell him to do. He screws over people, if what the media says is true, and he's been doing this for almost a year."

"No, Rae, that's not how Max explained things to me." *What if he lied?* I said I would be home in a couple of days. *No, Max wouldn't lie to me.* I hung up. *Or would he?*

I began to cry—hard. I demanded to go back to the hotel.

"What's going on?" Martin asked.

"Give me your damn computer, and I'll show you." I snatched the thing from his hands and logged on to Fox News. I shoved it back into his lap. He watched the clip and didn't comment to me, but said something in French to the two in the front seat. Claude shot back something quickly. Shawn was tight-lipped, but I could tell Martin had already known everything he had just watched online.

I felt awful. I knew something was going on with my blood sugar. I tried to get my glucose meter from my bag so I could check, but I was shaking too badly. Martin turned my bag around and found everything I needed. He put the strip into the meter. He stuck my finger as it continued to shake and pressed it until the blood popped out the tiny hole. Martin held the meter up to my little dot of blood until the strip sucked it in. My blood sugar had been perfect at lunch when I checked it, but now it was over five hundred. Martin asked what I needed. "Insulin."

He removed both of my insulin pens and held them up. "Which one, Livvy?"

I pointed.

"How many units?"

"Six, but I'll probably need more within twenty minutes." I was always afraid of bottoming out. Martin dialed up the insulin and asked

Shawn to check it. He took the pen from Martin and handed it back. "That's it."

I couldn't get my sleeve pulled up, so I lowered my jeans on my left side and turned slightly. Martin injected the insulin in my hip.

Within a couple of minutes, we were back at the hotel. Media people were everywhere. I was responsible for this mess because of a freaking lunch date.

Shawn removed his jacket and opened my door. He stooped down in front of me, threw his jacket over my head, grabbed my arm, and yanked. I sailed off the seat, and my feet hit the pavement in slow jog. Martin was right behind me. We were upstairs in the suite within minutes.

I began to cry again. I was getting sick, and I was hot. I managed to take my clothes off, down to my underwear. I leaned against the bathroom wall and felt myself slide down until I rested on the cold marble floor. I knew I was about to throw up, but with Addison's disease, this was not a good thing. I needed to check my blood sugar again. I shouted for help, but apparently not loud enough. I shouted for help again. Skinny came in the bathroom. I knew Skinny didn't understand me, but evidently distress is a universal language, and he shouted something in French. Everyone ran into the bathroom. Shawn was on the phone. He reached for my wrist and read my medical alert information from my bracelet in French. Claude left the bathroom, but quickly returned and dumped the contents of my bag on the floor. Martin quickly found my meter and checked my blood sugar.

"It's reading HI. How many units?"

"Ten, Martin. Give it to me in my arm, please." This time Martin didn't ask for anyone to double-check his dosage dial-up.

I tried to rise up from lying on the cold floor, but I couldn't. I pointed to the toilet. I had to throw up. Claude noticed my struggle and lifted me into a sitting position. Martin wet a cold towel for my head. I was crying as lunch came back up, but I wiped my mouth and told Martin I was sorry for causing trouble. He told me not to worry. That's what he and the others got paid for. "And after tonight," he added, "everyone is going to know Max Spencer, and that has nothing to do with you."

Skinny returned to the bathroom with a doctor. He asked in terrible English something about being "with child." Martin answered slowly in English, "She is not sexually active." Then Martin lowered his voice and said, "Sort of," in my ear. Shawn translated. They all were sitting on the floor with me, and my head was on Claude's lap. Claude said the doctor wanted me to move to the bed. I closed my eyes. Someone picked me up and carried me to the bed.

Skinny returned with a bottle of water. The doctor inserted the needle into my arm for an IV for fluids. I asked Claude to tell the doctor to speed up the drip, and I needed two bags. The doctor agreed. Skinny patted my hand occasionally, and he removed the lid to the water and handed it to me. I thanked him with a weak smile.

It was almost six, and I had at least fifteen minutes left to drip on the second bag. Oh Lord, I hadn't thought about what I was wearing tonight, either.

I heard Max's voice coming from the next room. "How is she now?"

I looked at Skinny, and then I looked at the doctor. *He's early.* "Take it out!" *Shit, he didn't know what I was saying.* Skinny certainly didn't have a clue. I nudged the doctor but not hard; I just needed him to move. I didn't want Max to see me like this. The doctor backed up. Skinny ran out of the room to get a translator.

"Take it out now!" I pointed to my arm, and then I finally ripped the damn IV out. I hurriedly began raking the medical supplies into a pile. I pointed to the doctor's medical bag, gesturing for him to clean up all of this shit. The doctor kept reaching for my arm.

Claude and Skinny ran into the room first, and directly behind them stood Max and Martin. I burst into tears standing there in my underwear, running my fingers through my messy hair. Max darted around Claude and met me with his arms open wide.

"I'm sorry, Max." I threw my arms around his neck. He held me tightly. I felt my feet leave the floor. I wrapped my legs around his waist.

"You haven't done anything wrong," he whispered. "Shh." The doctor was pointing to my arm. It was bleeding. I released my hold from Max and slid down his body until my feet were on the floor. Max lifted my arm and kissed it in the bloody bend. He held it steady for me while the doctor applied pressure until the bleeding stopped. The doctor placed a bandage on my arm, cleaned up the medical supplies, and left.

Max asked me how I was feeling. "Better. The doctor checked my sugar an hour ago—it was one eighty. It spiked because I was upset."

"I know," Max said. "Martin explained everything."

"I look awful. I could use Fred right about now."

"Why do you need Fred?"

I ran the back of my hand across my snotty nose. "He can put an outfit together, apply makeup, and complete a hairstyle in twenty minutes. But he can't make a drink to save his life." I smiled lazily.

"Do you still feel like going out for dinner, or do you need to stay in?"

"Out," I said. "Did things turn out the way you planned today?"

"Better. I finished early. Uh…you were right about Douglas, Livvy. I have one small detail I have to take care of, but I'll be back in a few minutes."

"I'm sorry about your suit. I know it's ruined."

"I'm not worried about my suit." He kissed me on my forehead and mumbled, "But damn, Livvy, those three men will never look at you the same, after seeing you in what you are wearing."

"They'll be fine. Claude held my head while I puked in the toilet."

"Oh." He traced my bra line. I turned around, unhooked my bra, and dropped it on the floor.

"By the way, you look hot in red, Livvy." I stopped at the bathroom doorway, hooked my fingers in the sides of my hipsters, peeled them off, and tossed them at him.

He caught them. "That's even better." He smiled wickedly. *Shit, no, he didn't.* "Smells like you, Livvy." Max added a few colorful words to his last statement and turned around, but continued to mumble. *"Sie hatte besser..."* *Is he speaking German? Yes, he is.* I guess I'll have to learn that crap as well. Max left the bedroom, but not without slamming the door and taking my red panties with him.

CHAPTER 19

I replayed my conversation with Rae repeatedly while I showered, now wondering more than ever what I had gotten myself into.

I flung open the bathroom door to clear the steamy haze, my hair tossed up in a towel twisted like a turban and another towel around me. *Dear Lord, what has Max done?*

Max coolly strutted in and wrapped his arms around my waist. "Max?"

"It was brought to my attention that you missed one very important stop today."

"Max, I wanted to purchase a *handbag*," I said, noticing Louis had taken over the entire corner of the bedroom. "I don't understand."

"It's a gift."

"A gift comes in a small box with a red bow. A gift does not take up an entire corner of a room unless it's a freaking elephant." I moseyed over to study the elephant. I lightly touched the Pegase 45 and 55, my finger traced the zipper of the Keepall Bandoulière 60, and closed my eyes when I gripped the handle of Bisten 50. A pile of smaller items flanked the top of a...*Oh you have got to be kidding me.* "It's vintage Max. The steamer trunk is vintage."

"I know. A 1910, I believe."

"Max, I cannot accept this." I said as a zippy organizer caught my eye. *Well, Fred would certainly insist that I keep that piece to go with the Palermo Tote.* "Send it back Max, all of it."

He popped me on my butt as he walked off in the direction of the bathroom. "We'll discuss it later. You need to get dressed, unless you want to wear that towel to dinner."

Lord, I thought, *what to wear?* As I opened the closet, I spotted a new addition and picked it up. The silk fabric was exquisite. The dress was black with a low V-neck and small, thin straps that would tie across my shoulder blades. The back would make a statement. It was completely open to the top of my butt. And the front—well, it made a statement on its own. The hem was six inches above my knee and fitted to show my figure. The shoes had a five-inch heel and straps that buckled around my ankles. Jewelry—one silver bracelet and a pair of silver drop earrings—also a gift from Max.

I sat down for a few minutes and studied the Louis Vuitton store. Max had to return these items. But then I saw one pair of heels I would love to keep. Everything *else* had to be returned.

Max came out of the bathroom wearing a towel around his waist. I thought I was going to slide right out of my chair. I quickly refocused as I stood up. I was about to say, "I'll step out while you get dressed." But suddenly I was in his arms, and he was kissing me. I couldn't breathe, but I was kissing him back. I gently and slowly pulled away, and our eyes connected.

"I have been waiting all day to hold you like this," Max said.

My knees felt weak, and my heart was pounding. I sucked air into my lungs. After a moment I managed to say, "Max, I'm afraid."

"Don't be," he said throatily.

We were quiet for what felt like an eternity while he dressed. "I understand why you're afraid. But I'm not Robert. I won't leave you wondering for three years what my feelings may or may not be for you. I'll tell you, and right now, I like everything about you. I won't let you go. I'm not like Crosby, either. I won't give up. Not this soon, anyway."

He had his tie draped around his neck, and I reached for it. "May I?" He dropped his hands and allowed me. I could tell he was staring at me while I knotted his tie. When I finished, I smoothed my hand slowly down his tie, and we both said, "Perfect."

Only Max wasn't looking at his tie. He was sweetly looking at me. I couldn't help myself. I reached up and touched his face with my right hand and draped my left arm around his neck. I paused only for a moment before I kissed him. *What am I doing?* Max was holding me tight, and I kissed him until he released me. He took me by the hand and led me into the living room.

"Good evening, Livvy," Martin said. I noticed two more gentlemen were in the room.

I hesitantly looked at Max. "I closed the business deal today like I told you. I felt better having a couple of extra people around."

"Has someone threatened you, Max?"

"C'mon Livvy."

"How many?" Martin took a step closer, as if I were the dangerous one. "I asked you a question Max."

"Three."

"This is some real James Bond shit."

"Do I get the girl?" Max asked more coolly than Mr. Bond could have. I hated all of this, but I was going to try to go with it.

"Maybe," I said with my red lips still parted.

"Range Rovers tonight," Martin told us as we stepped out of the hotel suite. He also said media was going to be a bitch. He told us to keep our heads down and to wear our sunglasses. I looked at Max. I had forgotten mine. Shawn tapped me on my shoulder. He handed me…oh, wait, these were new. Dang, I'd keep these along with the one pair of shoes I'd spotted earlier. I winked at Shawn. Max and I followed our instructions, even though Max's name was shouted repeatedly.

Shawn and the new guys took the first SUV. Claude, Martin, Max, and I took the second SUV. Both drove fast, barely pausing at red traffic lights. Both stopped in front of the restaurant. Max and I were quickly escorted inside. But the new guys remained with the vehicles. I was not surprised to see we were the only customers tonight.

"Livvy, just ask me," Max said. "I can tell you're thinking about something."

"I'm sorry, but it's about something Rae told me she saw on Fox News. I need to understand. They called you a handler. I told you earlier I was afraid. I'm trying here, Max. I need for you to understand my past is what it is. My being afraid is more about you, or maybe us."

I forced a smile and reached across the table. His hand met mine. "Us?"

"Maybe. But I need answers. Has anyone ever died as a result from your work?"

"I have a team of lawyers. Their job is to research every decision I make. They make sure I stay completely within the guidelines of the law, regardless of what country we're in. I've never broken the law, nor will I ever."

He didn't answer my question. I asked him again, "Max, has anyone ever died or been killed as a result of what you do?"

Max's eyes drifted to his wineglass, which he was twirling. "There have been three suicides that have been attributed to people losing their jobs. I am not proud of that. And there was one self-defense incident. I left the office late one night with Martin. A man jumped from behind a parked car and held a gun to my head. Martin demanded he drop the gun. He didn't. Martin shot him."

"Is there anything else I should know?"

He shook his head no, but he was staring at his wineglass.

"Look at me, Max."

"Cabo, the man that was murdered, did you—"

"No, I didn't know the guy."

I remembered he had taken off with his backpack. "But you thought—"

"Yes, at first."

"Thank you for your honesty, Max. I'm ready to leave."

He did that head thing. Martin quickly took care of the bill while Shawn and Claude walked us out. Max opened the door, and I slid to the middle of the seat. As soon as he sat down next to me, he wrapped his arm around me, but he was quiet.

Within fifteen minutes, the first SUV stopped in front of the hotel. We didn't stop. Martin was speaking in French, and so was Claude. Okay, I was pissed again. Every one of them spoke English as well as I do. Claude stopped at a different entrance. Martin got out and stood beside the door. Claude handed Max his jacket. He threw it over my head and grabbed my right arm; Martin took my left. I couldn't see anything as we ran.

"Don't stop until we have cleared the elevator doors," Martin said. "It's being held for us."

"We're on," Max said as he spun me around. I removed Claude's jacket from my head, and he whispered, "I can't wait."

Max kissed me roughly. I fell against the wall. The wooden molding dug into the center of my back. "Ah…Max," I grunted. He didn't back down. His hand quickly trailed up my dress with more force. "Max, you're hurting me," I whispered on his lips.

He buried his head in my neck and uttered, "I'm sorry. I thought after…what I told you at the restaurant, you would leave." *What?*

This was a side of Max I had not seen. He raised his head and looked at me, and I cupped his cheek in my hand. "Not tonight, Max. I'm yours if you will have me." I took his lips roughly. He firmly grabbed my hip with one hand and wrapped his other around me to hold me up, because I lost my legs somewhere.

"You two getting off?" Martin asked without a hint of irony.

Skinny handed me a drink when I cleared the doorway. Max had me by my other hand. Without stopping, Max told Martin to make arrangements for London early in the morning. I set my empty glass on the dining room table as we walked by. Max dropped his overcoat on the floor. He grabbed me before we ever turned the corner and yanked my sable off. While his arms were around me, he tugged the two thin strands of silk that held my dress on. It slid down my body to lie on top of my feet. I didn't have any undergarments on—the dress didn't give them any place to hide. I was standing in the entrance to the master suite, wearing only my new jewelry and those fabulous shoes. "Mother of God," he murmured.

"Come here," I said, pulling him close. I ripped his shirt, and yes, those damn buttons bounced everywhere. I snatched his belt, and he kicked off his shoes. I felt my feet leave the floor. He threw me gently on the bed and was now on top of me. I could tell he was holding back, gaining control of his actions. That disappointed me. He was making each move carefully. I wasn't being so careful. Oh no, not at all. I was touching him the way I wanted to be touched. He stopped me after he realized I had kissed him below his waist. He pulled me back to his lips. "I want you…and I'm thrilled you want me that way." He stopped. "But I want us to be in love first, even before we do that."

"Why?" I huffed, out of breath.

Max smacked my butt—hard. A jolt of heat pierced my core. I think I liked it. He rubbed my backside until the sting melted away. But the heat was still *there.*

"Either give me your hand, Max, or I will use my own."

He clasped my face between his hands and kissed me hard, then whispered against my lips, "My palm. But nothing goes inside you… understood?"

Our make-out session ended tonight in Paris without me getting the Max Spencer the way I desired. Dammit.

"Thank you for the beautiful outfit, the jewelry, and the pampering earlier this evening. But you have to return the other things."

Max never released me. I could feel his heart beating against my body. "I promise it was nothing."

"No. You must return the gifts."

"Shh. I'm not returning anything. Let me spoil you."

He kissed me again. I pulled away. "Max, please." He whispered an amount of money in my ear. I wasn't sure I understood him correctly. I rose up so I could see his face. In the dimly lit room, I focused on his eyes. I could tell I had not misunderstood him.

"My God, that is an incredible salary."

"No, I receive a bonus when I close a project. That's what I made today. My salary is ten times that."

I had to sit up. I looked over at the Louis store in the corner and said, "Okay, I'll keep the shoes sitting on top of the trunk, the dress, the jewelry, and the sunglasses because I've already worn them."

"No, you're keeping everything."

When morning arrived, Max got out of bed and reached for my ankles in a playful way. "I want you to always remember you kissed me first."

"You kissed me first in the airport."

"Doesn't count, remember? I didn't make your list then. You lip-locked me, baby, in the backseat of my car." He pulled me to the edge of the bed and lifted me off. My feet dangled until they found the floor. "Let's shower. You can lip-lock me in there, too."

By the time I dressed, Skinny had finished packing my things. I had to admit, the luggage was beautiful.

Max had already joined Martin and the others in the living room. I was completely happy hanging out in the bedroom. I was sure they were reviewing their strategy for the next James Bond shit, probably in French.

Max stepped into the bedroom.

"Please don't be upset," he said. "We have a few extra people this morning. The media is heavy at every exit of the hotel." He placed his arm around my waist as we walked into the living room. My stomach was doing flip-flops and not in a good way. I tried not to think about why they were there, but I counted seven men dressed in black, and I was certain they all had guns.

Martin took the lead. When the elevator doors opened, we were quickly surrounded by security. I was fidgety. Max slipped one arm around me. "Livvy, everything is okay." We slipped our shades on. "Three cars this morning—we will ride together."

The doorman swung open the doors and immediately after step-ping outside, I heard people shouting, "How did you do it, Spencer?

You took over the largest company in France. How did you do it?" A man in black opened the car door, and I sat and slid over quickly. I glanced around. *How comforting*, I thought, *ten men in black.* Thank the Lord I had my sunglasses on, because I had tears in my eyes. I could feel my bottom lip start to quiver, so I bit it gently.

I asked for my bag. Max watched as I checked my blood sugar. He leaned in so he could see the screen: 298. "I'll have Martin call for a doctor to meet us at the hotel in London." I told him I could handle this one.

Claude stayed on the bumper of the first car, and the third driver was on the bumper of ours. I was trying to give myself insulin, but good Lord, even with my seatbelt on and Max's arm around me, my hand wasn't steady enough. Finally I jabbed the needle through my slacks into my thigh.

"I would have done that for you," Max said. I popped the cap back on and tossed the insulin pen in my bag.

"I know."

As we arrived at the airport, the jet doors were open. Max grabbed my hand, and Martin opened the car door for us. We ran up the steps with Martin, Claude, and Shawn behind us. The remaining seven men in black loaded the luggage, and Martin joined the pilots in the cockpit. Joann disappeared, and from the looks of things, Claude and Shawn were coming with us.

Max was looking at something on his computer. He asked, "Will you take a look?" He moved his Mac to the oversized armrest between us. He told me he had a meeting in London with a real estate agent this morning, and he had narrowed his choices down to two apartments. After that, he had the entire day and evening free. I watched the virtual tour of the first one and told him it was beautiful. I wasn't sure what else I was supposed to say. Then he clicked on the second apartment. It was just as nice as the first one. I told Max I thought either would be perfect for him. He closed his laptop and handed it to Shawn, then he raised the oversized armrest between our seats and put his arm around me. Max unbuckled his seatbelt and mine and pulled me onto his lap. Claude and Shawn quickly joined Joann in her hideout.

"What do you think about the five- or six-month thing we discussed?"

"I'm good with it," I admitted shyly.

"How will I ever let you get off this plane tomorrow? I have wanted you since the first day I saw you in Cabo. I didn't think you would give me a chance, and now—" His phone rang, and Max never finished his thought. Max listened for a second and hung up. I scooted off his lap and reclaimed the seat beside him. After the plane landed, Martin came into the main cabin and chatted with the fellas near the exit door. I decided to keep my butt in my seat until I was needed.

Shawn picked up Max's bag and pointed to mine, which I was holding. I handed it to him. Max didn't say a word, but he reached for my hand. *Here we go again.*

Martin opened the door of the plane. Everything looked calm from where I was standing. Two Mercedes SUVs were parked by the bottom of the stairs. I was relieved when Max winked and said, "We're riding together."

* * *

The new driver pulled in front of a beautiful building. Max and Martin got out of the car, and a middle-aged woman approached them. She had to be the real estate agent. Max opened my door. "It's cold," he said. I grabbed my scarf, and he reached for my hand.

"Shall we?" The agent gestured to the door. She rambled on about how nice the building was as she pushed the elevator button, which she referred to as "the lift."

"There are six floors in the building," she said. The first three floors had three apartments each. The fourth floor had two spacious two-story apartments. And the sixth floor—one large apartment. We were viewing the one on the sixth. "You know, someone quite famous lives in this building," the agent said coyly. I smiled softly but didn't take the bait. Max and Martin could care less if anyone famous lived there. "But of course, he lives here only four, maybe five, months out of the year."

I grinned but still didn't ask. She finally said, "It's Peter Weston." I had to bite my tongue, then my lip. As we stepped off the elevator, I had a flashback of what Matt Bartlett said about Peter: my mom wanted him for the role of Ben Davis in *Finding Justice*.

We entered the apartment. It was spacious and beautiful. I never said a word. Martin said the security would need to be updated.

"Fine, but I want a new kitchen. Livvy is a great cook." I shot Max a quick, narrow-eyed look. But I knew better than to speak. Max told the real estate agent he would take it, and he wanted to close in a week. Martin said he would start the background checks on the building's other owners, contractors, and interior designers. Max had me by the hand and was walking toward the door.

I could hear the agent's footsteps behind us as she called out, "Mr. Spencer, you haven't seen the other property."

"Don't need to. Work out the details with Martin." Max still had me by the hand and pressed the elevator button with his other hand.

The door quickly opened, and Max pulled me into his arms. "Well, Max, we do have one thing in common," I said.

"What would that be?"

"Lack of patience for shopping."

He pressed his lips harder to mine and said, "I can think of at least one more thing."

He pressed the down button while I said, "Please don't renovate the kitchen for me, Max. We have to take this slow and see where things go."

"I told you I'm not going to let you go. You agreed we're going to talk for a few months, but I already know. I'm just waiting on you."

The elevator stopped. The door opened. The agent was right: Peter Weston stepped on. No one spoke, but he and Max glanced at each other, and they did that head-nod thing at the same time. I glanced at Peter's face and softened my expression, but I didn't smile. Peter Weston was taller than I'd thought he was. He and Max were the same height. He was less broad than Max, but he was built very nicely, and that hair of his was crazy. I loved it.

"Do you want to do anything special today?" Max asked me.

"Yes." I noticed Peter Weston's clothing. *Nice...modern.*

"What did you have in mind?"

"It didn't happen in Paris," I said. "So I'm thinking London."

"No, not yet."

"Why not?"

Peter Weston wasn't over the top with the modern thing. *But dang if he isn't handsome*, I couldn't help but notice.

"I'm waiting until you say it." The elevator stopped. I removed my sunglasses from the top of my head and placed them in their proper place. As Peter Weston stepped off the elevator, I thought, *Well, heck, he even smells good.*

"That's not happening anytime soon, Max Spencer."

"I have patience," he said.

Jeez, Peter Weston was not what I expected.

"I'm running out of patience," I said. "I'm ready."

Claude, Shawn, and the new driver waited outside. Max said, "Let's go. Martin's behind us."

"What will it take for me to get what I want?"

"You already know."

"Other than that. I've already told you—"

He butted in and said, "But I can tell you already do. You're stubborn, Livvy Hunnicutt."

I was aggravated and frustrated. "I can't give it away."

* * *

We arrived at the hotel, where a couple of news vans and reporters were waiting. "You know the drill?" Martin asked.

"Down pat," I grunted. "Heads down, shades on, and walk fast."

"Good girl."

Shawn opened the door, and Max grabbed my hand, pulling me slightly. The reporters were shouting questions, "Max Spencer! How does it feel to put a thousand people out of work?"

The question was repeated. "What was that?" I shouted. Shawn pushed me to the ground. Someone fell on top of me, knocking the air from my lungs. I saw Claude fall to the ground beside me. Gunfire was popping all around us. I was screaming from the top of my lungs. "Max! Max!" I was pinned down and crying. *Oh God, blood!* "Max, talk to me! Say something!"

He was still lying on me, covering me from the gunfire. He didn't move, but he asked, "Livvy, are you okay?"

"Yes! Max, I think Claude has been shot!" I reached for Claude. He was bleeding. I applied pressure to his upper arm with one hand, and he moaned. Shawn shouted, "Stay low, Spencer, but go now! Go! Get inside the building! I have her!"

Everything was happening so fast. Shawn grabbed me at my waist and lifted me from the ground. I had taken four or five steps toward the hotel when bullets broke the glass out of the doors. Shawn shoved me inside the hotel. I fell on the marble floor. Max dove on top of me, and then Shawn fell on top of Max. The shooter paused. Shawn and Max hopped up. Max stayed low, quickly grabbed me by my arms, and pulled me across the floor until we were safely behind a large marble column.

I was shouting for someone to help Claude.

Bullets began to fly again. Max dropped to his knees and held me in his arms. He let me go only to tightly secure my face in his hands. "Open your eyes." They sprang open on his command. I saw fear in Max's eyes. "Livvy, are you hurt?" I didn't answer. He shouted, "Answer me, Livvy." He wiped my face bare-handed and shouted again, "Answer me. Are you hurt?"

"No," I said, "I'm not hurt." The gunfire stopped.

People were running and screaming through the lobby. Max stood, then helped me to my feet and told Shawn to stay with me. Max turned and walked away.

"Max! Come back!" Shawn grabbed my arm. I realized my entire body was trembling. My knees buckled, and he caught me, wrapping both of his arms around my waist. I saw Martin walking in the front entrance.

"Martin, where's Max?" I shouted. Then I spotted him. He was heading into our direction. As soon as Martin approached me, he asked if I was okay and removed a handkerchief from his pocket and rubbed my face. Then he grabbed my hand and looked at it.

Shawn answered for me and said, "I think she's okay. That's Claude's blood. He's all right. Clean hit in his upper arm." *Thank God.*

"Get Livvy and Max upstairs to the suite now," Martin said.

I couldn't move. "I'll carry you," Shawn said.

But Max swept me into his arms. "No, I have her."

Max carried me until he placed me on the bed we would share tonight.

"Do not leave her until I get back," Max told Shawn. I needed to check my blood sugar. Shawn knew the drill, my drill, too well. "Livvy," he said, "your blood sugar is three eighty. What do we need to do?"

"Fast-acting insulin, five units now. I'll need to check again in twenty minutes. I also need two bottled waters."

Shawn dialed up five units. I checked it and lowered my pants a couple of inches on my right side. Max walked back into the bedroom and told Shawn he would do it.

"Mr. Spencer, Miss Hunnicutt said she would need to check again in twenty minutes."

Max gave me my insulin injection and adjusted my pants. "I'll check her blood sugar, thank you, Shawn." Max lay down beside me. "Livvy, I'm sorry this happened, but I need to know if you're hurt or if you need a doctor to help with your blood sugar."

"I'm not hurt, but I need to eat lunch. I know my blood sugar is dropping because my head feels better."

Max called out for Martin, but for now he didn't move. He didn't move when Martin entered the bedroom. Max asked him to order lunch and put a rush on it.

"Livvy, we need to get you out of your clothes." I didn't know what he was talking about, but I looked down at my hands and saw the blood. I remembered touching Claude. I could feel it on my face. I touched my hair; it was crunchy where his blood had dried. Now my hands were shaking, and the tears once again were streaming down my face. Max carried me to the bathroom and turned the shower on. He helped me undress, and then we stepped into the shower.

Max washed my hair and scrubbed my nails and hands until the dried blood had disappeared down the drain. He gently rubbed the side of my face and my forehead, where Claude's blood had dried, with a washcloth. "I forgot to remove your earrings," Max said. He turned the water off. "I'll get you a towel." He stepped out of the shower but quickly returned and wrapped a towel around me. That's when I realized he had not undressed. He was dripping wet, wearing his white shirt and jeans.

I noticed his sleeve, near his shoulder, had a two-inch rip in it and was stained with blood. "Did it hurt?" I asked, while tracing the bandage.

Max lifted my hand and kissed it. "Not at all."

Grabbing a robe, he wrapped it around me. "Hold on, Livvy. I'm getting your meter." I picked my brush up and ran it through my hair. When Max returned, I held my finger out, and he checked my sugar. It was 198.

"Hey," he said, pushing a stand of wet hair behind my ear, "we're okay. That's all that matters."

CHAPTER 20

With my hair blown out and flat-ironed straight, I applied lip gloss and mascara. I wore jeans, a pink hoodie cable sweater, and silver sparkle Converse sneakers. I was feeling better by the time Max and I ate lunch, but I was worried about Claude.

A short man knocked on the open door and entered the bedroom. Max introduced me to Henry. Henry quickly vanished and returned from the bathroom carrying a large black garbage bag. I was certain that bag contained our torn and bloody clothing.

I had spent the last two hours in the bedroom. Surely the men had finished discussing business. I turned the corner, and there on the sofa sat Claude. His left arm was in a sling, but he looked fine.

"Claude," I said, "southern girls like hugs. And you're about to get one." I noticed that the wound on his upper arm was head height on me. He had been standing beside me when he was shot.

"Max," Martin said. "We need you in the dining room." Max took my hand. The investigator said he had watched the hotel's security footage, and it appeared the incident was clearly an attack. As far as they were concerned, only one injury was reported. And as the shooter was dead, killed in self-defense, he was closing the case.

Max did that head thing. The room cleared.

"Max, you were shot today. I know it was only a scratch, but I'm worried." I placed my hand over his flesh wound. I could feel the bandage underneath his shirt.

"I'm sorry, Livvy. I promise I will never allow you to be in danger again."

"What about you?"

"Don't worry about me—that's Martin's job."

"Relationships come with worry, Max," I said, like I was some expert on the topic. "Shit, my phone will not stop." I fished it from my back pocket. "It's Mom." I plopped down on the sofa. She said they had seen the shooting an hour ago on the news, and she was in a complete panic.

"Here," I said, handing him my cell, "it's Mom." I made a beeline toward the butler's kitchen, but I passed it and didn't stop until I found myself at the elevator door. *I need fresh air,* I thought as the doors closed. *I need time to think.* I really didn't know what I needed, but I knew I could not get upset again. *Stay calm, Livvy,* I thought as I pulled my hoodie up to cover my head and exited the hotel through a side entrance.

I had walked about two blocks when I started to shiver. The fresh air idea was stupid. No coat, no money, no phone, no diabetic stuff. I took a right. That's when I paused at an open gate. A young woman scurried around me. "I like punctuality," she said to me. "Bugger." She whipped around. "Where is your coat?"

"Sorry?" I asked.

"Are you okay?"

My teeth were chattering, "Yes. I…"

She took a step closer to me. "I'm Kim." She pointed to the building behind her. "I work here in the afternoons." She touched my hand. "Come inside." We took a couple of steps. "You're not here to apply for the job, are you?"

"No."

"You're American?"

"Yes." We stepped inside the large open foyer. I pushed my hoodie from my head. Kim's eyes widened.

"You're the girl from the morning news. Shit, I'm sorry, but you are her?"

"Yes. I'm Livvy. Livvy Hunnicutt." She pushed back her shoulder-length blonde hair and adjusted her blouse.

"This place is for children—it's a nonprofit tutoring and exercise program, to assist working parents in the afternoon. The girls are in tutoring, and the boys are in the gym—that way." She pointed, then glanced at her watch. "They change up in twenty. Eight- to ten-year-old boys are playing basketball." She draped her stylish coat over the office chair. "I'm only filling in until the foundation hires another director. I thought you were—"

"Need help today?"

She laughed. "Know anything about basketball?"

"A little." The phone rang. I said, "You said that way?" She reached for the phone.

"Yes. Livvy, is there anyone I could call for you?"

Max. Oh God, he must be worried. "The hotel—"

"The Connaught," she said.

* * *

"Way to go, Nolan," I said, giving the little fella a high-five.

"Miss Livvy," Charles said, dribbling my way, "show me how."

"Charles, stand like this." I demonstrated. "Now, hold the ball like this."

I handed it to him and readjusted his hands. "There you go. Shoot."

"I missed."

"Yes, you did. But you were close. Let's try again."

And there he stood. In the doorway with his coat tucked between his arm and the hand in his pocket. I waved. He took a few steps in my direction. *Angry? I can't read him. He would have every right to be.* "Hey," I said.

He touched my arm. "You okay?"

"Max, I—" Charles handed me the ball.

"I'm Charles. What's your name?" he asked, tugging at Max's navy pullover sweater.

Max knelt down. "I'm Max Spencer."

"Want to play with us? Josh, that guy over there," he pointed, "he's not our regular person." Charles giggled. "He's our math tutor."

Max smiled. "Sure, I'll play." The little fellas cheered. I took Max's coat.

Ten minutes later, Josh called, "Time's up."

Nolan shook Max's hand. "Come back, sir. We had a blast."

Max reached for his coat. "Martin is out front." We cleared the front door. "Here, wear my coat." He put it around my shoulders. "You left, Livvy—why?"

"I needed air."

"Did you get enough?"

"Yes."

"If not, Martin will pull over, and we can walk together." He ran his hands through his tousled hair.

"Look, I know what I did was stupid. You were on the phone with Mom, and I didn't want to cry again."

"I was worried sick, Livvy. Damn, that was the longest forty minutes of my life. We had security cameras from the hotel downloaded in ten minutes. The investigator from this morning tracked you two blocks from the city's surveillance cameras. When you turned right, he lost you. You didn't even take your bag. Did you have money with you?"

I shook my head. "No." He pulled me into his lap and buried his face in my hair. "If you need to go for a walk, please take someone with you and your things, okay?" I nodded. "Thank God you told the girl to call." He nuzzled closer. "And I'm sorry for what I said to you earlier. I, uh, understand now relationships come with worry."

"Yeah, they do." I cozied up closer to him. "I'm sorry for worrying you."

* * *

"The kids were cool," Max said. "I'm glad they were labeled."

"What?"

"Name tags."

"Yeah, that was helpful." Henry placed our dinner plates down in front of us.

"It was nice seeing you laugh and play with them." My eyes drifted to my wineglass. "I watched you a few minutes before you saw me," he said, brushing my cheek. "I love your dimple." I blushed. "When you were younger, I always knew you would be pretty when you grew up. But today when you were laughing and playing with the children," he said, "I saw the real you, the beautiful you—"

"Max, I hurt you today. I'm sorry…I—"

"You took ten years off my life, but seeing you laugh, it was worth it. You like kids?"

"Yes," I said, looking at him.

"Good. I do, too. But I didn't know it until today." He smiled.

After dinner I took him by his hand. I needed to unwind. We walked into the bedroom, where I hit the on button to the XM radio. I let go of Max's hand and glanced over my shoulder. He was following. I went to the sink and picked up my toothbrush and his toothpaste. "You squeeze the middle of the tube?"

"Uh-huh." Max was still eying my reflection in mirror as he brushed his teeth. I pulled my hoodie sweater over my head and dropped it as I walked out of the bathroom. I unbuckled my jeans and slipped them off. I was standing in the middle of the bedroom wearing matching hot pink, comfy undergarments.

Max walked toward me, wearing the bandage on his right arm and his dark jeans, but his belt was dangling, and his jeans were no longer buttoned. When he was close enough, he embraced me, and we danced like I had never danced before.

"God, you have ruined me, Livvy." I took his lips and zipper. He swept me up in his arms and lay me on the bed. He stepped out of his jeans. I snatched my bra over my head and helped him remove his Burberry briefs. I hooked one side of my panties with my thumb as he pulled me back into his arms. He dampened my moment and not in a good way when he said, "Please don't."

"Please do," I begged. He grabbed me, and for a moment he was holding me so tightly I couldn't breathe. Then, with one hand, he ripped my panties off. I rolled on top of him and planted soft kisses from his neck to his happy trail, then aimed lower.

He whispered in a sorrowful tone, "Don't, Livvy. I want you to be in love with me first." *You have got to be kidding me.* He clearly desired me, but would not accept what I was offering.

"Give me your hand, Max, or I will use my own," I said once again.

Obviously my so-called purity was not sacrificed tonight.

"I don't know if I'll be able to let you go tomorrow," he sleepily said.

I didn't say anything, because it was as though my feelings for him were creeping up on me more heavily every time he touched me. I couldn't seem to make them stop, but I had to find a way.

Furthermore, I knew I couldn't do this life he had chosen. I couldn't allow myself to become upset like I had before, because I could die.

I touched Max's bandage. *He could have even died.* I knew I couldn't do this...fall in love and then have him snatched completely out of my life because of his job. No, I wouldn't. Not ever.

* * *

"Good morning," he said. "Sorry for waking you so early."

"I've been awake for a while now." I popped my head on his chest, and his arm folded around me.

"What's wrong?"

"I'm nervous about leaving the hotel."

"Martin informed the airport we would leave at noon today, but he'll change the flight time at the last minute to throw off any tipsters."

I wiggled free from Max's hold and said, "I need to get dressed."

I was stepping out of the shower when Max knocked on the door. "The water's hot," I told him.

"Livvy, talk to me."

"It's nothing really; don't worry." He got in the shower. *Thank God my hair was still good.* I ran a brush through it and applied mascara, lip gloss, and a light bronzer. I grabbed a dark purple wrap dress and flung it over a chair. I glanced at Max as he rearranged his computer bag.

White shirt and jeans again. I suspected it was becoming his uniform. He looked incredible. "Do you want to talk now?" he asked.

I shoved my diabetic things in my tote bag and noticed that Henry had taken care of everything else. "Really, Max, I'm okay."

He held his bag in one hand, planted the other one firmly at my waist, and inhaled deeply. "Livvy, you smell...so good. I need to speak to Martin for a couple minutes. Take your time." He walked out.

Max was standing next to Martin when I joined them. He slipped his arm around my waist. Martin said Max and I would not ride together this morning, but he would ride with me. "Who is riding with him?" I asked.

"Shawn." Martin removed my bag from my shoulder and dug around in it. He handed me my shades. "You should organize your bag. I can't find shit in it." *Me either, buddy.* I knew the drill. Max grabbed my hand as we stepped off the elevator. Our pace doubled within three steps. Martin grabbed me by my arm and told Max he had me. Max released my hand as the hotel's entrance doors flung open, and we never slowed down. The press once again screamed questions and took pictures. I never looked up. The back door of the car was open. I lowered my head and basically dove inside, with Martin right behind me. Within seconds, we were out of there, all four cars in a row. I rummaged through my bag, which Martin had tossed on the seat between us.

"Do you need something?"

"My phone."

He reached in and got it. "Thanks."

Max texted before I could text him: *Are you okay?*

I texted: *Yes.* ☺

He texted: *See you in twenty.* ☺☺

I felt a smile spring to my lips. *Stop it, Livvy*, I thought. *Stop. You have to let him go.* My smile faded.

After clearing the gates at the airport, I could see in the distance the jet had been prepared to depart quickly. Our cars stopped fewer than ten feet from the stairs of the plane. Martin grabbed my bag with one hand and my hand with his other, and dang if he didn't pull me across the seat. When my feet hit the ground, I stumbled. But he didn't release my hand until we had stepped on board the jet. Max, Shawn, and Claude were right behind me.

I asked Martin what time we were expected to arrive in Auburn. I needed to call my dad. Martin told me not to worry; he had spoken with my parents earlier. I didn't bother to ask any questions, because at this point, I figured I was better off not knowing.

While our luggage was being loaded, Joann appeared with simple continental breakfasts, prepared on trays.

An hour into the flight, I was bored with my iPod, but I had gotten tickled at Max. He was reading something that appeared to be a proposal. He cursed every now and then. I had to take a quick glance. He finally shoved the thick brown folder into his bag and said, "They're out of their freaking minds. Houdini couldn't make that shit happen."

"Carter is from Alabama, you know that, right? He lives in Singapore. I know you're looking at the clean energy part of his business. Watch it. He's an old guy, but he's shrewd, and meaner than an agitated rattlesnake. I know because he and Papa have been friends for over forty years."

I had to pee. "Excuse me."

Max stopped me. "What else do you know about Carter?"

"Oh, absolutely nothing."

I shared my iPod with Max. He laughed at some of my music choices. "Livvy, how many years did you take piano?"

"Ten, but how did you know?"

"Rae mentioned it once."

"I love when you sing to me, Max," I whispered.

He flashed his sexy grin. "Do you now?"

After lunch, I freshened up a bit. Max did that little head thing he does, and the guys disappeared into Joann's hideout.

"Can we talk for a minute?"

I felt my heart sink. "Of course."

"Livvy, I don't want to land in Auburn. I want you to go back to New York with me. I told you last night I wasn't ready to let you go."

I didn't say anything. I closed my eyes, because they were stinging from the tears that had pooled. They escaped and ran down my face. He asked me if I would think about it. I laid my head on his shoulder. He kissed me on the side of my head. The cabin phone rang. "Auburn for now," he answered.

Max walked to the front of the cabin, opened the door to Joann's hideout, and the men reclaimed their previous seats.

My voice shook when I whispered, "I can't go with you."

He didn't say a word, but he stood up, still holding my hand. He snatched me up from the sofa, and I stumbled a couple of steps as he pulled me behind him. I heard Martin, Shawn, and Claude move. Martin shouted, "Max!" Max glanced over his shoulder and only gave the three of them a quick, harsh look. Max paused for my feet to catch up with his, but he did not release my hand. He opened the door to Joann's hideout. Max did that head thing, and she hopped up from her seat. Max slammed the door, barely letting her clear the opening.

"Livvy," he said urgently. "Open your eyes. I am so in love with you, I cannot stand it. I fell in love with you the moment I laid eyes on you in Cabo and didn't even know your name. I know you now. We have so much in common. We tell each other everything, and it's only been a month since our lives crossed paths again. I know you feel something for me. Say it." Max was calming down now. He pulled me close to him. I was crying. "I know you have feelings for me, and you have since the day we left New York. You kissed me differently. But you held back again until our last night in Paris. I had to force myself not to make love to you."

"Max," I interrupted, "why didn't you make love to me?"

"You know why. I wanted you to tell me you loved me," he said, with tears in his eyes. "Do you love me?" he asked. I was shaking my head no, but my heart was aching for me to scream yes.

"Answer me." I was afraid to answer him. After a moment of silence, he ran his hand through his wavy, dark hair. "In Cabo I accepted your invitation to ride to the airport with you. I didn't need it. Martin was at the resort the entire time. I was supposed to leave Cabo the night before, but when you offered to share a car, I jumped at it. I bought a ticket to New York so I could spend an hour with you." *What?*

"I can't believe you did that." I took a deep breath. "I think I might be falling in love with you, but that's all I can say until I sort this out. You, your job, and your lifestyle scare me. I'm afraid—can't you see that?"

"Don't be afraid, and Livvy, I don't think you *might* be falling in love with me. You have fallen in love with me."

We were now sitting in the crew seats in the front of the plane. He put his arm around me. "I'm not giving up. I'm just as stubborn as you are. Come on, let's get you freshened up. We'll land in Auburn soon."

He opened the door, reached into a compartment, removed my carry-on bag, and took it to the bathroom for me. He turned to walk out, but he stepped back inside for a moment. "Do you have any idea how much I love you?" He kissed me tenderly.

I looked in the mirror. *Good God. Cher's team of people could not put me together again.* I did my best to look presentable. As I returned to my seat, I smacked Martin on the back of his head and asked, "How was your vacation in Cabo?"

"It was good," he said without batting an eye.

The cabin phone rang. Martin answered and announced, "Landing in ten minutes."

We landed and taxied to the complete opposite end of the runway, where the hangars were. When the plane came to a complete stop, Claude, Shawn, and Martin got out of their seats immediately. I peeked out the window and saw Dad and Noel leaning against the Hummer. The pilots were lining up the Louis department store beside the Hummer. My daddy was scratching his head. I pointed out the window, and Max grinned. "You can change your mind, you know," I said. "It really is much too expensive."

"No. But you can change your mind and come with me."

We stood up, walked to the front of the plane, and stopped almost in the doorway. Max asked if I would reconsider. I once again told him I needed to think. "You may be more than I can handle, Max, because of my health issues."

"But you love me, Livvy. I know it."

I could see out of the corner of my eye that Shawn and Claude were standing at the bottom of the steps. Martin ran back up the steps and stood in the doorway. "I will walk away from all of this today to be with you."

I didn't see that coming. I buried my face in my hands. "No. Max, you can't do that." I began to cry again. Max tenderly folded his arms around me. "I heard you and Martin speaking. Your contract with Global doesn't expire for two years. Besides, you said yourself you were hooked. You love what you do."

Noel demanded, "Let her off the plane." I looked to my left. I could barely see around Martin, but then I spotted Noel standing right in front of Shawn and Claude. Max still had a tight hold on me. Then Max kissed me. I felt my knees go weak and my head was spinning, but like a fool, I was kissing him back.

"Let me through. I'm getting my sister," Noel shouted.

Max released me and said, "I'll call you the day after tomorrow. But before you walk off this plane, tell me. Say it. Tell me you love me, and leave out that damn word *might*!"

"I think..." After a short pause, I closed my eyes and finished, "I love you."

Max picked up my bag. "Martin, help Livvy, please." He reached for my arm, and I turned back to face him. He kissed me, and I kissed him back. He said with his lips touching mine, "I will come back for you. I can be here in four hours. But you had better be ready to love me." I nodded. Martin took my bag from Max.

Martin was practically holding me up. Why couldn't I stop crying? I looked down as we stepped down the stairs, but I could barely see through my blurred vision. What I could see, though, was Noel holding a freaking shotgun, and he'd just cocked the damn thing. *Shit, don't shoot.* We've lived through that once already. "Shawn is staying in Auburn with you a few days until the press calms down," Martin said.

I interrupted, and through my sniffles, I told Martin this was Auburn—there would be no press, because football season was over.

About that time I looked to my right, and the entire fence along the main two-lane road was lined with people holding cameras and news crews shouting, "Livvy, look this way. Where is Max?"

Martin and I stepped on the ground. I turned to look back at the plane, but Claude said in his thick French accent, "Keep walking, and keep your head down unless you want to turn around and walk back up those stairs."

Noel swung open the back-passenger door, and Martin finally lifted me up and sat me on the seat, because I missed the running board with my foot three times. I couldn't see it because I was crying so hard. I could only scoot to the middle of the seat. The dang luggage had overflowed from the back. Martin sat beside me for few minutes. "Livvy, don't go anywhere without Shawn. I spoke to your parents and Noel before we left London. This is only to protect you. But if you change your mind"—Martin nodded toward the plane—"we can do a turnaround." He gave me a hug and made a mad dash toward the plane. Shawn got in the Hummer.

Noel paused to allow an electric gate to open. Someone jumped from behind a large oak tree, and suddenly a man slammed Shawn's door and pressed a camera lens to the glass. Shawn flung open his door, which knocked the man backward, causing him to fall. Shawn bent over and snatched the camera out of his hand, removed the memory card, and shoved the camera into the man's chest. The gate opened, Shawn hopped back in, and Noel made a left.

When the jet flew overhead, I knew at that moment—I wanted him. "Daddy," I shouted, "I've changed my mind! Turn around! Call the airport, Shawn. Do it now. Get Max. I want to go with him."

"When hell freezes over!" Noel shouted.

"Noel," I shouted, "it's my life." I slapped the back of his seat. "Turn around now. Daddy," I cried.

"No, Livvy," Dad calmly said, "we need you here for a few days. Kurt's at the house."

"Who?" Shawn asked.

"Her doctor," Dad answered.

Shawn sent an e-mail from his phone.

"I called Uncle Troy," Noel said. "If you had not come home today, we were coming to get you. He's investigating Max himself."

Two police cars sat at the entrance to my parents' neighborhood, and once we crossed the arched rock bridge, there were more. When we topped the hill, I saw the reporters. They were lined up and down the sidewalk on both sides of the street.

Even though the Hummer's windows were tinted, Shawn removed his jacket and covered my head. Noel pulled into the garage and lowered the door. "Miss Hunnicutt, all of this will be over in a couple of days when they figure out Mr. Spencer is in New York," Shawn said.

I hugged Mom so tight when we walked in the door. Rae, Andi, and Bradley were waiting on their hugs too.

"Everyone, this is my babysitter, Shawn, and he is an excellent bag carrier." My family introduced themselves.

Dr. Kurt asked to visit with me after I was settled.

I told Rae Shawn could speak in Spanish, French, and maybe Italian, but I wasn't sure about Mandarin. "Shawn here is quite a talker, and most of the time, I can't understand a damn word he says." Daddy apologized for my mouth.

Shawn greeted Rae in Spanish, but added he didn't speak Mandarin and admitted his Italian was not good; however, his French and Spanish were solid.

I knew I had to save Shawn from Rae. So after a couple of minutes, I interrupted their conversation. "Come on, Shawn. Let me show you to your room. Come on, Dr. Kurt, I know you want my blood." I pointed. "Bring that bag of fluids you're nursing, because I'm going to need it."

Shawn asked my father, "Is she always so—"

My daddy interrupted, "Yep, afraid so."

Mom shouted, "Livvy, wait." She told me she'd invited my friends over for dinner tonight. She said they had been worried about me. Inwardly I sighed, but I told her it was all right.

I showed Shawn to his room while Doc set up his mini mobile lab in my old fancy bedroom. Shawn immediately he asked to see my room. "Miss Hunnicutt, who and how many are coming tonight?"

"Five. Mom will give you the list of names. We'll eat dinner and probably watch a movie in the theater." I waved my hand. "Look around and get comfortable. I'll do as Martin asked."

Dr. Kurt pricked my finger. Whoa! From his expression he was pissed: my blood sugar was 360. Shoot! He spotted my black-and-blue arm. I quickly said, "Oh…oh, that. It was my fault. I snatched an IV out."

Dr. Kurt asked to see my other arm. I pulled my sleeve up and continued. "Shawn, do not call me Miss Hunnicutt. Call me Livvy. And if you slip up in front of my friends, I might have to borrow the shotgun Noel was showing off earlier. I'm a hunter, so I know how to use it."

Dr. Kurt snickered and asked if he should hang around.

"Yes, I understand," Shawn said. Then he laughed and walked out. He returned less than a minute later with a bottle of water, opened it, and said, "Here." He flipped my tote upside down, dumping everything on my bed. He grabbed my insulin pen, changed the needle, and asked, "How many units?"

"Four," Dr. Kurt and I said at the same time.

"I'll check again in twenty," I said. "Sometimes the fluids bottom me out."

Doc drew blood to send to the lab. He checked my temp and blood pressure. "Your pressure is low, seventy-seven over fifty. Let's get a standing pressure." I stood up. Dr. Kurt proceeded. Shawn stepped over and looked for himself.

"It's low—sixty over forty-two," Shawn said.

"Yeah, I thought so." I felt like a wrung-out mop.

"I want you to increase your fludrocortisone from one tablet to two a day, for a week," Dr. Kurt said. "Change from prednisone to hydrocortisone. I'll call it in."

"Aw, Dr. Kurt, hydrocortisone makes me puffier than prednisone."

"I know, but let's just try it." He patted my hand.

I told Dr. Kurt he could leave now. I would remove the IV when it finished dripping.

Doc pointed to my right arm. "From the looks of it, I will stay."

"Thank God," Shawn said. I told Shawn to leave, and he grunted on his way out.

Dr. Kurt laughed at him. I picked up my iPad from the night chest.

CHAPTER 21

Dr. Kurt's medical examination included a verbal spanking on how important it was for me to keep my blood sugar in a decent range of 75 to 120.

"I understand with your other medications, the range is difficult, and you'll always run a little higher," Doc said. "But try to keep it tight. Why did you need an IV while you were…um, vacationing?"

I told him everything.

"I'm glad you're home." He winked at me on his way out.

I took a short nap, showered, dressed for the evening, and joined my family upstairs. Mom, Rae, and Andi were gathered in the guest room on the main floor. I popped my head through the door, and Mom asked, "Darling, what is all of this?"

I shrugged my shoulders. "While in Paris, I was unable to visit Louis Vuitton. That was the only stop on my list that I missed. Max had those things brought to me."

Mom shook her head and walked out. "Good Lord."

I shouted to get Mom's attention and asked what was going on with the film.

"It's a go for sure."

"Who's gonna be offered the role of Ben Davis?"

"Matt was offered the role a few minutes ago, and the role of Tate Brown was offered to David Williams. The role of Clay Smith was offered to Scott White."

"Wow. What about the character Jane Morris?"

"We are hoping for Emily Webster."

Wow, she would be perfect. Petite, brown hair, and a nice smile. "Mom, you will never guess in a million years who I saw in London."

"I'm afraid to guess."

"Peter Weston. He's handsome." Mom grinned. "He's edgy, but in a gorgeous kinda way. He's at least six foot one, slim build, but fit."

"Where did you meet him?"

"Well, we didn't exactly meet. We shared an elevator."

She laughed and shook her head. "Peter Weston seems like a nice young man. Actually, I just got off the phone with him."

"Why?"

"Peter was interested in the role of Ben. I told him it was offered to Matt Bartlett only minutes before he called, but I said if it didn't work out with Matt, I would ask Teddy to call him personally."

"Oh, that's nice."

Rae and Andi were still admiring the Louis department store. Bradley thought the collection was tight. I told them they could all borrow it.

I also told them they should have seen the outfit I wore to dinner in Paris. It was to die for. Then after a second, I stopped in the doorway of the bedroom and said, "Oh, wait. Earlier that day, I got sick, and the next day we were shot at, so maybe it wasn't to die for. That was scary."

Rae punched Bradley on the arm and said, "Dang. In college Max asked me out twice, and I wouldn't go."

We all started laughing at her. Bradley said, "Baby, aren't you glad you didn't choose Max? You got me. You can just borrow all this shit from Livvy."

"And I got Noel," Andi said.

"God bless you, girl," we all said.

My friends arrived and joined us in the kitchen while my parents put the finishing touches on dinner. The five of them just stared at me. Luke touched my face, and I pushed his hand away. "What are you looking at?"

"On TV you looked awful. I just knew you were all scraped up or worse, shot. That guy pushed you hard."

"Well, meet the guy who pushed Max and me to the ground. But Claude is the one that took the bullet for me," I said with a *The Price Is Right* model introduction as Shawn cleared the doorway.

Everyone shook hands with Shawn, but Abby hugged him. "Thank you." I smiled at Shawn. He was tall; six feet maybe, with brown eyes, a nice white smile, and dark, smooth skin. A small scar above his right brow was barely noticeable. He had muscles too. I was glad to see he looked relaxed. He wore designer jeans and a great fitted button-down shirt. I liked his shoes, Dior sneakers. I noticed he was wearing fire-power on his right side when he slipped his cell into his back pocket.

Mother pointed us to the dining room. Shawn must have considered himself part of my group, because he sat beside me. He also took on the bartending job.

I even found myself laughing a few times during the evening, but good God, who wouldn't laugh at Jake? The stories he could tell about girls, and from the comments Tucker had made about Crosby, they were a lot alike, or at least used to be.

Luke had brought the funny comedy DVD that I referred to as my therapist. Shawn was probably the only black guy in the world who had never seen it, so that was a must.

After the movie, I was saying good night to my friends when Luke's phone lit up with Robert's name.

"May I answer it?" I asked.

He handed his phone to me.

"Robert," I said, "it's Livvy."

"My God, Livvy, I have been worried to death about you. I tried to call, but—"

"Robert," I said, cutting him off, "I think it's best if we keep our distance for now, but maybe we can talk soon. I wanted you to know I'm okay, but most of all…I hope you are."

"Livvy—"

I interrupted again. "Good night, Robert." I handed Luke's phone back to him and walked away.

I texted Shawn from my fancy guest room and told him I wanted to go to the gym in the morning. I said I'd meet him upstairs at five forty-five, but I also included the name of my gym, the phone number, and the address to save him the trouble of asking.

Shawn was waiting for me the following morning, but there was someone else in the kitchen as well. Another a black suit. Dang it, what is it with the black suits, white shirts, and the guns? Shawn was in gym clothes. I pointed to the guy wordlessly.

"Rick," Shawn said.

It was much too early to be nice, so all I could muster up was "Morning." I turned and walked in the direction of the garage. My babysitters were right on my heels. Shawn pointed to the Hummer and popped his butt in the backseat with me; apparently Rick was driving.

A small group of news reporters were still camped out across the street and an off-duty policeman was standing in front of a barricade in our driveway. He moved it over, and Rick waved at him as we drove past. Shawn asked me to lean over and get out of sight. I put my iPod buds in my ears. I wanted to sit up, let my window down, and give those reporters a finger gesture, but I didn't. Instead, after we had cleared the news posse, I slapped Shawn on his leg and told him I hoped he could keep up. He grinned and asked how far. At the least, five, I told him, but I would like to do more because I needed to vent frustration. I never looked at him, but I heard him mumble something in French. I was sick and tired of that. I decided to take German and French lessons to go along with my unpolished Spanish before the year was out.

The gym parking lot was almost empty. Strange. At six in the morning, this gym was always packed. Did Martin close the gym for a few hours? I decided it was best not to ask.

Heath, Greg, and Donna—the trainers—were waiting inside. I pointed and said, "Those two are cool, but that one will kill you." Without breaking my stride, I stepped on a treadmill. I was going to give it hell. I cranked up my workout music and completed a sissy warm-up. Then I hit the speed button; Shawn did the same. I ran and ran. Tears and sweat burned my eyes. After a while my tears escaped and trickled down my face. I didn't care. No one noticed, because the sweat was dripping as well.

When I hit five miles, I didn't stop. I went to seven instead. Then I pressed the cool down button. Shawn mirrored me. I asked Heath to help me stretch out my legs. He handed me a towel and bottled water, then pointed to the table. Donna helped Shawn out; he was panting as he drank his water. Donna pushed his leg back, and he moaned like she was killing him. Heath grinned. I wanted to laugh, but I didn't. I cranked my music back up while I lifted weights. From the corner of my eye, I caught Rick running toward us, holding Shawn's phone. I pulled a bud from my ear. Shawn picked up his pace to meet Rick and asked, "Who is it?"

"Martin." Shawn never said a word, but he was quickly at my side.

"We have to leave now," he said.

Donna removed the weights from my hand, and Shawn grabbed my sweaty, nasty arm.

We were about to exit the building when Rick stopped us.

Two men were standing next to the Hummer. Shawn threw Rick's jacket over my head. Rick shouted, "Back up!" and opened the door for me. I dashed inside. Before my butt hit the seat, Shawn said, "Slide, Livvy."

I never asked any questions. I returned my iPod buds to my ears. When we entered my parents' neighborhood, the media crowd had grown. I laid my head down on Shawn's knee until we were parked in the garage with the door completely down. When I removed the ear buds, I heard helicopters. I asked Shawn what was going on. He wanted to be all tight-lipped, but I shouted at him anyway and demanded answers. Shawn had me by my arm, helping me out of the Hummer, and I continued to bitch. "Tell me what is going on now."

Dad swung the door open and demanded an explanation. "You know, Mr. Hunnicutt, this is not about Livvy," Shawn said.

Pointing to the ceiling, Dad said, "She is involved in something, or there would not be helicopters flying above our home. Start talking, boy, or I'm calling Max."

Shawn reluctantly explained that Max and his team—with the help of the US government—had acquired a large bank an hour ago. It did not go as smoothly as he had hoped. My dad and I were nodding. Daddy noticed I was about to cry. He put his arms around me. "I can't tell you what to do anymore," he said. "You are an adult. But please don't go to New York. I'm not cut out for this kind of worry."

"Mr. Hunnicutt, we know for a fact the press only wants a good picture of Livvy, because they don't have any. She has shades on in every single photo the press has, including live news footage. I canceled Livvy's Facebook account." *Does "password" not mean anything to these people?* "Sorry, Livvy. I borrowed her phone too and spoke to her friends." *Well, thanks for asking.* "I asked them not to speak to anyone about her or share any photos, or Martin would pay them a not-so-friendly visit. One guy called me, though. His name was Robert. He told me I had better keep Livvy safe, or he would, uh…kick my ass. He mentioned something about making a mistake, but that was all he said."

"Well, damn," Tom spat, "why didn't he say something a month ago? We could have avoided all of this mess."

"Daddy, Robert doesn't want me. I know he didn't mean to hurt me, but I still don't understand what happened."

"You don't need anyone," Daddy said. "You are strong, independent, beautiful, and smart."

"I think dads are supposed to say those things to their children," I said to Shawn.

"In your case, Livvy, your father may be right. But if you repeat that, I will refer to you only as Miss Hunnicutt and Mr. Hunnicutt, bigger news will happen soon and the press will move on. It always does."

I told Shawn I was showering, and it smelled like he should too. My dad apologized to Shawn for my mouth again. But, my God, he was like me...he stank.

When Shawn appeared once again, he was wearing jeans and had made himself right at home. Mom and Dad were busy, so Shawn and I made dinner together and watched movies in the theater. It was early, but I went to bed and tossed and turned for hours.

Suddenly, I sat straight up and gasped. *What the crap was that all about?* I had had a dream. I never had dreams anymore. I flipped back over, but I couldn't sleep because of thinking about the stupid dream. I loved the yellow dress I had been wearing in the dream, and the spring lines were out. I would look for it online tomorrow. But Lord, I hoped the dreams didn't start again. I drifted back to sleep.

Shawn was right. The vice president said something totally ridiculous during an interview, and my parents' street was back to normal— dead as a doornail.

After breakfast I showered, dressed, grabbed my bag, and fetched Shawn. He beat me to the door. I think he needed fresh air too.

While he drove the big Ford truck to my little house, Shawn messed with my dad's radio. He reprogramed every damn station to crap I knew Tom would not like. Shawn laughed as we stepped on my porch. "Your dad's pretty cool, you know." He took my house key and left me standing on the porch. He came back out and said, "All clear." He leaned against the side of Tom's truck while he chatted on the phone. I changed into my riding gear and raised the garage door. Shawn was still on the phone, but he walked toward me.

"Wrap it up, boy," I said, tossing him a helmet. He caught it and quickly ended his conversation.

I removed the cover of my bike and straddled it. Shawn got his ass on, but he was fidgeting as he leaned on the backrest. I told him to relax. I turned the music on, and I felt Shawn's long legs tense up against my hips just a bit. I shifted into gear, and we were off.

Shawn and I rode for an hour or so; he never spoke. Back at home he got off, put one hand on his hip, and touched the seat with his other hand. "I might have to buy one of these."

The day crept by slowly, and after dinner, I decided to go to my room. I knew Max would call soon.

When my phone rang, I took a deep breath and answered. Max said he would be back on the plane tomorrow to get Shawn. He said he knew I couldn't go back with him right now, but he asked to see me.

"Yes, Max, I want to see you." But he was right; I could not go with him.

We both said, "Good night." Yet I couldn't press the end button on my phone, so I waited and waited until he did.

The next morning I hung out in my old fancy room at my parents'. Mom brought breakfast downstairs to me. I asked her if she would take Shawn's bag to the airport. I was taking him, but on the Harley. She was happy to, but she said she needed to speak with me later about the book tour and the movie thing.

I met Shawn in the kitchen and told him to put his bag in Mom's car; however, I would be taking him to the airport. He grinned. Obviously, he knew his method of transportation, because I was geared up in leather.

Martin texted the code to the back gate at the airport, and I forwarded it to Mom, who was ahead of us. The gate had barely closed when I pressed the code in again. The plane taxied to the same hangar as the other day. Mom stopped and removed Shawn's bag from her trunk and sat it on the ground. She got back into her car and drove away.

I parked a few feet from the bottom of the stairs. Martin met us. We removed our helmets, and Shawn strapped his on the backrest. I sat mine on the seat. I gave Shawn a hug. "Take care, Livvy." He turned and ran up the steps to the plane.

"I thought you were joking about the Harley." Martin gave me a hug and patted me on the back.

"You never joke about a Harley."

"I see that."

My eyes were drawn to the doorway of the plane where Max stood. He smiled as he walked down the steps. When he stepped on the ground, we reached for each other and hugged tightly. Max kissed me and took a step back. He reached for my hands and held them. "Now, this is definitely a good look for you," he said.

Without releasing my hands, he continued, "You were right. It was difficult for me to admit. I'm sorry your blood sugar ran high while we were together. That's not good for you. I spoke to Shawn while the doctor was with you. I'm sorry I upset you. Shawn said after you left the airport, you changed your mind and wanted to go with me, but Tom and Noel didn't agree. I know you love me and I love you, but I also understand why you don't want to say it, at least for now." I smiled at him with a stream of tears running down my face. "Livvy, please don't cry."

I slowly removed my hands from his. I reached up and kissed him, just as I had the day I ran after him in the hotel in New York. Right now I wanted to grab him by the hand and run up the stairs to the plane and never look back. But my family would never support me having a relationship with Max, nor would it be healthy. On that thought, I released him, and he allowed me to. In a broken voice, I said, "Thank you, Max, for understanding."

He had tears in his beautiful, sad hazel eyes. "You're welcome, Livvy."

I turned from him and had taken two steps when he said, "I will come back for you when you're ready."

I stopped dead in my tracks. I felt him touch my shoulders. I removed a glove, and reached back to touch his hand lightly. I could not turn around to face him, because I knew I would leave with him.

My hands were shaking as I strapped my helmet on and straddled my bike. I cranked my bike, lifted the kick, shifted into gear, and drove away. When I glanced in my mirror, Max had not moved from the spot where I left him standing. I blinked and didn't look into the rearview mirror again.

CHAPTER 22

I parked my bike in the garage and realized I was alone for the first time in days. I walked into my bedroom, fell to my knees, curled up into a ball on the floor, and cried. Hours passed, and I moved only once to check my blood sugar. I gave myself insulin and returned to my position on the floor. This time I didn't cry. I just stared at a tiny stain on my rug.

It was getting late. I remembered Mom wanted to speak to me today. So I got up from the floor, washed my face, and warmed up a can of soup in a saucepan. I skipped the bowl, grabbed a soup spoon, added crushed crackers, and called it dinner.

As I parked my car in my folks' driveway, I had a sickening feeling in my stomach. I couldn't talk about any of this to anyone, not tonight. I prayed this was not why Mom wanted to speak with me. I walked into the kitchen. Dad was tidying up after dinner. He pointed to the stove. I told him I had eaten.

I took a seat next to Mom at the breakfast room table, and she began to talk. She said Rae had an appointment in New York with a designer at the end of the month, and she preferred I not go. Mom didn't comment any further; she knew I understood.

She said she would start to travel to promote the book in mid-February, and she wanted me to go with her to five of the six cities on the schedule. I knew New York was the city that I was not invited to accompany her.

"We'll keep you busy," Mom said. "If you need anything, your dad and I are here for you."

Mom jumped to the next thing on her list, the film *Finding Justice*, which would be shot locally. They were having a difficult time finding accommodations for the actors and film crew, despite being willing to rent for approximately eight weeks, give or take a little. She smiled and said some people would start arriving in late May, but the film wouldn't start shooting until mid-June. I interrupted for the first time and reminded her about the new condos fewer than two miles from our lake place. None of the units had yet sold.

"That area will be perfect, because most of the film will be shot near the cliffs and in Dadeville." Mom grinned. "Would you call Ms. Fills, the real estate agent, first thing in the morning?"

"I'm on it, Mom, and thank you for officially hiring me." Mom was quiet for a moment. After she organized her thoughts, she said, "I'm sorry about encouraging you to go with Max. All of this is my fault." Mom hugged me. "Will you forgive me?"

"There's nothing to forgive. I would have gone anyway."

Dad walked around to where we were sitting. "Cookie, she needs to see what was delivered today."

"I know, Tom."

Dad opened the doors to reveal four large crates and a much smaller one. I read the return shipping address.

"What do you want us to do?" Mom asked.

"Mom, these items were tagged sold before I left the gallery in Paris," I said. "I need to call Martin."

Martin answered on the second ring. "Livvy, are you all right?" I didn't answer his question. But I asked him about the artwork Max had sent.

"Mr. Spencer said to buy any piece you studied for a long time."

"Martin," I said, fighting the urge to cry, "I cannot accept the paintings. Things are not going as Max or even I had hoped. I'm sending them to Max. I need his address, please."

"Hold on." He returned. "Will you talk to Max?"

"Of course I will." Max came on the phone.

"Livvy, I bought the artwork for you, and it's yours to keep. Maybe one day we can enjoy it together. Please don't. I can tell you're crying." After a long pause, he said, "Livvy, just say it, and I'll come get you." I closed my eyes.

"Max," I whispered, "what I want and what is good for me aren't the same."

"I love you and don't see that changing anytime soon. I'll let you go." He hung up.

When I opened my eyes, Dad was standing in front of me. I looked down at my phone. "I'm okay, Daddy."

Daddy wiped my tears from my cheeks with his thumbs. "No, you're not."

"I will be, and soon." *I have to get a grip on life, and I need to start right now.* "I promise."

I woke up early and immediately placed a call to Ms. Fills. She said all but three units were available. She would call the investors to see if they were willing to lease short-term.

Three days later, Ms. Fills called to say the investors agreed. She e-mailed the information. I looked it over and forwarded it to someone named Teddy for Mom.

My phone rang, and I answered it before I looked at the screen. A familiar and most welcome voice said, "Livvy." I must have lit up like a lightning bug. The first thing Crosby asked was, "Is it okay that I called?"

"Yes."

"Tucker and I have talked to Max about what happened. He answered our questions in detail, except for when you were involved. Were you hurt in London?"

"No."

"Max said you weren't, but I needed to ask. Tucker and I are upset with him for putting you in that kind of danger. I wanted to hate him for liking you—loving you, actually—but I knew he did the first day we saw you in Cabo. Then I wanted to be angry with you, but it's not your fault. Shit happens, I guess. Can I ask you one more thing?"

"Anything."

"Was Max a gentleman?"

I knew that wasn't what he wanted to know, but I would give him the answer he sought. It was nothing but the truth. "Max was a complete gentleman. But I think what you are politely asking me is did Max leave me the way you left me? All I can say is, my beautiful painting has not yet been completed."

"Thank you for sharing that with me."

"Crosby, I'm sorry I hurt you. I never meant to."

"Ah, you didn't do anything wrong. I'm still pissed at Max, though."

"You know, I couldn't give my stuff away."

"You'd better not give it to anyone until you're married."

"Undoubtedly, I'll die a virgin at the rate I'm going." He laughed, but I continued. "You wouldn't touch me because you thought that God would strike you dead with a lightning bolt or something. You know, I think you may have bowed out too soon. But I understand. I'm thinking about Bob."

"I know you've had lunch with Matt Bartlett, and you've met David Williams. Max mentioned you two saw Peter Weston, who, according to Max, never took his eyes off you. But who the heck is Bob?"

"I don't know Bob yet. But I thought about buying one. You know, a battery-operated boyfriend."

"Don't you dare pop that thing with a Bob. Shit. I gotta go, but don't do it. I'm going to call you a couple of times a week now to check on your cherry."

Tucker sent a text: *Little virgin Livvy. Don't do it. Forget about Bob. Wait, girl! By the way, thanks. I like Piper. And thanks for clearing up some details. I thought for a few days I was going to have to kick Max's ass.*

I texted back: *Happy for you and Piper! As far as Bob goes, we'll see.*

*   *   *

Mom kept me busy. It had been six weeks since I'd spoken to Max, but I talked to Crosby and Tucker every week. Of course, all Tucker wanted to know was if I had bought Bob yet. But Crosby and I talked about everything. Tonight he called and said he hadn't picked a girl up from a bar in three months. *Wow, that was before Cabo.*

Over the next three weeks, Mom and I traveled for her book. Yet for one leg of her tour, I had to detour. Dad met Mom in New York. Mom called with good news yesterday and said Max came by one of her book signings and apologized to them for everything. Mom and Dad forgave him, of course.

It was hard to believe that spring was here. It was cold in Chicago. As Mom's assistant, my voice mailbox was full, as usual. The messages were usually for Mom; however, to my surprise, the second one tonight was from Max. This was the first time he had called since we spoke about the artwork almost three months ago. I smiled as I listened to his voice mail. I returned his call, and we talked for over an hour. We laughed a lot. He told me he thought Crosby and Tucker had wanted to give him an old-fashioned butt-whipping. He thanked me for clearing things up. I told Max I was enjoying the beautiful luggage he had bought for me. As for the artwork, it was still crated, but I hoped one day I could admire it the way it was meant to be.

"Remember you only deserve the best in all things, and don't forget it. Oh, and one more thing—please do not introduce yourself to Bob. I haven't given up."

"You know about Bob?"

"Yeah, I do."

I huffed. "I'll think about it."

Before Max said bye, he asked if he could call next week. I said I would be completely disappointed if he didn't.

Rae's wedding was now only a month away. Andi looked like she was about to pop; the doctor put her on bed rest. She and Noel were staying at my parents' home, so she would never left alone.

Rae told me she saw a report this morning that said no illegal dealings had been found in the Max Spencer investigation, but they also ran every piece of old news footage they had, including ones of me in Paris and London.

"I could have told you that. He has a team of freaking attorneys who work around the clock."

"Why didn't you say something? I've worried myself to death."

"Big sis, you never asked."

Mom and I had a quick meeting. Ms. Fills and Teddy had worked out the living arrangements for our visitors. Unfortunately, two condos recently flooded due to broken pipes and were now unavailable. Two people decided to share a three-bedroom. Also, our lake house was going to be used for one person. Shoot, my plans seemed to be screwed, because I had planned to stay there.

* * *

After Rae and Bradley's wedding rehearsal dinner, ten girls spent the night with Rae at our parents' home, because Rae wanted to include Andi. Baby Riley had already attempted to make her grand appearance early into this big bad world on several different occasions.

A few hours after I retired to bed, I awoke, nearly hyperventilating and sat up in a panic. "I'm not the one getting married, Rae is. Why did I dream that?" I said aloud. I carefully rubbed my eyes. "Okay, focus Livvy." I switched on the lamp. "Who was that man, and why was he drawing…dear God, my wedding gown?" I fell back on my pillows, leaving the dang lamp on, 'cause I didn't want to dream again.

The next morning, I heard footsteps. It sounded like the bridesmaid posse was heading out for the morning, planning to reappear at two o'clock at the church. Oh, and I smelled bacon. I slowly got out of bed and made a low-key appearance in the kitchen. I made myself a plate and returned to my bedroom. It was Rae's day. I wanted Mom and Dad to enjoy her before the day got rolling.

I was excited and nervous. I would see Crosby for the first time since New Year's Day. I didn't know why I was nervous. We talked once or even twice a week, and some days we text-messaged each other three or four times. Tucker and Piper were attending as well. Thank God our bridesmaid dresses were pretty. They were classy black floor-length styles with an empire waistline. The fabric was silk satin, and the dress had a thin rhinestone band right underneath the gathered bustline.

I recalled my conversation with Max last week. Crosby had told him he was attending Rae's wedding. Max asked me how I felt about him coming. I said I was looking forward to seeing Crosby, but added, "You know, Max, I love Crosby and Tucker, and I'm happy with the direction our relationship has gone. Crosby and I know we will always be good friends."

Max had sighed. "Thank you for telling me."

It was nine in the morning. Max was in London. I did the math; it was afternoon there. I couldn't seem to get him off my mind, so I decided to send him a quick text. I kept it simple: *I know your apartment is absolutely amazing. I hope the renovation has turned out as you planned. Sorry you can't make it today. I'll save you a dance.*

He replied: *I'm sorry that I will miss an opportunity to see you. The apartment will be completed and ready for me to move in by the July deadline. The kitchen is large but will feel empty. Not quite what I had in mind. Don't give my dance away. I will claim it soon.*

I read his text five times, thinking, *I missed something.* I reread the text I had sent him. Then it clicked. Max had told the real estate agent the day he bought the place that I liked to cook. I had a flashback of the night we cooked together in New York. Tears stung my eyes. I shouldn't have texted him.

I wanted to call him and tell him his kitchen or anything would never feel empty, because I was on my way. *Stop it, Livvy. Don't think about Max like that. He's not for you.* I reminded myself it was over and I did not love Max.

I texted Max instead: *I'm sorry if I said something wrong. If you feel you shouldn't call for a while, I will understand.*

He texted: *You're kidding, right? I will call. Good news, though, this is a short trip to London. I'll be back in New York by early morning, and we're leaving for the airport now. Next week when I call you, I want all the details on Rae's wedding.*

I sent: *You got it!*

Time was ticking fast, and I needed to check on the bride. She was sitting Indian-style in the middle of her queen-size bed, chatting calmly on the phone. I laid her button-down shirt and comfy lounge pants on the foot of her bed. *Dang*, I thought. I would be a complete nervous wreck right now, but not Rae. She was as cool as fresh cucumbers marinating in the fridge.

When we arrived at the church, Aunt KK cracked the whip. My Lord, that woman could do anything. Aunt KK was a mixture of talents, a cross between Paula Deen and Martha Stewart. As far as her looks, I'd have to go with Diane Sawyer. You could sum her up as a real southern lady—a little loud, simply beautiful, and talented, with an enormous amount of confidence.

The spa people were on hand and working their magic. Suddenly, I started laughing. Rae asked what was wrong. I had never mentioned Fred in New York, Skinny in Paris, or Henry in London. I shared my stories about everything for the first time. We laughed, and some girls wanted to cry, but Danni told them they couldn't, because they would ruin their makeup and she didn't have time to start over. A few cried anyway. "Girl, if you don't go get your ass on the first plane out of here and go get that man, I will," Danni said.

"No, she can't," Rae said firmly. "She could die."

"That's right," Andi said, rubbing her belly with her feet propped up.

The room became totally quiet. You could have heard a pin drop until Aunt KK walked in and said, "Girls, get a move on now."

Mom stood on the left side of Rae and I stood on her right, holding her magnificent wedding gown. She stepped into it. Mom adjusted it as I zipped it and fastened the tiny hooks. As I stood in front of her, she didn't look real. She looked picture-perfect and as beautiful as my flawless angel. You know—unspoiled, timelessly untouched, or maybe the word *idyllic* would possibly describe her best.

Her gown was white but not too white. The illusion crystal neckline was embellished with just the perfect amount of stones. The gown itself was made from the finest silk and was completely stunning. Her veil was long, but it wouldn't cover her face.

It was time. We all stood waiting at the front of the church for Rae to make her entrance. I, however, was looking at Bradley. They hadn't seen each other today. The music began to play. I knew the doors had opened from Bradley's expression. A soft smile appeared immediately and was quickly joined by tears that slowly ran down his face as Rae and my father walked down the aisle.

"Who gives this woman?" Minister Chuck asked as Rae and my dad stood arm in arm, Bradley on my father's right. My father answered, his hands shaking but with a strong voice, "Her mother and I."

After the wedding ceremony, we were quickly rushed to the museum for the grand reception.

The wedding party was introduced to all six hundred guests, and then Rae and Bradley danced their first dance as husband and wife. I almost cried thinking her last name was now Davenport. I quickly decided not to cry because I didn't want to destroy Danni's masterpiece, nor did I lose a sister; I had acquired another brother. Come to think of it, I hoped my new brother was not as bossy as the one I already had. I would just have to trade his butt in.

I tried to make my rounds and speak to the guests, but crap, this process would take three days at the rate I was going. Everyone wanted to know who I was dating now. A few people looked at my face and said, "My, you healed up nicely." I explained it hadn't been my blood on my face.

I spotted Robert talking to a small group of our friends, and I knew it was time to speak to him. So I put my big-girl panties on and walked right up to him. "Thank you, Robert. I know today wasn't easy for you, but I know Rae appreciates you being here. She asked me several times if I thought you were coming. Please speak to her before you leave."

"I'll congratulate her and Bradley before I leave. After all, I was there when Bradley proposed." He lightly touched my arm. I said, "I remember."

I continued to circulate among the guests until someone tapped me on my shoulder and asked if he could have this dance. I smiled before I turned around. It was Crosby. His touch was familiar, but softer than it ever had been before. We didn't talk; we danced. After our second dance, I pointed in the direction of Piper and Tucker, and we visited for a few minutes.

It was time to send the bride and groom off. We hugged, kissed, and released butterflies, and they were on their way to start their new life together.

Most of the guests had left and the band had stopped playing, but someone had hooked up an iPod, and I asked my dad to dance. He grabbed my hand, and we danced the last dance of the evening.

CHAPTER 23

Every time I stirred during the night in my fancy guest room, I thought of Max. Now it was morning, but I still couldn't shake the longing to see him. My gut reaction was to get control of it fast, because my thoughts of him were eating me alive.

I kicked the covers back and joined my father in the kitchen. I ate and disappeared into my room. I whipped out my computer, checked flights to New York, and checked the time. I booked the thing. *Shit, what have I just done?* I sat on the floor, staring at my computer screen. I slammed my Mac closed. I tried to keep my mind off my late-afternoon flight. The rest of the morning, I read and tried to relax but found the relaxing thing made me tense, which gave me a headache. After a few hours of all that, I hopped up, took two Advil, and showered, still thinking and knowing this was not a good thing. I dressed and packed a few things in my overnight bag. Then I grabbed my Louis tote and threw a few items in it, knowing I could not tell my parents where I was going. I shouted from the back door, "See you tomorrow." With my bags hanging on my right arm, I left.

The entire drive to Atlanta, I had cursed myself for doing this, but it was too late now. My ass was now sitting in first class being served vodka and club soda with a lime. I would need a few more of these for courage, I told the flight attendant. Until that moment I hadn't looked up, nor had I removed my sunglasses since I boarded the plane.

In a faintly familiar voice, a flight attendant asked, "Miss Hunnicutt, may I get you a Bloody Mary to chase your vodka and club with?"

I lifted my shades. It was Dan. This was the third time I had flown with him. He said he had seen me on the news.

I lowered my shades and shook my head. "For God's sake, Dan, please don't remind me."

He laughed and walked away to assist another thirsty passenger.

I sat in my seat and listened to music, still cursing myself. Dan appeared and asked if I needed another drink or something to eat. He smiled and whispered, "I can tell you need a drink, and I'll bring you a sandwich."

Dan handed me my nerve medicine in a glass and a sandwich, then said we would land shortly. Crap, I didn't even have a plan. I didn't know if I could see Max, and I didn't think to book a hotel. Furthermore, I was tipsy.

I texted Martin: *Just landed in New York. Please call, ASAP! Livvy.*

Seconds later, Martin's number popped up on my screen. I pressed the green button, but before I could speak, he asked, "Livvy, are you all right?"

"Yes, of course, Martin. I'm fine."

"You don't sound fine," Martin said. "I'm on my way. I'll meet you at the carousel and help you with your luggage."

"Oh, Martin, I didn't bring any luggage."

"I'll meet you there anyway."

I found my destination with my Louis tote on one arm and my small Louis overnight bag on my other arm. Martin rescued me. He took my larger bag and grabbed my hand with his free hand, and I began to talk without filtering my thoughts.

"I don't know what's wrong with me. I couldn't get Max off my mind. So here I am. You know, I think I've allowed myself to have feelings for Max, and I don't want this. But I have, and I know it's a mistake. Martin, I don't know what to do."

When I told him no one knew I was in New York, he gave me a verbal spanking. I decided it would be best if I shut up.

As Martin helped me in the backseat, he said, grinning, "It is nice to see you, Livvy."

When we arrived at Max's office building, Martin got out of the car and Shawn got into the passenger-side front seat. "Good to see you."

I leaned forward and slapped him on the shoulder. "You too, Shawn."

"Are you drunk?"

"Probably." I lowered my sunglasses, forgetting it was eight in the evening.

"This oughta be good," Shawn said.

I wanted to grab my bags and run. But I knew my Louis Vuitton heels would never work right.

I heard Max's voice, and I suddenly felt sick. The car door opened. He was about to get inside, but he paused and looked back at Martin. I could tell Martin hadn't told him I was in the car.

Max sat down, loosened his tie, stretched his arm across the seat, and then pulled me closer. My heart melted. We still hadn't said a word to each other. Martin had driven a couple of blocks when Max said, "You didn't mention Livvy was here."

"I thought it would be better if you saw her yourself. Uh…she may need a cup of coffee," Martin said, ratting me out.

Max looked at me and asked, "Are you drunk? Look at me, Livvy."

Shamelessly I did but with my shades on. "What are we going to do?" he whispered with his lips pressed to my forehead. Martin didn't stop there—oh no. He told Max no one knew I came to New York, and I had only an overnight bag in the trunk. Martin was such a tattletale.

Martin pulled in front of Max's building. The media was everywhere. Max said he was sorry about the press, but we would get inside quickly. Martin instructed Shawn and Max to hold me by my arms, not my hands. Max looked at me. "Well, at least her sunglasses are still on."

We stepped on the elevator. Shawn released my arm, and Max wrapped his arms around me from behind. Martin went into Max's apartment first; Claude followed, carrying my bags. Max darted off right behind Claude into his bedroom. Martin asked me for my car keys. He said he was going to call Rick to make a copy and pick my car up at the Atlanta airport and take it back to Auburn. I handed him my bag, and he helped himself. I knew whatever Max had accomplished was big and possibly dangerous, so I would be escorted home.

I walked to a large window and stared out over the city. I shouldn't have come, because obviously nothing had changed in his world. To make matters worse, I still hadn't spoken one word to Max. I didn't know what to say to him. I didn't hear Max when he entered the room. He slipped his arms around me from behind and pulled me close to him. Max was no longer wearing his suit, and his bare arms felt good around me. "I'm glad you're here," he said. "Have you eaten?"

"I have." I leaned into him. "I guess you're wondering why the visit?" He didn't say anything. "I don't know myself, other than this morning when I woke up, I had to see you. I'm sorry I didn't call first." His arms remained around me. "I was doing okay taking it day by day, but yesterday you mentioned the empty kitchen. I replayed everything good about the week we spent together, and the conversations we've had these past six weeks. But now that I'm here, I see the things I ran from."

"Turn around," he said. "I don't care why you came and if you have to leave tomorrow. At least I have tonight with you." Max kissed me, swept me into his arms, and carried me to his bedroom.

It was as if I could not hold him close enough. I touched every part of his body. I wanted to memorize it as if he were a painting—created with intricate brushstrokes caressing a canvas.

Max did not allow me to do what I so desired, as usual. He whispered, with much hesitation in his voice, "Not yet." His words disappointed me, but did not surprise me.

He took control, because I was out of control. He was on top of me. But I noticed his touch was softer and slower than ever. And with the perfect music playing overhead, he too was memorizing my curves.

I was afraid to close my eyes, as was he. We knew without saying a word that tonight would pass us by and be gone forever. Max never told me he loved me that night, but that was okay, because I had never told him that truly I loved him.

Max and I slept only a few hours. I could feel him lightly touch my face, my lips, and even my shoulders at different times during the night. And a few times, when I noticed his eyes were closed, I touched him the same way. But it was morning, and he was now sleeping.

I eased out of bed and quietly showered and dressed. When I entered his bedroom, he was staring at the ceiling. I sat next to him. He reached for my hand and held it. "You are leaving so early."

"I'm sorry." I sighed weakly.

"I'll let Martin know."

"I called him."

He pulled me down to his chest and kissed me on top of my head. "Jesus, Livvy," he whispered into my hair.

I sat up and caught his sad gaze. His pain was deep. I lightly brushed my fingers across his cheek. "Max, I have hurt you more by coming than if I had stayed away. Please forgive me." I bent over and picked up his pajama bottoms from the floor and handed them to him. He slipped them on and picked up my bags, and I followed him. Martin was standing beside Max's beautiful baby grand piano.

Max sat my bags down and turned around. "Come anytime. But please let me send a plane to get you. I don't want you traveling alone." Martin grabbed my bags and left the room.

"This is more difficult than before," Max said. He kissed me softly and walked away.

Martin said the media was heavy this morning. He removed his jacket and covered my head. Shawn held my hand as we stepped outside. He quickly pushed me, and I fell forward, inside the car. *I guess I wasn't moving fast enough.*

I hadn't been home an hour when my phone rang. It was Mom. *I'm in trouble already?* "Hello," I said with trepidation.

"Andi's water broke."

"I'm on my way to the hospital."

Four hours later and nearly six weeks early, Victoria Riley Hunnicutt was born. She weighed in at five pounds even.

My phone rang. It was Max. He was checking on me. I told him I was at the hospital. "You were with me only a few hours," he interrupted. "What happened?"

I laughed.

"I'm glad you find it funny, but I don't. Tom and Cookie will kill me."

After he hushed, I explained that Andi had delivered the baby.

"Thank God. Call me when you get home."

After admiring my beautiful niece for a while longer, I headed home. I sank down on my fluffy sofa and called Max.

We spoke for a few minutes about the baby and the wedding. Then out of nowhere, he asked, "You're not coming back, are you?"

"Max...I—"

"For the first time, I regret..." He paused. "That I didn't make love to you. I made a decision today. If you come back to New York, be prepared to stay, Livvy, because I'm marrying you."

I gasped.

"I'll call in a few days." He hung up.

Max called five days later, but I took the floor this time. "You have eighteen months left on your contract with Global. After that, what are your plans?"

"Livvy, I will never ask you to wait. You waited once before, and it didn't work out."

"I asked you about your contract. It is my decision if I want to wait on you or not, don't you think?"

"Look, Livvy, my feelings for you haven't changed. If you want me, you know where I am.

"So that's it for now. We talk on the phone, send e-mails, and text until the freaking cows come home."

"I don't have cows, Livvy."

"Me either, Max."

* * *

Mom had me busy. Folks were arriving daily for the movie, and she worked me like a sled dog. I did have good news: Matt Bartlett would be staying in our lake cottage until the flooded condo was repaired. And, lo and behold, my parents thought I should stay there too, because I was hired as his assistant. I guessed an assistant, in this case, was nothing more than a fancy word for babysitter.

Matt had started calling me late last week, ostentatiously to talk about business, and we talked a few times a day. Our conversations seemed to always pick up right where we had left off before.

The first thing out of his mouth today was, "Hey, may I please give you a real kiss? Those freaking pictures of our lunch date were slapped on every magazine cover and ran on every news network because of Max for two straight months. Those were not impressive kisses, and I want to impress you."

"Dream on, Matt. I'm a pretty good girl, and I guard my lips and my heart as if they were Fort Knox."

He laughed and asked, "Well, how many guys have you kissed?"

"Not many," I admitted.

"I guess you are the kind of girl you would have to marry first," he teased.

"I've been told by two special people I should wait for love. But, Matt, don't get me wrong. It's not because I haven't wanted to."

"Okay, Miss Hunnicutt," Matt said. "I need to change the subject, because now I want to do more than just kiss you."

"Shut up," I told him.

He said they were wrapping up on the set tomorrow on the kick-ass movie he was currently filming and he would be in Auburn in a few days. "I'm taking you on a date. I'll kiss you and impress you."

"Good night, Matt."

I worked my butt off for a few days. I was still at Mom's every beck and call, because she was having a little meet-and-greet thing at her house in two days for eighteen people. The guest list included the main actors for the film, a few people on staff, and four of my parents' closest friends. But right now I was resting at the lake, because I'd just completely removed all my parents' crap from their bedroom closet and bathroom so Matt would be comfortable, even if it was only for two weeks.

My phone rang, and I checked to see who was calling. Damn. I shook it. My screen was black. "No!" I shook it again, like that was going to help, because the first time was obviously successful. I certainly wasn't about to answer it, not knowing who was calling. Who could possibly need anything at eleven damn thirty at night? I'd better drop by the mobile store tomorrow and take care of that problem.

I scrambled two egg whites, baked turkey bacon, and made some toast. I took my breakfast to the screened porch. I flopped down in one chair and propped my feet up on another, cracked open a book, and began to read as I nibbled on my breakfast.

I noticed the time. Crap! I had better get a move on. I was all caught up in Bill O'Reilly's new book. Bill either rubbed you the wrong way or stroked you just right. He hadn't pissed me off yet. I marked my page with a torn corner of my napkin and tossed the book on the coffee table as I ran past it to get dressed. I was out the door in fewer than fifteen minutes.

I took care of my mobile issue right away, because that black screen thing wasn't working for me. I swung by the grocery store and made one last stop at my house before my summer began. I loaded almost every item of summer clothing I owned into my hatchback and backseat, and I had more crap to put in my front seat on top of the groceries.

I arrived back at the lake cottage exactly thirty minutes after leaving Auburn. I unloaded the car, put everything away, and sat in a lounge chair by the pool with a tall glass of my signature Rock'n Lemonade. This was not just regular lemonade. This lemonade had a kick. I repositioned my chair to face the sun, applied SPF 4, waited a couple of minutes, and took a dip in the pool. After that, I collapsed in my chair with Bill's hardback back in hand.

I spent the rest of my day reading and relaxing. But dang, before I knew it, the next morning had crept right up on me. The bad thing was, I dreamed all night long. Crazy shit too, and it scared me. I was sick in my dream, and Max had been nowhere in sight.

The morning was almost a carbon copy of yesterday afternoon, but I drank plain sugar-free lemonade, because I had to leave the lake cottage at four for Mom's shindig in Auburn.

I was sitting at a traffic light when I realized I was not receiving e-mails on my new phone. Oh, well, I didn't have time to think about that now, because I had an appointment with Danni for my hair, nails, makeup, and waxing.

Two hours later, after a much-needed pampering and some undesirable abuse from Danni, I was feeling all shiny and looking prettier than my normal self.

"Let's see your dress so I can match your makeup," Danni said.

I unzipped the bag, and there it hung. The color was ocean blue. It had a V-neck that plunged down to meet where the empire waist gathered. It was shorter than cocktail length, but not too short, and the fabric was crinkled chiffon, sexy but classy.

On my way out, Danni noticed my Louis shoes, the ones that Max had bought me. "I want those when you are done with them." I gave her a huge hug and thanked her for everything.

I pulled into my parents' driveway right on time. I spotted the cars lined down the street. I checked the time again. Nope, I wasn't late. Ten till seven. I was technically early.

My heart was pounding. I could hear it beating in my ears. It was probably excitement from seeing Matt, I figured, along with meeting Scott White and Emily Webster. I had met David Williams once before, so that was no big deal. I reflected back on what Matt had shared with me. I couldn't help but smile as I stepped onto the front porch.

I had a great view inside the house through the large front door. I could see Scott, David, and Emily's back. I opened the front door and turned to close it. When I turned back around, I didn't see Matt. I swiftly scanned the room, looking for him. But wait, hold on…What was *he* doing here? And where the heck was Matt? I smiled at him and thought, *I am ringing Cookie's neck.* Peter Weston looked quite handsome, though.

I walked over and was about to introduce myself when Scott said, "You are Olivia Hunnicutt." He reached out to shake my hand.

I offered him mine and said, "Hello, Scott, nice to meet you, but please call me Livvy."

Emily was next, and David said, "I was about to give up on ever seeing you again. I, uh…thought about you after we met in Snowmass."

I smiled at David. Emily, Scott, and Peter all looked at him. He grinned.

"Is that right? I was excited to hear you accepted the role, David."

"I had to, because Matt wouldn't give me your number." He chuckled.

Everyone laughed but Peter; however, he pleasantly smiled and his eyes swept over me: head-to-toe. I repaid the gesture and offered him my hand.

"Pardon me for staring," he said.

OMG, I had forgotten he was British. At that point, he still had not taken my hand, so I withdrew my offer.

"Olivia, have we met before?"

Scott slapped Peter on the back. "You couldn't think of anything better to say?"

I thought it might be nice to come to Peter's rescue, but I was not about to sound starstruck. I played it cool and pretended to think for a moment. "Peter, we haven't formally met…" I paused. "Although I believe our paths crossed in London."

"Yes, you are right. We shared a lift. You were with my soon-to-be neighbor, Max Spencer."

"Yes, I remember. How could a girl ever forget?" I placed my hand back out, and this time, he shook it.

I cornered Mom for a moment. "What is going on? Where is Matt?" I said, never letting the smile disappear from my face.

"I sent you an e-mail," Mom said.

"My phone is broken. I never check e-mails from my computer."

"Matt broke his arm and had to have surgery. We were lucky that Peter was available."

I grunted but with a smile and said, "Oh." I mingled a bit with the other guests, while the small group of actors leaned on the baby grand piano as they sipped their cocktails. Unfortunately, I could hear every word of their conversation.

"Peter, what I would give to be in your shoes right now," Scott said. "You know that your condo is flooded, right? You are staying at the Hunnicutts' lake cottage."

"I'll swap with Peter," David said. "You can have my place."

It was almost nine, and Mom announced this wasn't a party; everyone was free to leave. Everyone cleared out within twenty minutes except my parents' friends, Peter, and me. I would be his assistant; how uncomfortable. I had no idea what he liked or liked to do. *Oh Lord, just shoot me now*. I had to start all over with my assistant homework.

He glanced around the house for a moment, and then he pointed to the piano bench. "Think it would be okay?"

"Sure."

"Olivia, what is your favorite music?"

"Umm..." I mentally pondered over my iPod playlists and said, "Everything."

"I like a variety of music myself," he admitted.

Before I realized what I had done, I sat down right beside him on the bench. But he didn't seem to mind, because he scooted over and allowed me more room.

"Do you play?"

"Yes, but not as well as you." He was playing a song that I recognized. He began to sing. I harmonized softly as he sang the chorus.

He glanced at me and sang louder. By now Peter had a tiny audience: Mom and her friends were leaning against the piano and slightly swaying. I realized he was staring at me, but to make matters worse, I was staring at him. My parents and their friends were clapping and complimenting Peter, but he didn't look up. I shook my head slightly to break the spell. "Oh, hell no," I said under my breath.

After that weird moment, I asked Peter if he was ready to leave. He was, thank God. Peter and I removed his bags from the guest bedroom. I totally forgot to say good-bye to my family. *What's wrong with me?* Then I remembered. My reason for the snag-causing, cockamamie behavior was that I drank only water that day. I would most definitely make that correction as soon as I got to the lake cottage.

I was backing out of my parents' driveway when Peter asked, "How long is—"

"Thirty minutes," I said as I shifted my SUV into drive.

Peter reclined his seat back and appeared to be comfortable. "How old are you?"

"Twenty-one."

"Ah, I would have guessed older." He asked me about college.

"I graduated early." I could tell he was looking at me again.

It seemed as if he was about to ask me another question. I didn't want him to, so I decided to jump in. I asked him how old he was. To my surprise, he was older than I thought. "Twenty-seven?" I repeated.

"Yes."

"What about college?"

"Oxford."

"Wow, Ivy League. Look where that has gotten you—smack dab in the middle of east Alabama," I joked.

"Yes, it did." We both chuckled.

Peter pointed to the radio and reached to change the XM station. I reached in my cup holder, grabbed my iPod, and tossed it to him. He connected it. I turned the volume up.

His phone rang, so I turned down the music. Peter glanced down at the screen and started laughing.

"You may lose service. Back roads suck."

"No problem. It's Matt Bartlett." Peter was still laughing when he accepted Matt's call. *What on earth will Matt tell Peter about me?*

Peter was responding to Matt with simple phrases, such as *yes, no way*, and *that's impossible*. He looked right at me and said, "Oh, really? Matt, are you kidding?"

Okay, according to Peter's expression, I knew exactly what Matt had said. Peter held his phone out to me. "Matt would like to speak to you."

"Put him on speaker; these roads are curvy. Hi, Matt. Sorry to hear about your arm, but when I see you, I am breaking your other one."

Matt and Peter were laughing. "Livvy, please forgive me, but what you told me is...well...sweet."

"Bye, Matt." Peter disconnected the call.

Peter didn't comment on anything Matt shared with him. I prayed he never would.

I stopped at the entrance of the drive to the lake cottage and pressed the code into the keypad. The gate began to swing slowly. "We're here."

"I thought you said thirty minutes." I pointed to the clock. "Time has flown, Olivia, but only because I was in such good company."

"Oh yeah."

He appeared to observe my every move, as if I was a mystery he was trying to solve. I wanted him to just say whatever he was thinking without hesitation, because right now that would work for me. But he said nothing as I parked the car and popped the hatch. Peter grabbed his guitar and his large bag. I reached for his smaller bag. "No, I got it," he said. "You can get the door."

I showed Peter to his room. He seemed to be pleased enough, although he was quiet as I showed him around the residence. I turned a few outside lights on to illuminate the deck, pool area, and the dock. We walked out onto the large deck and gazed out over the lake, which was still tonight. The moon was beaming down and reflecting off the water. Peter gestured for us to take a seat on a couple of loungers.

"How many summers have you spent here?" Peter asked. Before I could answer, he asked, "Olivia, is the lake always this beautiful?"

"Yes." Then it hit me: vino. "I'll be right back."

I returned with a bottle of red wine, two glasses, and a lightweight throw blanket. I was still wearing my ocean-blue dress, but I had kicked off my heels in the kitchen. I stood in front of him, barefoot and smiling, wondering if my choice of wine was okay. "Perfect," he said.

Peter and I sat quietly for a few minutes. I knew I had to tell Peter about my health. I wasn't embarrassed about it, but I was having a difficult time finding the words. I was on my second glass of wine when I blurted out, "Peter, there is something important you need to know about me." Oh, I had his attention now.

"What, Miss Olivia Hunnicutt, do I need to know?" I bet he was thinking I was about to elaborate on what Matt had shared with him an hour ago.

"You see, Peter...I'm diabetic." I waited for him to respond. He sat straight up and turned his body completely around to face me. I pulled my legs up to my chest, covering them with the blanket and wrapping my arms around them. He placed his arms on his legs and leaned forward. "I was diagnosed when I was eight. My sister was also diagnosed at age fourteen." I kept my voice low but steady, but now I was no longer looking at him. I was glaring in the direction of the lake. "My parents have always felt that if I was going to be alone with anyone, it was important they know at least the basic stuff." He was quiet. "I've had three life-threating episodes when I needed medical help, but the last time was over four years ago. I'm not counting the times I have needed an IV. That happens, often"—I glanced at him—"especially if guns are involved."

A faint smile touched his lips. "How would I know you needed help? And what would I do to help you?"

"It's unlikely I'll ever need you to do anything," I said, but I explained the signs of a low blood sugar. "I can handle them myself with juice, non-diet soda, and a snack." Then I described the signs of a serious one. "I would be unable to communicate, my skin would be pale and clammy, and I would be sweating. I could have a seizure, but to be honest with you, I don't know what happens, other than I'm cold and exhausted when I recover from a dangerous insulin reaction." I paused. "You can give me a glucagon injection and call for an ambulance. The address is on the refrigerator."

He pointed his finger. "Show me the injection, and teach me how to use it."

"I will before I go to bed. I'm sorry for having to share this with you. If you're uncomfortable with the living arrangements, I will call Ms. Fills first thing in the morning. We can figure something out. Or I can go—"

He cut me off in his most perfect British accent.

"Olivia, I think I can handle it. Besides, I like this deck of yours—the company is not bad, either." I blushed, because I had been thinking the same thing.

I stood up, holding the blanket, empty wine bottle, and my glass and said, "Come on, it's late." As we walked up the stairs, I asked, "Would you like me to make you breakfast in the morning?"

"No, thanks."

"I can cook, you know."

"That is good to know," he said. "I will have a short day tomorrow, so I'll grab something there. I will take you up on your offer the next day, though."

Peter asked again about the injection. "I always have one in my bag, and there is always one in the top drawer of the night chest beside my bed."

"Show me," he insisted, so we walked downstairs to my room.

I opened my top night-table drawer. "There it is." I took the lead, and we walked back to the kitchen.

He pointed to the red snap box that contained the glucagon injection and asked me to show him. I removed the vial that contained the powder and the syringe with the fluid, along with the instructions.

"That doesn't look so bad. Show me how."

I wanted to crawl in a hole, not because I was embarrassed of having diabetes, but good God, I just met the man. I swallowed my pride and explained what to do.

He watched and listened. "Is that it?"

"Yes. If you're uncomfortable—"

He stopped me midsentence. "No problem, Olivia. I got it."

Right before we parted ways for the night, he said, "Thank you for everything. I would be homeless or have to spend the next two weeks with David, or worse, Scott. I am grateful."

"One more thing. The long way or the short way to the set in the morning?"

"Always the short, Miss Hunnicutt."

"Well, then, Mr. Weston, do I have a surprise for you. See you in the morning."

"Yes, you will, Miss Hunnicutt."

CHAPTER 24

I kicked the covers back. *Here goes my first full day of being Peter Weston's personal assistant.* Mom had never explained what my job description truly was; but I figured I could wing it.

It was time to get my butt in gear. I needed to move one of the two Sea-Doos from the lift to the ramp, check the fuel, and find Peter a life vest that would fit him properly. I took a super-fast shower and applied sunblock and a small amount of makeup. I pulled my hair up in a po- nytail and quickly became concerned about what I was going to wear. I was having a swimsuit dilemma. I decided on the hot pink. At least the bottoms were wider, and the top wouldn't be an issue, because I would wear a life vest.

"Shit, where are they?" *I know I packed them.* I hurriedly plun- dered through the dresser drawers and found a skirt and a matching tank. I threw them on the striped chair in my room. I slipped on my Tory flip-flops, stopped by the basement storage room to grab two life vests, and headed out through the lower-level door to the boathouse. I uncovered the yellow and black Sea-Doo and checked to see if it would crank properly. I put my vest on and straddled the seat. I con- nected the kill switch to the plastic loop on my life vest. Then, without hesitation, I pulled the pin from the lift, pressed the lever, and lowered the watercraft into the water. As soon as it hit the water, I pressed the start button, pulled up the reverse lever, and slowly pulled the gas handle to back up. I cleared the boathouse and lowered the reverse lever and pulled the gas handle. Once I was out of sight of the cottage, I opened it up. It was running fine, and to my surprise, it had a full tank. I headed back and parked the Sea-Doo on the floating ramp. I tied it up and hooked my life vest on its handle.

When I headed up the steps to the deck, I glanced up, and Peter was looking right at me. Dear God, all I was wearing were two small pieces of hot pink fabric, sunglasses, and flip-flops. I offered up a brisk wave but no smile.

I knew I had to enter the house through the basement door. That meant I had to cross the deck directly underneath the upper porch he was on. Now he was leaning over the rail. I pretended not to care. I took one step onto the deck and said, "Good morning, Mr. Weston. Hope I didn't wake you." I shot him a quick glance from behind my Chanels.

"No, I was awake. But now I am wondering if *that* is what you meant by the short route to the set."

"Why, yes, it is."

The first thing I did when I entered the house was stop by my room and put on my skirt and tank. When I walked upstairs, Peter was standing at the top of the landing. He was smiling at me and said, "I am surprised about our means of transportation this morning. I had you figured to be more reserved."

"Reserved?" He was standing less than two feet from me. *My Lord,* I thought, *he was sexy.* Light-brown hair with natural highlights. Blue eyes, not just a simple blue, oh no. The color blue one can get lost in, sucked into, and never return. *I had better stay away from those.* Peter Weston must be one of the most handsome men I had ever laid my eyes on. And here I was, standing here, looking like this.

"I did not have you pictured as the outdoorsy type. I didn't mean reserved in an unflattering way, of course."

I heard him speaking, but I could not process what he was saying. I, for some reason, did not really see him until this exact moment, and it hit me like a lightning bolt. *Peter Weston is probably the sexiest man alive. Now what did he just say to me? I don't know, but he is waiting for me to respond.* Barely opening my mouth, I said, "Oh, okay."

I walked around him, and I didn't look back when I asked, "Are you ready?" I realized he was dressed in designer jeans. I asked, "Did you bring a swimsuit?"

"Afraid not."

A spring sprung into my morning step. "Come on." He followed me to the guest room. I opened a drawer and pulled out four new swimsuits. Each suit still had the tags dangling from them. I eyeballed them quickly and chose the royal-blue Ralph Lauren trunks. "I believe these will fit you." When I turned around, he was still standing there looking at me. I opened another drawer and said, "Choose one, but I think the white fitted one appears to be more your style. What do you think?" He removed the new white Polo from the drawer. "But don't put it on yet. You will need it when we arrive at the set." I tossed him a small bag and said, "Put your things in it. There is a storage compartment on the Sea-Doo."

"Thank you," he said. "You're welcome. I'll wait for you down at the pier."

I got to thinking about his "reserved" comment. He said he didn't mean it in an unflattering way. But how else could he have meant it? Oh dear, could he think I'm a frigid bitch? Or worse? Maybe he meant I was boring. Well, I was neither, and I would prove it to him. I would change Mr. Weston's opinion about me.

Peter changed quickly and joined me on the pier before I stepped onto the floating dock to untie the Sea-Doo. I quickly slung my vest on and tossed him one. "Peter, have you ever ridden one of these before?" I pointed to the Sea-Doo.

"Well," he said, his lips pressed together, fiddling with a buckle on the ski vest. I knew his answer was no.

"No problem. I think you'll enjoy it."

He slipped his arms into his vest, but the dang straps were hanging. I adjusted it for a better fit, but he never looked at my face. He was looking at my chest. I turned around when I was finished helping him and buckled my vest.

I straddled the Sea-Doo, and head signaled, "Get on."

He was trying to figure out what to do with his hands. I turned slightly, grabbed both of his hands, and put them on my waist. "So that's where they go."

"Yeah, or the tight strap that is across the seat, but your butt is on it."

I latched the kill switch to my vest and asked him to help rock the Sea-Doo. After a couple of side-to-side rocks, it slid off the ramp and into the water. I drove slowly at first, checking on Peter in the mirror. He seemed to be fine, so I accelerated.

As we approached the Cliffs, or the set, as Peter called it, I slowed and chose the empty space on the right of the ramp.

Before Peter and I could get off the Sea-Doo, Scott strutted across the dock. "Well, Livvy, I never would have pictured you as a nature kind of a girl."

"Is that right? That's the second time I've heard something in that vein this morning." I looked at Peter, who grinned at me. I snapped back, "You must have had me pictured as a *reserved* type of girl."

"No, not at all. But I can think of a few other things." Peter was still fiddling with the buckle on his life vest.

"I'll do it." I fanned his hands out of the way. When I finished helping Peter, I turned around and popped open the Sea-Doo's compartment. I tossed Peter's bag to him. "You might want to put those on."

"Livvy, I like your swimsuit," said Scott.

"Thanks, Scott," I said, lowering my sunglasses.

With my life vest buckled, I rocked the Sea-Doo off the ramp, cranked it, and slowly pulled away from the floating dock. Once I had completely cleared the dock, I opened it up and hit fifty mph.

I was home in six minutes. I had a lot to do. The housekeeper came to the lake twice a week, so this meant I had to tidy up five days a week. I also needed to think about dinner. The kitchen was stocked but with items from Matt's list, which he had e-mailed me last week. And now I had no idea what Peter liked. But for the most part, we would have to eat in or make trips into Auburn for dinner.

My phone was at my side all morning, and with all the chores completed, I made the decision for dinner. I hoped Peter liked tilapia.

The lounge chair by the pool was calling my name. I totally felt the need to respond, and I did for the next two hours.

When my phone rang, I didn't recognize the number. It had to be Peter, and it was. He said he would finish up in thirty minutes. I glanced at my watch, and it was only one thirty in the afternoon. What would I do with him all day? I wouldn't be doing much of this picking him up at midday, assistant or not. I would enroll him in Sea-Doo 101. Umm...I wonder if he drove a car. We could loan him one. Come to think of it, the day I saw him in London, I was certain he had had a driver. When I pulled onto the ramp, Peter and his three sidekicks were waiting. I greeted everyone, then opened the compartment, removed the life vest, and tossed it to Peter. This time he buckled up on his own.

We rocked the Sea-Doo; it hit water, I pushed the button, and we were off. This time I didn't baby him, and we roared across the lake.

I parked on the ramp and demonstrated to Peter how to tie up the Sea-Doo. I was about to walk past the pool, but spontaneously, I dropped my life vest and dove in. It was ninety-five degrees, and the humidity would kill you in Alabama. When I popped up, Peter was standing at the edge of the pool. "May I join you?"

Barehanded, I wiped the water from my face. "Please do." I thought of his pale skin. I swam to the steps and realized we did not have towels. I walked into the house dripping water, but I soon returned with towels and sunblock.

He smiled and asked, "Is that for me?"

"It is...unless you want to burn." He got out and dried off. I suggested he close his eyes, because he was one white man. I sprayed the front and the backside of his body from head to toe. I tossed the can of sunblock on the lounger, told him he needed to dry a few minutes, and I dove back into the pool.

He grabbed two rafts and threw them in the pool. We were both relaxing now.

I asked him about his day. My heavens, he went into great detail. Peter provided me with more info than I needed on that subject, but I listened. He then asked me about my day. "Well, Peter, you're pretty much looking at it."

He laughed. "Not a bad way to spend a day, from what I see."

"I totally agree, Mr. Weston."

"Olivia, do you like to travel?" *Talk about switching gears.*

I shifted into third and yakked on and on. However, I left out my recent forays into Paris and London, even though we had seen each other in London.

Peter enjoyed traveling as well. He chitchatted as much as I did. Wow, we had at least two things in common: talking and traveling.

We talked about our families. Good God, he was related to members of the royal family on his father's side. My mouth dropped to my chest. I quickly sat up, straddling my raft. I didn't comment; I only stared at him.

Peter caught the edge of my raft. "I have never shared that with anyone before." He smiled, but I almost choked on my own spit. I closed my mouth.

He had royal blood running through his veins? For the life of me, I could not think of a response, and he was waiting. One word popped into my head: "Oh." I was thirsty. "Would you like a drink?"

"A beer would be great, but I can get it."

"I got it." I raised my shades. "You're getting pink. Let's move to the porch upstairs. If you get burned, Sam will kill us both."

He got out of the pool and grabbed us both towels. As I passed by the XM radio, I turned it on and pointed to the porch. I made myself a Goose and club with two limes and fetched Peter a beer.

"Thank you. I will get the next round."

He and I talked for two hours on the screened porch. I forgot I had not dressed—I was still wearing my hot pink bikini, and he was still wearing his borrowed trunks and no shirt. As usual, after a few cocktails, I became quite the chatterbox. *Like I wasn't already.* Peter heard about my entire family, but I assured him, "No royalty here."

Peter said he had one sister, Mildred Brooke, but they called her Milly. "She's only a few months younger than you."

I smiled. His mother's name was Elizabeth McAlister, and his father's name was Edward Brooks. He said was named partly after his mother. I couldn't help but meet his eyes this time, and we both smiled. I could already tell Peter McAlister Weston was an incredible person.

It was already six thirty; no wonder I was starving. I asked Peter, with my fingers crossed, if he liked grilled fish. Time to freshen up and make dinner. As he opened the door for us to go inside, he said, "We can make dinner together."

"That would be nice, Peter…thanks."

After I showered, I saw my phone blinking from two missed calls, Max and Crosby. I would call them back later; I was sure they only wanted an update concerning Bob, even though I had promised them I would not dare purchase him.

I shrugged into a wispy floral sundress and pulled my hair back into a slick ponytail, and applied a touch of makeup. I slid my feet into a pair of white Gucci three-inch wedge heels and threw on some hoop earrings. I quickly looked for my single-stone Yurman ring. I couldn't find it in my jewelry box. Come to think of it, I hadn't seen it in a month.

I caught a glimpse of myself as I walked past the tall mirror in my bedroom. *Livvy, what are you doing? You don't need to chase anyone.* I reminded myself I had gone without dating for almost three years before, and I didn't get hurt until I had started dating again. *Lonely, hurt, or flirt?* Couldn't flirt—that didn't work with Crosby, so that one was out. Lonely or hurt—which was it going to be? I thought of Robert and Max. I quickly removed my earrings, rubbed my freshly applied blush from my cheeks, and wiped the gloss off my lips. That was better. I was going with lonely.

Peter was standing on the screened porch. He had made me another drink and had just twisted the top off a fresh beer. He saw me through the window. He didn't move, but his eyes followed me. I reached for the handle on the heavy sliding-glass door, but he pulled from the other side and opened it.

"Olivia, you look beautiful, just as beautiful as you did last night."

Snap, Livvy. "Thank you. You look handsome yourself."

Shit, that wasn't a snap. That was more like a dawdling turtle crossing a dirt road. Pitiful. Peter handed the drink to me. He pointed at my hand. "Oh, that," I said.

He gave it a rub. "It's sticky." He licked his finger. "Lip gloss. Did you not like the color?"

"No, the color was fine."

"Did you not like the taste? My tongue is tingling."

"No, I like the taste. I changed my mind. I didn't want to wear it. But, so you know, it is lip-gloss plumper, for lips, not tongues. I was about to tell you before you licked your finger."

He grinned. I was still in shock, because the man had just rubbed his royal spit on the back of my hand. Peter opened the door to the kitchen and didn't mention the lip gloss again.

We were making dinner together, the music was still playing from earlier today, and before I knew it, we were singing. I lit a couple of candles, and we dined on the screened porch.

I'm not sure when my filter began to fail me, but I warned Peter about it and asked him for forgiveness in advance. We finished eating. I hopped up and took our dishes inside, telling him not to move. I got us drinks and returned to the table. *Why is he staring at me again?*

I turned my chair slightly to face him. I sat down and, before I realized it, propped both of my legs on top of his. "Whoa, I'm so sorry. That filter thing. Sometimes I don't think." I put my feet back on the floor.

He leaned forward, picked up my legs, and put them right back where I had just carelessly thrown them up. We were quiet for a moment, but I finally opened my big mouth. "So, Peter, anyone special in your life?"

"No, not at all. As a matter of fact, my twenty-eighth birthday is next week, and I have seriously dated only two people. I dated the first girl in college for two years. Let's just say she wasn't for me. I dated one other person for about a year."

It clicked. I knew her, because their pictures had been slapped on the covers of every magazine a couple of years ago. "It was a long time ago," he said. "I knew and she knew that I knew she was cheating. But I was asked not to end it publicly until after the premiere of the movie we were co-starring in. Politics, that's all. It was her first lead role, so I agreed. Trust me when I say I have never given her a second thought."

"I liked you in that movie." He leaned forward and squeezed my knee. I giggled.

"I date," he went on to say, "but I'm selective. Mum says I am picky."

"Picky is good."

"Olivia, do you know what Matt said about you?"

I huffed. "Unfortunately I do."

"It is true, isn't it?"

"Jeez," I grumbled. "Yep, every freaking word of it. But don't you get all weird. It's not that I haven't wanted to have sex, because I have. I have had "my" clothes ripped off, "I" have ripped shirts, I've replaced lamps, and once we knocked a painting off the wall. But the kicker is...well, um...you see," I stuttered, "oh whatever, I've never had sex. I can't give it away. Three guys have said that I should wait until I marry, or at least until I'm in love. I've been in love, and you can see that that didn't work either."

I noticed he was rubbing one of my ankles with his thumb. I slid my legs from his lap. "I need a drink." I left the door open. He followed me inside. I was certain that the filter thing was totally turned off by now, but I didn't care. For the first time since I had emotionally spilled everything with Tucker, I was venting again. "Crosby wouldn't touch me, because I could not fall in love with him." I refilled my glass with club soda. "And it certainly wasn't because he isn't a great guy; he's wonderful. And my God, he is good-looking." I turned up the Goose and counted to five. "I was afraid but not from the making-out thing. Oh no, that was good...real good." I squeezed two limes and tossed them in my glass. Peter was laughing. Well, that was just too bad. He was about to hear more. "I was afraid to fall in love because of Robert." Peter was now biting his lip. Well, he could just bite the damn thing off, because I wasn't finished. "I dated Robert my last two years of high school. We didn't go to school together, because I was homeschooled. While we were in college, he never kissed me. This past December, he kissed me, and when I offered myself to him, he didn't take the bait. I still don't know what his problem was. He said he had to 'let me go.'" I twirled my hand in the air round and round. "And there is Max. You know Max. Everyone knows Max." I quenched my thirst. "I think I could have fallen in love with Max, or..." I paused. "Maybe I did love him. No, I loved him." *There, I finally said it aloud.* I threw my hand up in the air and continued. I didn't care; it felt good to finally say this crap out loud. "I wasn't afraid of Max because of the making-out thing either, because that was totally bitchin'." I sat my empty glass on the counter.

I was not finding anything funny about what I had said, but apparently Peter had, because he was laughing. I started to offer myself to him right then, but I was afraid he would say no, and that would mean rejection again. "You know, Peter, love is way too complicated, and maybe I am not smart enough to figure it out. But I do know one thing: Max's job could kill anyone, regardless of how many bodyguards he has. I know that for a fact, because I got freaking shot at!" Peter lost it, and he guffawed so hard he had tears in his eyes. I stopped talking and placed both hands on my hips. "Do you have a problem?" I asked imperiously.

Peter composed himself. "Olivia, you are absolutely the most in-triguing person I have ever met." *Intriguing? Me?* "I thought Matt had exaggerated when he first told me about you. You are beautiful. Obviously, you are smart and sexy-looking. I like that you are bare-foot right now; that's hot. And Olivia, I love it when your filter is not working. I can tell you right now—these next two weeks are going to be very interesting."

Crap, he's touching my dress. I didn't know what to do. I whirled around on my barefoot heels. "I need to go to bed. Good night!" I skedaddled out of there.

"I will see you in the morning, Olivia," he called out.

"That's right," I hollered without turning around. I wanted to use the four-letter word I liked so well, because I had forgotten to clean the kitchen. I would wait until he went to bed and then take care of it.

I returned Crosby's call first. He asked about Matt. I explained Matt broke his arm, and Peter Weston was my houseguest instead. "Try to stay out of trouble," he said. "I can tell you're tipsy." I got tickled. He knew me too well. We caught up on our week and said good night.

I called Max. He immediately knew I had drunk too much. I told him I had, but the last drink was only because I had had a meltdown.

He already knew Peter Weston had accepted the role and Matt was injured. Max knew everything before I did. He asked if he could send Shawn to hang out for a while. "Why on earth do you want to send Shawn?"

"Shawn misses you."

"Shawn does not miss me. You are up to something."

"Is the lake beautiful tonight?"

"Yes, it is. There's a full moon."

"Ah…that's nice. I'll call you tomorrow."

I brushed my teeth, washed my face, and slipped into a bright-blue cami and lacy boyshort ensemble. I heard Peter's footsteps. He was in his bedroom. I tiptoed up the stairs and flipped on the kitchen light. Peter had cleaned everything. The dishwasher was running, and he had even blown out the candles. I spun around and took two steps to reach for the light switch. I ran right into Peter's chest, causing me to slightly lose my balance. He steadied me by gripping my shoulders. "I thought you were in bed," I said. I took a step back, and he did as well.

"Thank you for cleaning the kitchen," I added, darting around him. I never slowed down until I was in my bed.

CHAPTER 25

My alarm clock buzzed; I slapped it. My head hurt. Oh God, I may have made it through college without a hangover, but since New Year's, I'd had two doozies. I showered quickly in hopes I would feel better. No luck with that harebrained idea. I pulled open my drawer and stared at the heap of swimsuits. I plucked up the one on top. After I put it on, I thought it ought to wake anyone up, including me. I did not remember it being this bright of a yellow. I pulled on a short skirt. I would make a trip to Auburn today and grab the one bag I had forgotten. I put a tad more effort into my morning makeup ritual and prayed I didn't look as bad as I felt. I was afraid this was a battle that even Bobbi Brown, my makeup goddess, wouldn't be able to help me with. I could only pray I didn't vent as much as I thought I had. "I made breakfast," Peter said, pouring a cup of coffee. I plopped down at the table, "That bad?"

"Uh-huh." Peter handed me two Advil and a bottle of water. We headed out to the pier, and I thanked him once again for cleaning the kitchen and for breakfast. "No problem," he said.

After dropping Peter off at the set, I tidied the lake house and put forth more effort in choosing an outfit than I had this morning. I wore white shorts, a black strapless top, and my wedge platforms.

My first stop was the mobile store, where I found that only a setting had to be changed on my phone. Then I stopped by my house and picked up that bag. It was sitting beside the front door, right where I had left it. Back at the lake, I unloaded the car and had put everything away when Peter called. He said he would be ready in an hour.

When I arrived at the set, I flashed the security guard my badge, and he said, "Yes, ma'am, Miss Hunnicutt, I didn't recognize you without your Sea-Doo."

Noticing his badge, I joked, "Sorry about that, George, I'll be on it tomorrow." I parked and proceeded to find Peter. A reporter shouted my name out a few times, I let roll until I heard, "Livvy! Where is Max Spencer?" My heart sank. The man repeated himself ten times, and each time he shouted louder. George was on it, though, and then I spotted Mom. She was running in my direction. David ran past Mom. My sunglasses were pushed back on top of my head, and I knew I needed to pull them down over my face. But for some reason, I froze. I couldn't move.

The man shouted again. My legs thawed. I twirled around and started to run toward the reporter. I felt someone catch my arm, and I spun around and slid, but he caught me, and we both fell. I landed on top of him. "Don't do it, Olivia," Peter said.

David helped me to my feet. Scott gave Peter a hand. Mom hugged me and whispered, "Do you want me to call Max?"

"No, he'll call. I'm okay, Mom, just furious."

Peter opened my car door for me. He walked around and got in the passenger's seat. "Olivia, I apologize for making you fall."

I laughed. "It's not the first time I've been thrown or pushed to the ground."

"I saw the news footage."

"You saw that?"

"It ran in eighteen countries. Today was a good day; no one was shot, and you don't have blood on your face."

"You're right—only a grass stain today."

"You are a fiery girl, and I like it."

"Ah…fiery is better than reserved."

"Olivia, the reporter had an iPhone. The pictures were probably posted on the Internet immediately—they always are."

"I know," I said, as I entered the gate code to the cottage. He reached across the console and squeezed my leg. At the same time, my phone beeped.

It was a text message from Max: *I hope you are okay. I will call later to check on you. Shawn will be there tonight.*

I texted: *How did you find out so freaking fast?*

He texted: *Martin has your name plugged into all news and Internet outlets. When your name comes up, he gets an alert.*

They stalk me. Shit. I handed my phone to Peter for him to read. "I'll have a babysitter for a couple of days."

"Good."

"What's good about it?"

I texted Max back: *Tell Martin to unplug me, now.*

"I won't worry now. So, Martin is the guy I need to thank."

"Well, don't worry about me. Yeah, I mean, no, you don't need to thank anyone. But, Martin is Max's guy, and it's part of his job to always be in the know."

I parked the car. Max texted: *Never.* Peter asked me to hold on. He got out, walked around, and opened my door for me. I stood up. "Here, allow me." He took my keys from my hand and unlocked the front door.

As we walked inside, I gestured to the sofa. I don't know why I felt like I owed him an explanation of what had transpired over the past five months, but I did. "I'm sorry about how I reacted today. I talk to Max a few times a week, but we don't date. That was the statement I wanted to give the reporter. I thought maybe people would leave me alone." I went on to explain why I felt so strongly about not dating Max, which included getting sick in Paris from becoming upset. That was when I mentioned my Addison's disease and how it affected me. I highlighted what had happened in London and the day Max had brought me home.

"Is that it?"

"Yes. I thought you should know since Shawn is coming. If you think you need to stay somewhere other than here, I will make that arrangement for—"

He butted in. "No, I want to stay here."

"Okay." I hopped up. "I got a jump-start on dinner earlier today, so it shouldn't take long."

"Wait, Olivia." He stood up. *Whoa!* He reached up and brushed the side of my face with his fingers. "Your skin is beautiful." Then he hugged me. "I thought you could use one," he whispered against my temple.

"Thank you," I whispered back. Peter put his things away, and then he met me in the kitchen. We finished making dinner together. He opened a bottle of wine, and we ate grilled chicken, asparagus, and salad. We sang, and I even danced in the kitchen as we cleaned. Peter got tickled at me several times, but I didn't care. I kicked my shoes off, opened another bottle of wine, and we sat out underneath a perfect blanket of stars on the deck.

After he finished his story about how he and Matt had become such good friends, I decided to go for a swim. I pulled my strapless shirt over my head and dropped it, then unbuckled my shorts and stepped out of them. I dove in wearing a bandeau and cotton hipsters.

I swam a few laps and looked up. Peter was standing at the steps, looking down at me and holding a towel "Olivia, I may not want to go to the condo…ever. I like it here."

I stepped out of the pool. He held the towel out and wrapped it around me. "It's nice having you here." I was about to step inside the house when I shouted back, "I'm showering; my babysitter will be here shortly."

I had barely slipped into my pj's and thrown on a wispy robe when Shawn called. "I'm at the gate." I gave him the gate code and met him at the door. "You look good. Where is that houseguest of yours?"

"He's asleep. Speaking of sleeping, upstairs or down?"

"Wherever you sleep."

"Well, down it is."

I showed Shawn to his room and indicated mine. "Good night. See you at seven." I stopped dead in my tracks. "Did you bring a swimsuit?"

"No."

"No problem," I assured him.

* * *

The next morning I plucked the brown swimsuit with gold rings out of my drawer. I threw on a wispy cover-up and tied a thin Burberry scarf around my head to hold my hair back.

I was making breakfast when the boys walked into the kitchen at the same time. "Peter, Shawn. Shawn, Peter."

"Thank you, Livvy. I like the trunks."

Peter glanced at them. I told Shawn I thought red was his color. "Breakfast is ready. Grab your plates."

I picked up a life vest from the kitchen counter and pitched it to Shawn. "You'll need that in a few minutes," I said as I poured a glass of juice and told the guys I'd meet them on the pier.

I overheard Peter ask, "Is she always—"

Before Peter finished his question, I heard Shawn say, "Yes, sir."

I moved the second Sea-Doo from the lift in the boathouse to the drive-on ramp while I waited for the guys to join me.

I watched Shawn as Peter untied the Sea-Doo that we had ridden the past few mornings. I asked Shawn if he had ever driven one before. He had. I still watched him as we all saddled up. Peter and I rocked ours, and it slid into the water. Shawn did the same thing; he seemed to know what he was doing. I went slowly at first to allow Shawn to get the feel of things, and then we both accelerated.

As we approached the Cliffs, I pointed to the ramps. I took the one on the right, and he took the one to the left. Peter got off and removed his bag. Shawn remained seated while I got off.

The media was standing near the barricades. Someone shouted my name. Peter leaned in and whispered, "Olivia, just ignore it. That's what I do." Shawn got off and stood at my side. I introduced Shawn to everyone. Mom waved from a distance but didn't join us on the pier.

"Hey, you're Spencer's bodyguard," another reporter shouted. "Spencer in town?" Shawn never moved from my side.

Leave it to Scott to speak up. "Livvy, I love your suit today. That's hot, girl."

Peter was about to say something when I said, "Don't. Just be quiet." I asked for his schedule for the day. He said they were going to a small town to film.

I laughed. "Dadeville."

He nodded and said they would return to the Cliffs later. Sam was hoping for a rainstorm tonight. Oh, I knew the scene he was referring to. I asked for a thirty-minute heads-up.

That idiot, Scott, said, "Livvy, Peter's gonna be busy tonight. Can I take you to dinner?"

Peter punched him on his arm. "She has a guest."

"How long are you staying?" Scott asked Shawn.

"As long as she needs me," Shawn replied.

I knew better than that. He was staying until Max gave him the okay to leave.

I smiled at Scott. "Thank you for asking, though."

"Yeah, you're welcome, but from the looks of it, that was probably my first and last opportunity to ask you out. What do you think, Peter?"

Shawn and I headed to the ramp before I could hear Peter's reply. I was off the ramp first and took off. I hit sixty mph before Shawn ever cranked his. I was all tied up and was propped against the railing on the dock when he came creeping around the bend.

After he tackled parking and tying up, I showed Shawn to the pool. It was only eight o'clock, and I told him I would be back in a few. I needed to order Peter a gift for his birthday. I returned to the pool and tossed Shawn a can of sunblock. He was on the phone, speaking in French.

I wanted to know what Max had done, but Shawn was not talking.

I floated in the pool and listened to music as it streamed through the outdoor speakers.

"Shawn?"

"Yeah?" he mumbled.

"You're welcome to help yourself to anything in the kitchen."

"Thanks, I will, but I'm fine right now. Can I get you anything?"

"No. I'm good." Suddenly my phone was flooded with endless beeps and rings. I waded to the steps of the pool where my phone was and shouted, "Wake up, Shawn. What the hell is going on?" A string of messages from everyone I knew all asking the same thing lit up my screen: *Are you okay?*

"Come here," he said as he reached for his computer. "It's running on every network." He clicked to CNN. It was a complete replay right before my eyes. For the first time, live footage was aired of me without sunglasses and Peter Weston was on the ground beside me.

Shawn said Martin was called as soon as it had appeared on the Internet. He wanted to make sure there was enough security around. "Livvy, the reporter from this morning is disappearing as we speak, but more will come."

"Why?"

"I can't say."

"Yes, you can, Shawn, or you will leave now."

"Max closed it."

"What did Max close?"

"The Carter deal."

I handed Shawn his computer, picked my phone up from the side table, and sent a massive group text: *I'm fine!*

"Let's go, Shawn. I'm taking you on a field trip." We walked down to the boathouse. I began to uncover the twenty-four-foot Cobalt boat. With a turn of a switch, it lowered into the water.

I stepped down into the boat and cranked it.

"You drive this?"

"Yep, with or without you, Shawn." He got his ass in. I pushed the accelerator forward, but I didn't open it up. Shawn did not look well.

When we arrived to my planned destination, I pointed. "It's called the Rock." I lowered the anchor, shut the boat off, walked directly to the back of the boat, and dove into the water. I swam to the Rock. After I reached the top of the sixty-foot climb, I made my stance and jumped. I tucked, flipped twice, stretched my body out, and dove straight in. It felt like a clean dive. I swam to the surface. When my head popped up, I waved to Shawn and continued to swim toward the boat.

Shawn was on the phone. He was shouting, pointing, cursing, and now speaking in French. When I reached the swim platform, I pulled down the ladder. I was about to start my climb when Shawn put his phone between his ear and his shoulder and tilted his head sideways. He bent over and snatched me up out of the water by my arms. My feet were dangling in the air until he set me down. He shoved his phone in my face. "It's Mr. Spencer!"

I was standing there dripping wet and out of breath. "What the hell are you doing, Livvy?"

"Hi, Max," I said, huffing. "I thought that would get your attention. By the way, that is my exact question to you."

"You have had my attention for six months. You could have killed yourself!" He shouted.

"That's the point I wanted to make!" I shouted louder. "Max, if you do not stop what you are doing, someone is going to kill you."

Max didn't say anything for a moment, but I could hear him breathing. "Let me speak to Shawn." I handed Shawn his phone. I lifted the anchor, stood in front of the wheel, cranked up, and pressed the accelerator down. Shawn was thrown from the front of the boat and landed on the backseat, but he never released his phone or ended his conversation. He was clearly bitching about something, but as usual, I could not understand him.

The remainder of the day, Shawn and I did absolutely nothing other than cover the Cobalt. It was almost dinnertime. I showered and put on a soft cotton sundress. I made pasta for dinner and popped open a bottle of wine. Shawn said he would clean up. I walked past him to turn the music up when I noticed my David Yurman stone ring was laying on the kitchen counter slightly behind the coffeepot. I had looked for that thing for weeks. I shoved it on my right hand and pressed the button for the XM radio.

After I polished off another glass of wine, Peter called. I thought it would be best if he spoke to Shawn. When he hung up, I told him he should drive tonight. "Come on, Livvy. Let's pick up your houseguest."

Well, Peter had been right. It was storming.

Shawn opened the back car door, holding an umbrella over my head. I reached forward between the seats to the front of the car and programmed the address into the navigation system. I told Shawn he was good to go after I pressed the last button to verify our destination. I quickly dozed off. I heard George ask Shawn who he was. I mumbled from the backseat, "George, Shawn doesn't have a badge, but he has a gun, and his is bigger than yours." I never opened my eyes. "Good evening, Miss Hunnicutt, it sure is a messy night. I'm glad to see you have company with you." I threw my hand up, offering him a lazy wave.

Shawn lowered the window. "Other side." Peter opened the back door while fiddling with something. Guess it was an umbrella. Peter asked Shawn if I was all right. "Yes, sir—too much sun earlier today."

My filter was not as fine-tuned as it had been earlier today, you know, because of all the sun. Without raising my head, which had been propped on the door panel for the past thirty minutes, I said, "Hey, handsome. How did your sexy make-out session go with Emily on the dock tonight?"

"It went well, Olivia."

"Damn that Emily." I yawned. "She's a lucky girl."

* * *

The alarm clock buzzed. I slapped it and heard it hit the floor. I slowly sat up and looked down. *What had I done?* I was wearing Shawn's white shirt. Why couldn't I keep my clothes on? I stood up and smacked the center of my forehead with the palm of my hand. I got nothing, but I was sure Shawn would fill me in on this tiny case of amnesia I was suffering from.

While I showered, a nightmare unfolded right before my eyes. *What if I'm stuck with a babysitter indefinitely? I've got to get a grip. This is my fourth freaking hangover, and the last three had something to do with Max. Stop it, Livvy! Don't think about him anymore.*

I noticed a note taped to the back of my bedroom door as I stepped out of the bathroom.

Olivia, I do not have to leave until noon today.
Peter

I fell across my bed. *There is a God.* I was not fired up about starting my day, so I postponed it until I couldn't any longer. I had to eat, or I would be suffering from more than a headache. I would have an insulin reaction without nutrition.

I made my way upstairs and noticed Peter was on the porch, reading. Shawn had prepared breakfast. I sat down at the breakfast table.

"Did I misbehave?"

Shawn walked over and handed me two Advil and a bottle of water. He walked away, then came right back with a bran muffin and fruit. "Hold on, you need protein and coffee." He still did not answer my question, but turned around again and came back with yogurt and a spoon. Shawn put his hands on his hips and finally said, "Maybe a little. You did speak what was on your mind."

I pushed the plate back and plopped my head on the table. "Why was I wearing your shirt?"

"That would have something to do with you dancing on the outside kitchen bar."

My head was still buried on the table. "I need more information, Shawn."

He cleared his throat. "Well, uh, you hit the XM control pad on the wall and shouted, 'Let's dance!' Then you ran out the door. By the time we caught up with you, you had turned every outside light on, and the place was lit up like a baseball field. The music was booming over the outdoor speakers. 'Shakin' Hands' was playing."

I gasped.

"We tried to stop you, but you hopped on the bar stool and were about to step onto the bar when your foot got hung up in your hem. Your dress ripped off your shoulder, and before the song ended, your dress fell off. We tried not to watch, but Peter said 'screw it' after about two seconds. I only watched because I was afraid you would fall." *Sure, he did.* "After you finished dancing and your feet were back on the ground—nice dismount by the way—I offered you my shirt."

Good grief. "Did I at least dance well?"

"Yes, you did."

I still couldn't look at Shawn. He asked about my blood sugar this morning.

"Good, one-oh-nine. What about last night, Shawn?"

"Two-twenty. I called Martin, and he did not recommend a bolus based on your activities."

I looked up. "You called Martin?" *Oh, it just gets better and better.* "What did Martin have to say?"

"Martin said he hated he missed your dance. But Livvy, you called Mr. Spencer."

I buried my face in my hands. "I did what?"

"Yep, I was checking your blood sugar, and you snatched my phone from my side and said, 'I have a question for your boss.' You pressed a button and said, 'Hell no, this is Livvy. Is your jet fueled up?' I put your things away for you, and when I turned back around, you were asleep with my phone to your ear."

"Oh God—why would I have asked him that?"

"Don't know, but when Mr. Spencer called back, that was his exact question. When I couldn't answer him, he demanded I wake you up, but you were resting soundly."

"No, Shawn. You can call it what it is…I was passed out."

Shit, Peter just walked in and was now standing in the kitchen, holding his homework. I looked up at him and returned my head to the table. *What did this man think of me?*

Peter pulled out the chair next to me and had a seat. Shawn disappeared. "Olivia, did you have a bad day yesterday?"

I raised my head. "Whatta ya think? I have had three hangovers in my life, and two have been in the past three days."

"I didn't picture this as being a regular thing with you."

"I'm awfully sorry and dreadfully embarrassed about last night."

"You do not owe me an apology. After all, I am ecstatic to know that you dance extremely well, and as a bonus, you are limber. I had no idea you were capable of doing a backflip…from the countertop of a bar."

"Would it be okay if we never discuss this incident again?" I begged as he was on his way out the door.

* * *

"Sorry to wake you, Livvy," Shawn said, tapping my shoulder. "Martin called and said I was needed in New York. I've already packed."

"Thank you for coming," I yawned. "Shawn, please keep Max safe. I do—"

"I know you do."

"I can't be with him, though."

Shawn sat next to me. "I am going to tell you something, but it stays between us. This last project turned out messy, but you knew that. Global will be a huge empire within a few years at the rate things are moving. Mr. Spencer is screwing around in technology with two of the largest companies in the world. These people are not taking it lying down. He delayed the takeovers for at least three months because of you. But they will happen, and when they do, they will be nasty. He has the backing of the US government for both. That fact will never become public knowledge, but he must finish them." He stood up and whispered, "You're doing the right thing, Livvy." He walked out.

I thought about what Shawn had said all day and worried about Max. Then I stopped myself, because I had already repeatedly tried to talk to Max and convince him to get out of the business. There was nothing more I could do.

Dinnertime was approaching, and I was bent over rummaging in the two bottom drawers of the refrigerator and singing loudly when Peter said, "Nice shorts." I jumped and flung the wrapped salmon across the kitchen. Peter snagged our dinner right before it slid off the edge of the counter.

"You didn't call."

"You needed a day off," Peter said. "Noel brought me."

"Oh. Well, you're holding dinner, and my babysitter left earlier today." I smiled and took the white package from Peter's hand. "You can go relax or whatever."

After dinner Peter and I were standing in front of the sink. I had just put the last dish into the dishwasher when he picked up the bottle of wine and his glass and headed to the deck. I grabbed my glass of wine and a blanket and followed.

Peter sat down on a lounge chair for two. I wasn't sure if I was supposed to sit with him or if I should.... oh, never mind. He did that head thing, so I sat beside him.

"Olivia, I have a favor to ask. I have been asked to write and sing a song for the *Finding Justice* soundtrack. Would you consider helping me?"

I thought a minute, and the evening sky grabbed my attention. I looked up and reclined my half of the seat back slightly. "I can try, but you won't offend me if I'm not the gal for the job."

"I would not have asked if I wasn't certain you could deliver. I will never listen to 'Shakin' Hands' the same way after last night."

"Jeez, Peter. I thought we were not going to mention that again."

"I never promised you I wouldn't mention it." I growled at him. He switched gears. "Shawn said you love art."

"I do."

Peter laid his hand on top of mine, which was resting on my leg. "We have something in common. I can spend hours admiring an excellent piece."

"It's getting late. We should probably get some sleep."

He stood up, but my hand remained in his. Peter walked me to my room, but he did not enter. "Good night, Olivia." He released my hand and walked away. I didn't understand why he didn't just call me Livvy.

CHAPTER 26

Mom texted early the next morning and asked if I would visit with her on set. *Whew! It's hotter than blazes out these days.* I rambled through my selection of light cotton dresses and decided on the white one. I took two-inch wedge sandals with white-and-brown plaid fabric from their box.

When we arrived to the set, I parked the car and got out. "Are you staying today, Olivia?" Peter queried.

"Thought about it."

Later that afternoon, we strolled underneath the shade tree. "Hey, Miss Thang," Scott called over. "I'm working tonight, but I'm free tomorrow night. How 'bout dinner?" he asked, glancing over his shoulder at Peter. Scott was twenty-six, but he acts more like six.

"Thought you played Xbox on your nights off," Peter said, gripping Scott's shoulder tightly.

Someone shouted my name from the direction of the barricade. My heart banged against my chest wall when she shouted again. "I will only take a moment of your time." *Ignore her,* my inner princess warned, but my warrior princess said, *go get her, girl.* I was fidgeting. "I'm not with the media," the lady said.

"Peter—"

"Scott, tell Olivia all about your Xbox," Peter said, laughing and heading toward the barricade. "George, come with me."

"Miss Hunnicutt, please, I would like to have a word with you."
Peter approached the lady. She handed him her card. George moved
the barricade.

"I play it live," Scott said.

"Is that right," I said. "Scott, what is Peter doing?"

"Dunno," he said, watching Peter.

"Olivia," Peter said, approaching, "apparently this lady would like
to have you photographed for her next swimsuit issue."

"Who are you?" I asked before she got too comfortable under our
shade tree.

"I'm Nancy Saxton," she said, handing me her card. "I'm a magazine editor." She said the magazine was wrapping up the final details
of its next edition. She wanted to include me, or at least get some
professional photographs of me and see what they would look like.
She said if my pictures turned out well, as she believed they would, I
would be in the next issue. "But we need to shoot within the next few
days," she finished.

"I'm not a model, and I don't look like those girls in the magazines." I shuffled my feet. "I'm short and, uh...I just don't look like
them."

"But you do," Scott said.

"I don't see myself that way."

I told Nancy I was flattered, but I wasn't interested. She asked me
to reconsider. I stressed to her that I was busy working and could not
leave town.

"You live on a lake. I think we can work with it."

"No one knows me, so I don't understand how this could benefit
the magazine or me, for that matter."

"Your name is popping up everywhere, and there are pictures of
you on the Internet in those cute swimsuits. When I finally got a good
look at your face, I knew I had to come and try to convince you in
person."

"No, thank you. You've wasted your time. You should have called
first."

"Miss Hunnicutt, I tried every way possible to get in contact with you. The few people who accepted my call said hell would freeze over before Max Spencer would allow this to happen." *What?*

Suddenly, words spewed from me like lava. "I'll do it with a few conditions. It must be done here, on my schedule, and if I make the cut, put my picture in the back of the magazine." I shook her hand, then pointed to my mother and told Nancy she needed to speak to that lady. I nodded at Peter. "And he'll work out the details."

I walked away and heard Scott laughing. I was using my favorite unladylike four-letter word, and I had paired it up with every other word I could think of. Peter was at my side, and of course, that fool was laughing.

I sat down in my car, turned the key, and asked, "Dear God, what have I done now?"

"As your unofficial agent, I will give you a recap. Olivia, apparently you may have your picture in the best-selling magazine of the year, and you will be wearing a swimsuit." I laid my head on the steering wheel and banged it lightly. Peter placed his hand on my back and rubbed gently. "Olivia, you are beautiful, and it is okay to show the world. Think about it like this: you having diabetes and Addison's could inspire a lot of people. Plus, your stories of your education, traveling, and your interests are incredible. You can allow people a peek into your life and show them that if you have health issues, it doesn't mean you can't live or set goals for yourself, and most importantly, accomplish them. I wish you would tell the rest of your story about how you have waited to totally give yourself to a man; that is a helluva story by itself."

I reminded him I didn't want to wait—it just hadn't happened. "I'm not beautiful. I'm cute. I'm bruised all over—that'll have to be airbrushed. I actually have a long list of shit—"

"No," he interrupted, "you have it wrong. First, you will wait, that I know. And you are beautiful, so throw your shit list away."

* * *

I tossed and turned all night, thinking about what an impulsive idiot I was. But I also thought about what Peter had said. He was right. I would take this situation and make something positive out of it. I would thank Peter tomorrow. I closed my eyes and fell right to sleep.

Over breakfast I mentioned to Peter I was going to take his advice about the swimsuit thing. He said he would call Nancy. He asked if I was going to hang out on the set again today. "No way. I can't seem to stay out of trouble there," I said. I didn't tell him I was throwing him a birthday party tomorrow, and I would be busy today.

I dropped Peter off and drove to Auburn. I met with the caterer about tomorrow evening's menu. Then, on a whim, I contacted a local, but very good, band. Tim said they would be happy to play. I stopped by the store and grabbed the necessary items for a small amount of decorating, which Aunt KK had agreed to help me with. My last order of business today: call Abby, because if I had a party and did not invite the group, she would die. I told her to arrange at least two DDs because no one could spend the night, and this little gathering would end at ten o'clock.

"Abby, would you please invite everyone?"

"Robert included?"

"Yes. Please invite him, but I'm afraid he won't come."

"Oh, he'll come."

When I arrived at the lake cottage, I cleaned out my car. I looked at all the crap piled on the great-room floor and wondered where I was going to hide it. I took everything downstairs and shoved it all into closets.

My phone rang. It was Max. *I bet he already knows about the swimsuit thing.* He did, but he was great with it and said he would buy the first available copy. I told him the only reason I agreed to it was because I had gotten pissed off, and if I didn't make the cut, I would be all right. "Hey, at least I can say I filled a day on my boring calendar."

"You will make the cut," Max assured me.

Max said Shawn had enjoyed his visit, other than me jumping off the Rock. I thanked Max for sending him and apologized for calling him so late the other night. Max wondered by chance if I remembered what I was going to say following my drunken question concerning the jet. "Max, I think we both know exactly where I was going with that."

"Yeah. How do you feel now about what you were going to ask me?"

"Max, I, uh…I don't…I mean…" I clammed up.

Max broke the silence at his end. "Livvy, Shawn thinks Peter is a nice guy."

"He is, Max."

"I'll let you go for now."

Mom said the photo shoot was scheduled four days from now, and it would take place at the Rock and the island with the white beach. The magazine folks would pick me up at eight. She said she e-mailed me a list of do's and don'ts.

This afternoon, after Peter had tied the Sea-Doo up on the floating ramp, he reached for my hand. Good Lord, I gave it to him before I realized what I had done. He held it as we walked up the steps to the pool area. With his free hand, he pointed to the pool. I released his hand and jumped in. When my head popped up, he was standing on the second step. I reached for a raft and hung on it from one side with my legs dangling in the water. He joined me on my raft, dangling from the opposite side of it, facing me. He touched my swimsuit strap, which was tied around my neck. "I like it," he said. "I spoke to Nancy today. She had no idea you are diabetic, nor did she know that you are only twenty-one and have finished college. I also told her you were well traveled, but when I mentioned you were a virgin…" He paused. "She is going to do something special with you. She is thinking on it." Peter touched the side of my face. "Olivia, everything will work out." I reached across the raft and threw my arms around his neck. I hugged him tight and realized his arms were around my waist. I thanked him for cleaning up after me.

Oh, hell, no, I thought, when the butterflies fluttered. I would not allow *that* to happen again. I let go of him and the raft, swam to the steps, and walked right out of the pool to take a breather.

* * *

The next morning, I'd been waiting for thirty damn minutes for Mr. Birthday Boy. If he didn't hurry up, I would have to serve him his hot tea and omelet on the Sea-Doo, because I had Aunt KK coming to decorate, and she was always early.

"Omelet okay?" I asked, nearly leaping from my chair when he walked into the kitchen.

"Anything," he said, watching me flip the gas on.

I whipped that thing right up and plopped the plate down on the table in front of him. "Eat before it gets cold." He pushed back from the table and was about to stand up when I pointed to the chair and said, "Orange juice to go along with your hot tea. Don't move. I'll get it."

I told him to meet me on the dock, hoping that might hurry him up.

I parked the Sea-Doo on the ramp at the Cliffs, and Peter got off, removed his vest, and reached for the compartment to get his bag. I touched his hand. He stroked the side of my hand with his thumb, and we were staring at each other. I broke the silence by saying, "Happy birthday."

"Thank you for remembering, Olivia." I felt that weird thing happen again. I looked away. He leaned in and kissed me near my temple.

Scott asked, "Peter, that's all you got? Jesus, man!"

Neither Peter nor I said a word. I straddled the Sea-Doo and sat down. I was once again staring at him. David asked if he could give me a push. I nodded. The watercraft slid into the water and floated out ten feet. I pressed the start button, my eyes still locked on Peter. The wind hit my face. I shook my head and said out loud, "Livvy, get a freaking grip." I didn't have time to dwell on what I had felt. I had a party to get ready for.

After lunch I let Peter know Noel would pick him up today, because I had a hair appointment and might run late. That may have been the first lie I'd ever told, but it was for a worthy cause.

He texted back: *Sure, but it is my turn to cook.*

I replied, *No, I got it tonight. Maybe tomorrow.*

The caterer had everything in place, and Peter's birthday cake was unbelievable: two square layers, one large and one small, stacked in a large, cream, modern shape with a rolled fondant bow, which gave the impression that the layers were being held together. The slick detail provided the appearance that the cake was a gift in itself, and this gift was made of chocolate, his favorite.

It was six thirty, and Aunt KK had done an amazing job. The ambiance would change as soon as the sun went down. Candles floated in the pool and lit torches lined the lake wall.

I paused in front of the mirror for one last glance. I adjusted my emerald-green gathered halter dress and pushed my hair away from my face. My friends had just arrived. I hugged each of them, and to my surprise, Robert had come. I took a deep breath. We hugged, but not too close, and released each other quickly. I had to walk away and process that for a moment. But on second thought, I didn't have time for that right now. I knew it would consume me.

Everyone arrived within minutes, including my new friends and the film crew. Being a weeknight, I knew we needed to get things rolling, even though Peter and Noel had not arrived yet. The band began to play, and the bartender was busy.

I returned to the front porch to welcome the guest of honor when it hit me. *What if Peter doesn't like surprises?* Then I was screwed. It was too late to worry about that, anyway—he and Noel had just pulled into the driveway. I suddenly got a knot in my stomach, but I plastered a smile across my face. As the distance narrowed between Peter and me, his smile grew wider. *Thank God.* He stepped onto the porch and said, "Your hair looks almost as beautiful as you do." He put one of his hands on my waist and leaned in as he kissed me near my temple. "A surprise party—"

"Just for you. I hope you don't mind!" Peter grabbed my hand and held it until we were standing on the deck. When the band ended the song, I released Peter's hand. I needed to make an announcement. Tim, the band's lead singer, loaned me his microphone. I welcomed all the guests and encouraged them to eat, dance, and plan to leave early. Then lastly, I said, "Happy birthday, Peter."

Everyone clapped and hollered out a birthday wish to him. Peter casually waved and mouthed, "Thank you."

I danced with a couple of my new friends and all of my old friends, including Robert. Emily and I were talking when someone slipped his arms around my waist from behind. I was afraid to move. But the British accent calmed me as he spoke. "May I have this dance?"

Peter took my hand, and we danced to "Something Beautiful." When the song ended, he dipped me and held me in that position for countless minutes. He looked at my lips. They parted. He sighed; his gaze caught mine. My heart pounded, and my insides quivered. My chest sharply rose when I filled my lungs. I swallowed hard. Peter smoothly smiled and eased me up. "Thank you for the dance," I mumbled and gradually took a step back. Frozen, I gaped at him. Peter wasn't frozen, though. He studied me from my head to my toes, nodding, with his hands loosely hanging in the front pockets of his jeans. "Livvy!" Abby shouted. I snapped my head in her direction. "We're leaving," she waved. I left Peter standing there nodding while those dang butterflies raged in my stomach.

All the guests had left, and the cleanup was finished by eleven o'clock. "Olivia, other than my parents, no one has ever done anything like this for me," Peter said.

Our eyes connected, and he carried on. "You are as beautiful as you were the first time I laid eyes on you." I'm sure I blushed an ugly shade of crimson. He took a step closer and said, "Thank you for everything."

We were standing in the kitchen with less than a foot between us. I reached behind me, picked up his gift, and handed it to him. Our gaze was not interrupted even as I said, "Open it."

He smiled and took the box from my hands. He popped the tape on all four sides, flipped off the top, and pulled the tissue back. He laughed as he removed each item from the box. "So you think I needed my own." We laughed. Now he had two swimsuits to go along with his borrowed one.

* * *

The next two days, Peter worked long hours because of rain and heat. I accomplished everything on my to-do list for the swimsuit shoot, which was scheduled for the next morning. By dinnertime I was a nervous wreck. Even Peter noticed. I passed on the wine—that was on my "don't" list—and I ate as lightly as I could while making insulin adjustments. Because of my diabetes, I couldn't do as heavy a fast as my "do" list instructed.

I headed to bed early. "Sleep well, Olivia," Peter said. Something felt odd when Peter brushed the side of my face. His touch felt distantly familiar, like he had done it hundreds of times, even though that was far from the case.

"Good night, Peter."

CHAPTER 27

I woke to One Republic's tune, "Good Life," blasting from my Bose. I slapped the off button. I loved the song, but nothing was good about today, other than I was breathing. *What was I thinking? I am going to make a complete fool of myself. And to make matters worse, I had invited Peter.* I wanted to cry, but that would only make my eyes puffy. I could scream and throw a good, old-fashioned hissy fit, but that would run my sugar up. So I went with a big huff and groan and kicked my covers back. I tried not to become mawkish for what I assumed would be a nerve-racking and, quite possibly, traumatic day.

While I showered, I had a couple of uplifting mental notes worthy of mentioning. I didn't have to shave a thing; oh no, my total body was as slick as a peeled onion. At least the hair thing was easy. My to-do list instructed to only wash and dry.

I snatched my soft, fluffy towel from the bathroom counter, wrapped it tightly around me, and darted out of the bathroom. I about ran into Peter; he was standing in front of my bedroom door, holding a breakfast tray. *How kind.* "I thought you might be hungry. You picked at your dinner last night." He sat the tray down on a chest at the foot of my bed. "Olivia, you will be amazing." He kissed me right in the center of my damp forehead. "I put your iPod in your bag."

"Oh, great, and uh…thank you, Peter," I said, gesturing to the breakfast tray.

I packed a small cooler with healthy snacks and my insulin pens. I glanced around my room to make sure I had everything when I noticed my BlackBerry was blinking. A text from Max. I felt happy for a moment. His text read: *Good luck today!*

I texted him back: *Thank you! I will certainly need it.*

He texted back: *Don't kid yourself. You will do great! Talk to you soon.*

I smiled as I put my phone in my bag.

I heard boats pulling up and loud voices. I took one last look in the mirror. Without my makeup and my plain-Jane hair, I was almost homely looking. However, I slipped on a great pair of Gucci flip-flops and an airy cover-up over my swimsuit, and I felt better.

The entire crew greeted me and shook my hand as I stepped onto the boat. One guy pranced right over to me and touched my hair. "Oh, thank you, sweet Jesus! It is fabulous." Then he plopped his butt down right beside me. Peter smiled and took the seat to my left.

When we arrived at the Rock, the two pontoons anchored as the drivers cursed and fussed. I got tickled.

"The boats will float around even though you're anchored."

The heavyset fellow wearing a Braves cap said, "But this is a lake. I thought lakes were still."

I had to give him a short Alabama history lesson. "Well, you see, this lake is an artificial reservoir. It was needed to generate hydro-electric power for the Alabama Power Company. The many natural streams and rivers can cause the current to be strong in areas of this forty-four-thousand-acre lake, and we are anchored in one of them."

The guy stood, picked up a rope, and looked at it. I grabbed the rope from him and said, "Get another one. We're tying the two boats together." I pointed to the guy that liked my hair. "Toss the bumpers over the side, please, so the boats will not bang into each other." He looked at me as if I had said a dirty word, but he tossed the bumpers over, and then immediately examined his nails. I tied the fronts of the two boats together. I grabbed the second rope and tied the backs of the boats together. Nancy then asked me to step into a makeshift dressing room, which was nothing more than towels strung together with string. Oh Lord. I noticed there were people from the crew climbing the Rock. I got tickled and said, "I could have shown them a better way."

Nancy turned around and looked up at the Rock. "Have you jumped before?"

"Many times." Nancy decided on the red suit after ten minutes of studying the surroundings and going through plastic containers of well-organized swimsuits.

In the meantime, Peter jumped up and pointed to the Rock. "You could have killed yourself."

"Oh, Peter," I said while the gay guy was fussing with my hair and makeup. "That's nothing." About that time I opened my left eye as he was applying eye shadow to my right. "What is your name?"

"God, I thought I told you, girl. But then again, I was a bundle of nerves. I hate the water, and I hate boats. I'm John-David."

I was about to step out from behind my strung-up towel dressing room when I realized the swimsuit bottoms were one of those little cheeky things. Half my ass was showing. "That's it, Livvy," Nancy said.

I took a deep breath and walked right past Peter. I stepped off the pontoon onto a Sea-Doo with another complete stranger and floated to the Rock. My sixty-foot climb to the top took less time than those of my four predecessors; however, they had been evaluating the sunlight or something. I stood there quietly and waited until Owen, the photographer, requested me. As soon as I stepped close to him, someone started pulling at my suit, making the needed adjustments. One wrong move, buddy, and I will fall over this sixty-foot rock, I thought.

Owen asked me to relax. *Relax?* Really?

I hoped I was following his instructions. After a few minutes, he gave me a break. "Livvy, we are done here, but I heard you can make a different exit. We would like to get it. Are you up for it?"

"Sure. I'll do it."

"That wasn't so bad," I said minutes later as I sat down beside Peter, dripping wet. Peter took me by surprise when he hooked his arm around me and leaned his head over, bumping mine. "Owen was nice. He talked me through most of the shots," I said, enjoying the closeness and starting to relax.

As we motored to our next location, I shouted, "Slow down! Raise the trim. You're about to run aground." I showed him the button. "Now park it."

Poor John-David was fussing over my hair and asked Nancy, "What swimsuit? I needed the color of it ten minutes ago."

Owen sat beside me while John-David dried and restyled my hair. "The sunlight on the sandbar is quite challenging right now. You have an hour or so to rest."

"Owen, I don't know what you're looking for, but before the sun sets, the sky turns a beautiful orange. The sky is already blue, so when the two are combined, it is beautiful."

Owen and Nancy exchanged a quick look, and then she said, "Save the ocean-blue suit. She'll wear it last."

Owen looked down at the swimsuits. "Put her in white, and the smallest one you have." He pointed to the suit on top. "That one. It looks like leather."

Oh thank God, my butt was covered. But dang, where was the rest of the top? Peter stepped off the boat and said, "Let me help you. Don't accidentally wet your hair—John-David will come completely unglued."

I was a tad distracted, because I could feel the mushy bottom of the lake squishing between my toes. In spite of this gross, annoying factor, I had to refocus, because Owen was ready to work. I blocked everything from my thoughts except the music that was playing and Owen. Fewer than twenty minutes later, Owen said, "Take a break."

Nancy met me with a towel. "Owen got what he needed. Go rest on the beach." Peter came over and joined me.

"Lie down." He patted his leg. "Rest until they need you." I took him up on his offer.

After the break, it was decided I would wear pink bottoms and a pink-and-black life vest. This time I had a prop, a Sea-Doo.

In fewer than thirty minutes, Peter met me on the narrow beach, holding the matching pink top and sunblock. "Turn around. I'll hold the towel."

As soon as the top was back in its proper place, Peter spread the large towel, and we sat down. "Your shoulders look pink." He held the can of sunblock up.

"Yes, please." I turned, and he sprayed my shoulders.

Nancy asked if she could join us. "I never would have guessed you had any health issues. You look so healthy. When Peter brought it to my attention that you also are a chaste young woman, it was a bonus. I would like a good friend of mine to interview you and feature your story. It would appear in a different magazine, but I trust her. Livvy, I think every young lady needs to know your story—what you must overcome daily and how none of your health issues have held you back. I think you could be a role model if we handle you and your story correctly."

I listened to every word she said as I drew circles in the sand. "Nancy, I'm not perfect. The reason I am a virgin is not because I haven't wanted to be with someone, because I have. I owe the fact that I'm still a virgin to three special men in my life who have respected me. I guess now I might choose to wait, but I don't want to make a promise that I cannot keep. I'll share my story, but I will be truthful."

Nancy said she wanted my story to run before the swimsuit issue became available. I went on to tell her this was the most difficult thing I had ever done.

"Don't kid yourself, Livvy. You made this look easy today, but I know it isn't, because I was once a model."

Owen was ready again. Peter hopped up and gave me a hand as I stood to my feet. I stepped onto the boat, and John-David touched up my hair and makeup. By this time, half of the dang curtain had fallen, so Nancy asked John-David to hold up one side of the towel. That nut looked over. "Girl, with a body like yours, I would never cover it. You do not have a freaking flaw." Peter was standing in the water less than a foot from the boat. Peter looked in my direction, slightly bent over from laughing. John-David dropped the towel. "Mr. Weston, my God, it is so true." I quickly reached for the towel. Oh God, my bruises. Everyone had just seen the real me: in black, blue, yellow, and even green, regardless of how tiny each dot was.

The sky had just begun to turn that beautiful orange color, and it was spreading into the perfect blue sky. Owen pointed where he wanted me, and I stood in his designated spot wearing the blue swimsuit. I tried to follow Owen's instructions, but nothing was working. I felt myself getting frustrated. "Can I try something?" I didn't wait for an answer. "Turn up the music," I asked.

I turned, ducked my head, and swam into deeper water. When my head popped up, I heard John-David gasp, but I could now feel what Owen wanted from me, despite the murky bottom of the lake. Owen snapped away for the next fifteen minutes and then said, "We're done."

Peter met me with a towel, and an hour later, we were back at the lake house. Nancy said she would call tomorrow with details regarding the interview.

Seven forty-five, and I was exhausted and hungry. Peter and I made a hearty chef salad, and I had wine. We ate dinner on the screened porch, and after we pushed our plates back, Peter apologized for not turning around when John-David had dropped the towel, but he said he had to look.

He smiled and squeezed my hand. "John-David was right—not a flaw."

"Oh, please," I said, rolling my eyes.

"No, I saw you. All of you today, more than once, I might add. But I swear you had my attention as soon as you put the red suit on and I saw half your ass. But when you dove off that damn rock, my heart about stopped."

"How was my landing?"

"Clean."

I stood up and squeezed his shoulder. "I'm going to bed." I leaned over and kissed him on top of his head. "Thank you for going with me today."

"You're welcome." I reached for our plates, and he said, "Let me tonight."

* * *

"The waffles smell good," Peter said as he entered the kitchen.

"Porch okay?" I asked and lifted the lid to the waffle maker.

"Sure."

"Nice trunks." I winked at him.

"Thank you. They are nice," he said, looking down at them. "A birthday gift from someone quite special."

I snickered. "Far from special, Mr. Weston, but I'm glad you like them. Now eat." I sat his plate down. "You're going to be late."

I dropped Peter off, headed back home, and parked the Sea-Doo on the ramp. I could hear my phone ringing from inside the watercraft's compartment while I fiddle-faddled around, disconnecting the kill switch from my life vest. Then I answered. Lo and behold, it was Ms. Fills. The condo had flooded again last night. She apologized and said she was looking for other options for Mr. Weston. I told her I would speak to him. If his current arrangements suited him, we would leave things as they were. I would let her know.

Peter called early; he was finished for the day. I grabbed my vest, and in no time at all, I was parked on the ramp at the Cliffs. Peter was headed in my direction. I stood a couple of feet from the Sea-Doo while Peter stowed his things. "Nice suit," he said. I smiled. He straddled the seat and sat down. I straddled the seat and was about to sit when he said in a low voice, "Ah...Jesus."

I looked back. "You okay?" He laughed and said he would be in a couple of minutes. He said he was trying to clear his thoughts from what had just flashed before his eyes. "Hush," I said, lowering my shades.

For the first time, Peter placed his hands differently on me, low, near my hips. Not at my waist like usual. At the cottage, as Peter was tying up the Sea-Doo, I said, "Funny thing happened today, Peter. Ms. Fills called. It seems as though the condo flooded again last night. She said she would try to find you something else. I told her if you were okay staying here—"

"Please tell her thank you, but I like it here."

CHAPTER 28

Max called the day the interview was released. He appreciated how I had answered the questions about him. I told him it was nothing but the truth.

Peter and I flirted every day, especially since we had danced together under the fireworks on the Fourth of July on the back of the boat. Talk about the sky lighting up—no, wait, that was probably me, but he had gotten into the Rock'n Lemonade. So I guess that could have explained his carefree behavior. It seemed when I was with him, I forgot about the promise I had made to myself. On countless occasions, I thought he wanted to kiss me, but he never followed through. *But did I want him to?*

I pan-flipped a pancake without a spatula about the time Peter walked in.

"Good morning." He had his homework in his hand. I pointed to the table and said, "I got it. You sit down."

I put a small stack of low-fat pancakes with sugar-free warm syrup in front of him. I sat down with my plate beside him.

I asked Peter if there was anything he needed. I was going into Auburn after I dropped him off in Dadeville. He grinned and said he didn't need a thing. I couldn't help but look at him and think, *What is my problem? Moreover, what the hell was his problem?* I caught him starting at me all the time, and he had almost kissed me more times than I could count. He held my hand every night on the deck. I didn't get it, but I was better off not going there, because he was leaving in less than a month.

I was picking at my food, drowning in my thinking session. "Olivia, what are you thinking about?"

I couldn't say *you*. "Dinner tonight. What would you like?"

"The salmon you've made a couple of times is good. Olivia, I would like to talk to you about something tonight, if that would be okay."

"Of course."

Peter leaned and placed his finger underneath my chin, gently raising it. He softly kissed my sticky lips. Then he pulled away, picked our plates up, placed them in the sink, and walked out of the room.

I didn't—or couldn't—move. *What just happened?* I was shaking and sweating; my surroundings became fuzzy and were fading into blackness. Suddenly I gasped and sucked air into my lungs. *Oh God... Peter Weston just took my breath away.*

Peter came back into the kitchen. I was still sitting but lost in a daze, staring out the window in the direction of the lake, when he asked, "Olivia, are you all right?"

"Uh-huh," I answered and shook my head to break my funk. I picked my bag up and asked briskly, "All set?"

The drive into Dadeville took twenty minutes. I was quiet, but I wanted him to talk to me. Screw after dinner. I was screaming from the inside, *Talk to me now.* He was voted the sexiest man alive this week, and now he was going to make me wait until after dinner to talk. I didn't know if he liked me or if he liked me but didn't think it was a good idea. Or maybe it was only the "let's be friends" thing.

Wait, Livvy, don't go there. Think about what happened with Max. It wasn't worth it. Then I had a quick flashback of Robert. All at once I felt a blanket of sadness cover me. I decided being friends wouldn't be so bad. With that thought, Crosby crossed my mind, and I smiled.

"Olivia, I never told you how impressed I was with your interview. I read the article the day it came out, and I can't seem to get it off my mind." *So this is what he wanted to discuss with me.* "You haven't mentioned the magazine. It's available today, you know."

"Actually, I forgot. It would be nice if everyone else has as well."

"Not a chance."

We arrived at the courthouse in Dadeville, and George moved the barricade. I stopped in front of the building. Peter sat for a moment, and once again we locked eyes. Peter leaned over and kissed me. He swung the door open.

"Remember—after dinner I want to talk to you." He trotted toward the building. I wasn't breathing. I gasped for air. *Oh God, what am I doing? Why can't my life be normal?* When my heart returned to a normal rhythm, I drove away.

I turned my radio up in an attempt to clear my head. I was determined not to analyze Peter or the two times he had softly kissed me. It would work itself out. As I approached the intersection, the light was green. *Wham!* I felt my car leave the ground. It was flipping. I could hear metal banging, along with glass breaking. When it stopped, my car was lying on its left side. My head was hurting, but I didn't see any blood. I screamed, "Help me! Get me out!" The SOS emergency assistance operator was speaking loudly through the car's speakers and informed me emergency units had been dispatched. I heard sirens. People were asking if I was all right. "That's Tom Hunnicutt's daughter," someone shouted. "Livvy, calm down. We will get you out." Someone threw a blanket on top of me and said they were cutting the roof. I heard the saw; it was screeching through the metal at a painful pace. When the noise stopped, a firefighter lowered himself down into my car and quickly evaluated my condition. I seemed to be fine. The windshield was removed so I could be placed safely on a stretcher until x-rays could be made.

Once in the ambulance and in route to the hospital, the paramedic told me as he started an IV that he'd contacted Noel, who was on his way. My blood sugar had spiked to 321. I was strapped securely to a gurney, which was hoisted out of the ambulance and rolled into the hospital emergency room.

"Where is Livvy Hunnicutt?" Robert shouted.

"Over here," the nurse said. Robert never left my side, not even when I was taken for a CT and an x-ray. Robert explained that Noel had called him, because he knew he could get to me quickly. I didn't speak, only because I was so nervous. I heard voices shouting again. It was Noel. He ran into my room. Peter, David, Scott, and Emily were right behind him. Peter grabbed my hand and asked, "Olivia, are you all right?" The nurse said three times I was allowed only two people with me. No one moved.

"Not a scratch," I said.

"No way," Noel said. "We saw the car. I'm going to speak to Dr. Watson.

Robert was standing at the foot of my bed. He touched my foot in farewell and turned to leave. "Robert," I called out. "Thank you for coming."

"You're welcome. If you need anything, call. I know your parents are traveling."

"I will," I said faintly.

Robert looked at Peter. "Bad place to meet up, but it's good to see you again, man."

Peter extended a firm handshake. "Likewise."

"Hey Livvy," Scott hooted. "Since you're feeling better, how about putting your autograph on this?" He tossed a copy of the swimsuit issue and a pen on top of my stomach. David and Emily each pulled out an issue as well.

"The nurse said, *go*." I told them take their magazines with them. Scott asked if I had seen it as he reached for his. "Not yet," I said with my lip twitching to smile.

He was laughing on his way out and said, "You didn't disappoint anyone, that's for sure."

I glanced at Peter. He smiled and said, "You told Nancy to put your picture in the back, and she did—the last eight pages."

I pulled the sheet over my face. "Oh dear Lord."

The doctor, a family came into the room and introduced himself to Peter. He patted me on my hand and said, "All your scans are fine, but I want to keep you overnight to monitor your blood sugar."

"Dr. Watson, how is the man that hit me?"

"He's lucky, like you. I just released him."

"Did he mention why he was in such a hurry?"

"His son was brought in—"

"I thought he was the only passenger. Sorry, I cut you off, Dr. Watson."

"He was."

"For appendicitis," a voice echoed from across the room. "I wanted to apologize for causing the accident."

"Your head."

"Helluva knot, but I'm okay."

"Your son—"

"Dalton. He, uh, is in surgery."

"How old is he?"

"Twelve," he said and shuffled his feet. "I'm very sorry. I, uh, have insurance—"

"I know," I said, noticing he was a humble-looking man. "I wish your son the best."

"Thank you. You too."

"Pardon me, sir. Does Dalton have an Xbox?" Peter asked.

"No, he doesn't."

"Would it be all right if a friend of mine drops by his room, in the morning? You know kids bounce back quick after this sort of thing. He might be bored."

"That would be mighty nice. Thank you."

"That is the perfect project for Scott," Peter said, when Dalton's dad cleared the doorway. I nodded in agreement.

"Livvy, your room is ready upstairs. An orderly will come to move you soon," the doctor said on his way out.

"Well, let's see it," I said, pointing to Peter's copy of the magazine.

"Move over." He tucked his right arm behind my back, then handed me his copy. "Open it, Olivia. You look beautiful."

I turned page after page and admired the gorgeous models, wanting to cry. There was no way I could ever compare. On the left page, near the back of the magazine, I saw my name first: "Olivia Sue Hunnicutt, but most people refer to her simply as Livvy." Underneath my name, a few more facts were listed, such as my age and hometown. Lastly, it noted I was single. And there I was in full color, wearing the ocean blue swimsuit.

On the right page was the same orange and blue sky, but my slightly covered backside was in full view of the camera with only a side view of my face. My top was thrown over my left shoulder. I turned the page, and there I was again in white, standing ankle deep in the lake. The light summer breeze had softly caught my hair and blown it gently away from my face. The sky was the most perfect shade of blue. On the opposite page, I was sporting the white bottoms only. Both of my arms covered my breasts, with my hands crossed over my chest. "Peter, wow, they airbrushed me."

"Maybe a little," he said, pointing to the picture, "but really, you look like this every day." When Peter turned the page, I was standing on the Rock, with my arms raised and my hands locked behind my head—laughing. In the picture to the right, I was lying on my back with my right arm slightly bent at my elbow; the back of my hand lay on my wavy hair, which covered the surface of the rock next to my head. My left hand relaxed on my hip. My left leg was almost straight and my right leg was raised slightly, bent at the knee.

In one of the last two pictures that made the cut, I was diving. On the last page, I was in the hot pink bottoms and the open pink and black vest. In spite of this, I was looking comfortable. I had been in my element, and it showed.

I handed the magazine back to Peter as the orderly arrived to take me to my room. Peter's three sidekicks caught up with us. "Have you seen it yet?" Scott asked.

"Give it back. I'll autograph it. And go buy an Xbox when you leave. You have an appointment with a kid in the morning." They all tossed their copies onto my lap while the orderly pushed my wheelchair.

"I'll set the kid up with a membership too, so he can play live," Scott said enthusiastically.

I had on one of those tacky hospital gowns, so I told everyone to stay out of my room until I was settled. Peter didn't listen; he followed me inside. I pointed back to the door for him to get out. "No, I'm coming with you." He held my IV bag and put it on the tall skinny pole while I climbed into that hard, crunchy bed. "Over," he said and sat next to me, about the time Noel walked in.

David and Emily hugged me bye, but Scott smacked me right on my lips. He knuckle-punched Peter and stage-whispered, "They are soft."

"Livvy, Mom and Dad were at the airport when they called; they wanted to swing home and see you, but I really didn't see the need. I told them you would call. Dad had me order you a new car. The salesman said he would deliver it the day after tomorrow."

"That could have waited, but thank you."

"Peter," my big brother said, "I'll take you to my folks' house. You can stay there tonight. I'll take you to work in the morning. Rae will pick Livvy up when the doctor releases her."

Peter kissed my hand. "Call me if anything changes."

When I was finally alone, I checked my phone. I had voice mails from Crosby and Max. I called Crosby.

"Are you okay?" Crosby asked.

"I'm fine, only staying the night. I'll go home in the morning."

"Thank God. By the way, I loved your pictures. The one with the blue bottoms and the top on your left shoulder was my favorite." I told him I remembered what I childishly had done in Cabo. He laughed, and then added I had changed his life, which was a good thing. I loved Crosby; he was probably my best friend now.

My cell rang as soon as Crosby and I ended our conversation. "Are you all right?" Max asked. "The accident is running on every network, but no one has released anything about your condition."

I assured him I was fine. After I updated him on the accident, he said he loved my pictures, and Martin, Shawn, and Claude wanted their copies autographed. I heard loud voices and suddenly my door swung open. I asked if we could talk in a few days. He said he would call. I took a deep breath and ignored my six friends crowding into my room. With all the noise in the background, I whispered, "Good-bye, Max."

"Bye, Livvy."

When I looked up at my friends, I saw they were all holding copies of the magazine. "I wondered what all the fuss was about in the ER this morning," Robert said. He tossed me his copy. "I love you in red." I smiled as I wrote him a message:

Dear Robert,
The hot summer day we climbed the Rock together, you stole my first kiss. I will never forget.
Livvy

Robert read the message and asked, almost in a whisper, "You mean, at sixteen you had never kissed anyone?"

"No." He left and took the posse with their signed copies with him.

I tossed and turned all night. Morning couldn't come fast enough. I called Rae and asked her to bring me a change of clothes. Mine had become scraps yesterday. I was lucky that my purse and phone had survived intact.

Rae dropped me off at our parents' house. I meandered to the front door, realizing how sore I was. A hot shower helped soothe my aching muscles, and I dressed for the day. I reached for the Hummer H2 keys and texted Peter. *I'm out! When do you want me?*

He texted back immediately: *Glad you are out! I'll take you now!*

What??? I reread our texts. *He's flirting! Peter Weston is flirting with me.* Shit. I sent a redo: *Very funny! What time will you finish today?* ☺

He texted: *See you @ 4. I'll take you then.* ☺☺

George did not recognize me in the big truck. I lowered the window, and he chuckled and let me pass. I parked in my usual spot. I was standing, propped against the Hummer, when I spotted Peter. He walked up, leaned in slightly, and kissed me softly on my lips. "Is this all you could find to drive?"

"Uh-huh, get in," I said, recovering from his angel kiss.

Scott was running toward us, shouting for me to hold up. He patted the hood of the Hummer as he approached my window and said, "This oughta keep you safe." Then he asked if I could drive a boat. I told him I could drive anything. He asked if I would take everyone tomorrow to see the Rock. I told him we could make a day of it. He tapped the Hummer door. "That will be fun," Scott said. "Right, Peter?" Peter was laughing but agreed.

I kicked my shoes off as I walked into the lake house. I suggested Peter get a head start on his homework for tomorrow. I pointed to the porch and said, "I'll bring you a drink." He nodded and walked out but leaned against the railing, looking back into the house. I turned the music on and made his drink. When I glanced back in his direction, he was sitting with one leg crossed over his knee, reading.

I eased out the door and sat his drink beside him on the table. He caught me by my hand as I turned. "Thank you."

I took a step closer toward him and said to myself, *Don't, Livvy, don't do it.* I bit the corner of my bottom lip for a second, and then I stooped over slightly. My hand remained in his. Why couldn't I listen to my better judgment? I leaned in, closed my eyes, and kissed him. I held my position for five or six seconds. I felt myself breathe in. I pulled away less than an inch and looked at him. I did it again. *What is wrong with me?* I pulled completely away this time and quickly turned away. I went to the kitchen, where I continued to spank myself mentally.

As we sat down to dinner, he reminded me about the songwriting thing. "I haven't forgotten."

He removed our plates and said, "Maybe we can work on it for a few minutes, but then don't forget, I want to talk to you."

"Sure." I had a gut feeling he was about to do the "let's be friends" talk, which wasn't a bad thing. We loaded the dishwasher, and he disappeared and returned with his guitar.

I refilled our wineglasses and joined him on the sofa. "What part of the movie do you need to write songs for?"

"The scene," Peter said, "where Ben wins the court case, his father's murderer is convicted, and he leaves the courtroom with the door swinging back and forth. Ben doesn't wait to see the murderer taken away in handcuffs."

"Yeah," I said, picking up, "Ben leaves the courthouse in a vicious rainstorm. Meanwhile, Jane is frantically searching Ben's home for him, hoping and praying he has chosen to be with her and not go for the big-city life. He just isn't home yet, but Jane thinks he's left town. She returns to the pier and unties her boat in the pouring rain. She believes it's over, and what would have been her forever has vanished. Her heart is broken, and she feels it never will mend, because her love for Ben runs deeply through her soul. Ben sees Jane's shadow in the gloomy distance, but only for a moment because the storm clouds cover the half-lit moon. Ben shouts her name; however, Jane believes she is dreaming. Out of desperation, she turns, and from the dim porch lights reflecting through the sheets of rain, Jane sees a mere silhouette. For a moment, she thinks what she is seeing is nothing more than a figment of her imagination. Nevertheless, she tries to wipe the rain from her eyes. She slowly realizes she sees Ben in the distance. They meet on the dock with their arms extended wide, and that is where they declare their immeasurable love for each other."

Peter was staring at me when I looked up. I had one tear trickling down my face. With the back of his hand, he wiped it away.

"Yes, that is precisely the scene I was referring to." He paused. "I didn't see it quite like that. I must have read the ending of the book ten times. I read the lines repeatedly. For the first time in my career, I didn't understand what a director wanted from me. Emily was having a difficult time too. But I get it now."

Peter and I worked on song lyrics for a while. He blew me away. I mostly listened to him, but I added a word or two here and there. After about an hour, I picked up my glass. "I need to think on it." I winked at him. "I'm going to the deck."

Peter joined me in the lounge chair for two. I didn't realize it, but I was rubbing one side of my neck. "Sit here," he said as he spread his legs apart, patted the seat, and placed his wineglass on the table next to his phone. I sat between his legs, but I didn't lean against him. But jeez, he gave a great neck massage. "You know, flipping in a car can make your neck sore," he said conversationally.

"Obviously."

"Olivia, I have wanted to ask you something for several weeks," he said, abruptly changing the subject. His phone rang. He continued to rub my neck with one hand while he answered it. "I apologize. It's Matt." Peter answered and handed me his phone. "He wants to speak to you."

"Hi, Matt."

"Nice pictures," Matt said. Peter laughed. I elbowed his stomach, and then absentmindedly leaned back against him. *Crap.* I quickly sat back up. Matt asked if I would send him a signed copy. I asked which one he liked. Peter pulled me back to lean against him, and he wrapped his arms around me, resting them nearly on my lap. He kissed the top of my head, brushed my hair to one side, and kissed my neck. *Hmm. Don't think we will be having the "just friends" talk. What did Matt just say?* "Oh, sure, Matt…I have to go to the post office tomorrow anyway." Peter brushed my hair to the other side of my neck. *"Now which one did you like, Matt?" Jeez…he's kissing my neck again.*

"The one with you wearing the white bottoms, no top. What is going on? You sound distracted. Let me speak to Peter."

Peter was kissing my shoulder when I rose up from leaning against his chest and handed the phone back to him. "Matt wants to speak to you."

"Not a thing, man." He pulled me back to his chest. *Jeez, he's good.* One playful, light sweep of Peter's tongue from my shoulder back up my neck gave me chill bumps from head to toe.

"Uh…Peter," I whispered.

"Yes, Matt, that is a good one. I'm busy. I'll call you later." He hung up, tossed his phone on the chair, and wrapped his arms around me.

"Olivia." He kissed the top of my head. "Will you…" His phone rang again. I handed it to him. "I'm sorry; it's Mum."

I stood up, walked over to the railing, and gazed out over the smooth lake. He walked up behind me as he was speaking to his mother and placed his free arm around me. "Yes, Mother, I know." I turned around and faced him. I didn't want him to feel he had to rush his conversation. "No, I will not return to London until we wrap things up here." I placed my hands softly on his lower waist, stood on my tiptoes, and lightly kissed him on his lips. I inhaled. *He smells like he did the first time I saw him in London. Clean, like fresh mountain air after a summer rain.* I backed away from him, but he quickly grabbed my arm and pulled me closer. He asked his mother to hold for a moment.

He kissed me softly on my lips. I pulled away and whispered. "Good night, Peter."

CHAPTER 29

I heard two soft taps on my bedroom door. I flipped from a comfy belly position to sitting straight up. *Dang it!* I ran my fingers
through my matted hair and blew my breath into my hands. Whoa, I
had some kickin' morning breath. I sniffed my armpit and mumbled,
"Whew, at least I had showered last night. Come in." I said sweetly,
sitting in the middle of the bed with my covers tangled around my legs
wearing a black and red fitted jersey cami and matching boyshorts.

Peter came in holding a breakfast tray and sat it on the edge of my
bed.

"Like your pajamas," he said.

I sheepishly grinned and pulled the breakfast tray closer. "Thanks.
Sit down."

"I'm sorry about my mum calling late." He tickled my feet, as he
sat.

I laughed and carefully shuffled my feet. "Cookie's timing usually
stinks too."

He smiled. "I still need to speak to you about something important." *Oh Lord.* I nervously ran my fingers through my tangled hair.
"We'll try again tonight." He quickly popped another kiss on my forehead and said he would meet me in a few minutes on the pier.

With my mouth full of wheat toast covered in sugar-free grape
jelly, I said, "Okay, and thanks for breakfast."

As we pulled onto the ramp at the Cliffs, Peter said there had been a package on the front porch, but he put it inside. "It's magazines. I would guess a hundred copies or so. Oh yes. Also, a package from Max arrived. I believe it contains—"

"Enough about the freaking magazines."

He laughed. "Don't forget to send Matt a copy. I e-mailed his address to you."

"Hush!"

Back at the cottage, I finished my chores and headed to the Dadeville Post Office. "Almost didn't recognize you with your shades on, Livvy. I heard you were living at your folks' place this summer."

I pushed the dang sunglasses on top of my head. "Yes, that's right."

He slapped a copy of the magazine on the counter and asked, "Do ya mind?"

"Not at all, Mr. Yates."

* * *

After I arrived back at the cottage, I immediately packed a cooler with a variety of beer and water, along with turkey wraps for lunch. I pulled the heavy wheeled cooler down the steps one by one. Then I stood on the pier thinking, how am I going to get this cooler on the boat? I removed the cover to the boat and turned the switch for the lift to lower the boat until it was completely even with the dock. I padded the edge of the Cobalt with towels, and I gave the cooler a shove. That sucker flew right over the edge and landed in the hull, spot on. The top flew open, and two ice cubes jumped out. I stepped down into the boat and closed the top.

I ran back inside the house and put on that fabulous red swimsuit with the cheeky bottoms. I grabbed a cute wrap and a red ponytail holder for later. All of a sudden, the phone rang. It was Scott, using Peter's phone. "I'm ready and waiting, girl."

I heard Peter say, "Give it to me." I laughed and said I would be there in a few minutes.

I lowered the boat into the water and cleared the boathouse, and that's when I realized I forgot my iPod. I checked the dash compartment, and Dad's old iPod was connected. It would have to do. I lifted my sunglasses so I could see the screen. I scrolled to an artist that sounded vaguely familiar, lowered my sunglasses, cranked up the music, and slowly pressed the accelerator. The first song finished, and "Cherry Pie" launched its reappearance after being incarcerated in the dash of the Cobalt. I turned up the volume and increased my speed. As I approached the Cliffs, I was at top speed. I was standing, singing, and feeling the music. Warrant was free at last, and I was rocking to "Cherry Pie."

The house at the Cliffs sat on a long, wide point. Three of the four sides of the property were surrounded by water. I was speeding along the lengthy side of the property, completely consumed by the music. My hair was blowing. I was singing and swaying when I quickly realized I needed to make a left. I turned too late and flew past the house, but I never slowed down. I gripped the steering wheel and swung it to the right. Then I gripped the wheel tighter and made a quick left, then looped back around. Now the house was in sight again. I never missed a word of the song, and I maintained my rhythm as I slowed down and parked the twenty-four-foot baby perfectly next to the dock. I was singing and dancing as I strutted over to the opposite side of the boat. I slung the bumpers over the edge, and then I grabbed the ropes and threw them onto the dock. With the music still blasting, I was about to step out of the boat onto the dock to tie and secure it when I looked up. *Oh dear mother of God,* the entire crew was standing no more than twenty feet from the dock, and they were all staring at me. I sang my last note as "Cherry Pie" ended.

"Livvy, that was totally hot, girl," Scott hollered. Most of the crew were clapping and whistling.

At this point, I was standing there looking quite hopeless, but then I heard the SOB shout from the direction of the barricade, "Talk to me, Livvy. Come on. Max is working on something big. Tell me what you know." My head snapped in Peter's direction. He stepped down into the boat, grabbed my hips, and in one swift move, he pulled me close. Then he cupped my face, capturing it between his strong hands, and kissed me. His lips parted, and good God, so did mine. One of his hands traveled with ease down the side of my body until he located my waist. *Jesus!* My knees buckled. He quickly steadied me by folding both of his arms around my lower waist, closing the already-narrow space between us. The next thing I knew, those dadgum butterflies had totally consumed me. I flung my arms around his neck. Cameras snapped, but I didn't care.

"Damn, Peter. Let her go," David said.

"Shut up, David," Scott howled, "it's 'bout to get good."

Peter slowly freed my waist but only to recapture my face again between his hands. He kissed me softly. The crew whooped and clapped again.

"I'm sorry, Olivia," Peter whispered. "I'm usually more private than what my actions have shown today. I wanted our first real kiss to be special."

"No problem. I'm sorry I didn't have time to put my cover-up on."

A cunning smile skirting across his full lips. "It's a little late now." His hands smoothly eased down my back until they covered where my cheeky swimsuit stopped. "I love your suit, and I am about to kiss you again."

Barely removing my lips from his, I whispered, "They're waiting."

Peter released me, turned to the gang, and asked, "Ready?" David stepped into the boat and gave Emily a hand. Scott hopped in. George held the ropes, then kindly assisted me by placing them and the bumpers into the storage compartments.

I was about to switch the blowers on and start the engine when Scott asked, "You sure you know what you're doing, Livvy?"

"Yeah, Scott, I do." I glanced at Peter and shook my head. "Most of the time." I cranked the music up, slowly accelerated to thirty-five mph, and pointed to the cooler. We anchored at the Rock within ten minutes.

Scott and David stood at the front of the boat looking up at the Rock, and said simultaneously, "No way."

"I saw it with my own eyes," Peter said.

The guys were relaxing in the lake, hanging onto foam noodles and enjoying their cold beverages. Emily and I were sunning on the swim platform, having a girl talk, when Beyoncé broke loose over the speakers. I grabbed Emily's hand. "Come on." Emily was like me; she liked to dance. Earlier, she had entered a drinking competition with David—and she had won. So that girl had some more moves. When our song ended, Peter asked if I would dance with him. "That could be arranged," I said flirtatiously. I dove off the front of the boat and swam to the Rock.

I never once looked back as I conquered the climb. I looked down. Everyone had rejoined Emily on the boat and was standing on the front, waiting. I proudly made my stance, pushed off, tucked, flipped twice, and dove straight in. I swam to the platform on the back of the boat and was about to lower the ladder when Peter reached down and snatched me out of the water. As soon as he lowered me, he whispered, "Olivia, you are amazing, but do you really need to prove it by jumping from that damn rock?" Then he kissed me, oh-so sweetly.

"Not anymore," I sighed.

After a light lunch on the boat, we lifted anchor and I gave them a tour of the lake. Soon, Scott was hungry again, so we put in at Frankie's Marina for pizza. They had more beer, and I was becoming quite the babysitter. Even though it was only nine o'clock, I decided it was best to leave Frankie's and take them to their condos.

Of course, they needed escorting up the stairs and inside.

When I returned to the boat, Peter was right where I had left him, laid back with his feet propped up and singing loudly. He continued to sing until I pulled into the boathouse and secured the boat.

During a serenading intermission, I said, "I hope they don't all have hangovers tomorrow. Sam will kill me."

Peter laughed. I fished for his hand to help him step out of the boat. "I hope I don't have one either," he slurred. Then he stopped on the pier, looked up at the sky, and pointed. "See the full moon? It is beautiful, but it doesn't compare to you."

"Come on, Peter, let's go inside."

I walked with him to his room and suggested he take a shower. He followed me into the bathroom and apologized for drinking too much. "It's all right. I should have warned all of you what the hot sun, the water, and a lot of beer can do. Besides, you've taken care of me. Do you remember?"

"Yes. I also remember the dance and the invitation you gave me."

"What invitation? Shawn never mentioned an invitation. What are you talking about?" I panicked.

"You asked me to come with you to your room, because you needed to lose something, and you were certain I was the guy that could help you."

My mouth sprang open. *Crap. No. Double crap!* I closed my mouth and hung a towel on the hook. I stepped into the shower and turned it on. When I stepped out, Peter was untying the strings on his trunks. I placed my hand over his, stood on my tiptoes, and kissed him. "I had a good time today."

Peter said he still wanted to talk to me, but he thought he should wait until tomorrow.

"Do you need anything else?"

"Only you." He was now removing his swimsuit.

As I made a quick exit to my bedroom, my phone rang. I took a deep breath and answered. "Hello, Max."

"How are you doing, Livvy?"

"Good. According to a hound reporter on the set today, you had a good day too."

"I suppose. Have you seen the news today?"

"I prefer not to watch the news. You know that."

"Take a look if you get a chance."

"Max, I'm going to ask you something. Please answer. I need to know."

"I'll try."

"After your contract ends with Global, will your line of work change?"

He didn't answer. I took a deep breath. "I didn't want to leave New York when I visited you in May. I wanted to stay, and if you will say what I need to hear, I will wait." He still did not speak. "If you think you will change your career path, I need to know now. That day on the plane you said you would walk away. I'm not asking you to that, but please tell me what your plans are." I began to cry. "Please say something."

"Livvy, I knew you fell in love with me, even though you would never say it." He paused. "I saw you look at Peter exactly how you once looked at me. But I will never ask you to wait for me."

He still had not answered my question. I tried again. "Will your line of work change when your contract is up, Max? Answer me."

"I don't know."

"You're a stubborn ass, Max Spencer. I need a yes or a no."

"Frustrating, isn't it?" he said.

"I will always love you, Max." He sighed. "But I think you could be right about Peter." I cried and paced the floor, waiting for him to respond.

"I know I am right, Livvy. But I have a question for you. When did you realize you loved me?"

"Max, please."

"When?"

"The morning you came to the Four Seasons and asked me to go to Paris and London with you...I'm pretty sure it happened when you kissed me."

"Thought so," he said flatly. "You are easy to love, Livvy Hunnicutt, but you are so damn stubborn. Peter is a good man. But I will ask you to stay true to yourself, because you are special. Do not ever forget that. I will not call you as often, but if you need anything, call me. One more thing—I love you in red." Remembering what he did with my red panties, I inwardly smiled. "But the first picture of you standing in knee deep water, wearing the ocean-blue swimsuit bottoms with one arm across your breasts," he sighed and carried on, "your hair wet, and beads of water dripping from your tanned body, with the orange and blue backdrop...that one is my favorite."

"Mine too."

We hung up without saying good-bye.

After I composed myself, I checked on Peter. His bedroom door was open. I quietly entered. He was asleep. I carefully removed the papers that were on his bed, laid them on the night chest, and pulled the covers over him. As I reached to turn the lamp off, I leaned over him, and closing my eyes, I softly kissed his lips and whispered, "Please don't hurt me, Peter."

CHAPTER 30

The next morning I included two Advil on Peter's breakfast tray. I tapped on the open bedroom door. I heard the shower running, so I sat the tray down on the foot of the bed and walked out. I was dressed and waiting in the great room. I thought the car might be a more pleasant ride for Peter this morning.

I was correct, because he walked out of his room, wearing only a towel, and said, "Just checking." I laughed, but he vanished as quickly as he had appeared.

He reappeared, dressed for work, and we left. "I enjoyed the waffles."

"Thanks. I'm going to Auburn for the day. Give me at least an hour heads-up." I parked in my usual spot. Peter opened his door and then immediately closed it again.

"I cannot think about this all day," he said. The next thing I knew, both of his arms were around me, and mine around him. Good God, my heart was pounding, my head was swimming, and my palms were sweating.

He pulled away from my lips. "I want to take you on a date tonight." He got out of the car.

After a visit to the spa, I had only one task left on my agenda. I changed into riding gear and grabbed an extra helmet in case Peter called before I finished my outing.

I rode for nearly an hour, pulling over at a country store to check my messages. I had just one, and it was Peter. I glanced again at my watch. He had called thirty minutes ago.

I pulled up to the barricade and when George realized it was me, he smiled and let me through. I parked, dismounted, and placed my helmet on the seat. I released my hair from a low ponytail and shook my head to fluff my hair. Before I turned around, Scott yelled, "Peter, man, you had better ask her, or I am."

Oh God, what if Peter doesn't like to ride? After all, he didn't handle the diving thing very well, seemed surprised about the Sea-Doo, and appeared to worry about me driving the boat. I took a deep breath and leaned against my bike, sporting my Tory aviator sunglasses. Trying to look cool, I asked, "All set?"

Peter pointed to my Harley. "Does that thing belong to you?"

I grinned and traced the seat with my fingertips. "Yes, it does." I tossed the helmet to him. "Get on. I'm taking you for a ride."

Peter put his homework in the saddlebag and ran his hand through his voguish hair. I pulled my hair back once more and gave Peter a hand, adjusting the neck strap to his helmet. I straddled the bike, and when my butt hit the seat, I lifted the kick and nodded for him to get on. He swung his leg over like a pro and sat down. I turned on the microphones, and music from the XM radio streamed through the tiny speakers in our helmets. I tested our microphones. "Doing okay, Peter?"

"Fine." The microphones passed the test. But I sensed a hint of irritation in his tone. *Guess he doesn't like to ride after all.*

Peter was quiet. But with several miles behind us, I felt his legs relax. I increased the volume on the radio. Train's catchy tune, "Save Me, San Francisco," pinged in my ears. I began to sing and seconds later, Peter joined in. When we arrived at the lake cottage, Peter got off my bike and asked, "Is there anything more I should know about you?"

"Nah. I'm going for a swim." As I walked through the house, I scaled back my clothing. I dropped my towel poolside and dove in wearing boyshorts and a sports bra. When I came up for air, Peter was standing next to the pool.

I swam to the steps and walked out of the pool. I felt my blood sugar was dropping, and fast. I grabbed the towel and wrapped it around me. "Olivia, what's wrong?" I couldn't find the words to answer him, so I gestured toward the house and continued to walk inside. As I climbed the stairs, I could feel my movements slowing. I made it to the top of the landing and leaned against the wall. I felt myself sliding down. "Olivia," he shouted.

Peter quickly poured a glass of juice, but I was unable to drink it, even with him holding the glass. He picked me up from the floor and quickly laid me on the sofa. "Olivia, I am getting the injection."

I was sweating and could feel myself twitching slightly every few seconds. Peter was back. He shouted, "Come on, Olivia," as he gave me the injection in my thigh.

I smelled the sweetest scent. I knew she was with me. At that moment she appeared. She was standing beside Peter. She was so close, I wanted to touch her. She was glowing with an unimaginable bright yet soft light. My angel was smiling, and then she spoke.

"Olivia, you are strong, and you will overcome this."

Peter shouted, "Come on, Olivia!" He was dialing the phone. "Come back to me. I love you! I love you, Olivia. I've been trying to tell you for days that I have fallen in love with you."

Peter was holding me in his arms as he shouted the address to someone. I could not speak, but I heard another voice, echoing. It was Robert. Peter asked him to get the doctor next door.

My angel was still with me. I stopped twitching. I was trying to speak, but I could not utter a word. My angel moved; now she was beside me. Peter looked up. *Oh God. He can see her.*

I heard Dr. Woodland and Robert speaking. Dr. Woodland was listening to my heart, and now he was looking into my eyes. Peter glanced at me, and then he glanced at my angel repeatedly. He answered every question Dr. Woodland asked him. She vanished.

Finally I could speak. "I'm okay. I don't need an ambulance." Peter was holding my hand, and Robert was kneeling beside me as Dr. Woodland made a call to cancel the ambulance.

"Livvy, I came to check on you to make sure you were all right from your accident a few days ago," Robert said. "I haven't been able to reach you by phone."

"God, I'm sorry, Robert. I forgot I had your number blocked. I will take care of it immediately."

Dr. Woodland asked me a battery of questions, but ended up attributing this incident to heat and stress from the automobile accident. He insisted I get a checkup from my personal doctor first thing in the morning. Dr. Woodland was on his way out when he told Peter to call if he needed anything. He bent down and pulled a copy of the swimsuit issue from the box that had remained beside the front door.

"Take it with you, Dr. Woodland," Robert said. "Livvy is on the last eight pages. Come back when she feels better, and she'll autograph it for you."

Dr. Woodland held it up and shook it. "May I?"

"Sure." I weakly grinned.

Peter and Robert exchanged phone numbers, and Robert left.

Peter pulled me onto his lap, "Olivia, you are wet. Come," he said, helping me stand, "let's find you something dry." I removed a lounge outfit from my drawer and shivered due to the low blood sugar. I decided to take a hot shower. "I'll stay downstairs until you are finished," Peter said.

The hot water made me feel weary. I began to cry. Peter had said he loved me, but after all this drama, he wouldn't want me. And how could I blame him? I knew better than to allow this to happen. I didn't need anyone to complete who I was, nor was I afraid to be alone. After I spoke to Max last night, I thought I knew what my feelings were for Peter. But I was certain of them after this morning. I no longer asked God for things, and if I wanted to ask him for Peter, it was too late. I sat in the tub with hot water from the showerhead spraying over me.

My heart was breaking once again, and I had no power to stop it. "Oh God," I pleaded. "What do you want from me?"

Peter knocked on the door. I answered, but apparently he didn't hear me because he entered. "Are you all right?"

I tried to answer him, but only tears came this time. Peter reached into the shower, turned the water off, and draped a towel around me. "Livvy, I'm going to help you up." *He called me Livvy for the first time.*

As I stood, he pulled me close to him while I cried uncontrollably into his chest. He swooped me up in his arms and carried me to my bedroom. "Peter, I'm sorry about what happened."

He sat me on my bed and handed me my clothes. He turned and faced the wall as I dressed. I finally stopped crying, and we sat on my bed together while I ran a brush through my wet, tangled hair. Peter took the brush from my hand and laid it on my night chest. He held me again. "Livvy, I planned for us to have our first date tonight. I'll cook for you tonight, but tomorrow I'm taking you on a real date."

"You called me Livvy." Peter tightened his hold, and we fell back onto the bed. He was kissing me, just as he had on the boat yesterday and this morning. He escaped from my lips but only to discover my neck. He paused, and our eyes connected. He smiled but continued his path down my neck. As he pulled my tank strap over, he kissed my shoulder, and then worked his way back to my lips.

He slowly rolled to his back, but one of his arms remained underneath me. "I don't have enough willpower to control my actions right now. I think I will go make dinner."

"I certainly do not have any willpower."

"Yes, I know. I read the article, remember." Peter went on to say that that was the only reason he'd not made a pass at me sooner. "Oh."

He pulled me on top of him, brushed my hair from my face, and said, "Livvy, willpower is the only flaw you have. However, after we marry, baby, you will not have a single flaw." He hopped up and walked out of my room, never looking back.

I sat up in a panic. *After he* marries *me?* I was in shock. Did he forget what had happened a few hours ago? *I did not frighten him away.* "Oh, thank you, God!" I toasted aloud. "I asked what you wanted from me, but you did something for me."

* * *

We ate dinner on the porch. Peter asked several times how I was feeling. He remembered me telling him that after a serious low blood sugar, I would feel tired. I assured him tomorrow I would feel fine.

Music was playing softly tonight, as always. Peter took our plates to the kitchen. When he returned, he asked for a dance. He kissed me several times during our dance. He kept his emotions contained, but I didn't. He started laughing, because he said he needed to clean the kitchen, when he really just needed a distraction. I sat at the kitchen bar and kept him company while he tidied up. I offered to help, but he refused. As he pressed the button on the dishwasher, he looked up at me and shook his head.

"What?" I wickedly teased.

He joined me at my barstool and hooked his arms around me. "You know what," he cooed as he tucked a loose strand of hair behind my ear and playfully kissed my neck. "Before I told you I was going to marry you, I should have asked if would like to date me." I sprang from the stool into his arms, and wrapped my limbs tightly around him. "Is this your way of saying yes?"

"Oh yes. And Peter, I think we *have* been dating a few days."

"Maybe for you, but for me, it's been longer," he said, popping my butt back on the stool, to take a call. He wandered into the next room. I scooted off the barstool, and when my feet hit the floor, I did a little happy dance. "I have a boyfriend, and he is perrrfect."

Peter snickered. He had caught me in hip-swinging motion. "Nice."

"Yeah, I thought you would like it," I blushed.

"I told my father I would call him later." He laid the phone on the counter and pulled me into his arms. "I have a girlfriend, and she will be completely flawless soon. Now, let's get you to bed. I want you to rest, because tomorrow we have a date."

He walked me to my room, but said he had better not come inside tonight. When he kissed me good night, I fell backward against the wall, because my dang knees went weak. "I cannot say I have ever had that effect on anyone before. Nevertheless, I pray it never changes. Good night, Livvy."

I was thanking God for Peter as I fluffed my pillow. At that moment I realized it was time to let go the bitterness that I had held on to for so many years. I knew I wasn't perfect, and Rae and I had challenges with our health. Today had been a bad day for me. But my life was important, and now my life mattered and mattered to someone whom I wasn't afraid to love. I hadn't told him yet. He said he loved me, but I don't think he realized I had heard him. I was fairly certain Peter saw my angel today, and even that had not frightened him away.

Amazingly, something felt so right about us, even though it was happening extremely fast.

Then it hit me. *He was a freaking movie star. Jesus*! The heck with it, I quickly thought, because it was simply too late to worry about the trivial stuff. I fell asleep.

I awoke, sat straight up in my bed, and gasped. Peter jumped to his feet.

"Livvy, are you all right?"

"What are you doing in here? You should be in bed, asleep. You have to work tomorrow. Were you sleeping in the chair? Why?" Peter didn't answer me. I ran my hands through my nappy hair. *Oh God.* "It's because of what happened this afternoon, isn't it?" I pulled my covers back, slid over, and patted the bed. I told him I would behave, but only tonight. He smiled and was about to lie down when I pointed and asked, "Do you always sleep in pajamas?"

"No."

"Well, don't start on my account." He smiled and pulled the string to his low hip-riding pj's. With little assistance, those suckers fell to the floor.

His head had barely sunk into the fluffed pillow when he scooped his arm around me and pulled me close to him. I rested my head on his shoulder, put one arm across his chest, and threw my leg across him. "You like to cuddle?" he asked.

"I do."

"I never have. But I like it with you."

"Good, because no cuddling could be a deal breaker."

"Well, we cannot have that." He pushed my chin up and sweetly kissed me. "No, we can't," I said, sensing he was not saying what was on his mind. "Peter, I don't want you to live in fear."

"I needed to be in your room with you tonight, not because I was shaken up about what happened today, even though I was. I am here because I have fallen in love with you. God, I loved watching you sleep." He breathed in. "I knew you were someone special the day I saw you in London. I glanced at Max right before I stepped onto the lift. I looked only at you after that."

"Really?"

"Yes. Matt had called me earlier that same morning and told me to watch the news. You were the girl he had taken to lunch. I watched the news all morning. There were a lot of pictures of you, but you had your sunglasses on in every one. Shortly after seeing the two of you, the shooting occurred. Blood covered your face, your hands, your hair, and even your clothes. You were trying to help the man lying beside you by applying pressure to his wound. You were screaming for Max to answer you. You never asked for help. You were only concerned about others. With all of that going on, you were still the most beautiful person I had ever seen." He nuzzled closer. "I was standing in my father's office, and we watched the news together," he said. "We stood less than two feet from the telly—"

I giggled. "Slang for television." I nodded against his shoulder. "My father asked, 'Who is she?' I remember saying, 'Livvy Hunnicutt, and she is amazing.' My father said, 'Probably short for Olivia.' There's another story concerning your name; I will tell you later. I knew that day I had to meet you. I also knew what you looked like, because on the lift, your sunglasses were on top of your head. By that time, I was in the running for the role of Ben Davis. I called my agent and asked him to do what he could to get me the part. He said Victoria wanted me, but you and Teddy—the casting director—wanted Matt. I didn't give up. I asked my agent to call Victoria and ask her if she would speak with me. Michael, my agent, got Victoria's number, but by the time I spoke to her, she said Matt was offered the role only minutes before. Victoria said if things didn't work out with Matt, she would have Teddy call my agent immediately." I smiled, because I remembered Mom saying she had spoken to Peter. "At this point, I knew I wouldn't get to meet you without going through Victoria. When Matt broke his arm, I got a call from Teddy, just as Victoria promised. Within two days, I officially met you."

Peter kissed me softly. "I've never believed in love at first sight until I saw you. The evening we formally met, every head turned when you walked into that room, including mine. When you introduced yourself, I asked you if we had ever met before. Obviously I remembered where, but I needed to know if you remembered. You said you were certain our paths crossed in London. Your eyes spoke before you ever said a word, just as they do every day. There is so much more I want to say to you, but I know you're tired. It can wait."

My words flowed easily.

"Peter, I love you." His arm tightened around me. "I recognized I had feelings for you several weeks ago, but I didn't want to. The morning you kissed me while I was sitting at the breakfast table, I couldn't breathe. In fact, I almost fainted. That same morning of the accident, you kissed me softly once more before you got out of the car, and I did it again. I still tried to fight my feelings, but on the boat, I knew I was in trouble. I was struggling with something, and I needed to…" I had to choose my words carefully. "I was torn. I had to make a decision to wait or find some sort of closure with my past."

"Max?"

"Yes. It wasn't easy, but I hope Max can move on now."

"I hope he can, too."

"Peter, this morning in the car, I was completely consumed by you. I don't know how you softened my heart, but you did. It was as if I had no choice but to allow it. After this afternoon, I didn't believe you would give me a second thought. That's when I broke down in the shower." I was quiet for a moment. "I heard you tell me three times you loved me this afternoon, but I could *feel* that you loved me while you held me in your arms. I'm going to ask you something, Peter. If I were not almost certain of your answer—"

Peter interrupted, "I saw her. She allowed me to see her, but I smelled her first. Her scent still lingers." He took a deep breath. "Livvy, you smell like her."

"Wow, I thought I smelled nice because of my expensive perfume. Guess I can remove that step from my daily routine and save some money."

Peter chuckled. "No, I can smell that too. I mainly smell the angel scent in the early morning hours. Your bedroom always smells like her."

"That was the fourth time I've seen her. My parents have felt her and smelled her, but no one else has ever seen her until today."

He lifted the back of my soft, fitted cami and lightly stroked my back with his fingertips. "Last night, I wasn't asleep when you came into my room. The bed would not stop spinning. You kissed me so sweetly. You taste good, by the way." He nestled his head to mine. "You said, 'Please don't hurt me.' I will never hurt you, Livvy."

CHAPTER 31

I ran my fingers through his hair thinking, *Thank you, Jesus, he's still here.* But wait, crap, the sun was blinding. "Peter, wake up. We overslept." He kissed my forehead, and we both flung the covers back. "Oh dear God! Peter."

He leaned over and smacked me quickly right on my lips. "Well, it is morning, and I held you in my arms all night with your leg thrown across me. Some things cannot be helped. Now hush and get dressed."

"I promise I'm not afraid of you. As a matter of fact, I would be happy to help you out"—I pointed—"with that."

"Thought you were going to behave, Miss Hunnicutt," he said as he cleared the doorway, naked.

"I did last night," I called out, "but all bets are off now, Mr. Weston. You are on your own."

George had saved me a parking spot close to the courthouse in Dadeville. Peter got out and walked around to my side of the car, opened my door, and lent me his hand to stand. I leaned against my car, and he leaned in closer.

"Livvy Hunnicutt, you are my girlfriend, and I am about to kiss you good-bye in front of God and everyone. Hope you don't mind." *No, no, not at all.*

My knees buckled like limp noodles. Peter tightened his hold around my waist and giggled under his breath while he kissed me.

The SOB reporter—who, incidentally, had already been run out of town once—shouted, "Livvy, is Spencer coming to town before he moves to London?"

Peter stepped back slowly and said, "Please come with me." He laced his fingers through mine and told George to follow us and bring his damn gun with him. Peter walked straight to the barricade, pointed to the guy, and said, "Get your ass over here." Peter looked at him, eye to eye. "Max Spencer is a good man, and you need to realize he is a businessman whether you like what he does or not. But obviously you are a freaking idiot, since you haven't noticed Livvy does not date him. But they are friends. Now shut your mouth, or George here is going to shoot your fucking brains out. By the way, the name of the guy who Livvy Hunnicutt dates is Peter Weston. You got that?" Peter shoved the reporter, and he fell on his butt.

Peter took my hand. "Come on, baby, we need to get you out of the heat."

"I'll sue you for assault, Weston," the reporter shouted.

"Bring it on, asshole," Peter shouted louder.

Mom walked over and hugged me. Then she stared Peter down. "So you're dating my daughter? Be good to her."

"Always, Victoria."

Scott hollered, "Way to go, Peter. It took you two long enough."

Peter stepped in front of me and asked Mom to forgive him because he needed to kiss someone very special good-bye, and he did.

"Oh, Peter," I whispered, "I liked it when your temper flared—totally hot."

He whispered in my hair, "You need to be quiet."

* * *

My first stop: Dr. Kurt. He gave me a complete checkup and determined what I had thought: the heat likely caused my insulin reaction late yesterday afternoon. However, he sent blood to the lab, and I would get the results in a couple of days.

I typed a text message to Peter, explaining exactly what the doctor had said. *Wow—totally weird*, I thought, reporting to someone other than my parents about what a doctor said. I pressed send.

Next stop was the spa. I had to see Danni, but thank God I didn't need anything waxed. She about killed me yesterday. Today was all pleasure, which was a rare thing these days. As I relaxed with my feet in a tub of warm rose-petal water, my phone rang. It was Max. I hesitantly answered, "Hi there."

"I like Peter Weston already." We both laughed. "I saw the news a few minutes ago. I hate I didn't see that in person."

"You would have enjoyed it for sure."

He said he knew he would have a tough time getting over me, but he would. I told him I didn't know if I would ever completely get over him. "Livvy, I am happy for you. You know, when I meet Peter, I'll tell him I saw you first." Max sighed. "But I will also congratulate him."

"Thank you, Max. I will always remember you saw me first."

"I know you will."

"Max, Crosby says you two are okay. Are you?"

"It took a few months, but yeah, we are. He's coming to London in a couple days."

"I'm sorry that I caused—"

"You didn't cause anything, Livvy. We pursued you. I'm boarding the plane now."

"Be safe, Max."

As I arrived on set, I strung my badge around my neck and walked directly into the courthouse. I spotted Peter. I knew what he was about to do; he couldn't care less that Mom and Dad were behind him. Yep, I was right. Peter grasped my face between his hands and kissed me. "Missed you," he said against my lips, "and thank you for texting me about your doctor's visit. Give me your keys. I'm driving." I handed Peter my keys.

Peter couldn't drive—he ran off the road twice. But I didn't criticize his driving, because from the looks of things, he certainly could not tolerate the slightest distraction. When he parked my car in the driveway, I laughed. "Well, it's good to know you have a license, but you need to work on your driving skills. They're not worth a damn."

"You are a smart ass sometimes," he chuckled, "but I like it."

While I unlocked the front door, I told him I had made reservations for us at the Summer House restaurant. I handed him my keys back.

"We're going to continue to work on your driving. By the way, do you drive in London? The day I saw you, I believe you had a driver."

"I live in the city most of the time, so I do not drive. But I do have a car." He popped me on my butt, grabbed my hand, and swung me around. "You are not going to behave, are you?"

"Never. What do you mean? Where else do you live?"

"My parents live in the country. I spend a great deal of time there when I am not working."

"Ohh…okay."

I analyzed my options, thinking the ocean-blue silk was my best choice. That was the same color I wore the night Peter and I had officially met. It was short and not too fitted, with one strap of crunched, gathered fabric over my left shoulder. Jimmy Choo would be needed tonight—the silver ones with four-inch heels.

Danni had covered the bases for hair. I decided to pull and secure it with a few hidden bobby pins and let it lay in soft curls. I wore one silver bracelet and matching earrings, both gifts from Max. After speaking with him today, I didn't think he would mind.

Peter was standing at the top of the stairs. I stood on the first landing with six more steps left on my climb. We both smiled at the same time. I knew at that moment, I wanted to marry this man and spend the rest of my life with him.

His blue eyes were inviting me to join him. I climbed a few steps, stopped, and stared. *How gorgeous he is.* My heart fluttered. No, that wasn't my heart. *Jeez…he hasn't even touched me yet.* Peter wore a white, tailored, but slightly modern-cut shirt, European-cut jacket and slacks, and a large, silk knotted tie. From the looks of his outfit, it was custom made. I climbed nearly to the top and stopped again. His crazy spiked and naturally highlighted hair was nothing but sexy-looking, and I loved it. When I topped the landing, I found myself immediately in his arms.

Peter suggested we leave, because if he kissed me again, we obviously would be unable to keep our reservations.

Dinner was delicious. My favorite was on the menu tonight: pan-seared chicken breast with creamed corn and greens. Peter went with the grouper and loved it.

Peter and I had a problem, though; we could not keep our hands to ourselves. He finally asked our server for the bill. But then he said, "Please don't walk away. Just tell me how much you think it is." The girl looked frazzled and threw a number out there. Peter handed her a wad of cash.

Peter didn't run off the road, but dang, that fifteen-minute drive felt like it took an hour. Peter parked at the front door, taking down a couple of shrubs. He laughed. "I'll call someone to replant tomorrow," he said and hopped out and kicked the door shut. He hurried around the car and flung open my door.

"Come on." He grabbed my hand, barely letting me clear the car door before he closed it. We made a mad dash to the front door. He locked his arm around my waist as he unlocked the front door.

"Push it, Peter." The door swung open. He spun me around when we stepped inside and backhanded the door shut. His hands never left my waist, but his soft lips took mine, wildly causing them to sting under his attack. And I liked it. I pulled at him and his clothing. His designer fat-knotted tie was nowhere in sight. He hoisted up my dress, causing it to tear. I grabbed his jacket and shoved it off his shoulders. He shrugged out of it. He yanked the zipper down on my ripped dress—it fell to my feet. I stepped out.

He took a step back and said, "Perfect." He returned to my lips.

"I'm not," I mumbled on his lips. I moved my hands across his clothed chest until my fingers disappeared into a couple of openings between his buttons.

"What do you mean?" he said into the soft bend of my neck. I snatched his shirt open. Those buttons hit the hardwood floor and scattered. *Will I ever learn patience?* I pulled at the cuff. *Crap, he wore cuff links.* "Pull, they'll pop off," he whispered. I yanked.

"Bruises," I whispered. He shook his arm out of his sleeves, one at a time. I unbuckled and jerked his belt. He tossed his tattered shirt on the floor. We bumped into walls and furniture. He finally picked me up and carried me to the bedroom. He tossed me onto the bed, undressed, and joined me.

Peter found the hook to my strapless bra and unhooked it with one hand. *Okay, I'm impressed.* His hands plowed over my body, with a lengthy halt at my breasts. Each responded quickly to his touch, and I moaned in appreciation. He swept across my panties and then lowered himself between my legs. He slowly tucked one hand underneath me and firmly cupped my bottom. I dug my nails into his back. "Sorry," I sighed.

"Don't be." He exhaled and took my lips captive again. He grabbed my wrists one-handed, pushed my arms above my head, and pinned them there. *Shit.* I bit his lip—hard. "Bend your legs." I did. His erection pressed against me, right there.

"Peter…a condom?"

He kissed me softly once more, then slightly lifted his upper body from mine and rested his weight on his elbows, next to my head. Peter's blue eyes pierced my dark-brown ones. *What? No, don't stop.*

"Your shoes." He moved from the top of me, grabbed my ankles, and pulled me to the edge as he stood. His jacked-up, sexy-crazy hair was poking up in every direction. He raised my leg and trailed his fingers up the outside of it and then back down the inside. "Smooth, Livvy." He unleashed his tongue and followed the same path his fingers took just moments ago. He stopped at the leather strap on my shoe and traced it with his fingers to the buckle, unfastened it, and dropped it on the floor. Then he repeated the process with my other leg and tossed that shoe across the room. He slowly and gently traced the front trim of my underwear. Then kissed me, right between my legs, *there. Oh yeah, score and with a man I love.* His breath felt warm through my lacy panties. I pulled his hair with one hand and tugged my panties with my other.

"No, Livvy. It stays on." *We'll see about that.*

He hovered over my body and kissed me as he ran his hand across my shoulder and stopped at the back of my upper arm. He kissed it softly many times. Then he took my other arm the same way. He trailed down to my abdomen and did the same thing. *He's kissing my bruises.* He moved to my left outer thigh. "Peter." I tried to cover the area with my hand. He slowly stirred toward my hip and gently began to kiss it.

"Livvy," he whispered, "they are hardly noticeable, but I have wanted to do this for so long." When he finished, he came back to my lips. "I love you, Livvy, everything about you, including your tiny bruises. But this," he kissed the dimple on my cheek, "is where your angel must have kissed you when you were born. To me, you are perfect."

I wiggled free enough to sweep my hand down his torso. I stroked him with my fingertips, then tightened my hand firmly around his length. "Ah, Livvy," he murmured. "I can't touch you that way, not tonight. I would not be able to stop. But somehow you will remain a virgin until our wedding day." *What?*

I felt tears sting my eyes, as hard as my sore lips burned. I blinked them away.

"I know you are disappointed, but I promise we will marry soon."

Peter was holding me in his arms with the covers twisted around us when I said, "I love you, Peter."

"I loved you first."

Peter eased the covers down and traced my thong again. "I almost ripped this thing off more times than I can count."

"Peter, we love one another. Please…"

He shook his head. "No, we are waiting." He reminded me he had always been selective when it came to dating and even more so about whom he slept with. "I have never had a one-night stand, nor have I slept with a virgin. I am not sure what the golden rules are with God on this one."

After a few moments of quietness, he said, "Livvy."

"Yeah?"

"My family wants to meet you. Milly called four times today. 'When will you bring her to London?' She thinks you are perfect for me. I asked Tom before dinner tonight, and he gave permission to ask you. Will you go?"

I didn't have to think about it. "Yes." I got tickled. "On second thought, I should play hard to get."

He laughed and pulled me on top of him. "I am telling you, we were meant to be together."

We repeated the same experience we had an hour ago, and dang it, my thong still stayed entirely intact.

"Why are we lying on the floor?" Peter asked. We sat up. The bedding was tangled and strewn across the bedroom, and both lamps were on the floor. "When did that happen?"

I turned to see what he was referring to. We both sat there on the floor, evaluating the situation. "I have no idea." Mom's window treatments were hanging in distress, ripped and drooping on the floor. Peter asked me to call a decorator to have the room repaired.

We threw the covers back onto the bed, and I reclaimed my spot next to him. "You need to check your blood sugar. Your skin feels different." He was right. I was getting low. Peter took off to the kitchen and returned with turkey on whole wheat, cut in half, and a glass of skim milk. I shared.

"I'll be back," I said, wiping my milk mustache away. I had to fetch my toothbrush from downstairs.

Peter was stretched out on his back with his hands behind his head. He said, "Oh, right." I had forgotten my toothpaste. He told me to use his. Getting up, he picked up the tube from the counter and stared at it. "You squeeze from the middle?"

"Uh-huh." I spat in the sink. "Told you I wasn't perfect."

"No, you are," he said as he brushed and spat in the sink. "Tell you what, you can squeeze me anywhere. But the tube?" I stood on my tiptoes and kissed him with toothpaste on our mouths. "You're not going to change where you squeeze it, are you?"

"Nope. Consider me flawed."

"Never, Miss Hunnicutt," he said, spooning up to my backside.

The next twelve days I thanked God every day for bringing Peter into my life and giving him the strength not to run when I was not at my best. I had asked God that day what he wanted from me, and even though he hadn't revealed his request, I knew it was coming.

* * *

In less than a week, we would leave for England, and I was getting nervous. Peter knocked on the shower's glass door. I pushed it open, and he asked if he could join me. I grabbed him by his arm and pulled him inside.

"What if they don't like me, Peter?"

"That's why you have been quiet today." He planted a long kiss on my wet forehead. He removed his drenched clothing and dropped it in the corner of the large shower, pulling me into his arms. "They already love you."

We lay down, and I scooted to the middle of the bed. I plopped my hand on his chest, then propped my chin on it and looked directly at him. We were thinking the same thing. His willpower was low tonight. We both laughed, because I never have any. So I got up and wrapped a blanket around me and told him I would be back. When I returned, I had pj's on. "Like that will help," he said.

I shrugged. "Don't know, but if you want, I could sleep in my room tonight, or we could…make love."

"No, come here. I want to tell you more about my family." I curled up next to him. "I'm sorry I have not shared something with you. However, it has been published for years, and at first I thought you might have known."

He took a deep breath and asked, "Did you know I had an older brother?"

"No…I didn't."

"He died six years ago, unexpectedly, from a brain aneurism. He was only twenty-four." Tears stung my eyes. The sadness in Peter's voice broke my heart. "I miss Edward Brooks every day."

"I'm sorry. I wish I had met him."

"I wanted to tell you about him when we first met, although I knew I wanted to share more with you …other than I had a brother. I needed you to know that my family is not strange, even though we have had strange things happen. I know you will understand now."

He tightened his arms around me. "I was a senior in college. One month before his death, Edward Brooks dashed open my bedroom door in my London apartment. He jumped in my bed, wearing a suit. He told me to break up with the crazy bitch I had been dating for two years, because he had had a dream. He said her name was Olivia, and she had a funny accent."

I wanted to interrupt, but I didn't out of respect. I was interested, but crap—*they* were the ones with the funny accent.

"That was Edward Brooks's only comment that day about his dream. I broke up with that crazy bitch that same evening. I'd already been thinking about it, anyway. The day before he died, we had dinner with my parents. Edward Brooks began to laugh and told my parents about the first dream. But he said he had dreamed again the night before." Peter now had my full attention. He took a deep breath and chuckled. "EB said not only was Olivia crazy hot, but she was smart, too. I mentioned to you that my father and I watched the news the morning of the shooting in his office. That was, of course, after Matt and David had told me about you. That was the day my father said he thought Livvy was short for Olivia. Two seconds later, your full name ran across the bottom of the television. I already knew about your Southern accent, thanks to Matt and David. So, I filled Father in."

I was in shock and told him that was an incredible story, but I was certain it was only a coincidence. "Maybe, maybe not," he said.

"There is one more thing I need to share with you. Your angel is not the first angel I have seen." I now lay completely motionless. "When EB died, our mother had a difficult time. One day I heard her speaking to someone, but there was no one present in the room. I called my Uncle Garrett, who is a physician. But then I felt something. A light breeze swept across the room, and a powerful, sweet scent captivated me. She allowed me to see her, just as your angel did. I was mesmerized and absorbed every word my mother spoke to her. But I could not hear the angel speak. Something happened to Mum that day. She discovered some way to live and laugh, but most importantly, she now cherishes the memories she is left with."

Tears slowly ran down my face, but a smile now accompanied them. As Peter wiped them from my face, I said, "I love her already."

Those were the last words I spoke that night. Peter and I fell asleep with our bodies tangled together.

CHAPTER 33

We had spent the entire morning together, and Peter's silence was bugging me. He's like me—he talked all the time. *Enough of this.* I removed his fork from his hand, tossed it on his luncheon plate, and pushed back. I sat on his lap, and with my arms draped around his neck, said, "Talk to me. What's wrong?"

"We should finish up tonight. However, Patti and Sam would like to reshoot one scene."

"Which one?"

"The last one. It's going to storm tonight."

"What's the problem?"

"I don't want to do it."

"Peter, this is what you do and who you are. If you think I have a problem with it, I don't." He smiled. "Would you prefer I stay home tonight?"

"No, I want you there. Emily better nail it on the first take." He pulled me close and kissed me. "After tonight I don't want to ever kiss anyone other than you for as long as I live. I'm thinking I'll change directions and do kick-ass action films or work in the office with my father. He would like that."

"Don't worry—just do it. We can talk about that other stuff later."

Peter parked my car in our usual spot, and it was already pouring. We ran holding our umbrellas until we were standing on a wraparound porch. We were on the opposite side of the house from which Peter and Emily would work tonight. Emily walked up to me. "I don't get it. The first one was fine; I just watched it."

I laughed at her. "Be good to Peter, Emily."

"Tell me what you told Peter, so I can get this right. I'm just not feeling it."

I was about to explain my interpretation of the book's ending to Emily when Scott, David, Patti, and Cookie walked up. Peter sat beside me, and Emily pulled a chair up. I took a deep breath and looked down while Peter held my hand. I spoke in a slow and moderate tone, totally unaware that my tiny audience was growing. "Ben leaves the courthouse in a vicious rainstorm…" I spoke for more than ten minutes, and when I looked up, there were twenty people standing and sitting all along the porch railing, staring at me. There was not a dry eye among them.

Sam asked if he could speak with me, and Peter gave him his seat. Everyone scattered into different directions. Sam thanked me for sharing and said he knew exactly what he needed to do now. He couldn't understand how he missed it before.

"Be Jane in the dark," he said. "Emily will do everything else, but I want you for the love scene on the dock. I'll clear the set—only a few people will be around. You're a couple of inches taller than Emily and your hair is longer, but we can fix that. We have enough footage from before that we can manipulate. Give it go, Livvy."

I looked at Peter. "Do it," he said.

I nodded. Sam shouted for Teddy to get the paperwork I needed to sign and hollered for wardrobe.

"I'll see you later on the dock," Peter said.

Scott and David joined me while Carla, the hairstylist, pulled and tugged at my hair. Kathy from wardrobe handed me a fitted tank and a short black lace skirt, plus two-inch platform Prada wedges. *Nice shoes.* As I got worked over, each complimented me on my rendition of the ending with Ben and Jane.

"Are you afraid to try anything?" David asked me.

"I was afraid to love, to fall in love again, but Peter made it easy. So no, there isn't anything."

"Too bad there aren't two of you," David said.

Carla was finished with my hair. I stood up and hugged David. "That was the sweetest thing anyone has ever said to me."

I disappeared for a moment and changed into Jane's cute outfit. When I returned, Scott said, "You seem a little agitated. I thought you weren't afraid of anything."

"I know this isn't a big deal, and Sam will only use part of the footage from the shoot, but I'm uneasy because I don't want to disappoint anyone, especially Peter."

"You'll do great, and when you finish, you can add stunt double for sex to your résumé. Just picture you and Peter alone, and go for it. No one gives a shit. Have a good time, and later, when you two get home, you can, uh…finish up."

I shook my head ruefully. His mouth fell open. "What do you mean, no?"

"Peter wants to wait until we're married."

Scott and David looked at each other. "No way," David said.

"Oh yeah."

Peter came around the porch corner, soaking wet. He grabbed me by the hand. "Come on, baby, I get to get paid to make out with you." Scott and David were laughing as I walked past them.

Emily was about to step onto the porch when I asked, "Where do you think you're going?"

"Inside. I'm cold."

"Bring your ass down to the dock, because I might chicken out." I was soaking wet by the time we were standing underneath the tent, waiting for Sam to give me instructions.

Sam asked me to watch the footage of Peter and Emily that was shot moments ago. Next, he had me watch the complete scene, which was shot over a month ago. Peter had Sam pause the scene and said, "This is where things fell flat. Neither Emily nor I could get it right."

Sam agreed. "This part is where you need to feel what Jane is thinking."

I pointed to the screen in two places. "I'm bigger. This will not work, Sam."

Sam looked down at my chest, then looked around at my butt, and said, "Tell you what—this is the only scene in the film where Emily's breast is exposed, and it only lasts a few seconds. So, Peter, the position of the camera will change here." Sam pointed at the screen. "This will allow us to get more of a side-distance angle of Livvy." Sam was holding his hands up as though they were the camera and pointed back to the screen. "This here is all about how Livvy holds you when you are lying on the dock. Peter, when you pull Livvy's shirt over her head and lay on top of her, make sure your hand is here." Sam pointed at my breast, and then he grabbed Peter's hand and popped it right on top.

My mother closed the gap between us—*totally awkward*—and said, "I'm leaving." *Thank God!* Peter, the crazy fool, still had his hand on my breast. Shit, he was holding it when he told my mother bye. Sam was still talking. "Livvy, only the side of your breast will show, and it will look smaller, I think."

He was staring at my breasts. I was dripping wet and cold. I gently pushed Peter's hand off my boob and crossed my arms over my chest. "Sounds easy enough."

Peter laughed. "Hush; or you and Emily can do the scene."

"No flipping way. I'm going inside," Emily said. "I'm freezing." Her little wet self strutted off. "Thanks, Livvy. I still don't know what the hell Sam wanted from me."

Patti shouted, "Closed set tonight, guys." People scattered in the pouring rain.

Peter and I were waiting when we heard someone shout, "Take one." Peter's expression changed immediately. He was now Ben Davis, and this would be a close-up of him. Not one person would ever see my face, but I gave Peter what he needed. The scene was a wrap, but dang, we didn't stop.

Someone cleared his throat and dropped a couple of towels beside us. "Livvy Hunnicutt, is there anything you can't do?" Peter cooed.

* * *

The next day, I invited Scott, David, and Emily over for post-wrap breakfast, which turned into lunch. Emily said rumors were floating around that David had all but shacked up with the set stylist.

In turn, David inquired about the rumors that Scott and Emily had had a fling.

"Yep," Scott said.

Emily laughed, "Lasted what, Scott—two weeks?"

"Sounds about right," he answered shortly. He was playing Xbox.

"Well, David?" Peter asked.

He laughed. "Great girl. No depth. But yeah, about a month. She left this morning."

"How did I not know this?" I said.

"I was there every day," Peter said, "and I didn't have a clue."

When we arrived at my parents' home, Peter and my dad dashed out to the courtyard. Mom and I set the table for dinner. "Livvy, I could not be more pleased that you are happy. But if Peter holds your breast in front of me again, I am going to smack him, regardless of who placed his hand there."

Spying out the window, I reminded her it was her fault—she had brought him here.

What on earth? Dad hugged Peter and came inside, but Peter remained in the courtyard. He was on the phone. Dad mumbled, "Ah... he'll be in shortly. He has a few calls to make."

Twenty minutes passed, and Peter was still in the courtyard. When he came inside, he wrapped his arms around me and kissed me in front of my parents.

"Do not touch my breasts again, because Mom will smack you," I whispered.

"May I later?" he whispered back.

"Maybe."

After dinner, I took Peter by the hand and went to the piano. I stroked the keys and began to sing. Mom and Dad moved to the sofa and listened. When I finished, I told Peter he would not hurt my feelings if he didn't like it or if it wasn't what he needed for the film.

"No, Livvy, I like it, but how—when?" Peter answered his own question: "Last night, on the dock, in the rain..."

"You inspired me, Peter Weston."

Peter played the piano better than me, so I scooted over, and he began to play. We sang the song twice, and he changed a few notes but no words.

As Peter hugged Mom good-bye, he apologized for not removing his hand more promptly last evening. Dad overheard and insisted on knowing what Peter was referring to. I pointed to Mom, because without a doubt, she needed to sugarcoat Peter's blunder. We left in a hurry. "Livvy," he said, pulling out of my parents' drive, "we won't be flying commercial. You can bring anything you want."

"Don't charter a plane. We can fly with Delta. I like them. But I do prefer first class for a long flight, only because my legs hurt. We think it's due to my meds. I'll purchase my own ticket."

He glanced over at me. I told him to keep his eyes on the road. "I am not chartering a plane. I own a jet. But even if I didn't, you would not purchase your ticket."

"You're an actor. Why do you own a jet?"

"It seemed like a good investment; besides, I can't keep my hands off you for that long. We'll need the privacy."

I smiled, but I was not quite convinced by his answer. "But you're an actor, and you're only twenty-eight. You shouldn't need a jet. A plane, maybe, something like a Cessna or Piper." Peter laughed. "What does your father do?" I blurted out.

"He owns a business."

I already knew that. "Successful?"

"Umm...yes."

"What does 'umm' mean?"

He changed the subject, a smile widening across his face, and said his family was excited about meeting me. Then he pursed his beautiful lips together and said he was sorry, but he could not change her mind. I asked Peter what he was referring to. "Mum—she is having a party the evening after we arrive. She wants to introduce you to everyone. I asked her not to overwhelm you."

"I like small parties—you know that."

"Yes, I know."

"Peter, thank you for owning a jet," I said, as I rubbed his leg, then leaned over, growled, and nibbled at his ear.

"You could care less about the jet."

This was our last evening at the lake, and it saddened me. We sat on the deck and stargazed. That's when he asked, "Are you okay, I mean, about leaving?" I told him I couldn't wait to start making more memories with him in England. He promised me we would split our time between England and here, because we both loved our families.

* * *

The following day we packed, and for the first time, I took Peter to my little house in Auburn. He told me my home looked just as he had imagined and smelled like my angel. While Peter loaded my bags in my car, I went back inside. I took one last look around and thought, *Life will never be the same.* I smiled and turned the key to lock my door for what I suspected might be the last time.

We were spending the night with my parents. I showed Peter to a guest room. He opened the walk-in closet door. "Artwork from Paris, still crated. I'm familiar with that gallery."

"Gifts from Max. He wouldn't take them back."

"We'll hang the paintings in our home, and when he visits, he'll know what they meant to you."

I felt the tears pool in my eyes. "Thank you, but we do not—"

He interrupted me. "Max and Crosby are your friends. And I am guessing Tucker might be related to you soon. Your relationships with them are different than anything I have ever experienced, but I'm good with it. I also have a feeling that before long, you and Robert will become friends again like you once were. I want to get to know each of them. Besides, I love great art. We have that in common, remember?"

Peter told me I needed to walk out of his bedroom, or Victoria would certainly smack him later.

I asked for a good-night kiss. He shook his head and did a silly little finger-wagging thing. "I can't. I know my limitations." I blew him a kiss as I walked out.

The next morning, my phone beeped. A text from Crosby: *We can't wait to meet him!*

I texted Crosby: *Thank you. We talked about you guys last night. He feels the same way.*

He texted back: *Love you.*

I texted: *You too!*

I could hear Peter showering. Oh, how I had missed him in my bed last night. I dressed in a lightweight summer pantsuit and Louis Vuitton four-inch, tan, ankle-strap sandals. When I joined everyone upstairs, Peter walked across the room to kiss me good morning. "You look beautiful this morning."

"Peter, Livvy is always beautiful." Dad smiled and winked at me.

We ate a quick breakfast, and my parents drove us to the local airport.

When we arrived, we pulled through the back gate. His dang jet was bigger than Max's.

"Nice jet you have, Peter," Dad said. Peter thanked him as the jet engines hummed.

"Thank you for everything, Mom," I said, watching her fight back tears.

She shook her head. "Livvy, you are an amazing young lady, and it would have happened regardless of me."

"Mom, you never said what photo you liked the best."

"They all are beautiful. But, darling, you melted my heart in the one in red, with your hands behind your head, laughing. It reminds me of how you laughed when you were a little girl." A twinge struck my heart, knowing Mom was remembering a time before diabetes and Addison's. I always laughed then. I was glad I had my joy back.

Daddy hugged me, then Peter, and said, "You know what I told you."

"I will keep my promise, Tom. We'll call you as soon as we land."

As Peter and I boarded the plane, I couldn't help but laugh. The crew of four was scratching their heads, not at all concerned with where to put my luggage, but probably wondering why anyone would need all that shit. They had my Louis Vuitton luggage store lined up, and it looked ridiculous. Peter looked back over his shoulder to see what I was laughing at, and he started laughing too. "I'll give it to him. Max has excellent taste."

Peter removed my bag from my shoulder, and we walked to two large leather seats. I glanced out the window as I sat down, and my parents were leaning against the car. My dad had his arm around my mother, who had her head lying against his shoulder.

Peter introduced me to Carolyn, the flight attendant. She asked if she could get us anything. I assured her I was fine. "Carolyn, Livvy is diabetic. We'll need a snack at ten and lunch around twelve thirty," Peter explained.

Once the plane was in the air, Peter stood up and led me to what I thought was a bathroom—but oh no, it was a bedroom.

I smiled and asked, "Can I become a member of the mile-high club?"

"Hell, no. But when we get married, we both will join."

"You've never had sex on your plane?"

"No, Livvy. You are the only girl who has ever flown on my plane."

"Good, Mr. Weston. I'm glad I am first!"

After a little tomfoolery, we returned to the main cabin, where a snack was waiting. Peter was chatty. He said we would stay in his apartment in London that night and shop in the morning. Then we would leave for the country and spend some time there. He laughed and said, "I need supervision."

"We do need supervision, because I do not want to wait any longer, and I am totally in love with you. However, if you deny me, I will definitely continue to misbehave, Mr. Weston."

He was quick. "I am totally in love with you, Miss Hunnicutt, but we are waiting. I asked your father for permission to ask you to marry me. He gave me his blessing, but I need to get a couple of things in order, because when I formally ask you, I want my timing to be perfect."

"You asked Dad? I'm with you. I'm not going anywhere. If you would just sleep with me, you can take your time about marrying me."

"No. I am marrying you."

"Well, then, you had better get a move on, or I will need to get acquainted with Bob, because I cannot take this anymore."

"I am going to be your first, not that. We will play with Bob later, and anything else you want." My mouth gaped open. "I mean anything, Miss Hunnicutt."

"Have you ever…you know, played with…things?"

"No. But I didn't like to cuddle either, until I met you."

"Oh—good. Well, at least touch me, like I touch you when we fool around."

"I can't, and that's different."

"No, it's not."

"Yes, it is. If you knew the things I wanted to do to you."

"Excuse me?"

"Livvy, your scent alone drives me crazy." *It does?* He traced my upper lip with his finger. "Your lips are crazy soft." *They are?* I bit the corner of my lip. "And you taste so good." *I do?* "Trust me, if I touched you, it would be like starting a wildfire. There would be no putting it out."

I moved from my seat into his lap. "Peter, take your time about proposing. I am looking forward to the day you ask me to be your wife, but I can't promise you that I will behave until then."

"If you behaved, life would be boring. I'm guessing we will never be bored."

I slowly batted my lashes at him and teased his lips with my tongue. "I still want you."

"I know, and I you."

"Do that thing," I said, slipping off my shoe.

"You know the first time I did this to you, you nearly bucked me off the bed."

His fingers moved across my ankle and then my big toe. I knew it was coming. Suddenly, he pressed his nail near the inside of my big toe, making the top of my head tingle. He dug his thumb deeper into the pad of my foot, but as he combed past the center of my foot, he pulled back on the pressure, lighting the sensation. When he hit the spot between the center and heel, close to the inside of my foot, he nailed it. I about came unglued. How in the hell can you feel that *there*? Whew, talk about making the little man in the boat stand up. I dug my nails into his shoulder. "Again?" he asked. I bit his lip and kicked off my other shoe.

"Shit, Livvy," he said when I clawed into back. With his eyes heavy and voice low, "You want me to touch you, baby?"

"God, yes."

"I'm about to—carefully, with these." He held up two fingers. "Let's go to the back."

Peter had his shoes and my pants off before got to the back of the plane. He pushed me backward. I fell across the bed. He hooked my panties with his pointers and peeled them off fast. He pulled me by my ankles until my behind was near the edge of the bed. "Keep your knees bent and don't move." He kneeled on the floor, firmly ran his hands down my stomach, and said, "You are so perfect." He leaned and kissed where his hands had been, but didn't stop until he kissed me *there*, for the first time with no barrier of fabric separating his lips from my flesh. The feeling was better than I could have ever imagined. He licked his two fingers and touched me where I still tingled from his warm kiss and playful foot massage. When I opened my eyes, he was watching me as his continued his smooth touch and careful caressing. I let go the bedding that I had been clenching tightly and slowly pushed them over my clothed breasts to my naked stomach. Wanting him, I reached for his shoulders. "No, I want to watch you. Let go, baby," he said. He then kissed my stomach, cupped me solidly between my legs, and shoved his other hand under my top and into the cup of my bra. He was watching me squirm with every squeeze, kiss, and eye-rollin' throb my body encountered.

"Peter," I moaned as I melted in his hands.

"Livvy," he said, pulling me into his arms, "I'm so ready to have you." I tugged at his belt. "Easy now. We're still waiting."

* * *

After lunch, another snack, and a movie starring Matt Bartlett, the pilot announced we would land in ten minutes.

I reached for my bag, and Peter said, "Leave your bags. Bradford will get them."

"Who's Bradford?"

Peter pinched his lips together and did that little finger-wagging thing as we stepped on the ground. "Have I not mentioned Bradford?"

"No." Two black Mercedes sedans were parked next to the plane.

"Uh, yeah, Bradford will take us home, but maybe you can choose a couple of those bags." He pointed. "We can send the rest of your luggage to the country with Hugh." He hugged me. "I promise your closet will be larger there." *Bradford and Hugh? He's up to something.*

I pointed to two bags. I knew I was missing something as I stared at the two men dressed in black and white. I saw no guns, though, so I was good.

I recognized the building immediately when Bradford stopped the car near the entrance. Bradford opened the car door, but Peter stepped out and reached for my hand. As we got into the elevator, he asked, "Livvy, are you all right?"

"Perfect. I had a flashback, that's all."

"Of Max?"

"No. You, Peter. The day I saw you on this elevator, you were wearing a black cashmere coat and a gray sweater. Oh...how I love Prada. The stitching around the front pockets on your jeans gave that one away. However, if I had known what the simple back pockets underneath your coat looked like, I would have definitely said hello, because, baby, you can rock a pair of jeans." I sighed. "Your Burberry cashmere scarf, not the traditional pattern—this one more gray—was draped loosely around your neck. In your left hand, you were holding your sunglasses, very nice, by the way. Tom Ford, I believe. I liked your leather boots too, and from the clean design, I am assuming they were Gucci. I noticed your coat sleeve was caught on the band of your watch. It was Cartier. The one with the thick, black rubber band. You've worn it a few times since. But I must say, the GMT-Master you are wearing today, I like just as well."

Peter listened to every word. The elevator opened, and he turned and kissed me. "I think maybe we fell for each other at the same time."

Peter unlocked the door and held it open as I walked inside. "Welcome home, Livvy."

I dropped my small bag. "Please tell me this is real."

"I was about to ask you the same thing." We stood in the foyer and held each other. He took a deep breath. "I knew you were the person I wanted to spend the rest of my life with the second I laid eyes on you. But when we first met, you seemed cynical and afraid. You changed."

"I told you, Peter, you got to me."

"I need to show you around, but I'll save our bedroom for last. I'm feeling weak right now." Peter held my hand as we walked. "We can change anything. Or if you hate it, we can purchase a new place. I want you to be comfortable, but most of all, I want you to feel at home."

After the luxuriousness of the jet, I knew his home would be awesome. The second floor hosted three spacious bedrooms and two large baths, although Peter wasn't kidding about the closet space—they were small. On the main level, another full bath joined his study. The bookshelves were lined with books, old and new. A wood-planked desk with thick metal legs sat strongly facing a large window in the center of an airy white-walled room. In the far corner of Peter's study was an accent table, which divided a pair of contemporary tufted brown leather chairs, with saber legs. I loved the living room—it was large, but the fireplace and the refurbished light-but-warm wood flooring made the room feel cozy. A commercial-style kitchen had every detail a cook could desire. The narrow but long dining room had doors that opened to a large veranda. His home was beautiful. It was airy, modern and just sexy. And Peter's taste in art was definitely à la mode.

I was staring at a light fixture, tilting my head to the left and then to the right, trying to figure out what it was supposed to be. I looked up to the ceiling. Next I leaned over the balcony and looked down to the first floor. I could tell Peter was watching me, but I didn't care. I heard Bradford come in and put my bags into *our bedroom*. I liked the sound of that. "We can change the fixture," Peter said. I didn't comment right away, because I was still trying to figure out what the purpose of the thing was.

I found a switch and flipped it up and down. Now I was thinking not only was that thing god-awful, but it also didn't work. I reached out to touch it, and suddenly Peter flipped it on. I jumped backward and shouted that unladylike F-word.

"I'll call a decorator to meet with you. I've never liked it, either."

That light fixture looked new and probably cost more than my ML350, but it was the ugliest damn thing I had ever seen. I used to guard my heart like Fort Knox. Well, that freaking thing could light up Fort Knox. "Is there anything else you would like to change? Or would you rather move?"

"No, I love your home. And I'm sorry that I do not like that. But it's ugly."

He kissed me. "*Our* home."

I was starving and needed to check my blood sugar. Peter reminded me that he had not been home in more than two months. He said he usually popped in a few times while working, but he had wanted to spend the days he had off with me. Luckily, the housekeeper had stocked the kitchen with basic items.

We ordered dinner, and I offered to go with Peter. He suggested I stay put and get familiar with the place. I thought Peter had left, so I jumped in the shower. He knocked on the open bathroom door, then did that silly, finger-wagging thing. "I forgot something." He stuck his head in the shower and kissed me. When he let me go, dang it, I almost fell. He chuckled as he walked out. "God, I hope that never changes."

I wrapped a towel around myself and opened the closet door. I now shared a closet; that was a weird feeling. My clothing choices were limited, because most of my bags had been sent to the country with Hugh. Who the hell was Hugh, anyway? Enough mystery. I grabbed my computer bag. I was going to do it. I was going to Google Peter Weston.

I decided to dress first. Barefoot for sure. The yellow chiffon sundress would work. I pulled my hair up into a messy ponytail and slapped on a bit of makeup.

I went to plug my computer into the outlet. Shit. I needed an adaptor.

Peter's computer bag was next to mine, but I couldn't Google him from his own computer. That wouldn't be cool. I couldn't use my phone, either—that sucker was dead. I needed a converter or a new cord. I was in the midst of my electronic issues when I heard voices.

I looked over the balcony, beyond that ugly chandelier, and shouted, "Oh my God, Max!" Peter and Bradford followed, carrying bags from the restaurant. I met Max in the living room. Before I realized it, I smacked a kiss on the side of his face.

"It's good to see you too." I asked about Claude, Shawn, and Martin. "They're probably in the hallway by now."

I glanced at Peter. "This is your home. Invite them inside," he said. Max followed Peter into the kitchen. I fetched the babysitters. They were on my barefoot heels and did not miss a step as they followed me inside. I introduced everyone; Peter and Shawn already knew each other, of course.

Martin told me I sounded sassier than ever, and Peter assured him I was. I asked Martin if he was keeping Max out of trouble, and he said he was, but Max kept him on his toes. "You know, Martin, Max is important to me. I am counting on you. Well, actually, I'm counting on all of you."

Shawn said he had bought a Harley. "There's nothing like it." *You betcha.*

The guys exchanged phone numbers and set a lunch date. Max said he spoke to Crosby and Tucker an hour ago. I nodded and started to say, "I, um…um…" My voice trailed off. I turned to get glucose tablets from the kitchen drawer, where I had placed them an hour ago. My sugar was dropping and fast.

"Livvy, are you all right?" Max asked.

Martin touched my arm. "She's clammy."

"Pale too," Claude said. Peter immediately poured a glass of juice, popped a straw into the glass, and sat me on the counter. I leaned against him while I drank the juice.

"Hey," Peter whispered, pushing my chin up, "are you okay?"

"I am," I said. His eyes were piercing mine. "Thanks, everyone," I said without looking around. "That sucker happened fast. I'm fine now." I touched Peter's cheek and nodded to reassure him.

Peter and I walked the fellas to the door, and Max said, "Call any one of us if you need anything. We will be in London until January."

Peter pulled a dining chair out.

"Sit, please. I will bring dinner to you." I sat. He picked up our empty plates from the table. "I like Max."

"Peter, I'm fine now. Please let me help."

"I got this one." He continued to remove the food from the takeout boxes and arranged it neatly on our plates.

Dinner looked delicious: salad with a cucumber dressing, some kind of fish in a caper sauce, and two vegetables, both green. Starches run my blood sugar up, so tonight it was roasted broccoli and crisp, steamed green beans. I watched Peter open a bottle of wine. "I understand why you love him." *What?* Peter placed the glasses on the table and poured the white wine.

"I do love Max, but I'm not *in* love with him…anymore." I reached across the table and touched his hand. "Does that make sense?"

"Yes, it does." A smile slowly skirted across the face of the sexiest man alive. "Can I get you anything?"

"Your lips." He leaned over and slowly licked his bottom lip, then taunted mine with his. My mouth watered, and my chest rose high with anticipation. He eased his hand around my neck and tugged my ponytail.

"They are yours…take them." And I did. "Now eat," he said.

Somewhat composed, I picked up my fork. "Dinner looks wonderful, Peter. Thank you."

"My uncle Garrett also lives in this building. He's a doctor. I programmed his number in your phone at the airport, along with Bradford's. I already have spoken to them about your health." Peter paused. "I'd prefer for you not to go anywhere in London alone. Bradford will take you anywhere you want to go, and if there is an emergency, call Max or the babysitters." Peter winked at me. "Actually, your parents requested that you not go anywhere alone and made me promise someone would always be close by. I had to respect their wishes."

I reached over, pulled him closer, and smacked him on the lips. He was chewing his food. "You're a mess," he said. "By the way, that dress is the sexist thing I have ever seen you wear. When I spotted you coming down the stairs, I wanted to show Max the door. You should know by now I am not a jealous man, but damn."

He also said he had let things go too far on the plane, because after I came in his hand and he licked it, he knew now what I tasted like and he would never be able to stop himself again. He blamed his behavior on the altitude.

Well, all I had to say was, "It was one downright bitchin' hour of making out, and baby, sign me up anytime."

Exhausted, I fell asleep that night with my limbs draped across Peter like a worn-out overcoat.

CHAPTER 34

I heard Peter downstairs in the kitchen making breakfast. After I brushed my teeth, I slipped on Peter's shirt, which he had worn last night, and I quietly eased down the stairs. I leaned against the wall and watched him. "Come here." He tugged me closer and sat me on the cool counter.

I gazed into his blue eyes. "I do not have an ounce of resistance left," I said. "I want you so badly that I ache for you, Peter. I know you want us to wait, and it would be wonderful to tell our children that we waited, but I love you."

Peter was kissing the side of my neck when he said, "This is not easy for me either, you know that. I want to do this right. I want it to be perfect. You said the first two times I kissed you, you stopped breathing. Livvy, I stop breathing every time you walk into a room, much less when you touch me, so I cannot imagine what our wedding night will be like." Peter took a deep breath. "Did you say children?"

"Ah…you caught that."

"How many?"

"Four." *Oh, shit. Maybe I should have mentioned this before now.* Peter ran his hand through his sexy morning hair. "My doctor suggested I birth no more than two," I weakly said. He nodded. Might as well say it. "But I would also like to adopt." Peter grinned from ear to ear. *Okay, we're good.* "You had better marry me fast, Mr. Weston."

I hopped down from the countertop and told Peter I was taking a cold shower. I grabbed a slice of toast and took it with me. I all but stomped out of the kitchen. He shouted he needed a cold shower too, but he'd wait until I was finished. "Livvy, I promise it will be worth the wait."

I pouted. "Yeah, yeah, I know. You promised soon, though. I'm holding you to it."

"Baby, I know you are."

I flat-ironed my hair and pulled it back into a slick, high ponytail. I dressed up a pencil skirt and blouse with a wide black leather belt and black heels. I was about to gather up my things in the bathroom to pack when Peter stopped me. "No need to pack anything."

"I'll need my makeup."

"Victoria e-mailed me a list of the things you like, and I forwarded it to Ruthie, um…a few days ago."

Ruthie? These people were coming out of the woodwork.

I gathered up my diabetic supplies and tidied up a bit. When Peter came down the stairs, I started smiling. "Bradford is coming up. He'll get your bag," he said. I dropped it.

"Peter, I love your crazy hair."

He folded his arms around me. "Your hair is beautiful too, but I love this." That fool had both of his hands on my behind.

"Good morning, Miss Hunnicutt." Bradford came in, took my bag, and walked out. Within a few minutes, we were sitting in the backseat. "First stop, Harrods," Bradford said.

As we walked through the entrance of the department store, I said, "Peter, what kind of party is this tonight?"

"Cocktail, but not black-tie."

"Okay, I know what I want." I walked into the beautiful dress department and approached the salesman. "I am not familiar with the lines that Harrods carries, but I like Preen, Herve Leger, Milly, and Vera. Please stop me if I mention a line of clothing that you have."

"We have them all, Miss Hunnicutt."

"Oh, thank God! Do you mind? I need a size two in the Preen." I blurted out the style number and added, "You're the best."

"I will get that for you, Miss Hunnicutt." I glanced at Peter. When the salesperson returned holding the dress and asked if there was anything else, I handed him my card.

"No, I am paying. I want you to shop. Get anything you want," said Peter. I smiled and told Peter I had everything I needed. Peter looked at his watch. "Livvy, please shop. You bought one dress, and it took you three minutes."

"Peter, you saw my luggage. If I needed anything, I would shop, but I brought enough crap to dress half of England."

The guy behind the counter was laughing, and Peter shook his head. "Yes, you did. And I bet there is not an ugly piece of clothing in a single bag."

That statement sounded familiar. I kissed Peter right there in Harrods and thanked him for the beautiful dress. "Let's go. I want to meet your family."

Peter said the drive to the country took twenty minutes. When I began to fidget, Peter slid his arm around me. "They already love you."

Bradford turned off the main road. A guard stood next to a lovely cottage. Bradford lowered the window. "This is Miss Hunnicutt."

The man looked at me and told Bradford he had been informed a week ago.

"Livvy, we have seven different security personnel here. All are former military, and they rotate. Each one is meticulous but cordial. They stay in that cottage while they are on duty," he said, pointing to his right.

"Oh," I said. I noticed the sides of the double-hung gate were attached to beautiful stone columns. On the right column was a large black plaque with the words "Weston Hills" engraved in gold letters.

The road was curvy, and the landscape was spectacular. In the distance I saw it. I closed my eyes and mumbled, "Holy crap." I raised my voice. "I think you left out a few details, Peter. That place is not a country house. It's a castle. Who are you?"

"This is my home," Peter answered. "I grew up here."

I remembered he was related to the royal family, but it didn't seem like it had been a big deal. "Somewhat related to royalty" would not explain *this*. "What does your father do?"

"I told you—he owns a business."

I must have looked mystified. He elaborated, "My father owns a large company."

"Be specific." I glanced at Bradford. His eyes were on me from the rearview mirror. "Businesses…my father buys businesses."

"More, Peter."

"We come in, take them apart, keep the divisions we want, and sell off the divisions we do not need." *We? Who the hell is we?* "But mostly we try to keep the entire company and umbrella it under an existing branch of the Weston Company."

"Weston Company, Weston Oil, Weston Banking, Weston freaking everything, even the tutoring foundation is yours," I said slowly. "I played with the children there once."

"I saw you. The day of the shooting. Kim called the office." *What?*

"You're *the* Westons?" I mumbled. Max had mentioned the Weston Company once. Max must know who Peter is. Why didn't he tell me? I never pieced it together. Peter was an actor—I never dreamed of him being anything more. "When you say 'we buy,' you mean *you*, don't you, Peter?"

"Only the interesting ones."

"You do what Max does when you work with your father, but on an even larger scale?"

"Basically, yes."

Bradford stopped the car. "You saw me that day?"

"You were leaving by the time I arrived."

I closed my eyes and mumbled, "I have jumped from the frying pan into the freaking fire." I buried my face in my hands.

Bradford opened Peter's door, and he stepped out. I didn't move. I needed to think. I picked up my bag and dug for my phone. I'd call Martin. He would come get me, and I could figure this out. I hit the power button, but nothing happened. I shook it—still nothing. "May I borrow your phone, please?"

"Give me your hand, Livvy," Peter demanded. I glanced at him and shook my head as I cursed at my phone and tossed the useless thing back into my bag. "I said, give me your hand."

"Give me your phone."

"No—"

"Bradford, I need to borrow your mobile, please," I said, almost in tears.

"Miss Hunnicutt, my battery is…dead." *Liar.*

"Livvy, your hand, now." It seemed I didn't have a choice. The damn car was no longer running, and I was melting in the heat.

I whipped my head around and looked at him. He smiled, but our eyes spoke fear. His said, "She's going to leave me." Mine said, "I have to leave." It was too late. I felt the world that I knew and was comfortable with crumbling around me. I closed my eyes and whispered, "I can't do this, Peter." I moved to the edge of the seat, knowing I was about to cry.

"Open your eyes, Livvy." I did and felt the gravel underneath my foot. "Give me your hand, now."

I stood without giving him my hand and locked my knees. I wasn't moving, not yet, anyway. He reached for my hands. "I'm sorry I did not explain things properly."

"Properly? When were you planning on telling me about all this? And I don't give a shit how you say it."

"Livvy, please." He wiped tears from my face.

"Do my parents know?"

"I told Tom. He assumed you knew."

"I see. You deceived me and my father."

"No. God, no. It wasn't like that. I thought you knew who I was… at first. Then after a while, it just didn't seem important."

Peter leaned close, touching his face to mine. "I love you. I never meant to deceive you. I will get on my knees now and beg for your forgiveness, but please do not give up on me, Livvy. I will spend the rest of my life making you believe in me."

"Peter, I love you. But I need to think."

"Think? Okay. Bradford," he said, without removing his eyes from mine, "take Miss Hunnicutt to our apartment and loan her your mobile. Stay in the guest room until she gives you further instructions." Bradford started the engine. "I have never loved anyone but you. I swear I will do whatever it takes to make us work. You are mine, Livvy." He feather-kissed my lips. "Go think. I will be here."

The gravel crunched under the tires as Bradford circled in front the Westons' home. *Who am I kidding, it's a castle.* Bradford handed me his mobile. I stared at it. *What are you doing, Livvy?* I thought as Bradford pulled onto the long, curvy entrance to Weston Hills. I couldn't help myself; only one thing mattered to me, and that one thing was—"Stop, Bradford," I said, wiping the tears from my own face this time.

"Miss Hunnicutt," Bradford said, waiting for further instructions.

"From here on out, Bradford, call me Livvy. And please turn around." Peter...I loved him, but most of all, I wanted to be with him. *My face.* I flipped my tote upside down on the seat next to me and grabbed a few items for a quick fix.

Peter was pacing the side lawn near the front entrance of the home.

Bradford stopped. Peter halted. I caught my breath, pushed my fear aside, and swung open the door. I reached for Peter's hand and stepped out, smashing my body into his chest, his arms around me where I belonged. I wiped his tears away, then kissed him. "Done thinking so soon?" he asked.

"Yeah. Turns out, it was a complete waste of time. I am yours, Peter Weston."

"Yes, you are," he said, taking my hand again. "You almost gave me a heart attack."

"I tried to Google you last night, but I need an adaptor for my Mac. But you listen to me, Peter McAlister Weston. The first time bullets fly, I will kick your fine butt. Do you understand?"

Bradford chuckled, and Peter playfully smacked him on the back of the head as we walked past him. "I have a feeling you can do anything, Olivia Sue, and kicking my butt is probably one of them." Peter's arm remained around me as we stepped inside his parents' home.

Milly, Peter's sister, quickly approached me. We immediately shook hands. "It is nice to meet you, Livvy."

I noticed Milly favored Mr. Weston, though her features were much softer. Her eyes were the same blue as Peter's, but her hair was darker. Milly appeared to be a couple of inches shorter than me, and her light pink sundress flattered her perfect figure. Ah...I loved her shoes. I reached to shake Mrs. Weston's hand. "Do you prefer Olivia?" she asked.

"No, please call me Livvy. It is nice to meet you, Mrs. Weston."

"Dear, please, I prefer Elizabeth."

I smiled once more and stepped forward. Mr. Weston was standing three feet directly in front of me, and from the looks of it, evaluating my every move. I reached to shake his hand.

"Livvy, it is nice to meet you," he said. He touched my wrist with his other hand, almost like a double handshake. Oh my.

"I was under the impression you exaggerated, Peter. But you have only spoken the truth about Livvy."

Mr. Weston hugged Peter. "Your mother is excited to have the both of you here. Livvy, please call me Edward."

I filled my lungs with air and nervously exhaled as Elizabeth reached for my hand. We strolled through the giant foyer. I noticed countless enormous, beautifully decorated rooms diverting in every direction. "Dear, it's your lunchtime. I spoke with your mother, and she had only one request."

I looked at Elizabeth. She smiled softly. "Victoria suggested it was in your best interests for our family and staff to properly be informed…" Elizabeth paused. From her expression I felt she thought she had insulted or possibly embarrassed me.

"Yes, that was an excellent idea," I said. "It is important for everyone to know." I was aware Brits are stereotypically less likely to show emotions, but Elizabeth stood still and spoke not a word. However, her eyes spoke…Peter was right. She already loved me. She knew… she knew everything. Peter had told her about my angel. I hugged her, but not too close. "Elizabeth, thank you for welcoming me into your home."

She hugged me back and carried on. "Garrett has educated everyone on what to do if an emergency occurs." She said emergency kits had been placed in every room, as well as the other outbuildings, such as the stables, the gym, and the garages. I thanked her once again. "Livvy, I feel as though I have known you for a long time." She made a gesture for everyone to exit to the veranda.

I was eating my first meal with Peter's family, but most importantly, I was enjoying myself. Elizabeth asked if I was *au fait* with horses. I told her I was, although I hadn't ridden in a few months because someone special had captured my attention.

"I thought you only rode contraptions with fast motors," Peter said.

Edward was smiling along with everyone. Elizabeth said her Gelderland had been delivered last week.

"Chestnut?" I asked.

"Yes."

"They are beautiful and easy. I love their high-stepping trot."

Elizabeth asked if I had horses.

"Yes, I have three. A Gelderland—she was a gift from my grandparents when I was diagnosed with diabetes."

"Her name?" Milly asked.

"Honey." Milly asked about my other two. Peter placed his fork down on his plate and leaned forward a bit. "Ace, an Arabian gelding; he was my equestrian horse. He is beautiful and good-natured, and I still enjoy riding him. And my colt is a palomino, an American quarter horse. Umm…he's a beauty, and he knows it."

I glanced at Peter, and he asked, "Does your beauty have a name?"

I took a sip of water, then cleared my throat and said, "Of course, Peter, his name is…Bullet."

The smiles turned into laughter, and when Peter reclaimed his fork, he asked, "Is there anything else I need to know?"

"Pretty sure that's it. So tell me, Edward, do you have hobbies or interests other than work?"

Peter looked at me and just shook his head. *Oh, crap, I must have said something wrong.* But then Peter laughed.

"Yes, I enjoy hunting and golf," Edward said.

"Is there a specific type of game you enjoy hunting?"

"Duck, geese, and pheasant."

"Oh? What type of small-game hunting rifle do you prefer?"

I heard Peter sigh as his father went through a short list. I was not impressed, although I tried not to show it. Edward smiled again. I took that as a green light to continue.

"Edward, I would very much like to take you deer hunting in Alabama on my grandparents' farm. I think you would enjoy it. There is nothing like shooting a ten- or twelve-point and field dressing it right on the spot. I have a Browning twenty-inch barrel with a nice scope I could loan you."

Peter put his fork down. "Are you sure there's nothing else I should know about you?"

"You're welcome to join Edward and me. I have several shot-guns—five to be exact. But Edward hasn't accepted my invitation yet."

"I would be delighted to go deer hunting with you. However, please withdraw your invitation from Peter, because he would try to save our kill."

After lunch Edward asked Peter to take a walk with him. As they stepped down stairs that led to a beautiful garden, I overheard Edward say, "She is not what I expected, Peter. Bloody hell, I cannot remember the last time I laughed until I cried."

Elizabeth, Milly, and I spoke for a few minutes about the party. Staff had begun to arrive and was buzzing around everywhere to prepare. Elizabeth said Peter had insisted the guest list remain small, because he did not want to overwhelm me. She added that she had arranged for help getting me dressed for the party. *What—a lady's maid?* We had started our climb up the grand staircase when Elizabeth apologized for the room. I hadn't seen it yet, but good God, from the looks of the place, I wasn't concerned.

She said Peter had insisted she give me this one. Milly opened the door. I had never seen a room so gorgeous and fancy. Not really me, but still incredible. The large, medium-wood, antique canopy bed was draped in soft, floral fabrics, with yellow being the main color. The furnishings were ornate but girly. Exquisite rugs covered most of the hardwood flooring. "Elizabeth, I love the room. Thank you for everything."

Milly showed me the closet and said Ruthie had put my things away. She pointed to the bath. I opened the double doors that exited to the upper veranda. Peter was standing against the railing. He strolled over to where I was standing, wrapped his arms around me, and said, "My room is next door."

Milly and Elizabeth were about to walk out when Elizabeth turned for a last word. "Livvy, if you need anything, please ask."

After they had left, I said to Peter, "Your family is wonderful."

"You made quite an impression on my father. Now I'll give you a tour of the house and the garden. Tomorrow Mum would like to show you the stables. Now tell me more about Bullet."

I told him to shush.

After I'd had my tour and met the staff, Peter wanted to take me somewhere. It appeared to be a tour of an enormous garage. He removed keys from his pocket and pointed to a black Porsche convertible.

"Are you driving?" I asked. He told me to belt up. I told him I couldn't—I wasn't even in the car yet.

He opened the door. "Belt up means shut up, baby." He kissed me and said if we were married, we would use the bonnet, because he fancied me. I told him to only speak American English, because my brain was tired. He laughed and said, "So you are zonked." I told him to belt up this time.

As soon as he turned onto the main road, he shifted and pressed the accelerator. Peter drove for maybe two miles before he pulled off the main road into a driveway. He parked in front of a charming but large home.

"I know we will maintain our apartment in London, and I realize we will need to purchase a home in Auburn. But I thought over the next month or two, we needed a project, so I bought us a home. After all, when we have our four children, I know we'll want to raise them in the country."

"Peter, it's beautiful. Please tell me I am not dreaming."

He brushed the side of my cheek. "You are not dreaming. I'm real. Feel." He placed my hand over his heart.

Peter said the previous owners would remove their personal items within a few days. He wanted an all-new kitchen, changes to the master suite, and a lift.

I got tickled. "So you think we need a project. I think it will take more than a little remodeling for me to keep my hands off you."

Milly was waiting near the back entrance when we arrived back at the castle. "Guests will arrive in two hours." I smacked Peter on the lips and ran off with Milly. She pointed to the elevator. "Your room is on the second floor, not the third. Turn left when you step off the lift. At the end of the corridor, turn right, and your room is on the left." Lordy, I needed a GPS.

CHAPTER 35

When I stepped out of the shower, I heard voices in the bedroom and a tap at the door. "Yes?" I said, wrapping a towel around me. One of the two girls flung open the bathroom door. Guess *yes* means *bring your ass right on up in here.* "You must be Miss Hunnicutt. Take a seat. The dress hanging on the hook in the dressing area, I assume, is what we are working with."

"Yes, it is," I said, tucking one corner of the towel under my arm.

"Love your accent. I'm Trish; I do hair."

I smiled. Those two chattered nonstop about boys, sex, and even discussed how sexy-looking Peter was. An hour later, Beatrice, the makeup artist, stepped back and popped her fat brush into the pocket of her leather makeup apron and said, "Bugger, I'm good."

The girls left, and I stood, staring at the dress. I wondered if my choice was appropriate. Where was Cookie when I needed her? She would know if the dress was right. I didn't want to embarrass Elizabeth or Edward. I needed a drink and a strong one, but I was afraid my filter would certainly fail me.

I removed the dress from the hook and stepped into it. As I zipped the dress, I realized it was four inches above my knee. The fitted black dress had one strap across my right shoulder. I slipped my feet into my jeweled satin Oscar de la Renta platforms and kept my jewelry simple: just silver drop stone earrings and two matching bracelets.

I looked in the mirror and felt sick. I needed some air. I flung open the double doors to the veranda and saw Peter leaning on the banister. "Livvy, you look amazing. May I kiss—"

I interrupted him with a passionate kiss. Pulling away, I whispered, "You never have to ask. I will always want you to kiss me."

As we ambled down the staircase and strolled through the enormous vestibule to meet the guests, I heard voices. Peter and I turned the corner and stepped through one of three sets of double doors that were opened to the veranda. I thought my chin was going to land on my chest. There must have been two hundred people there.

Elizabeth, Milly, and Edward instantly rushed to our side. In half a shake, Edward reached for my arm and escorted me to the center of the room. Peter was following, but I lost sight of Elizabeth and Milly. I glanced over my shoulder, and Peter smiled. *Small party, my butt.* I was going to shoot Peter Weston after I taught him some basic math.

"Sorry," Peter whispered. "Father is thrilled to have you here." I went around the room and shook hands, repeating each person's name back and saying how pleased I was to meet him or her.

Elizabeth darted from across the room. "Edward, darling, I must borrow Livvy." *I didn't know I was available for a loan.* Elizabeth turned while leading me by my arm. "Peter, come along. Livvy, you look stunning."

She paraded around with me on her arm for thirty minutes.

"Livvy, my brother Garrett," she said, gesturing to a man who looked *au fait*, and then she added, "and my niece, Rosemary."

I know this man. "Garrett, have we met before?"

As he shook my hand, he said, "No, I would have remembered."

I was not convinced. I told him it was my pleasure, and I thanked him for educating everyone on my condition. I extended my hand to Rosemary. She was at least Rae's age, and after speaking with her a few minutes, I was impressed. As a couple of bonuses, she was following in Garrett's medical footsteps *and* she was pretty. I eyed her ring finger. Nothing. I would keep that in mind as well.

Peter came to my rescue. He told Elizabeth he needed some air. We walked down the stairs to the garden, but he stopped only a few feet from the veranda. Milly joined us. Suddenly Peter had the strangest expression on his face. He did that silly finger-wagging thing, saying, "Milly, keep Livvy company. Do not let Mum take her."

As Peter left, I asked Milly what her interests were. She said she loved horses and shopping. I suggested maybe we could do both before classes resumed for the fall. I asked her about boys. "Boys?" She rolled her blue eyes. "Every time I mention my last name, they run. They're afraid of my father."

"Edward is nice," I said. "I cannot see that being the reason. I think the reason they run is because you are beautiful and smart. Boys get nervous like we do."

"No, it's because of my father. He's a loving father and adores Mother, but he's usually quite aloof, at least to outsiders. I cannot ever remember seeing him enjoy himself as much as he did during lunch today. He smiled and laughed the entire time. I want to bring someone home one day that Father will be proud of, like Peter has."

Milly seemed as though she wanted to hug me. I reached my right arm around her and leaned toward her. She, in return, leaned in my direction. With our heads tilted, I said, "I believe in God, and I think he has the person for us. When the time is right, your guy will walk into your life, and he won't care a bit about your last name." Milly dabbed underneath her eyes with her fingers. I tightened my arm around her.

"Thank you, Livvy. I'm twenty-one, and I had totally given up. But maybe he is out there, and he is waiting for me as I have waited for him."

I spotted Peter walking toward us. He apologized for his delay. He looked at Milly and did that head thing. "Oh—oh, yes, of course. I need to rejoin the party."

Peter and I stood quietly for a moment. I admired the garden from where we were standing. It was spectacular. The water from the fountain cascaded into the pool. Even though the garden was dimly lit, every star could be seen as they shone on the unspoiled lawn, which surrounded the manicured pathways and shadowed what remained of the fragrant summer blooms.

"This is a perfect evening."

"No, it is not perfect yet." That's when he took a step back, knelt on one knee, removed a ring from his jacket pocket, and reached for my left hand.

"I made you a promise, Olivia Hunnicutt, that it would not be long," he said. "Will you marry me?"

"Yes, Peter. Yes, I will marry you." Tears escaped from my eyes as Peter placed the ring on my finger. His hands were shaking, and so were mine. I barely looked at the ring, but it felt heavy. I grabbed his arms for him to stand. We immediately wrapped our arms around each other, and after a beautiful and perfect kiss, we heard guests applauding. We glanced up in the direction of the house, where a few people had gathered next to the banister on the veranda. Peter kissed me again.

I felt another arm slip around me from behind. I turned to see Milly, Edward, and Elizabeth. Peter and Edward hugged. I reached for Elizabeth, who hugged me. And then, my Lord, Edward hugged me. I used caution for a moment, but he didn't.

While Milly and Elizabeth were admiring my ring and Edward was congratulating us, my eyes were on Peter. He touched my face. "Livvy, now it is a perfect evening."

We rejoined the party. I noticed Peter began to smile, and then he started to laugh. Three young men about Peter's age were heading in our direction. "Who are they?"

The closer they got, the harder Peter laughed. "Old friends from college, and let me apologize now for their behavior."

I spotted immediately what Peter was referring to. Each of them had a copy of the swimsuit magazine and a pen. "Peter, what will your parents think?"

He laughed. "Livvy, they have seen it. My father has a stack of them in his study. He is too embarrassed to ask you to autograph them."

I smiled as I shook Peter's friends' hands, under the impression the British didn't hug or kiss. But dang, every one of them kissed me on both cheeks. Then the one named Jeffery grabbed me by my shoulders and smacked me right on my lips. He looked at Peter. "You're right. Her lips are soft."

"Are you going to carry those magazines all night, or do you want me to autograph them?" I teased.

When the party was over, I thanked Elizabeth and Edward for a lovely evening. Peter and I said good night, but right before we stepped out, Elizabeth asked if we had set the date.

"No, but it will be soon," Peter answered. Then he grinned and said, "I want us to wait until we are married, but it is difficult." They immediately understood what Peter was referring to. He looked at me and asked, "Six weeks?"

"Peter," I said, "I cannot plan a wedding in that length of time."

Elizabeth agreed it would be difficult, but it could be done. Edward had sat quietly until now. "September twenty-second is a Saturday, and it is exactly six weeks."

"That's my parents' anniversary," Peter explained.

"September twenty-second sounds perfect," I said.

Edward sat straight up, smiling. But I had a few wishes, and I was about to lay the law down. "I do not want a large or extravagant wedding, just an elegant, small church service and reception here, if that is all right." Everyone agreed.

I was excited. I asked Peter to borrow his phone. "Are you calling Martin to come get you?" he teased.

"No, I'm over that, but I would like to call Mom."

He handed me his phone and said all of my electronics would work tomorrow. I thanked him as I pressed Cookie's number. I filled Mom in on every detail about Peter's family and how he had proposed. After congratulating us and lots of squealing, she asked if she could speak with Elizabeth.

I smiled at Edward. Peter caught my expression immediately. He started laughing. "Edward," I said, "a little birdy told me you had a stack of magazines in your study. Would you like me to autograph them?"

Edward chuckled. "Yes, I would. The magazines belong to friends."

"Edward, I only agreed to the photo shoot because I was upset with a friend."

"Max Spencer?"

"Yes, that is correct." I paused for a second. "I hope that my choosing to do the swimsuit issue, prior to dating Peter, has not caused you or your family the slightest embarrassment."

Edward stood up and joined Peter and me next to the piano. "Livvy, I felt the interview was an eye-opener for young women. It is my understanding it has received more attention than the swimsuit issue. In my opinion, the issues that you chose to discuss in the article made your photographs more beautiful, if that was possible. I read the interview you gave repeatedly, and then I would stare at your pictures in the magazine, thinking, 'She looks healthy.' Then I realized two things had captured my attention: first of all, disclosing what you have endured during a health crisis could give someone hope, because tomorrow is a new day. Second, you challenged young people to wait for love, love and hope. Without them, what do we have? I do not think you realize what you are capable of. Nevertheless, when you discover it, things will change for everyone."

Wow. That was deep. Speechless for once, I managed to thank him for his kind words. Elizabeth ended her conversation with my mother and said my mom would arrive in a couple of days for a pre-wedding powwow. I told Edward I would sign the magazines tomorrow. We all said good night.

As soon as Peter and I turned the corner, I held my left hand up and really admired my gorgeous engagement ring for the first time. The stone was round, I guessed three carats, and from the way it sparkled, it was flawless. The band was entirely covered with diamonds.

"Peter, when? We have been together every day." Peter told me the same evening he had asked my father for permission to marry me, he had called his jeweler in London and requested perfect stones. The jeweler had e-mailed him the description of the stones and the setting choices. Mother had told him my ring size. He had put a rush on it, and the ring had been delivered yesterday.

Once upstairs, Peter and I turned the corner. I stepped in front of him, threw my arms around his neck, and he swooped me up in his arms. His room was the closest. He tossed me on the bed. He yanked up my fitted dress until it was bunched above my waist. He was kissing my stomach and working his way up to my neck. "Oh God, six weeks. Peter, this is torture."

Peter stopped kissing my neck and rolled over. I begged him, "Please marry me tomorrow. I can't take this."

"Me either," he finally admitted.

After a few minutes, we both calmed down and agreed. Six weeks. I kissed him once more and said, "I need a cold shower." He laughed and said the cold shower did not work for him earlier that morning, but he would try it again.

* * *

"I did not sleep at all last night," Peter said as he slipped under the covers with me. "I only lay in bed and thought of you. That will not happen again, so sleep in some damn clothes."

Less than an hour later, we heard a knock on the door. "May I come in?" Milly asked, peeping in.

Peter said, "Yes." I quickly returned to my prior position, spooning with Peter. I patted the bed. "Pajama party." Milly plopped herself down on the bed and fluffed the pillows. She reached for the blanket that was on the foot of the bed.

"So this is what it feels like to have a sister," she said.

"Yes, it is," I said. Peter wrenched me closer.

Milly asked me to go shopping with her in London and have lunch. She then quickly hopped up and said she would meet us downstairs for breakfast. I climbed over Peter, and when my feet hit the floor,

I said, "Looks like I will shop after all." I removed my lacy tank. I turned around and removed my panties. When I turned back around, Peter was smiling. I drew my G-string back between my pointer fingers like a rubber band. I released it, and that lacy piece of elastic traveled eight feet across the room. He caught it and shouted as I walked into the bathroom, "We are waiting, even if it kills me."

Over breakfast, Elizabeth explained there were several churches close by. "We could take a look this afternoon," she said. Obviously, with our wedding just six weeks away, we needed to start making decisions.

"Livvy," Peter said, walking me out to meet my shopping date, "I called my card companies. Your cards will be issued…" He paused. "Maybe I should have verified something with you first. Olivia Hunnicutt Weston, okay? I got your social from Tom."

"No need to rush with the cards, but yes, I like it."

"There is cash in the back zipper of your bag. Please use it."

"No—not until we are married. Besides, I have money."

I opened my bag, and he said, "No." He closed my bag. I told him I wasn't comfortable spending his money, nor did I want him to feel obligated.

"Obligated? Livvy, we are engaged."

Edward walked past us as he headed to his own car. "Livvy, spend Peter's money, or—"

Peter quickly interrupted. "Not yet." Edward chuckled as Hugh closed his door for him. Peter opened the car door for me.

I tossed my bag on the seat and sat down. "Peter, what did you mean when you said 'not yet'?"

"Nothing, really, but see, Father wants you to spend the money."

Milly dragged my ass to every designer store in London. Poor Bradford had bags hanging all over him, but he took it like a man. I found a few nice things for our honeymoon. Those were the purchases I was excited about.

After five hours of shopping and a quick lunch, I knew I absolutely loved Milly. She was different from me, but still wonderful and funny.

Peter was standing outside waiting when Bradford parked the car. Peter opened my car door and kissed me when I stepped out. "I love you, I love your sister, but I need a tall drink," I said. Bradford was unloading the car, and Peter was laughing. "What are you doing?" I asked. "Make yourself useful. Grab a couple of those bags, and don't forget I need that drink." I heard Bradford chuckle. Peter reached into the trunk and picked up a couple of bags.

As we walked up the stairs, Peter said he had spoken to my mom and was surprised to learn that I was not a fan of shopping, and he understood now why it only took three minutes to purchase a dress. "I love fashion, and I had fun today. If a shopping trip was what it took to get to know Milly, it was a small price to pay, because she is great." I fluttered my long lashes at him. "Oh, baby, you bought me some nice things." He swung a shopping bag and popped me on my butt.

While I freshened up, Peter left and returned with my favorite drink: Goose and soda with a lime. I drank it, then slapped him on the butt flat-handed. "Let's go find a church."

Bradford and Elizabeth were waiting in the car. Bradford drove a couple of miles before he stopped. I could not believe my eyes. I knew this church. As I stood in front of the church's double doors, I touched the large iron handles and closed my eyes. I described the inside of the church in great detail to Peter and Elizabeth. I opened my eyes when I had finished. Peter looked at me, seemingly in shock. "Your description is accurate; this is where I attend when I'm in the country," he said. "How did you know?" I didn't answer right away. The minister opened the double doors, and I gasped. The minister answered my question before I asked: "Two hundred twenty comfortably."

Am I dreaming...no, not this time. "This is our church," I said decisively.

"Livvy, we have not yet visited the other churches," Elizabeth said.

I smiled. "No need. I saw this church in my dreams many times when I was a little girl."

Peter slipped his arm around me. "Livvy, what else did you see in your dreams?"

I closed my eyes. I could see the dream perfectly. I told them I had not thought of it in years, but when I was eight, two days after I was diagnosed with diabetes, I dreamed the same dream repeatedly for more than a month. "It was you in my dreams all along. It has always been you, Peter. I only had to open my eyes to see it."

Elizabeth had tears streaming down her face as she took both of my hands in hers. "Livvy, I saw you in a vision, too—the day I saw the angel, only you were much younger. She said you were coming. Edward was right last night—you will change our lives, and we barely know you, although we have known about you for years, as you have Peter."

We all stood quietly for a few moments, and then Elizabeth joined Bradford beside the car. Peter wiped his eyes, and then he wiped the tears from my cheeks.

"Not for a second have I ever doubted my feelings for you. We know now who fell in love with whom first, but I will always love you more, Livvy."

After dinner every evening, Peter and I played the piano and sang together. I asked Peter if he remembered me asking Garrett if we had ever met. I continued, "I finally remembered. I saw him in a dream, but not the dream of our wedding day. I saw him in a dream the night before you came to Auburn. I never saw your face in this dream, but I saw Garrett's face vividly. I was lying on the bathroom floor in the apartment in London. I knew that room looked familiar, but I could not remember where I had seen it." I closed my eyes. "I can feel the cold marble against my body, and it feels good, because I'm hot." I opened my eyes. "I was sick. Garrett was sitting on the floor with me, and someone held a roll of tape for him in one hand and held a white stick in the other. I'm guessing that was you. Garrett was starting an IV." Peter's brow tensed, and worry burned his blue eyes. "Peter, in the dream, Uncle Garrett said, 'Everyone is different, but normally at thirteen weeks, it improves.'"

Peter sighed. "Morning sickness. Boy or girl?"

"Don't know. The dream ended. My room or yours?" I said, changing the subject. Peter laughed and said it did not matter, but I had better wear some damn pajamas. I told him all I brought and bought were things similar to what he had seen me wear since June. He asked if I had any ugly ones. We decided on my room.

While we were eating breakfast, which, my Lord, took forever, Elizabeth told me she had hired a wedding coordinator to help me. She asked if I had a gown designer in mind. I said I had always wanted my gown to be designed by Vera Wang, but I was flexible. I explained what I wanted: it was to be an early-afternoon wedding, so I did not want a fancy gown.

Peter walked past the dining room and waved, but quickly returned with my mother on his arm. I had been in England for just four days, but I had begun to miss her. We hugged, and she grabbed my left hand. In her sweet, southern voice, she said, "Oh my."

Everyone was introduced, and Mom was shown to her room. She rejoined us when the wedding coordinator, Deborah Wright, arrived.

I liked Deborah immediately, and after looking around the estate only once, she had wonderful ideas. She handed me an itinerary with appointments already scheduled and assured me everything would be perfect on our wedding day. I had no reason to doubt her, because she seemed to be a crackerjack, just like my Nonnie and Aunt KK.

Deborah had arranged for a wedding director, Allison Lucky, meet us at the church. Many decisions were made quickly, and we left for London to choose the wedding invitations. Deb put a rush on them.

My appointment with the gown designer was booked for the next day, but he was coming to me. During the appointment, we discussed fabrics and designs for the bridesmaids' gowns, along with the style of tuxedos.

No time to waste, Deborah would always say. So before the week's end, we had chosen the menu and flowers. Peter was in charge of the band—he had connections.

The next four weeks were crazy, but I made time to call and text my friends and family. I couldn't wait until Peter met Tucker, Piper, and Crosby. I knew he would love them. Max and I e-mailed or texted at least once a week, and he and Peter had lunch in London a few times. According to both of them, it was a friendship in the making.

My high point was when Rae, Abby, and Andi came across the pond for their fittings. As a bonus, Noel and Riley came, too. Elizabeth played with Riley most of the time during the day, and I couldn't help but think what an amazing grandmother she would be.

In the evenings after dinner, Edward and Peter would take turns with Riley. I could not believe it—Edward Weston playing with a baby. She even spit up on him. He simply removed his jacket and said it was his fault because he had forgotten to burp her.

Peter had fallen in love with Riley. There was something about Hunnicutt girls, he said; he couldn't help himself. But she liked him too. I told Peter it was because of that crazy hair of his. After watching those two, I concluded that Riley liked Peter because she was just like her Aunt Livvy—she couldn't help herself.

* * *

One week until our big day, and every decision had been made for our wedding. The minor remodeling was underway in our country home. Peter had contracting crews there 24-7 for the past month to ensure it was completed before the wedding. The biggest headache of all was deciding on a new chandelier for our London apartment. After I narrowed the choices down to three with a designer, I handed the final decision to Cookie and Peter. During that time I was also in the midst of deciding on the cake frosting.

The next morning, Peter was excited. He was lining up another project—like I needed more crap to think about. Peter said he had bought us a home in Auburn, right next door to my parents' home. After reviewing the pictures online, he wanted to make some changes. *Of course he did.* I thanked him for his thoughtfulness.

Peter did that silly finger-wagging thing and asked if I wanted to go London tomorrow and stay the night. At first I thought he was pulling my leg, because he was all about minor supervision, but he wasn't kidding. I promised him I would not behave.

* * *

I watched Peter while he slept. He whistled a little when he exhaled. *Cute.* His skin was smooth, even under his early-morning whiskers. God, his lashes were so long they curled. I had to use an eyelash curler for mine. *Well, that's not fair.* "Wake up."

He smiled and pulled me close. "Knock up."

"I'm not knocked up," I said. "You won't touch me."

"No, baby, *knock up* means to wake someone." I reminded Peter to speak my language, because translating English to English gave me a headache.

When Bradford parked the car in front of the London apartment building, the media was on both sides of the street and near both corners of the building. Peter pointed out that Shawn was standing in front of a car and Max was behind us. Peter asked Bradford to walk on my left, and he would walk on my right. We knew the reporters were after Max; however, Peter knew he and I would also be recognized.

Peter and I put our sunglasses on. Bradford opened the door, and Peter grabbed my hand. Max must have exited his car at the same time, because reporters were shouting his name. Then Peter's name was shouted repeatedly, and then mine. The sun was bright, even through my sunglasses. I threw my left hand up to shade my face when a reporter, noticing my rock, asked, "Peter, are you and Livvy engaged? Have you set the date?"

We stepped inside the building, and Max was waiting and smiling. "Livvy, it is good to see you." I reminded Max he had not returned his response card. He smiled at me and said all four were in the mail. Peter reached out and shook Max's hand and asked about having lunch again next week.

After sharing an old-fashioned southern hug with the babysitters, it was Max's turn. I stood on my tiptoes and hugged him. "Thank you, Max, for deciding to come."

He squeezed me, but not too tight, and said, "I think it will be a good idea to have Martin there." Max did that "I'm cooler than you" head-nod thing to Peter. "You know, in case you change your mind." Max reached for my hand and looked at my ring. "Livvy's ring is even more impressive than you described, Peter. It suits you, Livvy."

While taking the elevator to the fifth floor, Claude, Martin, and Shawn studied my ring. Peter and Max said something about business. I cut my eyes to Peter.

"You know what I told you," I said. The doors opened, and I grabbed Peter's hand. "Bye, guys. Make Max behave, would ya? C'mon, Peter."

Peter and I were truly alone for the first time in weeks. I kicked my shoes off and pulled my hair up into a messy ponytail. I strutted over to the new chandelier and viewed it from beneath, and then climbed the stairs, and admired it from the balcony. It was large but tasteful. Peter stood with his hands on his hips. "Well, what do think?"

"Peter," I said as I put more pep in my step to join him, "that one belongs here."

Peter surprised me that evening—he had made reservations at a wonderful, small restaurant a few blocks from the apartment. We decided to watch a movie in bed, for the first time. About midway through, Peter fell asleep. I turned the television off and flipped the side-table lamp on, gathered up my diabetic supplies, and headed to the bathroom. When I returned, I scooted next to him, claiming half his pillow. I was in deep thought concerning him when he sleepily mumbled, "You didn't have to get up to do that."

"I didn't want to wake you."

"What was your blood sugar?"

"Two forty-two."

"Did you give a correction bolus?"

"I gave Beetuhs juice."

"What?" he giggled.

"Wilford Brimley, you know, the commercial— dia-bee-TUHS."

"Oh…yeah." He pulled me closer to him. I felt the tears well in my eyes, and before I could catch them with the edge of the sheet, they dripped on Peter's arm. "Livvy, what is wrong? Talk to me, baby. What are you thinking?" He kissed my wet check.

"Peter, I do not want to wait until our wedding night."

"Our wedding is less than six days away. We can wait."

"No. I'm afraid."

He pulled me closer to him. "Why?"

"I'm embarrassed to say. My reason will sound ridiculous to you."

"Tell me."

"Every girl I know my age, except Milly, has had sex, and everyone says it's uncomfortable the first time, at least for a few minutes."

"Livvy, I don't know. But I love you, and I would never hurt you. I will be gentle. I promise I will not rush. I have waited to be with you, and I want our wedding day to be as perfect as you do."

"What if I'm not what you expect?"

"What if I am not what *you* expect?" he asked in return.

"I know you will be gentle, but I want everything to be perfect. You're experienced…I'm not. If we make love just once, I will know what I am supposed to do. It would break my heart if I disappointed you."

"Livvy, you have always known what to do, even before I ever met you." Peter pulled me closer to him and held me in his arms. "With each passing day, I become more excited about you. I am like a child with a beautifully wrapped Christmas gift I cannot wait to open. As far as any expectations I may have had, you surpassed them the first time I kissed you."

I heard what Peter said and I was still concerned I might disappoint him, but my willingness to please him was now greater than ever.

CHAPTER 36

"Peter"—I shook him—"wake up."

He grinned before he ever opened his eyes. "Baby, I'm sorry, but it is morning, and you are completely naked." He was rubbing my butt. "Where are your panties anyway?"

I told him he must have had a dream, because he snatched the things off me fifteen minutes ago, and it was only six forty-five. I had become excited, thinking he couldn't wait any longer and had decided to grant me my wishes. Well, no such luck with that. As I ranted, he continued to laugh. "Silver-spooned, related to royalty, a model, Oxford graduate, a businessman, a movie star, on the front cover of a magazine, and voted sexist man alive to boot. But you unknowingly reminded me you are just an average guy after all. Do you know what else you did?" I asked. He said he was afraid to ask. "Well, don't ask, I'll tell you."

Before I could tell him, he asked, "Do I need to apologize for something?"

"What part of the ordeal would you like to apologize for? Snatching my panties off, getting me all excited, or farting and then scooping me back into your arms as though nothing had happened?"

Peter apologized for all four, but said he hated that he slept through the first two. Then he asked if I had checked my recently reinstated Facebook page lately. "Well, no, I've been a little busy with all of my projects." The last time I had looked at Facebook, I changed my relationship status from single to dating.

"You have a generous amount of friend requests," Peter said. Before I could ask how many, he added out, "Thousands. My agent called to see if you wanted representation."

I shook my head. "All I want is an MRS degree. That one I'll use, unlike my Auburn University diploma, which, the way I see it, was a complete waste of my time."

"Nancy called too and asked you to call her. She wants to sign you early for next year's issues. I'm great with it. I like my friends to be jealous."

I snorted. "You're sick, Peter. What about your work?"

"I think I want to move in a different direction and try action films. There is a film coming up in late spring that caught my attention. I know I'll get the part if you are okay with it. We would get to stay in Italy for three weeks, and the film would wrap up in London in early fall."

"I want you to be happy, and I'll always support your film choices."

"I'm not considering any film offers right now, because I'm enjoying being with you. Yesterday, my father asked me to consult on three projects for two different divisions in the company."

"I like that you are going to spend time with me, but Peter," I grunted, "Weston? Come on."

"I know how you feel."

"Then why do it?"

"I like the challenge."

"Aren't I challenging enough?" I said, teasing his lips.

"Yes, you are."

"You are going to do it anyway?"

"Yes," he flatly said, biting my lip. "What about Sandy Lane?" Peter asked.

"You remember what I told you, don't you?"

"How could I forget?" he said, kissing the nape of my neck. "No bullets."

"The fancy resort in Barbados?"

"Yes, a villa."

"That will be perfect."

"We could spend our wedding night in our home in the country, and leave the next day."

"Peter, you've thought of everything." I scooted close to him. "You can hold me again. I forgive you for not granting my wish this morning."

"What are you talking about?"

"Peter," I said sweetly, "we were so close." He looked at me.

"I didn't mess up and miss anything, did I?"

"Heck, no."

"I'm begging you to sleep in layers of your little pajamas until we marry." I laughed. "Don't laugh. It would be catastrophic if we tortured ourselves for months by waiting to make love, and I made the plunge half-asleep. We only get one shot at this, and if I mess up, we can't get it back for our wedding day."

"Oh, for God's sakes."

"We are waiting," he sleepily said.

After a short morning nap, I sat straight up and gasped, "Peter, you must call Robert. He did not RSVP, but his family did."

"What?"

"Milly—I want her to meet Robert. Ah...I must check with Edward first."

"What am I supposed to say to him?"

I shook my head and threw my arms up. "Like I know. But get him here. I don't care how. I feel like I also need to speak to Robert about what happened between us."

It was only 7:50 a.m., and I was starving. "Come on," I told Peter. "I'm making breakfast."

At the kitchen table, he reminded me, "Your dad is flying in this morning."

Two days earlier than I had expected. I hopped from the table and smacked a quick kiss right on his lips. "I'm showering and getting dressed, because I am about to see the other most important man in my life. Hurry up, Peter. I don't want to keep Dad waiting."

While we sat in traffic on the way to the airport, I tried to strike up a conversation with Bradford. All I got was, "Yes, Miss Hunnicutt." Peter sent e-mails and made business calls about buying and selling stocks. Then he made another business call to Edward. Those two threw out numbers for the next ten minutes. I texted Crosby, Tucker, Abby, Rae, and Max while Peter finished up his next business conversation.

Then I realized the reason no one other than Max was responding to my messages—it was only 4 a.m. in the US. I extended two invitations to Max: one for dinner and dancing at the pub the night before our rehearsal dinner, and one to the rehearsal dinner.

Max texted back that he was sorry to say he was working in France the first night, but he would love to come for the rehearsal dinner. I handed Peter my phone so he could read the text. He smiled. "I asked him last week."

I texted Max: *Glad to know you were planning to come. Peter just told me.*

Max texted: *That's right. Still counting on you needing a ride.*

I laughed and handed my phone to Peter. He texted Max from my phone: *Not a chance. By the way, she saw me first in her dreams. Peter.*

Max texted: *Asshole. I know, she told me. Lunch tomorrow?*

Peter texted: *Not sure. I will call you later.*

As soon as Peter pressed send, I lit him up.

"Peter, you said you consulted with Edward. What you are doing is more than consulting. And by the way, I thought you were only an actor when I said I'd be your girlfriend." Peter was smiling, but I wasn't. "I love you, but I'm begging you not to get involved in any James Bond crap. I can't do it, Peter. Oh, one more thing that is bugging me. The last topic you discussed with Edward, concerning acquiring a particular American-based pharmaceutical company. You two don't want the entire company, though, only three divisions: technology, processing, and manufacturing. I thought that was strange at first, but now I totally get it. You need only those divisions, because you only want to enhance what Weston already has. I know Weston Pharmaceuticals currently ranks sixth among the big hitters, but you have set a goal to push them to the top. You want it all, don't you, Peter?" I huffed. "Well, let me tell you, I know Weston is already a powerhouse, mainly because of developing vaccines. Insulin alone is becoming a giant, due to the demand worldwide. If you accomplish what you are trying to do, Weston Company will become immeasurable. Sales should or may have already reached seven billion this year alone, if not more. Of course, you and Edward knew that." Peter was staring at me, but I had to finish. "I don't know where you received your information, but it is not correct. Recalculate your numbers per division. Your totals are off one-point-three billion in biotechnology the first year alone."

Bradford was staring at me in the rearview mirror and mumbled, "My God, lovely *and* smart."

Peter opened his leather-bound folder and studied it for a few moments. "You are right, Livvy. And you calculated the numbers in your head from listening to one side of a conversation."

I threw up my hand. "It's only math, Peter. Besides, I may not watch the news, but because Rae and I have diabetes, you can bet I have read everything concerning the disease, including information about the companies that make my meds."

He was about to ask me something, but I interrupted him. "I don't know shit other than the CEO of the American-based company you are interested in is my father's friend. Trust me, when you get the company to merge, you want to keep Mr. Jenkins—Dr. Jenkins, actually."

Peter was still staring at me, but his lips were pressed tightly together as Bradford parked the car at the airport. "Tell me more about Jenkins."

I once again threw my hand up and waved it in front of him. "Oh, Peter, I can't. This kind of thinking will give me a headache."

Due to my excitement, I was about to hop out of the car. Bradford stopped me. "Miss Hunnicutt, I think it is for the best if you stay in the car."

"Livvy, Bradford will get Tom."

"Oh, yesterday. The press. You go ahead, Bradford. I will sit tight."

Bradford soon returned with Dad. I hugged my daddy, and he proudly sat in the backseat next to me with Peter on my other side. Daddy struck up a conversion with Bradford. My Lord, Tom Hunnicutt broke through, and they chatted for fifteen minutes.

Dad asked Peter if I had been behaving. Peter laughed and told him I had. But then he asked Dad if he had ever noticed I could calculate or do equations in my head. I kicked my daddy's ankle. He looked at me, and I rolled my eyes. "Well, son, not sure I know what you mean." The subject was dropped.

Mom met us outside. She and Dad had not seen each other for five weeks. After introductions, those two disappeared.

Later in the afternoon, Peter asked Dad and me to take a walk with him. Dad winked at Peter as we headed to the garage. "Livvy, with Tom's help, I bought you a wedding gift. It comes with two stipulations." He opened the door, and there sat two of them. "The Softail is for you, and the Fat Boy is for Hugh," he said, referring to Edward's bodyguard.

Peter smiled and kissed me with my father standing two feet away. Daddy cleared his throat. "Sorry, Tom," Peter said, "Livvy never rides—"

I interrupted him. "Peter, you can ride with me."

"Hell, no," he said, but he didn't stop there. "That is the second stipulation. Never ask me again."

"I will never ride alone again," I promised. "But we have to do something about you not riding."

Peter shook his head and said, "No freaking way." He did that finger-wagging thing. "I enjoy riding horses, but as for motors, I will stick to the Porsche." Dad headed back to the house, and Peter and I detoured through the garden, where we had a quick, indecent make-out session. As we stepped onto the veranda, I stopped and asked Peter, "What on earth could I ever do or buy for you? You are always steps ahead of me. I can't think of anything special to do for you, because you have everything."

He put his arms around me. "You are the most precious gift I could ever want or desire. I tried to explain that to you last night. Livvy, it is you. I get to have you."

At that moment I understood this was what Crosby, Max, and Peter had tried to tell me all along. I was stubborn and spoiled. When they refused me, I tended to become angry and even pout. The gift Peter wanted was me. I kissed him softly and whispered, "Thank you for making me wait for you. I will not ask again. I will not pout or behave badly. I will wait for you, and our wedding night will be perfect."

After dinner Peter and I retired to the music room, as usual. As we sat on the piano bench, I mentioned that Elizabeth had said a few schools had called and asked if I would be their guest to speak to teenagers about my life. "Peter, you and I spoke about this at the lake. Even Edward mentioned it. I want to do it. I want to share my story about my health and why I have never let it hold me back from living. I'm not saying I was never sad, bitter, or even discouraged, because I was for a long time. I know I will be faced with many more challenges." I smiled at him. "Waiting to have sex has been my most recent challenge, and it has about killed me. So I will share that too."

"Livvy, do it. Then do next year's swimsuit issue. More people need to know you."

Peter called Nancy immediately. It was four o'clock in the morning in the US, but she answered. She was pleased to get the news. She asked about our wedding. Peter told her it was private and would take place very soon, and then handed me the phone.

Nancy thanked me for agreeing to do the issue. She asked me about our wedding. I explained just as Peter had. But I thought a moment. "Nancy, I would like to extend an invitation to you, Owen, and Janet to attend our wedding. However, the invitation comes with conditions that must be followed." I could hear her moving around. I had Peter's attention as well. I continued, "Janet may write about our wedding day for a future magazine article, and Owen may take photographs. But I must have your word nothing gets released until Peter and I agree. I am doing this because of *Finding Justice*. I realize the more Peter is in the press, the more people will want to see him, so this is good for him and my mother."

Nancy agreed to my simple terms. Peter e-mailed Nancy the information as I said good-bye. Peter told me I was quite a businesswoman.

Dear Lord, I promised Peter yesterday I would behave, and once again he woke me up excited. However, I told him I was getting up, not only because of his present condition, but also because the rest of my family would be arriving shortly.

I crawled across him, and as soon as my feet hit the floor, he grabbed me and pulled me back into the bed. He rolled on top, rested most of his weight on his elbows, and stared at my lips, then tried to kiss me. With this kicking morning breath of mine, I puckered up, but kept my lips tight. I warned him with what all he had going on, he needed to let me up, or I would need to break my promise. I once again darted out of bed.

My parents had booked a beautiful hotel just a few miles away from the Westons' home for our extended family and friends to stay. They would arrive in two days. I had invited only fifty-three people to our wedding. I realized Elizabeth would have liked a larger church, because she struggled to narrow her guest list to 167 people. I told her daily that I appreciated her tireless efforts to accommodate my wishes.

Our day and evening quickly passed, and by ten o'clock, my family members were tired—not only from their flights and the time change, but also all the sightseeing around the country. One by one, they disappeared for the night.

Peter and I made the turn at the top of the stairs, and from the looks of it, it was to his room tonight.

* * *

The next morning I carefully eased out of bed, threw on a lounge outfit, and kidnapped Riley. When I returned to Peter's bed with her, he was still. I laid my precious tiny niece between us. She was cooing. Peter opened his eyes, leaned over, and smacked me right on the lips. Then he picked Riley up and placed her gently in his arms. "She will be my niece in three days. I better teach her to say Uncle Peter."

I laughed and told Peter he was rushing her, but we played with her until she got fussy. "Uh, Peter, it's time to take her back." Peter laughed and handed her to me.

As soon as I stepped into the hallway, I spotted Elizabeth walking out of her and Edward's room. Elizabeth smiled. "Good morning, Livvy. May I?" She reached out and took Riley from my arms.

I stuck my head back through the open door of Peter's bedroom. "Meet me in the kitchen. I'm making waffles with Chef Nathan, and then we are going to the hotel. You are meeting the rest of my friends and family." Then I reminded him we were taking part of the group to the pub for dinner and drinks that night, and my parents were entertaining the others.

Peter and I arrived a few minutes before eight black Mercedes sedans pulled in front of the hotel and parked. I introduced Peter to a few of my parents' friends and family members as they gathered around.

Three important people stood beside the last car. I hugged Tucker and Piper and reached for Crosby. He gave me a huge hug. When he released me, I introduced Peter. Crosby immediately shook hands. Peter, Tucker, and Crosby exchanged phone numbers. I told everyone to get some rest. They were either going out with my parents or out with us. "Hey, Livvy, you letting your hair down tonight?" Tucker asked.

"You bet, Tucker."

"Count us in."

When we left the hotel, Peter put his arm around me and pulled me closer. "Livvy, I called Robert back at the hotel when I realized he was a no-show. I told him a ticket was waiting for him in Atlanta. He had better have his ass on the afternoon flight, or I was sending Bradford to drag him here."

After lunch, Cookie, Elizabeth, Deborah, and I had a three-hour meeting, and we reviewed every detail for the wedding. Everything seemed to be in order, and I needed to clear my head. I was about to disappear and take a walk in the garden when I noticed the time: five o'clock. I decided to make a cocktail to go along with my late-afternoon stroll.

I knew Edward had a great bar in his study, because I had sat at his desk a few times to autograph magazines for his friends—and enemies, according to him.

I flung open the right side of the double door to his office and looked inside. The coast was clear. I closed the door behind me and leaned against it. I closed my eyes, took a deep breath, and let it out. When I opened my eyes, Edward was standing in front of his desk. "Oh, Edward, I'm terribly sorry. I did not mean to disturb you." He warmly smiled, so I continued, "I needed a drink."

"A difficult day, I presume. What may I get for you, Livvy?"

"Goose and soda would be great."

"Will Belvedere be okay?"

"Certainly, and please make it a double."

He removed two glasses and said he would join me. "I rarely have seen you drink."

I told Edward about my filter problem. "I'm afraid to drink, because I do not want to embarrass myself or worse, embarrass Peter." Edward was still smiling as he handed me a big drink.

I immediately turned it up and took a large gulp, then apologized. "It's all right, Livvy. You must be thirsty."

I finished that one, and he took my glass and made me another one. Unfortunately, my thirst had not been quenched with my first drink, because my second cocktail went down just as fast, but not quite as smoothly. I think Edward must have taught Fred how to make cocktails, because they were god-awful.

Edward asked if I needed to talk about anything. I asked him if he was up for a walk in the garden. I took two steps when Edward decided to escort me by taking my arm. Guess he noticed my Gucci shoes were not behaving.

"It's Milly, Edward. She wants a boyfriend, but no one will talk to her. She feels everyone is afraid of you. What are your thoughts on that?"

He chuckled. "Milly is beautiful, and her mother and I would love for her to date. But unfortunately, she is right."

"Well," I said, "we need to do something about this."

Edward asked if I had any ideas. "As a matter of fact, I do," I boldly said. I just realized my damn filter had failed me, but it was too late. I had to finish. "I have a friend who should be on a plane as we speak coming from the US. He is from a fine family, and his name is Robert Blake. Now, I know you will have his ass checked out in an hour, but anyway…" Edward was laughing, and I had no idea why. This was a serious discussion I was having with him. "May I have your permission to introduce Milly to him?" Edward asked if this was the same man that I had once dated. "Yes, it most certainly is." Edward granted me permission.

I saw Peter walking in our direction. "Shit," I said, then followed that unladylike word with an apology. "Forgive me, Edward."

"Is Livvy's filter turned off?"

"Yes, Peter, I believe it is." *Just perfect.* They were both chuckling.

Peter asked Edward if he had mentioned it. "Not yet." Peter took me by my arm and told Edward to hold off.

"Peter, she needs to sign," Edward said.

"Sign what?" I asked. Peter said he thought it would be better to enter the house through the back entrance.

Once in my room, Peter turned the shower on and told me I had two hours before we picked our guests up. I pointed my finger at Peter. "Edward made me two drinks. They were doubles, but I am fine."

"Baby, if Edward made you two doubles, it is more like you drank six."

"Oooh, right. Guess that would explain a lot." Peter hung out in my room while I showered. He called the chef, who sent up a snack. After I ate it, I felt much better.

I stood in the closet staring at all the crap I had bought the day Milly and I had gone shopping. Screw it. I was wearing white. It wasn't fall until the day after tomorrow. After all, I was the bride.

I left my hair down and wavy. I slipped into my short, low V-neck, belted silk dress and buckled my sexy-strappy Jimmy Choos, and then I stepped out onto the veranda. Peter stood staring out into the garden with his hands in his pockets.

"You are so handsome, Peter Weston."

A grin tickled his lips as he walked toward me. Once I was in his arms, he asked, "Can we get married now?" He said he didn't want to share me tonight. I told him the day after tomorrow I would be all his, but for now, we were going dancing.

The small group was waiting in the lobby of the hotel as we walked in to fetch them—Luke, Abby, Bo, Jake, Patrick, Tucker, Piper, and Crosby. Rosemary, Peter's cousin, and Milly were meeting us at the pub.

Our four black Mercedes sedans pulled up in front of the pub. Peter took my hand, and as soon as I stood, he sighed. "Right back atcha, Peter." I kissed him, pulling him close and running my hands through his wild hair.

"Baby," he whispered, "go easy on me tonight."

Milly texted and said traffic was terrible in London, but they were on their way.

After an hour of eating dinner, drinking, and catching up, the band began to play. Bo asked, "May I?" and reached for my hand. I danced with him first. Then Jake caught me by my arm and said it was his turn.

Thank goodness, Peter had a cold drink waiting for me upon my return. After I recharged, Crosby looked at me and pointed to the dance floor. He dipped me right when I accepted his hand. It was a slow song, so we talked while we danced. Crosby said he liked Peter very much, but he knew he would because Max had told him how badly he had wanted to hate him but couldn't. He liked him too. I laughed. "Yeah, I know."

Crosby was my closest friend now. We shared everything. That was how I knew he had not met anyone special yet. When the song ended, he kissed me on the side of my head. As I turned, I saw her, and she was perfect.

Standing next to Peter was Rosemary. I stood on my tiptoes and smacked Crosby right on the lips. I thanked him for the dance.

"Come on, Crosby," I said. "You have got to meet someone." I walked up to Rosemary with Crosby on my arm. "Rosemary McAlister, Crosby Cooper. Crosby, Rosemary. Now ask her to dance." Crosby looked at me. "Well, what are you waiting for? Ask her." And he did.

I told Peter to order me another drink. "Matchmaking and dancing are completely exhausting."

Piper and Tucker were sitting next to Peter and me when Tucker asked, "Livvy, may I have this dance?"

We were on the dance floor when Tucker said, "Livvy, thank you for everything. I know we talk a lot, but I have never told you that you changed Crosby's life. He is a different man than he was less than a year ago, and you know what I am referring to."

"Girls."

"He was living dangerously, and now look at him. You may have done it again." We were quiet for a moment. "You waited, didn't you, Livvy?"

"Yes, Tucker. I waited, but only because Robert, Crosby, and Max loved me enough. Or were afraid of God."

"I knew you would." The song finished, and we returned to the table.

When the band cranked up again, Peter whispered, "My turn." He took my hand, spun me around, and added a dip with a kiss before we ever made it to the dance floor. He held me in his arms, and we danced until a band member toasted, "Here's to you, Peter and Livvy. Congratulations."

CHAPTER 37

We left the pub. Well, actually, I did not technically remember leaving the pub or going home, for that matter. I felt an urgency to pee. I was trying to open my eyes when I realized my head was pounding and I was hot, real hot. My chest felt heavy. I touched it. Peter's arm was a dead weight, wet with sweat and stuck to me. I reached to my belly. Peter was using it for his pillow. I tried to move my left leg, but he had his other arm tangled around it. *Jeez.* I got one eye open and fought the beaming sunlight by blinking. I smacked him on top of his head. "Where are my clothes? Peter, wake up." He moaned. "Peter, my pajamas. Where are they?" I fretted. "You told me after you almost granted me my wishes, I had to sleep in pajamas."

Peter laughed with his eyes closed, still covering my sweaty body like a well-insulated winter blanket. "Baby, Bradford and I got you inside the house and up to my room. I told Bradford to get you a shirt from my closet. I turned to get your meter out of your bag, but by the time I turned back around, you had taken your dress off and fallen across the bed. I covered you up, and I crashed beside you."

"But where are my panties?"

"You weren't wearing any." He laughed again.

"Oh yeah, I remember. You have torn every nude pair that I own but one. And I am saving that pair."

He said he was sorry about my panties, but my blood sugar had been good last night—128 and 109. I thanked him for checking it. Peter said he would forward my thank-you to Bradford. "What?"

"Yes, Bradford slept in your room last night. He's the one that took care of you. He was afraid with all the dancing, your BG might bottom out." I finally got out of bed and shrugged on Peter's shirt from last night. I scooted out of Peter's room and ran next door to mine. I tossed Peter's shirt in my closet, pulled on a lounge outfit, and brushed my teeth.

While I nibbled on toast from the breakfast tray, I read text messages from Tucker and Crosby. They thanked me for not disappointing them. And just in case I was wondering, they had spoken to Max. Within ten minutes Max texted and said he would never work again on a night that we were going out. He would have loved to have seen "all that." Now, what were those fools referring to? Peter had not said a word about anything.

Someone knocked on my door. Peter opened it. Edward stuck his head in and apologized for making my drinks a bit strong yesterday. He asked if he could step inside. "Of course, Edward." I pointed to the chair next to the one I was sitting in. "Please."

Edward wasted no time when he said, "Livvy, I have never met anyone like you." Peter was now standing in the doorway, and I was sure he was keeping an eye on me. But thankfully my filter was working.

I noticed Edward was holding a leather-bound folder. I pointed. "Do you need me to sign something?" Peter stepped closer to Edward and me.

"Peter, it's okay. I expected to sign a prenuptial agreement."

"No, Livvy," Peter said. "You will not sign a prenuptial. This is paperwork for banking."

"Oh," I said and glanced at Peter; he didn't look so well. "Well, give it to me, Edward." I opened the folder. "Do you have a pen?" Of course he did, a fancy gold one. "You know I can call and have my bank funds transferred here. It's not a big deal to me what country I have them in." I paused and looked back up from staring at the top paper. "Hold on. No, Edward. I can't accept this." I laid the pen down, and I swept my hand through my morning bed-head hair.

"I told you she would not want it," Peter said. He pointed to the table where the credit cards that had arrived four weeks ago were still sitting. "She also donated the money from the swimsuit shoot to the Weston Tutoring Foundation." Edward nodded as he glanced at the cards.

"Sign, Livvy." Edward picked up his fancy pen and handed it to me. "Use your new legal name but date the paper for tomorrow."

I took the pen from him and said, "I would rather sign a prenup. You don't owe me anything. I love Peter. I loved him before..." Peter and Edward watched me as I signed *Olivia Hunnicutt Weston*. That was my first time writing my new name. Then Edward flipped the page and pointed again and again until I had signed and dated ten different pages. I read only the first page. I could only assume the other pages were for transfers and drafts, but I didn't ask. I closed the folder and asked if there was anything else. I joined Edward when he stood, placing my hands on my hips. *Now what?* I made a hand gesture toward the folder and held out his pen for him to take. "Thank you, Edward, for the wedding gift, but I had planned to marry Peter for nothing."

"Livvy, it is not a wedding gift," Edward said. He took his pen and grinned.

"I know, Edward. I noticed the date. Those papers were dated the day I arrived six weeks ago, but it helps me justify your generosity, since I clearly do not understand."

"Point taken." Edward looked down for a moment and said, "Yes, there is something else. Thank you for speaking to me about Milly."

"You are welcome. Edward, I am not afraid of you. I will always say what is on my mind. I will also never let you make me another drink."

The two of them laughed. "I know, Livvy. But I think I have slightly underestimated you and your capabilities. Do you follow what I am saying?"

I was standing before him, barefoot with messy hair and crumbs on the front of my shirt from breakfast, and he was in a finely crafted custom suit. But I was going to hug him, and I did. Edward did not hold back. He tightly reached his arms around me.

"You are a breath of fresh air," he said. I pulled away, but I saw it in his eyes. I reached for his hand. As I held it, I realized I completely adored this man, and it had nothing to do with my new, fat bank accounts. Edward Weston was standing before me, trying to find the words to say he loved me.

"Edward," I said, just above a whisper, "I love you, and thank you for accepting me for the way I am."

He softened his voice from his usual tone. "You are easy to love, my dear."

"Oh, Edward," I said, "I also play golf. I have played since I was ten. My golf coach once won the Nike Tour, so anytime." Edward turned around and headed to the door, shaking his head.

"Livvy, is there anything else I should know about you?" Peter asked.

"Can't think of a thing." Before Peter walked out of my room, I asked if he was up for a run, because I needed to sweat.

"How far?"

"Four, maybe five miles. It's been a while, so ten is out of the question." He thought he could handle that.

I met Peter downstairs, and Bradford appeared out of nowhere with his running clothes on. I told Bradford and Peter to double-knot their shoes. I put my buds to my iPod in my ears and cranked it up to good running music. I slapped Bradford on the shoulder and Peter on the ass. "Let's go."

I led the way with Peter and Bradford following. I wanted to run by our home. I had been told the inside was off-limits until tomorrow evening, but I still wanted to see the outside. I smiled as we ran past the entrance gate and made a loop around the front drive.

I glanced at the time. We needed to head back; Danni would be arriving in a few minutes. I needed her help for tonight and tomorrow. I had been patronizing a spa in London for the last six weeks, but I wanted Danni to take care of me on my special day.

We entered through the front door. I felt shaky. I did not speak to anyone, but Peter recognized what was happening. He did not say a word, but ran past me. In a couple of seconds, he returned with juice. I was already chewing glucose tablets I had taken from my pocket. After I drank the juice, I looked up, and my entire family, along with the staff, was standing and staring at me. Ruthie was holding a Glucagon injection, but out of the corner of my eye, I spotted Danni. I stood up and slightly tripped over my own two feet. Everyone gasped, but I got my stride back, and Danni met me with open arms. I was sweaty and stinky, but she hugged me anyway. I turned and said, "Oh, I am fine, but thank you." Everyone went on about his or her business. I asked Peter to show Danni to my room. I walked over to Ruthie and placed my hand on her arm. "Ruthie, thank you. You did the right thing."

"I will put it away," she said.

Peter escorted Danni and I to my room, but I told him he needed to leave, because Danni and I had work to do.

A hot shower washed my stench away and soothed my aching muscles. I had to prepare myself for at least an hour of torture. That's right—Danni was set up and ready to go. I lay down, and Danni began with the Brazilian.

I shouted a nasty word after the first yank. Peter was knocking on the locked bedroom door. Danni bellowed out for him go away. He asked if I was okay, and Danni snapped back that I was fine, and sometimes being beautiful hurt.

I removed my dress for the rehearsal from the hanger—white again, strapless, soft-crinkled chiffon, daintily pleated. I removed the tissue from around the thin black belt and traced the jeweled buckle with my fingertip. I decided to wear my favorite black Prada heels, but I hoped it wouldn't be necessary to sleep in them as I once had.

I stepped out onto the veranda, and there he stood. "Peter, you are so handsome."

He placed his hands gently around my waist, kissed me softly, and said, "You look beautiful." He reached to hold my hand as we walked, and we met Bradford downstairs.

We were the last to arrive at the church, but we were not late. Allison, the wedding director, was in position. She instructed our small wedding party on what to do. We rehearsed twice and then dismissed.

At seven thirty sharp, our friends and family began to arrive at the big house for dinner. Peter and I greeted each one as they stepped inside the grand foyer.

After dinner and more mingling with guests, I discreetly let Peter know I needed a few minutes to collect my thoughts. I stood virtually motionless in the music room and stared out the window at the garden, which was almost in full autumn bloom, just as Elizabeth had promised. Robert was the only person I had invited who did not come, and that saddened me.

The doorknob turned, and I looked to see who had entered. It was Peter. "Someone would like to see you," he said. Peter turned around and reopened the door. Robert was standing there, and he removed his hands from his pockets when Peter said he would leave us alone. Robert joined me by the window.

With my thoughts somewhat collected, I thanked Robert for changing his mind. "I didn't have a choice. Peter threatened me."

"I am sorry. That was my fault. I told Peter to do whatever it took." After a moment, I said I needed an answer to the question I had asked him that night in Colorado. We avoid each other's eyes, both staring out the window.

Robert took a deep breath and sighed. "I believe I loved you before I knew what love was, and telling you I had to let you go was so incredibly painful," he said. "I thought I was going to die. That same night I lay in bed and repeatedly replayed what I had said to you.

Then, all I could think about was I had made a mistake. At that point I decided I would speak with you and try to fix things the next morning. But then I saw you leaving from my window. I shouted at you, but you didn't hear me. I chased the car until I could not run any longer."

"I'm sorry, I didn't realize. I thought that was what you wanted. Robert. Please forgive me. I didn't know you were hurting so deeply."

"I tried to call you. Besides that one time you spoke to me on Luke's phone, no one would allow me to speak with you. By the time I saw you in May at Rae's wedding, it was too late. I knew I no longer had a chance. As bad as that was, I realized it was a good thing. Livvy, there is nothing to forgive you for, but I need you to forgive me."

"I have forgiven you. But you still have not answered my question. I need to know what I did wrong so I will not make the same mistake with Peter I made with you."

"Livvy, I fought my feelings for you all those years, because I always knew you needed to do something more with your life. I didn't know what it would be or how you would accomplish it, but I knew for certain I could not give you what you would need. I'm not referring to material things. We both have all the crap we could ever want."

Robert paused and looked at me for a moment. "I know God created all things, including us, but there is something different about you. I have always seen it, but most importantly, I felt it, though I still cannot explain what it is. If I had held you back, you would not be with Peter, and none of this would be happening."

We once again stood quietly, and I recalled my childhood dreams. Robert was right. "Thank you, Robert." I faced him and reached for his hands. He allowed me to hold them. "I want you to know I will always love you. But most importantly, you must realize I am a better person for having had you in my life. Robert, you are special, too. Please don't forget it."

Peter opened the door. I asked him if he remembered the other reason I had wanted Robert to come. He did his silly finger-wagging thing. "Yes. I will be back."

"He is a nice guy, isn't he?" Robert said.

"He is."

We laughed and cried together as we reminisced of stories from our past, and shared our hopes and dreams of our future. When I was finished, we hugged. At the same time, we said, "This feels right." Then we hugged once more and stood in silence. Robert and I realized we would be what we were meant to be all along—just friends. Peter opened the door once again and asked if it was a good time.

Peter pushed the door open wider, and there stood my beautiful soon-to-be sister.

I smiled. "Mildred Brooke Weston, I would like for you to meet Robert Blake. Robert, we call her Milly." Peter placed his arm around me, and I said, "Milly, the garden is lovelier tonight than I have ever seen it. Why don't you show Robert?" Peter and I left them alone and joined our guests.

The long evening began to draw to a close when Peter tapped his wineglass, and everyone gathered. Peter thanked everyone for coming. "I do not need to stand here before you and say what each of you means to Livvy and what she means to you, because you already know. However, I want to thank a few people for coming."

Peter looked at Robert and said his name. I noticed Robert was holding Milly's hand. Peter called out Tucker's name. He smiled. Peter said, "Crosby Cooper." Crosby had his arm around Rosemary's waist. And then Peter said, "Max Spencer." Max was standing beside Edward and my father. Peter raised his glass and said, "Thank you all for being a part of Livvy's life and for the personal decisions you chose to make. I will never forget it. In addition to Livvy's family and friends, I am honored to now call you *my* family and friends." Peter turned and said, "Olivia Hunnicutt, I love you," and then he sealed it with a kiss.

I whispered to Peter, "Stop Max. He's leaving without saying bye. He must meet Allison, our wedding director." Peter started laughing and did that head thing. Shawn caught Peter's head snap immediately and stopped. I fetched Allison. She was about five-seven with soft facial features, and she wore her blonde hair shoulder length. She dressed flashy but had good taste and was tough as nails. *She could handle Max*, I thought as I introduced them.

Later Max hugged me and whispered, "I am happy for you and Peter, you know. I just hate that our cows never came home."

I took his hands in mine. "Max...I am so sorry."

"It's okay. The girl is all right. Not my taste, though. I'm guessing she will try to run over me like a lawnmower."

"You might be right. But go for it, Max. Her last name is Lucky. Besides, I don't think you have ever turned down anyone but me."

Max shook his head and mumbled, "Lucky," with that sexy grin of his plastered across his face.

After the guests had left, Peter walked me to my room. I told him Danni was staying with me. "What? No sleepover? I think you are wrong, Livvy, about Danni. She left with Jeffery."

"Thirty minutes. At midnight you are outta here," I said. "Now give me your shirt. I'm putting it on." Peter was giggling. "Do not follow me into the bathroom. There will be no making out tonight."

He gave me his shirt but not without saying, "We didn't make out last night. You passed out. But you danced well at the pub, and you sang with the band too."

"So that is what Max was referring to this morning."

I came out of the bathroom and crawled into bed. I lay in Peter's arms for the next twenty minutes while we talked.

He thanked me for what I had done for Milly and said he liked Robert. I smiled and looked straight at Peter. "Robert finally answered my question after all this time."

"Really?"

"Robert let me go so I could find you."

"I will thank him tomorrow."

We said good night while standing at the bedroom door, and Peter kissed me for the last time as Olivia Sue Hunnicutt.

CHAPTER 38

My day had arrived—the day I had dreamed of for so long. The most precious thing was that I was marrying the man in my dreams, even though my path to get here had not been easy.

I tried to open my eyes, but they were slightly stuck together from the added length of the eyelash extensions that Danni had insisted I wear.

I felt the opposite side of the bed. Whatta you know? Peter was right about Jeffrey and Danni.

Over the past month, I had gotten to know Jeffrey, and he was one funny character, but I liked him. Jeffrey was Peter's best man, and Matt Bartlett, Scott White, and Noel were the groomsmen. I couldn't help but smile and think it truly was a small world when I realized how our lives had intertwined.

I finally opened my eyes and stretched. My wedding gown still hung in the exact spot where Jim's assistant had delivered it yesterday. I had had several fittings over the past couple of weeks. I was immensely pleased with the gown Jim had created. The day I met Jim, he had walked in and shaken my hand. "Livvy, we have the gown you saw in your dreams, and we need to bring it to life," he said. That was it. Jim blew me away. He was my guy, no questions asked. We had each taken a seat in the garden room, and with a sketch pad and pencil in hand, Jim told me to describe my gown to him. I had closed my eyes, retrieved my childhood dream, and began to describe it.

"My gown is soft white, Italian silk, and strapless, with a slight sweetheart neck. The top is embellished with lace. It has a natural waist with a pleated sash a little darker than the gown. The sash ties and lies flat on my side. The skirt appears to be an A-line. My gown has a lace applique and is scalloped around the bottom, but not heavy looking. It has a chapel train, but it is not too long.

"My veil does not cover my face, nor is it lengthy," I continued. "It has a thin satin trim around the edge. My hair is down but pulled up on the sides, and it is wavy. I can see a clasp." I held my hand on the back of my head where the clasp was in my dream. "I can faintly see it through my veil. It has small stones in the most beautiful autumnal colors." I heard Elizabeth gasp, but I did not look at her. I opened my eyes. "May I describe the bridesmaid dresses?" Jim did not speak, only flipped the page.

I once again closed my eyes and said, "I will need four dresses. They are made of silk and almost to the knee." I touched my knee and then my waist. "The dresses have an empire waist." I touched my neck and said, "The neck of the dress is halter style, but has gathers and pleats with a ruffle standing up around the neck somehow. I see the dress in an autumn persimmon color. The flower girl is about six years old. Her dress is soft white with lace and has a satin sash the same persimmon color as the bridesmaid dresses."

I continued without opening my eyes. "The tuxedos"—I heard Jim flip the page—"are black. A slim European cut. The shirts are soft white, but the silk ties match the ivory color of the sash on my dress.

"That's all I have, Jim." Before Jim could speak, I told him our wedding would be small, but I wanted it perfect. If the gown I described would not be flattering for my body type, I would choose something else. I was firm when I said I wanted Peter to love my dress, so I did not want it frilly. I needed him to keep in mind that Peter's taste was modern, but I also wanted a soft, romantic look at the same time.

Jim smiled and said, "Your gown will be fabulous." As he closed his leather-bound notebook, he said, "You would look beautiful in a dish towel. Don't worry about anything."

Now my dress was hanging and waiting to be worn in a few short hours.

Someone knocked on my door. I looked down. I was still wearing Peter's shirt, but too late. Elizabeth peeked inside and asked if she could speak with me. As she walked in, Ruthie stepped around her with a breakfast tray, set it down, and all but skipped out. Elizabeth said Peter was downstairs visiting with my family, and she knew we planned to avoid seeing each other before the ceremony.

I apologized for not getting out of bed, but I wasn't dressed. I noticed she was holding a small box in her hand. She thanked me for the beautiful wreath that was being hung in the center of the foyer of the church in memory of Edward Brooks. She said I had described something once, and she wanted me to have it. I lifted the lid of the aged, red velvet box. It was the hair clasp that I had seen in my dreams. Elizabeth said if I already had something, she would understand. Choking back my tears, I said, "It is perfect, Elizabeth."

Her lips quivered but bore a subtle smile as tears slowly trickled down her face. "It belonged to my mother. She wore it on her wedding day, as I did."

I knew this was a precious gift Elizabeth had just given me. I let her know I would always cherish it and that I knew what it meant to her. I stood up and quickly apologized for wearing Peter's shirt. I straightened the collar. "I like wearing them when he's not around. It feels like he is giving me a hug."

She touched my hand and said that was one of the sweetest things she ever had heard. I asked her how Peter was doing this morning. She smiled.

"Waiting for you," she said.

My parents and siblings visited me one at a time all morning. My father melted my heart, because every time he tried to speak, tears would well up. "I love you, Livvy. I know Peter is a good man, and he loves you. I can see that I am releasing you into good hands." I hugged Daddy, and when I released my grip around his neck, he kissed me on my cheek and walked away.

Mom was too busy to get emotional, thank the Lord. On her way out, she reached in her pocket, tossed something on the bed, and said, "Sweetie, I believe you may need that." I picked it up, and we laughed, because she was probably correct. I thanked her for the bottle of lube.

Danni was on time and smiling from ear to ear when she pranced in from her night out. "That good, huh?"

"You bet it was."

By the time Danni had finished my hair and makeup, Milly, Abby, Rae, and Andi were all in my room. They were dressed and looking beautiful. Each of them thanked me, because they were afraid the dresses were going to be ugly, but they were pleased, and the Manolo's, which I had given them as gifts, were to die for.

It was time. Rae unzipped the bag that contained my gown. She and Mom removed my gown from the bag, and they both got teary-eyed as I stepped into it. My mother zipped it.

Bradford was waiting by the car. As we stepped down the massive front steps, he met us and lifted the short train of my gown without asking. "You will ride in my car, Miss Hunnicutt, with Mrs. Davenport," he said. "Hugh will ride in the limousine with the others."

As Bradford parked the car, I spotted Owen, Nancy, and Janet. Once Bradford escorted them over to where I was, all I said was, "Please do as I have asked, Nancy."

"We will not release anything until you and Peter give us permission," she said. "You look beautiful, Livvy."

Allison gave our wedding party the go-ahead to walk down the aisle. Then she closed the doors. Daddy and I stood and waited for the music to change for our entrance.

A few chords were struck on the harps and violins as the church doors reopened. Our wedding party stood in the exact spots we had rehearsed the evening before. Every guest stood and turned to look at me as the traditional wedding march played. I stood nearly motionless, trying to absorb it all.

The natural beauty of the church was grander that September 22 afternoon than it had appeared in my dreams as a young child. The flowers were not overdone for the simple reason that the church did not require it. Every candle was flickering perfectly, and the sun was dimly filtering through the magnificent stained-glass windows. I had memorized the guest list, and there was royalty at our wedding. But all those details seemed so small, because only one thing and one person mattered to me at that moment.

All at once my eyes connected with Peter's. My heart was pounding in my chest, and my knees were feeling weak. My father ever so slightly tugged at my arm, and with our arms chained firmly together, I matched his footsteps.

I could not take my eyes from Peter. I wanted and needed to blink but was afraid to because my fairytale might disappear, and I could lose Peter forever. *Oh God, no! Could this once again be a dream? No. Focus, Livvy. Focus on Peter. He is waiting.*

My father was standing next to Peter. "Who gives this woman to this man?" our minister asked.

My father answered in a tremulous voice, "Her mother and I." Dad took my hand and placed it into Peter's. His hand remained on top of ours. Dad kissed me on my cheek and whispered, "I love you." He released our hands. Then Daddy looked at Peter with a tear trickling slowly down his face. "Love her."

"Always," Peter whispered.

Our wedding ceremony continued. Peter and I knelt while The Lord's Prayer was being sung. Suddenly I was consumed by a peaceful feeling. Peter squeezed my hand, and our eyes met. Her aroma was all around us, and we could feel the coolness in the air from a slight breeze. My angel was standing before us. I gasped when she rested her hand on ours, but only Peter could hear. She vanished, though her scent did not.

After Peter and I shared our wedding vows, I had one last thought:

I do trust in God, and now I know my life is enduring when I am surrounded by family and friends who love me. Today I make a promise to myself: I will live my life praying and believing in he who makes me strong. I will be happy and healthy to the best of my ability. I will love Peter, but most importantly, I will allow Peter to love me.

The minister said, "What therefore God has joined together, let no man put asunder." At that moment I once again surrendered myself to the man who had captured my heart when I was a young girl. Only this time, I did it with my eyes wide open.

To the reader,

This past year, our twenty-seven-year-old son, Blake, was diagnosed with diabetes. He is doing well.

Our daughter, Brittany Rae, was diagnosed with Type 1 diabetes at age fourteen. She is now twenty-five and happily married to her husband, Russell.

Brooklyn, our youngest, was diagnosed with Type 1 diabetes at age eight. Other health issues developed over the next ten years, which made her diabetes very difficult to manage. Brooklyn is now twenty-two. Several months ago we purchased a diabetic alert service dog, Abby. Abby is amazing, Brooklyn's lifeline and best friend, and has made a positive difference in Brooklyn's life.

Please note: *Eyes Wide Open* was not intended for diabetes educational purposes.

Thank you for reading. I hope we meet again in my next novel, *In My Dreams*, to discover what further journeys and heartaches Livvy faces.

Correspondence for the author should be addressed to:

ag.acannon@gmail.com

www.ingramcontent.com/pod-product-compliance
Lightning Source LLC
Chambersburg PA
CBHW051434260626
47162CB00001B/98

Dios, y vuelvas con el tambien."

Tico knew this place on Bird Road that sold the best guava paste in Miami. It was no different from the rest sold anywhere else, same brand and everything — *Oya* — but for some reason, the *guayaba* there just tasted better. And anyone could attest to it, all you needed was a tin and some cream cheese. Silvia swore it was because the lady there was a *santera* from Anabacoa who worked the food with her charms, but none could be too sure. Tico said the woman seemed hardly cultivated enough to command spirits, she didn't even have an aura wider than her arm's length. Regardless, it was still his *Mami's* favorite, and as always, he had vocalized his intention before he realized it would have made a wonderful surpr —

"Virgen del Carmen!" he exclaimed. Angelica had emerged from the bedroom, painted and primped to perfection. "You are a *bird of paradise, mi amor."* They made to leave, but in a huff Tico scrambled back inside, cleaning the mango juice off of the floor and throwing the towels in the laundry bin.

"We're so forgetful, *corazon,"* she said, pulling him in for a long, soft kiss, *a bite of the heart.* Tico looked deeply into her eyes and feigned fatigue. She rolled her eyes.
"Come, let us go, *mi flor."*

~*~

Silvia finished using the bathroom and washed her hands, avoiding the mirror as usual. After drying them she decided that it had been awhile since she had looked at herself, and decided to take a peek. No. Wrung her hands. Looked up, her *bata* was pink. See, not that bad. Looked down again. *Ay, niña, it's just you!* Avoiding the mirror was silly anyway, everyone else saw what you were trying to hide from them even if you could manage to hide it from yourself. She thought of *La Virgen*, she sees me all the time. She looked up.

Ay, I...look fine. Her piercing green eyes still brought her olive skin to life—they would forever—and aside from the contemptuous crow's feet flanking her temples, she had few wrinkles on her face. She ran her hand over the smooth skin of her face, over her high cheekbones and across a neck that had just begun to betray her age. Down to her *bata*. The little lace frills bothered her for being so high up on her neck; she pulled them down to examine her collarbones. They were her favorite. Chiche called them *jaboneras* because he claims to this day that he could keep a bar of soap in there, *no prog-len meng*. They reminded her of her youth, her beauty, and she sighed at the rest of her body, which had only recently begun to reach for the grave. Old age, the slowest, most painful way to go. A few years ago had she found traces of grey along the outskirts of her hairline and proceeded to kill—dye—them as quickly as possible. Chiche told her not to, that he liked her as a *viejita*, but she shot him that look that could kill birds and he quit while he was ahead, turning his attention back to the TV without another word. A crow crashed into a glass door on the screen, so clean were the windows, call now and we'll send you two bottles for free. Plus the cost of shipping and handling. "You know my *telenovela* is on in 15 minutes, so finish up that show you're watching," she had said.

"*Negra*, I know it better than you. I love that Brazilian girl, the one with the eye that goes lazy when she's nervous. Don't tell anyone though, they'll call me *mariquita-maria* for watching *novelas* with my wife." He had smiled at Silvia's laughter. She was one of those women who enjoyed crass language, and Chiche flaunted it to pull her out of her...moods. "Why don't you make us some *café con leche* to drink while we watch it." He cleared his throat, and turned back to the TV.

Fucked it up, Chiche. *No pastelitos*. She had stopped right then and looked at the side of his head with contempt...John the Baptist on a silver platter...and she remembered the look he wore on his leathery face after looking back to the TV, that look that said so much — or so little, depending on how well you knew him — without words. It was a moist innocence in his eyes, one that betrayed nothing, everything, and she could not help but smile a little on the inside. He truly didn't mean to be a chauvinistic dickhead...*look* at him! He was like a puppy, a stupid little puppy. Smile back like a good housewife, who would I even tell anyway, the only people I talk to know that you watch the *novelas* anyway, and the others don't know shit about me, they still think we're happy because of this very smile. *Smile*, the mirror gave her the bullshit right back. She smirked, looking to the silver corners of her hairline in the mirror. 'Ugh, I was beautiful just seconds ago.' They agreed, old whores that they were. *Not anymore.*

"*Putas viejas,*" she spat at her reflection. "*Arrastrada de estas sinnnngadas me voy pa la tumba.*"

Silvia remembered that day well, the girl on the *telenovela* had betrayed her husband and ran away to Bolivia to live on her cousin's farm. She had made the *café con leche,* too. And though it was the day she had found her grey hair it was also the day she had decided to start dyeing it, which was something fun to do when the house became unbearable. She smiled into the mirror, and looked deeply into her eyes, shocked by their sudden beauty, their shape, the depth of her pupils. Happiness came only when she dove into her memories from behind a cigarette or before the mirror, never while they were happening. *Ah, cigarette...*she smoothed her hair back and fixed the Spanish bun she wore everyday, setting it where it felt right. Thought of her ashtray. She was at the point where doing her hair differently felt strange, and it made her feel anxious about going out, even to church. Silvia managed to go to *La Ermita de la Caridad* with her sister about once a month, about as often as she could remind Carmen to pick her up, and she always made sure to look good for *La Virgen* – or anyone else who might be there, you know how it is. She would dress herself up, do her hair in some way she thought looked okay on the news anchors that weren't little bitches, wear perfume from her little tray with the mirrored surface and put on a nice smile, at least for the first minute of church, that excruciating blaze of emotions and self-remorse where heads turned from the sermon to see who had just come in...and of course, what they were wearing. She could see the thoughts in their eyes every time:

"What...a fat bitch. Does she think she's still twenty-five? LOOK at those rolls. She had better switch to olive oil, Jesus...who would wear that to church? Is she trying to find a date?...doesn't she – AMEN – have kids? Isn't she divorced? Like three times, last I heard. Where's her man, he doesn't even come to church...some family they've got, and – *scoff* – those shoes...what a fucking whore...and her eyes are all puffy...AND ALSO WITH YOU, Father."

All the way to the pew. Her heart was pounding.
Cigarette.

Silvia heard the key scrape into the door uneasily, and she knew who it was by the way it happened. *"Mami!* What the *fuck* was *Papi* doing here so early? Oh my God he's *suchhhh* a hater!"

"What do you think, *niña?"* She stepped out of the bathroom and pursed the left side of her lips upon seeing her youngest daughter. Affection, in wolf's clothing. "He came for lunch," and she looked at the clock. 9:30 PM. "Early, I know."

"Well I dunno, I just thought he'd be done by now, you know? I sat through fucking Leopoldi's Saturday school just so I wouldn't have to run into him, *que* high-maintenance."

"No, *Yennifer,* he just came like normal, whenever he does. *Que,* did he see you?" Silvia grinned playfully. "Parents are supposed to *smack* you for cutting school, you know that? I'm

36

glad it still bothers you. You've still got a *soul*."

"*Que mierrrrrrrrrda.*" She threw her things onto the couch, running an exasperated hand across her glued bangs, being careful not to snag a bangle on her hoop earrings. Jenny arched her eyebrows high, Jenny wore apple-bottom whatever-the-fur jeans, Jenny showcased her boisterous *fondillo* like it was for sale, turning heads even at mass — *Jesucrísto!* — and Jenny was in the tenth grade. But that soul, it was pushing thirty. She was bothered, poor thing. *Pobrecita.* At first she would cut class and *not* come home, which made sense. At least she had *some* sort of...dignity. It had gotten to the point, however, where she no longer felt like going out for lunch:

"Those bitches eat *Rey's Pick-sa* everyday, that's why they're so fat — *heffuhs!*" So she came home instead to eat something healthier...like fried pork and *yuca* drizzled with garlicky oil and *chicharrones.* Well, it was free *okayyyy?! Dejenme vivir!*

> *Dejenme vivir!* That was Yennifer's slogan. Let me live!
> *Dejenme vivir,*
> > *dejenme en paz,*
> *dejenme llevarme el carro,*
> *dejenme ir al cine,*
> > *dejenme pintarme'l pelo como la Peenk,*
> > *dejenlo dormir aqui* — *Oye!* No, she was single.
> > > But not alone. *Ay mamá!*

She would never dare tell her mother, but she also liked to come home after skipping school because no matter how she tried to beat around it, she felt absolutely comfortable around her *Mami.* No sucking in when you're at home, un*button* that shit! *Ay, I don't know why I'm so fat, I eat healthy as much as I can! I get the apples with my happy meal, fockeen whatttt-everrrrr...*

It was no use, not in a Cuban household were Chiche Campos brought home the bacon...or *chicharrones.* The sweets stash, glimmering with *pastelitos, maza real, keke* and all sorts of pastries was positioned just perfectly so that anyone with the objective of trying to reach the fruit bowl had to pass by it first, like some kind of quest for the Holy Grail. Holy Grapes. But it was all in good sentiments, perfectly planned, for Chiche knew that Cuban secret of old, that being fat was being healthy. So their fruit was the filling of guava and coconut *pastelitos,* and you burned calories by drinking *café* and it's effects on the metabolism, *pin-pan-pun* and it's all squared, *vistes?* It was a worldview that still praised abundance in its most antiquarian way...tell me, have you ever seen a skinny Goddess?

Jenny would come home from school early, she would eat her healthy lunch with Silvia, wash it down with a *pastelito,* watch a little TV and wait for the inevitable to happen. She would pull out her cell phone, or *la cajita de mierda* as Silvia called it. The little box of shit.

"What—I'm tweetin' my bitches, *Mami!* God...nineteen-seventy-late."

They had this exchange everyday, it was clockwork. Jenny made her calls with Silvia criticizing her in the background and she would leave in five minutes flat, only to return sometime late in the night. She never ate dinner with the family. Silvia had begun leaving her a plate of leftovers in the microwave long ago, covered with a paper towel, and this unspoken agreement was the love between a Cuban mother and her daughter, beyond tradition and undisturbed as food in the microwave. Jenny would ride whatever buzz she was on at the same seat of the table, the rest of the house dark and silent, and in the light of the oven clock she would eat her plate of *Mami's* food and go to sleep, wiping her mouth with the paper towel Silvia had so tenderly placed upon her plate hours before, by then soaked through with grease. She would never tell anyone, especially not her friends—"Bitch you be eatin that *carne puerco* at two in da mo'nin! *Hefuuuh!"*

Mmhmm. It was never fun to be a heifer, especially not in Miami. And *especially* not after having wiped your mouth with a greasy paper towel. Perhaps the best part was that all of her her friends did the same thing. *I loff yoo too Mami – *muah* bechitos!*

Chiche had been pulling out of the driveway in reverse and saw Jennifer's little import sedan rattling down the block. She realized it was too late to slam her brakes and reverse all the way back to school so she merely crept up slowly, her soul bloated with fear, hoping that for some odd reason he wouldn't see her. Though the chances were actually quite high considering the man in question here, he did. He stopped the van, Silvia's cigarette hanging out of his lip as he leapt from his eyes into hers, through her brain and down her spine right into the depths of her little chongalicious heart. He made it snow there, and he whipped back into his eyes with a drag of Silvia's smoke, kicking the van into drive. That was it. The gears scraped loudly as he lurched off into the depths of their little Cuban *vecindario*. Jenny finally mustered to let go of the breath she had been holding the whole time. It was tepid, air heavy with the weight, the warmth, of her angst.

"God-DAAAmmit!" And then she walked through the door, by the rocking chair on the porch that swayed with laughter all by itself.

"*Bueno?* What's up *Mami?* What you do this morning?"

"The same thing, *mija.*" She pursed her lips. "The same thing." *He took my smoke, viejo maricon. I could kill him, Virgensita, I swear it.*

"You look tired, Mom. You should go outside. How long has it been since you went out the front door?" Silvia stopped what she was doing. She didn't know.

"Well, I went to *La Ermita* with Carmen last week, on Saturday I think, and I walked to 57th for some *arroz imperial,* but that was..." and her eyes lost their light as she realized, "last December, for *noche buena*." *Virgen Santísima*. She looked up to the ceiling. "What the hell's your problem, ah? *Yyyyyenniferrrr*...your friends don't want to see you today? Why'd you come here anyway?" She brought her gaze down with the wrath of the prophets, bearing into Jennifer with all the hatred she held for herself in that spiteful moment.

Jennifer met her gaze blankly, smearing an index finger full of lipgloss across her bottom lip, pulling at her *bemba* to get it all on, her frustration, her defiance, her defense. "To see you, what do you think." Warfare. She held her mother's piercing green eyes, thinking so many inappropriate things, tugging at her lip and moving up to the upper lip, and deep inside of herself she remembered how she used to suck her thumb. Silvia echoed what she had said in her mind over and over again, it was a silent battle of wits, Cuban wits, and neither of them gave in, nor would they ever, nor had they ever. But this time Silvia forgave Jenny everything she had ever done in her head as they stared each other down, Silvia sharp and green and Jenny dull, stupidly bright blue, for she wanted *so badly* to hear the inevitable and it was in Jenny's eyes already, wouldn't she just say it, Yennifer just finish smearing that fucking *cebo* on your lips and say it to me, say it *niña de mierda*, you know you want to, you know I need it, you know I will never crawl out of this ashtray if you don't help me right now, and she held her gaze into Jenny's empty eyes, waiting. Jenny pulled her finger from her lips, rubbing it against her thumb melodramatically before speaking.
   "You gotta go do something, *Mami*. What—the fuck." *Ay!* She needed a cigarette. "It don't even gotta be major. Just go for a walk or something low-key, *fuck* man, you know?" She followed her mother's eyes. "Yeah, I see that shit, start to buy your *own* cigarettes or something, just stop letting *Papi* do everything for you! God...he steals your smokes, anyway..." Silvia leered out the window.

"You ever wonder why he does it all for you? He makes it so you don't have to do *anything* except tend to the house...you'd think he didn't *want* you to leave or something." Silvia got a bad taste in her mouth. "Fockeen weird-ass *viejos*, both of you."

"*Santísima Virgen*," she said. She was speechless, her eyes darting about the room, unblinking. Silvia spoke out, to herself more than anyone. "Yennifer, what are you doing right now?" she asked. "You going out to *comer mierda* or you got a little time for your Mami?" Silvia smirked behind her tired eyes. 'Eating shit' was the Cuban term for messing around, *comemierda*.

"I'm..." and Jenny looked around uncomfortably, thinking of all of her friends, no, no, no, no, fuck, not him, no, don't even, *ahhhh crap*...before submitting, "not up to nuthin right now, why?" A coy look danced in her mascara-and-blue eyes. "What do you need, Mama-Chola?"

"Lets go for a walk."

"Well, you gonna change outta that *bata,* no? You can't wear Muumuus outside." Jennifer pulled out her cellphone. Hyper-scroll status updates, makes me look busy. "Do you...even *have* normal clothes anymore? Or did you send them all to Cuba?" Look, a monkey doing coke, *like.*

"*Callate niña!*" she laughed. "Let me go change into something." She walked off to the bedrooms, swallowing a smile. "I kept a *few* things for myself," and her laughter faded as she went down the little hallway decked left and right with pictures of *Santa Barbara*, a calendar from 1987 with San Judas Tadeo on it, Silvia and Chiche's wedding day, Mariza's *quinceañera*, Tico's college graduation, Jenny's first communion and a sublimely beautiful *Sagrado Corazón de Crísto*. She didn't look at any of them as she passed. It was like the mirror, she knew what was there.

~*~

Single story hurricane-proof houses sit happily, painted all sorts of tacky tropical colors gated with wrought iron doors and barred windows, lawns overrun with weeds, *Santos* in their alcoves with human hair to pay a *promesa* made long ago, all from behind chain-link fences since we're still in Cuba.

La Sawesera, we call it...*me oi'tes?*
Me entendi'tes, compadre?
Too many coconut palms and
Regal palmettos fan their leaves out like
Staunch green peacocks of the Caribbean.

Southwest Miami, home of the free...free Cubans.
Arrimese a este arbol y toma coco
Que aqui vamos bien.
It's as if all the *refugiados* end up somewhere here,
Where they have some cousins or
Aunties that got here before them,

You know,
    like

Manolito y Rigoberto, Daguito y Gilberto,
El que huele a perejil,
Kaky, Anaís, Martína, Francisca, Hernando Ibañez
Y su Rico Danzón,
Tio Pepe Guayabal, Barbarita Fernandez,
       El Cucúyo, Rafaelito,
Mariwanga Linares,
Anael o Papito, Chamaca y Albertico, Casquito, Lazarito,
Burufinda, Imel, Ariel, Reniel, Soriel, Mariel,
                que nommmbre!
Taíta Trucupey o Cachao, Bernabé,
El Songo, Mabongo, Bilongo, Mondongo y Borondongo

Aristide, Aquíles, Julio and Castellano Ferrer
...*trrrremeeeeennnnnda rumba que baila ese negro!*

Gutierrez, Miguelito el Ñoño, Aidel, Isabel, Moisé,
Papachango, Puchilanga, Burundanga
Que le hinchan los pies,
Bururú el maletero, El Padre Joaquín y su novio Alberto,
Juan-Crespo, Amaury, Anaíli, Janeysi, El Caimán,
Iliana-Maribel,
Mariluz, Luz-Maria y Pedro Navaja, *sorpresa te da la vida!*

Everyone was *someone's* cousin, you know? And it was
beautiful. The ones, then, who had bootstraps to pull on got out
of there and went to the rest of the *Nganga* of diversity we call
Ameri-sacarampeño, but many of them were comfortable right
there in *La Sawesera*, that fat auntie's kiss where everyone had
brought a little piece of Cuba where their hearts used to be and
planted it underneath their house, in the *bodegas* and *botanicas*, on
calle Ocho and into their cooking pots. Their hearts? Their hearts
were still in Cuba.

~*~

"So tell me *Mami*, where are we going?" Jennifer felt
strange walking around the sidewalks, Miami was for cars. She
looked away as people blew by them booming Pitbull's curled lip
service. *Dale.* Silvia, however, looked natural despite how long it
had been since she had taken to the streets. She had done a lot of
walking in Cuba. In her faraway past, she had gone to one of the
infamous boarding schools that came out of Fidel's revolution.
Communist or not, the education in Cuba was irrefutably good,
there was no denying it. The revolution provided this wonderful
'opportunity' for the children, to be educated for free, striving
always for *la patria, internacionalismo, libertad, unidad,* but there was
much more to their schooling than arithmetic or elementary

Russian. In exchange for a fine education, students were expected to contribute to the foundation of their country, to the roots of the revolution—quite literally.

Early in the morning, in the haze and heat of twilight the girls would wake with the crow of the roosters, who never failed to announce the impending return of the sun—*"Gallo de su puta madre!"*—and head out into the fields after taking their breakfast. It was always the same thing: a cup of burnt powdered milk, for they managed to burn it everyday, and a piece of Cuban bread. It had butter on it if they had butter that day. The walk to the fields was anywhere between one and three miles for these boarding schools were actually quite large, and the girls would trudge along in their work clothes, half asleep and poking fun at each other, burping up the ashy taste of the milk and gossiping about which boys the other girls liked.

Little Silvia was always at the forefront of the gossip chain, *chismeando* about everything and everyone as they walked towards the sea of cane stalks and royal palms, and this kept a steady crowd of girls around her the whole way there. She would tell them *everything*, every last juicy drop she had on the people back in town, and they would proceed to fill her in on the latest gossip of their own. It was an...interpersonal affair. Silvia loved the attention, though she knew the girls weren't her friends. Her only friend in the entire school was the *ovejita* who could always be found at her side, her lovely little sister Carmen, who took very much pride in being able to float in the cloud of *chismes* while at least three years younger than the rest of the girls. They all knew she was Silvia's little sister because only Silvia was allowed to throw the *taquitos* of dirt you made by rubbing your dirty hands together at her, and nobody else had better do anything because Silvia was known to go totally *guajira* when ruffled the wrong way. It was shameless, and she had already been chastised by the headmasters for whopping a couple girls in the head with her mountain-girl knuckles. Silvia hit with closed fists and everybody knew.

So Carmen was safe, confident even, to the point where she called the girls who got on her nerves *cara-chocha* or *comepinga*, knowing that Silvia would deal with them, and though Silvia hated her and her annoying round head grinning about nothing all *got-damn day* long, she felt obliged to protect her. Her *hermanita*.

Little Silvia used to smile all the time in those days.

When they finally got to the fields, it was time to work. There were tubers and roots to be dug up, *yuca* and *malanga* and countless fruits and vegetables, *platanos y maniz, tomates* and *frijoles negros*. Cane to be cut with long, rusted *guatácas*. Some tended to the land and others to the animals, running around with baskets of fresh dung from the cow pen or steamy grog for the pig troughs. The girls took their sickles and machetes up after the walk over to the fields, rusty veterans of the revolution glimmering in the skinny arms of innocent girls seeking knowledge — some on behalf of their parents, others on behalf of an unattainable hope. Freedom by knowledge, education. *Mmhmm. Plís.*

Singing songs to something beautiful in their heads and sometimes out loud, they cut and dug and picked all day, watching the blazing orb of the sun tickle the sky all sorts of colors until it laughed itself blue and baked the fertile earth mercilessly. Some would have to coax the chickens into giving them their eggs, and though it was never fun it was much better than stabbing the soil all day unearthing shiny brown *yuca*. Silvia remembered the scabs she would pick at during the afternoon lectures. The presumptuous hens pecked relentlessly at anyone who tried to stick their hands into their soft, speckled haunches to steal eggs, but they seemed to get Silvia more than the others, perhaps because she was too rough. *Anita* never got pecked, but it was because she sang to the chickens, and Silvia wouldn't be caught dead singing in front of other people, much less to chickens.

Around midday when the sun was at its highest, the girls would head back for lunch, making the girl with the lesbian shoulders carry the heaviest basket, always full of roots. They would enjoy the shade indoors as they took their lunch in the long hall with Spanish tiles on the roof and high ceilings stretching over long, shining walls that needed to be painted save for where the propaganda was, since you couldn't see behind it anyway. In that vacuous room the girls would sit on shiny wooden benches, the glossy paint reflecting the wood's every single scar and scratch in the light that poured through the doors. They would wait for the stoic *compatriotas* in green uniforms to come out from the doors on the far end of the hall and serve them their lunch: burnt *chicharos*, the awful split-pea soup that tasted of smoke, and rice, and sometimes sardines or a boiled egg. If it was a good day they got a glass of milk with their lunch. It wasn't up to them, however, to decide if it was a good day.

After an afternoon of learning they had to go outside into the humid evening and *dance* — "*Bailen, bailen, hecha un pie!*" — to the blaring crackles of a loudspeaker that spat tunes from America at them for an hour every night, after the sun had set. The Beegees, Beethoven, KC and the sunshine band, the Beatles (pronounced *los Be-AHT-less*), all sorts of songs that the girls could recite the words to but didn't understand a single one. Silvia remembered dancing awkwardly for song after song, by force, in the light of the lanterns with fuzzy wicks that burned brightly and made the moths burst into flame and spiral to the ground.

She smiled. "*Los Be-aht-les,*" she said, the words drowning in the rush of traffic.

Together they walked down the wide streets, mother and daughter each lost in their thoughts, of pending plans for the night and of morning walks through the cane fields outside of La Habana, until they arrived at the mini-mall that marked their destination.

"I'm buying my own cigarettes," said Silvia. Pungent incense swirled around the parking lot, and in the shadows within the doorway of the *botanica* next to her market Silvia saw a great statue of La Virgen with strange things littered at her feet, glasses of water, rattles, stones and candles. Toy ducks? She pursed her lips dismissively, casting it away with a swerving look at the mini-mall as Jenny swung into a parking spot. *"Ni pinga."*

The bell to the cigarette shop clanked awkwardly against the door as Silvia pushed it open, the corner tracing the greyish-brown arc of rubber smeared on the linoleum. She and Jennifer made their way into the air conditioning. They paused for a second and basked before acknowledging the cashier's presence. Would heaven be this refreshing? Scratchy talk radio tried to surface from the sea of AM static behind the counter, where the old lady Maribel leaned quietly, staring idly into the floor behind pink-tinted bifocals.

"Marlboro lights," said Silvia casually. "Five." The woman broke from her trance and looked up at Silvia, pausing for a second before she pushed herself off the counter and reached up above her.

"That's half a carton," she said, her hand up in the shelf. "You don't want a carton instead?"

"If I wanted a carton I would have told you."

"Asunto suyo. Aqui estan, Mama," she said, avoiding Silvia's eyes as she took the money. *Parlameng, aqui se acabo mi amor por ti.* It was what her brother-in-law Cuco had said the day

cigarettes went up to two dollars a pack. *'Parlameng,* my love for you ends here.' She didn't like Parliaments, it's what the kids smoked. That, and *marijuana. Dime tu...*

"Hmph." Silvia took her baggie from the woman. She didn't say thank you. The carton can thank her. It was one of those liquor store bags with a red rose on it and a bold-type 'thank you' on the side, colored with little dots like the pictures in the newspaper. She walked out of the store and swiped the wrapping off a pack of smokes in a swift motion that betrayed her experience with tobacconist culture. Tearing the shiny paper off from under the lid, she flipped the cigarette in the middle of the front row — for good luck — and took the one to the left, putting it to her lip as she stuffed the pack back with the rest of them. A soldier couldn't have assembled his gun faster. And she lit the cigarette, fresh in that liquor store way, a staleness you would get used to by the next smoke, drawing on it deeply. It ran over her tongue like cream.

"You know, Yennifer, I'm glad you told me to come out," she said with a flurry of smoke. "I'm gonna do this more often. I like going outside! I had just," and she shook her head, "forgotten. You know how that is." Jennifer smiled back to her silently, her thumbs ticking at her phone screen. "Do you remember Cuba, Yenni? You were just a little girl." The tobacco had fired Silvia up. She looked into her daughter's smartphone eyes, blowing smoke out the side of her mouth. She flicked her cigarette, ignoring the swirl of ashes that trailed behind her. "Do you remember that little store next to *Lissette's Zapateria* back in La Habana?" She smiled upon Jennifer's thinking so hard. "You know, *Lissette's,* where I bought you all of your shoes while you were still a little girl?"

"*Si Mami,* I remember, but not the store next to it." She put her phone away.

"It was the store where they sold clothes, remember? For

men, women, children." She smiled. "Everything." Jennifer's eyes suddenly came to life.

"Ay, si!" And the sparkle fled, quickly as it came. "What...about it?" She pulled out her phone.

"Well, do you remember the man who worked the counter at the store every day of the week? The one with the thin little moustache and the slick hair?" She smiled, putting the cigarette lightly to her lips. Jennifer slipped her phone back into her pocket without saying a word.

"Was it...Miguel? No...Marcos..."

"Antonio Sevilla," said Silvia with crystal clarity. "Antonio...did you know that before I met your father I had a passionate love affair with him?" Silvia brought a hand across her collarbone, her fingers running softly over her skin. "He was my first boy-freng." The words dissipated into the air. Silvia's eyes glowed with mischief. Jenny's grew as big as saucers.

"You *what?* He was your *boyfriend?*" Silvia raised her eyebrows as she took another drag, smiling coquettishly as she blew the flurry into the air above them.

"O, yes," she said to herself with a devilish smile. "It wasn't anything big, but it was everything while it lasted." She looked herself over, adjusting a ring on her aging fingers. "I just couldn't turn down a man who romanced me the way he did."

"Daaaaaaang, *Mami*, workin' the D! What did he do?"

"*Bueno niña*," glowed Silvia, "I'll tell you, that's what we do." She tossed her smoke to the curb, pulling a fresh one from her pack.

~*~

"Augustín! *Que paso, hombre!*" Tico swam through the sea of smack-talk and cigar smoke, pushing by moustached, seventy year-old *chulos* sharing *café* from old thermoses as they played *dominó*. A burly man in a *guayabera* and brimmed hat turned from his game, looking over his shoulder at Tico's slim, white form making his way over to him. Following closely behind him was Angelica, fearing for her life lest she lose hold of his hand.

"*Chamaco!*" shouted Augustín above the roaring chatter, extending a hand towards Tico as if to rescue him from the tumult. He looked at the table behind him, spying on another's rack with a shake of the head as he pulled the two lovers towards him. A *ficha* came down in front of him with a loud crack, jolting all three of them back into the game.

"*Vaya, nueve-nueve, que vale la pena!*" The heaviest bone had come off the racks, shit was getting serious. Tico slapped his old friend on the back, nodding to the others as they shot winks at Angelica sipping their drinks:

"*Mi flor!*"
"*Muñequita!*"
"*Corazón!*"
"*Mira pa'lla!*"

"*Buenas,*" smiled Angelica softly, blushingly aware of the shape of her body against the laughter that bubbled up from the table. These men intimidated her. Tico squeezed her hand reassuringly...*you're the cornerstone of her temple.* Seated around the rickety serpent of ivory pieces were the few men who Tico could consider friends of his. There was Osmani, a slick fellow dressed like a disco inferno, long collars, bell-bottoms and all, for he still thought it was 1974. He slicked his hair back with a sly grin. Next to him was Manolito, a skinny old man with gold-rimmed glasses and a slightly puckered mouth so that one would think he was always grinning...or perhaps he was, nobody knew. He held a perfectly white cigarette in his bony hand, swiping it across his rack and taking a drag before setting down his piece.

Rogelio *pssshhhhed* at his father's move. He was Manolito's adopted son, and his gums were the same color as the patches of piebald that mapped his black skin. He toked on a long *Romeo y Julieta* he had smuggled from Cuba on his last trip over. He and

Manolito would go a few times a year as mules, funded by anxious Cubans on this side of the ninety miles who gave them *maletas* and *maletas* of clothing, medical supplies and coffee to give to their relatives. Free as the trip was, they couldn't help but indulge in the luxury of coming back with the same suitcases full of contraband: cigars, rum, clothing, musical demos from aspiring artists in La Habana, whatever they thought people in Miami would pay for. It seemed that the two were a strange enough duo to make it through customs unscathed, over and over again, with their unbeatable mixture of luck and a knack for taking risks. Perhaps that was why Manolito was always smiling...*ah?* Nobody knew.

Augustín toked his cigar, looking up at Tico with drowsy brown eyes. "What brings you to the park today, *Bohemio?*" he asked as he set a piece on the table. *"Tres-tres – cantó el Pitirre!"*

"Nah, I was just in the area, you know?" He smiled out loud, pulling up a chair and facing Manolito and Rogelio. "Well, and, *tu sabes,* just checking in to see how you guys' trip went. You just came back, no?" *Oh, what a bad liar you are!*

"Si hombre," said Rogelio, setting his smoke into the ashtray. "Just got back the other night, it was some scary shit." Manolito nodded, bobbing his eyebrows as he eyed the *fichas* on the table.

"We were just through customs, our suitcases in our hands," he said, "and everything was fine. But the officer calls us back — *'Perdoname señor!'* — and asks to see our papers again." He shook his head. "We thought this was it, we're finally getting caught, they'll take our shit and we'll get blacklisted." Rogelio scoffed.

"Policias de pinga, they think they're running the whole damn show."

"So we turn back and show the lady our papers, and I can

see her looking at our suitcases, judging 'em with her little green eyes, and she asks us why we had so much luggage after going to Cuba only for five days."

Rogelio smiled. "So you know what I told her?" and he nudged his father on the shoulder. "I looked her in the eye and said *mi viejo's* on *el dialisis, pinga'e su madre!*" The whole table burst out laughing, even Angelica, who sat quietly wishing she could disappear. Flowerbuds close tight with the night.

The cold. "That's why we have all this shit, *mi amor*, it's my equipment!" And they laughed, repeating the punch-line over and over again, until they noticed that Osmani had gone quiet. He seemed to notice all the eyes on him and looked up.

"*Y a ti que te pasa?*" barked Augustín.

"*Bueno, tu sabes que, que* I went to the doctor's the other day and he offered me some of the *pastelitos* they had in the back room for the employees before telling me that I might have to do that shit one day," and he pursed his lips. "Dialysis." He uttered it like a curse.

"*Oye*, at least you can get shit through security without gettin' messed with, ah?"

"*Vaya*, that's ridiculous *meng*." *It won't happen for eight years.*

"Come on," said Tico, "it won't even happen for at least a decade or so, look at you, you're a picture of health!" Osmani looked himself over, and the light came back into his eyes when he saw his gold bracelet, the one that said 'OSMANI' in encrusted cubic-zirconia.

"Hell yeah, you know? A decade or so," he smirked, and he checked the pieces on the table dismissively, sliding a 3:4 across the table for Augustín to set at the end of the run. "Shit...yeah I'm fine."

"*Pero Manolito*," ventured Tico anxiously, "so you were, ah, you were saying that you had your suitcases full o—"

"*Ay, si!*" He yelled, pulling the cigarette from his mouth, "I almost forgot!" He hunched low over the table, as if it were a big deal. "Ah, Rogelio? What did we finally get for *Jose Marti* over here?"

"*Vaya,*" laughed Rogelio, "as if he doesn't know."

"*Ayyyyy!*" gushed Tico. "Let me take a moment to assure that this joy doesn't go to the wrong place!" and the men laughed, slightly confused. They didn't care, they liked Tico's bullshit. *They can not see these pearls of knowledge, swine that they are...*

"*Wah,* and if you see what *else* we picked up while we were there," smirked Rogelio, bobbing his eyebrows triumphantly at Manolito, who winked at Tico without looking at him. If anyone would have been paying close enough attention, they would have seen the Gardenia on the lapel of his coat pull open just a bit more. The old man put his cigarette out in the ashtray, raising his finger and shaking it at Rogelio with the dictum of a father, 'nah-ah'. There was silence.

Manolito lit a smoke and tapped the table with his knuckles. No bones. Next. Rogelio skimmed his rack with his eyes, and finally smacked the table with a huff.

"*Coño papi,* what's the matter? That's the coolest shit we brought over since that time you smuggled that *azulejo* in your pack of smokes." Tico swallowed a smile.

Immmmmmpeccable, this rogue!

Manolito kicked his chair back with a laugh. "Started singing on the airplane, piece of shit!" and the table boomed with laughter. "Had to whistle the whole flight over, people thought I was nuts! But no Tico, *de verdad,*" he said, in suddenly better spirits, "we got something this time that a guy like you would find," and he puckered his mouth, "quite interesting. That's all I'm gonna say about it." He took a drag.

"Listen up, you three," said Augustín, "as much as I enjoy hearing about all your stupid shit, we got a game to get back to," and he smiled around his cigar, "Manolo lags enough as it is, *coño'e su madre."*

"Ok, ok," smiled Manolito, "well Tico, your stuff is at the shop, go tell Bebita what you came for, and tell her to show you what we brought."

"And tell her to quit eating the *croquetas* from next door, ah?" cracked Rogelio. "I swear, she works there just because of that goddamn bakery next door, *andaaaaaaa,"* and he waved a hand into the air, *"pero cuadraaa!"*

"Sounds good, then," laughed Tico, "well my esteemed gentlemen, I think I'll making my way towards th—"

"Nah nah nah! Ni pinga!" yelled Manolito with a frown, shaking his cigarette 'no' with his bony hand. He looked at the gold watch on the same hand, keeping it out in the middle of everything, and he looked back at Tico. "You sit there, and your lady right there, and you two stay here and chat with us for a while since I know you ain't got nuthin to do anyway, okay?" He sat back. "Your shit will be waiting for you until you go get it, I *run* this got-damn show."

"Well," laughed Tico shooting a glance at Angelica, "I guess we could stay a little longer."

Augustín spoke. *"Bueno,* before you got here I was telling Rogelito over here that these cell phones everyone's got, they're just a lux—"

"Nah nah nah, no jodas!" laughed Rogelio, biting down on his *puro.* "You know what we were talking about and it wasn't no cell phones okay? That's from an hour ago, we're talking about why el *Castellano* is so late and you just want someone to help you out w—"

"Oye! Let me finish!" He paused emphatically, raising both of his hands high into the air, basking in the silence until he spoke once again. "Got-dammit."

"Ok *viejo*, what's you deal..." grumbled Osmani. He picked up a *ficha* and spun it across the table to the ivory serpent that curled between them all.

"That's the point, that I want someone smart like Tico, a youth of *la revolucion* to tell me what—"

"You're full of *shit!*" laughed Osmani. *"Comuniiiiiista!"* he wailed, pointing a ringed finger at Augustín who said nothing behind the thick *puro* in his mouth. *"Mira...*Augustín—" he spat his name—"listen here, okay? This was a conversation from an hour ago, but now that Tico's here—" he raised a hand to Angelica—"and his *muñequita* too, no?" He blew her a kiss. "We'll bring the topic back up to hear Tico's point *only because* Cachita told me one time that he writes books, and that means he's gotta know enough about things to tell other people about them, no? *Pues si."* He reached into Manolito's front pocket and took a smoke. Manolito nodded solemnly, taking a drag on his own.

"Okay then, so Tico, Tico, *mojame el pico,* tell me, what do you think? I was telling these ancients that cell phones are just a luxury, you know? That we existed long before cell phones did—"

"Before *cell phones?"* said Rogelio. "Osmani here existed before *condoms, meng,* you seen how many kids that guy has all over Cuba?" and he reeled back, laughing. Osmani shrugged, raising his bejeweled hands up in jest.

"Buuuuuuuuue'!"

"*Si, si,* I see what you mean, Rogelio, I mean, they—"

"*Aha!* I know exactly what the kid's gonna say, you see?" yelled Osmani with wide eyes. "He's gonna say just like I was trying to say earlier, you remember that time I got caught up under that snow bank when I went to visit my daughter in Tennessee?" He almost fell back in his chair, so high did he raise his hands. "I mean *black clouds,* Augustín, do you remember that? I told you at Rigo's barbeque, ah? Where he cooked those steaks that were like leather, disgusting as hell, *Jesucrísto!"* And he paused. "...but the *mojitos* were good. He grows his own *yerba Buena,* you know that?"

"*Si, si,* but the point you we—"

"So this storm kicks in out of *nowhere*, and we get caught in this *hailstorm* of all kinds of shit falling out of the sky, you know? *Tremeeeennnndo singete*, and what could possibly be worse than *bang!* Flat tire." He nodded with pursed lips. "*Mmhmm*, but *I*, alert and *empinnnn-GAO* as I tend to be, saw an overpass ahead through all the crap and drove under it because where we were, we were bound to get hit by some white-ass driving like crazy in the middle of that storm off his *wihhh-key*, which is what they drink," and he paused, scratching the little corner of skin between his nose and his cheek with a funny face. It was devilish tactic, allowing his point to gather strength in the silence.

"So what did I do?" He leaned into the middle of the table, his golden *Santa Barbara* hanging over the dominoes with a smile. "*Ah? what did I do, Augustín?!* Hah...I called my *cell phone*" – he pounded the syllables onto the table – "and got through to my *daughter* and told her we were gonna be *late*, since we were under an *overpass, okay? Me oistes?* And then I called the *Tres-A* and they came and got us out of the storm," and he slapped his domino onto the table with a definitive *bang* and said "*vaya, ocho y seis*," with an air of nonchalance. Augustín rolled his eyes at Tico.

"Tico! You seen my niece?" Osmani continued. "Swear to God, prettiest kid you've ever seen, *mira*," and he pulled a pharmacy envelope out of his front pocket, passing it to Tico.

"Oh yeah," said Manolito, "we've *all* seen the girl today," and he took a sip of his *café*, rolling his eyes.

"What's your *fockeen* problem *meng, ah?*" snapped Osmani, backhanding the envelope. "You haven't even seen the pictures yet and you're talking shit about my little *corazonsito de melocotón*, my *fockeen* niece? I'd like to see some pictures of your Rogelio when he was a baby, that'd put San Juan's finger up your ass," and no one said anything. Coffee, cigarettes, pursed lips. *Chismes* were brewing. Tico spoke, *out of the highest compassion...*

"*Mira*, she's cute, ah? And this one?" He grabbed the

stack. "*Ha*, look at you *hombre*, you hair was darker," and Osmani rubbed his full head of hair, staring at Manolo's balding head. Angelica tugged at Tico's arm quietly, whining at him with her eyes. He squeezed her thigh without turning from the conversation.

"She still in Cuba, or did she come over already?" asked Augustín, exasperated.

"Nah, they're still over there, they actually live on the same block as one of my neighbors did here...you know, the guy who got his kids taken away," and he sighed, messing with his bracelet. "CPS. See-pee-ess. I mean c'mon, you know? It's one thing to show your kids who's boss, but out in the front yard?" He shook his head. "C'mon, *hombre*, you can go to *jail* for that here, thinks he's still in Cuba. They just took the kids, though, he probably doesn't give a shit anyway if he was kicking their ass." He *tss*-ed and flicked his eyebrows at Rogelio, telling him to go.

Everyone nodded quietly at Rogelio's move. He was down to his last *ficha*.

"Man, what's happened to these people, *ah*?" Manolito gestured all around him. Chips, *chiviricos*, sweat pants and ghetto-fied youth. "I mean look, nowadays, you see these *Chusma* Cubans all *freneticos*, living all *guajiro-tumabayaya* over here, ah? They don't even give a shit, you know what I saw the other day in Hialeah? Got-damn goats in the street!" The table split with laughter. "Goats! Yeah, I mean, it was either some *compeinga Oriental* or some *Santeros* getting ready to feed *la Prenda* —"

"Waaaaaaaaaaaaaaaaaaaaaaaaaaaaaaaaaaaaaaaaaaaa!!!"

He took a drag of his cigarette. "I mean, you might be too young, Augustín, but Osmani — *you* remember the good 'ol days, when everyone was nice, and people used to dress up and the music was good and it had more *ritmo, caché*, and the *casinos* were alive with people, and even the races got along, you remember that?" Osmani nodded with a smile, fixing his tinted-glasses straight.

"*Si, tu sabes*, ever since the revolution, there's been all that racial warfare, discomfort, you know? White on black, black on white, everything in between, back in the old days they'd have the dance at the *Social Club*, and the *negritos* knew that they couldn't go, and it was okay, you know? They had their own dance, back at the *Cabaret*, and you know, they'd all be at each other's dances, *blanco con negro, negro con blanco*, but the point is that there was no trouble, ah? What happened to that? Now there's all this racism, you know *why*? Because Castro came in, and he said everyone was *eeeee-kwal, egalitario, bajo con la burguesía*, all that *shyet*." He said '*equal*' in English.

Tico raised a finger. *Mind your ego, Terpsichorean.* "Ok...*bueno*, I wasn't alive in the, as you say, 'good ol' days,' but I have read a lot of books about those very good ol' days, and even though I didn't live in those times like all of you esteemed souls — and trust me, I know experience is the best of teachers — I have to say that you are incorrect — "

"I ain't here to listen to no talk about that, huh?" touted Manolito, "last time I talked politics I got a tooth ache, now come on Augustín, play your *ficha*, Rogelio's ready to unload."

"I mean please, *caballero*," said Tico, "you're going to tell me that there wasn't racism, when the dances were *separated*? Perhaps the *revolucion* gave the people a *voice* and stirred all the *mierrrrda* — " *you've FAILED, curses!* "that had been simmering for a long time — " *You shouldn't be so profane, don't desecrate the temple of the Verb.*

"*Hmph*, we've got another *comunista* on our hands," said Osmani. "Typical, ah Augustín? And I heard his Mom's got the evil eye. Kills birds."

Tico winced. *Chismes!*

"*No, no*, so you *really* believe there was no racism when there was a dance for the whites and a whole separate dance for the blacks?"

"*Yyyyeahhhhh*," burped Manolito, "*because they both got dances*, Tico, this is what you're failing to see. That was equality, and everyone liked it."

"I can only imagine," smirked Tico. *Just leave it be, beloved.*

He paused, brushing his shoulder with a scoff.

"Listen," he said, his eyes narrowing, "I am absolutely sure that this whole idea of 'blanco y negro' was introduced right along with the slave trade, and that this is the whole reason for that silly notion of superiority the whites had, just because everyone's slaves were of a certain color, and that stretched itself out into being better than the *negros* as a whole, not just as slave-master dyads, *me entiendes?*" He cleared his throat. "It is a matter of interpersonal relationships."

"*Hmph*, you read too many books, Tico," said Manolito, brushing him off. Rogelio said nothing.

"*Si*, but that was the Spaniards who did that," said Osmani, "not us, ah?"

"*Bueno*, Osmani, *dos y dos son cuatro dedos de frente*, you know?"

Everyone laughed, everyone except Osmani, as Tico held four fingers up to his forehead in an adaptation of that old Cuban saying.

"The Spanish are the reason we're not *Indios* when we say we're from Cuba, you know *meng?*" He laughed. "Our ray is white. And yes, the scholars of the past hundred years have spen—"

"*Mi geeeeeeeente! Que peeeeeeeeeeeeste, la siento desde aqui! A quien le pica los hueeeeeevos!*" The entire park looked over at their table, and Augustín buried a smile into his closed fist.

"Son of a bbbb – "
"Aqui llego la fieeeeeeeesta, llegaron las Guayabitas del Pinar!"

Rogelio leaned over: "That's some of the best liquor in Cuba, Angelica, money-in-my-mouth."

"Castellano, que bueno baila usted!" exclaimed Tico, standing up to give the skinny Galician nut a hand across the tables of Cubans who had turned to look. *Chismes* bubbled in their eyes. He had said that 'the party had arrived' for he had a bottle of *'Guayabitas del Pinar,'* a liqueur from the province of Pinar del Rio that was made from the certain type of little guavas that grew there...even the children grew jealous, for they'd all heard the song. He gave Tico a hug, the bottle landing across his back with a thud as they turned to face their table. *El Castellano,* as they called him, was born in Cuba, but his parents were from Spain, having moved to the island in the sort of freedom that Hemingway was allowed to indulge. Who would want to leave Spain, one might ask? Why, someone who thinks Cuba is paradise, that's who.

"Who wants it, I even brought ice, and I've got some *bocaditos,* and why, you might ask?" He lingered on for a second, his smile hardly containing all of his happiness. "Because I *love* you assholes, *ha-HAAAA!* Come on, let's have a drink!" He screamed into the ceiling. "I got next game by the way" he winked at Osmani, "I can see Rogelio's about to unload."
"Castellano, you're gonna get us all arrested, *meng!* Sit-cher *ass down,"* said the disco inferno, slightly red in the face. Lowering his voice, he said, "and pour me some of those *Guayabitas, meng,* I haven't had that shit in years."
"Ha-HAAAAAAAA!" Castellano raised a finger to his lips, failing horribly to shh with snickers that made his face go red. Laughing with him, Manolito slammed his domino onto the table. *"Zero-zero, ambos liviano!"*
"Okay okay, listen up," said *Castellano,* pouring *guayabitas-*

on-the-rocks into the thinnest plastic cups he found at Ween-
Deesee. "I've got some *chistes* from last week for you assholes."
The banter died off in seconds. It was time for a joke.
    "I'll bet he heard 'em on—"
    "*Coño Osmani, callate chico!*" Okay. Now it was quiet.

    "So I heard they changed the vocabulary in Cuba to fit the
times," said *El Castellano*. "They call the bus *'aspirina'* now,
because you can only take one every four hours." Hahaha...*coño*.
    "And steak? *Bistec?* They call that *'Jesucrísto'* now,
because everyone talks about it but on on has seen it!"
Hehehe...*ay Mamá*. Rhymes in Spanish.
    "And the fridge," he said, "they call it *'El Coco'*, because
the only thing in it is water." *No, no...pero — psshhh! Aaaay coño.*
    "And Old Havana? They call that Hotel Carimao, because
if you take too long *te quedas enjabonao!*" Eyebrows rose.
    "You know, the shower, the water goes out—man, *fuck you
guys, goddammit!*"

    "Hahahahahahahahahahahahahahahahahahahahahahahaha!"

    "Ha-HAAAAAAAAAAA!"

    Angelica squeezed Tico's arm once again. He looked her
into her eyes and blew her a kiss. Her head spun and she looked
away, blushing. "*Bueno*, it looks like I gotta leave this party, eh?"
he said. "I gotta go see Bebita, remember? Plus," he winked, "*mi
jeba* has to pee, isn't she adorable?" Lica smacked him on the arm
with a frown.
    "*Maldito!*"
    "Let's go then, *muñeca*," he said, ignoring her jab.
Everyone said happy goodbyes, Osmani and Rogelio and
Manolito and Castellano and Augustín, who said:
    "*Bueno*, Tico, good luck with whatever awaits you, and
Angelica, enjoy your pee." He winked.
    "I don haff to *pee*, that's just Tico trying to play *machito*

around all of you *Cubanazos*, with his little flower and all. I tell you, it's probably *he* who has to pee, with all the *café* he drinks!" She slapped his butt with a vicious smile, and all the guys hooted and laughed—"*Colombiana, oistes?*"—as she shoved him off toward the gates, spilling over the crowded tables onto the heated blacktops of *Calle Ocho* once again. Tico grabbed Angelica, kissing her deeply before making for the crosswalk. He winced in pain as they stopped at the corner, rubbing his pursed lips. Angelica had bitten his tongue.

~*~

   "*Bueno muchacha*, like I was saying," said Silvia as she flicked her ash to the sidewalk, "he was skinny, with just a hint of grey peeking at the very tip of his hairline, and he wore the same suit everyday." Her words were riddled with smoke. "He would tell me he washed it every night and dried it in the heat, but I knew he just wore it until it felt dirty, like all of us. But *que*," she smiled, taking a drag, "I let him have the benefit of the doubt." The bag swung idly at her side as she walked, bumping into Jennifer every couple of steps. "It was too long ago to remember exactly when it all happened…all I remember was that the moon was so beautiful, rising right out from behind *El Malecon*, just a little more than half full. You could see the craters all over it, I couldn't believe how real it was." She rubbed a hand over her face. "I was on my way home from the park, it was Friday, and the little *conjunto* would always play under the statue of Marti, getting the tourists to dance and give them some money. It was there, right by the turn on the avenue that would have taken me home that he spoke to me. '*Ey, washyor neng?*' he said in English. 'Yarina,' I told him." Silvia smiled. "I never told the truth back then, it felt incredible."
   "He told me it was a pretty name, Yarina, and I laughed out loud. He asked why I laughed, and I told him it was because I heard it all the time. That was true, though, because I always

chose pretty names to lie to people with. He asked if I had been at the park dancing because of the way the sweat glowed on my skin, but I cast him off with a comment about the weather and that everyone was sweating. What did he want, you know?"

"I don't know, your number? He sounds kind of creepy, *Mami*."

"*Culicagada*," she scoffed, "he wanted *me*. He said that the moonlight on my neck made my ponytail horribly sexy. I smiled and thanked him, bringing a hand to my hair. It was clumpy and knotted in the heat. 'Can I walk you around the block?' he asked, and I'll never forget the way he did it. So forward, obvious, subtle...*ay Yennifer*," she sighed, "I have thought about it on the couch and at the stove for so long, and it is now that I finally see that it was love in his eyes, and he didn't even know me. I was just a girl. Do you understand that, *mija*?" She giggled. It was the first time Jenny had ever heard her mother laugh like that. "No, you're still too young."

"Well, we walked on and on, and finally, at a store window I stopped and decided it was time to go home. I didn't want it to end, but I didn't want him to know that so I turned around." She sighed. "I should never have turned, that was him, my love. But there I was, young and stupid, thinking that if God gave me this for no reason, he would give me something better when I decided to beg him for it." She stopped, picking another smoke out of her pack. "*La Virgen es milagrosa*, but I can tell you, *mija*, She's not always so generous if you ignore her blessings while they're there." Capricorn — a puff of smoke. Jenny cried alone, watching her mother with her swollen blue eyes, what about *Papi*, why are you telling me this, would I have even been born. *Mami* took a long drag of her cigarette.

"Was that it?"

"*Si*," she said, "that was it. No kiss, no sex, nothing." She laughed. "just...*amor*." She paused for a moment, looking through someone's screen door at the sunglassed *chulos* singing

Reggaeton on the TV. "But that was the closest thing to true love I've ever known, because it didn't have all the other things love brings with it." She tossed her smoke to the curb, almost whole. They walked in silence the rest of the way home, squinting in the sunlight all the way back to their house, where the neighbor waved hello as his dog squatted over their lawn, taking a shit.

~*~

Ofelia looks at her ball,
the phone warm with
the memory of her hands.
Something about the Toque last week,
Mabel broke down and
Light of the World was freed
from his prison.

The night sky, they tell her, is the
reflection of so many eyes
on this dark crystal.

~*~

Away from the domino park, little Havana wasn't as romantically Cuban — that sort of thing kept close to the domino tables, and the nostalgia shops. The old people. The rest of this busy little stretch was a new Cuban, and everyone was Mclovin' it. The groups of boys goggled like birds at *dat aaaaaass!* strolling up the streets, and the girls checked themselves out in the tinted store windows like it was their reflections that were 20% off. People left and right ate junk food both Cuban and American, washing it all down with those imported sodas that had enough sugar to stun a cow...*pero que rrrrrrico!* Pitbull, or 'El Peep-boo', jammed from one set of speakers, and across the street at another store blared Celia Cruz, answering to the call of the dying generation that would stay alive so long as people kept coming from Cuba. The streets were alive, with life, with passion, with cacophony and the highs of grease and sugar and subtle lusts. To be melodramatically confident, with the passion of a bull in heat, that was to be Cuban. Or at least to make it as one. Softies simply couldn't cope — they moved to Orlando or California and sipped mango mojitos at some watered-down restaurant with the rest of the wannabes. Cubanismo was serious as a ripe Catholic family out eating *bistec empanizado* with honey-wheat milkshakes at three in the morning.

If two Cubans talking about their new fence could make people think they were about to go apeshit on each other, then imagine, *imagínate!* What must it have been like at 3pm on 8th street that fine, sunny day, just a little too hot for comfort but still perfectly sexy? It was humid, sultry, and for the most part, like a better version of the same things we had in Cuba, for that's all it is, God save us all — *Rrrruueeeck-rrrickirrrrueeeck-rrrickirrrrueeeck* — *sazón criollo!* And it was good, better, better than yours, free to overwhelm you all the way to your God-given core in a 9-piece, brass mongering *orquesta*-of-a-wake-up-call to *life, you scoundrel!* If you didn't like it it's because you couldn't handle it, so get your shit to Fort Lauderdale and sip it through a fucking pineapple.

"Here we are, *mi flor*, I bow to your essence in allowing you to go first." Tico pushed the dark glass doors of *La Cuerda Floja* open, gesturing Angelica inside with the courtesy of three chivalrous men and the clank of an old cowbell that hung from the latch. The music of Beny Moré poured through the doorway as if in greeting, the slaps and open-tones of congas dancing over the familiar tune, '*Devuelveme el Coco*'.

Inside, the *negrito's* hands danced
across the *cueros* with
the reverent air one needs
to approach the voluptuous curves

of a well-fed woman — *muah*
'Wachappeng Mami?' —
and succeed.

Anyone who knew how to
play the congas could tell you that it was easy to go to town and
beat the hell out of them, but they made music only when touched
the right way...any woman could agree with *that*, no? To kiss a
nalga the size of Cambodia took fierce control — nay, divine
intervention! — and it was precisely this that made the *conguero*
such an important part of all traditional music in Cuba, he took
directly on the *rumba* that the *clave* brought out from the skies, one
click at a time. Patterns emerged, and Goddesses were stirred
from their languid naps, surrounded by honeybees and bushes
laden with citrus fruits. Without the *conguero*, you were left to the
pendejerias of a Bachata, and we all know how *that* shit sounds.

"*Ay, pero mira lo que me han traído los Reyes.*"

Tico turned to face the glass-top counter, behind which sat
Bebita, the *mulata* who ran the store. Her hair stuck out in all
directions, and she stopped caring about makeup years ago: *que
chusma.* He looked up at her — "Bebita, *que cuentas!*"

"*Hmph*," she smirked, flicking her eyes toward Angelica.
The ashy skin around her armpits glistened with sweat, hair
follicles caught in the goosebumps of a forgotten shave. "You
know, the only thing worse than people who laugh alone is the
ones who talk to themselves. And you're too much of a *mariquita-
maria* to be on drugs." *Ay, was that the pejorative?!*

"Ha, I was just sorting some things out. Listen, Bebita, I've
don't think I've introduced you t—"

"Oh, I've heard." Bebita smiled at Angelica. "*Buenas,*
you're just as pretty as they tell me."

"*Hmmmmm*, well," laughed Tico nervously, "Bebita,
Angelica, Angelica, Bebita. I am slave to the charms of

formality...she, this beacon of a *mulata*, runs the store here, a muse amongst melodies, indeed, my favorite place to frequent the spirit of music."

"*Vaya*, he'll always be a poet," scoffed Bebita, sticking her pinky into the air. "Like I said, too gay to be on drugs." Angelica looked to Tico, but he was caught in a stare at Bebita's neck, swollen and riddled with the deeply set lines of obesity. He blinked, mouthing something to himself. *Runs in the family...*

"Mira...Bebita," said Tico, pulling out his handkerchief, "I was just with Manolito and Rogelio at the park, they told me th—"

"*Ay!*" she looked into his eyes. "*Si.* Roge was excited about this one." She rolled her eyes. "Those two can't lay off the *marimba*, ah? *Tres pares de cojones que han de tener*...but yes," she said, her eyes down to the ground, "I don't know if I should give this to you..." She flicked her gaze back into his eyes. Wink.

"*What*, the...guiro?" asked Tico innocently. *Apt feigning of perplexity.*

"Oh, *that's* right here," she said, the smirk on her face contorting into pain as she bent down, probably further than she had in years. She emerged, out of breath. "This what you were looking for?"

"*Ayyyyyy*," said Tico, trembling with reverence, "the signature of Crispín Garcia." He breathed into the moment. "It is beyond words."

"I got a word for you," she smirked. "Cris-*PINnnnnnnn-ga.*" Tico choked. Angelica scoffed. *Tersssely.*

Enemies, from the beginning.

In Bebita's gentle, stroking hands was the most exquisitely crafted *guiro* one could ever behold. It was made of the finest wood, painted and glossed over with reds that faded into the pink spines, glowing like roses in the depths of the ocean, set with leather ringlets in the holsters and, indeed, crafted in the shape of a red snapper. It was sunset, sunset for dinner, sunset for music.

He made to grab it from her, but she pulled it back with a snort, her eyes insulted and wide.

"*Ni lo pienses!*" she gushed. Winked. "You need to give me a kiss first." Angelica's core tightened with a stifled growl.

"Tico, I think we're done here."

"Easy, easy, *blanca nieve*, dont worry," Bebita laughed, "we finished that shit long ago, *pegatarrrreando* is impossible with your *girlfriend* in the room...no?" Tico bolted around, taking Angelica by a hand that she snatched away.

"*Lica, Lica, mi tocinilllllito del cielo,*" he whined, "this is how we always speak with each other, it's a game as old as our friendship —" and he turned back to Bebita with a scowl— "Bebita and I have never...oh...please, please take no offense." Angelica *rolled* her eyes, turning to the *negrito*, who had stopped playing at the mention of *pegatarreando*.

"*Y que tu quieres?!*" snapped Bebita. The man tipped his hat and went right back to the drum. "Si, Tico, just a game, only now we play with words and not our bodies," she smiled. "*Mmmmmm...*"

And that was enough for the bird of paradise.

"Look what you've done, Bebita! This is no way to stay on my good side." Tico turned to watch his lover, who had gone to flit through the vinyl.

"*Ay pero Tico,*" Bebita said, leaning over the counter, "you have *nothing* but good sides," and she enjoyed a bobbling laugh lit by the illuminated panes of glass underneath, all to herself. Shadows danced about her well-fed figure.

"Ok *mira*, that's enough, *stop*, please," he snapped.

"Can't a girl play a little before you take your things and leave...like that?" She tilted her head to the side. "They come, and they go, and all poor Bebita can hope for is that they come before they go —" she laughed, watching Angelica bend over the records. She looked at her own ass in the security mirror. Pursed her lips. "But the good ones never come...just bastards like you," she said, watching Angelica bring a record to her face, smelling the old vinyl. *Angustia, de La Sonora Matancera.* "Did you know there are two hundred and sixty two records back there? *Hmmmph...*" she reached over to the register and grabbed a pack of cigarettes, setting one in her mouth before continuing. "Lath week people vough nine of 'em...amm poor Vevita'th here to keep track of efery, ffingle, one." Her lighter clicked loudly, and she brought the flame to her face.

> *A puff*
> *of*
> *smoke*
> *rose*
> *from*
> *thick,*
> *freckled lips.*

"*Mira...*" she said through the smoke, "Manolito and Roge are a little crazy, you know that." She took a long drag, her eyes coming alive with the slightest flash of mischief. "I mean...they would bring anything into the country just to get that...*tingle* in their balls, you know?" She laughed a long laugh to herself. It was the spirit of rum-running smugglery, as old as Cuba itself. The perennial rush of thieves somewhere up in the family tree. A pack of illegal smokes for your nephew, a bottle of the good ol' days for Chispa, they'd all remember you when you died. "But this time?" She paused, blowing smoke slowly through her nostrils. "This time I think they've gone too far. Make's *my* balls tingle, *shyiiiiiit.*" Tico's eyes glossed over with confus—"Just listen," she said, gesturing him closer with a look at Angelica. He leaned in. "I know you're quite..." and she searched for the word, "...*espirituaallll*, but even this freaks me out a little bit...." She blew smoke out the side of her mouth, away from Tico. "I know about this shit, and I don't think they're giving it the respect it deserves."

Rrrrespect...rrreverence, born of fear.

Tico's ear pricked. "Well what *is* it?!" he pressed, scratching the side of his head. "That's the only way I can muster to see if you're right. Until this very moment, my respect is yours, indeed, Schrödinger's cat can be in there as far as—"

"*Hold on.*" She waved her hands about her ears, cracking her gaze at the man at the drums. "*Señoooor,*" she smiled disdainfully, "*y piensas hacerme mercancia?*" He smiled, looking Tico over from head to toe.

He nodded. "*Si, mama, pero atiendelo a el primero,*" and he stood, making his way out of the store with a tip of his hat.

"*A el, a esssste,*" scoffed Bebita, bringing her gaze back to the Bohemio clad in white. "I'm sick of you, Alberto Campos. You and your, your....*ay, que va,* I've been here for too long," she exclaimed with a stretch toward the ceiling. "Unnnnnhhh..." she groaned, picking up her cigarette up from the ashtray. "*Oye niña,*" she called across the empty store, "*ven pa'caaaa...*"

Angelica looked to the kindest, freckliest smile for a good three seconds before slinking over with her nose in the air. Bebita turned to Tico and said, "I only trust a woman's intuition." *I—I say!*

"*Y que?*" said Angelica, a coastal flare in her eye. Fire, fought with fire!

"*Mira mami, dime...*are you a...religious person?" Angelica thought for a second, and looked at Tico.

"*Bueno...on my good days.*"

"Good enough. *Mira,* I've got something I don't want to give to your *mari-novio* over here, even though he's crazy for it." She winked. "I'm sure you know what we're talking about."

"No, no, I don't, Bebita, I don't even want to imagine," she said, swallowing a swell of nausea.

"Very well, I'm going to let *you* decide if I should give it to him, because I know just as well as you do that we—women—are the only people who should be making decisions in this world," and she blew smoke into the air for a long, drawn-out pause. "Because the men have two heads to think with...and the smaller one tends to run the show." They both enjoyed a long laugh together, at Tico's expense.

Angelica turned to him with a smile. "*Ay, si*, I know that all too well. The smaller one." Tico felt as though he was surrounded by wolves. *Maintain awareness, the moment has come...and yours is perfectly normal, sweet pie, worry not.*

Tico smiled out loud: "*Si*, the smaller one. *Que lindas son...*"

"So let me see, *niña*, I've got it...right...here," and from beneath the counter, after another heave and groan, she pulled a bundle of tape and thick paper, as big as a loaf of bread. It was as if the air recoiled from the room in a wave of unnoticed...respect. "This right here might be the stupidest shit Manolito and Rogelio have *ever* brought from the other side, they should have left it there but it's too late, and I don't want it on my hands if the rumors are true. So you'd better think about this well, because I want Tico to have it just so it'll get the fuck outta my store."

"*Bueno?*" sighed Angelica, feigning boredom. "And what might it be?" Bebita, shaking her head, unwrapped the bundle, layer by layer, and the smells of Cuba emerged from the wrapping paper, giving both Bebita and Tico a breath of nostalgia.

"*Ay, Cuba,*" sighed Tico.

"*Mmhmm*, this is Cuba alright. *Revolucion, religion y rrrrechusmeria.*" She brought her hand into the bundle, raising its contents for all to see, her sunken eyes flinching as if she herself couldn't believe she was actually handling it. Between Tico, Angelica and the *mulata* hovered a long, glistening machete, black as the slaves that had cut cane on the island for so many years.

"Look at that shit," grimaced Bebita. "The *fuck* were they thinking."

Tico's head began to spin, and he bobbed himself upright again, his jaw slightly agape. *It...it is...the sword! The signs, the dreams! B-behold, the Venerable —*

Bebita looked at Angelica: "Now tell me, *caramelo,* what could your little *bohemio y poeta* possibly do with this, that would be better than throwing it away?" *B-BEHOLD, initiation is at hand! The Goddess Herself has manifested the mountain onto the physical plane, maintain awareness, I told you!* Tico's head began to spin with dialogue, awe, and a sense of intuitive guidance that told him above all things that he had finally been initiated into a battle as old as time. And his weapon, beloved, was hanging a foot from his eyes.

"*Ay —*" cringed Angelica — "that thing is absolutely disgusting, look at it, it's rusted over, what were those two thinking?" She turned her wrinkled nose to Tico, whose eyes were fixed on the blade. "My Tico wants nothing to do with something like that."

"I...I must object," laughed Tico nervously, pulling at his collar. "This...is perfect. I'd been...looking for one of these...for a while, actually." High in heaven the angels enjoyed a long laugh together, clinking glasses made from the finest baccarat.

Bebita shrugged. "That's not rust, *mijita,*" smiled Bebita bashfully. "But *guad-eh-verrr*...they did say it was specifically for you, so fuck me and just get it off of my hands." She winked at Tico. "That one was an accident."

"*Cuidadito que tengas!*" hissed Angelica.

Tico swallowed a smile, beyond himself, bewildered. Heard none of it — *the blade of Shekhinah, Pallas Athene, inches from your attainment! The Goddess made of fiery liquor awaits her spear, it is here, the next phase of the path, beyond these guardians of the ninth threshold —*

"That...seems most appropriate, that they brought it for me, actually" he smiled triumphantly, bowing his head with the humility of a knight. He took a breath, stroking his head — "for whom and for when, you know, it's somewhat of a serendipity, believe it or not." His eyes hadn't left the blade.

Angelica was suddenly beside herself with a wave of

anger...and a strange dizziness. *"Ay Tico, ya deja la estupidez,"* she said, grabbing at her head. Drop the bullshit. She was sharper than the blade. Coastal heat.

"You don't understand," said Tico into the air. He was engrossed. "This is..."

"Bueeeeeeno," smiled Bebita triumphantly, "I gotta tell you the shit that Rogelio told me about this thing before you take it, at least. You both look a little loopy this morning, so be careful — you just might shit your pants. *Blanca Nieve* will *chess lofff it."* English. She lit another smoke, glancing at her phone. A friend had checked into a mini-mall nearby — *'pan con empellas #aceeeeeiiiiteeee!'*

"So Rogelio shows me this thing and I'm like what the fuck. You know? They don't even make 'em like that anymore. I'm like, this nigga seen the revolution, you know what I mean? *Old* ass shit. So I asked Rogelio what exactly the fuck he was thinking when he was decided it would be a good idea to bring it home. And he tells me what, that it was good luck? *Fuck* that, that mufucka can support three *heavy-ass* bitches with his good luck. Never gets caught, *shyiiiiit...*" She took an exasperated drag, rushing it out into the air. "Says he saw this kid he hadn't seen in years, Casquito, sprouted a beard, right outside of the cathedral, tourists everywhere. He was showing the goddamn thing to some *jineteras* in nightclub attire at three in the afternoon. This thing, right here! *Y que,* what does Rogelio do? This mufucka decides to walk *towards* the assembly of *children, weapons* and *prostitutes* to go see what the commotion is all about. See, that's where I, a sane woman, you know? would've gotten the fuck out. You with me? I know." Another drag. "And this was outside of a *cathedral!"* Smoke blossomed around the sacred word. "So he sees the girls are into the thing, *ay it moss be so esspeeeensiifff,* they like it, he likes it, and what? He gives the kid twenty bucks and takes it, like a fockeen prize. Stealing candy from *putas* — *Oye papi, you wanna use that thing on me?* And the kid got twenty dollars! He could take all three o'them call-girls out for a flat-iron steak dinner with that kind of *fula*, and he's a goddamn kid!" she shouted. "That little shit, he threw my *durofrio* in the dirt the day before I came here, I remember that kid. Look at him, pushing weapons in Havana!"

"*Jesucristo,*" said Angelica, looking to Tico.
"Get it out, *belleza!*" answered Tico, breathless.

But Bebita hadn't left Angelica's gaze. "And that's not even it, *mijita*, you got me going now, it's not even three and that's when Jesus died." She snuffed her smoke in the ashtray. "The kid stops him, and says wait, I gotta tell you something about that machete, *señor*, and Rogelio said what, and the kid says I stole it. And there's Rogelio thinking what the hell is going on, and suddenly he's surrounded by children and prostitutes again. Trouble, I swear. The kid tells him the knife's special, that he heard the people he stole it from say it had magical powers. See, right then, *mijita*, *right then* was when Rogelio should have dropped that shit and ran, but he didn't. You know what he told me? He told me that was *the fockeen moment* when he realized he'd made a good deal! You kidding me? *Pero Dios miiio!* A magic machete, twenty dollars CUC—it's not bad, actually...you see, that's Rogelio and Manolito's problem, they don't believe any of it, all they see is the value, the big fat dollar sign that fucked everything in world to pieces already. To them, it's just a gift for Tico...*ay*, I see you want it even more now, look at you! Remember me when I'm dead, Tico, remember me when I'm dead, the bringer of your good tidings..."

Angelica met Tico's gaze, which spread slowly into a smile. *Escandalos, escandalos* are brewing!

"And Casquito told him straight up, it was just last night, a couple of university kids with American money eating on the plaza, talking about their thesis with hamburgers by the fountain.

Something about war and religion, you know how the
government gets 'em all studying politics. Casquito said he was
sitting there and heard them going on about how they were going
to get rid of it, especially after what had happened to that one
kid's dad. And one of them says what happened, and you know
what? I don't even think I need to tell you," she laughed,
"because *Blanca Nieve's* already scared, I can see it. I don't wanna
be blamed for startin shit between you two..." and she took a cool
drag of her smoke, turning the radio off. Static, that whole time?

Angelica looked to Tico and Bebita, wide-eyed in self-
defense. Cant hide a lie from Cubans. "She's fine," said Tico
hurriedly, "...well come now, what happened? You can't leave us
hanging like that."

"Okay...*bueno*, then listen." She shrugged disconcertingly
at a quickly reddening Angelica. "He sat there with his back
against the fountain, listening to these overly confident, naïve and
oblivious *universitarios* talk about their project out loud in public,
on war and religion, how they say Fidel came to power with the
help of *brujeria* — you know, the doves on his shoulder before the
morning of the revolution? All that shit. Well, then they're
talking about the *machete*, which Casquito hadn't seen yet, okay?
Remember that. He was just getting his kicks, fishing around for
chismes he could use to get a can of *Bucanero* the next day while
telling the story. And they're talkin' about how it was cast for war
over a hundred years before, and had passed through some weird
shit on the way to this kid's thesis, apparently someone cut off
someone else's head with it — fockeen *what*, right? — and it's got
some kind of power now or something. These college kids were
talking about the possibility of *brujeria* here too, see? War and
religion."

Tico blinked. "Indeed!" *The initiation of the scorned apostle,
pinnacle of the first mountain, rejoice, neophyte thou art no longer!* "I
know *just* what to do with all of this. War and religion, the
revolution of the dialectic!"

"Oh yeah?" smiled Bebita. "Well guess what, I'm trying to tell you a story so shut the fuck up." Tico's eyes became tea saucers. Angelica's narrowed into a sweet, vengeful smile. "Well *anyway*, they start talking about this *kid*, a couple of years ago, who brought the knife home one day on his bicycle, if this was the one. Said he had found it with a bunch of other ones on the steps to the church. Now I know what that means, people ditch their shit there once they get too freaked out by some spiritual shit and turn back to Jesus." She waved the knife away with a hand, taking a drag of her cigarette. "But this kid, he up and stole it because his mama had to do all the cooking at home with a butter knife, and that's some bullshit right? Apparently he didn't think it was a problem to steal shit from the stairs of a church, especially something he needed, but look, you'll see, what goes around comes around…so he brings it home, running it across his sleeve before showing it to her to make it shine, and *oh* was his mama a happy woman. So was his daddy, but the guy was always up early in the morning moving milk cans between San Roque and Cienfuegos, so he didn't give much of a shit. He was on his way to his afternoon nap and didn't really care, and I mean come on, the only thing the guy had ever cooked was *café*. He didn't get it. His mother, though, was ecstatic—*imagínate!* Never again would she have to cut up the pork and *platanos* with a butter knife. Can you imagine that? *Carajo,* only in Cuba, *rrrrrrecoño.*" Angelica pricked her nose into the air—"*ay niña,* whatever. Then they said three days later someone stole the kid's bike in the middle of the night." She turnd to Angelica. "Now look, *mijita,* you gotta understand that in Cuba, we don't have much of anything anymore, and we have even less to be throwin' around, so to have a bike, even the shittiest, rustiest piece of work, was a *luxury,* and to get it *stolen*? To get your *luxury stolen*? *Muchacho, sacrilegio!* And he knew he wouldn't get another one for *years,* so he decided he was going to get it *back.* Someone had to have it, and it's a pretty small town, San Roque, so he knew that whoever had it couldn't live too far away and had stolen it shamelessly, without thinking. Hunger can make anyone stupid, I mean, look at me, I skip lunch and I'm a fockeen crisis." She threw her head back, her chins bobbing with glee. "Ay, mama...he knew they'd ride right by soon enough, he *prayed and prayed* for the chance, and suddenly his plan fell out of the sky and into the back of his mind. He went to the shed and got a long piece of rope, tied it on the street sign across from his porch, and kicked a bunch of dirt over it, praying, praying, praying as he set up his trap. Then he went inside and grabbed the *machete* and sat on it, waiting for the little *hijueputa* to ride by on his bike."

"The kid waited *all damn day* on the curb in front of his house, praying, praying, running thoughts of vengeance over in his head thousands of times in the name of God. Praying that he could get a chance at this *thief*. What goes around comes around, you see...? The sun set, but the kid didn't get discouraged. He figured that the culprit would ride the stolen bike at nighttime at first, around the general store and the palm trees in the square so people could all see his new bike and he could get used to him riding it like it was actually his." The woman's eyes lit up. "And...he...was...right! It was half-past midnight, and his mother had just brought him some *chocolate* with Cuban crackers to drink, thinking he was simply musing about some girl he had fallen in love with. He was sipping the last of the cup when he heard the familiar grind the gravel made against his tires — it's like Mama-bird, you know what I'm sayin, knows her babies from a tree *fulla* finches. Fockeen *magic*. He knew, it was *his* noise, *his* bike, *his moment*! Off in the *black* of the night he saw the familiar chinking of his signal-light growing brighter and brighter, and his heart wrenched with metallic excitement he could taste on the back of his tongue as he sat up and grabbed the end of the rope. He held his breath, clenching his teeth, his eyes fixed on the blinking light, the only light in the whole scene, and *chhhhest* as the tires came to the pile of dirt he pulled at it with all his might, launching the thief from the bicycle with a yelp of surprise, and taking the street sign down along with it. *Instant* shit-show. The culprit came crashing to the ground with everything he had balanced on the handlebars, and in a matter of three seconds, the kid had jumped from the curb and cut off the thief's head with a tuft of hair in his hand, *todo por la revolución, pin-pan-pun, y cantó el manizero.* '*Cuuuuuuche p'alla!*' Bebita shook her head with tightly pursed lips — "Mmm-*mmmm!* And as he caught his breath, the purple blur in his field of vision coming into focus, he saw with eyes rattling back and forth that the ground was littered with empty milk cans... and his heart fell from his chest into the dirt as he realized he had just killed...his own...daddy. *Waaaaaaaay, pal carajo!*"

"*Sssssssssssssssss!*" hissed Tico with a mighty wince in. Angelica cupped her hands over her mouth. The anger was gone. Replaced. Respect.

"Goddamn, *Got* damn, ah?" laughed Bebita. "Shit...he fell to the ground, and he wailed loudly into the night, blood smeared all over his face as he hugged the headless corpse of his father. Knife don't fuck around, you see that? Three seconds. He picked the knife up again, and yelling '*Papi, coño, papi!*' stabbed himself in the gut." The woman laughed, basking in the expressions the two spiritual birds, pure as celery, wore on their faces.

"And imagine, *imagínate!* What must that poor woman have thought upon coming outside! *Pero niññññooo!* And that wasn't it — the woman ran off to get her neighbor's husband to deal with the horrors that lay on the street, I can't believe she didn't faint right there, and by the time she returned the whole block had come outside to see what had happened. And after everyone had finished crying and telling the story over and over again to all the newcomers and giving their opinions of what should be done and how, the dark corner became quiet once again, and everyone went home, *calabaza calabaza todo el mundo pa' su casa*...and the knife was nowhere to be found." The woman took a deep breath, holding her side. "*Ay – coño...*" She probably hadn't talked this much in a long time. She lit a cigarette. "Somehow one of these kids got ahold of it, complete with all the rumors of where it had gone to, and when the other kids asked where it was, the kid pulls it out of his bag! That's when Casquito couldn't handle it anymore, he must've been squirming over there behind the fountain! He started walking towards the table, and he said the kid knew what was going to happen, they locked eyes for a good three seconds before Casquito rushed him and tore the knife from his hands, running into the dark little alleyways of *La Habana Vieja*, perfect for taking that drunk Yuma out for a breath of fresh air and a kiss...and *PAN con aceite! Se acabo.*"

"*Whuuuyyyy!*" Tico flicked a bead of sweat casually from his brow. "Well, honestly, I can see why Rogelio picked it up off the kid, if anything it truly is an island legacy! It's got a little of everything Cuba's about, and like I said, I know just what to do with it, I know exactly why Rogelio said it should be given to me...I'm," and he brought a hand to his brow, "a spiritual being. I can handle such a thing. Just, ok, wow, what a story, this is too much, I'm honored frankly –"

"Tico, *no*. Take your instrument and *let's. Go.*" Tico shot a glance at Bebita, who wasn't saying a word, smiling at the two of them.

"Well ok, that's enough, then. I already told you, I've business to tend to!" Tico bowed his head down and froze the space. A breeze passed into the room. "Do pack it with my things. The sun has passed its Zenith."

"*Ay!* Are you *stupid?*" piped Angelica, "we're not taking that thing with us! That's your stupid friends and a bunch of ghost stories that I don't want messing with us!" Tico took a deep breath, looking to his shoulders and sighing up at the two lovely ladies. Goddesses.

"Twenty dollars?"

"Twenty dollars...yeah, for the *guiro* stick, put it up your *ass* with *twenty dollars*. The *guiro's* forty-five...stick included."

"And...the machete?" Tico tried to sound cool in the midst of Angelica's wrath. The heat of a bonfire glowed at his back.

"Hahaha," bobbled Bebita. "Look at you two, it's funny how things work." And she looekd at Angelica. "*Mija*, it's true, they brought it just for him, something must be going on, *dejaselo en las manos de Dios, que sabe lo que hace.*" Leave it in God's hands, he knows what he does. "And yes, Tico, *mi corazon de melocoton*...that'll be sixty, for the risk." Tico winced.

"Sixty?! Sixty total, right?"

"Yeah, sixty tot—*no*, fuck you! What you mean, sixty total? That's the craziest shit I've ever heard, *you cheap shit*. Roge's trying to make a deal here, I told you, he sold it for twenty and needs a return for getting it off the island. Now you give me a hundred dollars plus his recovery fee or I'll call him up and keep this shit 'til you figure it out with *his* black ass." Tico hovered in the silence. *A bird in the hand...*

"Ok...ok, ok, here." He pulled a wad of bills from his coat pocket and slid them across the counter. Bebita grimaced at the machete and wrapped it up again, putting it next to the *guiro* in a paper bag and handing it over with a smile for Angelica.

"*Buen provecho*, it's like this for all of us sometimes, *mijita*," and Angelica looked at Tico with the most disdain she had ever felt towards him. He said goodbye to Bebita and made his way out of the store, muttering things to himself.

The woman winked at Angelica—"*Cuidenseeeee!*"—and waved her out of the store.

"Goddammit..." she said to herself as they walked out of sight in a frigid silence. Lit a smoke. "*Poncho pilate.*" She turned the speakers back up into the empty store. It was Celia Cruz and the Sonora Matancera. *Saludo a Eleggua.*

"Why'd you really buy that knife?" Angelica finally asked in a huff.

Tico looked deeply into her eyes, holding it for four drawn-out seconds, and listening to the voices that coursed about his head in visions of rapturous spirituality, he said, "it...is an initiation. I tell you because we make love...I can trust you." Angelica tried desperately not to roll her eyes. It was the most serious thing in his life...*religion*. He looked serious. *Is* he serious? Rituals and old bearded men trying to make lead into gold, tricking themselves into becoming the universe. *Hmph*. She thought of what the hell he could possibly have meant by that, what kind of stuff is he up to, is he dangerous, why are clowns dangerous, am I in danger? It was all interesting at first, mother told me to pick a good one and settle, I'm living with this one, it's about finding love and joy and leaving suffering aside, and we do that, but what the hell is this he's really scaring me right now...his eye, it's twitching. There's no end to a mystic. Opening mysteries, of my little fragrant heart...

"Hmmmm!" she growled into his face defiantly. "An initiation, how cute."

He pulled her in and gave her a restless, violent kiss. Pressed together, they wrestled, fought, she beat him with closed fists, over and over again and he comforted her, assured her, consoled her angst, her ceaseless fire dancing about the both of their auras, and up they squeezed it all, hugging tighter and tighter until the fight was over. They sighed together, relaxing their chests into a tremendous opening no one around them would have noticed, and merged in this way they pressed their lips together and breathed it back in once more. Opened their eyes. *Bingo, linda.* Tico smiled into the distance behind Angelica. It was done.

"*Ay Tico*, I could kick your ass."

"I love you."

"I love *you*." She looked to the sky, exasperated, defiant—
it was a blessed tension. Rolled her eyes. "I could kill you
sometimes." Brakes squealed in the distance...and nothing. They
had both listened for the crash.

Back by their car, Angelica took notice of a little black boy
playing with a shard of glass in the dead yard of an old house,
stabbing the old butt of a cigar over and over again. He looked up
with bright, mischievous eyes and caught her stare, throwing the
shard under the porch without breaking her gaze.

Angelica said to the boy, "You shouldn't play with glass!"

"*You* shouldn't play with *me!*" he shouted back with a
smile, and he ran inside with laughter trailing behind him,
slamming the screen door.

"*Laroye!*" shouted a voice inside. "*Que Dio'te ampare si te
veo tira' otra puedd-ta, coño!*"

~*~

Mio, es mio,
soy feo, destino,
Abrecaminos, rompesaraguey,
la paz que queda despues de
holas lentas y espumosas.

Azufre y resinas achicharradas, ruedas de cobre,
uñas pintadas color de mi corazon,
precipitado rojo con polvo de ajo,
y me ciegas en la luz de tu sol.

El fuego arde del fondo hasta mi piel, y doy retorcijones
sobre raíces de troncos ancianos,
Ochosi y su Siguaraya,
viendo visiones

del desgraciado pasado
lleno de hoyas de hierro,
tragandome la lengua sofocada,
hinchada, bofetada,
candados en el alma de la gente,
batalla de muertos a la distancia del odio,
y solo la luz en los ojos del loco,
cocos, cocos, plumas de pollo,
presiones orgasmicas sobre
semillas de corojo
quedan como testigo
de los tiempos cuando mi sangre
era algo nuevo, celebrado.

Ofrendas a lo unico que me
detiene de la sobresaltada rutina
de cada dia, el santo trabajo de
vivir como si todo fuera normal,
dandole a la gente como misión,
mata-indios, malditos mata-indios,
una moneda por lo que no tiene valor,
y quedo asi como un pez.

Frio, pero con hojos abiertos.
Ruegame, Santome, que te hablo con
caracoles sonrientes.

Hijo, de mi madre La Sirena! con
faldas de olas espumantes
y un mantel casi igual sobre mi mesa,
como yo el pan de cada dia,
cada dia mas viejo!

Cada dia mas viejo.

~*~

*...and take the sword, and turn it there, yes, just as the text instructs and imbues...*Tico sat in the light of dusk, having conducted preliminaries just as the sun set to catch the plunge into night. *The scents, the subtle body, the Pentalpha! Imminence is here in the sphere of Netzach!* His eyes glazed over as he performed rituals with the sword, assuming poses and chanting incantations before a grisly image of geometrical cacophony that shone golden in the light of seven white candles. *"Jachim, Boaz, Elohim,"* said Tico, swiping across the sides and signing himself with the Star.

"Aaaaaiiiiiiiiiiiiiiiiiiiinnnnnnnnnnnnn Soooooooooooooooophhhhhhhhh Auuuuuuuuuuurrrrrrrrrrrr," he sang into the electric mist all about him, engulfing the room with a resinous charge.

> *We...*
> *have entered the imperium*
> *of High Magic. Mmm...*

The smoke curled tight all about the room, sighing into languid sheets that fell about the space and disappeared into thin air. And high up in the sky millions of years away the tiniest little star popped out of existence, leaving nothing but a hovering cloud of dust in its place.

"Bingo, linda," said the Kabbalist, his shadow dancing about the walls.

> *Indeed, the blade of the shining ones has entered thy fateful grasp.*
> *But votary, knowest thou not the subtleties of surrender?*
> *The blade is the serpent with no tail, she who gave*
> *you life — pray, she accepts it and fights the great*
> *fight for you. She is your Master, your*
> *innermost star of light and being.*

"Amin-Ram," answered the Ecclesiarch. *The acolyte.*

And the night passed, and
it was day once more.

~*~

"*Vieja! El café!*" shouted Chiche as he walked through the
doorway. He threw his jacket onto the couch. "I sold three
vacuums today, *que me digang que no!*" He kicked his shoes off
and gave Silvia a kiss on her stiff, immobile cheek. Silent
resistance, fancy lotion. She smiled at him, smelling the tobacco
on her lips and turning back to the kitchen. Chiche turned the TV
on from his favorite chair. He took his wallet, a lighter, and a wad
of folded papers from his pocket and set them on the table, as
always, pulling his shirt off right after and scratching his feet in a
tanktop and khakis. "*Vaya...*" he groaned, scratching himself into
a trance. "*Ñoo...ahi mi'mito, ñoh...*" Silvia grimaced from her place
behind the counter, rinsing the *cafetera* extra well. He turned the
TV on, pressing three buttons without thinking: it was his favorite
channel. Well you know, one of 'em. Walter Maricado was on the
TV, giving the latest astrological forecast: "*Y para todos mucho,
mucho *muah!* Amorrr! Bye-bye, Capricornios!*"

Silvia snapped her gaze to the TV, where bejeweled fingers
waved at her, one by one, most gingerly. She pursed her lips,
digging a spoon into the dark, earthy espresso. She basked in the
crunching sound.

"*Eso'h una mied-da,*" said Chiche out loud. "*Las planetas,*
how is it that 8% of all the people, all the people here, in Cuba,
Brazil, Africa, *Europa*, even *los Chinitos de poralla*, are gonna do the
same shit?"

"*Ay* Chiche, I don't know," said Silvia to herself, spooning
an extra bit of grounds in with the rest. *There* it is. *Bingo, linda.*

"*Y* where's *Yenni?*" asked Chiche from his chair.

"Upstairs on her computer," said Silvia as she pressed the
espresso into the little tin piece of the percolator. She put it in the

base full of water and screwed the top on, placing it on the stove next to the quiet bubbling of the pots and pans on the rest of the burners. In a few hours there would be *ropa vieja,* white rice, and *mariquitas. 'Su maaaadre, estas acabando, niña.'* She lit the flame under the *cafetera.* It would be precisely five minutes and twenty-or-so seconds until the very first drops of the black nectar would ooze out of the top and into the spout. She got the sugar ready in the mug.

"*Y que,* how was your day?" she asked from the stove, looking at the reflections on the wall.

"I already told you, *negrita,* it was wonderful." He turned his neck uncomfortably to face her. "You gotta listen to what I say to you, it could be important." Silvia went to say something but got cut o — "It was the lunch you made for me, I know it. It tasted extra nice today. I know last night you were in a good mood. That means I'm gonna make good sales the next day, I've thought this out...and I did! *Trrrrreh bakyoon-kleene' en* one day?! I did the light trick, *negrita,* you know, where I showed them all the dust coming out of their old vacuum with the flashlight, sells em like *perico,* swear to God." He sat back and laughed to himself as a commercial for a weight-loss product came on the TV screen. "*Perico...coño...y tu?*"

Silvia had to stop and think. And me? What have I done today? Woke up, smoked some cigarettes, cooked, some TV...

"*Yo...aqui. Tu sabes...*" her voice trailed into nothing. Drummed her fingers on the stovetop. *Brrrap. Me? I'm here.* You know that.

"*Yeeeeeeeeeeeeni! Beng pa'ca, coño!*"

As the first drops of *café* trickled out of the percolator Silvia hardly realized her mind was going through the same motions it did five times a day. The thoughts and things she remembered while making cafe were the same everyday, nonsense she had ground into her mind and percolated for the last twenty something years. 'The first drops, the *very* first drops, go in the sugar —' Carmen showed her how to do it in a muffled, foggy voice, black stringy liquid failure over andover again, thick foamy victory —'no more than five or six, any less, you're finished, and any more, you're drinking it black.' The black woman from that commercial, Celia Cruz sang for the other one, *café Pilon!* *Llave's* better, *Bustelo's*...She poured the little trickle of *café* into the pile of sugar and whipped it with the spoon vigorously until it turned into a frothy, tan pulp. *Bustelo's* so good, is that someone's face on the label? Heart, every single time. Red and yellow McDonalds. The gas station. The sound of the cup on the stovetop, clanks scraping spoon. Buchito's scrap shop, metal clanking all about. My teeth, that *dentist*. Named like a sip of *café*. *Un buchito.* And by then it was always ready.

She turned the stove off right when the bubbles came to the tip of the spout. She would get angry if she let it spill, it was all her fault. She had cleaned the stovetop enough times to know. *''Detras palante, y por dentro pafuera,'* and she poured it in, stirring the sugar into the *café 'y dime tu! Espumita.'* The espresso had the signature creamy foam at the top that made it *Café Cubano.* All of Chiche's criticism, he only makes it when he wakes up before me...it's hard at first, to catch it all just right when making *café*.

"*Neeeeeeeegraaaaaa...*" said Chiche, scratching his head into the TV. He didn't even notice.

Silvia thought into the reflections on the wall. She looked at the *café*. 'So easy once you get it.' Wives flashed through her mind, young and old, making *café* was as essential as knowing how to cook...and she took a deep whiff of the hot coffee steam, laced with the fragrance of sugary bliss. It cleansed her nostrils with hot, earthy clarity. "*Ayyyy...*" she sighed. She glanced at Chiche on the couch. Now he had his hands in his pants as the girls danced to some *merengue* on a comedy show. "*Oyeme, negro depravao!*" she snapped. Chiche chortled in surprise, sitting upright.

"*Suuuu'to que me ah' dao, negra, cuidao con el corazon!*" He cleared his throat. "*Coño...*" he said, rubbing his fingertips blankly, "*y el café esta listo?*"

"*Café, si, beng, dale.*" It was a ritual incantation, so many times had she just it just like that, right there, in the same tone of voice. *Café, si, beng, dale.* Four words, the temple is open. Chiche could find his *café* in a cave full of screeching bats, so reliable was their system.

He sat at the table, took the little cup by its tiny handle. Thumb and index finger, a-ok. It was a secret handshake amongst the elders, take a sip and it's a-ok. Swallowed the perfect *buchito*, mouth, throat, cheeks came to life and swarmed with sugary heat—*con espumita, vistes?* He nodded at her with a smile, and this meant it was ok. Truly, she couldn't care less whether he liked it or not. She wasn't gonna make more, and he'd never asked for it. Just rituals of the temple. Bells and whistles...but she waited for that nod every time, it was true. It was part of the ritual. The call, the preparation, the little *buchito* and the nod, *café, café café* everyday, *negra negra negra*, it's what held us all together. *Lo que nos mantiene vivo. Café,* that is. Indulging in the routine was the only way of getting away from it's looming presence, the emptiness behind it, and it made Silvia sick to her stomach day after day after day, but she never noticed it. She blamed it on eating cold leftovers.

"What's the matter, *vieja*? You look like you got *un peo atravesado.*" A fart stuck up your...

Silvia laughed cynically—"Ha. You'd never believe me."

"That's right! I don't ever want to hear about that kind of shit, *coño...chucheria de mujeres.*" He snorted. "Women. To me, they should never be associated with anything that has to do with the bathroom, except for make-up and mirrors, *me entiendes?*" He set his *café* down on the glass-top table with a definitive clunk.

Popped the sip. *"p-AAAAAhhh*...speaking of which...have you showered today?" He looked half serious. "The house smells like sleep." He sniffed pompously, authoritatively. Silvia's guts writhed like serpents. She looked at him, feeling the ruffles of her *bata* suddenly puff into the expanse of the room. Hurricanes, palm trees slamming onto flimsy roofs, wrathful ocean spray.

"No." There was silence. He knew better than she did that she showered every other day. "I showered yesterday."

"Well Jesus, open a window or something, this is gonna kill us all before the tobacco." He looked to the TV screen.

Silvia kept her eyes on him as he disappeared into the screen. He pulled out after three seconds—*"Baaaaaayaaa!"* he cried. "*Ay Negrita,* I forgot to buy you your cigarettes. Fijate..." he pursed his lips, shaking his head into the wall. *La Virgen's* eyes went wide. Chiche made a clicking sound with his mouth...it must have made things better for him. A crack in the silence. She wanted a cigarette. Filters, in the ashtray, pecked with smudges of brown. Buffaloes and Indian chiefs. Chiche, however, was busy going over all the times when Silvia did not have her smokes, and he was about to get up and book it to the mini-mall when Silvia spoke.

"*Ay, pero* don't worry about it, *mi vida,*" she said frigidly, "I went out and bought my own today." She cracked a smile. Couldn't help it—"See, it was *la Virgen* who made you forget," she said to the picture on the wall, "and *fuck you,* what do you think about that." She stood, walking to her pack on the glasstop coffee table.

"You went *out?*" Chiche looked like he had been hit with the most thinking he had to encounter all day. He sat back, stumped. "You didn't tell me that," he laughed. "*Si claro,* it's—well, I, *coño*...why'd you...go out? W-without me?" He fidgeted with a piece of lint on his pants. "You don't know what it's like out there," he said, confused. His voice was shaking. He looked up at her. The emperor, gazing into his harem of one. Knew not what to do. What to say...

89

"Ay Chiche plllíssss." She bit her tongue at him.
*"Yennifer...*came too." Silvia folded the dish towel on her lap
neatly and didn't say another word. Her smile was enough. The
Virgen behind her, too, smiled in silent sepia. Smoke blossomed
into the air as Silvia reached back and slid the window open. The
curtains bellowed up in response.

Chiche huffed and sat back in his chair. *"Chucheria de
mu—Yenniferrr!"* he screamed, without moving an inch. He was
the only person Silvia knew besides his own mother Barbarita—
Bab-barita, peace be upon her—who could raise his voice so much
without moving a muscle. For most, it took a considerable effort
to yell, or at least some kinesiology of sorts, some movement,
strain, but for Chiche...it was easy as talking.

"What *is wrong* with you," shouted Jenny's muffled voice
from upstairs, "I'm right here!" Clunks and shuffles.

"Come down here, I haven't seen you today." He said this
as if to the remote. Three buttons. It was the same channel.
"Shit." Flip flip flip flip flip flip...

Upstairs, Jennifer thought about the car thing earlier, how
he probably would've forgotten by now...no more reason to avoid
him than usual...she thought herself over, her eyes, her pockets,
sprayed herself with perfume and went downstairs. She came
down the clanky steps to Chiche's joyful commentary and gave
him a hug and a kiss. *"Que paso, a'onde esta mi niña, eh? Beng paca,
coño, muchacha'e mierda, culicaga'..."* Then she stood up, went over
to Silvia and gave her one too.

"Why'd you kiss me?" she retorted, her dishtowel up to
her heart. "I've been here for the past three hours..." She shook
her head, a look of surprise on her face. It was as big as her smile.

"Well, its because...I love...you I guess...? *Man, what the
fuck, Mami!* Can't I give you a kiss? That was precious fuckin
moment, Jesus!" They had gotten her when she was vulnerable.
"Lil' *babies* with their big-ass *heads*..."

"Well okay, then, let me have one more!" Silvia flashed

another smile, this one out of spite.

"Oh my God *fiiiiine*," said Jenny, groaning with a smile, and she plopped another kiss on her mother's cheek, squeezing her suddenly and farting furiously into the small of her neck — "*Ay niña, no, no!*" bellowed Silvia laughing, swatting at Jenny with her dishtowel.

"*Mami, Mami, Mami!*" wailed Jennifer into her mother's face. "*Te quiero, Mami Chola,*" she grinned into Silvia's exasperated smile. She could have been six and toothless. She squinted mascara and blue into Silvia's eyes, playfully. This is *our* thing. Chiche smiled from the couch, watching Silvia squirm.

"See?" said Silvia to Chiche, holding their daughter to her side. "It was nice today." She shared a genuine smile with her daughter, and that very instant of clarity was the best moment of Jenny's week, though she'd never tell anyone. Especially not *them.* "Alright, I'm blowin up — "

"*Niña,* sit here with your father for a minute, come on, I forget what you look like," and he patted the cushion next to his, turning his gaze from TV only when he thought Jenny was ignoring him. "*Ay* fine," she said, plopping onto the couch next her *papi.* He threw his arm around her and sat back once again, giving her ample room to pull out her phone as Silvia made her way back into the kitchen and cleaned the pans that had been soaking in the sink.

After a silent pause, during which only the oblivious TV kept making noise, the three of them were awakened once again by the smell of *ropa vieja* wafting through the house. "*Ay,* it's finally starting to settle, you smell that?" Silvia stood up and shuffled off to the other side of the counter in her *bata,* holding the dishtowel in a closed fist. "Oh, I'm cooking *ropa vieja* tonight by the way, Chiche."

"Yeah, I could smell it." Silvia looked at her pack of cigarettes. The ladies in the room waited for the inevitable.

Logical conclusions, grinding through his shining cranium...it took longer than they suspected.

"...Tico's coming?" Beef.

"*Hahaaaay si! Tico, Tico, mi carita de pico!*" Silvia smiled with all of her teeth, and Jennifer caught her out of the corner of her eye. She smiled herself. It was sort of like the crying thing.

"He bringing *la Colombiana?*" he asked gruffly.

"Why wouldn't he, *Papi*? They're probably going to get married," and she made to go upstairs. "And her name is *Angelica...Papi.*" Popped the P's.

"*Si, si, La Lica,* I know, another mouth to feed, now come back here and sit with your father!" cried Chiche childishly, without moving a muscle.

Dammit! she mouthed to herself. *Thought I had it.* Jenny turned back and pursed her lips playfully, plopping onto the couch next to him once again. *I wasn't trying to escape, Papi...got twenty bucks? No, don't even ask. The ice is thin, saw me cuttin.* She pulled out her phone. *Omg the red light's not blinking wtf.* He rubbed her head to the sound of cracking mousse. Her eyes popped into saucers as she stifled a scream.

She appreciated the attempt at affection, but now she'd have to go do her hair all over again. She plucked her thumbs into her phone: 'w/e omgggggg.' She would have done it over anyway. *Chui's comin' out tonight...nigga got dem grapes! Brown paper packages filled with my trees, boys and my chucks and my fav MP3's...*

"OMG I'm tweetin' that shit." She ran upstairs.

Chiche pursed his lips.

"*Tss.*"

~*~

"Voy pa casa Tía Conga' comellll yuca frita, y arroz blanco, y un poquito'e ca'ne asa'!" The door blew open to the lustrous sight of Tico and Lica — *aceeeeiteee!* — he knew it would be unlocked. Everyone exclaimed something at the same time, and they made their way in to make sense of it all.

"Buenas noches," smiled Angelica to Silvia and Chiche, and Chiche said hello back but was waiting for Tic's eyes so that he could tell him the song it was that he was singing. It was a contest they'd had between each other for years. Chiche, though a humble man, had a rather cultivated palate for music, and he flaunted it in the presence of his educated son. Tico called him *'El Caballo Viejo'* because of this.

"Que dice el Conjunto Céspedes, ah?" yelled Chiche after waiting long enough. Tico turned and exclaimed his hello, making his way over and giving his father a kiss on the cheek and a man hug, *pat pat pat.* He stood upright, clearing his throat to the buzzing of his chest. *Father's love, right in the unstruck chakra!*

"Claro que si, Papi, an old favorite of mine, and yours too, ah? I heard it today down on *la Ocho. Ay,"* he said, turning back to the ladies present, "and that smell must be the delicious dinner *mi madre* is cooking, no? *Ropa vieja, con sazónnnnn! Criollo!"*

And free of pork! A true marvel at a house like yours...

He made his way over to Silvia, who had been waiting for him feigning anger. Her arms, crossed around her wooden spoon. "Muah! You have a nice day, *mami?* Thank you, thank you for cooking for us tonight. *Como te quiero, y extraño."* And he gave her a kiss on the cheek, pulling back with a gaze that only Bollywood baad-shahs could rival with their odes to motherly love.

"Pues deberias pasar por aqui un poquito mas, si te pone tannnn," and she tapped the air in front of his nose with her spoon, *"sentimental."* Well, then you should stop by more often if it makes you so...sentimental. Silvia, you see, could not be bought

with words. Especially not Tico's.

"*Ay, calculadora! Pero no ves, que hay que ser como yo, Bohemio y poeta!*"

"*Tener sentimiennnntoooo!*" crowed Jenny from the fridge—

"*Y ademas corazon!*" laughed Silvia, smiling the way she only saw in the mirror.

"*Que patrulla,*" grimaced Chiche to himself on the couch, flicking his eyebrows at Angelica.
"*Oyemeeeeeeeeeeeeeeeeeeeeeeeeeeeeeeeeeeeeee...*

...aaaaaaaaaaaaaaaaaaaahhhhh...

...TICO!"

shouted Chiche from across the house, "*y que con el merenguito'e la vida, eh?* How's life? You been waking up at noon still?" Didn't matter. "As for the people with…real jobs, this one right here sold three vacuums today."

"*No jodas* – sign me up, I'll make it four!" He looked at Silvia, who waved her spoon into the air dismissively. "Work is virtue, I'm glad you're reaping the fruits of your labor, *Papi.*" An abrupt knock at the door silenced all the small talk and drew everyone's attention to the front of the house, where after an idle second, the doorknob flickered and pulled open to the tight red hourglass that called itself Mariza. Her hair was sprayed into perfection, her thighs in full flare, and somewhere behind her was a man. She lifted her arms into the air, posing in vogue:

"*Ay, pero que me dice may fameeleeee!*" She made her way in, flinging her purse around and onto the chair covered in plastic. She looked up at Angelica and paused, pursing her lips. "Oh and hello *An-heeeelica,* how's…que, Bucaramanga?" and Chiche's laughter was too loud to let her answer. The women ended up holding mutual smiles in the noise: 'I hate you with my *teeeeeeeeeth!*' Chiche shot a glance at Silvia, who smiled back at him. Yes, she had invited them all. He usually would have showered and shaved on such a night. Silvia smiled a little more. She loved having the whole family together, *Ave Maria*.

"*Y tú, Ricardo,* how are you?" asked Silvia as she carried a steaming pot to the little doily in the middle of the table.

"*Coñó!* Just in time!" said the burly Cuban in his stylish *guayabera*. "I heard there was *ropa vieja* tonight, so I made sure to wear some *ropa nueva* with a couple of extra sizes for your cooking." His hair was slicked back, his moustache pencil-thin over his lip, and he looked like was ever on the brink of a wink.* Ricardo Chamaquín was his name — no, I swear — and he had straight teeth, a leased sports-car, and shiny, shiny shoes. Always.

Pobre Juan.

"I'm fine, Silvia, *muy, muy bien,*" he said, sliding a few bottles of wine onto the dinner table. Fuck if he knew the vintage, 45 a pop and you're makin' people happy goddammit. "Thank you for offering to cook dinner tonight. Truly," and he put his hand to his heart, "it made my day to know that I would get to come over as soon as I found out. My own *mother* can't live up to your cuisine, and I mean that."*

Chiche leaned over to Jenny: "This guy would make a good communist."

Jenny giggled. Ricárdo darted his gaze at her.* The sixth sense, Cuban *e*style. Many don't even know they have it, but it's always there. Fire behind the eyes, African sun. It made the gossip that much hotter, and the only thing Cubans liked more than *chismes* were *chismes* about people six feet away. *Mmmmm.* A giraffe grins toward the top of a tree. Checking out the leopards. Chewing leaves, chewing leaves, chewing leaves —

"*Pa' la meeesaaaaa!*" yelled Silvia above all the chatter, "dinner is ready!" She crossed from the counter to the table holding a heaping plate of *mariquitas*, freshly crispily bubbily greasily yellowy goldeny-brown fried, to the table. The whole lot sat down as if bowing to Silvia, smiling and acknowledging the food with their hearts and souls, and above them all watching with her spoon was Silvia, looking over the spread of the table and the family with a pair of eyes that knew not what to do with such fervent emotions. And Tico helped himself to a clump of *mariquitas* that had stuck together. These were his favorite. Jenny, appalled, complained immediately.

"Why does *he* get to taste them before dinner is served? You get on *everyone's* case about that." Mariza sighed reproachfully.

"*C'mon* Jenny, you know our little *Tiqui-tiqui* gets to do whatever he wants around here. He's the...oldest?" She scoffed. "*Whatever, niña, it's fockeeng mariquitas...I'm ku, look at my figure, that's why, gordis.*"

"*Ay plís nigga,*" said Jenny with eyes wide as idols, "*I will kick yo' ass right now, falta'e pinga!*"

"*OYE YA NO FALTEN DE RESPETO, COÑO!*" bellowed Chiche, and they both said one more thing to each other at the same time before Silvia *hmph*ed at the two of them and they were quiet. They looked to Tico at the same time, who swallowed and looked to them as if nothing had happened.

Chiche looked to Jennifer's mascara-and-blue eyes and smiled. "Well, you know I love the three of you just the same. I've never played that game," he said. It was true. But a father's love is very different. It is free-flowing, pure and consistent. Unconditionally safe and distant. A mother's love, on the other hand, was complex and unique as a snowflake. Ashes, falling from the sky. *Mmmm,* thought Silvia to herself, looking through the door at her pack.

"Tico, say a prayer," insisted Chiche. Tico didn't even care anymore. For years upon years did he complain for always being delegated to say the prayers at the table, and when he was younger, he used to bounce it back and poke at Chiche's fear of praying out loud, but he had finally accepted it. No one could talk to God with so many blossoming words as Tico, and his publications proved it to a sickeningly sweet point. He had accepted this fact and bowed his head, smelling the gardenia on his lapel suddenly as he sought the words with which to begin. He felt the mist, swirling across his brow and across his lips, tipping them with the most delicate kiss one could ever imagine.

> "Father in heaven, holy Virgin Queen,
> beloved Verbal Fruit of God,
> Spirit of Omnipresence,
> we thank you for this evening spent together.
> > Half of us are in the midst
> > of trying to start our own
> families, and you, Divinity, have given us such a
> wonderful model upon which to base our hopes and dreams.
> > I think of my past and lose count of the blessings you have
> rained upon me…
> > on behalf of all present, I'd like to glorify your holiest of
> holy names, and in that very name
> > I'd like to thank you for our food, for the conversations yet
> to be spoken, for the nourishment, and for the lofty ear with
> which you listen to my simple words.
> > Look upon us, oh Great Architect of the Universe! And
> take us
> > to
> > where
> > we should be.
> > In the name of the Father,
> > the *Mother*, the Son and the Holy Spirit
> > we pray, Amun-Ram-Io!"

Tico opened his eyes to a speechless table. Contempt. Repressed giggles. Shaking of heads. Chewing.

"Jesus," said Jenny.

"*Precisamente*," smiled Tico.

"You are such a bad Catholic," said Chiche stabbing a tomato, "throwing words where they don't need to be." He stuffed it in his mouth. "*Mffffhrrrfff...*"

"Well, I mean think about it *Caballón*...why does the Holy Spirit get two touches of the sign of the cross? Throwing *la Virgen* in evens things out, you see? I'm simply a pragmatist." Tico smiled. "Besides," he said as he spooned some rice onto his plate, "Every son has a *mother*, right *Mami?*" and Silvia looked up at Ricardo bashfully. Chiche simply shook his head at all of it, focusing instead on the better task—a forkful of rice and black beans...into his mouth. "*Frrrrry Fico,*" he said, and he chewed and swallowed. "*Que Dioh te ampare.*" *Ay Tico.*

The *romantico* looked to his left: *Indeed, God save us all!*

"As if he were *el Santo Cachón*," said Mariza. Chewing, chewing leaves.

"*Pssssssssssssssssshhhhhhhhhhhhhh,* that's not even the right line," said Chiche, looking over to Tico. Ignoring him, Mariza raised a fist into the air and said, "*Tico, hermano mio,* you don't need no forgiveness, you're into all that weird shit and you know what?" She looked around, got serious. "I still love you. It's true, fuck it I even believe you!" Jenny choked on her food, laughing. "Yeah, bro, power to you, I liked that prayer. Remember us all when you say 'em, maybe we'll end up alright." And *that's* how you pull out of that and stay alive. She looked to Chiche. "Are *you* a good catholic...*Papi*? Last time I remember you going to mass was the day after you swallowed a fishbone and thought you were gonna die."

"*Waaaaaaaaaaaaaaaaaaaaaaaaaaaaaaaaaaaaaaaaaaaaaaaaaaaaaaaaaaa!!!!!*"

"I got my *Santos* in the room, Mariza, you know that." He

stuffed a hand into his shirt, balancing the food on his fork. "And look at 'em right here around my neck," he said, pulling out his chaind and showing off the gold.

San Lazaro.

"Nice."*

"Yeah. I don't need to go to no church to be Catholic." Another fork-full of rice and beans, innocent eyes, vulnerable, hard, soft, chewing, quickly. San Lazaro.

"*Papi*, you're *such* a bad *Catholic!*" Mariza said sarcastically, mimicking his comment only seconds ago. She bit her tongue and winked, looking back to Tico.

"Let's eat, my God I'm starving!" she sang. "See, that's *Jenny*'s prayer."

"*Ayyyyy comepinga!*" laughed Jenny, dropping the handful of *mariquitas* she had been trafficking to her plate. But no one noticed, they had become too busy with the food.

As the family began to mow through their plates and stock up on second helpings, Silvia looked across the table again and felt the same joy that had overcome her twice already today. Yet it was all-too familiar, this joy. It was the stuff of their souls. The conversation would be typical bullshit: two or three of them at once, intersecting each other crazily over the steaming plates of food, interruption *tras* interruption, asking for this or that, some throwing in their two cents from chairs pulled up from the living room since they couldn't all fit at the table, and forkfuls of playful insults, harmless over-exaggerations that made for loud, loud banter and laughter that echoed in the pit of their bellies until they had finished dessert and sipped on their *café*, suddenly feeling sad. It would all be over soon. That's the moment where reality sets in once again with the sugary kick to the spleen...and it's over.

Pray it might happen again next week. As it all began to unfold, Silvia couldn't help but smile even wider on the inside — '*te la comistes, niña.*'

"*Pues si,*" she smiled to herself over the scene. Indeed, her cooking had come a long way since she was a young, newlywed señorita, and behind this whole situation was a very interesting story.

~*~

Silky black beans,
wafting swirls of garlic
and soft strips of
aji verde that
dissolve in your mouth,
I spit on the whole thing with love.
Comino, laurel, crumbling leaves of
oregano that make
the mouths of the ancestors water
still to this day as they help me cook,
a pinch of azuquita
for those who wait on the island,

Oya, Oya,
Santa Muerte amargada y dulce
si es Oya tiene que hacer bueno.
My past is my cooking pot,
where stories of today
arise in plumes of steam
and never come out the same
twice, as unique and alive as
each cigarette I smoke while cooking.

My table is the extension of my watery heart,
the family, it's thick, red lifeblood.

~*~

As it turns out, Silvia's famous cooking was once not-so-famous, if only for being burnt and grainy. This was never a problem for her, though, because her *Mami* was an amazing cook and had provided for the family in this way for years on end since little Silvia was a baby. The moment she stopped suckling at her mother's breast she was eating blended concoctions of *ñames*, *malangas, bistec* or *higado* and *chicharos* or something along those lines which was always so delectable that the whole family would compete over who got to feed Silvia just so they could eat half of it along with her. But she didn't remember any of that, of course. She was just a baby.

All through Silvia's childhood she ate well, for Cuba was in abundance back then, and there was always enough to buy at the *bodeguitas* on the corner, and there was milk and meat and the coffee wasn't cut with lentils or anything, it was all natural and wonderfully fresh, like the island itself in its nostalgic past. *Mami* kept cooking right on through the revolution and *oye*, this lady could cook it all! Some cousins from Las Villas were coming over — no problem, *Mami* would cook up some breaded steaks, *potaje de Garbanzos* with fresh *chorizo* and a big ol' *Tasajo* from the butcher, *tostones,* sand dollar-esque abstractions of the plantain, *arroz, Yuca frita,* and the classic Cuban salad, which was simple: chopped cabbage, sliced tomatoes, sliced avocados and onions and perhaps some roasted red bell peppers, all covered with olive oil and vinegar. *Voila* (That was French, *mi amor*). And the *primos* would go back to Las Villas *begging* for a lonely little burp, just to remember the night's exploits once more.

Si, food was the staple of Silvia's youth, but in her upbringing it was lunchtime that held all the notoriety, for the whole family would get together around the big table just near the kitchen fire to eat some of *Mami's* home-cooking together. Dinner was always there for whenever people got home — or hungry — but lunch was obliged, sacred, ritual. Everything went into the day's lunch, *everything*: the *Pan Cubano*, the fried pork, the *platanos*, the rice, the beans (*negros*, of course), all of it was there, all of it was good, but the *best* part, the *best* part, was the cheese. *No, no,* not the kind you eat. The *chiiiiiiiiiiissssmes* – gossip. Everyone in the family was spread out enough about town to know about what had happened that morning, and in sequence, or more often, cacophonous unison, everyone would talk about the daily slander and drama as they ate, filling the whole family in on the world, which only went as far as the town's end. Russia became part of the picture only years later. This was how *Mami*, who hardly left the house, knew that Cachita was cheating on Julio with Rodolfo down the block, who had cheated on *his* wife with Daguito's niece when she came to visit from Guantanamo – and she was *sixteen*! You see, *Mami* knew all this even though she had never met Rodolfo, though she knew that his sister had married some guy just to get a ticket to the USA and that he sold bad car parts off as new somewhere near 8th Street. *Mmhmm*…this cheese tasted better than all the rest – and it didn't even make you fat.

Dinner was somewhat similar, except that after eating you didn't go back outside into the scalding heat of the midday for more work or school after taking *café*. Instead everyone would move out onto the porch and talk, and of course, someone in the family played guitar or did something entertaining, since this was before TV or hiding from the *partido*, so people would light up their *puros*, crafted from the finest leaf in the world – don't tell the Turks – and toke them slowly as the crickets chirped into the night and moths ticked over and over again at the porch lights. There, with softly strumming guitar-strings the family would chat idly and surf the occasional evening breeze that came down from over the hills like a spirit in the night, caressing their faces and necks like the living breath of the first book. It was divine. Silvia would never forget how the breeze showed her exactly where on her face the beads of sweat were, she played this game late into the night, feeling her smile from the inside as she watched moths find their way into the lightbulb and die. She didn't talk much in the evenings. She would stare at the stars, pretending they were the lights of a distant city in the sky, and listen to chatter fade into silence, every night. It was so beautiful.

People walking around in the evenings would get called over by the family and they would cross the wooden fence and make their way through the tall grasses in the yard over to the porch, where they would exchange gossip and hang out for a while, smoke a cigarette, take some *café*. In this way, everyone in town was practically family, or close enough, linked by the soul-felt bond of village gossip. Blood-relation was a secondary detail: family was knowing someone's business, and loving them still.

The time came, then, when the girls in the family started to grow up and get married, and Silvia was no exception, ending up with a formidable young *chulo* who had a back good enough to support a family. His name was Orestes, and Silvia fell in love with his eyes. There wasn't much dating. The fact was that Chiche's parents knew Silvia's, and the rumors went around that the families had kids that needed to be married...so it wasn't outwardly arranged, but in some ways it was. Small worlds are simpler worlds, and they all have less choices. Silvia never cared enough to raise a fuss about it, for she had the strangest way of dealing with things: she was known for her vicious temper, her fiery wrath, but when it came time for her to fight for the things that were worthwhile — not the last slice of guava paste in the tin, or whether or not it was too late to go into town — she did very little and simply went along with it. She hoped that people would notice her *lack* of arguing and see how dire the situation was, but they never did. Married, then, as Silvia suddenly found herself, she was forced to provide food for her husband every day like a good wife...as well as other things that he seemed to take care of perfectly on his own.

It was food that caused the first tensions between the

newlyweds, who had settled into a small square-shaped house with lime-green stuccoed walls just across the street from Chiche's family. There is an old saying in Cuba, that when one messes things up, you've made an *'arroz con mango'* – rice with mango. The grainy pulp, the clashing of worlds, of sweet soft fruit and hearty starch staples; it was simply absurd, or more so, for the sake of south Asian cuisine, it was simply vernacular. But imagine the look on Chiche's mother's face when the poor thing told her that his brand new wife – and they didn't do the *divorcio* thing, only if there were bruises involved – had actually served him *arroz con mango,* for dessert!

"*Ay Mamá,*" said Chiche, "Silvia made *un arroz con mango* for dinner."

"*Que QUE?*" What the hell? She snuffed her *cigarillo.*

"*Arroz con mango, Mami, arroz con mango! It was for dessert!*"

"*Hmph...ay Chiche,* I'll see what I can do," and she laughed out loud in her rocking chair.

It was a dire situation, and it put the matrimony off to the worst of starts. Silvia suddenly found herself inundated by her in-laws all the time: commenting, criticizing, *correcting, cajoling* her to do things this way, that way, move aside so they could cook in *my* kitchen. She quickly learned to hate them. Sadly, the times Silvia *had* stood her ground were when she defiantly refused to come into the kitchen when her mother called her, come join Carmen, Silis, we're cooking together, it's such an important part of being a woman...and she would scream at them, running off to the square to flirt with the boys, for *that* was what being a woman was really about. Later in life, in the ashen remains of that horrible accident, she saw from behind her cigarettes that her mother was right – Silvia had confused being a woman with being a young, stupid girl. This mix-up reflected itself sadly in her food, in her marriage, her future. Her ashtray.

The thing was that Chiche was a nice guy though, and

never did he complain directly to Silvia about the food...perhaps this was the second half to the problem. This was all because he had quickly learned that Silvia refused to accept any criticism, neither from him or his sisters or even his own mother Barbarita who always came with the best of intentions—or a *fuente* of *Arroz con Pollo*—trying to help her cook, teach her, but she always rejected her because some part of her knew that by cooking like the Campos family she would become them, their family, their property, their *blood*, and it was too late to go back to her family and learn. Never had she realized it until just then, it weighed down on her shoulders and made it hard to breathe. It couldn't be taught so quickly, she thought to herself, I've been asting all this time, I...I missed the bus. She had thrown it away, she had been given away before becoming who she was supposed to be, now she was *supposed* to become a member of a different family, there was nothing she could do and the regrets filled her soul with the same charred lining that clung to her cooking pots every time she overdid a watery mess and called it *potaje*.

Hear now wisdom, that the child of virtue is born by the womb of misfortune. Laments and wails, high-pitched shrieks and swollen eyes, garbs of black, sallow tunes coming from strings loosened with lolling remorse. The entire family stood naked in the cold despite the torrid waves of humidity that hovered around like inattentive sheets in the atmosphere. Their seam had come undone, *Mami* had died in the middle of the night. No one saw it coming. Everyone thought of their last goodbye, what it would have been like, what it really turned out to be, their last looks into their eyes, what she could have been doing in the *Mas-alla,* stories of the good times, stories of the bad times, of the wet kisses she would give you on the cheek, of her tired glares before going to sleep. Chiche and his family brought Silvia over and dispersed themselves amongst the mourners, looking at the ground, the women with tears in their eyes, the men feeling awkward at being around so many souls in pain. It wouldn't be until literally weeks before leaving Cuba that Chiche would feel the pain of losing one's Mother, 'for leaving to America' and then for *good*; until then, he was just a broad shoulder to lean on, sure I'll go make café, it'll give me a chance to *breathe*... Together on the porch they all wept, leaving her chair empty and rocking by itself in the breeze of that cloudy grey afternoon, as if she were sitting in it, watching them all cry for her with the same tired glare.

The time passed, and though Silvia had been doing a lot less talking and absolutely *no* cooking, things always end up taking their course, and little by little, by the grace of time itself, even the worst of pains settled down to the depths of her soul, as sand inevitably returns to the ocean floor. There came a time when Silvia couldn't help but feel better, something she felt guilty admitting to herself, and at that point, when the memories of her mother brought her joy instead of grief, a primal urge to *cook* arose within her, an urge to *make*, to *feed*. To provide, nourish and aliment. Paired with this was a strange sort of thing, an emotion or thought that was just beyond her understanding, and it goaded her on to the pantry, where she saw things meld together into elaborate dishes she knew not how to prepare. Her eyes quivered with awe at the visions in her mind before the open pantry, and she jumped inside, jamming her hands into the beans and rolling her fingers through them, her face pressed against the pile of *boniatos* that sat there waiting for Barbarita's hands. *Barbarita?! Peace be upon her.* She consoled the pantry with that feeling, that feeling she prayed would never leave her, and pressing all of the ingredients to her chest, she set them upon her counter and began to work, inspired. Before she realized what had happened she was dipping her ladle into a pot of silken black beans, their aroma bringing tears to her eyes. She set the table, and when Chiche got home with the usual load of food from across the street, she seized it from him and walked them back across the dusty road into The Campos' perennially open door.

"*Barbarita, jamás necesitamos de su cocina,*" she said. Barbarita came over to her with questioning, leering eyes, pulling her *cigarillo* from her lips.

"*Y que van a comer, Silis, arroz con mango?*" And what'll you eat, Silis, *arroz con mango?*

"*Ven,*" Silvia challenged her. "*Ven y come en mi casa, mmmmi caaaaaasa! Que al fin soy esposa de tu hijo, ya que al fin es mio.*" She *popped* the last word: *mmmmio.* Come and eat, in *my* house! For I am finally your son's wife, now that he's finally mine. *Mine.* Barbarita pulled on her *cigarillo,* her eyes fixed on Silvia, and nodded, accepting the challenge. The declaration. Neither said anything, but something started right there, and it was behind the looks they exchanged from that day onwards. She called for the family to go across the street for diner, without moving an inch.

"*Dale,*" she said, gesturing towards the newlyweds' house with her lips. "*Vamo'a ved lo que ahh immmbentao, mijita.*" Silvia bit her lip with a smile.

"*Vamos,*" she said, laughter in her voice.

Ay, pero niña!
   Mi China linnnnda! No te ob-bideh de mi, te lo dije yo!
      No te han dicho que tu cocina era un arro' con mango?
   Cojehhhta candela, y metele addd Mambo mijita, pa'que vean quien soy yo:
                  Frrrrrrrrriiiiijjjjjoles negros espezos como la madre que te parió, oi'teh? arroz blanco esponjoso y caliente, tostones crujientes y bistec sofrito con cebollitas y bastante grasita, que es lo unico que sobra por aqui: black beans as thick as the mother who birthed you, fluffy, spongy white rice, twice-fried crunchy plantains and sautéed steak with onions, bell peppers and just the right touch of you know what,

all of it
   waited
      for them
         at
            the table, and the glow was ravishing, nobody could deny the power that they sat down to at that table. Everyone looked at each other, unable to name the miracle that hovered all about them, and bite by bite it all seemed like it was more than a dream, and they took on a new liking for Silvia without even realizing it, as if it were indeed only then that she had become Chiche's wife, a real woman...and they were finally there to let her know. It was then that the families truly mixed together, and this is a very important thing to know, for there is much more to a marriage than newborn grandchildren. But everyone was too caught in the glow of the moment to think about such things, they merely happened behind the light in everyone's smile, and Silvia couldn't tell a soul how it had all happened, for in truth, it was beyond her comepletely, she was glowing the brightest of all. She had seen it unfold before her, her hands merely flowing with the motions of those distant instincts, impulses that she swore voiced themselves – *'not so much!'* or *'let it brown a little more, give it a handful of water...'*

       'Vino seco, vino seco!' Y un poquito de café,
           quehhhloque noh mantiene vivo niña.
     Silvia, always having been a little superstitious, took the thoughts to heart happily, for her mother had always said that women possessed a wisdom that came from giving life and she thought that perhaps she was finally entering into the society of womanhood. Until just under a year ago she had been but a girl living in her parents' home, chasing boys. It was Chiche, and his mother – *ay,* peace be upon her – who got her to finally grow up. Acceptance of pain, and cooking. *That* was a true wife. That was Silvia. *Aaaayyy...*

    "*Oyeme Silis, estos frijoles e'taaaaaaan!* – " but Chiche never got to finish his exclamation of praise, for he had already spooned another heaping pile of rice and beans into his open mouth. Never in all his *Guajiro* vernacular could Chiche have come up with a better end to that sentence. Silvia would never forget it, it flashed in her mind whenever she held her tongue and tried to remember why she loved him. Just like when she went to look up at Barbarita to find she was already watching her. It was there, and neither said a word. Chiche was already on another bite.

"Silvia, I know where I've tasted these beans before," he said, using his fork as a pointer. "These beans taste *just* like your *Mami's*, 'bout time you started cooking like your family." Silvia took a backwards-dive into the depths of her mind and the possibilities, the sheer *impossibilities* unfolded before her, but she accepted them without thinking twice. Goddammit. She was a real woman now. All of this, all the women know it better than me, this is what was missing all along, its so *simple*, it's right *here*, it's *this*...perhaps her own Mother had undergone the same initiation long ago. Did Carmen? She smiled out loud. Within a week, she was the talk of the town, and the people, who itch to weave things into village lore, were convinced that it was Silvia's *Mami* who was helping her cook from the *Mas Allá*—and though the town began to tell the story to others, only Silvia knew it was true. Still, people would tell her in passing that she should do this, do that, where do you have the ashes, put them outside that's bad for her, put this by your bed so you can sleep again at night, take this holy water, I asked the priest to bless it just for you, all of it, over and over again and to this day in her hometown the people *still* talk over afternoon beers and a greasy *dulcemaní* about hot-tempered Silvia, *la atrasada*, whose got her man's heart through the love brewing in her cooking pot. But Chiche never bought the story, he loved hearing people talk about it so he could correct them in a loud voice so that everyone in the square could hear. 'He wasn't into any of it, not him *or* his brother, you hear me, Goddammit?' He was absolutely sure, as he was with his every opinion — *of course* — that in all the mourning she had done back at her house, her sisters had merely taught her some things she had finally cared to ask about. *Pim-pam-pum. Ya nos sobra el tiempo, vees, cuentame algo mas.*

"*Chismosos,* the whole lot of them," he would say to Silvia back at their house, and that was it. He touched the *Santo* on his heart nervously, without thinking. "*Coño, meng.*"

~*~

Together they ate, enjoying both the food and company. Everyone got their fix of bullshit somehow at the table, Jenny and Mariza's jokes, Silvia's feeding Lica too much, and Ricardo too little, Chiche's purveying the scene, chewing slowly, chewing slowly.

"So yeah, I swear, that lady had these *mazas* hanging off her arms that you could've put on bread and sold at the *zolar,* you know?"

Tico laughed, goading his dad to laugh with him as he liked to do. He spat clumps of *congrí* all over the table, laughing like he hardly ever did. "*Ay, coño.*" The ladies looked on quietly, and Mariza smiled to herself. It wasn't about Chiche, though...she simply thought fat people were funny (because she was petrified of becoming one).

'*El cobarde llora con carcajadas,*' and it was true. Cowards laughed their tears.

"And the *guiro* I got?" Tico continued, "Plays just like it should, *mmhmmm*...you know, I only invest when I'm sure its worth my while." Chiche rolled his eyes.

"*Coño* Tico," he said, running his tongue across his molars at a piece of stringy meat caught in the back. "Keep doing what you do, *guiros* or writing or whatever other *marañas* you're up to, because to work without a boss, and to make good money? *That's America right there Goddammit.*" He pointed his fork at the boy. Authoritative silence. *"Que pasa USA, me oi'teh?"* he laughed, looking to Silvia, for they used to watch that show together, *Que Pasa USA.* She glared at him, biting into a crunchy *mariquita* with enmity.

"So as I was saying," Silvia continued at her end of the table, casting Chiche's lingering gaze aside contemptuously, "then Tanya said to him, *'A mi nadie me pega lo' tarrrrrros!'* and she left him, right there. 'Good for her,' I said to Lidia, because you know, cheating on people is just about the worst thing you could do. Look at what I'm stuck with" — Chiche's eyes darted back over the table — "but you don't see me messing around town. I have morals."

"*Mami*, even if you tried, I don't know what you'd manage to tap with that *bata* on," cracked Jenny. Both Mariza and Angelica burst out laughing, and Silvia shot an eyebrow at *La Lica*, who stopped right there and bit into a piece of *yuca* on the end of her fork.

"I've got some nice clothes, okay? You *sinvergüenzas* forget what your mother is capable of, I was just telling *Yennifer* about that earlier, *no, mija?*"

"*Si Mami*, she was a little somethin' somethin' back in her day, Angelica, I'll have you know that." Angelica feigned amusement, chewing on her *yuca* for as long as possible. It was like a life raft from the rip-roaring currents of risky dialogue.

"So yeah," continued Ricardo, "I've been selling more and more radios, because the people in Miami have realized that CD's just aren't doing it anymore, and they're all lazy — we're all lazy, like anyone else — and we don't wanna change our CD's, no?" Ricardo had put down his fork, gesturing with his hands, and Mariza looked at him ravenously from the other side of the table. *Ay*, a man with *pasión! Que rrrico!**

"Señor Campos, you know just as well as anyone else that

CD's can get all scratched up and all, you know? People are sick of them, they don't want to deal with skipping anymore, and at the same time, they've found a solution. Everyone's got their MP3 players now, you know? That's the future, and it's here among us right now." He smiled as only a businessman could. "That's some deep shit, ah?"

"*Aw haaaaaayll yeah!*" shouted Jenny across the table, reaching for a slice of bread. "I got my shit on *tap*, during history class, *ya hearrrrd?*"

"*Precísamente*. You see, Chiche? Its all over the *juventud*. The youth craves it."

"Like those fucking *pastillitas* the kids like to pop at the disco," said Chiche, scowling at Jennifer. Ricardo coughed. "and *drive home*," he continued. Jenny went red as the *aji* in the *pitipoi*. This was the only way he could make her see. It's true.

"*Ah…si, si,* the youth love these new things for music, it makes it easy, and you have all of your music with you, always, its amazing, incredible." He paused, for emphasis. "But *then* you get in your car, and you're stuck with CDs, and people hate this. You scratch them, they skip, they're all over the place, and some people even get their cars broken into for a pile of God-damned CDs." He raised his hands higher into the air. "I mean, come on, are you serious? Are you?" He suddenly beamed with a smile full of sly, flashy teeth. "So I, on behalf of my company, have patented a radio that accommodates your MP3 player *into* it, so you don't have to buy one of those adapters that picks up all the funny low-frequency stations or the scratchy, low-quality ones that have the bulky tapes hanging off one end. Its clean, the sound is good, and it sells like the little *croqueta* sandwiches on *el malecon de la Habana,* remember those?"

"I like this guy," said Chiche to Mariza, ignoring his commentary altogether. Well shit in my cup if Ricardo didn't blush right then, ah? *Cojones,* he wanted in on the fun. "*Bueno* Ricardo," said Chiche, turning back to face the clean-cut businessman, "I'm glad the business is going well. My trade doesn't change much with technology, though. Everyone's gotta vacuum their floors—but," he grinned, "I gotta tell you something. This *negra* right here, when she cooks me lunch, sometimes when its really good, I swear I sell more vacuums, it's like she's back there doing a little something funny to the food, you know?" He smiled at Ricardo.*

"*Oye*," said Silvia, leaving her own conversation hanging, "I don't mess with that stuff. My *Santos* are from the church, okay? And I got 'em here in the house, that's how it is, *y si fuistes tu, aing sorry for joo.*"

"You should tell 'em to redecorate the place," said Mariza, slurping up a fork-full of *ropa vieja*. Jenny cracked and hid her smile deep into her plate. Giggles.

"*Hmph*. This place is fine, but *you!* You need to go and confess, *culicagada*. And make sure the priest doesn't know Ricardo when you do." This time it was Mariza who was left out of the table's laughter.

"*Mmhmm*," she replied after a heavy second, "like some old man is going to help me out on my, what is it, Tico? My 'spiritual journey?' *Psshhhhh.*"

"Don't make me pull your pants down and give you three *chancletazos* right here, *niña*." Silvia reached for the *mariquitas* with a matriarchal nod.

"Be careful, *Mami*, Ricardo might like that a little too much." The clean-cut *Cubano* slapped the table with his hands, rattling all the silverware and booming with forced laughter as he nudged Chiche nervously. "Ah, ah?! Might like it HAHAHAHA!"

"Oye Mariza," Chiche softly asked with bulging eyes, "come on, ah? Drop it. Ricardo," he continued, "I'm sorry you have to sit through this whenever you come to my house. I always said the dinner table is a sacred place, but these people *all* need to go and confess. Or something, I don't know." He suddenly seemed clear of remorse. "You know what? To hell with all of it," and he spooned another heaping serving of rice onto his plate, as if to propitiate his nerves.

"Look *Mami*," said Jenny to the table, "Mariza's giving *Papi* the diabetes again."

"*Señor Campos*," said Ricardo with a tension-breaking sip of his beer, "I assure you, this family is a beautiful thing, I swear. Know what?" he smiled, "makes me miss Cuba, the good ol' days. How about that? *Damn*," he sighed nostalgically. "All mine are still back there, and trust me, if anything it gets worse at our dinner table. I am honored to eat here." Chiche smiled, messing with his plate-ful of rice. Deep inside himself, Ricardo sighed deeply, and made a mental note to be extra rough with Mariza later. It would be a better solution than confession — 'at least for her,' he thought. 'It's the only time *I've* heard her call out to Jesus...'

"Hell yeah."

"*Bueno dime*, Angelica," said Mariza, "how long have you been in Miami?"

"*Pues Mariza*," smiled the Colombian blonde, "I left Cartagena for the USA just over two years ago, and when I was deciding where to go, I knew I had to find a good Spanish-speaking community, so I picked Miami, more for the beach than anything else. I do like Cubans, though," she giggled, grabbing Tico's hand under the table.

"Oh, so you wanted to find a good Cuban man here, that's what you're saying?" she said, with a devilish grin. "*Hmm? Un Cubanito que te de tres vueltas?*"

"No, no, Mariza, it's not like that...it's more about...the...*ambiente*. 'El Cubaneo', as Alberto calls it." Silvia nodded silently in agreement, smiling softly as she plucked a few *mariquitas* off her plate. "It's Latino, no matter what flag you're from."

"Oh, you call him 'Alberto'. That's cute."

"Mari-mari, why don't you stand up and recite '*los Zapaticos de Rosa*' for us?" said Tico. "That's pretty cute too." Mariza said nothing, reaching across the table for some *mariquitas*, making sure to linger long enough so that Ricardo would notice she was showing him her tits. Chiche saw the whole thing, stabbing a slice of tomato over and over again under his lowered gaze, wondering if his blood sugar really was soaring.

"*Vago*," whispered Mariza to herself as she sat down.

"*Y tu*," said Tico, right on the money. "At least I do *something* for my money...what *you* do I do for free." Poor Angelica blushed red as a rose.

"*Ya, ya, no se fajen*," said Silvia with an air of finality.

"We're not fighting, Mami," said Mariza coolly, "we're just discussing life. *Filosofía*, right Tico? *La Piedra Filosofal*, the center of gravity, you're stupid flower on your jacket—"

"*Rrrrrecoño!*" said Chiche, a piece of rice clinging to his lip. "*Ya*." Enough. There was silence, broken only by a quiet muttering of '*Guaricandilla*' by Jenny. Chiche's fork scraped across his plate, heaping up more rice into his mouth.

"Whenever a conversation goes silent, it means an angel flew by..." Tico grinned quietly. "One can only imagine what flew over just now." Slowly, the room was filled with the tinkling of silverware on plates, until the ladies resumed their conversation quietly, as if in secret.

"So Jenny, tell me what you plan on doing once you graduate," asked Angelica softly.

"*Bueno*," she said, "I don't know where exactly I want to go, but I need to find a rich man I can travel with. That's step one. This booty aint goin' to no college, I'm goin' to Brazil!" and Mariza laughed hysterically. Tico knew that people laughed at things they identified with, and this made *him* laugh, which Jennifer appreciated, since she often felt that Tico was above the family, lost always in his traipsing thoughts and fragrant gardenias. It all worked out at the dinner table though, like the unseen force of something great that people couldn't name but Tico called love. How else could people argue and nag each other, and then do the same thing at the dinner table with smiles on their faces, in good spirits? Was it just the food? It couldn't be. Was it the *Cubaneo? Nah, no jodas.* There was something special about the dinner table, and whatever it was, it made the love flow strongly there, right along with the hate. But it was family, so it was good hate. Loving hate, the pleasure of life. Tension...and release.

"...and the *sala'o* was *this big, Chiche!*" shouted Ricardo over the rest of the banter.

"*Coñooooooo!* You cant be serious." Chiche played along.

"O yeah, swordfish the size of the boat, *meng*! I still got steaks in the freezer, you should come have one sometime.* They're like freakeen hubcaps, *meng*." He nudged Chiche on the arm. "I'll teach Mariza how to cook before, though." Everyone laughed. Everyone, of course, except Mariza.

"Maybe we'll have the barbeque when we get that new place on the beach you've been talking about for months, *hmm?*" said Mariza right into Ricardo's eyes. Plates tinkled with silence all over again.

"Yeah, I don't know if Mariza has told you, Señor Campos, but we're planning on moving by the beach as soon as I'm done with some projects I'm working on right now," said Ricardo.

'Yeah, like those thirty kilos under the fish,' thought Mariza silently. That was a line she *wouldn't* cross.

"...and that's my idea for the new book," said Tico. "To tell that story, but from a different perspective, from the other side of the coin, you know?" Everyone nodded half-heartedly, half-confused. "Don't tell anybody though, they'll steal my ideas." They didn't care. Things, it seemed, were winding down. Tico was taking about his books.

Everyone ate their fill soon enough, and as they poked at the bits left on their plates, Silvia came out of nowhere with a crystal dish laden with fat slices of guava paste and cheese for everyone. The smell of *café* filled the room as they ate the dessert from 8th street, and Tico smiled to himself with every bite as he wondered over and over again why this guava tasted better than from anywhere else. It was the best question to ask in any circumstance, 'Why is this so good?' As if reading his mind, Silvia reminded him as she wiped cracker crumbs from the corner of her mouth:

"*Santos, Santos, Santo Padre Celestial,*" she said with a delightful smack of her lips. Tico laughed, but he knew it was probably true. Even the Catholics in Miami respected the *Santeros.* The traditions of the Yoruba people were very present still in Cuba and Miami, all over the world, in fact, and it was very, very real. *Santeria* was a very…tangible religion, and everyone knew that the *Orishas,* and thus their children as well, were not to be messed with. Power, of course, carried its responsibilities, and that was the cause of all the fuss. People were afraid of the power of the *Santeros* garbed in white, their beads ravenously colorful, their smiles eerily confident. They feared that smile, the boon of *Aché*…for it could be used for good, and just as well for bad. It was all a matter of responsibility, of consequences, of determination and sometimes, sheer hate.

The men took their *café* and Ricardo, being the man he was, pulled three Cohibas straight from the motherland out of his coat-pocket and offered them to Chiche and Tico, respectively. They went out on the porch to talk, and Angelica squeezed Tico's hand silently as he stood up to go outside. He gave her a wink and took off. The dreaded was about to happen.

"*Ay,* girl talk!" squealed Mariza. She exchanged that same smile with Angelica once again while Silvia made her way to the kitchen, where she began to do the dishes, one by one, thinking of how nice it was to suddenly be where she was, and not at that table.

"So tell me, Angelica, what's the deal with you and Tico, have you been hinting at a ring or what?" asked Mariza as if she were on her side.

"I'm not looking for anything like that. I mean," she fumbled, "it would be nice, but really, it would just be a sort of confirmation on Tico's part that he likes what we already have. I feel like it works between us, and that's alright for now."

"*Hmph*. I think you're lookin' for a ring if you ask me," said Jenny nonchalantly. Mariza laughed louder than she should have.

"Leave her alone," insisted Silvia from the sink. "You want some tea, *mija*? See, I remembered your tastes. The other day at Solano's I bought some tea just for you." She made to get up, but Angelica assured her it was ok. They would enjoy it another day, she insisted.

"Wow, Mami, you got her tea...where's my tea?" asked Mariza, twirling a curl of her hair with a frown.

"Yeah Mami, we're, like...your like, kids, you know..." Jenny had pursed lips.

"Ay, stop it, coño, I was just trying to be nice!" growled Silvia, showing the box of tea back into the cabinet.

"Aww, she's embarrassed, you're such a bitch, Jenny."

"ME? You the one gettin' turnt off dick ammm-money!"

"*Niñas!*" spouted Angelica, "don't talk that way in front of your mother." She couldn't help it. Silvia smiled, though she had no idea what had been said. English.

Jenny and Mariza shut their mouths, tongue in cheek, and just looked at each other. *Mmmhmm. She di'nt.* They were suddenly sisters again. And no one spoke for a few seconds. "I'm sorry," said Angelica dismissively, "it's just all the bad words, I don't know. Forgive me." *Mmmhmmm...she can't play us, she ain't gettin in on this.* Silvia felt a wrenching in her gut. She hated *talking, talking* in this way. They were talking about her, defending her, caring. Pretending. Each in their own way. She was spilling herself to these people who didn't need to know a damned thing. She wanted to be alone. She felt empty. She wanted a smoke. She looked down at the ice-cubes melting in her glass.

"You okay, *Mami?*" asked Jennifer.

Silvia smiled, more to herself than anyone else, "*Si, niña,* I'm fine." She kept grinning distantly, watching Jenny toy with a piece of cheese on her plate.

"Whatever, Mom."

Outside, the three *hombres* sat on the porch chairs, smoking their cigars and talking about...manly things...which Tico found rather difficult. He was more of a spectator then, like the Holy Grail at the round table of King *Arturo Fuentes.*

"So I think I saw a cage back there, Señor Campos, what you got goin' on in there? *Palomas o que?*" Ricardo laughed. "You haven't been gone from Cuba long enough to forget about a good ol' *Palomita,* ah?"

"Nah, *meng,* we don't gotta do that here anymore, but you're right, nothing reminds you of Cuba like the sight of plucked doves and a big boiling pot of water, no? *Coño!* I miss Cuba every Goddamn day."

"*Awwwww,* come on, Señor Campos, you're telling me you weren't part of that famous plaza across Miami at the beginning of the Mariel?" Chiche laughed out loud, shaking his head as he milked his cigar. "Señor Campos, come on! You can be honest with me! I know how it is, *meng,* I just got off the boat, my uncle Chucho used to catch doves in a trap in the backyard so we could have something to eat with our rations, you know?" He drew on his *puro.* "I know the story. That plaza, full of doves, and the white people didn't know what to think when all the doves disappeared...*HhhhhhAAAA!*"

"*Palomilla? No meng, Paloma!*" laughed Chiche. He sighed. "*Pal carajo, meng, pal carajo...*"

"Señor Campos, I can—"

"Ricardo," said Chiche, sitting up in his chair, pulling the cigar from his mouth. "You can call me Chiche."

"*Coño...*" said Ricardo, more to himself than anyone. He was in. He sat back in his chair, setting the moist tip of the cigar between his teeth triumphantly. The grin was inevitable.

"And yeah, they're for canaries anyway, the cages. *Canarios, y Azulejos.*" He lingered on the 'S's. "I catch the *Azulejos* when they're on the move to Canada. Then they're blue, but up there they turn brown. Beautiful, ah?" He smiled. "Better here."

"Oh, yes! *Si, si!*" chimed Tico. "The *Azulejos* perch on my balcony in the virgin spring and make my heart overflow! *Ay, que belleza...*" Both Ricardo and Chiche looked to him with smiles on their faces, their erect cigars jutting from their manly grins. Men...men...will be men. *My heart ain't what overflows, mijito...* "*Bueno*, I'm gonna get going, let me go say my goodbyes to everyone," and with that he snuffed his smoke out and saw himself inside.

"*Los azulejos, ya tu sabes,*" said Chiche, letting his gut out just a bit further under the flickering ember.

Silvia was wandering around the living room pretending to tidy things up when Tico came through the door. "*Mami*, come here, I want to show you something." Silvia looked at Tico, who smiled at the three young women across the room, absorbed in their conversation.

"What is it?" Silvia asked, feeling her guts churn—Jesus, was it the food?

"*Mira*, I'll show you." Silvia grew confused as he made towards the bedrooms. Silvia followed Tico past the beautiful sepia picture of *La Virgen* on the wall, and into the end of the hallway. He didn't turn on the light. Neither did Silvia. Tico squatted down and grabbed a bundle on the floor at the foot of the door to their bedroom.

"Tico, what is all th—"

"*Shhh, Mami*, I have a gift for you." In the dark, she saw a hand rise past the gardenia and point to the sky. *"La Virgen*, she has a gift for you." Silvia said nothing. Slowly, Tico unwrapped the bundle, layer by layer, wafting hints of tropical must and aloeswood into the air.

"*Ay, Cuba,*" said Silvia. Tico smiled.

"*Si, Mami,* I am merely the messenger, though this is indeed, mine." He lifted the machete from the wad of paper, letting it shine in the little light that was about them.

"*Ay, Tico, y que' eso, un machete?*"

"*Si, Mami,* it came to me and I must give it to you. It's so that you'll always be there to protect me." Light flashed in Tico's eyes, and Silvia saw it. She said nothing. Like so many Alchemists before him, Tico was making the dire mistake of taking allegory too literally, and it was the enthusiasm that goaded the whole thing on as if it were truly magical. *Goddesses,* I tell you, he made them feel like Goddesses, all of them! "You need to keep this safe, and let no one see it, or know about it, for its power will keep both of us safe. It will bring us both happiness—"

"Ay, Tico, this stuff scares me, it looks like bruje—"

"*Mami, no!* I forsake black magic with all of my heart! This is just a protection for me and for you, everyone who truly becomes a philosopher does it, you will use it to strike the stone, you see, but that's all complicated stuff. You just need to keep it safe for the both of us, and it will make us both very happy. I *promise.*"

"Ay, a philosopher, what prestige, I will tell all my friends, my son is *un* philosopherrr. *Unggg Pee-Eyshe-Dee,* they won't know the difference." She looked over her shoulder. "You said La Virgen?"

Bingo, Linda.

"*Si, Mami,* in philosophy we're all *La Virgen,* so this is why I'm giving it to you, because in my life you're my mother, you're

La Virgen, you were the first eyes I looked into, and if I am *La Virgen* as well, then I am giving this gift to my Goddess, and She is giving it to herself as well. I know, It's complicated—"

Silvia took the bundle into her hands. "Ay Tico, you're such a beautiful child."

He could say nothing through his tightening throat. *She speaks to me.*

"Look how you care for your Mother—"

"Forever, Mami, that's why I was born."

Silvia went to make a joke about striking the stone with it, but behind them, Mariza had pulled the knotted chain on the ceiling fan, trying to turn it on—she looked up at it's inaction. Pulled again. Snapped her head to the left.

"T-Tico? Mami?" She squinted into the dark hallway. A white suit. "What the hell are you guys doing?" Out from the hallway emerged Tico and Silvia, their eyes as bright as stars, and wet with tears of love. Silvia's guts roiling over each other, but she wouldn't tell a soul. They were all about to leave, anyway...

"No, *niña*, Tico just had to tell me something."

"Yeah," answered Tico in English, "don't worry about it, I got it covered."

Mariza looked unconvinced. "Well...I'm starting to choke on that nasty *smoke* from outside, I was trying to get some ventilation in here. This thing looks broken," she said, grabbing the chain again.

"Don't pull on it again, Mariza, that doesn't solve every problem," said Silvia, cracking a smile. "That thing's been broken for years, you never noticed?"

"I never had to breathe that nasty *shit* here, so *no. Coño, Mami*," she said, frowning at Tico.

"Yeah, see?" he said briskly, "don't worry about it, Mariza, I got it covered." And they made for the dinner table, where Silvia and Tico kept looking at each other throughout the small-talk. She couldn't stop thinking about the Virgin, and the machete she had given her. Her gift.

A few minutes later, right as Tico mentioned he was getting ready to go, Jennifer said that her friend was about to come pick her up and she went to her room to get her things, suddenly distant. "That was weird." Angelica offered to clean the table up before they left, and Mariza helped her out, leaving Silvia in a chair, fumbling with a crumpled napkin. *"Pues coñito,"* she said to herself with a smile, looking at the picture of the Virgin. She was *smiling*. She looked around the room, at the two ladies moving the doilies to the sink and wiping the table down, and she thought about the men left outside, what they must have been talking about, that's why poor Tico probably got up and left, Ricardo talking testosterone and Chiche probably complaining about something. Tico's a good boy, a sensitive soul..."*Viejo de mierda,"* Silvia mumbled to herself at the thought of her balding caretaker, "always complaining, always talking such shit. I swear I could kill him."

With that passing statement, uttered by her so many times before, in anger, in vain, in playful jest, her eyes glazed over with something deep and thick, evoking memories before her mind of the first time she had made love long ago. Something indescribable and new, enjoyable and alien, it overcame Silvia with such power that her leg kicked out in a vicious twitch that shook the table. She began to laugh, repeating to herself, "I could kill him, I could kill him...*lo podrrria matarrrr,*" and she gasped a long, endless hiss up into the top of her head, smiling like she hadn't in years. Her giggles became uncontrollable laughter, hysterical, breath after breath, stopping Mariza and Angelica in their tracks as they watched her double over in her chair all by herself.

"*Mami,* are you alright...really? I mean, you seem strange." She stuck her tongue out in jest, her eyes slightly concerned.

"*Ay mija,* when you're married you'll understand. *You,* though," she said to Angelica with her crazy smile, "you won't, you'd better not!" and she narrowed her eyes into two hellish slits. "You'd better not," and she burst out laughing once again, rolling around in her chair with deep laughs that sent tears down her cheeks, until she finally calmed down, wiped her eyes with her wrist and stood up. "*Ay...*" she paused dramatically, hunched over with a leering smile, "I need a smoke, though. I'm just *happy!*" She giggled, running her hands across her arms, over and over again. Gliding over to the glass-top coffee table, she grabbed her pack and pulled out a cute little cigarette. It was so small, so perfect! Everything was perfect. It had been her first orgasm in years.

"*Ay, Virgen Santísima,* forgive me for forgetting what it's like to be happy," she sang to the picture on the wall with a smoke hanging from her lips. The Virgin Mary smiled at her like always, holding the Child and a golden cross, flanked with the stories of Cuba, and she lit the cigarette with her Capricorn lighter, looking back to the two girls as she plopped onto the couch triumphantly.

"*Que quieren?*" she said, blowing smoke around the cigarette in her lips.

Jennifer's cell phone rang as she came back into the living room. The hottest Reggaeton jam blasted for the three seconds it took her to silence it. She looked to her mother, and to the ladies by the sink, thought to herself for a second, and shrugged it off, clicking a text message into her phone.

"*Mami,*" she said curtly. "*Me voy.*"

"*Ay, chatack,*" she said. Shut up. She smiled with hot, rosy cheeks. "It's my *family,* girls, you're my *family,* it's all in the family, you, me, everyone, and we live together, we die together, here, there, anywhere, and it's all so beautiful *mija...isn't it?*" Her glossy eyes twinkled as she took a long drag of her cigarette, beaming with a happiness she hadn't known in a long time. The cherry grew longer and longer with each satisfying pull on the tobacco. *Silis, we shall make you happy. I will light your heart.* It was as if her wrinkles slowly traced back into her lips, back into the corners of her eyes, across her forehead, around her nose, and she sat there, smoking like the *señorita* she once was. Would Tico have been jealous of such Alchemy? *No jodas.*

~*~

After Tico and Angelica and the rest of the kids left, Chiche came back inside and headed to the bedroom to sleep with nothing except for a casual bob of the eyebrows as he passed by. *Good night, wife.*

"Your pills," Silvia said into the ceiling.

"Ah, *caaarajo*," and she listened to him shake the pills, fill a glass of water, check his blood sugar, and shuffle over to the bedroom after the satisfying beep of the little monitor. He was fine.

Silvia sat alone in the dark room, the shadows flickering to motion of the TV she ignored. It was some *telenovela* in Portuguese, and though she had gotten through them before with her Spanish and its limited semblance to Portuguese, she couldn't even concentrate on the TV, not even on the mismatched dubbing, which never failed to catch her attention, but only when she tried to avoid it—*'That's not her voice, carajo!'* Besides, someone had told her once that speaking Portuguese was as easy as putting a potato in your mouth and speaking Spanish...but what was this to say about Cuban Spanish? The curls and loopy knots that made Spanish distinctly Cuban was enough to make people in the motherland scream at each other every once in a while—*"Niño, sacate esa papa de la boca!"*

'Child, take that potato outta your mouth and SPEAK, Goddammit!'

"*Quiet. I'm theenkeen.*" She lit another smoke.

It was one of those nights where she just sat and thought about things until she got tired and went to sleep, sometimes on the couch, sometimes into bed. There was too much to think about, and too much time to do it. Silvia lay with her head back, her eyes lost in the sparkles of the ceiling, thinking about what she had said at dinner over and over. '*Viejo de mierda, I could kill him, I could kill him, I swear...lo podria matar...*" and after a while she woke from her trance to find her gaze resting on the picture of *La Virgen*, flanked by the stories and faces of Cuba, the Child Jesus' face as beautiful as baby Krishna. *Horus. Heracles. Mithras. Quetzalcoátl. Ay, I like this game...*

"Ay *Mamasita*, what has come over me tonight..." Silvia whispered into the silence with a coy smile. " Who are all those people? *Unh...*" she whined, "I'm going to kill him, *Virgensita*," she said, laughing at herself. "Am I? Can you believe that? *Mmhmmm, si Mama*...with the very knife Tico got me, with Cuba, I'll cut off his head...and his balls, too. His *balls. His little red cojones de su puta madre.*" She made to laugh, but her thoughts interrupted her: '*Calm yourself, mija, it will all unfold in due time. You're so beautiful when you're happy...*'

Silvia sat in the silent darkness, overjoyed at the words the Virgin whispered to her, she could tell no one, it would all go away, the happiness would go away...she watched her fears project themselves in the dark like curling tentacles, rapists and fire, strangling the little fledgling of joy she had felt tonight, her anger kicked them all in their little red *cojones*. Chiche, *Chiche's the trouble in your life. Your anger, your sadness, your age! You'll die before him, he's killing you with the tangled knots of repression!* "*La Virgen* is with me, fuck you." Smiles, sickly satisfying smiles, right only because they could bear to exist in so much wrong. Nothing was wrong. "Fuck you, Chiche, *te voy a matar.*"

Nothing was wrong!

"I swear, if I didn't know it was You talking to me, *Mama*," she replied, "I would think I was crazy." She giggled. *You're crazy? Let me tell you something, florecita...* "But I'll have to think about it, Mama. It seems too crazy. *Too messy.* I'll have to think about it, make it look like an accident. I'll go to jail...what then? *This aint Cuba, Mamita,*" she laughed, clearing her throat. "*Que*

Guajira. A horrrrible accident, Silvia, horrible." She took a deep breath, laughing at how she talked to herself. *"Santa María, madre de Dios, ruega por nosotros pecadores, ahora y en la hora de nuestra muerte, Amen."* Holy Mary, Mother of God, pray for us sinners, now and at the hour of our death...Amen. She touched her fingers with their cigarette to her brow, her heart, her shoulders...and she lingered smiling. "El Espiritu Santo," she smiled, touching the filter tip to her nipples, one by one. They stung as they tightened stiff. "Amen, Jesus. Amen, Jesus." *Consummatum est.* She kissed her hand, and took a drag.

She soon got up to go to bed, her bones aching through her muscles. She turned the TV off and walked into the darkness like she did every night, and the air always felt thicker then. She would normally find her way to her bed by Chiche's snores, but tonight she saw everything behind her closed eyes, she was alive as the world around her, and it was as if everything in the room glowed with a heat that helped her find the room like bats do their perches. The bed glowed brightest of all. She paused. The *machete.* The image of the bundle conjured itself into her mind, nestled behind the curtain rolls and plastic mattress wrappers that has been under the bed for over fifteen years. Chiche roared like a bullfrog off to the right, and she shook her head, thinking of the pills dissolving in his stomach. *I could do it right now,* she smiled. *No, no, Silis, it's the journey, the journey that counts,* and her base churned once again with that tingling heat, that velvety pleasure that squeezed at her insides. Once she opened the door the hall was filled with moonlight. *'Look at him, just sleeping like a Goddamn...Hmph!'* She tiptoed into the room and slipped into the sheets, holding her *bata* down to avoid flashing her sheets as she did every night. She settled in, pulling the sheets over herself she lay down facing Chiche, the machete beneath them both, like the Holy Spirit at a middle-school dance. She stared at his snoring head for a few minutes. Into the pitch black of his ears. An icepick, slowly...*into his brain.* "Malandro," she whispered softly into the dark. She touched her tongue to the roof of her mouth, aching with pleasure as she ran it back toward her throat, over and over. She leaned near to his face, grinning happily as she did when she used to pull him over to make love. She kissed the tip of his earlobe, the softest peck, brushing her lips down to his earlobe and whispering, *"Comepinga...te voy a matar..."* He chortled in response, choking on a snore. He sighed, and resumed his snoring once again. Snoring, snoring all these years when he should have been holding *me*. He doesn't know love, we married in heat, we were rats in the spring. Starving, young, hot-blooded. She closed her eyes, leaning back onto her pillow, smelling the tobacco on her lips. Pursed them in the dark, kissing an imaginary face hovering atop hers. Gentle company, intimacy, they were all figments of her imagination. *Ay Silvia*...it felt good sometimes, to be surrounded by so much frustration, so much anger, so much sleep. It was a warm lullaby...she was never alone, never cold.

She smiled to herself in the dark in her thoughts until a gust of inspiration stirred her to move, and she found her hand moving down her body as if on its own. Slowly down the stiff cotton of her bata, slowly across her stomach, her haunches, her loins, down to the triangle of her aging sex, over the scrubbing fleece of her old age and, with an exasperated gasp, onto her warm, anxious sex. She let it rest there, feeling the heat of her passion, her awakened joy, the moistening of her dire, dire circumstances. Clenching her teeth, she pulled her hand away, drew it out of the blanket high up into the air, and watching it tremble in the darkness above her, brought it down firmly onto Chiche's face. He screamed in surprise, to which Silvia did the same—"...The fuck is wrong with you?!" she yelled at him, squinting her eyes in the darkness. "What were you dreaming about, your mother Barbarita?"

He shook his head, grabbing his cheek, running his fingers together, smelling them. "What the hell, I'm gonna go get a glass of water. I was having a nightmare." He stood from the bed with a groan. "About you, of course. You were bitching about something." She listened to him chuckle to himself as he made for the kitchen in the dark. Once she heard the faucet turn on, turn off, *'p-AAAAhhh'*, turn on again, repeat, three times, only then did she hear him ask quietly: "You want some water?" She feigned sleep, and listened to him walk back to the room. Plopped into bed, farted. Groaned. Only the moonlight knew where her smile was, and the soft white light played across her lips in the darkness as she squeezed her thighs over and over again, basking in the pleasure. She was the woman she used to be. She smiled like that all night long, even long after she had fallen asleep.

Far off across Miami, the old man sat before his tablet of *Ifá*, tossing his *kwele* onto its surface with cackles of ancient knowledge. He stopped after a throw that left him with wrinkles in his brow, and tapping one of the nuts, it moved over onto its flat side. He smiled. Throwing the chain again, he asked them if they would tell him why, and they all stood on end. Brushing his arms thoroughly, he asked if he could throw them once more. He touched them to the four corners of the tablet, spraying *aguardiente* to his back, where a wide-headed little idol smiled blankly in the candlelight. This time the *kwele* rolled off of his hand and fell into a pattern that left the man stroking his chin.

"*La pobre*," he said. "There is light in the darkness, and darkness in the light."

~*~

Lo voy a matar, lo voy a matar, viejo manganzón! Lo voy a matar, como que nunca supo todo lo que nos hizo con sus estupidezes y el mizmo tiqui-tiqui de siempre, los días sin television…lo voy a matar, lo voy a matar, viejo de pinga sala'o! Jodi'o calbo de su puta madre Barbarita como las croquetas en las playas…las orquestas en el cine del Gallego, cigarros de maleficios y buen provecho, bien hechos, bien dichos, fumados, prendidos, Orquesta Aragon y la Sonora Matanzera, cocos

*secos...y...senos ardientes...plateados con los terminos de su
sonriza...maleficios de los mal-hechos fumando cigarros contra la
humanidad...te hablo de los mejores Cubanos como José Martí
con...su...cabezita de rosas...cardo y...ortiga...fumando cigarros con una
mano blanca, mano franca...leer...andar...borrar y limpiar...matar...
matar...matar...fumar...matar...fumar...amar...matar...fumar...am
ar...Maria...mat-re mato
matagallos...matar..mat..ar...ma...ma...ma....mama...matamoros y luces
de las culebras...sanguina...semilla...matar...via de la muerte ida y
venida...secreto fijo y corto que te digo y nunca de darás cuenta mijita,
mi niña bonita...mirala que se durmio. Matar las frutas podridas de
donde se viene el fuego del alcohol...susúrren tenebrosos maleficios del
fondo me mi mente, y tú...tú ni sabes lo que te espera,
mijita...Silis...tengo hambre, y usted, Doña Silvia, estas dormida...en paz
descanzes, y comeras tambien. Mire, mire mi amor...bienvenida a su
destino, tan fino, te loy doy como una linda flor.*

Toma.

*The ring boy came forward in his white suit, a carnation set on
his lapel, a frilly white pillow in his hands. Silvia, beautiful as ever, took
the ring and looked back to her mother and her father, who embraced each
other and cried. The priest, his greying hair combed neatly to the side,
slipped his thin metal-framed glasses onto his face and opened the little
book. He read:*

*Do you, Silvia Perez, take this man, Orestes Campos, to be your
lawfully wedded husband? She nodded, and looked to Chiche, his eyes
dark and grey, encircled by ashy rings, and she slipped the ring onto his
finger. There was only one, one ring, for him.*

Silvia opened her eyes, the ceiling vibrant with the last
embers of the dream she had seen. "My father didn't cry at my
wedding," she said. "And of course he'd forgot my ring." She
sighed with a smile. "Even in my dreams he's an asshole."

She tried to fall back asleep after this, but thoughts about the dream, the details, the people, the clothes, the teeth shining inside of everyone's mouths — especially Chiche's, so crooked and perfectly white. He had nasty teeth he hid under his wide, curling lip, but not in this dream. They were shining and white, set off by the rings under his eyes — there were two of those. It filled her mind with all sorts of things, worries, predictions, sanctified omens and rumors of old about dreaming with teeth. It was death. Her mother always told her that dreaming with teeth foretold death. The world was behind her, La Virgen knew, it was an omen, she felt it in her heart. Her heart tingled, she squeezed her thighs, breathed deeply. Was it all in her head? *Is this all in my head?* Was it a message from the above…*an okay? Okay! Okay! Or a 'watch out'? Puta que eres! You are blissful, happiness incarnate, look at yourself! The cross has been placed into your hands, my child. You can end it all, right now if you wish…all the wrrrrrong! he's done you. Goddammit. God damn it all, damn him…*she cast it all aside upon remembering her new quest, her new *joy,* and it made her feel giddy, it made her insides churn with excitement, happier than she had ever been in a long time. And that couldn't be wrong. *Happiness is not wrong!* Feel it, feel the joy of the Virgin. *'Yes, yes, it is right to be happy, and I am happy.'* Still, though, she couldn't sleep. She stood and went to have a cigarette outside.

Out there in the thick air of the porch, she filled the still air with the fragrances of tobacco, and it almost smelled sweet all around her — tangy…she wondered if other people felt that way as they smelled her cigarette smoke. She remembered hating the smell — until she started smoking them — she cracked a laugh all alone on the porch. Whenever she would walk by someone taking a drag, she would inhale deeply and smile as the little white sparkles all over the place filled her visual field like it did when she held her breath for too long. It was negligible, but it was there, that smoke, those sparkles, the flittering of joy, and she blew her drag out slowly, letting it rise right before her eyes. A curl of smoke caught on her eyebrow, and she blew it off, jutting her lower lip out the way she did to get things out of her eye.

> *'...The sting of smoke in the eyes*
> *Is the startling reminder*
> *Of the responsibilities that come*
> *With harnessing fire, Doña Silvia.'*

A kiss...upon her brow? Another drag. *"Mosquitos de su pinga."* The moon broke through the heavy clouds that loomed in the sky above her, and her ample face stuck out to the solitary girl on the porch as if she could reach out and touch it, a perfect half-moon smiling down to her, light and dark at once. The little girl blew a waft of smoke towards it, teasing it back into the clouds. Her eyes darted below.

"Hmph – Cagar Parao, what's he doing out so late?" Her neighbor was out for a midnight walk, as he liked to do every now and then. His name was Emilio Gándara, but in her family they liked to call him *'Cagar Parao'* because he had a nose that curved to the side giving him a perennial smirk and a boil on his head the size of a tennis ball. One day while gossiping about him at the table, Silvia baptized him with the name on accident, because she said at the table that, *"Ese viejo e'ta ma' feo que cagar parao!"*

"That guy's uglier than a standing shit!"

The family laughed so hard that the name stuck. Ever since then, whenever someone would see him they would say, *'Coño!* There goes *Cagar Parao!"* and laughter would invade the scene like clockwork. Silvia would catch him occasionally on his walks while smoking quietly on the porch as she was just then. It was a strange relationship that they had, for he participated in it just as much as she did, even if only by being there. They were friends who had never been introduced. *Ay, Silvia. Those are your favorite, no...*

He pretended not to have seen her and she did the same thing, looking over to that house down the block, which had suddenly become very interesting...

"*Okay, he passed,*" she whispered to herself happily, releasing the air from her lungs. The smoke had been absorbed into her beating heart. She took another long, long drag, just a little too much, crossing her eyes to look at the ember sneak down the end of the cigarette. 'I'm anxious,' she thought to herself. 'Look how long the ember is,' and she flicked the tip — *wah*, a rain of ashes. It made her smile. '*Lo vamos a matar,*' she remembered, smiling out loud. She giggled, biting her lip at the effervescence in her sex. 'This is why the Virgin is smiling,' she reflected. 'She's always like this. *Like me.*'

There she sat, alone on her porch with her cigarettes and her thoughts, until she felt sleepy and went to bed. Across town, Ricardo stared up into the spackled ceiling, thinking his debts out. The night was hot, the AC was off; sex hung in the air. Moonlight poured through the windows, playing across Mariza's frizzy black hair — she'd die if he told her about the snoring. Far off in the distance, a dog whined into the night sky. 'There goes that dog again. It's been at it all night,' he thought to himself. He laid a hand on Mariza's exposed breast. She clasped it without waking, smacking her lips lightly in the sticky heat. 'Ay, those old *Guajiro's* tales never get beyond me,' he thought, shaking his head. 'Here I am, a grown man in the USA, and I still think about who's gonna die every time I hear a dog whine like that.' He stifled a laugh; the bed shook a little. 'Do they know about that here in the US, too?'

~*~

Silvia reached for the phone without moving her head from the pillow, her eyes closed to the morning light. It was an antique phone, made to look as if it were crafted with care and precision, as they used to do with things a long time ago. She tried to open her eyes, but only one opened — the other was crusted shut. She would end up pulling at it with all her strength, using muscles she didn't even know she had around her eye and after a few seconds of tension it would *pop!* open and hurt for a bit, but today she laughed it off as she put the receiver to her ear with the look of an angry sailor.

"*Dime.*"

"*Herma*, you're still in bed? *Dale*, it's Sunday!" Shit. It's Sunday.

Silvia imagined being sick for a second, if I were feeling ill I would say...go *see your mother!*

"Okay, let's go." She popped her other eye open and slinked out of bed with only 4 cracks of her aching back.

"Ok, I'll be there in 20 minutes. Have you looked outside?" Carmen sounded excited.

"I can't reach the window from here, but I'll check in a minute." Silvia looked at the lace curtains from her side of the room and she noticed how full of sunlight they were this morning. "It looks nice." She smiled. "No, no, I'm excited, let's go."

"*Bueno daleeee*, the service is at 11! I gotta go cleanse myself in front of *La Virgensita*, I've been dreaming with lots of teeth lately, it's got me worried." Silvia wrinkled her brow in thought. "Silvia?"

"*Hmm?*"

"You remember, right? What that old lady next door always said...what was her name?"

"Miosotis."

"Yeah, her, remember how she always used to say to be careful when you can see people's teeth in a dream? It's bad, bad, remember Silvia?"

"Mmhmm."

"Yeah, I'm thinking it's Reynaldo and the cancer, I'd better light him a candle, but either way, something bad's going on, we'd better get there. Come on, mass is in half an hour!"

"Mmhmm." She hung up the phone.

Silvia placed the receiver back on its little hooks and looked the old phone over for second. It *was* beautiful...she'd forgotten how beautiful it was. She took a deep breath and stretched, crackling her lungs open into a new day:

"Ay, por Dios!"

In and out of bed;
the two times a day
when smoking seemed
like a bad habit.
'Coño...gotta smoke one before Carmen gets here.'

She went and took a quick shower, dressing up in the clothes she had laid out before hopping in, and right as she walked into the kitchen she heard Carmen's car roll into the driveway — she knew better than to honk. *'Su pinga!'* She looked at her pack, and up at the clock. It was wrong. *'Shit.'* Silvia grabbed the empty purse she decided to bring along and checked her hair one last time in the mirror, messing with a strand towards the back before remembering that Carmen was still waiting. She checked her breath and winced, pulling a pack of tic-tacs from her other purse as she made for the door. She shook the pack as she walked, asking for two, settling for seven. Bringing them to her mouth, she snapped her head up instead: Carmen was flailing her arms inside the car. "No no no!" she yelled, muffled by the windows of the import sedan. Silvia froze in her tracks.

"Que?" she shrugged.

Carmen motioned to her mouth. "Oh. *She wants to keep a fast. Que linda.*" She looked down into her hands, at the little white *pastillitas*. Ten seconds went by, Silvia thinking the hardest she had ever thought about tic-tacs. She was sure that if *San Judas Tadeo* himself was next to her, he'd probably have had one too. It seemed ok. It was silly. But she didn't eat it.

She put them back into her purse and walked over to the car. Her insides churned with excitement: 'this morning is alive, *Virgensita*! I pray for illumination — *and grace!*

'*Ave Maria, llena eres de gracia,*
El señor es con tigo. Bendita tu eres
Entre todas las mujeres, y bendito es
El fruto de tu vientre, Jesus.'

She got in the car.
"*Pues tengo peste a boca, jodete.*"
"Ay niña, who cares — you look so *beautiful* this morning, Silvia! What happened?"

Silvia smiled out loud. "*Que?*"

"Si, *Herma*, you look, I dunno, something is different with you, fresh...ay, I know — " and she looked over to her sister. "You quit smoking, didn't you..." Silvia's smile faded.

"*No.*" Pursed lips. "In fact, *dale*, roll my window down, I haven't even smoked today, you've had me on my toes for the past twenty minutes."

"No, not in the car, it *stinks*. Wait 'til we get there."

"*Carmen, mira, no comas mierda*, I smoke in this car all the time, and you kn — "

"*Ay niña*, just quit it, wouldn't you? Haven't you seen the commercial for that new pill they have, it makes it so easy, all you do i — "

"*Don't* get me started...*Carmen*. We're going to church. Now roll down my window and let my soul breathe." *Su pinga.* You see, the button on the passenger side didn't work. Carmen said nothing, but did nothing either. "*Caaaaaaarmen*," Silvia crooned impatiently.

Carmen smiled.

"*Carmen.*" Frown. "*Oyemeeeeee.*" She cocked an eye to the

left over clenched teeth, boring into her sister's round head. "Carmen! I swear, if you —" and there was suddenly light in her eyes. *Obviously*...she relaxed, suddenly inspired. Her lighter clicked.

"*Ay, por Dios*, are you crazy?!" yelled Carmen, rolling the window down. Silvia blew the smoke out the window. "Ugh, second-hand smoke, it kills children!"

"Nope." She laughed into the morning light, over Carmen's exasperated sigh.

Silvia always wondered how a person could be so poor, so simple, so restricted, repressed, yet still so happy. Happy as the smile on her round little face. She scoffed smoke out the window. It was as if her happiness had nothing to do with the frustration welled up in her unmarried guts, churning about every bite of food, every thick swallow of fried, sickeningly sweet *platanos* sliding down her gullet, every musky whiff of pheromones and *Tabaco* cologne from men in front of her in line, every pulse of her blood rising up into her head with passionate kisses she saw on the *telenovelas*. Every bite into juicy — *ay, stop it, niña! It's Sunday for Christ's sake.* She flicked her ash. She would have hated Carmen if she wasn't her sister. Her and her round fucking head.

"You know..." she said, smiling into the breeze, "I just had a really good time at dinner last night," she said, flicking her ash out the window again. "That's what it is. The kids all came over, and the *ropa vieja* turned out nice, and...I don't know. It was just nice. Rejuvenating." Carmen smiled into the windshield, and Silvia squeezed her thighs silently.

"Didn't I tell you what a beautiful day it was?" Carmen responded, oblivious. She extended her hand towards the windshield, as if to try and touch the sky. '*Goddammit. She had the personality of a fucking mushroom. Just tell her you're going to kill him too, she'll talk about the Food channel.*' Silvia had been too busy thinking about tic-tacs to even notice the weather. *Herma* was right. She breathed in deeply. Even the air seemed clean this morning, as if the ocean had taken all the junk out of the city and cleaned the city out for the people on this golden day of rest. The sky was the bluest of blues, and only a few fluffy clouds dotted the horizon, far off into the open sea. Coasting down 17th, Miami seemed relaxed, the people seemed to walk a little slower, the sidewalks were bright and open and full of surprise. Silvia felt the church would be full on such a beautiful morning — an empty church was never fun, but a church full of Cubans? She smiled, flicking her ash out the window. Carmen spoke.

"*Y que*, how's Chiche?" she asked.

"*Hmph*, he's there. Still selling those vacuum cleaners, you know, same same," replied Silvia through pursed lips. "I left him in bed. He was still sleeping, like *un bebito*," and she stifled a laugh in the silence. *'Still as death. Oh, I saw this recipe last night, Silvia...'*

"Well, I'm glad you didn't ask him to come like you did last time. You know how I like *La Ermita* to be *our* thing."

"Ay niña, I was just waking him early, messing with his mind. This *is* our thing." A woman screamed into her cell phone as they pulled around a street corner in Carmen's little import: *'...You fucking asshole! Comepinga, get the fuck out of my house!...I'm on the corner of the street you fucking dickhead!...That's right, I'm walking back right now you son of a bitch!...Yeah I fucked Carlos! Fuck your welfare!...Ok malpinga, I'm 'bout to...'*

"*Y la niña?*" asked Carmen.

"Oh, she's fine...well, *tu sabes*, I'm fine with *her*." She waved her cigarette in the air dismissively.

"*Esa niña...esa Yennifer esta salida del plato!*" Si, si, she knew. The girl was 'off her plate', an obstreperous meal that wouldn't do what it was told, scandalous, rebellious, out of hand, and all the time. Silvia knew it all too well, but it was no use...she was fine with *her*. She had tried explaining it to her sister a million times already, and every time Carmen would recommend the age-old remedy of Cuban mothers, the *chancleta*. They say that a Cuban mother always has one sandal ready to kick up into her hand and allow justice to prevail once again. And if that didn't work, there was always Carmen's next suggestion, *el tacón*, to which Silvia would reply, 'high heels?! You want me to hit her with high heels?!' Carmen would always remind her then of the tack-marks that Juanito from next door always had while they were growing up.

'He became a doctor, Silvia, you remember that.'

'*Hmph.*' Things like this made Silvia miss *El Coco*. Back when her kids were younger there was nothing, no one, as effective for getting kids to listen as *El Coco*. She could make them go to sleep whenever she wanted, she could make them clean up their messes, come to her while she was talking, anything: all with the threat of this fabled monster. 'you'd better listen to me, or I'll call El Coco!' *Ay*, this trick was the Cuban mother's cream in her cup, and even though he was supposed to be *El Loco*, conjuring images of some crazed lunatic with a machete coming through the door, children in their toddler-babble had spread rumors of *El Coco* instead, making him 'The Coconut'. And it was that much scarier. Absolutely horrifying. Just thinking of *how* this Coconut would carry out its dirty deeds, or what he even *looked* like, was enough to scare any child into obedience and morality, and every single child had their own version of what it was that he would do. '*El Coco*, you haven't *heard*? He comes if you don't listen, and makes you rub his back until all you have is stumps for hands'...'well *I* heard that all he does is look you straight in the eye, and you die from the shock. That's why I always go home when the pumpkin on TV says so, *calabaza calabaza todo el mundo pa' su casa*'...'No, you're both wrong. I heard that when you're in your room all by yourself, *that's* when he comes, and he punches you in the face while you're sleeping'. To Silvia, it was a reminiscence that evoked both fear and laughter, for though she used him with her kids, she vividly remembered how her father would go out around back and come knock on the door, three times—'He's here, Silis, let me go get him!' her Mother would say.

Waaaaaaaaaaaaaaaa! El Coco!

Eventually they drove by the gas station with the restaurant next door, *El Carajo*. What a name for a restaurant. Gorgeous. *'El Carajo'* was an old sailor's term for the top of the mast of a ship, where you'd go 'look for land' if no one wanted you to be around. It was also, more appropriately, a slang term for hell, in a vulgar way, though, the way you would tell someone to go to hell: "*Vete pal carajo!*" She didn't know how the food was, but she figured most people ended up there the first time only so they could tell their friends they were 'going to hell' for a late lunch. They crossed the street and were officially out of the good part of Miami, and into what most *other* people called 'the good part'. Here the houses got nicer, full of Spanish architecture, leafy yards full of palmettos and bougainvillea, lavish fountains, wrought-iron birdcages and sporty cars. It was nothing like '*La Sawesera*'; it was set apart for a whole other socioeconomic stratum who went out to the house music clubs on weekends and sipped Sangria dressed all Mondo Bahama and thread-slacks. Miami beech...trees. Bottomless mimosas and a crew of gardening Haitians. It all came as a package. 'Here the money talks, and the bullshit walks to 57th for the real *chicharrónes*.' A few more turns, to the left, to the right, cut the bus off, drive past the Catholic school, and there they were, right on the water: *La Ermita de la Santísima Virgen de la Caridad del Cobre*. The circular shrine stood at the oceanfront always, weathering tropical storms while wafting prayers to heaven on the wings of ocean breezes and thunderhead clouds — that Miami might stay in one piece, *ay Virgensita!* This shrine was home to the heart of Cubans both in Miami and the motherland, and it had a beautiful story behind it.

~*~

At the time of her apparition, Cuba was referred to as 'the Island of the Ave Maria', for the Goddess-worshipping natives found no problem in loving their Mother in different clothes. The rest of Christianity was a leap of faith, but the worship of the Virgin came as easy as the rising sun. The three Juans were no exception; they had paddled far out into the *Bahia de Nípe*, all the way to a little key in the middle of the bay called *Cayo Frances*, to collect salt. On the way out that day, however, the sky grew glum and grey, and dark swirls began to roll thickly through the clouds, blowing the winds into a choppy mess of froth and spray. By the time the three Juans were near the key, heavy rain had begun to fall and the waves bared their teeth at them, biting down over and over again on the damp wood of their creaking dinghy. The ocean grew more and more restless in the pouring rain, dropping sparkling sheets of static onto the turbulent waves. They looked back to the tiny palm trees far off on shore and grew fearful of what could happen. There was only one thing to do – they began to pray the *Ave Maria* the priests had taught them as they paddled furiously, sprayed in the face over and over again by the reckless waves, vicious winds howling hymns of fear into their ears.

"*Mira, Mira!*" Juan screamed into the wind, "what is that out there, to the left?"

"It is a light, a light in the surf!" screamed Rodrigo, "keep praying, she has answered our call!" The other Juan kept praying fervently as he heaved the oars back over and over agan with all his body, all his heart, all the hope in his soul.

They steered towards the light, and as they got closer Juan screamed, "I see! It is a great bird, with wings stretched from the shore to the sky, let us approach this blessed sign of salvation!" The boat rode a wave inland, heading closer and closer to the light, and the two brothers Juan said at the same time, "No, it is a young woman, hovering over the waters..." and their hearts swarmed with emotion as their canoe tossed in the storm, which mattered to them no more. The light grew ever more effulgent, and suddenly the vision opened unto them in its full splendor. Clad in a cloth embroidered with golden patterns of sunlight and stars, the Virgin Mary held the child Christ and a cross, smiling benevolently upon a pedestal that read '*Yo soy la Virgen de la Caridad.*' I am the Virgin of Charity. The three Juans felt safe and cared-for in Her presence and she told them in a soft, ethereal voice to build a shrine for Her so that the devotees may worship, white and black, brown and yellow, all colors wrapped around the same red blood, and with this she opened the way to shore for them.

"Worry not," she said lovingly, her eyes shining like honeyed flames, "I am the end of fear, the end of evil. I am the Mother of All."

The sun broke through the clouds, shining down upon the still waters she had made for them to return to the shore. The foam around them sparkled, and Mary filled their boat with three loads of salt as they made their way back to the port. The Virgin disappeared into the light that played off the reflections in the sea, Her child reaching up and giving her a wet kiss on the cheek as they dissolved into the sparkle of the sun.

The people on shore were shocked to hear the story: *Imaginate!* The Virgin Mary Herself appearing to the boys collecting salt! Some didn't buy into it—especially not the priests—but the devotees felt encouraged and built the shrine for her anyway, naming Rodrigo the *capellán* of this *Ermita*. People came and worshipped *La Santísima Virgen de la Caridad* for many years, but late one night, after praying his rosary, Rodrigo went to say goodnight to the Virgin and did not find Her in her alcove. His heart raced at seeing Her sweet pedestal littered with flowers to be empty, and his night was filled with worry and fear, robbing him of the little sleep he mustered as the chaplain of the newly inaugurated shrine. She returned, however, to her proper place in the morning. This happened, to the shock of Rodrigo, over and over again for three nights, until he was convinced that *La Virgen* wanted to go somewhere else, speaking in that mysterious language of divinities, rife with signs, omens, and portents of auspicious tidings. She was moved to the city of Cobre, where she was installed in the Parochial Temple of the city. Here she began to disappear also, and it was after the third time again it became obvious that luxury was not the home of this Virgin Mary. She did not want to be in the Parochial Temple, she wanted to be somewhere else. It was only then that news got into town, that a little girl who frequented the church in Cobre, named Apolonia, saw *La Virgen* up on a hill in the *Sierra Maestra*. She had climbed the hill to the mines where her mother worked, and in the lush surroundings of leafy trees and creepers, surrounded by butterflies and flower petals, she had seen the little Virgin Mary holding Her Son, looking no older than sixteen. Many dismissed it as gossip and lies, but the devotees knew what needed to be done, for this news came at the same time as the Virgin's repeated disappearances from her shrine. *La Ermita* was thus moved to the hill where Apolonia had seen *la Virgen,* and her burgeoning worship at this spot led her to be crowned Queen and patroness of Cuba by the church. Because of this she became the Virgin of Charity, of Cobre.

A long time passed before she ended up in Miami. It was not until the politics in the Americas got out of hand, and revolutions broke out in the name of various political corruptions that she left the country in silent exile. In the midst of the revolution, with so many Cubans fleeing the country, a group of devotees were inspired by the Holy Spirit and took the illustrious Virgin from her shrine, smuggling her to the Italian embassy. Panama was placed in charge of getting her to Miami, and the escorts managed to cross the waters without any problems. She was eventually installed in the *Ermita* that stands today, and, like the many Cubans who had also left in exile, *La Santísima Virgen de la Caridad del Cobre* stands by the waters, facing Cuba with the memory of home, and generations of hope behind her, all around her in her circular shrine shaped like the very mantle that saved the three Juans from drowning an awful death that one fateful day hundreds of years ago.

Since Her installation on the shores of Miami, she had never left—or disappeared—for any reason at all, that is, until she was taken out in a procession before the body of the late Celia Cruz. Nobody mustered even the slightest hint of a complaint, Celia was just as much a patroness of Cuba as *La Virgen* was...and in a similar way she held a loving place in everyone's heart. Who else but Celia was at every Cuban child's birthday party for as long as they can remember? It was Celia who taught us all how to dance, who moved the currents within our spines with her *azuuuucar!* It was she who smiled upon everyone during our celebrations of life. Celia, you've never died, you live in the skins of our drums, in the hearts of our celebrations...*La Virgen's* presence at the head of the procession made Celia's passing all the more meaningful, for the community saw it's Queen leading a ray of light back to the sun whence it came.

~*~

"Would you look at that view," Carmen smiled softly as she shut off the ignition. The vast expanse of ocean gaped before them into eternity, glittering with sunlight and sparse mist, and gentle waves crashed softly onto the stone wall at the shoreline. It was 11:08, and the 11 o'clock service was about to start. People unloaded from of their cars, yelling at their frantic children to get back from the water's edge, don't scuff your shoes walking in the sand, don't climb the coconut palms, you're no *Rompecoco*. The people headed for the front doors of the circular building, their cars beeping goodbye for now, by the bathrooms painted with *los tres Juanes* and the Latin verses flanking the entrance: 'This is you mother', and the sisters Silvia and Carmen moved along with them all the way to the entrance. They kissed the hands and feet of the life-sized Sacred Heart of Christ upon entering, squeezing past all the tumult and commotion to find seats. They found two in the back, at the edge of a pew, and sat down right as the procession began. No one had noticed, no one they knew, and they looked to each other with a smile as the music began to play on the speakers. We've made it.

Two children made their way up the aisle first: a boy dressed in slacks and a white *guayabera*, wearing all the gold given to him by his grandmother, and a girl in an antique Cuban dress with a big frilly pink skirt and poofy shoulders that made her look like a spring blossom, or a *petit four* you could eat sitting amongst such an idyllic garden. Her shiny white shoes kissed with little golden buckles and leather heels clicked softly on the linoleum floor as she walked up the aisle next to her brother. The two must have been no older than seven. The boy carried the same ragged bible that was leafed through at every mass, and the girl cradled a thick wooden rosary that looked hundreds of years old and had beads the size of golf balls. Their parents would bring the gifts of bread and wine up later in the mass. Behind them came the altar servers, carrying the binder of incantations for the priest to sing during the service, and the golden staff topped with a crucifix. They looked sullen and somber, as if they would rather be outside, but their expressions seemed fit for the occasion— Christianity, in itself, came from the staunch stoicism of Ancient Egypt. The priest walked next, holding nothing, and next to him walked the layman, holding the papers that would guide the servant of the Lady throughout the the mass. Silvia liked the children best, for they seemed the most innocent out of the whole lot, and the mass began, as usual, with songs where only half the people actually sang the words and the rest inflected their voices in the general direction of the woman on the electric organ by the altar. The song ended, and the people settled down, chattering as the priest rose to the lectern to speak. "Today we will focus on the communion of death and rebirth, two facets of the holy mysteries of Christianity. As you might know, Our Lady hold in her hands a cross and the child Christ..."

'Ay Mamá, think on the virgin.' Silvia smiled to herself in the pew.

From that moment on she lost the flow of the mass, for she didn't like the whole bells and whistles thing about Catholicism anyway...she was there to see the Lady standing at the base of the looming mural of Cuba's history, complete with happy Indian slaves and moustached colonial scholars of politics, poetry and prose. The Virgin stood at the base of the towering mural like a little girl, the most elaborately dressed doll you could ever have seen, her quaint figure hidden in layers and layers of the finest silks. Upon this Virgin did Silvia fix her gaze, standing and sitting in turn as if she were actually taking part in the droning service. She stared ceaselessly at the Virgin as the mass went on, and while people contemplated the Gospels and answered the priest as if speaking to their father, Silvia eased her way into a trance that filled the entire church with swirls of sparkling purples, shimmiring mists of silver and blinking lights. The only thing she would mouth to *la Virgen* throughout her hour-long monologue to her was, "*lo voy a matar, lo voy a matar*", but this was only because such words roused her to the point of breaking the trance. The Virgin would answer softly, every time, '*Be wise as a serpent and gentle as a dove,*' the first time through the mouth of the priest. This phrase resounded through the whole of the mass for her, it haunted her prayers, filtered through the haze of morning thoughts and gospel commentary, swimming around her mind behind closed eyes. She knew that her prayers were being answered in this image of birds and serpents, life and death. The Virgin was guiding her away from a horrible mess, a horrible accident. It was her secret, and she would tell no one lest it be taken from her. She couldn't tell a soul, how ironic it was that happiness itself is the secret of the wise. She smiled at the thoughts that flowed through her head from last night, urging her to squeeze her thighs together in her pew, her breath wavering as she whispered enlightened thoughts to the bloodied Chiche in her mind's eye. *Su pinga.* She wanted a smoke. A man in the back of the church stood up that instant, quietly, and stepped outside. The aroma of tobacco soon made its way through the frankincense and mini-mall perfume.

That fucking asshole. She felt for the pack in her purse, letting it go upon seeing how the Virgin smiled at her cravings.

"…and this, good Christians, is the link between death and true, sacred birth in Christ; the power of spirit, that you may all feel the endless love of God as the very freedom we inherit as his children. Go in peace, to love and serve the Lord Jesus Christ, Amen." Hundreds of bracelets clanked, assuming the sign of the cross over plucked brows, tasty hearts, refluxed solar plexuses and tired shoulders, lips, nipples and souls.

By the time the mass was over, Silvia was messing around with a piece of the communion bread that had stuck to the roof of her mouth as she walked to the car with Carmen, whose eyes glowed with joy. "O, how I love coming to Sunday service! *Ay* — wait, I forgot something. *Ven,* let's go to the back room — I've got to light a candle for *San Lazaro,* remember? You can't delay your promises with him…his miracles are not for free…" *San Lázaro* had the notorious reputation of messing with your legs if you didn't pay for your promise. Sure, he'll cure that ulcer, but you'd better don some burlap and make your way around that church on your knees…or he might break 'em. "*Dale, Herma*! The promise I made, you know, for Reynaldo?"
Silvia nodded. "Yes, yes, what is it, cancer?" She pulled out a smoke.

"*Oye niña*, are you kidding me? '*Cancer, Cancer,*' like its nothing? Reynaldo can't even walk around anymore! He can't keep a meal down! Does that not get under your skin, your thick, thick skin? *Ay*, never mind," she scoffed, turning away from her. "Smoke your cigarette here, and wait for me." Carmen frowned. "I'm leaving the car locked," and she turned, making for the church once again. Silvia simply looked at her cropped hair bounce with every click of her half-inch heels, bringing her lighter to the smoke in her lips without breaking her gaze.

She turned to the ocean. It was true. She didn't care. Death was like nothing to her, something so simple, so minor, meaningless as life itself. '*People fear death, they have no idea what freedom it brings...wise as a serpent, gentle as a dove.*' She went to the water's edge and flicked her ash into the shallow water. A school of fish swam by, scuttling through the submerged tricycle that had been rusting away for what seemed like years. She took a long drag, and as the breeze whisked the smoke away mercilessly she turned to a group of children playing a few feet away. They stopped in their tracks, looking at her, and ran away. A baby bird fell from a palm tree, hitting the ground with a squeak. "*Santisimo!*" Silvia screamed. She looked up to the top of the tree, where a bird leered down at her with its beady eyes. They held their gaze until Silvia was finished smoking. Then the bird propped up and flew away.

The little piece of bread loosened itself from the roof of her mouth, and she nibbled it between her front teeth as she made her way back towards the car. The food on her tongue made her look over to the stand across the parking lot, where some reverent Cubans had skipped mass to fry *croquetas* for the hungry masses barreling out of the doors with squinting eyes and fatigued palates. Hot *croquetas* on Cuban crackers or a thick slice of bread, dazzled with mustard and a pickle. Stave off the hunger for lunch. She wouldn't support them. It wasn't fair that they got to miss mass. *Fucking bitches.* She turned, looking back at the baby bird, who hadn't made another peep.

"*Ay Mami,* only you understand me," she said into the wind as Miami came to life over the waters with the passing of a cloud. "I mean no harm. I have only found joy once again, bless me," and she smiled into the reflection of the morning sun on the water. "You're in my heart, in my ears, praise you. I don't need a building to love you, have my heart instead," she smiled, leaning against the car. The water sparkled across the dancing waves, and the glare extended all the way to the bridge across the way. '*Mija, your joy is my joy. Forget the rest of them, they know not what they do.'* She popped tic-tacs into her mouth, watching the people eat their *croquetas.* They crunched louder than the laughing children, and she smiled to herself, sipping the cool wisps of air until Carmen emerged from the church, looking obliviously into the sky.

"Amen," said Silvia to herself, propping up from the car with a backward heave of her ass. She thought of 57th, the people, the antics, the *lunch!* A family passed by, the little girl holding a plastic Virgin from the church store. Silvia admired the girl as she made her way past, looking up into her eyes and waving the statue into her face playfully, biting her tongue. *Ay, Virgensita...*Silvia stuck hers out right back. Wide-eyed, the girl pulled the Virgin back into her arms, her laughter like tinkling bells. She took her mother's hand with one last look back. *Crazy lady,* she said with her eyes. Silvia smiled. *Si supieras, if only you knew.* The little Virgin would soon assume some place in their house, holding her pink Christ-child up to her mantle adorned with the night sky.

She would never understand
why *La Virgen* was such a beautiful, bronzed *mulata,*
but the kid was always white. A car
drove by, playing Roberto Anglero's *Si Dios Fuera Negro:*
'If God were black.'

"*Jesucristo!*" laughed Silvia. "You have a sense of humor."

"Ah?" asked Carmen, unlocking her door.

"*Nada...*" smiled Silvia to herself, looking over to the shiny black car where the family had boarded, the little girl in the back seat playing with the Virgin as if she were a doll.

"*Vamonos, que estoy 'bolaaa!*"

~*~

Silvia opened the door to her house, thankful to be in her nest once again after so much time outside of the house. They had skipped lunch, because Carmen was still upset at Silvia's insensitivity. Silvia said nothing, but smoked another cigarette on the way home, forcing her sister to open her window. Starving, Silvia made to change into her bata and eat some of last night's *ropa vieja* when —

"*Oye Silis*, wachappen!" Her body tightened with a jolt of disdain, her jaw tense. She spoke without looking over towards the table.

"Cuco...*buenas tardes.*"

"*Y que*? Where've you been? We need *café, dale.*" He laughed. "I was just telling Chiche about Manolo, the fisherman from Rancho Luna, you remember that guy?" Before Silvia had a chance to answer — "The bastard had been fishing for lobsters since he could walk, ah? You knew that. I knew that. Come on." He raised his stubby hands into the air about a yard apart. "*Big,* big lobsters, you remember? They would *shit* out lobsters like the ones they catch around here. Come on, you remember the guy?" Silvia made t — "Of course you do! He lives down the street with his wife Magali, you know? The lady who makes the best *pudín* this side of the river Nile, you know that river? It's in Africa. Flows upwards, that motherfucker. Saw it on the TV the other day. Floods every year, got crocodiles. Best *pudín* since Africa, swear to God." He kissed his thumb and forefinger, and touched them to his heart. Silvia leaned against the doorframe, her shawl still on her shoulders, her hair still tied back in her Spanish bun, her purse still in hand, her heels *still* on feet, a fart up her ass, her face...the same. Tired. Smiling. Subtle. Starving. And Cuco had decided to come visit. The Lord's day.

"The guy's been living off his catch since he was a little kid, you know that? Swears on it for health, you know?" He smiled, exposing the gap between his teeth. "Yeah...bull-*shit*. We all know how bad the cholesterol is, you know? *Colessssssteróllll, Mádre de Dios!* Lobsters, crabs, they're full of that shit, you know? Yeah, of course you know. Look at Chiche, this guy eats well, I've eaten here before, *Dios mio!*"

"So this guy swears to God that lobster's all he needs, it's all he eats. He'd go fishing, sell his catch over by the 7-11 off Flagler, you know, by that stoplight that takes forever?" He touched his fat finger to his temple. "The guy *thinks*. The *slowest goddamn semáfaro* in Miami—sells his catch right there. Lobster right to your car window! That's America, Jesus Christ!" He gasped for air, looking to Chiche for affirmation. There was fear in the poor bastard's eyes.

"The guy never paid for food. Water bill—check. Drinks are done. Milk for the kids, cha-cha-cha, whatever. But the only thing *he* would eat was *thirty lobsters a day*. I swear to God, thirty lobsters a day! Did you *hear that*, Silvia?!" She wanted to slap the *shit* out of him. "*Santísima Virgen, thirty fucking lobsters a day!* And he would eat 'em like nothing, like it was his job—" and he looked over to Silvia, straight-faced as a judge. "Because...? It *was*. God *dammit*." Silvia swallowed a smile. Her ass purred, and she walked over to the kitchen, settling her elbows across the counter, pressing her finger on some stray breadcrumbs.

"*Y que?*"

"So Magali calls me the other day in tears. She tells me 'look, Cuco, I need you to come over.' Of course they need my help, right?" He looked at Chiche. "They don't call me when things are good, but when there's bullshit in the air? *Cuco, Cuco, ya tu sabes.*" Chiche pursed his lips, looking to Silvia. "She says, 'After Manolo finished his dinner, he had trouble breathing, but you know, he had just eaten a lot, *thirty lobsters, right?* So he went to sit in his chair, but he only felt worse. So he went off into the room to pray...and,' and then she paused there, and I was like what the hell does she want, and then she says 'and I found him there, dead.' Dead, she said. 'On his knees...praying.' Holy shit, Silvia! Holy shit! God took him in heat!" He had his hands up in the air, beads of righteous sweat all over his face.

"So I had to go over there and console her, and take Manolo outside and figure things out from there, I used to be a pallbearer back in Guanabo, but I tell you Chiche, you see? *That's* why pig-lard is better than olive oil. That's what we were talking about before you came, Silvia. That shit is *full* of Cholesterol, don't feed it to my brother! Full of it, those little goddamn olives. I mean, all you gotta do is look at the sides of the pan to see, that's my mark of proof, I'm not asking you to *beliiiiieve* me, right?" Silvia swallowed a smile. "Olive oil—" and he cringed as he rubbed his fingers together in the air—"that stuff *clings* to the sides of whatever you put it in, but *pig-lard? Hmph,* that shit runs *clean. Clean,* Silvia." He took a sip of his water.

"*Oye Negra,*" asked Chiche, "make some *café* for us, ah?"*

"*Hmph.*" *As if Cuco needs café.*

Silvia felt the ground fall away from under her, fearing for her innermost thoughts, as if everyone was able to *see* them, for it was one of those moments when someone, by sheer coincidence or by the intercession of some greater being, happens to answer the exact question that was flowing through your mind. "Silis, I'm serious, I drink *café* at night to sleep better, swear to God. What kind are you guys brewing anyway, *Pilón?*" Cuco grimaced. "*Oyeme,* Silvia, don't let this guy buy that crap anymore. *La Llave* is the best kind. Hands down. You know why they call it la *Llave?*" Cuco paused for dramatic emphasis, letting his eyes dart around the room to make sure everyone wanted to hear what he had to say. "Fuck if I know—*comemierdas!*" and he slapped his knees with a snicker that purged all the garbage out of the depths of his lungs.

He spent the next thirty seconds laughing alone. "I'm gonna have a smoke. Silvia, you still smoke? You know, that stuff's bad for you. Our *Mami* used to smoke no less than 120 cigarettes every day," he said, "*seis cajas diariamente.* Ain't that right, Chichón?" Chiche nodded, it was true. "You see? She would wake up and light one right there off her nightstand, and she would keep that same goddamn flame going until she went to bed, lighting tip to tip all day. It was like her clock." He grinned. "Time *flew* when she was pissed, ah, Chiche?" *Waaaaaaaaaaaaaaaa!* they laughed. Silvia suddenly felt healthy next to that bird of prey, that Barbar*ita* she kicked out of her kitchen. She smiled.

"*Si, oyeme*, on that system a book of matches would last her 20 days, even though that was what—2,400 cigarettes? *Su pinga!* You would wonder why she lived to be so old, ah?" He laughed as Silvia ran the math over in her head from the other side of the counter. " It's cause she switched to cigarillos, and she smoked way less of those. She didn't inhale 'em, either, then. But you know, that was back in Cuba, the good old days, when smokes were worth less than a fistful of dirt, you know? Nowadays it's stupid, I don't got time for that shit, cause time is money, ah? Think about it: when I saw that smokes got more expensive than two dollars, that's the day I quit, you remember that, *Chichóng*? I told you how I looked at the sign, and it said $2.65, and I said to it, '*Par-lameng, aqui se acabo mi amor por ti.*' And that was it. You remember that I told you that one day, I know it. Coño, meng," he said, laughing out loud to himself. He stood up and pulled a pack of Marlboro ultra lights out of his front pocket, excusing himself out of the glass door.

"On that note," he said, his voice disapearing behind the glass...he mumbled something as he lit his cigarette, puffed it twice lightly, and proceeded to smoke it in three drags. It was a matter of ten seconds:

Rrrrrrrrrrreddddddddd...gggggggrrrrreeeeeeyyyyyyyyyyyyyy... and *poof,* to the ground. 'Jesus *Christ,* I would hate to be his cigarettes,' Silvia thought to herself. She thought of the brown stains in the gap between his two front teeth, and how he must have smoked with his jaws clenched. *Uggghhhhrrrrrrrrr...*her ears rang with the tightness. Silvia had clenched hers without realizing it, and she shuddered as she crammed *café* into the percolator, moving her jaw from side to side.

"We brew *Bustelo,* Cuco," she said as he sat himself back in his chair. *Ay, that fragrance!* she thought to herself, *that lucky son of a bitch just had a smoke.* He nodded slowly in silent approval, *that's right Goddammit, I know exactly what you're thinking.* That *fucking* smile! Silvia couldn't help but laugh out loud. Chiche would never understand, the *fragrance.* "How's Melva?" she laughed angrily, diverting the attention from herself. *"Ay, Dios mio,"* she sighed, fanning her tear-filled eyes before chiche asked what the joke had been about.

"Meb-ba? Meb-ba's fine, strong as ever. Goddamn *ox,* that woman." Chiche cracked into a snicker that held out for no less than ten seconds, a perfect backdrop for Cuco's pendulous crocks of bullshit. "I told her one day while I was taking a shit to stop taking those pills, they were wrenching her guts from the inside-out. The woman was constipated, out of breath, achy, sore, her pee burned...*pal carajo,* she even had diarrhea, you're family. It's ok. *Mira,* so she finally did, and she's feeling way better, though her original problem is back."

"The diabetes?" asked Chiche.

"Nah, the kidneys, her blood. Some crap the doctor was talking about. You know, those guys don't know shit. I swear to God, last time she was in there, I told the guy exactly what was wrong before they ran those tests on her." He touched his finger to his eye. "Trying to charge me money for using some fancy *machine*...I know, I can see that shit with my eyes closed. And I don't read no books about it either. Books are for the uninformed," he scoffed. "That's why they read the goddamn things in the first place."

"You know, Cuco..." laughed Chiche, and he took a bite of a Cuban cracker. "Whatever." He tapped his cracker on the tabletop, pressing his finger into the crumbs.

"Man, I feel good," Cuco continued. "Slept in a little bit, my diabetes is good today, I'm just sitting here with my *hermanito, tranquilito*." He winked at Chiche, who reached out and patted Cuco on the back of his unbuttoned shirt. The hairs on his chest plastered to his skin behind an old tanktop and a thick golden chain with *Santa Barbara* on it, encrusted with rubies. It was quite beautiful...the medallion.

"*Oye, oye meng*, have I got the news for you. You know I finally got my diabetes to go away. Kicked that bitch outta my life. You know, that shit used to have me by the *balls*," and he crunched the air in front of him with a fist that could hardly close. "But I figured it out. I didn't even know what was going on until I went to the doctor and told him to check on me. He told me I had my diabetes at 1,242."

"1,242? *Carajo*! I feel like I'm gonna *die* when my diabetes gets to 300-something! You're—lying!" Cuco's face grew somber, his eyes wide with shock—*insultado*.

"*Hermano*...I'm insulted. Come on, would I lie to you? My own Goddamn blood? *Mira, no jodas!* 'Cuche palla, Silvia, you were there—remember the school in Cienfuegos by the plaza? They gave me an award for honesty when I was six years old. Never missed a day of school."

"Cuco, you've never been to Cienfuegos."

"The *hell* I haven't! I know everyone there, all the old *bohemios* who sit around near the square like they ain't got nothing to do! Remember *el Gago*? *El G-g-g-gago*?"

Silvia burst out laughing from the stove. Cuco smiled triumphantly.

"*El Gago!*" she sang. "I wonder if that guy is still alive, shit!" Everyone around town knew each other, but *El Gago* was special. He had a notorious stutter that everyone knew about, and for this reason he was called *Gago* – 'the stutter'. Silvia never knew his name – well, aside from *El Gago* – she was pretty sure that no one else did either. He was a good guy, but that stutter, shit, it was just too much. "It took the guy five minutes to ask you how you were doing! Do you remember his mother, Silvia? She was the only one who had the courage to *smack* him out of his tics when they went too long, *coññññó!*" and she reeled back in laughter until the espresso maker spurted and chortled with the noise that brings Cuban households alive to this very day – swear to God.

"*Ay*, smells nice, don't put any sugar in mine Silvia* – " and he put his hand to his throat – "I don't eat sugar anymore. Got over it after the diabetes got to me. Can't even eat bread anymore. You know what I did to get rid of it?" He scoffed at Chiche. "Muchacho, I haven't even told you, you're messin' with my head, *meng*."

Chiche shrugged, smiling. "*A ver, dime.*" Tell me.

"*Muchacho*, I changed my diet, all the way. I got sick of sugar, right? I tell you, this is what I got Melva doing for hers too," and he held an invisible something in his hand, nodding silently as if he had just told them. Silvia clenched her fist, thinking of the slap she should give him.

"Apples, Chiche, apples." He tossed the imaginary apple over his shoulder. "You know how good those things are? I eat eighteen. Everyday. Rain or shine. But they're *red*, Chiche, *red apples.*" He pointed a finger right into Chiche's eye, squinting crazily. "*Red* apples. The secret is that they *have* to be red." He nodded victoriously, as if waiting for their applause. "Eighteen apples, I eat some when I get up, when I go to work, when I get back from work, hell, sometimes I have more than eighteen, like thirty or something. *Hehehehe*, thirty lobsters, thirty apples. The guy at Solanos gives 'em to me free now. Says he feels bad chargin' me...nice guy." Silvia set their steaming demitasses

156

down on the table in front of them, on the doilies that never moved. *"Sin azúcar*, Cuco."*

"Ay pero graaaaacias mama." He raised the little cup to his lips and slurped a sip. *"Ay, y rrrrrico que e'ta!"* — Oh, and how tasty it is! *"Que buchito, hombre,"* he said, looking to Chiche as if he were talking about Silvia.*

The *buchito* was an unmistakably Cuban phenomenon. Somewhat of a quantification of a sip, a *buchito* was less than a shot, but enough to 'hwwwet your whistle,' a slurp, just enough, that perfect amount that fits right in between your thumb and your forefinger when you answer to how much you want to drink—but that's only if you weren't feeling like a whole lot, yet wanted some for the sake of the flavor but *coño*, come on, I didn't ask for a *drop*—just enough to taste it and get back on track during the day without getting all caught up in the *siestas* of the other Latinos. The *buchito*. *Ay*, what satisfactory perfection can be found in the ambiguity of the *buchito*. There was silence for about one minute, save for the sips of the two men drinking their *café*. *Café Bustelo*, the kind Silvia hated but the kind Chiche bought. She never told him, but she liked *La Llave* better too. She wanted a cigarette.

Cuco banged his knee against the table, tipping his empty cup over as he clutched for his pocket in what seemed more like a fitful seizure of sorts. He pulled his cell phone out with a grimace and put it to his ear. *"Meb-ba! Que paso Mama,* I'm at Chiche's, *si, si, no, no no no* not that Chiche, my *brother*, Meb-ba! My brother, Chiche! *Mi hermano!"* He smiled silently at everyone else in the room, shaking his head as if to reconcile her error.

"Mmhmm…mmhmm…no, no, it's in the freezer; *dale*, Meb-ba, Christmas Eve was six months ago! Why would it be there?" He twirled the demitasse around with his finger, but Silvia came by and snatched them both away with pursed lips.

"Mmhmm…si, si, I bought some too, it's under the

stove...see, I know my woman, I know you *Meb-ba*, hahaha...the years rub off...no, no, its only *vino seco*, we used the *adobo* on the pork, remember?" He scoffed. "The one...for Christmas Eve...for *Noche Buena...coññññoooo*...yeah, yeah, *si, si, mmhmm*...okay, okay, and don't put it in the microwave, that shit's bad for you — and if you *do*, don't *look* into the Goddamn thing, *Meb-ba!* How many times I gotta tell you, *Goddammit!* Yeah, yeah you know how I tell 'em what's goin on...mmhmm, mmhmm...okay, okay, you too, *bechito bechito* – *muah muah*,*" and he put the phone back into his pocket.

"*Coño...*" he grinned, "it was *Meb-ba, ya tu sabes.*" Chiche shook his head. "*Pues si*, the wife's thawing some pork from Christmas Eve for dinner..." and Cuco trailed off into his own thoughts, nodding back and forth with squinting eyes for a moment before continuing on. "You know, I'll tell you right here, right now, that pork came out *reeeeal* good. Damn, it's because I know how to roast 'em. You know, last Christmas Eve I killed, cleaned and roasted twenty-five pigs, I ever tell you that, Chiche?"

Chiche clicked his tongue against his teeth incredulously: "*Tsssss*...twenty-five pigs? Cuco, Cuco, it takes six hours to roast a pig, and that's if you do it right. To have the *lechón* come out all nice and right, in a pig-box? Six hours, maybe even eight."

Silvia shook her head. "How, *how* could you have *killed, cleaned, and roasted* fifteen pigs in one day, Cuco?" She bit down on her smile. "You're *lying!*"

"*Vaaaaaya*, I'm outta here, that's it." He paused, thinking of how to explain it to these people. " *Mira*, they were sixty-pounders, too, Chiche. Swear to God." He fiddled with a piece of food on the tip of his tongue, making him look as if he were suckling an invisible something that no one else could see. "Ey, you don't have to *believe* me *meng*, but I'll tell you, I get shit done, okay? I didn't leave Cuba to come flick my bean in Miami. Shit...I don't even need to sleep anymore." Silvia threw her arms in the air, turning to the sink. "You know I work the night shift at the concrete yard, ah? *Si*, okay well look, I go to work at 9, I *work* 'til about 9, since it evens out nice, and then I go home and eat breakfast with *Meb-ba*. About noontime I take a nap with her on the couch." He squinted in thought, puckering his lips as he tapped the table quickly. "Yeah….about three hours, since we get up to watch '*He Dicho!*' at three o'clock. *Ay*, Dr. Ana-Margarita Colón, that *beacon* of a woman!" Silvia nodded in agreement. "See? *I aint lyyyying*, three hours of sleep." He lifted three fat fingers for emphasis. "*Uno dos y tres — caso cerra'o!* And *that's* how I do it, I aint around to waste no time. And I tell you Chiche, if I get anymore than those three hours, I feel like I could take a *machete* and cut someone's head off!" Silvia's guts spilled to the ground, her eyes wide with shock. Cuco fished his phone out of his pocket again.

"*Que, Mami, que paso?* Mmhmm...oh...*pero pa' que? Silvia?* Oh, ok ok stop it I don't need to know that shit, *si, si*, she's right here," and he looked up into Silvia's green eyes with an air of suspicion as old as gender itself. "Here…it's Meb-ba." Silvia came around the counter and grabbed the phone with a smile. "You know," Cuco said as Silvia took the phone back behind the counter, "that right there is the first cell phone to come to Miami."

"*Melva?*"
"*Buenas*, Silvia, it's Melva, how are you?"
"I'm surprisingly well lately, thank you for asking."
"Well that's good to hear…" she had trouble sounding authentic. "*Oyeme*," she said, "do you think you could help me out with something?" She paused, brining her voice down to a whisper. "Chiche and Cuco can't...hear about this." Shadows came over Silvia's face — she turned toward the fridge. The two men looked at each other and flicked their eyebrows simultaneously, resuming their conversation.

"Yeah...woman stuff. Jesus."

"*Niña*, I have to tell you something, and I need your help

okay?" Silvia swallowed the lump in her throat.

"Okay, okay, *dime*."

"*Ay*, Silvia, I'm sitting here at home with some *lechón* thawing in the microwave, and I can barely stand the pain, Silvia…it's my feet, they're swollen the size of footballs, the American kind…" Silvia hesitated.

"The American kind?"

"*Si niña*, American footballs, and Cuco keeps assuring me it's just my diabetes acting up, but I know it's not. It's, it's—" she sobbed, "—it's something bad, Silvia, something very bad." She broke into tears on the other end of the line.

"Well, what is it?" insisted Silvia.

"It's my *primas*, Silvia, my cousins in Cuba. They did something to me, I know it." There was silence. Silvia wrenched her face after a few seconds of that torturous hiss of phone silence and gave in—she knew it was her place to say something. No one saw it, but the fan twitched, moved an inch, and the door pushed open just a sliver. A *breeze*.

"*Alavado sea Dios*…you really think so? You know…" and she pursed her lips, thinking of all that had been going on lately, "I believe you." She mouthed a great '*pinga!*' into the sidewalk. What did she want…

"*Ay* Silvia, I know it is, I know it. You see," and she blew her nose from the other end of the line, "I've been sending them money for years, ever since Cuco and I came here. But I know what it's like in Cuba, and their demands kept getting more and more extravagant. I mean, Silvia, it's one thing to want American dollars to be able to buy bars of soap and chicken, but *Tony el Figer*? You know…that *marca* is the kids wear…" Silvia thought of Jennifer's big Cuban butt with a smile… *ay*, these Cuban women. Even *they* must know they're botching their English. *Happy Sengeeveen.*

"They want these nice jeans and the Nike shoes, and *Silvia!* They think we're rich over here—you know what I mean?" She squealed. "*Ay* Silvia, I need you to help me." Silvia, like Melva, did not have many friends outside the family or neighbors, and she only knew Melva through some holiday dinners and things. She felt Melva's desperation in opening up to her about something like this, *brujeria* and all. People tended to keep that kind of thing to themselves. It made her feel bad. Who would *she* tell if she was bewitched?

"Silvia, I need to go see one of those ladies who can tell me what to do, that's why I'm calling you." *Padre Santisimo.* "But you know Cuco, he'll never buy it, he would purposely stop me from going to see someone like that...I think he's just scared of it all. He's *seen* it in real life, he knows it's not fake. Can...can you find a way for us to go? Do you have a car?" Silvia thought about who she could sell this cheese to...it was *fresh.*

"Hmmm...*bueeeeno*..." Silvia thought for a few seconds, clicking her tongue against her teeth. "Chiche is Cuco's brother, you know that...he's just as bad as Cuco with this stuff...but don't worry Melva, we'll figure something out." Silvia smiled, putting a cigarette to her lips. "Wasn't Barbarita into all that shit? Those dolls in her house...*pues mira, Yennifer* will take us, okay? I'm sure of it." She could feel the relief through the receiver pressed to her ear. "She'll be excited to go, it's one of those things I tell her not to do. Those are her favorite things, you know?" They both laughed. "*Muchacha de mierda.*"

"*Ay, gracias, Silvia!* Virgen Santisima...truly, I'll make it up to you, I swear. Let's go as soon as possible, do you know any good ladies around here?"

"I've never gone to see one," she said, taking a drag of her cigarette, "I haven't been fortunate enough to have clever enemies." She flicked her ashes to the ground.

"*Ay,*" she groaned, "this is horrible, my feet hurt so much, what would the doctor say to this? Please, we need to find one immediately."

"I'll talk to Jennifer about it, *no te preocupes.*" She took a drag. "And Melva," she said, "I wouldn't worry about those *hijueputas* over in Cuba, ok?" She took another drag. "We'll figure this out."

"Ay, Silvia, they're my *primas*, my family! How could they do this? You think it was really them? Do I sound crazy?" She whined on the telephone. "Maybe I should just go see the doctor."

"*Hmph!*" said Silvia, with a puff of smoke. "Melva, listen to me, *okay*?" She took a drag, gesturing with the cigarette in her first two fingers:

"There's respecting people, *respetándo*, and then there's giving them the respect they deserve, as human beings, *el respeto*. Those bitches might be related to us, but as for *respetándolas*, giving them actual respect, based on the things they do—to the people they claim to *love?*" She laughed. "*No, no, hermana. They—are—un—excremento*. Do you know what that is?" She picked up her smoke. "*A pís o shyet*." That last bit was in English. She took a drag.

"*Ay, ay!*" laughed Melva. "*Si*, it's true. Thank you for helping me Silvia, *que Dios la bendiga*."

"*Y La Virgen. Igualmente*, I'll call you back...*buenas tardes, Melva*."

Silvia dialed Jennifer without looking at the phone:

"*Ay Mami*, of course I'll drive you guys! I know the *best* lady to go see, too..."

"Of course you do, *mijita*." A smoky sigh of laughter.

"Ok well I know for a fact that she doesn't work on Sundays though, so if it's that bad we have to go tomorrow. We can go in the morning—no, wait—more like...ten-ish?" Silvia shrugged. "Yeah, I'll cut at break and we'll head out. I got a test before that I gotta take. You know, education Mami. And besides, I mean...you two *viejas* don't got anything else to do anyway...."

"*Tres chancletazos, Yenni...te voy a sazonaaaar...*" she smiled into the phone, "Ok, *don't* be late, we have to go pick up Melva and they live in Hialeah."

"Oh, and *Mami*..." she hesitated, "I'm glad we're doing this...you know, like...*us* you know?" Silvia smiled, tapping the ashes from her cigarette gently as a dove.

"*Ay, si!* And I almost forgot..." Silvia's voice fell to a whisper. "Your father can *not* know about this, okay?"

"Aaaaa Mami!" laughed Jennifer. "Welcome to the club, I'm the queen of tricking Papi—"

"*Mira, niña!*" laughed Silvia in a hushed scream. "No, *pero* I'm serious...yes, it's our thing, ok?"

"Mom..." and there was silence on the phone, "don't worry, we got this." Silvia could feel her daughter smiling on the other end of the line. So was she.

"Okay," she laughed, "see you for dinner."

"Okay *Mami* peace in da middle eeeeesss! Love you *muah*muah* besitos!*" and she hung up, snatching the blunt from her *chongaleechous* girlfriend:

"*yall niggas skipped me, I'm campin' on dis shit.*"

Silvia put her cigarette out on a little ant. "*Su pinga.*"

~*~

Tico rolled over onto his back, exhausted. Moonlight poured in through the window. Angelica grinned next to him, her cheeks red as pomegranates, cuddled close with her head on his shoulder, her long blonde hair splayed across his side. It felt heavenly, Tico was sure that he wouldn't be able to sleep without it. "Sometimes when I'm falling asleep, I can feel you leave your body, like you say you do," she said, stroking his chest idly. Tico smiled. "I...want to be part of it." She buried her face into his armpit bashfully, and Tico laughed, squirming around.

"I saw it long ago, that fire in your eyes. Therein lies a Goddess, waiting to be born." He smiled. "I just have to teach you."

"I don't think I'd ever be able to sleep with another man who spills his cup, but" and she raised her face to his, "I don't think that will be much of a problem." The lovers kissed. An owl screeched into the night.

"*Ay*, did you hear that?" Tico said, sitting up.
"*Si, una lechusa, no?*"
"*Si, si,* symbol of Athene with the shining eyes...but it is an ill omen. Portent of ill-fare. My mother always said that an owl screeching in the night means death." He shuddered. "The tribunal is ever busy — I wonder who they've chosen this time." He lay back down, thinking into the ceiling as Lica resumed her place on his shoulder. He felt her twitch as she fell asleep, aligning her bodies until she floated gently into the world of dreams and the winged masters of light.

~*~

The three Cuban ladies — one with swollen feet, the other singing as she drove, the third glaring out her window at the passers-by — blew down Flagler, changing lanes three at a time to the radio's booming basslines. The sun beamed brightly that Miami mid-morning: the cheese was fresh, and Silvia had the cow in the car to prove it.

"So Melva, tell me for real," asked Jennifer innocently, "do you really think this is...a spiritual thing?" She smiled back at Melva, "You know..."

"*Ay Yennifer*, I can't even wear shoes anymore, look at me...*ay*, I feel like they could burst at any minute." Silvia rolled the window down.

"*Mami, no!* No smoking in this car, I just got a new air freshener and everything! See? Look..." and she grabbed at the pair of plastic cherries that hung from the rear view mirror, reflecting sunlight in red rings around the car. The car smelled like chewing gum.

"*Mira*, I *know* that you and your friends probably smoke more than *I* do in this car, and probably those *cigarritos de marijuana, que Dios te ampare si yo te —*"

"*Okay, okay, Jesus!* Smoke if you gotta, but out the window, ok? I just don't want to ruin the new car smell...and *no, Mami*, I don't smoke those *cigarritos.*" She grinned into the windshield. "I smoke *blunts*, there's no *marijuana* in those, don't worry..." Melva *hmph*ed from the backseat. "*They're tabacitos, tabacitos con sabor a miel,* come on!" she laughed confidently.

"*Si, mija,*" chirped Melva, "you look like the type who would enjoy a good *puro* in the evenings."

"So...do you, like, actually know what you're doing today, Melva?" said Jenny, changing the subject. "I mean...in terms of what to expect, what to do?" She watched Melva purse her lips 'no' in the mirror. "It's not even—damn, *Mami*, you jealous or something?"

"*Eh?*" Silvia had been thinking out the window.

"Look at the tip of your cigarette, it's burning all lopsided. You're jealous."

Silvia laughed. "Come on, it's just the wind..." Silvia thought about it. Jealous...*nah.* "What is this thing all about, then, ah?"

"Well, I mean, there's lots of stuff that can happen. The thing to do here is to just sit and let her read the cards. She'll tell you all the rest. I get *my* readings done at least once a quarter." Jenny smiled guiltily into the windshield, and Silvia raised an eyebrow out into the passing buildings, pursing her lips. "It's just to show you two *viejas* that I know what to do at this place, ok? *Asi que mira*, the lady will tell you what's going on, but the cool thing is that it's not her who knows the future—" Jennifer paused for emphasis—"it's the *muertos.*" Melva's face went taut.

"*Hmph!* Melva, you be careful with all of this, don't give into anything these spirits say!" warned Silvia. "I know how that kind o' *shyet* is, when the...the...when the *Santero* gets their...*muerto* or whatever you call it." She blew a long billowing tail of smoke out the window, leaning her head back inside. "They get possessed by it or something," she shook her head blankly. "You never know what you're going to see, or hear, it's...different, but real."

"Dang *Mami* where'd you hear about all this? I thought you weren't even into it."

"*Niña*...don't forget that '*I an frong Cuba*'...you can't get *away* from that shit! If you don't want to be part of it you just close your eyes and pretend it isn't there."

"*Shit nigga*, that's legit."

"What did she say?" chirped Melva.

"You think I know, Melva?" said Silvia, rolling her eyes. "Something English."

She continued. "Well, so I had this neighbor when we lived by the train station...and I would hear their music going on into the night, their Santo music, all that rattles and gourds shyet, and drums and 'wirikikere' this and that. I had no idea...and you know, I'd see all these old people come in with chickens and goats," and she smiled into the window, "but none of 'em ever came out again...the animals, you know." Silvia's smiled as Melva signed herself with the cross:

"Virgen santisima..."

"And I remember Melva, every once in a while the lady would start screaming, *screaming*, Melva. In the middle of the day! You could hear it through the walls, from outside, and everyone would say 'the lady's *Santo* has descended' and close their doors." Melva had begun to pray *Ave Marias* in the backseat.

"And she would burst through her screen door, Melva, you know, since she always had her door open because of the heat. She would come out into the hallway and scream *boberias*, all this crazy Afro-Spanish *colando la cafe pancontimba* shit, I don't even know...and I remember talking to her, she didn't know any African or whatever that language is, she was just like us, and her eyes would glaze over when she got descended on, she would light these *big* cigars, *hmmmm!*" shuddered Silvia, "and Melva...*Melva*...she would smoke them backwards, *niña*, I swear. She would stick the fire in her mouth and blow smoke all over the place and *bite* down on it, spitting fire all over the ground and her clothes, and she wouldn't even notice! Well, remember...same same." *Jennifer, Jennifer, hellooooo? Jesus, we're driving the speed limit.* "*Si*, and then she would head back into her room, stumbling around, breaking things and you know, all of us kids in the building, whenever we would hear her going again you could hear all of them boom up and down the stairs to my floor and we would all try to peek inside to see what she was doing, and once we saw her drink an entire bottle of rum, an *entire bottle*...all at once, just like that—*clack, clack, clack*—and she would keep going like that until she collapsed onto her olive green couch, this one with velvety square cushions and big buttons in the middle, I remember it like it just happened yesterday, Melva, and after a while she'd get up like nothing happened and drink a glass of water. You know, back to the usual, '*Que pinga quieren, muchachos de mierda, EH?! AH?!AH?! Larrrrgense de aqui!*' You know, a pure *negra Tomasa*." Silvia looked over to the both of them, her green eyes wide with excitement.

"Dang, *Mami,* you never told *me* that story," said Jenny. Silvia laughed to herself. She hadn't told *anyone* that story.

"Well maybe I should have, so you would have known what you were getting yourself into, visiting all that shit without telling us, *hmm*?" She pressed a ruffle out of her skirt. "You can't play with this shit, it's real." The scars on her shiny calves and shins seemed more prominent with the color of the skirt. She could see the pores of her legs, too. It bothered her. "*Bueno*, just so you know, then, Melva, I don't think this is what we'll be walking into today, right?"

"Yeah, Melva," sang Jennifer, "trust me, it's nothing like that. This is America," she laughed. "Well, Miami. Close enough. It's chill, trust me."

"I trust you," Melva crooned from the backseat. "Thanks for bringing me." She raised her face to the rearview mirror, holding back tears. "Frankly, I'm scared shitless." She clutched the shoes she brought with her, a pair of nice, white leather sandals with intricate straps...the woman was hopeful. "I don't really know much about all this stuff, but I know that if this is what did it to me, this will probably undo it, right?" and no one said anything.

Jenny's head jerked over towards the window: "Look, *Mami*, I know those kids, that's Panchita from Uruguay and her boyfriend Luis, fucking pervs." She laughed as they drove by, Luis throwing an empty bottle of soda at the girl in her jeans and puffed white shoes. "They decided to take the *long* way to school today." Silvia shot her *la Timbita*. Jenny saw the look and rolled her eyes.

"I liked that bird," she said, pursing her lips playfully.

"I didn't kill it, Yennifer," she snapped, reaching for her cigarettes. "That's how *chismes* start, with bullshit lies."

"*Queeee?*" gasped Melva. Jenny told her the story against Silvia's ceaseless will, and somewhere across Miami, an older woman in a bathrobe walked into her kitchen to find her *Galletica* on the bottom of the cage, still as death. *Galletica's* eyes were still slightly open, glossy and black, empty. She clutched at her robe, calling for her husband: *René!*

"*No...*" said Melva in disbelief. "Really, Silvia? That's the evil eye, you know. *El mal de ojo.*" She signed herself with the cross. "You should wear an *asabache*, especially if you're giving it to other people—or animals, even worse!" and she looked out the window at a lady walking her dog. "*Definitivamente, Silvia...*I have one I can give you. Poor Timbita," she sighed.

Silvia pursed her lips and lit another cigarette. *Poor Timbita...poor fucking Silvia! Calm down, calm down, wise as a serpent, gentle as a dove. Actions, mi Silvia, are louder than words, you know that...*she smiled at the memory that came to her mind. "*Ay, Cuquita,*" she mumbled into the wind, blowing smoke around a long, lurching left turn.

A few years back Cuco had inspired his brother with the idea of fattening a goat for San Lazaro's feast day. Chiche had fallen in love with the idea immediately, remembering his past in Cuba as a make-shift farmer raising chickens and goats in his backyard, making cheese and growing vegetables until the revolution began to tally them for redistribution (to the tourists). He told Cuco to get the goat and bring it to *his* house, because nobody would be able to raise the goat like he could. And it was true. Cuco did as he was told and brought a skinny, sickly-colored goat to the house, where Chiche tied it to a post in the middle of the backyard and had it graze on the tall grasses and palm stalks and even the occasional bush from the neighbor's yard. The fence wasn't intact, you see...soon the grazing was out of control, for the goat was eating its way back to health and devoured everything it could with gleeful bleats and that sheepish grin, and it bleated ceaselessly for more. Chiche had never looked so pleased. The yard was *immaculate*.

He began to take Cuca, which is what Silvia had named her, to the marshy lots on the side of the highway after coming home from work. In a matter of days the clever goat was hopelessly conditioned to the love that Chiche showed her: she bleated happily whenever his van pulled into the driveway, for she knew that this meant it was time for a ride on the Palmetto.

Chiche would come out back and caress her, escorting her to the front seat of the van, whereupon he would roll down the window and let the merciless, sweltering wind beat her beaming face all the way to the fields by the exit for the Turnpike. Her tongue would flap happily out the side of her smile the whole way there, attracting honks from laughing passersby that made Chiche glow with native pride. *"That's right, Goddammit, I'm a Cuban farmer in 21st century Miami. Sue me."* Goats were renowned for their wise grins, but Cuca...Cuca *smiled*. And so did Chiche. Silvia shook her head every time she saw him barrel through the house without saying hello, his head forever cocked at the angle of that crick that still hadn't gone away. Tending to the goat as if it were his firstborn child.

"*Hmph*," she would say to herself, "I'd cook the *both* of them for San Lazaro if I got the chance," and she would pull on her cigarette like a banshee, fondling her Capricorn lighter on the couch. Watching. Watching them through the glass door.

Smiling. As the time passed, Cuca's coat turned a dark, chocolate brown and her eyes grew fiercely green. She would prance around the backyard and bleat happily when it rained, skipping about and shaking herself off under the awning over and over again. When December finally rolled around, Chiche began to grow nervous whenever the subject of the feast came up, and he started to tell the family little by little that he thought they should buy another goat for the feast...he didn't think Cuca was fat enough for the *chilindrón* that Silvia had been planning since October. "Are you kidding me?" Silvia spat back when he told them. "If I took a knife to that goat right now I'd drain enough lard to fry for a year!"

"Not in *my* house, *coño!*" he shouted back. "*Jamás!*" he said, invoking his masculinity, "*Jamás se habla de mi Cuca asi en esta casa!*" and he stuffed a spoonful of *frijoles* into his mouth, his hand trembling as he set it back down on the table. "*Mi Cuquita, coño...a matarla asi, a huevo', me cago en diez cabrones...*" and that was it. '*Never again* will anyone talk about killing Cuca in this house...my Cuquita, killing her just like that, mercilessly...'

Soon enough, the 15th came and Manuel, Mariza's *pobre Juan* at the time, had not come through with the cuts he said he could get 'real cheap' out in Homestead. In *el Hon-ste.* "Don't worry, I'll take care of it," said Chiche cooly as he took his breakfast. Silvia smiled, glancing to the picture of *La Virgen* on the wall. That evening, Chiche returned home triumphantly with a slab of goat-meat across his shoulder, fresh in a clear plastic bag smeared with bloody drops of water. The mass hit the ground with an empty thud as Chiche fell to his knees before the sight in the glass door. Silvia had even skinned the poor beauty by then, and what was once Cuca the smiling goat hung upside-down by her hind legs, her ribcage splayed out like the wings of a fallen angel, dripping the last of the blood that had once given color to her coat, and life to Chiche's day. Silvia was collecting it in a basin underneath the goat, to make *morcilla* for new years eve.

"Don't you *ever* scream at us like that again!" she screamed through the glass, pointing at him with her machete. "Look what happens," and she slapped Cuca's hairless ass with the side of the blade. "*Chilindrón, malllllPINGA!*" Chiche's spirit went completely black, and he stood up quietly, holding back tears as he made to go lay down. The next day, the whole family came over and enjoyed the fragrant *Chilindrón* together, spiced to perfection and colored a delightful red, all in honor of *San Lazaro*, the old man on crutches covered with leprous wounds and surrounded by quivering dogs. Chiche's *Santo*.

Chiche's *Santo*...didn't come out of his room until the next morning.

When the family asked why he wouldn't come out for dinner, *San Lazaro* is his *Santo*, is he okay, Silvia told them his diabetes was acting up, and to keep eating. They had a happy evening, and the statue of *San Lazaro* beamed with life all through the night, surrounded by purple candles and yellow flowers.

~*~

Chiche drove around Miami in the van with the happy vacuum-cleaner on it. The look on his face was static, turned inwards. It was the harmless scowl that most people have while driving, a look that reveals nothing save for the person's state of autopilot, that hoary trance of pre-learned, pre-conditioned traffic laws and random thoughts, turn-signals, twist the wheel, slow down, stop, go, gas, brake, pedal, wait, red, green, gas, thinking, thinking, thinking...gazing, glazing, waiting. He made his way through town with the drone of AM static at the back of his afterthoughts, too low to listen, too high to drown out, traipsing about his garden of mental *musarañas,* spiderwebs of unconscious thought, as the scenery crept on by.

The sun played across his leathery face, shining off windshields and store windows, car mirrors and shiny spinning rims too nice for the cars they hung from. The light ahead turned yellow, and Chiche slowed down—he was proud of himself for it, it was his demonstration of self-control. Three cars honked in perfect harmony as he slowed down before the light. A sedan with a bumper from another car cussed him out as it sped around and through the light, which had turned red by then. Chiche smiled. *'Why rush?'* Ahead, the sedan veered two lanes to the right, passing a group of cars right under an billboard advertising auto-insurance: 'Don't pay for that ticket!'

"Comemierda!" shouted a man in a truck next to him. He turned his head to the right, looked him right in the sunglasses, and turned back to the flurry of cars before him. There was something extra special about today, everything seemed to be going well. He felt warm inside, contemplating the tumult under the ambiguous sky. The sun was out, but not like in the summer. It wasn't one of those mornings where the sky was bright blue at 7:30 AM; the sky was an odd color, a greyish sort of mixture between all the colors at once. The sky wasn't exceptionally bright, but it still hurt your eyes to look up at it. A morning like this was best just about now, between 10 and 11 AM. He didn't know why, it had just come to him with age.

"*El diablo sabe mas por viejo que por diablo,*" he said to himself with an air of finality. The devil knows more for being old than for being the devil. So be it. He felt the sunglasses on him again. *Vaya,* once again the people catch him talking to himself. He rubbed his head dismissively, shining opaque in the hazy glow of the morning, and the light turned green. 'Thank God,' and the van accelerated, but he *slammed* on the brakes, letting another red light runner fly by. "*Maricon!*" yelled the sunglasses, revving his engine and taking off down the eight lane road. Right then it struck Chiche like lightning — *coñññoooo!* — that was it! He knew why he had started the day off so well. He suddenly realized what he had seen when he got out of bed this morning — his *Negrita* was smiling. '*Pobresita,*' he thought, 'the poor thing never smiles.' He drove off, dodging a mass of black feathers and cardboard in the middle of the street. "*Goddamn brujos,*" he growled, swerving back into his lane.

He examined his clipboard with one eye on the road. "Just around the corner," he said to himself. *Tss.* Potential clients filled out raffle tickets at the mall, or had been recommended by friends who bought a vacuum — everyone was required to give at least five addresses they could sell to. It wasn't obligatory, but most people listed close to ten; they were, more often than not, signing their friends up for a free vacuuming of their living room. Or a surprise knock on the door, *pa'que no me joden.* Before stopping at the next house, which was just around the corner, Chiche pulled over to the coffee window and parked his van by the air pump — it was also a gas station. He got out, dodging a puddle of oily rainbow-water that had collected in the concrete, and walked up to the window. He ordered himself a *coladita,* a fresh pull of *Café Cubano.* It came as perfect as could be, with the *espumita* and everything, strong, bold and perfectly sweet — so sweet, in fact, that it was more like nectar than coffee. There is a strange phenomenon, with *Café Cubano.* Too much sugar in your coffee could often ruin the whole experience, but with this way of preparing espresso they seem to have breached some sort of threshold, practically spiritual, surpassing which the coffee tasted good once again...better, even. Perhaps it was so much sugar at once that the tongue could do nothing but assume the sensory assault to be pleasing. Perhaps it was a mild epileptic shock to the papillae of the gustatory palate, setting them off erratically in response to the sugar and anticipated dose of caffeine. Whatever it was, any Cuban woman behind the coffee-window — *la ventanita de café** — knew how to surpass this threshold with the utmost and effortless precision, and this made every trip to the *ventanita* a journey into the happiest regions of one's mind, where sensation reminded one, if only for a minute, that everything was, or should have been, alright. Silvia never made *café* like this anymore, not since the diabetes had gotten to him. She had weaned them both away from the sugar over time, serving him black, bitter coffee in lieu of the liquid thrills that other women could give him so liberally.

He waited for his *colada* along with the rest of the customers, half of whom had probably been there for hours, eating *pastelitos* and *croquetas* between *colada* after *colada*, bullshitting about Castro and the most recent news off the island. Cellphones, *Moringa*, Raul's a child molester — *que comepinga.* Chiche eyed a fat, old *chusma* of a lady in tweety-bird sandals who had everything to say to a skinny little man who had been educated in Cuba before the revolution. Chiche could tell these types from the rest, for they were as full of shit as they looked. A lexicon, of the Castilian variety, glasses and all. Taxi drivers, a local term for 'regulars', leaned into the counter around the corner, trilling advances at the coffee-maids like children at the zoo. Beware, *niñitos*, birds bite back. The old man looked at Chiche from behind his bristly salt-and-pepper moustache and Tuscan nose, a hint of snide bullshit in his eye. Chiche smiled and nodded out of courtesy, and right then his coffee popped out the window — "Aqui esta, mi amor,"* sang the blonde coffee-maid.

Chiche made to smile back, but he then realized he was already smiling. *Café*...he turned around triumphantly, coffee in hand, smiling at the old man and the lady in the tweety-bird sandals, and the old man was still smiling from behind his glasses, and the lady said *"what?"* and everyone stopped.

Coño...tss.

Chiche popped the little square off the top of his cup and snapped it onto the lid. He liked those tops. This was the only place they had them anymore. Plumes of steam curled out of the cup and dissipated into the high-octane morning air. *Ay, la vida...* Chiche reached into his pocket and paid with one hand. 'Off to the next conquest,' he smiled to himself, and he caught the fat lady scratching the inside of her calf with her other foot out of the corner of his eye. She groaned in a mixture of pleasure and pain, laughing at the old man's perfectly punctuated bullshit. Tweety's head bobbled above her curled toes as she scratched, purring softly as the old man prattled on. He left them both, dodging the rainbow-puddle as a woman told the taxi drivers in a throaty drawl that they could put it up their mother's ass, and twenty on #8, *porfavor*.

~*~

You bring a smile
to the face with cowrie eyes,
that mischievous child Elegguá
who smokes cigarettes behind
his mother's back
and sits by the crossroads.

~*~

The ladies had arrived at their destination. It was a little *botanica* in the far left corner of a mini-mall a couple blocks off 84th street, and it was very subtle, one couldn't simply stumble

175

upon it. You had to know about it to go...*Botanica Fururú.*
Though there were iron bars drawn across all the windows as
though it were closed, the door had no bars on it and was cracked
open a little, making the little sign that read *'Open: Abierto'* click
against the door with every passing breeze. Jenny parked right in
front. Theirs was the only car in front of the *botanica.* Melva
voiced her fears: "You know, Yennifer, it doesn't look open, we
could just...come another day...no?"

Jennifer turned to her. "*Oye* – I brought you here and
made the appointment and everything, ok? And yeah, it's open,
look at the door – it's totally open." And she smiled. "Melva...are
you still nervous?"

"*Ay ok ok!*" she whined. "*Vamos.*" Jenny saw her rub her
hands across her face in exasperation through the rearview
mirror. Silvia tapped her fingers on the door handle.

"Can we go inside? This heat is starting to get to me," she
said, rolling her eyes at Jennifer.

"Well ok, but what do I do with these?" Melva held up
her shoes and a pair of white socks. "I can't put them on, but if
that's impolite I can squeeze them on," and she winced, "I don't
know how these people are." She pouted, looking at the day care
center across the mini-mall. "You know..."

"Melva, it's ok, just can come in like that, that's what
you're here for. *Dale*, come on! We're late anyway." And they
shuffled for the door in a bundle, the two ladies perched behind
Jenny's shoulders..though they acted as if that were perfectly
normal. Dignified, even.

The sign cackled against the glass door.

Thick with the fragrance of resins and gum-benzoin, the
air inside the *botanica* was crisp and cool. The saints sat still, stoic
as statues watching the ladies made their way inside. They found
themselves surrounded by gourds and rattles and shelves lined
with foggy jars and baskets full of all sorts of oddities, railroad
spikes and ladders, powders and insects, candles shaped like

lovers and skulls, lizards, feathers, beads, Indians and Gypsies and thousand-armed Buddhas, thousands upon thousands of icons from every religion in the world. At the foot of the door, an egg-shaped stone with cowrie-shells set in as eyes, nose, mouth and ears sat in a dish full of dried mackerel covered with grungy brown powder, bright orange palm oil slathered atop everything with its rancid viscosity. Sweets and bitter coffee sat next to the food offering, by a half-smoked cigar, old-fashioned keys and a little glass filled with clear liquor. The stone greeted them at the entry with a smile: "Elegguá," whispered Jenny to Melva, who whispered 'Santísima Virgen' in return, grabbing Silvia's wrist. As the wise ones say, age alone does not stop one from being a child. For better, or for worse. Silvia snapped her gaze to the left—a pile of pennies slid off of a stern Indian chief's foot. She looked up at the statue, who was looking her in the eye.

"Maferefún Elegguaaaa!" laughed an old man behind the counter, motioning toward the stone. "He's spoiled, mischievous! But very powerful. Bara, suwayooo!" he shouted into the hanging coconuts with glee, and outside the sun broke through the clouds as if something peculiar was in the making. "You see?" he laughed, looking outside. "Echu Bara, good morning to you!"

African robes and tapestries hung behind the counter and coconuts., framing the old man with an aura that smacked of the diaspora and its silver lining. He was no younger than fifty, happy, skinny...and white. Thousands of colorful beads hung around his neck, under a yellow and green hat that sat atop his head like a lid. He greeted them with a smile of yellow teeth that curled against a grainy white moustache. He stood behind a counter that housed copious bowls and feathers, rusty iron nails curled around each other and thousands upon thousands of beaded necklaces colored for the different Orishas under buzzing fluorescent lights. Jenny spoke quietly to the man, who gestured toward the back room* and smiled to the older ladies as they nodded their greetings.

"This is Burufinda," she giggled as she led her mother and

Melva to the consultation room.

"*Bueeeeeenas...*"

"And this is my mother Silvia, and Melva, who are here to see Ofelia today."

"*Buenos dias,*" they both sang in unison, following Jenny toward the sign above the door in the back above all the aisles, an old sign surrounded by glittering stars and pyramids that read '*Salon de Consultas.*' They passed through a screen of beads that slid across their shoulders, tickling their necks like the tendrils of happy spirits.

Before them, in a dramatic display of mystic grandeur, the wise Ofelia sat at her chair like an African queen, clad in flowing purple robes and bedecked with dozens of colorful *collares.* Her hair was tied into a multitude of braids that were thrown up into a great mass atop her head, tied tightly with a golden turban. She sat, ominous, voluptuous, before at a wide table topped with a white cloth. Silvia expected Walter Maricado mysticism complete with rings and golden globes and crystal lanterns—*muah baby!*— but it was not so, and upon the table were her various tools for contact with the beyond, the *Mas Allá.* A censer ran-over with thick smoke that hovered over the table and slithered down to the ground, or out into the surrounding air and up, up toward the ceiling. A cigar sat in a crystal ashtray, smoking coolly from its ashen tip, and a pile of white shells sat next to the ashtray, along with a deck of unusually large cards and a few little images of *los Santos.* In the background, various Catholic saints stood silently, observing all with their sullen eyes between wooden Orishas striking rigid poses in the smoke. Wide, bulging eyes and smiling lips looked at them from everywhere in the room, idols smeared with pastes and dyes and robed with elegant sashes, their feet littered with powders and seeds, cigarettes and rubber ducks, coconuts and cloudy glasses of liquor. Silvia shot her eyes into the corner where she could have sworn she saw the smoke *swoosh.* It happened again by the ceiling. Indians, feathers and seashells, curls of smoke, colored necklaces, black women in white robes smiling from the wall, coconut shells and stones distorted in glasses of water caked with minerals and years of crusted egg whites. *Swoosh..."Sientense, porfavor,"* said the woman at the table, her eyes deep and wide like onyx set in ivory. Smiling onyx.

She gestured to the chairs on the other side of the table. There were three—who knew? The ladies sat down, Jenny between Silvia and Melva. Jennifer stroked her glued-bangs coolly, darting her gaze to the ladies, left and right, with a mischievous smile: *we're here, bitchesss..."Buenos días, Ofelia."*

"Buenas, Yennifer," smiled the oracle to the three of them. Silvia looked to Melva with raised eyebrows.

"Ok, so like I said, *I'm* not here for a reading today. But I'll call you next week,"* she smiled. "What we're here for is my aun—"

"Basta, basta!" and she raised her white palm into the air, calloused with age. "Would our Melva like to have her reading alone?" She looked from Silvia to Melva, waiting for an answer.

Melva shook her head with fear in her eyes, saying shakily, *"si,* they can stay," and she laughed nervously. Ofelia leaned out to the side, spurting a swig of liquor to the images behind her and dipping her finger into a glass of water with coins, a corn-cob and a little cross inside of it.

"Very well. Then let us hear the *barajas* speak..." said Doña Ofelia calmly, and she grabbed the deck, sticking the lit end of a cigar into her mouth and leaning the deck open in her hand. She blew smoke into the cards, yellowish coils sizzling into into every nook and cranny of the deck in her hands. Melva watched mystified as Ofelia, bowing her head, spoke prayers under her breath and drew them back in with a quick gasp, slapping the cards onto the table. Smoke flew up in all directions, and Silvia felt a raucous shiver go all the way up her spine and out the top of her head. "This woman here..." she said cooly, looking to Silvia, "kills birds with her gaze." Three pairs of eyes went wide at the ground, feigning calm.

"*Mami...*" cracked Jenny, "*damn.*"

"They sell *azabaches* here..." insisted Melva.

"*Hmph*," said Silvia, brushing the comment off. She did not acknowledge the oracle.

"We can talk about that later," Ofelia said, spreading the deck out with her left hand. The cards unveiled their strange symbols, clubs wrapped in ribbons and women standing atop orbs and balances, twins and skulls and kings and golden coins, all sorts of marvelous things. The woman pursed her lips, squinting slightly for a second before she grabbed the smoking cigar and tapped it on the ashtray, its bright ember emerging from the cracking ash. She toked it slowly, looking into the cards with eyes narrowed into slits.

"*Mmmmm...osogbo...*they tell me there are...three women doing you harm, my Melva. I see three women. Do you owe someone money?"

"*No, no!*" cried Melva with fear in her voice. Her chin was full of pouty wrinkles, and she brought her hands up to her face in despair. "I don't owe anyone anything."

"Don't worry, Melva, relax, there's nothing to worry about...we'll sort it all out. Now..." and she moved a card to the side, "what is this, how can it be that someone *feels* like you owe them and yet you do not, because they have strong convictions in the harm they've sent in your direction." She smacked her lips. She nodded into the haze..."They feel like they're right."

"*Ay*, Doña Ofelia, it's my cousins in Cuba, I know it, they—"

"They want their *Tommy* jeans, no?" The *Santera* cocked her brow up to the ladies seated across from her, smiling ominously. Blazing onyx set in ivory. Melva gasped with a smile of disbelief, but said nothing. It was Silvia who spoke, meeting her eyes with her own gems of fire.

"And what have they done to her?" said Silvia, holding the

Santera's gaze.

"Much more than those swollen feet she's got, *mijita*, I'll tell you that much." Silvia threw her gaze down. *Goddammit.* "There's some eyes on you, Melva, eyes you can not see, but they see you...the *Santos* brought you here *just* in time," and she leaned back in her chair. "Melva, *mijita,* how long has it been since you've checked your blood? Get it checked...and with a new doctor, that last one didn't need to give you a breast exam," she said, shaking her head. "*Aprovechados.*"

She flipped another card, turning three toward each other. Up she looked, into the ceiling, closing her eyes and speaking with an aethereal smile: "*Si...si,* Melva, we'll take care of you in no time. The sun will rise tomorrow to healthy feet, doest that sound nice? *Mira,*" and she pointed to one of the cards she had flipped. The hell if they knew what that meant. "Ochún is going to take care of everything, she's with all three of you here, sweet as the light of the sun!" Silvia smiled to herself — *La Virgen* was the same as Ochun, she had been told long ago. They changed names with each other. "And I don't want you eating anymore *pastelitos* for now, that's something you should nip in the bud. Your blood's sweet enough, *me entiendes?*" Melva took her face out of her spotty hands and nodded childishly, her eyes round with shock. "God, everyone here in Miami has the Santos telling them to take it easy on the sweets...but it's hard with a bakery right across the parking lot, ah?"

"*Coño,* and they've got those new *mamey* ones, too..." She looked to Silvia and Jenny, and back to the cards. "*How...how do you know all this?*"

The oracle shook her head, laughing to herself. She gazed deeply into a glass of water across the room in a windowsill, rubbing her chin with a very puzzled look on her face. "*Melva...*" she said with a look of contempt, "don't you send these *villalobos* anything ever again. I don't care if they're family. They're not. These are spiteful women, lazy, evil, witches in every way. I can see them here, they live better than *you* do *Melva*, with all you've been sending them. Bless your heart, Melva, isn't—that—something." She enjoyed herself a long laugh before going on. "They're not family. They're...*un excremento*." Silvia gasped, feeling intruded upon. The oracle laughed out loud again, this time louder than before. "*Ay*, we're cooking now. Melva, you've been the victim on both ends of this situation, cut them off, cut them off! No matter what they say, they'll call you with stories, Melva, they'll curse you and call you insensitive, you're over there and we're stuck here with the *Moringa!* There's no shaving cream, mayonnaise, whatever they say, just ignore them. These *rrrrekete-bitches* don't deserve to look into your beautiful eyes, and your spirits aren't letting this happen any longer. That's why they've brought you here, thank them Melva, thank with a bouquet of white flowers." She paused, and there was silence for a drawn-out minute of dissonance and disbelief.

"I'll...take care of them for you..." The words lingered in the air. "But it's not free." Melva said nothing. The silence was broken by the clanking of the bells on the door out front. "Customers," said Ofelia. "I love customers."

> *And musing in her thoughts, did she,*
> *The soul of Silvia Campos, see*
> *Her husband, bounds with cords of dark-*
> *ened blood — 'the knife's possessing thee!'*

But angel mine, who listens to a passing thought?
   "*Tin, Marin, y dos Pingüe, cucara-macara-titere fue. Vamos, que tengo sed.*" Silvia

                              yawned, thinking of
                              heading outside for a smoke
                              with *the Virgin.*

From the corners of the room, soft vocals began to rise and sing in harmony, over and over again—"...*Ven a trabajar, Cachita,*

Cachita, Cachumbambe..." Silvia began to grow uncomfortable in her seat. No one else seemed to notice, was it all in her head? Soon she was sitting on a fiery beehive. *Come to work, Cachita, Cachita, Cachumbambe...*Ofelia danced softly to the beat of the *canto*, looking Silvia right in the eyes. Silvia's eyes betrayed her bewilderment, her uneasiness, the beehive between her thighs.

"You seem as though you sense things in here you can not see, Silvia..." Jenny and Melva looked up at her, confused. Silvia shrugged it off dismissively, waving a hand around her head – "the incense, it's playing with my head," she smiled. The bees churned with ardor in her base, and more voices joined in, more and more spirits, and there was no fear, Ofelia was right. Silvia looked around as Ofelia continued speaking to Melva and Jennifer as if nothing were going on, and no one noticed that she had begun to dig her nails into the cushion of the chair. *Ay, ay, ay...ven a trabajar, mi negrita, mi viejita...y como te quiero, como te nememememeemeesssssssssssssss...*and the sounds threw themselves into pitches higher than she could comprehend until the hive burst open with a flurry of wailing shrieks and cries into the chair, onto the floor below her, out of the top of her head and into the air. She filled the whole room, sitting still in her chair so that no one would notice. Her breath moved all of the smoke in the room, back and forth, swirling all around her, up into the air, in through the windows, it was as if the very sky were pouring into the room to suffocate her with the hyperventilation of concentrated glory, and nobody noticed, for they were dancing, dancing, dancing in their chairs to the song of their routine, of social propriety, and Melva was the best dancer of all. Everything was perfect, just then. No one noticed how perfect they were, how perfect everything was. And the room was full of bees, full of ethereal spots that churned about, sparkling with laughter and reverence for their holy hive seated across from the oracle.

Jenny leaned over and whispered to Silvia, "I told you this lady was the shit. She's got you seeing stars." Silvia winced and nodded, wondering if Jenny had *any* clue as to what was really going on. "Come on *Mami*, get ahold of yourself, it's just spirits, they're how it all happens."

"No, no," said Ofelia to Melva, they won't be able to do a thing, you'll see." A grin came across her long lips, "*San Lazaro* is saying that he'll help you do some things, in addition to what we'll do next week when you come back." She looked to the three of them, making sure that they were all listening.

"My Melva," she said, her voice thick with power, "what you need to do is find a nice, thick branch of *Rompesaragüey* and have someone give you a nice *despojo* with it from head to toe, and then put it in a bag and take it to the shore of the ocean in the dark, dark heights of the night and set it ablaze, and then run off — and *don't look back!*" The woman's nostrils flared as she paused for emphasis. "This is to be done once, tonight, and that's it. It is Monday, the best day for *limpiezas* besides Friday. *Melva,*" she repeated, "*don't look back...*and for the next nine days, I need you to pray the prayer to *San Alejo* nine times in the light of a candle, to send all that nasty stuff away with the power of *God, oistes? Dios Todopoderoso.*" she raised her hands toward the ceiling. "And..." she looked at the three women, a sudden grin coming to her face, "take a black chicken, and have someo—"

"A *what?!*" piped Melva.

"Did I stutter?" Melva took a long, hissing breath in.

"*Ay...ayayayyyy, por Dios...*I've reached my limit with this."

"*Ay niña,*" Ofelia said with a brush of the hand, "how many times have you made chicken soup for your husband?"

"He..." Melva's face flushed. "He says chicken soup's—"

"*Pero forget Cuco for once, Meb-ba!*" snapped Silvia, annunciating the C's with a pent-up vigor. Her inner-*guajira* had slipped out.

"Ladies, ladies, it's just a chicken. Have someone clean you with it, snap its neck and throw it in the bag with the *Rompesaragüey.* It's eas—"

"And *we* have to do it?"

"That's what the *Santo* says, I *wish* I could do it for you. Shit, these landlords have me doin' backflips."

"Hmph," scoffed Silvia. "*Mirala.*"

"And...we still do the same thing to the bag, even with the chicken?" Melva looked to the ground, at her feet, thinking hard.

Ofelia glanced over to the water by the window. Paused. Smiled. "*Si, si* just like that." And she laughed to herself, muttering something about monkeys and coconuts.

"*Por Dios,*" sighed Melva, looking to Silvia. "If that's what it takes for these feet to come down..."

"I'm busy."

Ofelia sat back in her chair watching them, smoking her cigar. "You haven't even seen the beginning of what they wanted to do to you, you know that? It's good that you came today, Melva, how much can I tell you, they wanted you in a wheelchair, I see it right here, it's coming through so strong..." She toked on the cigar, the smoke billowing up her face in three thick puffs. "So put it all in the chicken and you'll thank me later. No really," she smiled, ashing the cigar, "you will."

She threw some powder on one of the *Orishas*, muttering a prayer. "Don't worry, Melva, you do what I say and you'll be fine. My husband has already begun to prepare these things for you in the back room," she said. Melva looked to the beaded curtains behind her, confused: indeed, there was no one at the desk. Ofelia took a sip of water and continued. "Do this, and you'll see that you'll be fine." She bore into Melva with her eyes for a few drawn-out seconds, to Melva's growing concern. And then she smiled. "And don't forget to offer your love to Ochún, she's always looking over you, even now, Melva. Look at her!" she said, gesturing behind Melva with her lips. "It was She who brought you here today," she woman smiled. "She'll sweeten your life in turn, *linda que es.*" She smiled, and so did Melva. From somewhere in the aisles of the *botanica*, Burufinda's voice sounded into the room: "...touch that and he'll slap the shit out of you. Go ahead, try."

"And for good measure, Melva...put some water by a window at the front of your house. That'll catch anything they try and throw at you from now on." She sat up in her chair, with an air of finality.

"*Omío Yemaya*," she said, putting the cards back into the deck. "Now, I've sensed a certain *vibra* from this woman over here, with the piercing green eyes, Jenny's mother Silvia." Silvia raised an eyebrow, over flushed, bewildered, confused cheeks.

"What do you mean, *Doññña Ofelia?*" Silvia asked, hints of sarcasm in her voice.

"*Oye, oye,* you have no idea what might follow you home if you insult me, you hear me?" Burning embers of onyx pierced Silvia's eyes. Silvia backed down, looking to the ground.

"Well, *Doña Ofelia*," answered Jennifer, I'm sure that my mom could use some advice too, I got her *consulta,**" and she smiled at her mother.

"Yes, I should...definitely see her," she said, "the situation is, well...can the both of you leave me here alone for a few minutes with Ms. Silvia, let me talk to her while you two go and get Melva's things ready, no?" Melva nodded and walked off with Jenny's arm in her hands, back to the main room where Burufinda sat quietly, smiling to himself from ear to ear. *Doña Ofelia* motioned for Silvia to take the middle seat. She shifted over and sat face to face with the mysterious *Santera,* whose eyes teemed eerily with powers unknown. As Silvia looked up to the oracle, the beehive in her womb became obvious as the sun. Silvia tried to hide it, her thoughts, her feelings, her eyes.

She looked down: "*Y que,* what do you need?" said Silvia apprehensively.

"Miss Silvia, *porfavor,* let me remind you once more of the favor I'm trying to do you here," and she looked through the beads to make sure that the others were out of earshot, bringing her voice down to a whisper. "Because I don't think it is a laughing matter that you would like to kill your husband." Silvia laughed out loud. Doña Ofelia waited patiently for her to look back into her eyes.

"*Si*...no laughing matter. Are you serious about it, or should I send you home to watch your *novelas* and keep fantasizing about it?" Silvia frowned — *challenged*. "I see this ugly knife, shining like the black *machete* of Yemaya. This is no laughing matter."

Silvia kept her eyes to the ground, nodding slowly. "If anyone, *anyone* else knew about this, I'd call you a charlatan, but truly, Doña Ofelia, not another soul knows." She shook her head in disbelief, her eyes betraying a slight sense of defeat. "Tell me what you see."

"*Ay* Silvia, I assure you, *many* souls know." The *Santera* smiled mischievously. "But that's nothing to worry about. Not right now. All you need to know is this: the *santos* are laughing, for the future in this case is left short of destiny, short of fate. It is surely the play of Elegguá. So be careful. They are waiting to see what you do...tell me, what are your motives?"

"I don't want to talk about it."

"Silvia..." Ofelia's tone softened. "I can *help you*...I'm seeing lots of tension, stress, all sorts of things, this seems like too much at—"

"*I don't want to talk about it.*" She went to stand up. The *Santera* slapped the table with an angry '*Hmph!*' scattering smoke everywhere. Her nostrils flared, and her eyes bore into Silvia with the penetrating gaze of Oyá, the Lady with the flashing eyes. Silvia's head popped up to the *Santos* behind the woman. Had their eyes gone just as wide? She glared back, angrily. *No, this is between me and La Virgen.*

"*Oyá yegbe iya mesa oyo orun afefe,*" she heard in the background, smothered voices from the room next door. "*Iku lelebi oke ayaba gbogbo loya oninrin oga mi ano oga mi gbogbo egun orisha ni abaya oyu ewa oyansan oyeri gekua iya mi obinrin ni kiukuo le fun*

olugba ni olofi nitosi wa, ayaba nikua moducue," and in the silence
that followed Silvia found her gaze upon a Goddess in the back of
the room, holding a brush of horse hair high in her hands and
robed in garments of every color. She wore the sun around her
neck between two full, black breasts that shone with the polish of
well-worked ebony, and posed in dance, her eyes shone with the
power of lightning, even in dark, smooth wood. Doña Ofelia
sprinkled some water over the image and sat back down,
brushing her white robe gently as she turned back to Silvia.

"*Coñó*...look, *Mija*, you don't understand..." Her tone of
voice had softened again. "I can...*help help* you." Burning hot
onyx, set into the finest ivory, bore into her eyes, into her beehive,
which had begun to buzz once again. Her gut convulsed, and that
raw, sexual pleasure ran all up and down her spine and through
the hairs on her head. *The wise come in with sharp senses and leave
with their arms full.*

"I can give you what you need. But those things don't
come easy," she said, and with that she ran a hand over her neck.
"To kill someone costs a lot of money in the world of *Araonú* — let
all who have ears listen to *that.*"

"*Hmph.* What are you talking about here?" She looked
behind her shoulder, making sure that Jenny and Melva were still
in the aisles. Ofelia *smiled* at the question.

"Give me...nine hundred dollars," she said, "and some of
his hair, so I can make it."

"Ay niña, I don't have that kind of money...and
besides...he's bald." The thrill left her eyes, and she made to stand
up: "My show's gonna be on soon, and that cigar has made me
want a cigarette since the moment we walked in here." She
pressed the ruffles out of her skirt. "So...*si*, as it should be...*que
Dios te bendiga, Doña Ofelia.*" She turned to walk out, but a
piercing pain stabbed her at the base of the skull as she turned.
She remembered that old superstition, that one should never turn
their back on a witch. She grimaced, clutching at the back of her
head and turned around, her eyes wide with rage. In the next

room, Jenny pointed to the door. A little bird fell out of the sign, right outside. Melva shuddered and looked into the beaded curtains across the room, signing herself with the cross.

"*Silvia*," Ofelia growled, "*Stop*. They...they *want* me to help you. *Sit down, would you?*" Silvia looked back through the curtains—the other two had begun to chat with Burufinda. She sat, staring at the sacred heart of Jesus with contempt. "Let me at least give you this, Silvita—for you're a daughter of Ochún just like me. Don't worry about paying for it, consider it...a gift from God." The *Santera* got up from her table and scattered offerings before all of the *Santos*, touching all of their feet as she walked over to a wooden chifforobe she had in the corner of the room. There she paused, saying a few mumbled words before opening it, and having pulled the doors of the chifforobe open, Silvia beheld the smoke in the room churn vigorously, whirling around and whooshing cold wisps of fragrant air all over her skin. Goosebumps pricked all over her body, her shoulders, face and arms, swirls of timorous vibration chittering through her legs and arms and neck, her face and out to the tips of her fingers.

Inside the cabinet were piles of feathers and straw, dolls that looked like little African slaves and Indians, and jars filled with strange, strange things, all under the apparent supervision of a conch shell with a face painted on it with dried blood, slanted eyes and a long nose lingering over an eerily childish smile. The *Santera* dug through a drawer she pulled open, and Silvia could hear the clinking and scraping of hundreds of vials and things. Doña Ofelia approached her with a little glass vessel filled with a substance that looked like tobacco and sand mixed together.

"What you've got to do, *mija*, is give the potion what it needs: *Aché*." Ofelia let the words hang for a few seconds. "You see, right now it is in a dormant state. This little vial holds power that must be called upon from the *Mas Allá, entiendes?*" Silvia nodded. "It is not difficult to do, but I need you to prick your right ring finger with a needle," and her eyes bulged, "a *new needle, Silvia!* And from there you shall squeeze five drops of your own blood into the vial, and cap it once again." Silvia nodded her consent. It seemed simple enough...and with that Ofelia continued and told her what to do through to the end.

"So that's it?" Silvia asked. "I just prick my finger and sing a song?"

"*Ay Silvia,*" sighed Doña Ofelia, "you say it as if it were nothing. To the one who simply pricks, or simply sings, it is just that, but you and I, *we are working.* And you, *mijita,* you are quite lucky, for not anyone can turn such simple things into great work. Ochún likes you, and that, *niña,* is where you're power comes from, from Ochún, *la Santísima Virgen de la Caridad del Cobre.* You know that, and I know that, and because of Her I am helping you, nothing more. You're no charmer." The *Santera* sat back down in her chair, closing her eyes for a minute before continuing. "*Si, si,* your Chiche will...fall asleep — but *fall fall* asleep....for your benefit, *mija.* The slaves used to use it to get themselves out of bondage, but today its only used by the Haitian *brujos* who raise the dead to make them their slaves." Silvia smiled with disbelief. "But away with all that." Silvia's eyes glowed.

"I'd give it, *hmm*....fifteen minutes, and the *malandro* will be out cold. Make sure he's wearing pants, for this potion..." and she blushed, "it does strange things to men." Silvia looked confused. "It is then that you can do whatever you want; with this much, he'll be our for precisely three days."

"*Jesucristo,*" said Silvia, her mouth agape. "Three days?"

"*Si,* Doña Silvia, think about that. Three days in *Araonú?* But it shouldn't take you three days to..." she smiled softly, "...and you wouldn't have to look into his eyes. That would get to you, *amorsito,* I know it, you're human like the rest of us." Silvia thought of his eyes, hollow pupils looking into hers as she ran the blade along his neck. He gagged and sputtered blood for only seconds before spitting up his ghost. Silvia bit her lip, her eyes rolling in a mixture of fear and arousal. *Tobacco and sand.*

"*Bueno*," said Silvia with a smile, "*muchas gracias, ah?*" She took the vial from Ofelia's hand. "Oh, and, hmm..." Silvia paused for a second, trying to phrase what she was about to say nicely. She sighed. "Is it...right? What I'm doing?"

The *Santera* smiled. "That's up for us to decide. What I was offering to you would have been a tip into the *caldero* and '*buenas noches Babalu*'. He'd never even see it coming. But you don't want it, and I'm not even charging you for this little assistance, you know..." she winked. "You're a working woman, I like it. Ochún egúa Iyá mío, iguá Iyá mío," and she touched her heart. "But I will say no more, I've done *my* work here, and any other advice will be...well...nine hundred dollars." She smiled into Silvia's frown. "In case you've never thought about it, that's not too expensive for *a human life.* Come now, Melva still needs to pay me for the consultation," and her eyes lit up with mischief. "*She* should know better than to owe a *bruja*, hmm?" *Virgen Santisima.*

Silvia made to leave, but turned around. "Doña Ofelia," she asked innocently, "and what is that you have going on next door? All that noise?"

"*Niña*," laughed Doña Ofelia, "the other side of that wall is a shoe store."

"Com iya, com iya!" shouted Burufinda from behind the counter with immaculate timing. Ofelia escorted Silvia back into the *botanica.* The old man watched Silvia emerge from the door of beads, a few strands clinging to her jacket, sliding down her neck. With a frown Silvia cast them off of her and readjusted herself. She was a new woman, with new intentions, a new focus and clear motivation, a slight smile across her lips, across her eyes. Clear as crystal. Green with vengeance. Doña Ofelia followed her out, looking peaceful and ethereal, grinning lightly behind mystic eyes in her flowing robes and turban.

"Seelvya, I haff something for you, but all will enjoy, yes!" said Burufinda from behind his counter with a large, toothy smile.

He made it difficult not to smile back. Perhaps he too was aware of this, and used it to his advantage. He motioned for Melva and Jenny to come out of one of the aisles, Melva holding a brown paper bag that rustled with the snap of twigs. The other ticked every couple of seconds.

"*Jesucristo*," said Silvia, meeting Jennifer's gaze. Her eyes were wide as a chicken's.

"I haff hat the sodden inspireshon to spik to all of yoo of a storee from my tyme of yooth," said Burufinda with a wide, wide smile. His eyes suddenly shone with a gloss that seemed euphoric as he summoned the story up from the depths of his mind. "Aha, yes...so lung ago, I woss yoss a chile, a lido, skeeny chile, no?" (For he spoke Spanish with such an accent as if he were from Nigeria, though he was white as an *akwa*, an egg.)

"And de woss this two brothass in my town...names? Taíta and Mabongo." The *Santero* leaned over to Silvia and whispered loudly, for show. "Taíta would giff me de essssstra meat when I wen to de market," and he smiled widely again, touching his heart with one hand and pointing up with the other, "*Babalu Aye*. Ah, yes, so dis men, de boochass, Taíta and Mabongo, dey woss de boochass in de market, and Taíta woss mah friend, he would giff me de meat! An one ting bout dem bot', woss dat dey bot' weren't having de first too fingez of de lef hans, ah?" The man raised a left hand and pulled down the index and middle finger. "Missin dem." Melva whispered to Jenny wit—

"*Ah-ah-ah!* Let Burufinda tell de storee!" and he laughed a long time before continuing. He turned back to face Miss Silvia and Doña Ofelia.

"Ah, yes, so dis men, dey were bof havin de fingez missin on deh lef hans, and you know what? Taíta, he woss mah friend, and he tol me wot woss hapnin fo dem to *bot* bee dis weh, with the same fingez missing *mmmhmmmm!*" and he stood up straight once again, his wild eyes dancing within deep, hollow sockets, to and fro, up and around. "An Taíta tol me wot is hapnin, an it woss dat Mabongo lung lung time ago, he bring de *machete* down on his fingez of de lef hans when he woss cutting de lamshonks." Silvia spoke.

"The *what?*"

"De *Laaaamshonks.*" Jenny laughed out loud: "*lamb shanks, nineteen-seventy-late!*"

"Yes, yes," he said, "so dis one, Mabongo, he hat loss his two fingez in de market, and to his soprise, the company gifft him lots of money! Lots of lots of money comin in to Mabongo! Money fo de injury at work, money fo Mabongo, and Mabongo wass ok, he could still cottin the meats, and he didn't needs all the fingez for it, so he woss happy an rich now, wit dis money."

"Time pass, and Taíta woss comin' roun low on the money, deh poor-man problemz, of course, what you essspec' in Cuba?" and he smirked. "Effffryone haff de poor man's problemz in Cuba," and the smile returned once again, "but Taíta," he said, with a happy inflection, "he woss havin de plans..." and Burufinda laughed to himself before continuing once more.

"Mah brotha, mah brotha, Mabongo! said Taíta as he ronnin in one mornin. 'I nid you to do me some good favors todeh,' and Mabongo says 'of course, Taíta, you are my brothas, an I am always hoppy to do you de favors.' *Taíta smile.* 'Ah, yes,' he said, 'I wan you take the *machete* an I gwaan put my *hans* down on the wooden cutting board, and you will be *cottin* mah two *fingez* off de lef hansss, like you was havin on de lamshonks, yes?' But Mabongo looked at Taíta like he woss met, like he woss cresee. 'Mah brotha Taíta,' he said, 'you dun haff to do dis, I am hoppy with mah six fingez and two thoms, I am not jealous, but Mabongo is hoppy dat you honor yo brothas so, my good brothas Taíta."

"No, no, Mabongo, it is nut dis, but now you mek me fil bad. I am haffin de poor-man problemz an I nid de money, like you, I dun need all the fingez like you, Mabongo, so I am puttin my hans on de wooden cutting board, and you are choppin off mah fingez on de lef hans like your on de lamshonks, so I collec de money too."*

"Mabongo grabb Taíta with hiss six fingez an his two thoms round de sholdass, an he look him right in de eye and he say, 'Taíta! You—are—craaaaaayseeee! I am *nnnnut* gwaan do dis to ma'own brotha, undastan?' but Taíta woss de little brotha an he woss annoyin all de life to Mabongo an he *whine* and *whine* an finally Mabongo say 'ok ok Taíta, puttin de hans de on de wooden cuttin board an I will cut off yo fingez like mine on de lamshonks so you are collec' de money an no more havin the poor-man problemz, ok?' and Taíta smile wide, wide smilin eyes wit dem huppiness." Burufinda smiled just like Taíta would have, but not even he noticed this.

"Hmmm....so Mabongo grab de *machete, long and black* — " Silvia tensed with wide eyes — "an he lif it op op op into de eh, an he say 'ok on tree, ah?' an Taíta say 'wait, wait, you are droppin on tree, o tree an *den* de cuttin de fingez?' Mabongo sigh an say on tree, Taíta, on tree I am droppin it, wan too tree and *tak!* Iss ooooovah."

"Ok Mabongo, he say and he tek a dip breath," and Burufinda leaned over toward Silvia once again, for show: "he woss haffin lots o dem feers, ah Silvia? Scared dem, Taita woss." Silvia pursed her lips to Burufinda's laughter.

"So Mabongo...he count loud dem loud to tree an he say 'WAN...TOO...TR—' but Taíta *tek* hiss hans way from de wooden cuttin board an he laff loudly dem, 'WAAAAAAAAA! HAHAHA o Mabongo I am sorry, so sorry ok one more time, I am haff the feers, ok?'"

"Ok, Taíta, I dun haff all deh, I gotta get de meets ready for de pipol. Yes, yes, so he raisin the *machete* op op op in de eh once more time an he say, 'Ok Taíta you reddi?' an Taíta say, 'Ok Mabongo, I am de reddi,' and Mabongo counted, 'WAN...TOO!' and *tak!* He cotted the fingez off on TWO!" The skinny old *Santero* fell back into his counter with laughter. Melva, white as an egg, held her hands up to her mouth in angst, and Jenny laughed like the girl she didn't let anyone else know she was, her smile large

and awkward, deliciously real. Silvia, Silvia simply shook her
head with a tight grin she pulled back on with all her might as she
bore into the Santero's laughter with her eyes.

"So den the two off dem are havin de same fingez missin,
an bof dem say were from the lamshonks, so de buss? De buss
dun buy no mo' lamshonks!" and Burufinda fell back once again
reeling with laughter. "I like dem lamshonks...Taita giff em to
Burufinda fo free..." he sighed nostalgically. "Ah yes, ah yes,"
and he rubbed his stomach as he propped himself behind the
counter once again.

"*Orisha* teach de lesson, ah? Fire done, 'ccept de burn," he
said, his smile fading. "If you back up fo tree, Orisha *tak-tak* an de
too! An you still loosin de fingez, cos you call Orishas—" and his
eyes went dark with foreboding—"an dey no *wesssss* de tayme,
like Mabongo." His eyes narrowed further: "*Meeees Seelvya!*"
screamed the man, "*Follow tru o tak-tak on two! Orisha kind—you
assss...dem ansah, see dem? No playin wit fayah, only maferefún
Eleggúa play,*" and his smile disappeared, "*dun waste 'isss time.*"
Jenny and Melva wore faces of confusion, but Silvia stared deeply
into his eyes with stone cold crystals of emerald fire.

"*Gracias,*" she said curtly. She walked outside, giving a
particular nod of thanks to Doña Ofelia before stepping out the
door, and the little bell jingled as she did so. Burufinda reminded
Jenny and Melva of what to do, giving the bag a good pat before
sending them off. It was Melva who cried out. They smiled their
hesitant goodbyes to each other as Doña Ofelia retired once again
to the place behind her curtain of beads, which clung to her
turban as she passed through.

"It has been done," she smiled to the conch shell on her
shelf. "Just as you said, *Laroye,* you sent her to me, and I have
done my part." The sun broke through the clouds: "Customers,"
she smiled out loud.

Silvia lit a cigarette in silence by the car, fumbling with the
vial in her pocket as she stared into the sudden light of the mid-

day. "Fucking birds," she said, looking to the mess on the ground.

~*~

The brakes whined as Chiche pulled the van with the happy-vacuum cleaner on it to a stop. Checked his clipboard. "*Llego...el manizero.*" Tss. It was a typical house, yellow in color with white trim, though it could have used a little touch here or there. A typical house. It had playground-fencing around it, three feet tall, keeping the weedy lawn from the sidewalk as if doing it a favor. An avocado tree bore ripe fruits from one corner of the yard, dozens of bumpy, black breasts swaying gently in the morning. Chiche grew jealous. Why didn't *his* avocado trees ever grow breasts? For years, *years* he had been through the same hoops: he would eat a ripe, buttery avocado and feel so inspired that he would make Silvia fish the pit out of the garbage and wash it off. He'd take the clean pit, give it a kiss and put it in a glass of water, praying to Mary, Jesus, San Lazaro, God, *anyone*, to let this be the one. After a few days it would crack open, a touching display of natural wonder, and a thick, white tentacle would grow out of the avocado pit, reaching blindly into the water like a newborn nymph. Chiche would rejoice and head out to the garden after consulting his brother Cuco (who grew the *best* avocados in Miami, swear to God!) and plant the seed accordingly, making sure to do everything right, planting it the right *depth*, giving it good *water*, but not too *much*, and '*lots* of sun, Chiche, *lots* of sun!' He added, of course, all the necessary fertilizer that it needed — one time he had used miracle-gro, one time a husk of corn and leftover fish from a show he had seen about thanksgiving, and just this last time a frothy tea given to him by a neighbor who practiced *Santeria* and said to douse the potting hole with it and blow on the seed three times before covering it with dirt.

The plants all grew! But they were just plants. Just *señoritas,* never the robust *Doñas* that had ripened and matured into regal women with their seductive and delightful fruits, *aching* to be picked. No, never. They always sat there in the soil, drinking water with their lanky roots and eating the sun for free like they were on *'El Plan Ocho'*. There was *one,* however, that had excited Chiche beyond belief. Imagine, just *imagine, imaginate!* that after so many failures, so many years of desperation and masculine integrity on the line, one of your avocado trees should suddenly sprout little buds the size of olive pits. How would you feel? Would you be excited enough to throw a party? Well, Chiche was.

He invited all of his family and friends over, but made the unfortunate mistake of letting the neighbor, who was a gossip anyway, invite the old lady who lived on the other side of the fence along as well. She, of course, insisted on bringing her new *'boy-freng'* Rafaelito along too. *Rafaelito*...was fresh off the boat from Cuba and had *mal de ojo* like it was high-noon-halfway-to-La-Habana. But no one knew that...Silvia can still recall the hot tingles up and down her arms and across her brow when she saw him in the doorway, his eyes piercingly bold, mysteriously dark, lined with ashy rings and thick, red lids easily mistaken for a drinking problem. He entered through the doorway, ominous, forever clenching his teeth, with his old white girlfriend from the keys: "and they were both strangers!" Chiche still yelled to Silvia when telling the story. She reminded him that frankly, she had nothing to do with the decision. It was the neighbor who *Chiche* had decided to invite to his avocado party, but somehow it was still Silvia's fault...for letting them through the door, for greeting him with hospitality, for not telling Chiche she had felt the tingles all about her. She told him that 'oh yeah? well he gave her the same shit, so get the fuck out of here,' and that was usually the end of the story. But there was more...there's always more to a story. That's *chisme* law #3.

In came these...*distinguished* guests, and as the couple was
being taken to the backyard where the plant was, the guy says,
"*Ay* Silvia, what a marvelous vase, my mother had one just like it
in El Santo," gesturing to a blue crystal piece in the living room
that indeed, Silvia's mother had left her when she died years ago.
The next day *Yennifer* knocked it over dancing to Jamaican music,
and it shattered. He moved on, and before reaching the backyard
he took a deep whiff and said, "*Madre de mis hijos!* Are those
garbanzos that I smell, *Mama*?" And to this Silvia replied with a
smile, "*Pues si,* they are Chiche's favorite," and without thinking,
her head full of pride, she walked around the counter and pulled
the lid up off of the *caldero,* giving the new neighbors a good, long
look at the bubbling glories beneath a flash of steam that boomed
languidly up onto the ceiling. They were colored like the ripest
and most luscious shades of pumpkin and orange, warm, sensual
fruits bursting open to reveal their immaculately ripe flesh —
indeed, autumn incarnate. And the smell! They all took in some
of the plumes of steam from the bubbling *caldero* with closed,
smiling eyes and reveled in the aromas (Silvia reveling in the
compliments as well) before the lady of the house put the lid back
on and escorted the neighbors off to the backyard to join the party.

Now one can call it coincidence, but this household
certainly knew it was the evil eye, *mal de ojo,* for as Silvia put the
lid back on, some miserable corner of her apron caught on the
little knob of the burner and turned it up to high as they walked
off towards the backyard. By then, of course, most neighbors
knew about or at least had heard of Silvia's cooking, but of course,
no one knew why — that was a family secret, a mother's love.
Silvia's cooking was just about the only thing people knew about
her, besides the incident with *Timbita.* Imagine, then, *imagínate!*
the shame of running into the house to put out the smoking mess
that a *caldero* full of overflowing *Garbanzos* could make. She
looked upon them, her jaw trembling, *cllllenched,* seeing that the

whole bottom inch of the *potaje* was charred black and the rest of it tasted like smoke. She could have brushed it off and told everyone that the *Tocino* was extra-smoky this time around, but the biggest *rrrre-puta* of a neighbor had smelled the disaster and of course, had already *yelled* it across the yard in her nasally trill of a voice so that everyone at the party watched Silvia run off and tend to the mess. They would, of course, talk about it later over the phone while watching *novelas*. That was law #2.

"*Su pinnnnga.*"

As soon as Silvia and the neighbors had originally gone outside, however, which was before the *garbanzos* had burned and before the vase had broken—in other words, when all still seemed well—Silvia took them to Chiche, who had been keeping post by his beloved avocado tree with a drink in his hand. He stood proudly by the young tree, about seven feet tall with its little budding fruits, covered in tinsel that Chiche had brought out of the Christmas box. *Rafaelito* came up to Chiche and gave him a hearty pat on the back, shaking his hand. Upon seeing the tree he said, distinctly, mythically, poetically, so that all in the yard turned their heads to look:

"*Pero que mata mas liiiinnnnnda, carajo!*"

And what a beautiful tree it was. The tinsel fell right off. Chiche, not a superstitious man himself, bent down to pick it up, for it was *obvious* that this strange man, being the *guajiro* he was, had groped his beloved tree's tresses too roughly and the tinsel had simply lost its grip.

"*Si*, nice tree, Chiche," said Reynaldo, another neighbor, "I got two in the backyard, they've been giving fruit for ten years now, but that aint even half as long as my *guayabitas* have been goin, ah, Mari?" His wife turned from the circle of *chismes* on the other side of the yard:

"*Eehhhh?*" she said with a confused frown.

Chiche took a sip of his *Cuba Libre*. A perfectly green leaf fell from the tree, and Chiche swallowed his strong drink with a trite gulp, clenching his teeth.

"*Que va,*" he said to himself, pursing his lips. *Psshhh.* There's no way. *Cuba Libre,* and he took another sip. He became a believer the next morning.

Every single leaf had fallen off the tree, and the house smelled like burnt *Garbanzos*. Chiche went outside and, with tears in his eyes, caressed the supple buds of the once-burgeoning plant with his calloused fingertips, for they were the only thing that remained on the tree, save for the bark itself. They had dried out completely and looked now like those strange, coniferous little balls that one usually finds sitting amidst the dry bitterness of potpourri mixtures. He wiped his eyes and went inside once again, and Silvia gave him a hug—for he deserved it, the poor thing. He sobbed, he truly did, and hearing her father in such a dark place, Jennifer put down her new Major Lazer mix-tape and went to go see what was wrong.

Chiche gazed, through the haze of all those memories, upon the sweet curves of the avocados, taunting him with their robust health as they swung around one another in playful fun. And it wasn't even windy. *Goddammit.* With a couple of hesitant glances toward the front window of the house, he walked across the lawn and plucked one of the biggest ones off the tree. It was just a little smaller than a football, the American kind—'*claaaaase de aguacate!*' he thought to himself with a happy grimace. The ripe, mature beauty tucked under his arm, he tiptoed back to the van and set it down right next to the driver's seat—not only would he enjoy it with dinner sprinkled with a little olive oil and salt, but he would keep the pit and plant a new tree, he thought with a smile. It was time. He took a deep whiff of the morning air, his left nostril screeching with glee:

"Caaaaarajo! Que viva el triunfo. Y su puta
madre la necesidad."

He walked through the playground-fence gate once again,
up the cracked walkway painted over in a glossy red that was
missing patches as if people had ripped them off and taken them
home to their own. He rang the doorbell, gripping his black
duffel bag nervously. Nah, they didn't see me, relax, I can just
compliment the tree if they say anything. They'll buy the vacuum
and give me three more, *pssshhh*. But nothing happened. He
looked at the ringer: was it broken? He knocked. Shuffles from
inside — and *silence*. The faint whisper of a voice. Chiche could
feel the tension from the other side of the door. The woman, for
Chiche could tell by the steps, had walked up to the door and seen
that it was a stranger, deciding to wait it out with an eye stuck to
the little lens in the door. Experience is the best teacher. It was
worse, he mused, shameless even, when they looked through the
window and then did it. It was a game, though, and they always
had the winning hand...what could he do? Nothing, he'd won
this game many times as well, opening the door minutes later to
find a copy of *Watchtower* rolled up in the door-handle.
Something in his gut told him he would vanquish this woman,
however. That, or he had taken his *café* too quickly. He prayed
for the first. *San Lazaro, coño meng...*

He knocked once more, right where he imagined the
woman's face would have been — he caught it out of the corner of
his eye. A little kid in the window, the curtain had moved and the
little head had popped in and out, but no one was too fast for
Chiche, not even a little *culicaga'o* whose heart beat to reggaeton.
Now was the time to work the shame, for he knew that the
woman, her eye leaned up against the little lens in the door, had
seen him look at the kid in the window. He shook his head a little
and...three, two, o — *"Salllla'o, largese de aqui!"*
And the door swung open. *'Victoria.'*

"*Buenos días, Señora* – " and he looked to the clipboard – "*del Socorro. Señora del Socorro, Orestes Campos, como estas.*" He slipped his foot in the crack of the door.

"*Bien, bien,*" said the woman, "how may...I help you?" She looked like she would have been very young and beautiful if she weren't so sad. It hung from her eyes like a burden she thought she was hiding.

"*Bueno, Señora,* I was recommended to come talk to you about my services, my product, the *Huracán* vacuum-cleaner. May I come in?" Chiche employed a technique he had learned at the office every time he asked this question. He looked deep into her eyes, grabbing hold of the very decision-making cells in her brain and twisting them into a nod. He had noticed, though, that it only worked if the person was particularly susceptible. Like hypnosis, and timeshare presentations.

"*Bueno...entre porfavor,* I don't have much time, but I'll listen for a little bit, I actually need one." *Ay,* admitting defeat from the beginning! Chiche's asshole seized with glee. She opened the door and her little son scurried off from behind her legs. "*Mi vacuum* (which she pronounced *bAH-kyoong*, as did Chiche) actually broke just the other day, *será el destino.*" It must be destiny. He stepped inside with his duffel bag, a little sad at how easy this would be, and let the woman show him to the living room.

The walk there was short but very interesting. The house was full of pictures of the family: the father, a robust Cuban man with streaks of grey in his hair and a wide jaw. The mother, this very woman, much happier in the pictures, smiling even. And the child was different in each one, for so were children in pictures: growing from baby *guayaberas* and *azabaches* to sunglasses, silver and Mami's hairspray. The house was quite clean for a home with children, but more because it seemed as though things went untouched. They looked dusty, but without any dust. The cabinets held all sorts of dishes and china, but the woman was so unkempt, so defeated and undone in her little white nightgown, that she looked as if the house were drowning her.

"*Ay sientate, mira aqui esta el sofa.*" He sat on the furthest edge of the velvety green couch. Chiche felt bad that she was letting him in so easily. He felt no resistance from her. Usually the clients were so *skeptical*, it was as if you were convincing them to buy swampland. But it was always the 'clincher', the peak moment of his demo that got them to buy into the joy of the *Huracán*. This was the part where he took their old vacuum cleaner and turned it on, dusty devil that it was, holding the flashlight up to it so the people could see the dust just *billowing* out of the old burlap sacks of uselessness they were convincing themselves they had been cleaning their houses with. *Mmhmm*...from there they'd always at least think about the superior product. It worked well, that move. All the salesmen in town used it. He would see the shift in the clients' eyes, that shift from skepticism and business-defensive to interest, an hazy ripple of a *need* for what he had in their eyes, a need to be rid of inferiority...his was the superior product, the *Huracán*. But this lady, del Socorro, she didn't have that skepticism. He probably could have sold her the thing at the door.

The kid walked back into the room, a backwards baseball cap on his head. He had a bright orange toy gun in his hand, and though he looked timid and scared, he snapped into cop-pose and shot Chiche repeatedly in the face with little bursts of air. Thank God he had lost all the little sticky-darts already. He smiled at the kid, who growled at him and kept shooting until his mother shooed him off with embarrassed laughter and a platter with two cups of *café*.

"*Ay, perdon, ya haz de saber como son los niños,*"

"*Que si se?*" he scoffed. "*Si te digo que tengo tres, y me han deja'o calbo los cabrones.*"

The woman laughed, pulling a tuft of hair behind her ear. Why would she hide a smile like that? He took a demitasse triumphantly between his thumb and forefinger, killing the *buchito* in one flick of the wrist. She laughed again.

"What is it, did I forget to toast?" asked Chiche with a coy smile.

"My husband always used to do that. He'd make the same sound as you did, too."

"Ay, I'm sorry about that, I've always taken *café* like my grandfa—oh, he used to...?" and the dust in the house echoed into the reality of what he had just walked into. In the flash of an instant, he saw the vacuum cleaner fly up and away back into his van. The woman pursed her lips, shaking her head as she looked to the floor, her eyes welling with tears. Chiche screamed a loud, prolonged '*Coooñoooooo!*' in his thoughts.

"Martin...is dead." She bit her lip. "But don't let that get in the way, you're trying to sell me something, go on." She wiped at her eyes with the hem of her nightgown, bending forward on the seat so a hint of her thighs showed as she daubed at her tears. Chiche's mind went into dissonant conflict—the guy's *dead, por Dios!*

"Well," he ventured, "as you may know, your friend Amaury Marchena recommended that you listen to this short presentation after he himself bought one of our famous *Huracán* va—"

"Amaury was *his* friend!" wailed the woman. "*His* friend!" She broke into tears, and the rubber band in her hair slipped off, letting her dark hair fall over her hunched frame like a dark veil. Chiche, who had his hand halfway into the bag to pull out the first diagram, let the laminated page go and sat back up in his seat. *Goddammit*. He drew in a long breath. Thinking of all the better places he could be, he remembered what the woman had said about destiny and reached out, patting her on the back softly. It evoked a fatherly sensation, and he made the *tss* noise with his mouth as he looked to the wall hopelessly, apologizing to the picture of Martin. The kid appeared in the doorway. Chiche turned his head and the kid shot him a couple more times, disappearing after his mom sat back up with a scowl. The woman threw her veil back over her head and pulled it into a bun once again, clearing her stuffy nose as she breathed deeply, taking her *café* from the tray.

"I'm sorry. It's just that you remind me of him, that's all. I was fine until now." *Mmhmmm*...Chiche looked to a picture on the wall and took the hair off the guy's head.

"*Coño*, you're right," he laughed. " A little bit. But he kept the hair." He cleared his throat. "But *mija*, really, I'm not here to make you suffer, I can leave if you want, I've got plenty more houses to make it to before I go home to my lunch..."

"*No, no, Señor,* please stay, I am interested in hearing *why* this vacuum is so good, I mean, why *this* one? Why did Amaury buy it?" Chiche felt the yearning in her words, and it made him feel so terribly sad. Wanted. No one, *no one* had ever wanted to have the thing sold to them—but she wanted *him*. He thought of the kids, of Yennifer and Tico, Mariza, Cuca, Silvia...of the crying *dama* right next to him...he couldn't. But he didn't move.

Chiche smiled and said, "*Ok, bueno.* Let's see, where were we...Amaury, *mmhmm...si,* so the reason he bought one was because of the demonstration I showed him with his old vacuum," and Chiche went on to explain the 'clincher' right off the bat to get this woman to agree so he could leave. This place was making him feel very strange. He explained it to her, and she feigned interest behind those tired eyes that didn't leave his gaze and asked to see what the vacuum itself looked like, if it was easy to use. Chiche started to swallow frequently. Finally, as he ran the model over the floor tiles as if cleaning with it (which he hadn't truly done once in his life), the woman broke into painful laughter and shook her head in disbelief.

"You know, I'm sorry. I've been a mess here in front of you, but *coño*, you just remind me of him so *much*, and he hasn't even been gone for over a year. It seems like just this morning he left for work that...last time." She looked at the picture of the three of them on the wall. "We had been arguing the whole night before, he left this world at odds with me, Orestes, we were mad at each other," and she broke into sobs once again. Chiche kept vacuuming, as if it would suck up the heaviness in the air as well. After a few seconds he turned it off, sitting back down and looking her in the eyes.

They were two roses wilting in an icy bank of snow, strewn across the hopes we keep from the rest of the world. If you can die before your dreams, this is what we pray. Chiche swallowed, moving to rub her back once again. She scooted closer to him, leaning against his side.

"He and I," she crooned behind sobs, "we would always fight, over *tonterias*, stupid things like why the light bill was higher this month than last month, or whether we were going to church or not on Sunday, where we would go and eat after leaving *Martin-yoonior* with the neighbor...and then we wouldn't even go!" She pulled at her hair. "*Ayyyy*....we would even fight because we didn't want to fight in front of *el niño* and show him how messed up our marriage was, but it was too late. Our whole marriage was one big *fight*." She took a deep breath and looked up to the ceiling.

"Whose parents would we go eat with on Christmas Eve?" she said, more to herself than Chiche. She stuck a hand out at the wall, as if arguing: "Whose parents would pay for the wedding? He had money when we were dating — *right?* But as soon as I got pregnant with *Martin-yoonior*, things changed, he got cheap, started to complain about the bills." Chiche shrugged, swallowing with a nod. He saw a flash in the window — a bee tapped twice on the glass and flew away.

"But you know what, Mr. Campos? I loved him. That's why we fought so much, I think, because we loved each other, and we wanted to make it work. I wouldn't argue with someone I didn't love...we could have gone and gotten divorced, but we wanted to stay together for the house, for *Martin-yoonior*..." And she pursed her lips hopelessly, "for each other. We...just didn't know how to move on, that's what it was, two Cuban opinions—"

"A cock fight," rang Chiche—

"but he would never listen, he wou—*ay, coño!*—I would have killed him before that damned bus!" She wrenched her *bata* between her fist, spotted with more and more of her tears. "But God...*el destino*, whatever you want to call it, got to him first, got to *me* first. To the both of us. Perhaps he would have realized the same thing if *I* would have gotten in that horrible accident." She frowned at the wall. "It should have been me. Look at this," she said, gesturing over herself. "I'm a mess. He would've been like this, and I would've been the one smiling in the pictures, free from all this pain," she sobbed.

"*Ay*, I know he feels the same way up there where he is, the only difference is that death took him somewhere else. I'm still just here, in Miami, *con calles de oro*." She played with the hem of her *bata*. "I hated my life...and now I miss it, Orestes. I miss him—*coño, Martin!*" she yelled at the picture with tears in her eyes, her arms trembling with tension. "I'm sorry...you don't have to listen to this, I just don't have anyone to listen."

"*Mi amor*, that's what we're here for. Forget the vacuums," he smiled to her, and rubbed her back again. Her eyes smiled brightly behind their veil of tears, and she plopped her head onto his shoulder, sighing a long, comfortable sigh. He looked, wide-eyed, at the picture of Martin, shaking his head— "*Coño meng*, I didn't do it!"

"I just..." she said, pulling up off of his shoulder, "I just wish I had another day, just one more day with him, to set things straight, Orestes. That's all it would take. *Otro día*. To say goodbye. Then he could go back to his new home, and I would feel clear." Chiche nodded in reflective silence. *Tss*. His father had told him long ago that women sometimes needed this, to just talk and that's it—so he nodded and waited. She raised her eyes, puffy and red, into Chiche's, and there she was met with that childish innocence he couldn't put away, not even for a moment of grief. She laughed.

"*Ay*, Orestes, I'm sorry to have put you through this. Just give me one of those vacuums, *dale*. You've got other customers to get to, I know." Chiche reached for the bag with a trite, refreshing breath he felt press against his gut. His father also told him never to let emotions get in the way of business. Sra. del Scorro walked into the kitchen with the tray of *café* and Chiche listened to her dig through her purse, click a pen and write a check, ripping it out a little too quickly and walking back into the living room with a teary look of seduction on her face. She gave him his check, and he gestured towards the the vacuum, looking her in the eyes. He stood from his seat and placed a hand on her shoulder, to which she closed her eyes with a sigh.

"*Señorita*, look, I'm not a religious man, but I can say to you: talk to your husband, he'll hear you. I don't believe in all that stuff people talk about on TV, hotlines and all that, but I remember there was this lady in my home town who could look into a bowl of water and see the *muertos*, you know? In the reflection, like ghosts." Her pupils dilated. "People who had lost their loved ones would go and see her, and she would talk to them, speaking her loud, resounding words into the bowl where the little sparkles in the water would turn into the light in the spirits' eyes and they would answer her." Señora del Socorro smiled.

"And you know what they always said?" Chiche had a new glow in his eyes. "My mother told me this when my *Papi* died—saddest day of my life—she said that those dead people always said that they could hear everything their loved ones said to them, it was like they had all these voices in their head while trying to get through their business in the *Mas Allá*...but still, I'm sure they didn't mind those kind of interruptions—at least I wouldn't." Chiche smiled and touched a hand to the woman's cheek, stealing a tear. Her eyes went tenderly wide, and the toy gun went off again behind them both. They laughed—it was time to wrap things up.

"*Bueno mija*," Chiche said with a bob of his eyebrows, "I've got other people to sell *Huracánes* to" and he smiled—"lets hope they're all as nice as you were, ah?" He laughed. "*Pues si. Buenas tardes.*"

"Orestes," she said, taking his hand once more, "I've never felt so happy talking to anyone about my husband..." She looked into his eyes. "Your...phone number is on the business card," she said, biting her lip. "I might need another vacuum...?"

Chiche grinned bashfully, scratching his head. "*Coño, mi amor*, that sure makes me feel special," and he laughed, squeezing her hand. "You see, though," and he pulled away from her, raising his eyebrows, "the thing is...my husband gets really jealous when I see other people...even women."* Chiche's *muertos* fell back onto the floor behind him, rolling with laughter.

"*Ay*," she said, blushing with confusion. "I see, I'm...I'm sorry, never mind." She shook her head, laughing to herself bashfully. "*Bueno, se lo agradesco. Muchisimas gracias*, now I can vacuum *Martin-yoonior's* mess..." He took her hand into his, and pulled it up to his face, giving it a light kiss.

"Destiny brought us together, and now it keeps us on our way." She grabbed him by the collar, pulling him inches from her face—"Oye, oye, muchachita!" laughed Chiche, grabbing her wrists and pulling them down to their hearts, where he squeezed her hands, holding her gaze for a few seconds of silence. Their eyes finished the conversation. She saw him to the door, and he scowled at the avocado tree as he walked back through the yard and into his van. The interior smelled like scented chemicals and avocado since the gigantic fruit had been baking in his supply-ridden car for quite a while now. He turned it on and drove off, waving goodbye to *la viuda del Socorro*, that poor widow, as he drove away. Once off her street, he hooted out his open window,

shouting *"Maricón! Todavia te queda! Todavia te queda!"* and he
laughed at himself all the way to the next house on his clipboard.

    "Coñññño!" he screamed, slamming on the brakes.
      A car blew around him—*"comepinnnnga!"*
        He had forgotten to get addresses from her.

    He thought of going back, of ringing the doorbell before
ravishing her avocado tree with all the juices he had left in him,
kicking the kid out to the neighbor's for a cup of *melao*. But he
pulled over, scribbling down a few addresses onto the tally sheet
and kept to his business. It was futile—he already had a wife to
come home to, 'and we've got plenty of days to figure it all out.'
"Martin," he said into the air, "your wife's a marvelous creature."
He gripped the avocado. "But mine's got *sazón, mi hermano!* She
wouldn't need a God-sent bus to get rid of me." He kissed the
fruit, pulling out from the curb. It was time to go home for lunch.

~*~

Como sirenas en el mar,
Llamando los marineros con
Sus dulces canciones,

Se estallan los inocentes
Sobre las piedras de
Indiferencias humanas,

Promesas sin fondo;
Se ahogan los marineros
Muriendo en lamentos por creer

Las dulsuras de esas caprichosas
Cantando a la orilla del mar;
Nos llaman con serenatas de belleza,

Veneno rodeado de miel
Y yo, un pobre marinero de esta vida,
Oigo las canciones para dartelas a ti.

~*~

Now sit, children, iss time for da lec'ture o de day:
Too Much Coffee(house)

"*Mi amorrrrr!*" yelled Tico from behind his booth,
bordered by the finest mahogany. Angelica turned from her
conversation with a group of women she had just met by the
crescent-moon bar — they were passing through from Colombia.
Tico, his arms up in the air, stood out from the plush
surroundings...*white petals on a dark, black bar.* Angelica raised an
eyebrow:

'*Que quieres,*' she said with her eyes.

The coffeehouse, *le Croissant Fécond,*
was full of old ship-rigging and paintings of *la Fée Verte,*
reminiscent of the Absinthe-tinged days when writing was still
considered prolific. Belle epoch, in the *belle aujourd'hui.*
Surrounded by booming banyan trees and idyllic statuary, they
could've been no place but Coral Gables. "*Y estas seis lindas*
Cubanas?" he sang across the room. And these six lovely
Cubanas? "I've yet the pleasure of meeting them, and yet I know
their names already —" he raised a hand to each of them — "*Pinar*
del Rio, La Habana, Matanzas y Santa Clara, tu ves?!" They smiled,
raising their eyebrows one by one. He winked at the last two*:
"*Cuando llego a Camagüey, Oriente me llama!*" Only Angelica knew
it was an old Cuban song he had quoted. Supper-clubs and
casinos, that's what one would find in Tico's brown paper
packages tied up with string. That, and temples found in
Kabbalistic dreams. She rolled her eyes as they walked over
towards his booth.

"These ladies *I've* had the pleasure of just meeting are from my hometown—"

"The beautiful Cartagena!" chimed the shortest one. Tico felt that familiar Colombian fire in all of their eyes. Hot, bottomless cups of coffee. He bid them sit down. *Mind...your lusts, o initiate of the seven lights. The Venerable Masters purvey in silence.*

"*Ay, claro que si,*" he said out loud, to himself—"*Bueno,* let me at least fill your cups then, *amores,* no? Who, I say, *who* rivals the people of Cuba in their love for *café,* if not the mountainous blossoms of *Colombia*?" He smiled, rising to his feet: "*Ay, café, café, cafetero! Dulce diosa bujanguera,* sweet nectar of creativity! Bless us all with inspiration, o Lady of the Deep Brown Eyes!" He ran his hand along the length of the booth, crooning, "O Anael, surrounded by your love I am! Watch me pass through the fire unscathed," and he left the ladies with looks of confusion on their faces, dancing off to the barista's dwelling where a hip, dreadlocked youngster bobbed his head to the reggae music that played in the background. He made faces at himself as he wiped the silver tusks of the steamers clean:

"*cuz-a-reggae music*
is-a-ghetto music
an-a-ghetto music
is-a-rebel music
say reggae!"

"*Oye, oye, Toots-I,* prepare for me no less than seven mochas, and another *espresso* for the one who will pay for it all!" The kid turned his head and looked Tico inattentively in the eyes for a good three seconds before raising his eyebrows and smiling: "*Jah seh! Roff-a-roff-a-reggae!*"

"That kid," muttered Tico as he walked back to his booth. "Talk about a dub-plate."

"*Dob- pleeeeeuht!,*" sang the barista, "*a-reggae staaayl!*"

It was one of many booths along that far wall, this one, large and velvety with red cushions that unfurled like a great seashell and ferried the immaculate Goddess Aphrodite across the frothy surf and to the shore in a resplendent aura of light...just perfect for this terpsichorean bullshitter, no?

"Quite," he nodded to himself. He may have had a condo with an ocean view, 'but this', he smiled to himself, glowing over the scene, 'this is my home. The place where visions turn to ink.' He picked up the paper he had been scribbling across for hours now, frowning at the flower who had begun to look it over as they waited for their coffee. He copied its contents onto another sheet, clean as could be. "Excellent." He caught the girl looking again and stuffed the paper into the pocket behind his lapel.

"Hmph."

At that precise moment the dreadlock-barista shouted, *"Far-I an-I say Rasta vah-breee-shan make-a-dem perco-leeeeeshan, seven mocha-an-a-coladah-Koo-bana, bambo klaat!"* The Colombians eyed each other in a mixture of horror and confusion. Tico stood and fetched their drinks, set neatly on a silver-plated tray, carrying them to the table where unbeknownst to him, the Colombian women had immediately begun gossiping about him with Angelica: he looks just like Simón Bolívar, come on you know that's why you snagged him, did he pursue you or did he **giggle** come to you, does he have any brothers, cousins — like-minded colleagues...? — and his hair, did you see how he brushes it back with a hand deep in thought, it's so sexy, did you see how he took that paper from Rosalinda, he's so sic-retive! Ay, those man are my favor —

"Selaaaasie-I!" sang the barista at the tip in the jar. He'd just noticed.

Tico smiled as he set the tray down, eyeing the ladies one

by one, brushing his white suit off with an air of suave that made the Colombians buzz with desire. He saw it immediately in their widening pupils, and pounced on the opportunity — *watch me, Anael, watch me pass through unscathed.*

"Would my seven Colombian beauties like to listen to the latest of my inspirations?" He kissed the flower on his lapel. "I've written a poem," he said stoically, suffering, starved. Smiling. The women gasped and crooned in each others' arms, and Tico looked deeply into Angelica's eyes, assuring his *muñeca* that there was nothing to worry about, he was just having fun — but those two bottomless cups of coffee burned with all sorts of things, charred grounds and smoky notes of cedar-wood, but amongst them was that fierce love that they shared, the boiling water that pulls the essence out of all things put to fire and brewery. She wanted to kiss him then and there, to slap him, bite him until he bled, in bed, in front of these women, surrounded by all of them! But she calmed herself, beckoned him fetch the poem as she felt her breath slide past her nostrils, and sat back in her chair, calm once again, throwing her arm around the girl to her left. *Two can play at this game, chichipato...*

He gently reached into the lapel of his coat and pulled out the paper that he had stolen from the eyes of sweet Rosalinda. The ladies smiled to each other, nipping at the whipped cream set atop their mochas, adorned with the slightest sprinkle of bittersweet chocolate flakes, commenting excitedly on how nice this Tico was as to buy them all drinks. And he *did* look like Simón Bolivar.

Little did they know that Tico bought *everyone* he met at *le Croissant Fécond* a drink: it was his custom, for he knew the secrets of merit and charity. And so he brushed a hand over the paper he held in his other hand and cleared his throat, saying, "This poem, like all of my inspirations, is dedicated to my beauty, my pearl of the Antilles, the beloved Angelica." The six Colombian flowers cooed her as the muses like to beseech Athene, reminding her always of her brilliant eyes. Tico cleared his throat and began:

"I call this the Perfumed Garden.

>Full of grace,
>An idyllic playground
>Found in the midst of
>Marvelous worlds all around

>The sweet garden
>Flowing with nectar and
>Blissfully delightful ambrosia,
>A perfumed garden of Romance
>Under the smile of a jasmine moon
>Where Gods sport and recite and
>Lovers find themselves —

>Making offerings to
>The sacred fire of Love

>Dressing Her with garlands of affection
>Invoking Her with the comforting warmth
>Of ineffable yearning, fulfillment
>From Her open palms

>The incense of sweet songs
>Lingers softly around
>The curl of love's tresses

>And the flickers of oil,
>Love's potent flame
>Lit in vocation
>To the heart of the Gods,
>Burning brightly in the garden
>Reaching always, up into the stars,
>Tendrils of awakening rain
>Upon everything in Grace

>The rites of the garden
>Romancing the stars

Aetheric vibrations
'Tween Venus and Mars

Colorful skies give in to the
Endless worship that these Lovers
Possess, infinite showers
Of virgin blossoms,
Lady petals
Upon the Lotus feet
Of the benevolent Goddess
Burning forever in all hearts:

The regal dove,
Ave Maria.

"Que poeta!" shouted the ladies playfully, boisterously, overly congratulatory. Tico didn't think it boisterous at all. *Mind...your head, you'll hit the ceiling.* Angelica said nothing, sending vibrations of praise to her beloved with her eyes. They had been practicing the lover's gaze for months now. He caught her gaze and fell back into his seat, feigning fatigue.

"Yes, yes, thank you, I wrote it just now before you came to listen." He stuffed the verse back into his coat. "I said it once, and I'll say it again, with all of you beauties of Bolivar's Colombia as my witnesses, that I am completely, hopelessly, *desssssperately* in love with this one, the Goddess with the Shining Eyes, Angelica, this effervescent work of art!" He looked to the ceiling: "All of ye souls, forlorn, lost, confounded and found, ye that seek the simple joys of happiness seek nothing less than the ray of love, the perfected magnetism of essence calling all back into blissful reunion!" And he pulled her out of her seat, slamming her into his chest with a deep kiss that merged all but the couple's individuality into its sensual locking of lips. The six beauties wailed with glee, their eyes turning circles, fanning themselves playfully and looking at each other as if they had made the right choice in stopping for a coffee at *le Croissant Fécond.*

"Your verses are inspired, but they are full of shit," said a voice from the corner. The muses fled the scene in horror, and Tico let Angelica go with a look of shock across his slender, poetic face. The Colombian beauties all turned toward the voice with jaws agape, their eyes wide and their tresses swinging to the left in a flurry of every color. The comment had come from a sallow man slumped over a paper cup of coffee, sitting at a little round table all alone.

"Why must I liiiive thiiiis liiiife aaaaloooone," sang the dreadlock-barista.

He took a sip, lifting his gaze to Tico. It was a challenge, a defiant weakness characteristic of all troubled souls and the rings around their eyes. His face hung from his skull, as if an atrophied smile had spread to the rest of his head. He wore a scruffy black peacoat covered in weeks of dingy life inundated with shadows and long-haired cats who didn't like company at all. The man set his cup back down threateningly, stained with running drops of coffee and a great splotch where his lips were. *A light touch of watercolor...across the thick paper of his cup. Remember that down, chap.* To the artsy types everything was art, even coffee stains. He wiped his nose and nodded with unflinching eyes, as if waiting, *begging,* for Tico's response. And hopefully it would be angry. *Troubled souls thrive on such things – but you must know that.*

"Well, thank you for listening, *querido ser,*" said Tico. "I always appreciate feedback. It *h-wwwets* the sword, you know." Angelica grabbed his hand reassuringly. *As if he would be provoked...come now, girl! He knows this is all a test! The Masters...purvey in silence.* "*Estimado Don Critico,* though I appreciate your criticisms, I must at least know your name in order to address your scathing commentary." *Scathing, a wonderful choice of words.* His gaze was focused. "I've never seen you here before, and I must come here more than the owner does. Tell me, then," said Tico, walking in his direction, "*what pains you so?*"

The man's pupils dilated. No one else noticed, but he had also choked on the sip he was swallowing. He tensed, holding coffee in the middle of his throat, rasping air down his throat and into his lungs so that he might clear his throat, swallow the coffee and answer. So much goes on behind steady, narrowed eyes. Tico heard him clear his throat, and the man swallowed, and then went to speak.

"*Ay, se trago un gargajo,*" said Rosalinda, turning away from the scene.

"Forgive me for having interrupted. Please go on with your poetry, impressing the ladies as you do so well, just don't mind me." Angelica shuddered at the cryptic rhetoric of this strange, shadowy man. The beauties sipped at their mochas, watching the confrontation as if at the movies.

"*Señor*, I insist, please do tell me what pains you, for though my verses may be full of shit, I am not. I wish to help you, if only just now and never again, for I can see the pain clearly in your eyes, and every gaze is a reflection of one's own." The man set his cup down on the table and looked even further into Tico's eyes.

"Get your goddamn flower out of my face or I'll...*ay*, I don't even care." He smiled. "That's my pain, I don't care. I await death." He said it like a challenge.

"You know not the perils of which you speak, my friend."

"Oh I know," he said with a glimmer in the shadow of his eye, "and this is why I haven't done it already, gone and thrown myself off a bridge, or taken death by too-much-opium and brandy, but instead I raise my hands to God—" and to this Tico's eyes went wide—"in anguish, for these circumstances I take upon myself have me shackled to the pangs of iniquity. *Thus* are the debts I find myself paying in this most horrible of lives."

"At least you are aware that you suffer debts, and not evil," said Tico cooly. "This is wise. And you speak like a poet."

He smiled. "This is beautiful. Tell me then, friend, what is your name?"

"I've read many things, and they've all shown me how miserable this world is, again and again. There's no way out, just consolations that numb the pain. People like to laugh and pretend everything is okay with their surroundings of quasi-opulence and external comforts, but I can not shake myself of the anguish present *everywhere*, for it accosts me without cessation." Tico's eyes softened.

"Good Sir, do you not see that everything is in the control of the Venerable Masters? There is a great force, bright like the Sun and dark like the back of the moon, that brings all good and evil into the world, balancing it out equally amongst those who deserve it, and so do good things come to the good, and bad to the bad, and vice versa to those in the midst of purgatory." Shaking his head, the man— "Purgatory is no waiting room—it's here now, the very fabric of circumstance. It can be the death of the noblest of men, the end of John the Baptist at the will of the treacherous Salome, who knew nothing but to have the other, in love or in death. To the yawning mouth of desire there is no end, and through such a mouth does time swallow us all whole—lest we act nobly, in harmony with the Way!"

"I'd like to go along with your metaphysical dribble, your banter and prattle," said the man, "but I can not help but think that any God who would let evil fall upon his children could be loving as well. If we are made by God, he is an *imp*—" *Oh, you winced!* "He spills the blood of his own children, and then washes it for us with the waters of reason and philosophical abstraction, letting us all go on our ignorant way, *consolations*, I tell you! This is precisely what I mean. The worst of us are the ones who buy *in* to this *shit*. Blood is thicker than water, as you poets like to say, no?" He smiled. "Well, then your God is a fucking tar pit."

"*Deeeumn nicka,*" said a girl into her cell phone, bursting through the door. "Sell that shit. *Yeah nicka, dat nicka jus got paid!*

Sayo. Dat. Shyit." She slapped her phone closed.

"Late ass bitches," she said to the Barista, poppin her eyes out.

"Treeeee minutes!" laughed the barista, *"Seeeeeeeriously easygoin."*

Tico turned away from the distraction, his jaw agape from the audacity of the past few seconds. "But my esteemed sir, cream is thicker than coffee, and yet it rises to the top. Act with your own heart, and you will see that the answers will come to you before the questions. The intellect is full of twists, turns and tall trees, tales and tribulations, and it is oh, *oh* so easy to get lost in such...*shadows. Such thickets."* Tico looked deeply at the man, who caught the insult without flinching. "The blade of the philosopher will be no use to you in this forest of life, of the mind, I've learned this already and my hair hasn't even begun to turn." He raised a hand to the sky. "Come, then, drink to the coming of tomorrow's Sun...and I don't mean that metaphorically, *Señor Nietzsche."* He smiled. "Times are changing for you, look at this very debaucle the universe has brought you, *hmm?"* The man did not look in the least bit pleased.

"And what is the blade of the philosopher?" he asked monotonously.

"It is," and he raised his eyebrows ominously: *"hhhh-why."* The man looked down, and slowly began to nod his head. The hint of a smile came across his face.

"Aha! It's been a while, ah?" laughed Tico. "Happy or sad, a smile is a smile, it's a much better blade to work with. One must be careful with philosophies born of the intellect and not the direct experience, they would turn a Socrates to Baudrillard. Now come, let me introduce you to these *seis lindas Cubanas,"* and he stood up, turning to face the women. Angelica cocked an eyebrow — *bringing him here?*

"They look Colombian," said the man from beneath a wrinkled brow.

"They are! Oh — never mind," laughed Tico. *"Ay, Mama,"* and he patted the guy on the back. *"Ay, Mama."*
  You rogue! And you'll even buy him a drink!

~*~

Cuco had fallen asleep on the couch, twelve red apple-cores at his side in a plastic bag from Solano's. It was a daily occurrence; he would eat six more before leaving for work, no lie. Seeing this, Melva's father Pito came over to the kitchen in his little blue sweatpants and a worn-out undershirt through which you could see his gold chains, his heavy *Santos* over a heart flanked by frail ribs. He had developed a cute little belly in his old age, though he had always been a skinny man, a city-dwelling *bodeguero* who made his bread socializing and selling everyone their *frijoles, papas y aji.* His cocoa was notorious, people would come from all over the province just to sit at his counter and drink the incomparable *chocolate*, together with his freshly-fried, sugar-coated *churros.* No, no, they were sugar-laden. *Y ya tu sabes lo que sigue — toma chocolate, paga lo que debes.* He extended a frail arm in Cuco's direction, and waving his hand about a few times, coughed as well. *Nada.* Coughed again — *Ahhhhhh-AK* — *"Se durmio,"* he whispered to Melva, chewing his lips with the unavoidable simper of one who has taken out his teeth. He's asleep, *se durmio.*

  "*Dale, dale!*" she said, a bit stressed. "It took long enough, and tonight of all nights." She looked her husband over, his jaw succumbing to the pull of gravity, slightly to the left. "He'll be awake soon — you know how he is."

  Pito bobbed his eyebrows: *"Dale."* Melva couldn't lie about feeling a little flustered. She had tried to defer the work until Friday, for she had yet to digest all that she had heard. She was still scared shitless by the pronouncements of the oracle, but her father wouldn't have it any other way — "Tonight. The lady even said so." She had, of course, told him the whole story upon

221

getting home—it was Pito who had recommended she go see an oracle to begin with. The thought of witchcraft hadn't even crossed her mind with Cuco's incessant diagnoses, pompous pronouncements made with the confidence of a typical Cuban bullshitter: *"Ponle' cuño que eso te paso por andad muy fre'ca con migo Meb-bita...pongle cebo, remedio Chino e infalible. Y te lo dije yo, pa'que te acued-de'."*

"Okay okay!" whispered Melva in a harsh tone. *"You* have to do this, ok? You know what to do with this...this *branch*." Pito walked up to her and set a hand upon his daughter's back, right behind her heart. He was smaller than her, more frail, weaker and more in need of her than she was of him, but truly, few things trumped a reassuring hand upon a daughter's back. Pito, to Melva's surprise, was very excited about all of this—it had been a while, but he still remembered what to do. Growing up in Cuba, he had learned quite a bit about spiritual work, if only by default. Pito had learned, as it were, from spending too many late nights visiting his brother Asiago, a self-proclaimed *curandero* who would help people with their 'spiritual needs', white or black.

He improvised half-baked rituals based upon what he had seen while trying to make his fortune in Pinar del Rio. El Pinar, where the guavas are the size of bonbons and sweeter still— *guayabitas del Pinar*, Castellano's drink of choice.* Asiago had left home in a huff after an argument with his family, taking things all-at-once as he did with everything—obsessively. Inspired by a story someone told him at Pito's *bodega* that afternoon at 3:08 PM about a woman named Panchita and a pair of sneakers from Korea, he packed his things and told Pito and the rest of the family to go to hell and that he would be back in a few months— when the money-making had peaked, plateaued. Panchita. Indeed, he returned just as he had prophesied, but for reasons he cited hastily as *'La Nueva Inquisicion Religiosa'*. This inquisition had only one victim, it turned out. After settling down and finding a job, Asiago floated around town and stumbled, one

fateful day, across the mysterious spectacle that had always made
the nape of his neck bristle with joy. A *Bembé*. It was December
3rd, the night before the feast day of Santa Barbara-Chango:

> *"Maferefún Arufina Chango,*
> *Santa Bab-bara Bendita!*
> *Nuestra oracion favorita,*
> *Con su'arina y kimbombó!"*

When engaged in rituals, especially those involving the
happy farm-animals, the *Santeros* kept to themselves behind
closed doors and frequent glances over the shoulder — Big Brother
was known as '*La Comité*' in Cuba, and would have everything to
with Chino's *prenda* wanting a bull for its birthday.

Bembés, however, were
a *celebration*, a conscious vibration of exaltation for the Cuban
spirit's collaboration toward harmonization, revelation, inner-
exploration and, of course, the hyper-amelioration of a broken
nation's spiritual desolation. Open to anyone who had the *Aché*
born of radiant, smiling ancestors...or to those who simply wanted
to *hechar un pie*. It was an open invitation to come and dance, to
give energy and anticipation to the powerful African rhythms that
could churn the aethers with the poly-rhythmic soul train of
intricate drumbeats carefully designed to be noticed from the high
heavens where the *Orishas* dwelt in wise, peaceful repose.

He went home that night unable to sleep.

Asiago frequented that stretch of town on every feast day
he could think of, finding every *Bembé* that he could — *Santo Niño
de Atocha, San Lazaro, San Francisco de Asís, La Santísima Virgen de
Regla* — and eventually, the *Babalawos* took notice of that same
sketchy face, wide-eyed with wonder and dancing awkwardly
amidst the *esqueletos rumberos* who would thrust their chests
forward and back, sinking down low into the hair-raising
Guaguancos that reverberated all through the *barrio*. They

whispered to each other softly from behind their beads, contemplating him to the shakes of their rattles and gourds, commenting on this stranger who was all but a stranger by then, and at the end of the ceremony they approached him, deciding to test his soul.

The officiating *Awo* of the ceremonies, Yamaloro Mapfumo, who had eyes so wise they were set in a perennial squint, asked Asiago with a mysterious smile if he would like to partake in a highly secretive ceremony that would end up taking the life of a woman so her barren sister could keep the twins. Asiago, *honored* at the prospect of working with such esteemed priests, nodded his head eagerly in response—"but I'm not yet initiated, I will leave the dirty work up to your auspicious demeanor."

Yamaloro Mapfumo set a hand on Asiago's shoulder and said, "I never want to see your face around here again, *oistes?*"

Shocked, disheartened, *cheated!* Asiago

went home,

his

tail

bet-

ween

his

legs.

He laid in bed until dawn, running over the exchange over and over again. And plans emerged. He stopped shaving, and with every passing day his neighbors saw his beard grow that much more, and soon it covered his face with bristly black hair, for Asiago had ancestors from Andalucia—*sangre gitana*. Together with a *pachanguita* he had bought at the store nearby, he looked like a completely new man, save for those beady, anxious eyes, itching ceaselessly for affirmation. The love of God. Looking himself in the mirror one Friday evening September the 7th, he gave himself a firm nod and

donned his jacket, walking across town to the *barrio* where the
Santeros were sure to be throwing their heaving *Bembé* for
Yemaya, *La Sannnnntísima Virgen de Regla* — it was time. And
indeed he found it with ease, for the earshot went out for an entire
mile.

'Yemayaeeeeeeeeeeee olodo awoyo Yemaya!'

he heard in the

distance, soul-shattering rhythms swaying in a regal three. "I can
assure you," Yamaloro Mapfumo said, fluffing an imaginary
beard under his chin, "that this is no place for *Judios*." Black
magicians and their evil spirits were — and are still — referred to
under the derogatory moniker of Jew. "I thought I told you never
to come back. No respect." Those squinting eyes had seen right
through him, through his beard, his intentions, his *pachanguita*.
Yamaloro Mapfumo then raised his voice and shouted, "*Mira el
Judio, bota el Judio!*" to the rhythms that were already steaming the
marrow in everyone's bones, and the rest of the assembled joined
in, spurning Asiago with that fitful cheer, "*Mira el Judio, eeee-aaa,
bota el Judio!*" Asiago ran off to his place,

his

tail

bet-

ween

his

legs.

He packed his things

and shaved his beard, leaving his *pachanguita* a crumpled heap at
the doorstep of his apartment. He had made his fortune. He
thought of Panchita and her sneakers all the way home. But the
stories, the stories he told of that trip, they would have you think
he was the foremost Babalawo in all of Cuba. And Pito was
always on the other side of the tall tales, sipping his *café* with ears
wide open. He thought of his brother, long-since dead, as he held
the branch of *Rompesaragüey* in the darkness of the kitchen,
reassured by Cuco's every snore.

Melva went to her bedroom, where San Lazaro stood in the corner with his crutches and his dogs, a bouquet of yellow roses bursting open aside him. A candle was lit next to the little *santo*, hobbling forever on his crutches and surrounded always by two starving street-dogs who would lick at his leprous wounds. *"San Lazaro, milagroso San Lazaro,"* she whispered as she opened the chifforobe and pulled out the paper bag with all her things for the *despojo.* *"Ayudame."* Help me. She sighed into the darkness, waddling on her swollen feet past the smiling image of *La Virgen* and into the backyard, where Pito waited for her in the darkest corner, contemplating the moon.

"I told you it was a good night, *mija.* Look at that moon. Come on, all this will be over after tonight. *Malditas,* I can't believe I have to clean up my own nieces' *brujeria.*"

"Doña Ofelia said they were *a pís o shyet.* And not to send them a cent."

"I told you before," he whispere—

"Ay Papi no empieses," snapped Melva. *"Dale,* the grass is wet."

She stood in the freezing grass, wet from the rain earlier that evening, and waited for Pito to clean her off with the crispy branch from the *botanica.* But nothing happened. She opened her eyes.

"What is it, come on, clean me off!"

"Bueno...I," and Pito gestured towards the paper bag, "It's not..." and he thought for a second...and then he winked.* "I know what we need." He disappeared for a minute, leaving Melva with nothing to do but pray. *"Ay San Lazaro, Ay Virgensita..."*

Pito showed up with a cigar in his mouth and a bottle of booze.

"That's what we need? A Goddamn party?"

"That's right.* A party." He set the bottle on the ground with a slow, groaning laugh and rubbed his hands together, reaching into the bag. He pulled the branch out, shaking it in the air before them. It unfurled from its compressed crescent shape, into a shaggy, shooshing bundle of leaves and twigs. It...it almost...*leered* at Melva.

"*Ay*, be careful, it's losing leaves."

"*Oye, no jodas*," smiled Pito from behind the cigar. "I just remembered some things." He laughed the same slow laugh again, making the branch shoosh in response. He lit his cigar, Melva looking back to see if Cuco would notice the sparks, and soon puffs of smoke rose into the night, black against the light of the moon. He whirled the cigar around, sticking the lit end into his mouth, and blew all around him, to his left and his right, and then firmly into the mess of sticks and leaves that was the leering branch of *Rompesaragüey*.

"Why did you blow it all around?" whispered Melva.

"It's for the ancestors...I think," he said, pulling the ember from his mouth. "*Pa' lo' mueddd-toh*." He winced, smoke in the eye.

"*Hmph*," she replied, looking to the branch. "Well tell them to hurry up."

"We're doin' jussss fine, *Meb-bita, mijita*," laughed Pito, unscrewing the lid from the bottle of booze. "*Dale dale Cachiiimbambooo...*" he sang to himself, tilting his head back for a long swig and *shhhhoosh!-ing* it onto the branch in a sparkling flurry:

"*Pfffffffffffff-FFFT!*"

"*Papi*, this becomes you, I've never seen you like this before," smiled Melva.

"I didn't say much, but I watched Asiago, I watched Asiago do his things." Carefully he turned the branch over, giving it more *tabaco* and another spurt of liquor, and only then, when he picked it up off the ground, dripping droplets of *aguardiente* that caught the light of the moon and trailing wisps of smoke behind it, did it look ready. The branch was *alive*. And it leered at Melva.

"Come on, stand up straight like I taught you when you were a girl. Company's coming over." Melva propped herself stiff and closed her eyes, hearing the branch rustle and snap all the way to her head, where Pito then brought it to the ground in one swift motion that *popped!* it onto the ground:

"SssssAH!" he winced —

"*Oye, coño,* not so loud!"

"Ay, Cuco sleeps for two hours, and *deep*," he said, grabbing her by the shoulder and spinning her around. The next ten seconds saw the world spinning for Melva, a dizziness surrounded by swirling streams of lunar orbs and icy drips of aguardiente all over, garden sheds and *pop!* after *pop!* after *pop!* in the ring of light made by the sparkling grass as she spun, spun, spun around.

"A-sssssssAH! *Llevatelo Mama!*" groaned Pito, shaking the branch terrible across Melva's feet. He slapped them, over and over again, beating the *brujeria* out of her poor, swollen feet. Propping himself back up right, he puffed triumphantly at the cigar as he caught his breath, his mouth in the unavoidable smile. He *shooshed* the branch between the both of them again, shaking off the rest of the liquor before cramming it into the bag. He tapped the cigar with his index finger, the ember burning brightly once again. And with that, the electricity dissipated.

"*Bueno...y ahora hay que...*" he raised the cigar back to his mouth. Now we've gotta...Melva's eyes went wide, looking over to the bag behind the lime bush, which had been sitting just there all afternoon. It ticked.

"*Ay Papi,* let's just get this over with, we already started." She looked down at her feet. Wiggled her toes — *wiggled my toes?!* "*Dale,* go get it, we have to do it right now!"

"*Ay si,* says Melva, why don't you go get it? *Caaaa-rajo,*" said Pito, puffing at the cigar nervously. The ember glowed brighter with every pull, it could have been his heart. "You go get it — I'll do it."

"Just go get it! Come on, you're the *brujo* here," she said, cracking a smile. Pito looked himself over.

"*Me cago en diez cabrones*," he said, walking over towards the lime bush. The bag ticked. Twice. He grabbed it by the folds and *shooshed* it as the sound of claws slipping across the paper began to go crazy in the darkness. Lifting it up hesitantly, he walked it over towards the shed, putting it down on the ground between them.

"Let me go check on Cuco," said Pito.

"Okay," said Melva, just as quickly. She watched bag silently. Nothing happened. Pito came tiptoeing back, the smell of *tabaco* about him as he passed by.

"*Bueeee –* " he said, wincing. He pulling on the folds of paper, hearing the staples crack open and reveal, fold after fold after fold, the pitch black inside the bag, broken only by a tiny beam of moonlight that fell onto shining, black feathers. Tick. Pito looked up to Melva, grinning, and set the cigar on the ground.

"Go on, take it," he said, nodding towards the *puro*.

"What do you mea—" snapped Melva, but it was too late. Pito had jammed his hand into the bag and wrapped his fingers around the chicken's head, to which the bag began to pop and rustle as he lifted it out and snagged it by the scabrous yellow feet. Pulled it taut. Tick.

"I'm holding it, you give it *tabaco* and *aguardiente*," he said, panting quietly as he watched it look blankly towards the sky. Melva winced.

"*Ay...*"

"*Dale, niña!*" he whined — "it's a fucking *pollo, carajo*, look!" She took a deep breath and looked at the ember hesitantly, grimacing, looking back to the glass door before she closed her eyes tight and wrapped her lips around the warm, oscillating waves of heat that rose from the tip of the cigar. She clenched her throat, feeling the smoke trail back, trying to choke her. She reached her head towards the chicken and blew with all of her might, opening her eyes for a a split second of barreling smoke flying in all directions. She shook her head, getting it all over the chicken:

"*Sopla!*" laughed Pito, "*caaaarajo!*"

"Holy shit," said Melva, pulling the *tabaco* from her mouth. She looked down at the bottle of aguardiente, grabbing it and taking a swig just like her father had, bringing her face down at the chicken and *shooshing* it just as he had.

But it *brrrrab-b-brrr-b-ed*
through her lips,
dripping off of her chin
and onto the grass.

She opened her eyes, shocked, her mouth hanging open, searing with liquor as she looked to the ground. Tick.

"*Rrrrrr!*" she growled, wincing.

"*Mija,* you have to '*Pffffft*' when you do it, you have to make your mouth say that," and he repeated, "*Pffffffffft.*" Melva looked down at her feet.

"Pffffffft," she said to herself. "*Pfffft.* Okay." And she took another swig, closing her eyes before giving off the biggest PFFFFFFFFT Miami had ever seen. The chicken *kAAAAAwk-ed!* out loud, and when she opened her eyes, wiping the drops from her chin, she saw that Pito glistened in the light of the moon, his moustache twinkling brightest of all.

"*Mira,* let me see that," and he let go of the chicken's head, letting it hang upside down—instinctively, it opened its wings and hung, still, motionless. Like a ceiling fan. Pito took a swig and *pffffffffft-ed* it onto the chicken, handing Melva the bottle again and grabbing it by the head. It didn't move.

"Okay, stand up straight again, like I taught you—"
The glass door slid open.

Pito and Melva's glossy eyes showed each other the moon. Hearts hit the ground. Freezing dew. Cuco's eyes were puffy with the ghost of sleep, squinting out into the darkness, where he saw his wife with her pants rolled up to her knees, a cigar in her hand, Pito with a bottle of booze and a...is that a...

...no one sees the ceiling fan...

The chicken *rrrrrrrr*-ed a nervous whine. *Nicka help me!*

"*Y ustedes...que hacen aqui afuera?*" ventured Cuco. What are...you guys doing out here...but he answered his own question with silence, shrinking into his eyes and creeping behind the door once again.

"Roots run deep," Pito said into the darkness. "He's scared shitless, went back to sleep."

"He's gonna kill me," shined Melva.

"*Que que?!*" scoffed Pito. "Look at him, his dick almost fell off. Come on," and he swung the chicken up onto Melva's head, planting it on her upside-down so its wings splayed out atop her skull like the top of a mighty, animistic caduceus. He prayed, empowered, Oedipal, having defeated his father-in-law by the power of his own half-baked sorcery. *Asiago.* Melva watched as his eyes rolled back into his head, exclaiming incoherencies as he grabbed her shoulders and began to spin her around once more, wincing, this time to the accompaniment of ticks and *rrrrrr*-s. He swiped the chicken up again and again, until her whole body had been run over by the bird, who now took on the illness that Melva had borne only seconds before. He lifted it up into the air after finishing, and looked Melva in the eye—"Before Solanos, we made soup like this"—and he raised the chicken above his head, sweeping it around in three great arcs that made the chicken's neck go limp in his fist before throwing it to the ground, where it writhed and stretched for five drawn-out seconds of clenching claws and tight *seizurrrr-rrrr-rrr*...Pito and Melva watched the chicken raise a foot into the air, and to their horror it grew, grew, swelling like a marshmallow in the fires of hell, first here then there, and soon it looked like a cluster of lobes on the end of a stick. And it stopped. Relaxed. Gave up the ghost. Jesus Christ at 3PM.

"The hell?" said Pito.

"*AYYY!!!*" yelped Melva. It popped.

"*Santo Cristo...*" he said, easing over to the chicken, whose gentle eyelids were cracked open as if squinting into the light of the moon. "I've never seen that before...*su madre,*" said Pito, throwing the bag over it and swinging it all upright. He rolled it shut, holding it up between the both of them before dropping it onto the ground. "*Bueno*...we're done. That was a sign."

Melva hadn't moved an inch. She finally seemed to come to, looking around in disbelief, at the ground, the cigar in her hand. Confusion. She took a puff. Coughed. And it fell to the ground, tapping her on the foot.

"Look at that shit, Melva!" Pito pointed to the smudge of ash on her foot.

"What—another sign?"

"A sign?! No, your feet!" They could have been those of Mother Mary.

And the ashes fell away with a pattering tear. The bag gave one final tick, and as if in perfect synchrony, the ember of the cigar succumbed to the dew that was all around it, going out into the darkness all around it. The electricity dissipated.

"*Se acabo.*" Pito grabbed the bag once again. "I'm gonna go drop this off at the beach...the beach right?" Melva nodded. "Ok, go inside and say your prayers to San Luis Beltran, I'll see you later." And he slinked towards the side gate:

"*Cachimbambo...*"

Melva eased her way toward the back door, where she brought her face to the glass and peered inside. Cuco was asleep on the couch. Still had his dick—*whew*. She straightened her hair out, took a dignified breath and ventured inside. He didn't stir.

She passed by him and made for the kitchen table, where she lit a candle and sat in the darkness watching the flame grow huge on the tip of a long wick. Light fell upon the grainy image of a Catholic monk surrounded by angels. She had never felt so fresh, so *open*, it was a holy vigor that hovered about her, and with this she prayed,

"Once mil virgenes..."

Cuco cursed his ancestors to the sound of his thundering heart.

Basil in water under the bed, for nightmares.
Bab-barita.
Six packs a day.
It's all a dream.
"She'd never...how..." sleep, mijo,
you've got work in an hour.

Across town Pito had arrived at the beach. It shone hazy and blue under the light of the moon. Only the foam of the waves could be distinguished from the darkness all around. He got out of the car, walking through the cool air that gossiped to the leaves of the palm trees, and felt the cold sand crunch under his *chancletas*. Armed with the bag and a barbeque lighter, he made his way to the shore, where the waves crashed every few seconds with sounds that reminded him of Cuba. *"Patria de Maceo y de Marti,"* he sighed. He set the bag down on the sand, and— *"Yemaya, aqui esta su mondongo,"* —lit the bag on fire. Slowly, the flames danced about the thick brown paper of the bag, first on the rolled bundle up top, then down the sides. The paper turned black under the mantle of flame, and the *Rompesaragüey* caught on the inside, casting the whole bag into a burning ball of noxious *burundanga* in no time. Pito, superstitious as he was, turned his back on the whole deal, running off toward the car, daring not to look back.

"Waaaaaa!" growled an ashy *hong-lés* who popped out of nowhere, running towards the blaze.

"Santísima!" shouted Pito, kicking up more sand as he ran.

"Don't touch that! It's dangerous!" he shouted into the palm trees above him, but it was no use, for the *hong-lés* had smelled the chicken, which was surely roasting deep inside of the bewitched conflagration, and he leapt upon the blaze crazily, stamping it out and tearing it apart hungrily. If Pito had looked back to the scene, he would have seen the vagabond crouched over the smoldering pile of ashes and sand, poised over the half-burnt branch and scraps of brown paper, gnawing at the blackbird dripping with ash and bloody, sticky sand, but he didn't. He knew better. He slammed the car into reverse and sped off, signing himself with the cross. Spectacles-testicles-wallet-and-watch. *Asiago.*

And just as he feared, imagined, the beggar had picked up every bit of black magic that was in that bag, and crazy as he was already, he devolved into something primal, something that made the glazed tick in his eye all the more dangerous, vile and sandy as the grimy locks that dripped about his head like wax from a black candle. He had lived on the beach for years, haranguing tourists and living off the coconuts and seagulls that fell from the trees. In time, he would come to be known as *El Chango* after attacking a group from Mazatlán that got interviewed in the *Herald.* They said he was like a giant, ferocious, enraged *changuito.* Even stole their bananas. More dangerous and less predictable, even, than the *Chupacabra* that plagued farmers all across Latin America, and crazed like 'El Coco,' this poor bastard — *El Chango* — who was guilty of nothing but being crazy and a little hungry, would forever remain toasted along the dancing tides on the beach, but from the inside-out. Look out for him if you're ever in Miami, children....

Waaaaaaaaaaaaaaaaaaaaaaaaa! El Coco!

~*~

Across the amber of city lights, the peacock blues of street signs and searing halogen high-beams, Silvia sat quietly, fumbling with the little vial in the dark. The winds were picking up outside, thunder rumbled in the distant caribbean skies. Her countenance was peaceful, like saints on the votive candles at the supermarket, and without moving she turned the vial over and over again between her fingers, watching its contents glisten in the darkness. Tobacco and sand. The powder inside ticked with patters that whispered of death, power, *Aché*. It smiled at her, *leered*. She looked up to the picture of the Virgin on the wall, bending forward to pick up the needle she had set down on the glasstop coffee table. Took a deep breath. Her nails clinked across its surface, and she tapped it twice, reveling in that familiar sound, the hollow raps that had accompanied her in all of her loneliest moments, her self-created void of cigarettes and TV commercials. She pinched the cold needle with her fingers and rolled it between them, bringing it close to her face where it seemed to reflect light that was not there. Light from outside, too much light. The moon, the night sky. Lightning flashed for a dim second, and there was silence for seven drawn-out seconds before the air around her oscillated with the energy of nature, compressed tension released all around her as sound. Thunder...it was ethereal, surreal. The whole world was around her, and only now did she notice it, she was so small, so great in the magnificence of the world around her. She set the needle onto her tongue, piercingly cold, and pressed her tongue to the roof of her mouth, swallowing the itch in her teeth the metal caused her. The tip of the needle pressed against the soft skin of the roof of her mouth, and she rolled it around, feeling it scratch across the bumps and ridges as she gazed in the direction of the hallway, the bedroom, where Chiche slept silently. *Ay Chiche, in that very bed would you lay to* rest, just like tonight. The evening news, a full stomach, sleep thrown about you like a shroud. *The Virgin wears the night sky*...she smiled.

Silvia undid the top of the vial, showed it to the Virgin, and cleared her throat, beginning to sing, softly, to herself:

Awo, awo, tutu pa' ti,
ven a bailar mi pasito mambi,
Keke, Mafefe, siempre seran,
tome su vino, denme mi pan...

And singing it over and over again, feeling shivers come about her arms and spine, she pricked herself on the word *'vino'*, feeling her life go into the pain, her eyes rolling back in her head, and an orb of blood grew into a little black pearl at the tip of her ring finger, whose end she began to pull on to make herself bleed. She pulled and pulled at it, her uncle yelling at her from across the yard, pull on the teats until you have half a bucket, Silis, come inside when you're done so we can make *café con leche*, but the pearl stood still, no matter how hard she pulled, pulled, squeezed, twisted. Nothing. Her heart shuddered at the mistake, it hadn't been deep enough, she had been scared, you'll *ruin this if you keep pulling back, this is no fucking joke, Silvia! Mijita....*her mother rubbed her tired head, the little sleepless child plagued by nightmares. She sucked on her finger, tasting the iron-y-sweet ribbons of blood swirling between her teeth, swallowed it all. Pulled her finger out, slowly. *Let's try this again, they're...waiting. There it is, by the whorl, look it's a little tiny slit. See it?* There. She turned her finger in the light behind her, the amber streetlight, and keeping her gaze fixed on the slit, brought the needle to it once again, setting it at the perforated skin before singing the song once again. *Vino, vino, vino,* she winced, easing the needle in once again, sinking into the waves of pain that ran through her body with trembling breaths, a clenched throat, a perennial swallow, locking poison from the rest of the body, the rest of the world, waking everything inside of her up with sheets of electricity that she wedged open, further in, digging it in and around, around, no turning back now, and blood began to overwhelm the space around the needle. *Bingo, linda. I'll never do this again.*

236

She pulled it out. *Efficiency reduces toil, mija, don't forget this pain.* She took a breath and relaxed her navel, which had grown tight with the anger that was bubbling up inside of her. Leered at the needle. Sucked the blood off. She wanted to bite it, snap it in two, swallow it and feel it scratch her insides, *buckets and buckets of glass pouring in, ay! Stop.* Stop. The droplet grew in size and began to tremble. Silvia moved it to the mouth of the vial, letting it ease gracefully into the mixture, which drank it up like thirsty soil. She was nursing this little child, fruit of her innermost cravings. Again, from the base of her finger a droplet gathered at the slit, and she pulled, pulled, milking the teats and feeding the children. *Two...three...four...*five drops that Ofelia had ordered, dissolved into the powder. She stuck her finger in her mouth again, pressing it to the fleshy roof with her tongue, sucking the iron-y-sweet ribbons back into her throat, swallowing, swallowing again. It glistened in the streetlight, and she grabbed the vial, holding it into the stripes of light that glowed through the curtains. It was moist and black, clinging to the sides like it had grown, drinking the aliments she had poured into its tiny little mouth, round like the glass of the vial. She crooned the vial with the soft music she had been humming all this time, *Keke, Mafefe, siempre serán...*soon enough it would be time, and she set the cap on it once again, showing it to the Virgin, whose eyes flashed with a second of lightning. *Aprovado, she is here! They...are near.*

Singing the little song out of habit, she made her way to the bedroom, where Chiche's snores and calloused feet created the same ambiance that serenaded her every night on the way to bed. *It's his day...his time,* Silvia thought to herself. *Si,* she replied. She set the vial on her nightstand, just as she had been told, behind the telephone.

"Keke, Mafefe, *buenas noches,*" she sighed, and turning over, she proceeded to fall asleep...

...sueños...

     ...susúrren...

~*~

      ...sleeping dreams...whispering
softly...the...sound...of...sssssss...

    ...ssssssssssssss...ssssssto...

    tac-tac-tac-tac-tac-WHOOSH stovetops! Fire, Fire, FIRE engulfs the scene, hazy purple veils pulled aside, consumed by shrieking flames and brilliant laughter shriveling in horror, more, more, more! so many more...they burn, they writhe and fall, serpents hiss and kiss each other in braids of sweet longing...can you see?! Are you feeling alive yet?! Yet! See the ribbons, ribbons hover in oil, flecked with the gold of youth, happiness forgotten until old age, liquor spurted across the searing flames of time WHOOSH the smiling sounds of an untuned thumb-harb come forth from everywhere at once, dancing to and fro, to and fro, back and forth, back and forth, popping, stomping Mbiras...tumbling tumbling African masks, eyes so real slender noses echoing into the eternity across thick, freckled lips...they dance, hunched, arms flailing back like the wings of celestial birds, and up they leap, to and fro, up they leap, to and fro, back on ground, up in sky, the sound of Affffrikaanssss back and forth, back and forth...HOO! HEE HEE!

    AAAAAAAA-WO! AAAAAAA-WOooo-HOO!

"*BOGBO!*"
    "*OooooSOGbo!*"

  "*Abbakuaña!*"

      "*Araye!*"
    "*Arun, aro!*"
        "*Iku!*"

  "*ArrrrrASSSStres!*"

"Ano!"

"Araye!"

"Achelu!"

"Oniketa!"

"OFO!"

"EeeeeeyO!!!"

"Eeee-eeeeh...malpinga!"

"Hacía tiempo....pero ya llegue!"

"Maricon! Llegamos!"

"Salamaleko!"

"Malekosala...Salamaleko!"

"Maleko-SALA! Aye, aye!"

"Babawaye, waye!"

Keke and Mafefe

they have

come

to

play.

Palm husks and crackling gourds, liquor
and blood spattering and sizzling across the hot tips of searing tobacco
embers...Would you like to dance? "Come...I'll show you..." Shrieeeeks!
of joy, deep, wise laughs at my movement, the spheres dance around
ME – stars bear witness and it is done in blood, done to you...pulling at
my dress, tearing it off, they laugh at my nakedness, I dance with them
back and forth, laughing, back and forth, to and fro, eyes so real, eyes so
real...Mbiras popping my heart's joys, clave clicks cracking into the
nerves of my teeth, I throw myself to the floor and heave with pain,
seizing, twitching, writhing, giving birth to their child...they pull it from
deep within my spinal cord and blow it out, up, off into the air, vibrant
expansion of colors all around us, veils of fire, back and forth, braided
serpents whipped about their straw hair...rattles shaking all through my
body and I, I become the colors, Keke, Mafefe laughs from down below the
ground, laughing this great primordial sound, and the two mischievous

spirits light me to their hymns, eternal memories of what I have always been, giant eyes in the sky, irises like rainbows, smiling down smiling down, back and forth, back and forth...temple bells and palm oil smeared about me like kohl, collyrium palm trees and beads of sweat swaying across sagging black pearls, black breasts, his drooping orbs, come to Mama breaking with laughter, back and forth, back and forth, and crystal ribbons cry down to us, as if from the sky...Chiche's sagging breasts growing thick black veins of remorse and decay, rotten avocados that I scream at him, scream at him, they scream and the ribbons pull tight all about him...wAAAAAAAhahahahahahainnocent eyes awakened, no what is this, make it stop surprise and drunk with stupidity...I dance with his naked body, wrinkled like leather, hairless, pressing it to my chest with brotherly love, this time I will get you back, you murderer, I married you for it, you married me and my brothers dance around us, shaking their hips, arms flailed back like celestial birds, back and forth, back and forth...masks smiling, hearts popping into stars all over the walls, as if from the sky, my child, she is everywhere, and the rainbow eyes frown upon us as we tumble through veils of coconut cackles crackling shells, bitter, oily chunks spat at the feet of idols falling falling laughing laughing tangled in ribbons, and the two sit down to take their toddy in mid air, feet splayed before them and take a deep breath....smiles, smiles, cheese and goat-herds back and forth, back and forth, swaying, bra-a-a-a-a-a-aying ribbons around his neck, tighter, tighter, tighter! His eyes bulge and glisten, drunkenly, stupidly, veins of remorse and stupidity bursting, swelling under crackling eggshells and spilled turtle bowels he calls and calls but nothing, nothing, no one hears, and the ribbons go taut, popping him three feet above the ground and STOP. Still.

"AAAYYYYYYYYY!" screamed Silvia, sitting up in bed.

Her insides roiled, and her body seized over and over again in the seizures of an horrendous orgasm. *"AAAAY-AAAAAY-AAA-AA-A-AYYYYY! AAAAAYY!!"* Chiche whooped and snorted himself upright.

"Me cago en — what the hell was that — *Negra!"* he shouted,

disoriented. Silvia turned her head, bewildered, into his eyes, gasping with her mouth wide open. Her heartbeats sent streams of light into the dark with every booming pulse. She cast her eyes aside and there, on Chiche's pillow, was the vial. Silvia threw herself towards him and grabbed the vial. It was empty. Her face slammed into his chest, and her womb seized, over and over again, boiling, unfurling more and more thick, vicious bliss everywhere inside of her. The room swarmed with angry bees.

"A-a-a-a-aaaaaaa-*aaaaaay* Chiche!" She wailed, clutching the vial in a tight fist. It ticked in her palm, the glass cracking into the muffled void of her hand.

He sat upright, moving away from her.

"The hell is *wrong with you?*" he said, his voice trembling.

"*Ay*...I don't know...it was just a dream." She took a deep breath and looked into the ceiling, where the black bees sparkled and popped into the darkness. Spiders scurried into the corners.

"Bad dreams, ah?" Chiche scoffed, rubbing his face with exasperation. "It's all that shit you watch on the TV. Put some basil under the bed, Cuco told me it cures nightmares."

"*Hmph.* Go back to sleep, Chiche, I'm fine." Silvia turned to the side and stuck her head under the sheets, waiting for her eyes to grow into the darkness. She opened her hand. The warm stickiness was enough to tell her to get up. Chiche was already snoring. Slowly she got out of bed, her fist tight against the broken glass, she *liked* it, *no one knows it but me*, and made her way to the bathroom, where she let water run over it, staining the sink with pink splashes that eventually ran clear. She squinted her sleepy eyes in the yellow light, pulling her hand away from the bubbling spout. It was fine. She looked at the wad of toilet paper in the garbage can, checked it again. Blood and glass. Where's the stuff. *The fuck is this*...she looked at her hand once more, turning it over in confusion. Nothing. Fine. She poked her head out of the bathroom door, looking into the living room where the Virgin stood in her frame as if nothing had happened. Lightning flashed. Ashtray. It caught the corner of her eye, the smooth, polished glass. She scurried over to the table and fished it from the cigarette butts. Just as she had left it, tobacco and sand. *Did I leave it here? Did you? I put it by the night stand. Then why is it here?* Silvia's neck snapped tight with a shudder. Her eyes landed on the Virgin. *Mija...don't worry about it, put it in the fridge. Am I making this up, going crazy? Why would I think of the fridge? Shouldn't I do what doñ – THE FRIDGE. And go to sleep.*

"*Dios mio, that was real.*"

Something scratched at the wall. She seized with fear, looking outside. Nothing. *The fridge.* She walked over to the fridge and opened the door. Winced in the light. Whirring motors, mist. *The papaya.* What about it. *Put it in your papaya.* The papaya? *Your papaya.* Laughter scurried behind her. She whipped her head around. Nothing. The *fuck.* The *fuck. The papaya. Put it in the frutabomba. In the frutabomba?* In *your frutabomba. My papaya? God dammit. She winced at a sharp pain in her neck – ayyyyy, she whined, Virgensita is this real? Dios mio, this is real, I'm going crazy...the machete flashed in her mind, lo voy a matar, lo voy a matar,* and Silvia's eyes glazed with the same primal joy that had overcome her so many times before. Her guts roiled inside of her, and she lifted her *bata* in the light of the fridge, easing the vial into her papaya. *Virgensita,* she whined. "*Keke, Mafefe...*" It was already moist. Bees, swarming inside of her, all over the kitchen. In her ears. She winced, over and over again, swatting at the bees, and clutched the vial tight inside of her, where the pleasure took over her loins once more and she seized with pleasure, biting her lips with tears, was it joy, was it fear, was it remorse, it was all of them at once and she didn't know what to do. *I don't know what I'm doing. You're perfectly fine. There's no turning back, Silis,* her mother kissed her on the brow. *Wise as a serpent, gentle as a dove...*and she took a deep breath, feeling her insides buzz with thousands of hummingbirds, their wings quaking the earth into piles of dust. The beehive swarmed with pleasure, and everything calmed down, like the confusion at the end of a storm, as she set her eyes upon the faded glare of the black metal in her mind. She cleared her nose with a deep breath and wiped her tears away. Took it in her hand. Inches from her face, she looked at the grainy metal of the machete: *"lo vamos a matar,"* she smiled, in a voice that was not hers. *Vamos? Si, mijita, vamos, let us smoke a cigarette, sleep and tomorrow it will be ready. Tomorrow he shall dance. We shall dance. Let's...have a cigarette. Si, Virgensita, I love cigarettes. I know, mija. Let's go. Vamos.* And she whisked her hand to the left, watching the knife fade into darkness.

She smoked a cigarette on the porch. Leaning back and forth, feeling the vial, smoking nervously. *The child, in your dream...ribbons of blood...smoke another one.* Drops began to tick at the ground, one by one, and within seconds it had begun to pour. She pulled on the butt and flicked it to the ground, where the cherry snapped out of sight instantly next to the first.

~*~

Your sleeping face reminds me
of the day I fell in love with you,
seeing you happy,
seeing you with eyes closed in peace.

You found this very feeling in me,
and we promised before
God and the Virgin
to be with each other forever,
in life and in death,
take refuge in that feeling,
in that sleepy forgetfulness of young love.

Today I wake and dare not touch you,
give you a kiss on the forehead or
on your perfect collarbones,
only so that I may give you that feeling once again,
the sleepy forgetfulness, eyes closed in peace.

Your love, it is my fear of death,
the solace of my trust in you.
You can close your eyes,
I'm here with you.

~*~

It was noon. Chiche had woken up alone and made himself breakfast, leaving Silvia alone in bed clutching her hand. Jenny had left without saying anything. In the silence of the empty house, Silvia got up and walked into the living room, confused. The air was stale in the house. It's too quiet. She lit a cigarette. Turned on the TV. *The vial.* "Dios mio," she whined. The ceiling fan leered at her from above, watching her rub her hand over and over again in confusion. She snuffed her cigarette in the ashtray on the darkwood coffee table, going to bathroom once again. Blood and glass. The *fuck.* The faucet hissed, and Silvia washed her hands again and again, daring not look in the mirror. The vial sat in the soap dish. She rubbed her hands together furiously, watching the vial, fighting the burn of scalding water as if her hands were wrestling, fighting, rather than trying to clean each other. It was satisfying, to push so hard. The battle flushed her face, and she felt the blood rush to her cheeks as she tensed her arms harder and harder, her hands writhing together harder and harder, one against the other. The forces slipped in the chaotic frenzy and her left hand *slammed* into the white bowl of the sink—"*Pinnnnnnga!*" she yelled into the mirror, snarling into her own reflection. Rings, around her eyes. "Dios mio..." Her rage calmed down. Her eyes, her eyes, they were oilslicks. She growled, pushing at the rage in her stomach until it broke from her chest into a scream that echoed throughout the bathroom. The silent house swallowed it whole. She was out of breath, her heart thumping in her chest, and she felt her pulse in her hand, running blood all through it, the cuts were gone, the *fuck,* the *fuck,* the *fuck* is going on, is this working, am I wrong, is this all wrong? *Niña...*She sighed, turning the water cold to ease the pain. *Calm* *down, mija, think about what you need to do. Everything's fine. Keke, Mafefe, siempre serán...*she took a deep breath and let it out slowly, wiping her hands on the little towel that no one in the house used since it was the nice one, for show and for guests, but she didn't care. It felt good to use the pink towel with the lace every once in a while. She pressed it into her eyes, scraping the rings away into the towel. Looked up. Oilslicks. She wanted a smoke.

"Fuck you," she said into the mirror.

Her eyes...forget the rings...got no sleep...today they had an extra flair to them, it was thrilling, mysterious, fearful. They pierced the mirror, pierced her eyes. They were so ugly, surrounded by those awful bags, but so beautiful inside of them, the eyes themselves, they were...*beautiful, mija, calm down.* She smiled. Her pupils dilated as she stared. Tonight, the stars will shine on your graces, you will see...thoughts of dinner peppered across her mind like divining-shells, how had Melva been with all the treatments she had to do, what about Jenny, she didn't say hello, goodbye, she just left, why did Chiche leave, why am I alone, all alone in the house. Her pupils shrank in fear. Rings, oilslicks. Chiche would be home soon for lunch. Oh, God. She had to cook something for him. Oh God.

"*Ay Virgensita. No, no,*" said Silvia out loud. "Not tonight." Her voice seemed loud in the bathroom. The *machete* appeared before her in her mind, sending tingles throughout her whole body. Her loins itched. *Gentle as a dove, a dove, the dove of the spirit, bringer of la paz, paz eterna. Of course it's tonight. Eternal peace* that she would give to Chiche, gentle as a dove, in his sleep. Gentle serpents, suffocating him as he slept. Wise doves perched on the blades of the ceiling fan. Squinting eyes, the perennial squint. The unavoidable smile. She saw him there, in his bed. His eyes popped open, black. Her heart skipped a beat and hammered twice as fast; her guts roiled, filled with shit. She gasped into her reflection in the mirror, squeezing her legs together. Beating of hearts, in her head, in her ears. *Those eyes, those eyes, staring at her as she pierced his skin*, that soft, vulnerable skin on his neck, riddled with little bumps like salty chicken fat, *brujeria* on your front porch. *Filled with shit.* She took a deep breath and relaxed. *He'd reach out for her, grab her by the neck, and she'd slash at him more and more, getting blood all over his bald head, all over his face.* He would be asleep. She needed a smoke. She would have to do it quick, the blood would go everywhere. *In the backyard, then, niña, the backyard.*

"No, in the bed," she said into the mirror. *The bed, the bed, the bed. Filled with shit.*

"But the neighbors will see," she said to herself, "the fences are low, those assholes will call the cops after telling everyone in the neighborhood—then what?" She leaned against the sink, moving closer and closer to the mirror, looking deeply into her own eyes. "*Then what?*" She could see the back of them. The void shone golden deep inside her eyes, ethereal, a mysterious cave. *I'll eat him. I'll buy dogs. Pigs. Tell the kids he drowned. Throw him in the ocean. I'll call Ofelia, she will help me. Will she? Right? I'll go to jail. I'll run. I'll hide. I'll win. Lo voy a matar, lo voy a matar. The kids. Fuck the kids. Make him lunch.*

Have a smoke first. Si...si, have two. You're hungry enough.

Don't you want him to see you do it?
       To know why you are doing it?
Pupils.
All those years, Silvia, years of putrid shit, sitting at home and fucking your time, your age! What is your life?
       You are old, you are ugly.
Pupils.
You are the hollow inside of a housedress, a little mannequin for the shitty clothes he makes you wear.
He doesn't even buy you clothes.
       Fucking greasy food you don't even want.

Show him what you are...all those years of complaining, and his stupid mother! She NEVER liked you, always thought you were a failure just because you couldn't cook. But you showed her...now show him.

SHOW HIM!

She rubbed the rings around her eyes.

"*Santísima Virgen,*" said Silvia, looking deeply into her eye. "Who are you?"

"*Quien soy? Quien ERES...resingada.* You're the one going crazy. It's your Mother, the one who brought you to this world."

"No, *you're* going crazy. This...*this is wrong.*"

"What about the kids? Yennifer? What if she comes home? *Mijita...*"

"*Have faith, wife of Ibrahim, the Lord provides.*"

She nodded into the mirror. Sighed. "*Okay. Mi Viiiirgensita,*" she whined, "it's you I trust."

"*And I trust you as well,*" she said into the mirror. She poked her head out the doorframe and looked at the picture of the Virgin. Her eyes, they were alive, smiling, smiling..."*Si, Mami, I trust you.*"

"*Youuuuu...*" Her bowels relaxed, silent laughter rolling about their depths. "Remember the *joy*, Silis, you're just getting scared. Cut that shit out, it's bad for you. They all get scared before they do it, *before the great challenge.* It's the price of victory. *Don't shit your pants now* – she squeezed her legs together. "*Ayyy...*"

"*Don't do it....*" laughter echoed around her as she squeezed her legs, waiting for the wave of uneasiness to pass back upwards. She let out an exasperated sigh into the cold, fake marble top of the sink. *Squeezed* it.

"Who...what am I doing, I'm so...there's so much going on, I—" and her pupils dilated in the mirror—"*I'm gonna kill him.*" Her lip twitched. A rush of thoughts poured through her head, screams of frustration, joyful cackling, the pleasures of laying back while making love, spackled ceilings and sweaty chest hair, rearing children, dilations, contractions, fears, hope, dreams, nothing and everything...and all over it, that *sick* face, poking her in the nose, shit balling up in her gut, '*eating his congrí and staring stupidly at the wall'*, making me do all these stupid things all my life, living it for me! He wants me to *rot here! I kill him because he has been killing me slowly for so many years...THAT'S WHY, SILIS, I am the saint here, it is la Virgen who has brought joy back into my life, and he must die. Don't forget that, he dies, or you do. Lo voy a matar, lo voy a matar, lo voy a mat—"*

"*Negra! Donde andas?*" Her knuckles were white on the rims of the sink. She let go and her hands were stuck that way. Open, close, stretch, palms up, palms back.

"You're old, useless," she whispered, putting the vial into her *bata.*

"*Y a ti que te imPORRRta?*" she snapped from the bathroom. *Mira que este viejo habla pinga, Ma...*

"*No, nada,* I just didn't know where you were." She heard shuffling steps into the kitchen. "*Buuuueeeee...*" he said, with a detached inflection, "*Y...el lonche, que?*" Of course he wanted lunch. *Su pinga...*

"*Si, si,* I...slept in, I didn't know you were coming so early today," she said into the mirror. "Just sit down." *Screw him, let him swallow his tongue. Que coma pinga. Fucking lunch, everyday. And he doesnt give you*

"shyet!"

"*Que?*" said Chiche, recoiling in his chair. "*Coño*...early? I'm an hour late! Don't worry, *negrita,* I'll kick back while you cook, no problem. You wouldn't imagine what happened to me today, I sold this old couple a—" he opened the door to the bathroom — "whoa, *que te pasa?*" .

"*Que?! Que quieres?*" snapped Silvia, her eyes wide and surrounded by rings. "Ah? I can't even shit in here without you coming in? What's with that little smile?"

"*Nada,* you're just standing there, I don't know. That's not how I shit." He shuffled off back into the living room. "Well, you gonna cook something or what? Come on. Let me know when it's ready."

Silvia heard the couch groan as he plopped down onto it and, she assumed, closed his eyes to listen to the TV. *If only he knew...you want lunch, how about dinner, come home maricon, just show him the machete, just show it to him, see what he says, he won't say shit, he doesn't know shit, let him wonder what that look in your eye is, maybe he'll get up and make his OWN* — and she smiled at the idea of it, her taunting him with the *machete. I'd kill him right now, tumbar ese resingado con un vuelo de el machete, malDITO!'*

Ay...niña...hurry up, he's going to wonder what's...gotten into you. Would he beg? Would he make her promises to change? Does he know he needs to change? *Of course not.* What would he say? *'Ay Silvia, estas loca!'* Damn right I'm crazy, you son of a bitch. Or *'Silvia, put the knife down, please, Negra, what are you doing,'* Ay, I'd tell him right then what I was doing. He'd never hear the end of it, the *malDITO!* and she gasped.

Her hair was unkempt, she realized she was making a scene, acting strange — *coño,* he knows something was up...does he? He does. No, he doesn't. She composed herself, stepping out into the living room. Napping. *He don't know shyit.* She raised an eyebrow and looked at him for a good three seconds before walking over to the kitchen where she uncovered the little containers she filled *every* night with leftovers. The same leftovers, he always wanted the same thing. What do *you* want, Silis? do you even know? I do. She dumped the leftovers into the skillets with a little handful of water for reheating. *Tac-tac-tac-tac-*

whoosh, and the stoves turned on — four clicks today, she always counted them.

She cut the *pan Cubano* and set the *cafetera* up with a fresh pull, heading over and pouring some milk into his mug and setting it in the microwave for 2 minutes and 9 seconds; this was the exact second before it would spill over if she filled it to the precise point she had found in his mug. It would beep three times, and she would let it sit until the *café* was done — by that time, the *nata* would have developed on the surface of the milk, that little skin that she always used to fight with Carmen over in Cuba. *Ay*, the simple pleasures. She would take the mug out of the microwave, twirl a spoon in it, wrapping the *nata* around it and stick it in her mouth, steaming. It burned, and it felt so good. She did it every time she made *café con leche*. She would suck the *nata* off the hot spoon with her tongue and swallow it without chewing, it drove her crazy. And it clung to the back of her throat in a way that gave her pleasure.

But today she just waited, waited for the *café* to percolate, waited for the *congrí* to start popping in the skillet, waited for the microwave to beep, and she tapped her fingers across the stovetop, making that surprisingly loud hollow metal noise *brrrap. Brrrap*. The four fingers, over and over, and over — "*Negra!*" yelled Chiche. Silvia pulled her hand back instinctively. She tensed up. *You fear him! You're scared of him! He's got you trained like a bitch! A whining, little — be FREE from those shackles, that communist piece of shit*, and she kicked her shoes off in frustration. The floor was cold against the soles of her feet. Sticky tiles. Chiche snorted. How could he fall asleep so fast? And *what the hell did he want?* She spat in his food. Her eyes, she could feel them, they were puffy. Oilslicks.

"*Ay, pinga*," she sighed.

Silvia stared out through the glass door. A palm tree swayed in the wind, its long, shaggy locks moving to the rhythm of the wind. *Anaíli. Tia Anaíli.* Silvia smiled as she remembered her childhood trips to her auntie Anaíli's house. The swaying palms, the peaceful breezes of innocence, of childhood in Cuba, the joy of vacation, the best *chilindrón* on the island! *'Cuca,'* she laughed to herself. And no oilslicks. Everyone was happy there in the country, where they rode dried palm leaves down the hills like sleds and skinned their knees, and Carmen would always cry, it was so beautiful…

"Silis! Come here, the lemonade is ready!" Madelai always looked out for Silvia, like a sister. Carmen? She was too nice, she wandered around the *viejas* who did the cooking like the ugly girls who couldn't get married, and they all cooked and cleaned and talked about the important things in life…or just shared *chismes* with each other. Silvia, however, who had a reputation from her boarding school that everyone knew about, got to tend to the fun chores with her older cousins, and on the ranch in the lush hills of Oriente, there was always much to be done. Chores abounded. Who liked to do chores, though, right? Silvia knew what it was like to run errands on the *ranchito* with her cousins, especially Madelai, who treated Silvia like a little sister. They cleaned the stables and tended to the animals, cleaned the yard, sweeping dust around the pens and drizzling fodder all about for the animals, or else they collected vegetables from the garden. It was *fun*. Not *chores*. Silvia smiled as the *congrí* sizzled and popped in the skillet.

The lemonade — *ay, that lemonade!* — it was one of those things that she could hardly describe to city-dwellers. It was her childhood, it was Cuba, it was *gross*, but it was so good when it was all you had…*imagínate,* the freshest lemons, straight off the tree, squeezed into a *jarro* of water drawn straight out of the *tinaja,* the big clay amphora that kept the water surprisingly cool in the heat and gave it that sweet taste of earth. The lemons were squeezed into the water, and then everyone had to get ready quickly, because they would get some baking soda and pour it in and *stir stir stir* and *"Dale, dale, toma, toma!"* the lucky soul would have to take it all down before the fizz died off and it was flat again. The belching that ensued was inevitably hideous.

This was what Madelaí was screaming at Silvia for, she had gone off towards the bushes looking at a colorful lizard that had skimpered across the gravel. She ran back to the *tinaja* where her cousins were gathered round, from pre-teen to post-teen, and they all smiled fiendishly as Silvia grabbed the glass and kicked it back, streams of fizzy lemonade trickling down her face and her neck into her shirt and the girls all laughed as she gulped it all down. There was always too much baking soda in it since everyone wanted bubbles so the lemonade tasted like bitter mineral water, the *cal* off of the walls. It was good, it was bad, childhood. And she would belch like it didn't even matter, laughing it off with her cousins, distinguished ladies that they always were. Carmen, all the while, would chop tomatoes in the kitchen with her puffy hair and the old ladies. *What a bitch.*

The microwave beeped. Silvia reached over and lifted the lid off the *cafetera*. The black nectar dribbled down the little tower inside the chamber, bubbling into that delicious brown foam that went so well with the black of the coffee. Silvia was never really a fan of *café*, perhaps a *café con leche* if it felt right, but she absolutely loved the smell. No one could take that from her. It was one of the reasons she made it so often for Chiche without ever complaining, for she too had a secret joy from making *café*. He got to drink it, and she got to smell it and delve into her past, watching the trees sway in the breezes of her memories. 'Buttered toast,' she smiled to herself, 'that's the smell of good coffee.' It was a good day, she felt sharp—those times were the best, when your thoughts were clear, when you finally nip something off the tip of your tongue, when you finally get at that little piece of something caught in your teeth. It was the joy when you finally catch that bothersome little piece of skin on your lip that you've been working at for hours. *Brrrrrap.* She poked at the *congrí,* evening out the cooked part and pressing down on it firmly with her spoon so that it sizzled loudly. She smiled. Pulling the mug of hot milk out of the microwave, she whisked a little spoon from the drawer and twirled it along the surface of the steaming milk getting the *nata* all caught up around the spoon, and she lifted it to her lips, wrapping her mouth around the steaming metal and everything flashed for a second as it touched her tongue. It burned, but it was so good. She smiled around the spoon, pulling it out slowly and dipping it back into the milk as she poured the *café* into the mug. She swallowed, and her insides roiled with pleasure. She stirred and added a couple spoonfuls of sugar — she had been killing Chiche this way slowly for years now. She added one more today, it didn't matter. Her heart seized in her chest. She was *alive.*

Setting everything on the greasy doilies, she called for Chiche to come eat, and he did, smiling strangely as he walked over. The world froze in shock as Silvia beheld what happened. She saw it from above, hovering about the whole scene like a silent ghost. It happened in slow motion...Chiche walked over to her, leaned in, and grabbing her forearm awkwardly, perhaps so she couldn't escape, gave her a peck on the lips. It tingled, it bore up her cheek into a an uncomfortable grimace, it buzzed and made her smack her lips. It thundered in the room around them, this kiss, and in its wake, Chiche sat down with a boyish grin and stirred his *café con leche*, picking up the spoon set next to his plate of leftovers to eat with. Silvia's jaw had dropped.

"*Y que fue eso?*" What the hell was that? She went off to her room to change.

Dressed in her favorite *bata* and some slippers, Silvia went red in the face as she saw Chiche toss a fresh pack of Marlboros by her pack on the table. The door closed, and Silvia shuffled over to the darkwood table with the thick glass with the green edges and grabbed her smokes and her Capricorn lighter, and it made that pleasant noise scraping along the glass as she picked it up. Walking hurriedly to the kitchen, she grabbed the *café con leche* that was left and rushed for the glass door, lighting her cigarette before she sat down on the plastic chair outside. The grass was yellow, sickly, like Cuca, and she felt how hard and dry the soil was under her slippers. She loved the thin soles, they reminded her of the ground's eternal presence. A cheatsheet for going barefoot. She drew heavily on the smoke, *ughhhh*. Little bits of paper fluttered off the tip as the cherry burned brightly and pulled back towards her lips, sizzling as the air flowed through and transformed the tobacco to sweet, smoky nectar that filled her completely. It stung; she held it, let it out...slowly. *Ugh.* Slumped there in the chair, she sipped the lukewarm *café con leche*. *Ugh.* The dirt and grime on the chair, speckled with the dried remnants of rainwater, were probably all over her *bata*, but she didn't care. *As if I don't have another one to put on...*

"*Mmhmm*," she said as she took another drag, pulling her lips tightly around the paper filter. "*Virgensita, I'm scared.*" She stared off into the blue, blue sky. A couple of little clouds sat still in the distance. "They do nothing with all that freedom, they just sit there, *nuves de mierda*." Stupid clouds. She took another sip from the mug, swishing it in her mouth before swallowing tightly.

"Mmhmm."

Tonight, mija, esta noche, we'll show that hijue'puta what's coming to him. That's what we did before Cuba went to shit, we would kill the enemy with machetes, we fought for freedom with their bare hands. Juttthhhhtithia!' Silvia looked again to the sky, her cigarette jutting out the side of her mouth. *You know you want to watch as the life leaves his eyes,* and her loins tingled with temptation. Fuck

the vial. He would look into my eyes and ask, *why, why?*
Porque, Negra?

He was crying. She slashed his face, and jammed the blade into his gurgling throat. She spat onto the ground, scraping her front teeth across the surface of her tongue. Another sip, another drag, a deep pull into the lungs. *I'm alive,* she said, *I'm happy.*

She was far from done smoking. This flimsy little smoke had done nothing, *nothing* for her. "*Smoke another one, niña, come on,*" she said out loud, and she pulled another one from the pack, bringing it to life with the cherry of the other. She tossed the half-smoked cigarette into the grass. The motions of throwing snapped her arm stiff, and the smoke hardly flew past where her toes would've reached if she tried. It landed in the dead grass right in front of her, as if it were a plastic bag, heaved with all her might.

'You're weak, you fucking prisoner. Starved.'

"*Maldito cigarro!*" she growled, standing up with one swift movement and pounding it into the ground with her foot over and over again. Chiche's nose broke, blood spattered everywhere, and it hurt her to see him so defeated, big and old as he was, and she stopped, exhausted. The butt was dead, covered with dirt and streaks from her sandal. She leaned on her thigh and heaved hoarse breaths into the void around her. She set her smoke into the side of her mouth, and there was silence as she smoked it softly, hunched over in the yard. Her face was contorted like *Popéye* and she milked the smoke gently from the side of her mouth through clenched teeth, standing up slowly and feeling the top of her head tingle as her blood caught up with her. *Uggghhhh!* Her lungs begged for air, and she punished them with smoke, with what *she* wanted. What *she* wanted.

"*Mmhmm,*" she mumbled, letting the smoke out through the other side of her mouth and taking a deep breath through her nose. She walked around, peering into the dirty birdcages caked with white, splotchy turds and wispy feathers, old seeds and hollow broccoli, the rolled tarpaulins with their translucent fibers jutting out of the tears like ribs in the ashes of a funeral pyre, littered with the shells of birdseed and string, and it angered her so to see all this *crap* everywhere. She lifted the great blue roll with all her might, but she could not lift it, and she pulled up harder and harder, squinting like *Popéye* from the smoke in her mouth effortlessly stinging her eye, like water drowns one, mercilessly, effortlessly. Her back popped shooting pains up into her neck as her grip failed her, and she flew backwards into the dead grass with a squeal of pain, her back, her *bata* fondling the years of urine all over the ground from the stupid neighbor's dog who was nowhere to be found, full of nothing but blank looks and piss.

"Fuck you, fuck you," she said, pleased that she hadn't lost her smoke. She let out an exasperated sigh, watching the tendrils of smoke ease their way towards the sky and die trying. *You'd never have made it anyway.* Silvia stared at the sky, that vast expanse of blue that was ignorant of her plight and everyone else's, shining blue regardless of how bad she felt, of how pissed she and countless others were, and she knew it didn't care. *Fuck you, you selfish piece of shit. Si, niña, this is your dessstiny. There's nothing you can do now.* The ash fell from the tip of her cigarette and onto her face in the most uncomfortable places all at once, her eyes and the tip of her nose, the skin around her nostrils, and in a huff of anger and hazy laughter she inhaled the ashes through her nose, fucking herself, fucking everyone, that she should take them all down with her torrents of rage, and as her nerves tightened with hatred all through her body she suddenly found it within herself to relax, letting it all course through her like a poison...*I deserve it...this is my destiny, look at me,* every day a day older, every day a day closer to *kicking the can*...no one saw, no one helped.

You see, mija? You're all alone except for me. For ussssss.

Chiche, hijue'puta! she thought to herself, and as if in perfect, cadenzic response a shaggy grey blur came out of nowhere and put its tongue to her eye with a chortling sound of slobber and spit. She recoiled in shock, dropping her smoke as she gagged and screamed *"Maldito perro! Resinga'o! Sala'o! Comepinga! Te voy a sazonar con Oya!"* she screamed, tears streaming past the slobber on her face. The cigarette burned her neck as it fell to the grass. *Rrrrrrrrrr!!!! Look at your power!!!* She stood up on sheer instinct, wiping her eye with the sleeve of her sweater, wide-eyed with hatred, her vision blurred with fitful tears, and she kicked at the dog but missed. *My power, goddammit!* It scuttled away towards the bushes in the corner of the yard, its tongue hanging out of its mouth. It was *laughing*. That son of a *bitch. Powerless! You can't even kick a fockeen dog!*

"Hijo de puta!" she screamed at it. *"Hijo de tu puta madre!"* She screamed at everything, at the dog, at the house, at herself, the clouds, the virgins in her head, none of it made sense, and it was all a son of a *bitch*. She snuffed the dead cigarette out with her *chancleta*, stamping on it over and over again with tears streaming down her face, and she brushed the dead grasses off of herself, sobbing. It clung mercilessly to her sweater. *Everything I do fails, life's strangling me! Fuck you, fuck you, fuck you!* She rubbed at her sweater furiously, but the grass did nothing, and growling she tore at the wool, pulling patches of forest green and strings of lint from the little sweater she had worn over her *bata* for years. Seeing her body under the ripping fabric she cried even more, digging her fingers into her *mazas* of menopausal fat over and over again, moaning helplessly like the little child she'd never outgrown, and with each blow she slowly came to her senses once again, standing up straight. *No, no , stop...*she said to herself, taking a deep breath, ignoring the little fucking *tinkle* of the dog's collar around the corner. *Perro de mierrrrrda, it's probably licking it's*

own asshole. She listened, feeling her body like never before, stinging sensation all over, and in such a flurry of energy all over she suddenly found it absolutely and disgustingly audacious that the *dog* should even be in her *yard!*

She *whipped* her head around: it was taking a piss by the birdcages.

"*WAAAAAA!*" she screamed, flailing her arms as she ran towards it. She thought of all the weak animals on TV, how they used silly methods to scare the enemies away. This dog could turn on me, bite me, make me recoil into my house with antibiotic cream and two weeks of scabbing, and what could I do? Juss *kick da mufucka!* It scurried into the bushes as if its very little insignificant life were in danger, pissing all the while. She heard it scrape through the hole in the fence, *scr-scr-scr as hard as it could,* scraping like it had never before, and she landed on the fence next to it, booming on the wood so that it yelped and got all the way through.
"*Resingaaao!*" she screamed.
"*La tuya!*" screamed a voice from somewhere beyond the fence. Silvia hunched low, her eyes wide as could be. *Me oieron,* she whispered. *It's ok it's ok it's ok keep going.* She whipped her head to the left, trying not to smile. *The tarp. Put that shit on the fence, plug the hole. God, youcould have done this yeeears ago!* It's like everything, like *tonight,* and *look*—it's *done.* She grabbed the tarp, and pulling it away from the bundle of garbage inch by inch, she could already see where she was going to put it, shove it into the bushes, plug the hole. Plug the hole. She pulled, and pulled, and suddenly the whole assembly, the bird cages, the garden tools, the boxes, tarps, chicken-wire, all of it fell to the ground.

"*God daaaamit!*" she screamed, dropping it all. *Fuck you, neighbor.* Didn't say a word. Her face clenched tight with a tear-filled grimace, and she welcomed the dog back into the yard. Go ahead, come back inside, I don't care, do what you want, you win, you win, I can't win at this, I need a smoke, I don't even want to smoke, what the hell is going on, and she looked up into the sky, where the clouds ignored her as they traipsed across the blue field of freedom where there was no rent, no bills to pay, no need for food, nothing. Nothing at all. "I do nothing at all, and look how unhappy I am." The bees stirred in their hive, *oh, the pleasure is there, Silis, right here, come, forget this, let's sit and have a smoke. Mmmmm. Seal the deal. Finish this, finish him, and we'll go inside and cook. You'll see, you'll see it'll be so much fun.* Disco lights went off in the back of her mind. *"Los Be-aht-les,"* she said to herself, squinting into the patterns of wood on the fence.

Silvia went over to the chair once again, poised and elegant like a lady. Her gaze tight, fixed, narrowed. She extended her hand nobly towards the arm of the chair, letting her fingertips fall onto it like the they would tell her to when she was posing for pictures as a girl. *Dale,* Silvia, just like that, look up there, hold the telephone to your ear, talking on the phone so modern, the Yumas will ask you out to the casino, to do just that. Sit and look pretty. A clean spot in the shape of her back could be distinguished on the white plastic — *Are my hips that wide? Look, mija, dirt don't lie —* and she bent over, a hand on her aching back, to grab the mug of cold *café con leche* she had set down. She lifted herself once again and walked inside. *"That's it. I don't give a shit,"* she growled. *"It's happening tonight,"* she whispered to herself upon seeing the kitchen again, smiling at how angry she was. Laughing. *Seal the deal.* No more fear, she thought of what she could do to keep it going, to keep the fear at bay, to fuel herself with this anger, this pain. She lit another cigarette. *I could kill a dog...mmmhmmm....just don't miss this time. Mmhmm...he'll be...asssleeep.* She smiled. Ofelia and the vial: it all turned to joy, the ashes scattering inside the house, the long drags that hurt and suffocated her, the freedom she had rediscovered, to determination. *You still feel angry. I feel alive! I'm alive, I feel it everywhere, everywhere, this pain!!! Do you feeeeeel the paaaaiiiiiinnnn?!?! It's exhilirating. Powerful. Cut through it and fffflex it into your intentionnnnsssss!* She blew smoke all over the house, blew her drags and ashed her smoke wherever she pleased. *"Uggghhhhh..."* she moaned, looking around.

Oilllslllicksssss...

> *You're so fucking weak.*

> *Come, little dog, come in*
>> *and piss right here,*
> *I'll clean it up for you.*
>> *On my tiles.*

Come!

> *Come.   I don't care.*

I'm done.
> *I could kill a dog...*

Just don't miss this time...

> *Stupid bitch.*

> *You killed a goat last time you got pissed enough.*

Her eyes went wide with surprise.

"Goddamn SHYET! I'D KILL HIM RIGHT NOW!" Her teeth crackled into her skull as she bore own on her jaws, it felt incredible, everywhere, everywhere this pain. *I'm aliiiiiiive Goddammit, I'm happy, feel it.* She felt herself taking a deep breath, as if it weren't her doing the breathing, and it filled her up to the brim of her lungs, they stretched and remembered how it felt to choke, soaking the pain of her tightly clenched jaws into the entirety of her being. Everywhere was this pain.

"Ay....pinga," she sighed. "Empty promises, that's all there

ever was." She sat down on the couch, lighting another smoke. 'That's all this *viejo* is, empty promises....you know? *Mmhmm.*' Long ago it seemed, but still, memories of the past stretched their spindly legs all the way into the present, where Silvia tried ceaselessly to smoke them out of her mind, drag after drag. *Yeah, chew on this shit for a little bit...*She was getting dizzy, her body stung, it hurt all over, the grass scratching her, her nail-marks across her abdomen, the stink of dog shit all over her face, it was a happy day when Chiche announced that the family would be leaving for America. *You seemed so happy then...*she laughed a mouthful of smoke into the living room, coughing as she ashed her cigarette on the table. *Fuck you, ashtray.* Out of the sweaty darkness of repression, after decades of pitiless squalor, out of the musky stench of tropical death to the spirit, after an eight year-old engorging boil of choleric soullessness — law after law, slogan after slogan, death after death — all that Chiche had promised them was a dream. Gone like that; it was never there. Grabbing at the memories only made it that much more real, *pero niña get ahold of yourself you stink like shit*, let us keep fantasizing about America around the dinner table, it was a game to him, something to pass the time with the emptiness of hope — *negra, negra, negra,* the best of musings, a vision of the future! For everyone, for *us.* Aren't you happy now? At least until the end of the movie? Then it's back to reality. Remember it, *mija*, remember the joys then. But then one day he came home with papers in his hand; beautiful eyes can't tell a lie. *"Are you serious, Negro, you finally came through on something?!"* Celebrations ensued at everyone's houses, dinners of *Jamón Serrano* and *boliche, arroz imperial* and dozens of *platanos, dulce de guayaba, cafe.* Chiche was emptying his coffers onto the dinner tables of all the neighbors who had kept the dream alive with him all these years. Hell, even *Pepe y Lola Gutierrez* came over one time, and they were red as Russian beets. Nobody cared, everyone was happy, it would all be over soon. For the Campos', that is. Silvia saw the same looks of unbelief come across the eyes of the poor wives in every household, the most complex emotion of all. When one came over and proved that dreams could come true, and then you realized it was not you who was leaving, it became difficult to be happy for them much longer. The sadness would sweep across the smiles within an hour, Silvia discovered; there was not a genuinely happy woman in her entire neighborhood. They all saw Silvia as the one that could have been them, and the sadness would turn into anger, and longing for Silvia's shoes—would she leave them for us when she takes off for *la Yuma?* And this would churn into sadness, and back into anger again and again, and it would slowly cook into a *bola* of *envidia* that was quite probably the most disgusting thing a human being could produce. Envy, green as pestilence. Their eyes could not lie, Silvia saw it in every single one. It was a pestilence of the soul that began to surround her, in the fabric of her very society, the neighbors who turned to hating her for wanting to leave, and the rest who hated her because she was not them.

But Silvia did not care, all of it made her smile. This unfurling, this sweet unfurling of her innermost flower.

They would be gone and Fidel could wipe his bony ass with their days of starvation, drinking water to numb the pangs of endless hypoglycemic labor, of having your poverty handed to you, of people waiting in line for it, sleeping on the floor next to your uncles and aunties and all of the kids, and waking up covered in greasy sweat that made each day begin with an unconscious wave of dross, of breaths smacking with the sulfurous lack of toothpaste, it was suffocation between the sweaty breasts of tropical communism. Come to Mama...it wasn't your fault, no Cuba, you're beautiful. It's the law, justice's ugly sister corruption, this is the one who throws dirt at you so you can sink down to her level. She's the bleeding Goddess of those who took you from us, Mami, the lawmakers playing with our fates like it was a giant game of living chess, suck it up and look happy to the rest of the world, we're in this *together*...the communists...with their red condoms full of poverty and flawed philosophies, reciting the manifesto as they thrusted impositions left, right, and up, up, up into the very rights that the plush intellectuals called unalienable in their manuscripts. It's pain, perpetual pain; rape is about control, not sex. Every cigar he lit burned with the tears of Cuba; the searing embers of endless hunger. Life and its tithe of suffering for all, a thousand-and-one novels written for the inquisitive; this place among us, a true canvas for the Goddess of Beauty. Joy is in our nature, if you take it away you've smothered our souls. You've smothered our freedom. I haven't even been able to speak all of this until now, and my journey to the *Yuma* was the longest of all. But the adulterous wolves write with the pen of politics and sharpened quills that shear the very locks of Nature from her head. My mother is sick and bald, the people are hungry, and equality got lost in translation. The manifesto should never have been penned into Spanish.

Look into the eyes of Cuba, beyond the pride and palm trees.
Under the weight of humanity's worst, there is
Still light. Light so bright it can't be seen.

For years, Chiche worked in a *bodega* with a rather prosperous business, fair until the beard came along. With the revolution, and then the hunger, people had to unite...and not under the flag, if you get my drift...to make their own way. Night-robberies ensued left and right; trains, trucks, ships were pillaged for the *real* revolution! It was an entire language of whispers and eyes. You want an operable government? Pull the rock of communism up from the ground, and beneath it you will see the network of ants in the darkness. The black market, put to the test of survival, becomes a natural humanity stronger than an oath to God. What is true to the words of Marx, if not the revolt *against* communism, the reactions to it? Chiche came across this fine booty, grabbing it happily for they were leaving it all. Crumbs for the Queen! The people needed to eat, and behind the ration-stamps at the counter, Chiche had his real business — chicken, beans, canned sauces — the black market gave people food to eat. Powdered milk was the *perico* of this black market, *comino* and *cafe* the *marijuana*, pots and pans the weapons of a nationwide *Guerra Criolla*. *Pssst* — you buyin' beans? I got beans, black beans, yo mama gonna like these beans. Go talk to Laly by the green bike over there, look like she sellin ice cream huh. She see you comin, you got a bag? Store aint got no bags either.

And the people ate — don't tell *Ratoncito Perez* down the block,
$\qquad\qquad$ he's with the *Comité*.
$\qquad$ And the petals stretch as wide as they can,
$\qquad\qquad$ and my golden core shines black.
$\qquad\qquad$ This, Silvia, is the cup of your life.

$\qquad$ "*No Mami*, what I'm sayin is that we have the papers, they just have to be cleared — why don't you take another flan down to the office?" Silvia had stopped letting him below the waist after the third years of waiting. All he had was his little *monito* when he curled up next to her to sleep. "*Get the fuck off*, Im trying not to sweat before I fall asleep. Fuckin *tits*, he can kiss my ass." They had gone broke. The neighbors' wives hissed their smiles at Silvia every time they saw her — *Ay pero hello, niña, I see you're still here...muah muah bitch.* First three, then five years of waiting, waiting, *waiting*...you can wait for the *potaje* too, *sala'o!* Goddammit, everyone was pissed. The freedom parties were a mistake; she winced every time she remembered them. Letting herself be happy, what a waste of time. Counting chickens, cooking them night after night with no eggs to hatch. It's like the wisemen say, if you want something to work out for you don't tell a damn soul. Makes you shake your head at people telling you their dreams, we spilled it out for the world to see, here's the dirt, and there's the seeds...oh shit. Hams were once again saved like golden eggs for the holidays, sugar used sparingly, little chips of soap picked up from the floor and pressed into balls after months of frugality, just like before. *Silvia's voice quivered in her mind*—I let myself buy into Chiche's fantasy, and it fell through, took me with it. I started to hate that man. It fizzled, our dream—an explosion that could have been ninety miles of fuel. Was it my fault too? What is worse, to be a slave in peace, or to be teased with the prospect of freedom? To let yourself be happy when you know it's against the laws that bind your soul? It's the uncertainty that kills you, *mijito*, if your fate is sealed you can come to terms with it and die a slow death with your loved ones around you in the same defeated peace. And even with all of this back-and-forth in the family, Chiche still could not be shaken from his hope, there was nothing that could kill his soul—"I know we're gonna go, *Negra*, I can feel it, you gotta believe me..."—and only Tico could find it within himself to join in with his songs of freedom. But it wasn't because he cared about America. Tico had already been singing for years, he thought nobody could hear him, or went through his things. I'm Cuban, you son of a bitch. I know my kids better than they do.

Tico's song had set him free long ago—the surroundings don't matter to the inspired, the truth is on the better side of the skin—all when he came across a set of dusty volumes in the archives of a library. As it turns out, the librarian who's private collection Tico had pilfered was part of some ancient church that revived in Colombia after thousands of years of transcultural allegory and misappropriated mysticism. 'The Movement,' as he called the group, was rooted in the wisdom of Ascended Masters in the plane of the dreaming and dead, and had been brought back to life—to the *essence* of the times—under the veil-piercing wisdom of a Seraphic man they called Samael Aun Weor. Peace be upon him. Seeing the sparks fly in Tico's eyes, the librarian didn't beat him out of the back rooms when he caught him, but instead gave him twice as many books as he was trying to steal, to devour at home, in the moonlight of an open window or off in the fields under the shade of a mighty Siguaraya — *Siete Rayos que tiene esa mata, Siete Rayos!* — while the other kids played baseball with no shoes on and bats made of Tia Yarina's old broomstick. The librarian sent Tico away with as many books as he could carry, the one on top brushing his chin all the way home. Rubbing the dirt from his chin, he noticed the cover of the first book: it was an igneous flower, caught in the still life of poorly printed literature. The real shit, the stuff money can't buy. With the pillar of wisdom given to him did the eager boy learn of Mayan mysteries, of the Tree of Sephiroth, Alchemy and Egypt, three great mountains and unbridled Christianity. Goddess-worship and the sexual trance, checkered floors and books once set to burn into the vacuous sky. "Bake under low, low heat, and bake, bake, bake again." Tico, however, was much too young for such...seminal practices...and the books served instead to open his spirit to subtleties that didn't bear much fruit until he went traveling through the foothills of the Himalayas. *That,* beloved, is another story. It's where he met the woman who changed his life forever, not even he knew her name. The knowledge itself, however, was marvelous. It made his mind churn with questions and doubts until he tore himself into two and began his own branch of the work, offering sacred vows to the Gods in secret, a true revolution of the dialectic, praying like a fiend deep into the night behind closed eyes and a perfectly straight spine, wearing white and talking to the local *Babalawos* who had fed their own spiritual needs with the only mystic system publicly available to Cubans at the time. The *Santos* didn't appeal much to Tico, however. He welcomed them into his worldview, and indeed, he was amazed at how well the syncretism between Catholicism and *Santeria* boiled itself out, eerily precise, but what he truly liked most was going to the village *Padrino's* house on feast days for a good *Bembé,* where he could see all of the regular people remember their essence for at least one night. The names of God didn't matter. To Albertico Campos, at least, devotion knew no names. Or perhaps too many.

When Chiche came home with the *actual* papers hidden beneath his work shirt, stuck to his chest with the sweat of oppression, there was finally reason to give him credit, but after eight years of semi-valid lies, jubilation was not in question. With a simple smile, Silvia said quietly from the table where she sat sorting the little rocks out of the black beans one by one, *"Gracias a Dios. When do we leave?"* Chiche simply smiled. Her lack of emotion was not a stonewall, but a gift, a boon. Kiss the snake, there is nothing to fear. And the neighbors all grew suspicious of the activity in the Campos' home those last few weeks before they left. Silvia was smiling again, but not with her mouth, she kept it all in her eyes. She had learned this over the eight years of holding back from everyone around her. And they didn't tell a soul this time. They were so secretive that even the *chismes*, fluid as smoke, could not get through that doorway until one day they saw there was nobody home. Beautiful eyes can not tell a lie. They had taken a boat at 3AM, with baby Jennifer wrapped in blankets and covered in jewelry like the rest of the family. Within the folds of the blanket, like a secret mantle, went the one thing Silvia could not leave behind, the picture of *La Virgen* that adorned the walls of her house to this very day. Everything else was left behind: they had turned their money into lavish but impersonal bracelets, rings, necklaces, encrusted medals of the *Santos* and earrings, for the complication of immigration and assets was not worth the efforts of dealing with men-in-uniform, or of trying to learn English — there was no time for that. *"What part of 'just put that in this basket' don't you understand, Señor-a?!"* Sweet Jesus, there's no way around the fear. On that fishing boat, packed with hundreds of Cubans legally leaving the country, the family stepped on board, wearing nothing but the shirts on their backs and the life-savings that shined over their most sensitive parts, expecting a leisurely trip to Key West that would take no more than eight hours.

Twenty-two hours and thirty-nine minutes later,
they stepped off the boat.
Silvia, naturally, was *pissed*.

The waves churned all the way over. *'Eso va a pasar,
hombre, eso no es nada...un peito tropical...'* The people watched the
palm trees swoon and lash about each other in the warm drizzle
of the wind. Indeed, storms did come and go all-too-easily in
Cuba, but this one followed them all the way to Miami, just what
you'd hope wouldn't happen, and it made the trip over a living
hell. Who would have known that hell was so wet, so frigidly
miserable? It's a blessing just to feel your entire body at once, it's
like the frigid deck sucks the little life you have left out from your
skin, the rain keeps all of it flowing and clean. A slow, painful
death. People were sick over the side of the boat the whole way
there. Those last bowls of *sopa de platano,* the last touches of
guayaba y queso and the last one-peso *tintítos* of *cafe* all saw their
way into the ocean; *Maferefun Yemaya muchacho, que wirindinga, que
mondongo que se va pal mar, deja que te aguante el pelo.* Perhaps, in
better light, it was indeed a final purge of the communist
nightmare before starting over in America, a rite of the threshold
perhaps. And bitch and moan as they did, they finally saw the
waters grow shallow once again. Hammerheads and manatees
swam in the passing blurs of reefs and stacks of boulders, spotted
with nervous little fish flirting with the surface, and the waters
burbled with foam as waves began to form in reaction to the ever-
approaching slabs of land and coral. It began to feel like gypsies
were thrashing at their guitars with every crash of waves across
the spearhead of the bow. The trip was finally beginning to look
like what they had expected it to be, even the skies had cleared;
Silvia's grip finally loosened on the little bundle held ever-so-
tightly to her the whole way there. It was Jennifer. People started
singing once again into the sky, making everyone smile and laugh
and clap along, and others pulled out the *dulce de leche* and flasks
of *Havana Club* and *pastelitos de carne* they had stuffed into their

pockets for when they knew it was all for real, that they were guaranteed to get there. When they finally got to the Keys in the glorious haze of an approaching dawn, the welcoming embrace of the United States of America was not poetic at all. It was cold as steel balls. Of course, it was also freedom, and they didn't complain, but still, to see the soldiers posted there with no compassion and a general affect that betrayed a sense of zoo-keeping humbled the songs of the Cubans as they got off the boat, seasick and waterlogged. *Omío Yemaya.* Name. Papers. Mmhmm. Ok go to this line. Cavity search. Drug test. Of course, you signed for that right here. The dogs. Health check — the one smile in the building, in his white coat. Mariza would never tell anyone he touched his icy stethoscope to her nipple, softly. She couldn't look into his eyes for the rest of the check-up. She didn't know it, but she was this close to being detained, for 'health issues'. Power corrupts. Clothes, from the church. Secondhand. Secondhand smoke. Oh, my poor cousins back in Cuba... A bar of soap, a foggy little bottle of shampoo. Throw it away when you're done.

"Ehhh?!?"

Seeeee, Miss...*Camp*-Ohs. Like a Goddamn cereal. Throw it away when you're done. Uh, bah-soora, yeah? *See.* Right there. Atta girl, contamination prevention. Next. Food...*Food!* It was no *Noche Buena* feast, but *coño*, after so long, food for free! And no ration-cards! They ate happily, enjoying the interesting taste of American cuisine, corn and mashed potatoes, meatloaf, pudding. Everything was a little square. Throw away the sporks and little riblet knives. Cots. Sleep, it's six in the morning. We'll see you at 3PM. Yeah, you'll hear the line from your cots, don't worry.

Y el sueño...susúrre.

Some of the people stayed in the camps for weeks, until

they could sort out housing, welfare, whatever it took to get them settled into the God-Blessed USA. Chiche, however, had some *Tias* and *Tios* in Miami already and they moved in with them immediately, driving that lush drive across the Keys into Miami in a charter bus that dropped them off downtown. "*Los Estados Unidos,*" they all said to each other, taking in the buildings, the commotion, the cars that were younger than 30, the people eating ceaselessly. Only when the kids went and bought a candy bar and a Coke each did it really sink in. 39 grams of *libertad, moth-er-fack you Fidel!*

> "*Mami, Mami, mira! Chocolate!* The legends are true!"
> > Silvia
> > > relaxed her muscles with a
> > > > sigh.

She held back her tears so easily, smiling back at them with the softness of what one would mistake for wisdom. She was finally here, but she still felt the same way. It was as if nothing had changed. All of the hatred, it wasn't Cuba, it wasn't communism. It had followed her here too. And her eyes, they could not tell a lie. "Oh, what *beautiful* eyes you have," a nurse has smiled to her as she went through the motions. Silvia didn't know what the hell she had said. She smiled back and pretended to laugh — "*Ay senk you mees ley-dy.*"

Nah nah nah, that's just how you tell the story. You called her 'Mees America,' and that lady almost shit her pants.

~*~

Otro Dia

The day love stopped being a vice:

Peace be upon you, and upon me as well.
A twisted, gnarled romance we are,
driven crazy by painful
passions that leave the palate
filthy and unsatisfied,
peace is mine every time
I beckon a kiss from your earthy lips.

You give me so much when I ask,
and only now do I see that slowly,
tactfully, you have taken your share
every time
and so much more, when the debts
are counted out.

I count them.

White stones, black stones,
my pile is
a mouthful of black pepper.

But pepper is black, and white as well.
A little savors life, too much drives you insane.
You are like God to me, in your absence is my suffering..
Your tangled brown locks
leave my fingers raw
with the marks of unrivaled fantasies,
and tumbling in our thin white sheets
we revel under a facade of poverty.
The people think we are nobody,
But richness is ours.

Forever dissipates meaninglessly,
you tell me with every passing breath,
as we lay together in each other's thoughts,
over and over again

A curl of smoke lingers
still as death, grapes
curing into searing spirits that
move with beauty,
sublimating sex into art, and death.

Into beauty, the price is your chastity.
You know the sacrifices I've made for you.

I take you again and again until I am satisfied.
For this reason I never leave your side.
I am in love, and because of this
I am never satisfied.

A dry smack of the lips and another cigarette
lit at the end of earthy lips that
belong to that mysterious smoke-filled aura, that
man who gives me life every time I ask.
He walks down the avenue forever, my
only memory of him the kiss he never gave me,
the kiss he gives me behind closed eyes,
My neck tingles and I smudge myself with death,
a bath of ashes from the inside out.

Here I leave my mark on the world.
I press it with my foot as I walk on.
I am in love, and because of this
I am never satisfied.

~*~

"*Mami?* Yeah...totally....no, I'm fine, just telling you that I'll be out tonight with Mercedes...yeah, wait, what?...that's fine?....ummm ok cool I guess...umm yeah we were actually going to go see her boyfriend in Tampa, apparently he's been cheating with some white bitch...we're gonna go b—uh, talk to her, yeah, I know...I'll wear my seat belt. I know, I know, I saw that on the news last night, yeah, O I know, ok, ok, ok Mami, ok, ok...ok. Ok. *Bechitoshhh,* *muah!* Ok. Ok. Ok! *Te quiero mucho.* I know. Ok bye."

She slapped her phone shut. "Jesus Christ, did you get that handle yet or what, I'm on the fuckin phone! Yeah, I'm good, I'm good for it, that was my Mami. Nah, she's watchin all the *novelas* with my Dad, you know, just the same, typical shit." She buckled her seatbelt. "Lezzgo, I *want* me this white bitch!"

"*Unbelievable,*" smiled Silvia, looking at the picture on the wall. "*It's time, wife of Ibrahim,*" she whispered to the flames bobbing on the stove. "*It happens now.*" The fire danced with glee. It never ignored her. Silvia prepared dinner when the shadows on the floor looked like it was dinnertime. Today, her insides danced like the flames as she prepared to make this fateful meal for her beloved husband. Olive oil, a couple crushed teeth of garlic, onion, some green bell pepper, *comino, oregano,* and *laurel,* plenty of cilantro, and some *puré de tomate.*

"*Sofrito.*"

She stirred it round in the old-style pressure cooker, the *hoya de presión* that topped with its shiny steel lid would sing its irresistible song, the *tssss-tsss-tsssss-tsssss-tssss* of the swiveling *bab-bula* that filled so many Cuban households with spraying cadenzas of steam. It was a phenomenon that told you the cook in the house was old-fashioned, and thus seasoned with experience—the best of salts. It took wisdom, a *finesse criolle*, to cook Cuban food home-style. If not, you might end up serving west-coast modernity at your dinner table...'mango salsa with chicken breast and black-bean paté-a-la-bullshit' instead of *bistemmmpanizao con moros y maduros*.

'Ñooooooo!

Te la comistes, Negrita.

"Claro, y aue tu crees?" smiled Silvia into her cooking pot.

Silvia listened to the ingredients sizzle and sputter on the hot surface of the pan, imagining what it would be like to be thrown across a hot surface like that, tossing and seizing around on a bed that was so hot it didn't even feel like anything in her thoughts. She winced in her mind, clenched her teeth, stop thinking about it, but she couldn't. Hissed inwards, *sssssssssssss*. Wince. It persisted in her thoughts, every 'stop' was another, more grotesque image of her pain. The smell of vaporizing skin sticking to the pan with long rips off of her arm, up from the hot surface of the pain clashing with the smells of *sofrito*. She thought, eerily, of some big, dark chef wearing a colored mask above her on that hot skillet, burning her skin and throwing *comino* all over her, into her eyes, all over her lips, stuck to her teeth and up her nostrils, and drowning it all with *vino seco, waaaaaaa!!!*

"Stop it, ya!" she said out loud, clearing her throat of the caky powders. She darted her glance at the picture of La Virgen on the wall. *Her eyes, they're glowing—*
"Ochún, Ochún!" she heard herself say.
The fuck was that...
Car-horns blared with gut-busting laughter.
Eyes to the cooking pot. Mmmmmmmmmmmas ajo,' she thought, biting her lip. *Si, si, mas ajo, que hay que esssconder la*

*preciosita...el juguito de papaya, ya tu sabes que...*a few more teeth of garlic, for 'taste.' She smiled out loud, this would mask the flavors of the vial. *Just let go and everything will be just fine...*Bit harder, it felt good, gnawing, gnawing, how hard to draw blood. *Mmmmmm...ay, niña don't get me started on blood. That shit grows on you.* The garlic danced into the pan playfully, spattering *sofrito* on her apron. *Carajo.* She let go of her lip, feeling the blood return it to its normal shape. Wiped the apron off with her finger, leaving orange streaks to complement the rest of the stains. Licked her fingers. Thick, spicy blood. *Sangre criolla.* Spread across her lips. They tingled with cumin.

"Salt, Silis," she said. "*Sal, y pimienta.*" She stirred it up and let it sit for a bit on low heat while she went outside and smoked another cigarette, shooing the neighbor's dog away when it approached her. *What the fuck is that dog even doing here,* she asked herself. She glared at it, laughing at the thought of the dog dropping dead right there. "It's not true..." she smiled to herself. "Timbita, Timbita, it's all a bunch of bullshit lies." She put the butt out on the side of the chair and set it down with the rest of them, her backyard smokes.

Back inside, she added the chicken and let it sauté for a while. She looked at the clock, that little sunflower on the wall that had been telling the wrong time since they moved for more than 20 years. The chicken was bubbling in the *hoya*; it was time. She set the rice in the cooker and pushed the orange button that lit up when you pushed it in, heading back to the stove where she uncovered the *hoya de presión* and added some cooking wine — *vino seco* — and some Spanish olives, the kind stuffed with *aji,* to the *sofrito.* She ate three during this step, just like always. It was the good sort of bitter, she thought. *You like every kind of bitter, diabla.* Lick your lips. Peel me some potatoes, chop them up nice and big like he likes it, add them to the *hoya*...and simmer. "*Mmhmm,*" she mumbled. That's done. She put the lid on and moved on to the next task.

The pan full of frying oil was always in the oven. She reached behind her and pulled it out. The little black crumbs submerged in the oil swayed around passively as she turned around and set the pan on the stove. Medium heat, four on her little dial. She went and turned on the TV. Too quiet. She had missed the beginning of her *telenovela*. "*Coño*," she sighed. "Of course." She pulled out a couple of green *platanos* out of the bottom drawer of the fridge. They were long and gnarled, like the tusks of some tropical beast, cold from their time in the fridge. She peeled them, *arduous* work that it always was. Cut the tips off, run a long slice all along the peel and rip it off the plantain, one of the most satisfying sounds that exists. Bits of the starchy peel got caught under her nails every time, everyday. *Every fucking day.* She *hated* it, but how else were you going to peel *platanos*? You *have* to peel the *platanos*. Everyone did it, every good Cuban wife put up with it. *Starch* under the fingernails. Plantains, frying, washing and cleaning the grease off of *everything*, husbands, the sky, the four greasy walls of my house, myself, the little fucking lizards that didn't do shit on the walls outside. She chopped them up into chunks for *tostones* with extra force, with satisfaction. *A free fuckin ride.* Lizards, plantains. Into the frying pan. They hissed a flurry of bubbles and popped under the thinning grease. Chiche fried in fifteen little pieces, slowly. *Su pinga! Chicherrones.*

Plumes of steam rose from the *fricasé* and she chopped the tomatoes and—'*Santísima, what a huge avocado!*' she thought to herself. She held it up to her chest, smiling as she looked down. It made her breasts look like sacks of potatoes, 'with only one miserable *papa* left in each one...*Madrrrre que me pario.*' She cradled the avocado with one hand, guiding it to the counter behind her with an air of reverence. Tomatoes and avocado, some chopped cabbage, a drizzle of olive oil, some salt. *Ensalada. Cuban ex-tyle.* She ate a slice of tomato, rearranging the rest on the plate and setting it aside. The *platanos* were ready, just a *little* golden.

Spurts of steam flew around her: *tsss-tsss-tsss-tsss-tssss-tsss-*t-t-
tonight the sound made her nervous. She ate another tomato.
The paper towel she laid on the plate welcomed the *platanos*
happily, going translucent in three seconds with all the grease
they dripped as she set them down. They still bubbled on the
plate, it was always surreal. She reached into the drawer and
pulled out that big black stone she had since she got married, just
about as big as the avocado. Ask any Cuban woman where the
cornerstone of her marriage is and she'll tell you, "Third drawer
from the left, under the piece of bread I leave at New Years for
luck." *Boom!* rattled the counter, she pounded the *platanos* into
silver dollars. *The coffers will never be empty with that bread there,*
you see? The color contrast was strangely beautiful, this dark gold
of the outside flanking the virgin yellow of the stars inside. She
smiled. *La Virgen.* They were all done, and she tossed them back
into the frying pan on high, high heat. They fizzed and sizzled so
furiously that the flurry of bubbles occluded them from view, but
she knew they were okay. *"Mmhmm. He'll be okay when I'm done*
with him." Twice fried. Like the *platanos.*

Ya llego la hora del interperio.

"Que qu – "

Chiche opened the door. *"Negra!"* Her heart splattered
across the walls.
As if I wouldn't be here waiting, negroemied'da! Ya este tarrú
me esta cayendo mal...
"Hmph." Her heart gripped her tightly.
"Que paso, estoy vola'o!"
"Y que? No hueles la comida? No me ves aqui cocinandote
como todo los dias?"
"Claro que si, pero es pa' que lo sepas, mi negrita." He
enunciated his words, for patronizing emphasis. *"Eh-toy bo-*
LAO!" He came into view, smiling as he unbuttoned his jacket.
"Well, you know it'll be ready soon, drink some water if

you're so damn hungry." Silvia smiled tauntingly. He looked up at her: he remembered. "Can you smell what I'm making?"

"*Bolíche*." He said it with a tone of finality, sitting down.

"*Fricase de pollo. Y callate ya, coño, como si lo supieras todo, viejo de mierda...*" Thinks he knows it all...She lifted the top off the pot. A flurry of steam mushroomed to the ceiling, dissipating near the greasy paint above that looked slippery to the touch. Drops of condensation ran down the inside of the top; she shook it off into the bubbling of *fricasé* in the pot: *Goddammit Silvia, why do you do that?* Her Mother's voice echoed in her head. In the orange-colored cacophony, pieces of potato, chicken, bell pepper and olives surfaced and swirled back down, mixing about like sharks feeding on one of their own. She set the lid back on. "*Si, si,* almost ready."

Chiche had gone to the bathroom. She heard his urine flow into the toilet, thick and frothy. Cringed. It stopped, and there was no flush. She waited, waited, stirring the *platanos*, messing with the salad, shifting around with the heat on the stove. She huffed and stormed over to the bathroom, where she saw Chiche standing there holding his old manhood, '*and that Goddamn freckle on the head.*'

"*Y que, le estas haciendo un cuento?!*" she snapped. You tellin' that shit a story?

"You ever get that thing where there's just a tiny bit left, but it won't come out?" Nothing. Contempt. "Yeah, I'm workin' on it. It's a *man* thing, *cosa de hommmmmbreh,* forget about it. *La prohhh-tata, Negra, dadle graciahhha Diohhh...que la tuya no te molehhhta.*" She bore into his moist eyes for a few seconds, and walked away, spatula in hand. *Was he being serious?* His eyes, they can not — the toilet flushed.

"Wash your hands!" she yelled from the stove, shaking her head with exasperation. "*Goddammit, coño'e tu Madre...*"

"*Ay Negrita,*" he said to himself out loud, "*como me conoces.*" It sounded weird coming from the bathroom, echo-like and hazy. *El Mas Allá.* He walked out and went off to change without looking over to the kitchen, where Silvia was toiling and troubling over greasy bubbles of steam and vapor.

She watched him walk through the living room into the hallway, past all the pictures of the *santos* and the kids. She felt their eyes on him, it was as if she too could see him, through the tips of her fingers. The eyes of the Gods, of the Saints. She reached into the pocket of her apron and pulled out the little vial, giving the brown *picadura* a long look. Rolling it about her fingertips. It very well could have been tobacco and sand. *Mmmmm.* She undid the top and went to smell it — *niña, estas loca?!?* She recoiled and dumped it into the *fricasé* hastily, though she really wanted to smell it. Something about the flavors; she still appeared to be cooking, she was treating the mixture like a spice, part of a far greater picture. *You always smell them before you put them in.* It spread out into a thousand flecks and bits and specks, floating all over the top, jumping over bubbles and gathering round the ends of the boiling fury. She scraped at the edges of the pot, mixing it in with everything else. Slowly but surely it disappeared into the food. *'Coño! Forgot to taste it — looked good, too,'* she smiled to herself. Leaving a ring of water on the counter, she lifted the lid and put it back on. She grabbed the dishrag and wiped her hands off on the *trapo,* stained with *puré de tomate* and grease. It was wetter and dirtier than her hands. But it was also a habit. "*Poncho Pilate,*" she said to anyone who may have been listening. She looked at her hands. Wet, but clean.

> There you go, there's no turning back now.
> "Of course there is, if I—"
> Silvia winced as her neck snapped forward.
> "*Ay!*"

"What is it, you watch too much TV while laying on your side again?" Chiche walked out in sweatpants and an undershirt, his feet in sandals. "Bad for your neck, gotta do something better with your time." His pants were black — he always wore blue ones. Always. "You've been walking though, that's good I guess."

"That crick in your neck is for being so goddamn stubborn...*y que*, what's with the pants?" Silvia had a strange tone in her voice, a false sense of passing interest that made her sound nervous.

"*Nada*...they were on the top of my drawer...*y que?*" he said, looking at her nervously. "She even wants to tell me what *pijamas* to wear, '*cuche p'alla*...'" He plopped on the couch with a quiet "*yo te digo...*" that questioned everything. Rubbed his clean pants. He fixed his gaze on the TV and disappeared. Silvia tended to the *tostones*. A puzzled expression came over Chiche's face, as if he suddenly weren't master of his little world. He sat up and pulled at the blinds: "*Oye*...did Tico say he was coming? Why don't you tell me these things, I wouldn't have gotten ready for bed so quickly, *Negra*." Silvia's heart fell into the boiling grease, screaming sizzling cadenzas of invisible profanity. Her voice faltered, echoed into the aethers. *Su puta Madre:* "N-n-nooooooo," she croaked with a grimace over the stove, rubbing her throat. "No. No, why, *he's here? He's here?*" Fear filled her eyes. Wife of *Ibrahim! Goddammit.* Her heart sank into her stomach. What now, Ma, what now *Mi Virgen*, am I wrong in all of this? What am I doing? *CALM DOWN.* Cigarettes. No, no, '*Ay, Virgencita, what am I doing?*'

> *Am I wrong in what I do? Her heart cringed again,*
> *A grape forced into raisin by the heavy heat of remorse.*
> *Ah, but in this pressure is the sweetness the most strong.*
> '*Get it together, this is all in the air, you can*
> *still work it out, life's more unplanned than an improvisation...you came*
> *to the show expecting a guided improvisation, and forgot once you*
> *snapped into the trance...look at him, watching TV...just send these little*
> *birds away, they're trying to fffffuck with our shhhhhhit!* Silvia
> *frowned into her thoughts, oye cuidaito con mal-decir mijito...don't be*
> *weak, Silis...*' Her eyes lit up. "*Ay, pues claro que si.*" Insight bites. She grabbed her smokes on the way outside. Chiche bobbed his eyebrows as she glided by and swung through the door with

hardly a sound, like a passing wraith. 'They'll come inside,' he thought to himself. Back into the screen.

"*Ay, pero Mami,* we were just on our way in!" gushed a flamboyant Tico, locking the car doors as Angelica smiled her greeting with a hand upon the passenger side. *She truly does look like a flower, Silis, you know that's what he thinks of her...*"everything's ok, right?"* Laughter blossomed in the back of Silvia's mind. *He wouldn't imagine.* The Capricorn lighter burst into the twilight, gone as quickly as it came. Cherry flickering, and a plume of smoke out the side of her mouth. *Now we can talk.*

"*Ave Maria, Ave Maria,*" smiled Silvia, "*y es verdad lo que me dice el Tico, que usted luce como una...fllllorecita...*" Angelica shifted nervously, smoothing a ruffle out of her dress. Silvia seemed strange. Heated. Happy. *Pissed.*

"*Pues Gracias,*" she smiled curtly — appropriately — looking at Tico with a flicker of fire in her eyes. Tico, however, was confused. He looked over at Silvia with suddenly thoughtful eyes, curious, inspired. *Inspired.* A two-way mirror. *Behold yourself, these eyes can not lie.* Silvia held his gaze and took another drag of her smoke, watching the plumes curl about his figure in her field of vision.

"*Pues ven y darle a tu Mama un beso, coño!*" she smiled, her form still palpably between them and the door. She shifted her weight to the left, in unison with Angelica's trying to peer behind her. *That's right, you come give me a kiss. I'm the Mother here...* The lovers looked at each other, and then back to Silvia. Tico made his way over, his eyes fixed on his mother.

"*Algo...algo aqui estaaaa...extraño,*" he smiled, his drawl revealing a gold tooth at the back of his mouth that was not there. *El Bohemio.* And the smoke passed through his eyes and they glowed fiercely white — if only for an instant. *Mmmm.* Silvia noticed. And the beehive began to churn with red lights as if in response, red lights she could not see but could feel all through her insides, what the hell is all of this, it's like a shiver and a stomachache, a feeling she could only call red, *this,* swirling about her and letting her *relax, relax...relax into the pain...*but she could say nothing, nothing came to mind, only those flickering white eyes, what the hell is going on, relax *niña, here he comes, here he —*

and Tico leaned in, softly, like a poet, and gave her a kiss on the cheek. Pulled back slowly, found her eyes, and holding them, lifted a hand into the air between them, two fingers, like the sword, like Christ and the Venerable Kabirs, and he made for Silvia's —

"*Ay, pero que's eso, niño!*" Silvia wailed, laughing out loud toward Angelica. She took his fingers into her calloused fist, tossing the light to the side like a little firefly. She laughed as Tico snapped out of it and back into himself, placing herself between him and the door...and then, with no intention or forethought, she reached out and set a hand upon Tico's chest. It was *electric*. His eyes, they went wide, and he swallowed, and was still again. Looked into her eyes, confused. Smiled. "Mother's love," he said to Angelica. "Only *Mami* can touch my heart like that."

Silvia smiled brightly into Angelica's confused smile. "*Ay, si,*" ventured the Colombian blonde.

"Tico, Lica, look, let me tell you something." Silvia took a long, ominous drag. "I don't know why you're here right now, but I've —"

"Mami, you look tired, have you been alright?" Tico's eyes were on fire.

Oilslicks — ugh! "*Si*, I've been watching this show that's on late, it's an old one." she rubbed her eyes instinctively.

"Hmm..." murmured Tico, and his gaze snapped over Silvia's right shoulder —

"*A ver...y queh'ehhhhhto aqui afuera...que hay fiehhhta singgg mi?*"

Hijole! Ahora si se jodio la cosa.

"*Mira lo que noh'an traido los Reyes,*" Silvia smiled, flicking her ash to the ground.

"*Papi*, what's up with the pants," laughed Tico, "you always wear blue pants."

"*Pero que lio tienen ustedes con mihh —* "

"*Ay Tico,*" answered Silvia, "they were on his top drawer, everything's a little... funny tonight." She smiled to herself. Tico saw it. She remembered the stove. Eyes went wide — "Hold on, I'll be right back!" and she ran inside. *If there's one dish you can't burn...Jesus Christ. And his smoky tocino.*

"Yeah, a little funny..." said Tico into the open door...he looked to Angelica for a long second, but she didn't look back. She missed it. The house glowed yellow inside, lamplight and the flickering of the television. The pungent smell of *sofrito*.

"*Y que, que hacen aqui, buscando jama?*" You guys lookin for a handout or what?

"*Como siempre, Papi,*" smiled Tico.* Like always.

"*Buuuuue — Sib-bia ehhhta cocinando un bolíche, asi que ha de ver pa todos.*" Still on the Goddamn *bolíche*. There was a moment of silence, while Angelica thought of something to say, she felt like it was her turn to say something, but there was a tension in the air that didn't let her say a word, until Silvia appeared once again in the door with her wooden spoon. It glistened with steaming *sofrito*.

"Doña Silvia," said Angelica, and that was all. She wanted to leave.

"I'm cooking a *frisasé* tonight," she said casually. Tico frowned and looked to Chiche. And it hit Silvia like a lightning bolt — it had all been autopilot, fight or flight in fear, when in doubt indulge in routine — "*pero sabes que...*you know, it's not a lot, I made it with the last of the chicken *en el freeser.*"

"*Ñooo Negra, a negarle un plato de comida a tu proprio hijo! Pero coño,* we can all sit i—"

"*Chiche. Ya,*" spat Silvia. "I'm the one who's cooking, I know how much damned chicken there was in the *freeser,* there won't be enough, *callate la boca si no sabes lo que decir.*" *This sonnn, of a bitch.* Tico stepped in with a wave of the hand.

"Please, please, *Mami, Papi,* it's no problem, we were just passing through the neighborhood and decided to stop by." He looked to Angelica. "We just ate, actually, it's fine." Images of Silvia and Chiche writhing about under the sheets flashed across Angelica's mind.

"*Ahh,*" she said to herself, surprised. Looked to Tico, who shot her a wink.* *She's comin around, beloved.* Then came the grimace. And then the sigh, she was hoping to get another taste of Silvia's cooking, she could never figure out what it was that gave it that touch, that touch that she couldn't create on her own. 'My Colombian food always comes out so good, though... 'Ugh. Only he'll be tasting it tonight—*ay, bollo de pescado, por Dios!*'

"*Eso esta extraño,*" grimaced Chiche, "that's weird, that there's not enough food at my house. I don't like it, I don't like it at all." He looked to Silvia: "There better be enough for my lunch tomorrow. I don't wanna see you at your cooking pot in the middle of the day."

"*Ay, Chiche,*" smiled Silvia, but she held her tongue. She didn't want to send him to hell in front of the kids. "*Este Negro si me quiere,*" she smiled, and smacked the wooden spoon against her open palm without thinking. This nigga *shooo love me.*

Smack. went the spoon, again. *Smack. His fuckin face.*
Get these niggas outta here.

"*Bueno,* you guys want some *café,* something? I can't send you away without having something, come on, let me go get some *chicharrones.*"

"No *Mami,* Mami calm down, *calmate,* it's ok, really, we were just stopping by to say hi, we're on our way downtown for a pot of Japanese tea." Tico looked to Angelica again. He took a deep breath, swallowing a smile. "*Mmm,* I can just *smell* the romance cooking up, we'll be on our way." He continued, hiding the tension in his voice. "That's good, you two, it's beautiful, like Garcia Marquez."

"*Por el rio Magdalena,*" chimed Angelica, suddenly looking

to Chiche's tanktop and *Santos*, his belly, his lanky arms and moist, innocent eyes, and letting all of it go, just like that. *Por Dios.* 'That must be love, I suppose, to connect even when the years have made you old and grey. *Ay Magdalena*, there's no such thing as ugly, I keep forgetting.' Tico was lounging on the couch when he told her that, she remembered it clear as day. Silvia's guts began to roil—everyone was thinking about her having sex, she wanted to scream—but she let it go. *There's your Cuquita, your scapegoat. Fuck it.* Fuck *him. Be sexy, niña,* it'll drive them away. She smiled.

"*Ay...pero este naufragio?*" she cackled into the evening air. "He'll be lucky if I serve him his food tonight."

"Ah, but you guys don't know what happens when I rub her feet," grinned a suddenly 'in-the-know' Chiche—

"*OK Mami, Papi,* we're on our way out of here," and the *Bohemio* took Angelica's hand, bringing it to his lips for a quick kiss. "I'm sorry, but we've got our own evening to tend to, Venus just squared Saturn and we've been practicing our Mudras, right *muñequita?*"

"I...thought we were going to go downtown?"

"Ah! The Grove, indeed. I mean...the Garden." And the flower blushed. "We're all in the Garden tonight—ok *si*, we'll be on our way out," and with that they said their goodbyes— Angelica was always too kind during this part, like how the happiest part of mass is that last sign of the cross, the light of God, the back doors opened up to let us *out!*—closing the car doors behind them with a rattle that was both empty and whole: life itself, the Gardenia would have said into Tico's ear. And the car pulled out of the driveway, the lights flicking on. And stopped in its tracks. Tico rolled the window down, bit by bit, pointing those two fingers out right into his Mami's heart and spoke directly to her, as if everyone else in the world had disappeared:

"You see? Remember what we were talking about the other night, this is a gift from heaven." And with that the car roared away and around the corner right through the stop sign onto the eight lanes of the River Flagler. Both old birds listened to the sound of the engine dissipate into the rest of the noise. The kids fleeing the nest. And she sighed a long, long sigh, her eyes fixed on a streetlamp. She felt like crying.

"*Coño...*" said Chiche. "What the hell was that, *Negra*. You know they came to eat something. You're actin weird tonight, *Negra, cuidate*, you be careful," and the imaginary threat of a backhanded slap across the face followed him into the house, where she heard him plop onto the couch and change the channel around six times before coming back to the same one that had been on before. And she felt him disappear once again.

"*Goddammit*," Silvia said, wiping her brow. 'That was rough, but you made it. I made it,' she corrected herself. A gift from heaven...it's an omen, they think we're gonna sprawl, and what they don't know is that my gift from heaven will my freedom from his bullshit. 'That's a good fuck right there.'

"It's tough sending him away like that," blared Chiche from inside the door. "I can't let it go, I feel bad, I wish he would have stayed. *Coño*, I've never seen you do that, *Negra, me ha dejao medio nervioso...*" It's left me a little nervous...he turned towards her figure, which had appeared in the frame of the door. "You ok?" He looked up. "Why didn't you just whip something up for them, a goddamn *tortilla Ethpañola*?" Silvia stood and walked back to the stove. "*Etho ethhhebolla y jamong, un tiempo ganao...*"

"I think, he was right...*mi amor*. Tonight feels like a night for just you and me. Yennifer's in Tampa—"

"*Que que?*"

"*Ay Chiche*," laughed Silvia, turning around to reveal a writhing smile: "*Shut up, you know I'm kidding, your Huracán hasn't caused a storm in years.*"

And she made her way to the stove, listening to a speechless Chiche rant about time and work and the kids from before and remember Cuba and this is how it works, that novel was a lie, it's the diabetes, Cuco told me about this pill they've got now and eventually he stopped on his own... Chiche more than anyone had learned to quit while he was ahead. And that *Goddamn* freckle on the head.

The Television serenaded the silence until Silvia broke it with her song.

"*Dale*, come eat." The declaration was definitive. The space shifted, the food was ready, the kids were gone. It was time. It hung in the air, the declaration, the *sentencing*, passing through her loins, stirring them with such force that she leaned onto the table with a heave, and her face beaded with the essence of a cold sweat. *Get. Yourself. Together.* It's finally happening. She thought of the empty vial. Took a deep breath, one that was not hers. *There's no turning back, I'll kill you instead, you'll kill someone else, just THINK of that feeling, sssssssssssssssssliccccccccing through his neck, seeing his blood spill, oh, my God...* Her sex grew hot with the stir of awakening bees, drones coming out of their hive by the thousands. *Flowers called, full of nectar for the Queen.* Silvia took a deep breath. Chiche turned off the TV and there was silence. Oh God. It roared throughout the house, more present than the air itself. She heard his footsteps, the *crack* of rubber gritting across a clean slate as he shuffled across the pinkish-white tile floor *step* by *step* and headed to the table, to the same plate he ate from everyday, the one with the faded little flowers on it, waiting on the greasy doily covered with creases and crumbs from that morning's *pan Cubano*. It was all so perfect, so normal. Seamless. On it was a mound of white rice, and on the doilies in the middle of the table she had set the salad —

"*Si, hombre, there's that avocado,*" he said, smiling at the thought of the sultry widow. 'Still got it,' he thought to himself as he sat down. "*Mmmmm, coño, aguacatico que he ha dao la vida.*" Silvia stopped in her tracks — but he was talking to himself. He picked up a piece of the avocado with his fingers and popped it into his mouth. "*Y que shabrosho e'ta, Nefhrita.*" Silvia came over with the plate full of hot, fresh *tostones* sitting atop the translucent paper towel and followed it with the steaming plate of *fricasé* that would have been so good had it not been teeming with *burundanga*. Tobacco, sand, papaya, blood. *Jesus Mary and Joseph* it was time for Silvia to be coy. She went back to kitchen, fumbling with some dirty dishes. *The fuckin ball's in the court now. Y niña, smile – you're a natural.*

"*Negra, y no te vas a sentar?*" Chiche looked up at her, puzzled. Her loins reeled again, pulling her insides close to her spine with such force that her breath pulled her throat shut.

"*No, no,*" she said cooly, smiling. "I had some *café con leche* just now while I was cooking, I'll eat some leftovers later, for when my show's on, the Brazilian one. *Come,*" she insisted. *Eat. Eat, eat, malpinga. Dale.* He held her gaze, suspicion crossing his face. Silvia's gut swarmed. He took a whiff of the steaming plate before him.

"I'm telling you *Negra,* you're getting weirder and weirder tonight... You...expect me to eat this..." he said, and this time with the same old bullshit pause came a thousand answers, questions, accusations and ruined moments, food out the window and into his face, *sangre criolla* splayed across the heavy glass door, upheavals, suspicions, revolts, thundering angels of right and wrong, blowing on long trumpets and churning oceans of fateful fury all over Silvia's mind, "*...sin un tenedor?*" The Goddamn fork. *You'll go crazy, I swear! Relax!*

"*Ay, Chiche,* you stress me out...*coño.*" She went off and fished through all the mismatched silverware until she found the thick, heavy fork. It was his favorite. She set it down in front of him.

"*Mmhmm,*" he said, happy to have food before him. Another piece of avocado with his hands. Sucked his fingers. *Cerdo.*

"*Mmhmm,*" he said said again, and she replied with the same *mmhmm,* happy to watch him finally take a bite. *Traigo su vino, denme mi pan...*

"*Coooojones!*" shouted Chiche. "This is *good,* Tico should have stayed to have some! Oh, better tonight than ever, I might call him—" and he put another forkful into his mouth. "This is why I married you, *negrita*, right here, for a night like tonight." Silvia stood there behind the sink, watching him eat, so gluttonous, so happy. *Un puro marrano.* He looked to her— *"Me estas vigilando?"* —and Silvia jumped, washing the dish she was holding once again. " *Negra, I'm telling you...eso es falta de alimento...ven, come."* Silvia cringed. Thought of her rolls, the scratch-marks on them. No, she didn't need to eat more. And none of *this*.

"No, no, *Negrito*, I told you, I'll eat later." She went outside and lit a cigarette, leaving his presence. Out of earshot, out of mind, isn't that how it goes in marriage? *Ay*, the evening was *alive!!!* She swatted at a nasty-looking bug on her arm she hadn't seen since Cuba. It flew away, bobbing into the night sky. The tip of her cigarette was long, phallic. She felt that crazed itch in her womb that seared whenever she used to think of her school crushes, and it sent hot shivers up her spine. *Ay, Virgen Santísima!* Oh, it's happening, it's happening, you feel it? forget the memories, the feeling's reality. Mmmm, we're cooking, look, look at him. On the other side of the door, Chiche yawned over his food. He— *ay, padre santisimo, oilslicks!* He rubbed his eyes, cast around with dark, ashy rings that hadn't been there minutes before.

"*Negra,*" he said into the glass door, "leave my plate here, I've got to"—he yawned—"I've...got a stomach...sleepy for the...bed, I have to...*mmmmmmmuayyyyy...*" and he looked into her eyes, and she saw that he was no longer there, it was startling, horrifying, *ñoooo ehhhto lo ha padddtiiiio sin pensallll-lo doh veces niña!!!* His pupils had gone as wide as they could and she could see every color in them, like the glow around a crystal in the dark, glowing emptily from all the way across the room and through the door, imagine what was going on in there, this is real, it's too real, it's scary, it's *sexy*, this isn't good it's witchcraft, it's *hot*, this shit is real and flashes of Ofelia's dark crystal came across her mind and the ribbons and strings and stove-fires and dreams,

African masks and talking Virgins smiling to her over her
shoulder, she frowned into his empty eyes with her piercing green
eyes, *aquellos ojos verdes*, he was there no longer, he's gone already
look at him, and she took a drag of her cigarette, listening to him
groan and babble more and more incoherently about his sleepy
stomach without saying a word, without breaking his empty gaze,
and after hovering about his plate of food in a stupor he groaned
with a nod of finality and heaved himself up out of his seat, he
was going to take care of it himself, *es cosa de hombre*, and his
breath scraped heavily as the chair slid across the back of the floor
and he stumbled off first towards the bathroom, and then to the
hallway, smacking his lips past the pictures of the *santos* and the
kids to the bedroom where Silvia imagined he collapsed onto the
bed behind closed eyes into that deep sleep Ofelia had told her
about, the false death of the slaves, burping up hot fumes of *fricasé*
and *burundanga*—*what the hell are you thinking, you don't even know
what you're doing. Think about it.* Serpents and doves. *Slit his
throat, he's not dead yet, it's finally time, think of all that freedom, all the
bullshit, are you really scared now?* Ay, no! *Be free of your sick, pitiful
life! Now, now, it's finally time! What are you doing just standing
here, it's fucking time, you can smoke another cigarette, take this one
inside you're stressing me out, you did all this work and the moment has
finally arrived, are you fucking serious right now?* The beehive was
reeling, there was a swarm about her, churning the quills of
smoke into nothing *and look it worked fast, huh...wow, Silis, too fast, I
don't think I'm ready, you ready? You better be ready it's time, this is
your moment, your gift from heaven, we're going in oh my god I will
drink this blood, the spittle across the blade of the machete will be my
fingers across thick, freckled lips mmmmm...Jenny's in Tampa, what are
you gonna do, how you gonna do it? Hmmmmm? Easy, niña, you
wanna smoke another cigarette? That's what you'll do, you'll clean it
all up and go throw him in the ocean. All of it, has to happen tonight.
Pigs will eat all of him, you don't got no pigs, just throw him into the
ocean, it's going to storm tomorrow remember the weather report?
Night time will pull him out to sea. Sharks will smell the blood. Go.
Hammerheads, tigersharks, reefsharks! We're fine, Ave Maria, Ave*

Maria, Ave Maria...Mother of God, ruega por nosotros pecadores, now and at the hour of – will his heart really stop? *'Is he really dead?'* No! *Matalo! Matalo!* Kill him! Go now! A rush of cold air came over Silvia's body, and she began to tremble. *'I'm...'* and she sighed a long sigh, *'scared,'* she thought, wanting to cry. A sharp pain came over her, from her stomach up to her head, to her toes, and she lurched over herself, dropping her cigarette. *Fucking shit! Let's GOOOO, and do it you're fucking it up at the pinnacle moment* –

"I. Need. To EAT," growled Silvia into the glass door. She hissed into the half-visible glare of her eyes on the glass. Focused into the house. Still life. The same shit for twenty three-years, is it twenty-six? *"Madre Santísima,"* she said, pressing a hand to her sex. She *gripped. Ay, Madre Santisima...* Thoughts of the knife inside of her womb. Birthing into freedom, remember the moment when they were finally born, the *release,* O God, the machete, drinking blood, breathe, breathe deep, drinking blood that's what we do...her hand tingled with pleasure, feeling with her fingertips, electric velvet, her insides coming alive with more and more bees, thundering growls booming across the back of her mind, and the heat rose to her chest, and up through her neck into her flushing face, and she gritted her teeth, crackling crystals into her skull with the frenzy of a thousand wasps. *I'm getting pisssssssssssssssssssssssed...* Her eyes went wide with rage. Into the door again, she saw the living room reflected in them, eerily green. They stung her from the inside-out, thousands of drones, wasps, hovering, setting it down gently like a syringe, driving it in, everywhere again and again, she couldn't shake it off, it was all so real, and the pleasure melding with the pain, there was no difference. She shook with a thundering shudder. *Ughhhhhh....*she growled. "Come, let us go. I am the Mother of Charity, *Virgen de la Caridad.* Your storms end here, upon the crystalline path I have made for you, let us walk, let us walk, it is finally time, remember those dreams as a little girl, you do, you do, you were born for *this very moment!"* She bent over to grab her cigarette, drawing on it like a banshee, harder and harder, but it had gone out.

"Feel it, I feel it, I'm alive, it is destiny, here, on the edge of time,"
she said, hunched over, bobbing like a slave.
She snapped her head to the right.
Eyes can not lie.
Eyes smile.

"Haaaaaaaaaay!" she yelped in surprise, shooting herself upright. A bird had flown right by her face, perching itself on the wooden fence across the yard. *Inches* from her face. It was a grey dove, two of them, one of them, two again, and it looked at her with its beady, black eyes. The air shifted, and Silvia stared at the bird for a long, drawn-out moment until it twitched and flew away. Another shudder, her arms whipped about and were still again. She turned, sliding the screen door open and walked into the smells of a happy household. Absolutely still. She tiptoed gracefully, scared of stirring the blissful silence all about her. Warmth, flavor, home is where the heart is...a bubbling pot of blood set in the hearth. Chiche, we're going home.

The dark red *fricasé* had coagulated in the middle of table. A wave of shame came over her, it's really happening, I shouldn't have listened to that *Santera*, look at this shit, and she thought of feeding the rest to the neighbor's dog. Smiled, rubbing her eye. She took a deep breath and frowned. "I am free." *Fuck La Virgen – winced.* She growled, repeating to herself, "No, no, no...She is my Mother. *Fuck La Virgen. What am I doing. I m not saying this...si mija, look how little you know, you gotta piss her off, you gotta make it happen, get her to come down and kick your ass, her attention is all you need, it's the power, this fucking cunnnn-t, come down you little bitch!"* "You *slut!* Aaaaahhhhhhh!!!" she screamed. "STOP! STOP IT! STOP! FUCK HER, FUCK YOU! AAAHHH!" She could feel it from here, he was out cold. Stings prickling all over, thousands of tiny legs tickling her every inch of skin, lines of them crawling up her ass and out of her ears, she opened them into her throat, oilslicks writhing in agony, it's time to go inside, make it happen, I'm coming I'm coming Oh my God it's finally time you've been so good until now...the house, the entire house was out cold. *Ay, se aparecio la Quinceañera, tirale una foto que de aqui solo se pone peor la cosa.* It was the freezing space around the blazing sun, breathing deeper, heavier breaths. *Mmmmmm....* Heat from the kitchen, freezing breezes, the smell of old, musty crap everywhere, stale cigarette smoke and freshly cooked food, Television toothpaste commercials and the push and pull of cold winds and humidity, all of the senses were bulging open into the true squalor of the moment, open the windows open the window, all these horrors are surfacing past the perfumes in the wall-plugs, the ripening fruits, the sweets, the coffee, everything was nauseous, overwhelming. The darkness is blinding me, eyes become *vacuous slits* —

"Wise as a serpent...gentle as a dove," she tiptoed, gracefully.

Across to the living room and into the hallway with a long, slow turn, *la Quinceañera,* past the *santos* looking at her with piercing eyes, high priests in a court of dark art. The light is the *bess disquise, mmmmmm....* Eyes shining like beacons, onyx encased in searing ivory, every color at once. Glycerin drool, clinging, clinging to your beautiful lips... She made her way towards the end of the hall, step by step, toe by toe, smiling, squeezing the joys in her gut tight, tight, the beehive furiouser and furiouser with every heavy breath... Slow and luxurious it was, this promenade, this elegant reverie past the closet full of blankets and bed-sheets and into the bedroom, *ahi viene la Quinceañera,* whose door lingered seductively open. Beyond the doorway the air was hot and still, the lights eerie and yellow — just like always. "Look at those lamps, I'll have to dust them off in the morning." Chiche was sprawled across the bed, face down. She tiptoed over to the mirror and looked at herself disgustingly, poising high as she took a bottle from the mirror-faced perfume rack and touched it to her neck, twice. She sniffed, and set it back down again.

Posed. Once in a lifetime, *mija, gordita*, drink it all in. It was a moment of glory. Ran a hand slowly down her *bata*. Ready and waiting, she would have said to him if he could hear. Ready and waiting, my Chiche. *Mi amor.* She approached the bed carefully and lay her hand on his stiff shoulder, rolling him over. His eyes were white and glossed with every color, like a bubbly film of glycerin in the sun, rolled back into his head. *Tico. Fabada. Cigarro. Matalo, matalo* — and she squeezed the handle on the blade. Empty fists. The walls chittered, clicks and creaks. *Animals* outside. *Fffffffear.* Ancient stories, *mijita*, that's all we are. Chiche was limp and passive, heavy, *'for the last time, malpinga,'* she growled from the depths of her mind. She smiled, aroused by the excitement of the moment.

"*Ay*, this is so *real*," she stretched into the emptiness with extended arms and a long breath back, smiling, her stomach trembling with nerves, excitement..."*traigo su vino, denme mi pan...*" She crouched down and peered under the bed, where the electricity was booming in every direction, enticing, velvet *acccccccc*id echoing everywhere from her chest, this heart has never been so alive as it was just then. Her heart trembled, palpitated as she reached for it, her entire body tingling with the opiate of raw, vulnerable sex, it was ecstasy. *Mmmmm*...goading her on, guiding her every motion. She brought her fingers slowly around the hilt of the blade, ran around *tight* with leather that had begun to crack, and squeezed with all her might. Knuckles popped, joints cracked into a grip of steel, river rocks pounding on years of plantains. Surges of power flowed through her — grip a weapon of death under the pangs of bloodlust and feel it for yourself — and she pulled away, pushing herself up with a mighty crack of her back. One-two-three-four-fivesix pops and a breath into a straight spine. "*Mmmmmm....!*" Rolled her neck around, wielding the knife like a powerful, vengeful Goddess. *Ochun, Ochun!* she cried out in her thoughts, but the answer was in the silence, all about her like a sacred shroud. She is here, *la Quinceañera...* Her head snapped back, taking a long, deep breath in. It was rich, thick, filling her entire being with its presence. She laughed. He *sssneezed!* –

"*Aaaaayyyyyy!*" she screamed. He fell backwards onto the bed, eyes back into his head, and he was still again. Limp. "*Jesucrísto,*" she said, sighing. She grew angry. Squeezed the handle. "*Goddammit!*" laughed Silvia in shock, gripping the knife again with a new fervor. "I...I can't do this, what am I—*dale.*" Her voice grew gruff. Her eyes fell over with a foggy resolution, dim, dark, and she moved closer to him, edging herself onto the corner of the bed, into the merciless pit of bloodlust. War, and religion. Religion, and war.

It's our past, it's humanity, it's love.

A spindly mosquito-eater hovered silently across the room, bobbing its way

> onto the corner of the
> ceiling lamp.*

"*Chiche...Chiche...negro...*" whispered Silvia nervously, hoarsely, her voice trembling into the charged air. Nothing. The room was enormous, cold. Smile. She crawled onto the bed, on all fours, and hovered over him. Kiss the knife, Chiche *mi amor, mmmmmmm...* She yearned between her legs, hot and ready for *man,* for *anything,* for a hot *pinnnn...*to fill it all in, I can drink the ocean into this empty heart, fill it all in, fill it all in, and she looked down, startled, pulling her *bata* up to see his sweatpants. She had been seizing, gripping him, straddling his undead body. *Es cosa de hombre,* it's a man thing, below the faded black cotton his manhood writhed and bulged itself into shape, twitching with the unconsciousness of every sleeping heartbeat. It grew before her eyes, coiling itself around his groin to the left, pulsing every few seconds like some newborn creature. "I've never understood these things," she said out loud, slightly horrified...*mmmmmm...*she grabbed at the sweatpants with her hand and closed her grip tightly around the bulge; it jerked and pulled itself tight with blood, and she looked up to his face with

wide raging eyes, you've freed an *Amazon*, breathing heavily.
Eyes still white. She touched his face, hissing inwards with
gritted teeth. Nothing, nothing across his face. Just his manhood.
That's all I need. I need, need, *mmmmmmmm*...the beehive churned
and churned, harder and harder, with every pound of her her
racing heart. She touched his lips softly, the rings around his
eyes, almost expecting the lids to flutter softly, like the petals of a
flower, an anemone thumping shut at the bottom of the sea.
Nothing. Undead. *Nsambi.* She felt like a little girl, hovering over
the lifeless body of her husband. He had finally become her toy,
the women weren't lying, it's absolutely blissful. But I'm done, I'll
kill him and find another. This power is intoxicating, toxic. She
ran the tip of the machete across his still eyes, across eyelids that
could flutter no longer. Trapped. Straddled by your wife,
brandishing a machete over your lifeless face. Helpless, lost in
hallucinations. What a little child, can't dress himself in the
mornings! A hot rush passed over her feet, *ayyyyy*...something
slithered over them. Swatting behind her in alarm, there was
nothing there, of course not. *Goddamn mosquito-eaters.* She turned
back, her eyes wide, unnerved. A smile betrayed her lips, her
flushed cheeks, and she looked back at Chiche's face nervously.

She passed the *machete* across her stomach, and her heart
skipped a beat. She breathed in deeply and set it down,
mmmmmmmm... His mouth hung open, his gold teeth shining dimly
in the back of his mouth. His tongue was swollen and smeared
white with God-knows-what, and all the buds across its surface
splayed themselves out, vulnerable, confident in their detachment
from the pain and suffering of this reality. *Arousal.* She squeezed
his manhood again, gripping his core with her strong thighs, she
squeezed as hard as she could, she would smother him to death
with her *papaya*, he would suffocate and squirm as she reeled with
pleasure until the moment of *connnnnsummmation...mmmmmmmm...*
She swallowed dryly, her throat sticking to itself. Ripping his
pants down, she exposed his balding mess of peppery hairs, a
greasy bed of straw, of her most carnal of instincts, the disgust,

the oilslicks, the shame, her Amazonian hunger, and she reached around the pants and took it into her cold hand, feeling a rush of heat, a rush of relief, pour through her like a frigid undertow that washed her with the joys of so many years ago, everything she had deserved all her life at once, here and now. Everything was hers. The beehive, it oozed with honey, the Queen was swerving about with rolling eyes. She rolled with the white current into the depths of the dark, moonlit ocean and was lost in the moment, letting herself be taken up and across his body, washed across his chest, and she put him inside herself, it happened on its own like magic, and she sat up straight with a gasp, a lightning bolt straight up her spine and out the top of her head, feeling his searing rod brand her insides with the heat of a thousand red stars up into the core of that frenzied beehive, this connection is so perfect, so *sacred*, and it emptied itself all over her body, screaming bees released into the infinity within her, her dry, empty garden of withering weeds. All of it was set ablaze, the beehive itched with blazing fire, and the point of sensation was brighter than a welding torch, blinking, blinking like fireworks on their way to the ground. Charcoal fell all about them. Dust, and crumbles. She screamed with angst, with remorse and pleasure, clawing at his chest and pulling his lifeless body up to her by the saints around his neck. Chew on the mouthful of dirt... Shrieking curses, at the world, at the clear blue sky above. Clouds in the night, waves breaking on the slowly moving ocean of stars. Thousands of red stars, pouring all about in lifeless circles, rhythms forming at the basis of the universe. Her *bata* was halfway up her waist, porous unshaved legs and calloused feet defying the thick air of the room with their unworthy presence, her stomach and stretch-marks free to dominate the room, she was ugly, she hated everything and it all felt like bliss, like the Virgin, the *Quinceañera*, the very first time, her old body pulling his into hers by the forbidden fruit — she would swallow him whole. She would drink the ocean, she would drink the seven seas and all of their stories of fame and fortune alike, oceans of blood, plagues of pestilence. Death to the firstborn son of the Pharoah, it was absolutely disgusting, never more real, and the waves tossed her to and fro atop this sacred fire that had been left in darkness for so many years.

And she took a deep, long breath into the stillness,
the silent darkness all around this blazing fire.

Her eyes poured into the worlds behind his closed eyelids with the heat of a panthress, her teeth bared angrily, her eyes tight as slits, throwing him around and sucking on the droplets of blood that bloomed from the scratches. His chest touched hers, and she pressed him to her sagging, swollen breasts, to her swollen heart, pulling at his head, scratching his face, embracing him in her femininity. Kissing the blood across his cheeks, his lips, smearing the saliva with stringy ribbons of blood. Squelches and writhing hisses issued forth from her bowels, and they grew full of thick serpents of her hatred, her past, her failure at life, gripping the beehive with force that sent more and more of the sickening, sweet sensation through her body, to her fingertips, to her open mouth. Her ugly mouth. Her ugly, beautiful eyes. Her pulse played across her lips as she jerked herself across her husband's body, over and over, over and over. It was horrible, the only sound in the room under the shrieking of her ears, the peals of ringing bells that smothered the silence that would have disturbed any fly on the wall. Mosquito-eaters. Wasps. *Spiders.* She looked up to the yellow light above her and pressed herself down onto him deeper, deeper, her body seizing, her heart wrenching with so many years of pent-up aggression, hundreds of soap operas and shitty magazines incinerated in the heat of her moment. She touched her navel, flattened by age and repulsing decay, and let Chiche go, his lifeless body falling back onto the bed with a boom that pulled him into her a little more and she moaned, drawing her nails across the skin of his thighs. She grabbed the *machete* that danced across the bedsheet with a leering smile. Frigid hands clawed at her from behind and she *laughed, slapping at her shoulders and swinging the blade behind her, awake and empowered. She moved in fitful gasps, expanding in every direction, her bata torn from her body, her breasts dancing in an eternal arc of graceful freedom, the dance of the seven veils has shown itself to its wrathful core, riding him over and over again, every man in the world, every drop in the ocean down my throat, swallowing dryly, scrrrrraping against sticky crystals of syrupy honey, it was the ride she had never allowed herself to in the past, don't stop, keep it going, don't stop now, don't fail me now, don't fail me now Negro, just like that, just like I showed you...* She had never been on top, she had never bought her own cigarettes, she had never gone outside on her own. "Mmmmmmmnnnn..." *she whined, biting her lip. Pulling, pulling, whence shall come the nectar, the blood? The tables have turned, my little Chiche, the tables have turned. don't stop, don't stop now, keep it going, just like that, you're being so good, mmmm...* The side of the *machete* ran itself across the blood seeping from the scratches, across his chest, his stiff nipples, his bobbling gut, his face. Biting her lip, she drew the blade to his neck, feeling her arms flex with tension, with laughter, and she shrieked with the hatred of fallen angels as a thick jet of hot fluid filled her insides with fiery embers, molten sulphur at the bottom of the dark volcanic ocean, and the *machete* flew across the room, smashing into an image of the Virgin on the wall.

"*AAAAAYYYYYY!*" Silvia hissed in agony, throwing herself off of her limp husband and to the dresser behind which the frame had fallen. She threw it to the side, crashing it to the floor with the strength of an Amazon, the strength of a mother, a Goddess, in heat. Glass littered the floor and stuck into her feet. She screamed over and over again, tears streaming down her face, her body aroused with the black remorse of sexuality, of sin, *what have I done? what have you done?* And there behind the dresser she saw the Virgin, torn across Her womb, looking at her with the *machete* splayed across her body, her eyes still, unrevealing, as if Silvia had walked in on their promiscuity, between her and this machete. Stay *out of it*, didn't you see the sock on the door you little *slut?* She heaved with a wave of nausea, her throat sticking as she swallowed it all down into her stomach.

"*Ay pinga, ay pinga, ayyyy, mi Virgensita, mi Virgensiiiiiiiita!*" she cried out in shame, her knees bobbing back and forth, marching quickly in stillness, going nowhere, slap me is any of this real, it hurts, it hurts, the reality. It was her Mother's picture, it was all she had brought over from the island and she had destroyed it, desecrated it in the heat of sin. She took the picture to her breast, hugging her beloved Mother, hugging the torn Virgin, sobbing in a pile of broken glass that cut into her knees, the only reminder that all of this was real. She closed her eyes, and her tears stopped, her body going unfathomably numb with an emptiness that had crept up from her knees to the top of her head, and it swallowed everything.

There was silence.

Blissful, blissful silence. Her blood flowed through every inch of her body, pulse by pulse, as she lay and let the darkness consume everything, her womb full, finally complete. She seized, and was still again. *Relax, niña...and giggles echoed into the darkness around her, the bubbling laughter of tightly pursed lips...*

She felt herself dissolve further into the broken glass, deeper and deeper, I'm not dying, the fear makes no sense, the fear of pain, it's all an illusion, onto the carpet littered with shame and months of un-vacuumed dust, a powdery sigh of oblivion, and thoughts...surfaced...with a lucid clarity.
Blood...glass...witches and pearly semen, long draughts of potions and oblations to treacherous spirits, tears across the face of the machete, Chiche's blood, Chiche's tear-filled soul dripping red and white onto her naked body, squealing pigs suckling at their dead mother's teats, disgusting violations of sexual taboos smeared with ashes and shit in cremation grounds, African masks and ground-up unborn children, what do you need I can do it for

you, but everything comes with it's *priiiiicee*...corpses, screams and laughter in the distance and she couldn't find it in herself to move any longer, she couldn't she tried, she didn't want to, didn't need to, didn't care to...it was everywhere now, the hatred was bigger than her, it was she who would die, it was she who wanted to die...*children*...the *machete's* eye stared blankly into the ceiling, eyes cannot tell a lie. She moaned as a hot tear slid down into her ear. It blocked the sound of the silence, and she heard her body churning all about behind her plugged ear, her heart lolling its sloshy beatings of blood encased in constricted veins, pulsating everywhere at once, trying to escape its prison over and over again for years, refuse and bile, childhood emptiness, Anaíli's aged palms, old memories curling across her calloused skin black and white, and black sparkling stars of purples and greens...the most beautiful eyes of clear, blue light...so quick it's a memory and not an image, a thought...remember I was here with you, I am here with you...and she swirled into the death of sleep without even realizing it.

~*~

The air was damp and still, and the sky hinted at the emerging violets of twilight. Alone, Silvia found herself walking along a deserted path of rubble and sand, approaching a crossroads at whose intersection loomed a great tree. "Siete Rayos tiene esa mata, Siete Rayos..." Getting closer, she saw that it had seven great roots reaching into the soil, this tree, and the leaves hovered majestically upon the boughs of the powerful trunk and core, splaying themselves into seven branches of staunch repose. She looked down the four roads, one at a time, confused by the smell of burning tobacco, and saw nothing in any direction, making her feel alone and scared. Who's smoking, it's right here, I can smell it... Nervously, she made her way around the great tree to see if she would find anything, and at the foot of the tree she found a little black boy sleeping, with a straw hat over his face, and she noticed his feet, tiny and calloused from all the walking he must have done. He wore a red vest and black pants that sat loosely rolled up over his plump thighs down to his knees, and his limbs were soft in the grey morning light. Fearing she would wake him, she tried to make her way by unnoticed, but he stirred and pulled his straw hat up onto his round head: he had been sleeping with one eye open. He smiled, at Silvia, at the tree, the sky, and he jumped up, placing a lit cigar into his mouth. Hmph. Silvia thought he was much too young to be smoking.

"What? Age is a number, come here Ma, I have something to show you." The boy extended his hand in her direction with a mischievous grin. Silvia took his warm hand and noticed, in the little light there was, that his right side was tinted with a subtle sparkle of black, like charcoal in sunlight, and his left side was tinted an earthy red, like the clay of roof tiles under the same hot sun. Together they walked in silence, Silvia and the little black boy, down the road into the light of the approaching dawn. The boy began to hum a song as he smoked, the rhythm going with the steps he made with his little playful legs, one and two and three and one, bringing Silvia feelings of childish joy from out of nowhere, it was like her thoughts about Cuba, if only these could so easily bring the joy out of nowhere, this invisible joy nowhere to be found until it finds you first, and a smile soon came over her face without even realizing it.

It is here, the joy. It's you —

"Do you see that?" the boy asked Silvia, pointing off into the fields. "Over there by the large grey stone." Sure enough, there was a flickering white light all alone in the dead grasses, by a large grey stone. "Let's go see what it is," smiled the boy. Mischief attracts mischief. Silvia, soft and comfortable in the boy's singing, agreed. Together they walked in silence through the grasses and the flickering light grew brighter as they came closer and closer, making the boy pull harder on Silvia's hand, for he seemed to be more anxious to see this interesting sparkle of light than she was. As they came within feet of the light, Silvia saw that it was a coconut all by itself, in the field of rocks and trees that bore nothing close to coconuts. Its eyes glimmered like diamonds under the light of a full moon. It grinned at them, staring with its entrancing gaze, and the boy let go of Silvia's hand, leaping down and crouching before it, his eyes moist, innocent, and wide in the flickering light. He turned to Silvia and gestured for her to come close: "Come here, Ma!" Silvia caught up with him, laughing at the impatience of the little boy, and she too crouched before the coconut, looking into its brilliant eyes. He tapped the ash off from his cigar and crossed his arms, smiling.

"Would you tell my Mother that it's true, that we've seen Obi's shining eyes?" asked the child. "Make sure to tell her I was here with you," and he snuffed the butt of his cigar into the dirt between his feet. "But nothing else." * He smiled up at her from under his straw hat, his eyes two gleaming cowrie shells, bigger than she had ever seen. Silvia screamed, and looked to the coconut, which had become Chiche's lifeless head, its eyes glimmering just as brightly as they were seconds ago. She leapt up with an even louder scream to the boy's great delight, and the ground disappeared beneath them both, but only Silvia began to fall, shrieking as she went. "Remember to tell my Mother, Ma!" the boy yelled at her, laughing as she fell down into the smoke. Thousands of puffs of smoke surrounded her on all sides, blowing into her face and all over, and she felt hot spurts of searing liquor all over her body, clouds of powder in her face, flowers and cinnamon and honey and cloves, bay leaves, oregano and eggshells and thick slaps of palm oil crusted into iridescent orange pearls and chicken blood stock, ancestral soup of debts and memories and generations to come, until she landed in a pit of mud littered with spits of old cud and weeds and dead grass. She looked at herself and saw herself clad in burlap, her body as slender and young as it could ever be. "Mmmmm..." She was sexy and lithe, rubbing her feet against her silky legs in disbelief, it's just like Cuba, but looked about in all directions nervously wondering where she could possibly be. Ran her hands up and down her arms: where's the boy, he didn't fall here with me? Where am I, what is going to happen to me? As the fog retreated from the space, Silvia saw an old man sprawled across a bank in the mud patch, tattered and beaten, covered with bandages and sores. He fed a band of scraggly dogs who whined at his swollen feet, licking them nervously. Scraps of bread, one by one, fight for the little that's given to us all. Give us this day o...a smile came across Silvia's face as she sat up in the mud, making her way towards the tattered king, the fallen soldier.

"Lazaro Santisimo," she said, tears in her eyes. "Milagroso San Lazaro, ay mi Viejo, que merezco yo el honor de verle el rostro a usted."

Her hands went up into the air in salutation, and before she knew it she fell to one knee, her arms crossed up and touching her shoulders, her head bowed. She touched the ground near him, her brow, and said in a voice that was not hers, "Moforibale."

"Y que asi sea," answered the old man, tossing her a piece of the bread. She stuffed it into her mouth with the piety of one who had just spoken with God. The man extended his gaze towards Silvia, his eyes bruised and blackened, resplendent with wisdom only the devil could rival. "Mas sabe el diablo por viejo que por diablo," he said to her, "por eso te han mandado al pie de este viejo, a ver si te puedo hablar de algunas cosas, mi niña." The devil knows more for being old than for being devil, for this they've sent you here to the feet of this old man, to see if we could talk about some things, my little girl. He continued to feed the dogs, smiling at them compassionately as she sat in speechless silence. They licked lovingly at his leprous wounds, quick little laps of healing and hope, and Silvia made her way to his feet at the behest of an urge from the depths of her very soul, huddling at the mass of dogs and proceeding to wash his feet with her tears, cleaning them with her burlap robe, her honor, her pride and pudor, her hair. Huffs and chortles filled her ears, whiffs of air all about her, and never was her heart so close to the meaning of it all.

"Salamaleko-Malekosala," said the old man with a wave of the hand, and there was peace. "Con licensia." He called Silvia's eyes up into his.

"The dog has four legs, yet takes but one path," he said. "You have come a long way, my child, we have been watching you." Silvia broke down and cried like the little girl she had been the whole time, all her life since youth, since Cuba, and tears streamed down her face and onto his bruised, broken feet...it was as if they left trails of pure gold, over age-spots, scars and bulging veins, you've been here the whole time, Lazaro, we waste so much time away from this, this joy we seek in all the wrong places. "Your path has come to a tremendous crossroads, and for this have you seen Elegguá — I hope he was not smoking — who brought you to my side." He took a dog under his arm and began to scratch its head. "That little boy is older than I am," he smiled to himself. "I would like to ask you, my child, why you wish to kill the man you once felt fit to

marry." He paused. "My child." Silvia's knees went suddenly weak.

She sighed a long, long sigh. "Lazaro, you who know it better than I do, I have been brought to a happiness that I forgot long ago and this is all I know, it is my testament and my will, the happiness all around us here and now, it is palpable and I feel it, and it came with the Machete my son gave to me."

"The son you drove away tonight."

"Lazaro," Silvia whined, tears welling in her eyes, "it broke my heart, I – "

"What came back to you was not happiness, it's what we all mistake happiness to be. And that was not your son, it was I who came to see you, in the heights of your perceived splendor." He held her gaze. "Your creation."

Dark rings fell about Silvia's eyes, and it was as if the muddy pit about her looked more alive than her then. The light fled from her being, and she became dense, dense with shame. And to this Lazaro extended his long arm, and placed his broad, bandaged hand on the front of her head, his thumb across her brow. And the light poured into her being, and she was bright once again.

"And I saw...that all was well, Silvia, for there is always more at hand than what one takes things to be. Proceed, you've set something in motion, and it is like all of you, it shall not stop until it is satisfied." Silvia's blazing green eyes rose, slowly, from the shadows of her bowed head.

"All...is well?" She thought, confused, of the picture of the Virgin on the wall.

"But you're at odds with one who does you well," he said to her. "You've been looking up the wrong branch of this mighty tree, my child, your family, the problem is within you, not him. And only because of this do you see it in your home, for your home is a reflection of your soul. And only because of this do you see it in your life, for your life is a reflection of your soul. And only because of this do you see it in the one you wish to kill, my child, for your husband too is a reflection of your soul."

The sun broke through the clouds and bathed them in morning light. Lazaro smiled at this. "Bring this light about us to the four walls of your prison, and then you shall see who the treacherous one really is." He paused, a little too long for comfort, for emphasis. "And be careful what you say about us dirty old men," he smiled. "We're not all bad." Silvia smiled, playing with a clump of dirt between her fingers.

"So what should I do, Lazaro, what should I do? Why haven't you helped me until now, until all of this has happened?" Her face went halfway to tears. "I've made such a mess, you could have come to me before — "

"God doesn't need you," said Lazaro with a wise grin, letting the phrase hang in the silence of Silvia's downcast eyes. "You need God. And you're the one, not I, who's showed up just in time. I could talk to you for seven days and nights and still you wouldn't understand what is revealed to you in everything that happens to you, one deed at a time. Your life is your soul, both the answer and the prayer at once. Live, and live again, victory shall be yours, Silvia Campos-Guerra."

"I am still at a loss, Lazaro, I don't want to leave your sacred presence and still not know what to do!" she said, her eyes wide, hopeless, alive.

"Indeed!" Lazaro laughed. "I would be at a loss as well, you think it's the Virgin who speaks to you." Silvia looked deeply into his eyes, and burst out in wide-eyed horror, seeing everything at once.

"I don't let evils fall on my children. There is no question, go in peace." Silvia's eyes were wide, with light, inspiration, insight, confusion.

"Wait, wait, Lazaro — "

He simply raised a palm of blessing between himself and her, and prayers began to swarm around them both, filling the sky with sounds, voices, chattering and moans, and pleas and promises and little crutches made of gold and lavender flowers that dissolved into the essence, the faith, the universe, and the experience returned from the edges of existence into its original, pearl-sized shape and set itself into the head of Silvia Campos once again. "Tell my mother I was there with you!" And she woke.

"Your best friend can be your worst enemy," she heard, from somewhere in the next room,

"But more importantly, your worst enemy can be your best friend."

Her eyes, they were fixed on the light of the lamp, wide as wisdom as she sat in the truth.

~*~

"My God, how dark everything is, Virgen Santisima!" screamed Silvia, jutting up onto her feet. Blinking, stupidly, in disbelief. Looking about. Glass, stuck into wounds all over her knees. She thrashed at her knees in fitful seizures and bursts of disgust, shooting herself back up into a long pull back on her hair with upraised arms...hair which had remained in its perfectly-tight Spanish bun. *"That's right, Goddammit."* And with this she stopped — smiled. 'It was all real,' she mouthed to herself, "it was *real,"* and — she bolted about in an explosion of righteous disgust — *"it was real, UGH!"* Her face contorted into wrath. *"Puta Madre!"* she screamed behind gritted teeth, and she began to claw at the shooting stings at the back of hear head. *"Vayaaaaaa!"* she growled. *"Haz vihto un fannnntahhhma?!"* and Silvia reached for the floor, brandishing the *machete*, which jerked itself away from her in three great heaves that took her across the room.

But then it all stopped,
and the light shone bright yellow once again.
"The fuck," she whined, baring her teeth.

And there was silence. Silvia looking everywhere with wide eyes, her breath the only sound in all the house. The silence was never more horrifying. "This is all real..." she huffed, swallowing the knots in her throat. She looked about, left and right, and the waves of disgust swelled in her again as she looked up into the world around her, everything was so *dark* here, so *dark*, so *dull*, the ceiling light was gritty and yellow, a reflection of the imperceptible darkness that hovered everywhere in the room, in the house, in Silvia herself, and only now could she feel it all with the clarity of a dream. She stood, like a rat, in the middle of the mess she had made. It was everywhere. "And this is the most treacherous evil of all, to make the victim think it is their own doing." Her eyes were wide as saucers. Her mouth dropped agape. "It's the light that plays across the shadows! You see?!" she screamed, growing angrier with the waves of shock that coursed through her. *"Fuck you!"* she gritted, she winced, she spoke, she listened — *"Not the other way around..."* And she screamed again, angrier than she had been in all her life, it had been decades of silence, of unconsciousness, of being poisoned slowly from the inside out, plate by plate, smile by smile, thirty mosquito-eaters twitching on the wall, but the light is within them all just as well. *"Look —"* All of them burst into the air at once, and the light began to flicker once again. She swung the machete all about her in disgust, as if the hoard of insects were real, as if they were evils that she herself had called upon to bring her into this pit, thirty years of desolation, *denme mi pan, denme mi pan,* fodder for this old *witch,* and the flickering yellow light grew brighter and brighter, as if there was a great revolt, and it was Silvia's, for the first time in thirty years. *'Silis, the ti —'*

"NI PINGA, AQUI SE ACABO LA FIEHHTA!" screamed Silvia. *"Virrrrrgen Imaculaaaada,"* she spat, "you have played with my stupor, you have taken me into this pit of darkness, and now I know who you are, I can't believe you, *rrrreputa Madre!!!"* She heard herself breathe, growl, breathe, *growwwwwwlllll,* her heart beating steadily, and she smiled. Silence. The picture of the Virgin on the wall. The next room. The *beehive.* The ceiling fan. Mami's picture — *"Mami!"* she gasped. "Oh my God, *Mami,* why..." Silence. Her eyes wide. *"Mami!!!!"* she whined, and the picture sat there, crumpled and defeated, her womb torn across to the head of the third Juan. *Snapped,* it did, this horrible acident that got brought over from Cuba in the picture of the Virgin, it had been there this whole time. And immediately she was shot into the height of the light. Rings of ash fell upon piercing green eyes. *"Maaammmmiiiii..."* she growled, suddenly furious, clenching her teeth. *"Cooking for him,"* she hishhhhed, *"it'shhhthe way into a man'shhhheart, hmmm?!"* She grrrowwwlllled – *"The way into hishhhhoulllll...mmmmmmm..."* and the beehive began to writhe with the hum of millions of tiny wing –

" – MAMI!" she shrieked. *"Rrrrresingaaaada! Rrrrreputa Madre!"* and she tossed about in blissful, seizing circles about the room, pleasure she no longer wanted, it was disgusting, it was the problem, it had tricked her from the inside of her own mind, from wall to wall, like a crazy chicken clutching her own head...for the whole ordeal was too much for her to bear, it was as if the world had been torn open and all that was left was the bitter emptiness of utter reality. And like that, her head snapped to the left and her eyes fell upon Chiche. Chiche, closer to the dead than ever. Closer than Silvia...*Mima, what have I done*...Silvia looked up into the light of the ceiling lamp, and it grew brighter, flickering with more and more electricity, and with every flicker the images came into her mind, and she saw what she needed to do, it was like magic, and La Virgen was suddenly Goddess of the Sun, of the light. She was the bright, golden radiance that had surrounded her in her dreams, and the light grew white before her, and in the corner of her perception she began to see the faint outline of shapes and sparkles that were shooting about the room like a swirling wind. And she felt it, she felt it, she did, over in the corner. *Lazaro*, he had said it: "Mother's love."

And she snapped her gaze into the corner, where there as nothing, save the purple splotch that blurred her field of vision in a rhythmical array of swirls and pulsing light.

"Veo, Madre, Mi Reina, Mi Virgen Imaculada," she spat. *"Por fin te veo,"* she said, and her smile washed over with hot tears of remorse, misunderstanding, traumatic indigestion of experience welling up in her eyes. *"Te veo, por fin te veo."* Silvia breathed deeply and looked at Chiche again, her chest heaving, *what the fuck is all of this, I was so happy, I was so happy,* so long ago, she

309

wiped the tears from her eyes. The room was vacuous, consuming. So much *density*, so much *darkness*, inertia...spindly mosquito-eaters bobbing about, in one place and then another, they were here and they were beyond at once like little busy souls. She felt the light being sucked from her, from the room, her house, her life, her husband — *"He's mine now, it's too late,"* she growled, and shrieked in response — her experience so divine, all taken so easily with every step forward that she took? It can not be taken this easily, *"Dame la vista, give me the light Lucero, que no veo, que por fin te veo ya ni se lo que veo hay que no veo!"* and she seized, looking up into the ceiling light and making it brighter with every fiber of her being, doing what she had never done before, and it was her mind, it was making the light, a star would die if it didn't light up the darkness all around it. *'But Jenny will come soon, you have to —'*

"Go to hell!" Silvia screamed. *"Back to hell...que Dios me ampare, what the fuck is going on..."* She signed herself with the cross. "O my God, what about purgatory, what is all of this, where are you, where am I?" she said aloud, "was I going to kill him and have Jenny come home? *Jesucrísto, what was I thinking?"* She had no time to think. Insects, crawling from her shadows and across the room, into the corners, under the bed. "What were you thinking...through his *stomach...te voy a matar...lo voy a matar...hijole! He's finally mine now, es mmmmmmio..."* and with another wave of disgusting nausea Silvia shook herself over, whipping her limbs about with a fire she had never felt before, and snapping into a straight spine by the powers about her, She looked with wide eyes to her poor undead, unconscious husband and leapt onto his half-naked body, his pants at his waist, his arms rigid at his sides, eyelids half-open to pearly white vacuity, a mouth hanging open with sleep and death, *sofrito* breath. She grabbed him and straightened him out on the bed, putting him under the sheets as if he were sleeping, pressed his eyes shut and grabbed the knife off the floor. *"Puta Madre, lo que te voy a sazonar, vas a ver!"* she screamed into the yellow flickering light. *"I know what to do, thirty yyyyyears, thirty fucking years!"* She pulled the blade up near her face—*"ya se acabo ehhhta mmmiEDDD-DA!* I know just what I need to do—*by the grace of God! I'm gonna send you back to hell, you evil bitch!"* She slashed the blade around the room in maniacal, swerving arcs that pulled every fiber in her arm wincingly tight.

"Goddammit! God damn YOU, you bitch!" she screamed, clenching her teeth with decades of rage. She felt it all deep within herself, it could have been the very power of God, so intense was the drive within Silvia. It culminated in a release of ancient tensions into the present so great that it filled the universe completely: serpents all over the world opened their mouths wide and bore their smiling fangs as Silvia screamed, and the black contents of her soul spilled all over the walls around her, into every nook and cranny of the waking world. It was a lunar eclipse, a passing shadow that everyone felt and nobody commented on: "Yo Jerry, that an earthquake?" She screamed and screamed and screamed and tasted infinity, tasted herself. And far across Miami, the old man laughed happily off in his dark room, his eyes fixed on his round tablet, kicking his yellowed feet into the air: *"Ifa, Ifa!"*

All of it had come into place in seconds, it made her dizzy, it made her world spin, it made her *scream,* playing on her evils to drink blood and spread death throughout the universe, evils that were never hers, never her own. Lazaro's boon. And they had taken over the house. *She* had taken over the house. The beaded string on the living room fan shot down to the ground with a shatter that sent thousands of tiny beads everywhere across the floor. *"Rrrrrrr!"* Silvia snapped hear head toward the dark hall at the sound. Lamps and *bucaros* smashed onto the ground. Spiders pouring from the shadows, from her mouth as she screamed, screamed it all into sight, into light that was fire in the darkness, light so bright it can't be seen... She jumped to her feet with tears searing across her face and stomped on them all like cockroaches, all over the floor, the years, the demons, the spiders and shadows and *freeloaders* all over her skin, *evils too dense to move onwards* crawling up and down, skittering across the walls like tiny armored insects, black knobbly demons that flicked their tongues at her and stabbed her in the ears, in the womb from the other side of the room, whiplashing from black bullfrogs on the wall with leering, wall-eyed stares, entrails and flashes of putrid smoke drowning her peripheral vision and filling the room with darkness, darkness, thick black smoke, shooting pain and black, clotty blood all over the room.

"*La Virgen* is so much bigger than all this shit, I will prevail, you have no chance!" she screamed, feeling herself being pulled to the ground, doubled over, and she heaved thick vomit from the depths of her core. Heeeeeeeaved, *heeeeeeeeeaved,* coughed. "*La Virge –* " it was a mess, watery phlegm and cle – *heeeeeeeeeeeeeeave!! Heeeaaa – Heaaaaaa –* and she pushed with all of her might, her eyes stinging with blood, as if her eyeballs would explode, and she pushed, pushed, "*heeeeeee-aCHHHAK!*" and there it was, plopped into the pile of milky vomit. What it was, she did not know, but it looked like a little *bulto* of moldy spinach, and it had the shape of a little dead bird. Thrown from its nest, a fall into oblivion: *chhhhak.* "Ugh..." she whined, strings of saliva gliding to the pile of sour *café con leche.* "Ugh!" she seized, she sneezed, scoffed, strings of saliva trailing across the side of her arm as she wiped her mouth clean. "Ugh!" She pulled her head back and took a deep breath in, vomit running up through her clearing nose, her eyes watering, her ears ringing, shouting in the background, nonstop, in pitches too high for humanity, feeling the black claws pulling at her hair and shooting through her body, oh God it won't stop, it won't stop, tearing mercilessly through her skin. "Ughhhh!" and she stood, scratching her skin, dizzy, trying to pick out the demons, and she saw this one on the ground, this little bird, and she grabbed the *machete* and raised it high above her head, and brought it down with all the force in her being, and the puddle of vomit spattered everywhere five feet around the dirty carpet, and nothing happened, the little dead spinach bird simply creased and had shifted position. This was not the magic, this was not the task. *Proceed, Wife of Ibrahim! We're here when you need us most!*

And then the beehive erupted, not with pleasure, but with *fire*, with stings and swarms of red and black ants running pearly white eggs all about her body in waves of furious fire, spreading all about. Writhing, wretched electricity lashing the trillions of tiny fibers into contractions of the most heated *shame, lethargy, hatred, sadness, rage* and *death, death, death* flashing in the back of her mind, in the sparkles that defibrillated through her visual field like a throbbing headache. She clawed at them furiously, at her sides and her arms, until bloody slits ran themselves all over her body. A heat filled her head with mind-bending dizziness, her face a thousand pounds, brittle dragonfly wings buzzing all about as she slumped to the floor, weakened and beaten, roaring insects crawling into her ears, fighting to get inside first, *get back inside, get back inside!* pressing, blazing with hot irons of white fire, she was drowning in an ocean of air, nobody would believe any of it, even if I showed them the scratch-marks. *"Stretch-marks –* " and she began to laugh in the midst of all of it, the crying, the screaming, the fire and pain. With hundreds of insects filling her mouth and picking at her skin, she said in a muffled gag, remembering Lazaro's words, "victory shall be mine..." and she shook all of it off with a tremendous breath out — *"Se acabo, que si La Virgen es Madre mia!"* — a heaving sigh that filled the room with a tempestuous wind. She *blew, fearless,* and everything faded away. Silvia growled, the dark taste of everyone's blood and vomit in her mouth.

"Ay..." she laughed, catching her breath slowly. "This is so sick, *Virgen mia,* what would the neighbors think, to see me dancing around in a puddle of vomit," and she laughed with relief, looking at the cabinet, the glass, the torn picture of the immaculate virgin, the bed, the blood, the little bird. "It's over..."

she laughed. "It's over now, Goddammit, I see it all, you evil thing, and I'm done with you, ah? Ah?" She raised her voice. "*Si*...this war is over, for you don't scare me any longer, Chiche doesn't scare me any longer, Chiche doesn't scare me *any longer!*" and she fell to her knees, for the light came over her and she felt as if the entire universe was standing by her side. "*Ave Maria, llena eres de gracia, el Señor es con tigo, bendita tu eres entre todas las mujeres y bendito es el fruto de tu vientre Jesus*...I was so scared, I have forgotten how beautiful you are, all around me, all the time." She sobbed, saying over again, "You've opened my eyes, *it doesn't matter than it took thirty years — NO!* You've opened my eyes, you've opened my eyes," and she found within herself a tremendous power awakening, smothering the shame, the anger, the remorse. The evils, the insects, the gritty sound of dark and silence. The house had hovered with dark and dense emptiness, and through Silvia it had bloomed into a cleanness that began to pervade the entire space. All became a breath of fresh air. It was still. "*Santa Maria, Madre de Dios, ruega por nosotros que tenemos el yo pecador, ahora y en la hora de nuestra muerte, Amen Jesus, Amen Jesus, Amen the house,* this house, it isn't empty, it isn't silent, it's clear! *Santísima Virgen de la Caridad, it's clear!*" she yelled, "*Feeeeel it! Cachita, Cachita, you are here, you have saved me from the darkness, you have been here the whole time!*" and she lifted her hands to the heavens, the thoughts, the voices coming at her again, scratching at her feet to what she found to be great delight. She screamed at them, stomped at them, laughing, destroying them, it was so easy now, her eyes went wide with wisdom. She felt them writhing away, for she was bathed in light, and it was the light of the sun, shining through everything in the dark of night. Light so bright it can't be seen... The craziness sent shudders all through her spine, and it was blissful, these stomps, this destruction of all evil at *Her* behest, the righteousness of her heart, of her best friends for the past thirty years, the thick cloud of ashen smoke and the dross of disdain, of effortless negativity, *the charred remains of a horrible accident,* and the whole world unfolded below her, the entireties of Earth and its hells, its sanctuaries for dark beings and communes of evil, and she stomped upon them all, destroying them all, consuming everything in sight and beyond sight, for she had birthed them and destroyed them all in the *contrapunto* of her dance.

And without realizing it, she leapt into the air with an arc so large that it was hardly human at all, and she came down upon the little bird with a force that resounded through all the hurricane-proofed windowpanes with the timbre of a gunshot. *"Holy shit!"* she gasped, popping her eyes open. She looked beneath her, and whatever it was had turned the puddle into a licorice red that curdled into ribbons of *pure de tomate*, of *comino* and minced cloves of garlic, silky ribbons of *aji* and curdled blood for the *morcilla*. *Baking soda fizzing down your throat. Anaíli, feel it —* but she was pulled up with a hissing breath in, and her eyes shot up into her skull as she swung the blade about and hopped on one foot, over and over again, the Thunderbird, triumphant, engorged with lucid lucid light, she could have drawn the entire ocean into herself again, she was a living being, a Goddess, brandishing a whip of fire from her lolling tongue. The *machete* swung about her in praise of the Illustrious Mother of the worlds as she sang Her name, too great for words, over and over again, it was a humming, a roar, a rod of thunderous lightning, the name of the wind that stirs the primordial waters into the storms of life, rebirth, *transformation. Transformative change. Transformative change. Transformative change. Transformative change. Transformative change.*

"I am here, mijita," a voice said, in the still eye of it all.

Transformative change, she danced. And her pounding heart was the drum, the spurts of laughter and shrieks the *clave*, the chorus ten thousand angels and demons deep pouring through this mighty hole in the veil between worlds, this mighty chasm bridged by the ladder of enlightened fire that whirled and whirled about like a fiery, white star.

315

Es el relampago claro de la verdad, ruega por ella,
Madre preciosa, ruega por ella,
Madre cariñosa, ruega por nosotros,
Madre de Dios. "Ruego por os."

"*No hay fecha que no se cumple, ni deuda que no se cobre,*
Virgen, Imaculada, del Cobre!" She reeled wildly, teeming with
powers she could not understand, and the eye of the machete, the
eye of the *huracán*, she was the sun, the sunlight, the star, she was
its salvation, its end traced back to its very beginning through
living, conscious light, and again it would come back, again and
again, this darkness, for its is the oldest game in the world, the
pretext for every battle, of will and wit, of love, and war. The
turning of the light creates the darkness in its wake, and only then
does the Beauty mean something to us all. She swayed with the
movements of her swinging *machete* like a gypsy, *una gitana*
inttthhhendia in the hills of *Andalucia,* clapping to passionate flares
of flamenco and *bongó,* some ancient slave *screaming* at her captors
from an altar to *Oyá, Oggún, O-CHO-SI,* brandishing a whip of
fire, the frenzied gaze of a mounted witch. *Lash!* — another dead
insect, another dead bird. *Waves of crinkly wings curling up into*
tight little balls, their legs withdrawn into the light at their core.
Breathing heavily, her hands on her thighs, she saw flashes of
light all about her, pulsing in the darkness like the flavors of a
primordial soup, she smiled at the thought, making to move out
and *proceed, mijita, they have told you to proceed.* A last mosquito-
eater bobbed along the wall silently— "son of a *BITCH!*"—she
slapped the face of the machete onto the wall with a pop that sent
cracks three feet out in four different ways. "*Mmmmmm...*" Silvia
growled. It was intoxicating. She grabbed her smokes, her keys
and her Capricorn lighter, wrapped the *machete* in a bundle with a
towel from the bathroom, and stormed for the front door,
slamming it shut behind her. Chiche would be fine until she came
back. If she came back.

There he lay, *Pobre Juan,* what did he do, in the empty

room with the silence of death, surrounded by hundreds of crinkled spiders all over the floor, all of them smothered, smashed, like the picture, like the boudoir. Twitching. A house in shambles, you can create only after you have destroyed. And in the living room the chair rocked itself back and forth, back and forth, the smiles lacing themselves through thick flurries of invisible smoke.

~*~

Something was bothering Tico. Something in his mother's eyes earlier was strange, and it had thrown him off into existential thoughts, biting philosophies that spat in the face of poets and would never have bled from the tip of his pen had it not been for the hisses of his muse who saw everything and knew even more. His soul, it bled, into tears at the eyes and words on the page, nasty splotches of deeply-seated garbage of the soul. It was growth, its beginnings. Something was bothering him, and it was heavy, this one.the last thing he could do was sit in peace. He stared at the scrawled words, spat across pages he had already torn from his notebook, in indecision, in shame. And with Angelica in the bedroom, stilled in meditation, her long blonde hair flowing over her delicate frame like the tresses of a young Sibyl, he bore over his thoughts once more, deciding whether or not to throw them all away, no need to remember this awful mood, it too shall pass. Thoughts of his Mother's sadness brought tears to his eyes, his heart was heavy, why did he feel this way, if he had finally brought light into the house, into their marriage? It was a gift from heaven, he wished for nothing more than the both of them to grow old in peace and smiles. Thoughts of Chiche's heart flashed across the mirror of his mind. *Love* lives there, *love*. It was high magic, a once-in-a-lifetime opportunity to bring mortals into the ray of Theurgy. Perfect transmutation, a blade into a sword. He swallowed his doubts, his fears, tears, and tried to clear his emotional center with the appropriate mantrams, but it

still left him as sad as he was before. This was more than a
misplaced impression. Stammering with his overwhelming
feelings, he roiled with discomfort, his gut instincts writhing like
serpents around their prey. *It is not in my nature to feel like
this...amphora of salvation, materialism has no strength next to me.
Come, sit by my side, Bellilin.* He grimaced upon looking back to
the paper, for they were horrid reflections of himself, inspired by
something he could not see, something he did not know. Was it
all a farce? "Have I acted in the wrong? Was it wrong to give it to
her, to bring this out of their marriage, of our family? Ugh,
something must be happening, this is excruciating, are they
making love, or have they begun to fight? Did *he* find the
sword?" and his eye went wide with the possibilities, it could be
so ugly in there. "*O, face of the Sphinx, Goddess of the rolling eyes,
Divine Mother, take this horrid ego away from me, let the light prevail in
all places, times, minds, and spaces, faces...'*

"*Oh, sweet one, you are tired, let us call it for tonight and go to bed,
there is nothing to worry about, of this be sure.*"

He read, with a fluttering sigh,
"lest I throw it all away, *in a huff*, old sport:"

> *I've seen, that what people call
> stability is very fragile. It is a house of
> cards held up only by people's fear of it
> falling down. We work to have a house
> and a job and things to do and eat, but
> there is something else which people fear
> constantly, the void of blind, merciless
> death that the house of cards exists in,
> the imminent, ever-lasting failure
> behind it all, and people don't want to
> know it, for it is what they hide from
> their children, what they pretend is ok so
> the little ones can stay ignorant of it for*

as long as possible as well. It is our task as human beings to maintain this illusion. It is a fat old man in red, this life. It is a lie that we all wink at each other as we push it up the chimney of our family life, the home in the hearth: "Have you been naughty or nice?"

"Naughty or nice." They are all the same, bulbs across one great billboard that shows the world what God would do in ignorance, in blissful forgetfulness and irresponsibility. This is the human condition, a failed experiment in the power of love. And this is precisely where it shall all go, to the shitter, the void whence we have come, the love itself, the hard way. Oh, that the fish would struggle upon being pulled from his tank, only to be freed into the ocean!

The freedom, it would kill you. Kill you. Woe, to those who act in goodness, for they are sheep amongst wolves! This is the human condition, to shine in the midst of perpetual darkness.

The needs we have aren't real. More, they aren't necessary. What is necessary is to act, and that it be something that contributes to our collective understanding of 'what' and 'why'. This helps us all to dissect the illusion into the love it is, and not the darkness. The moon is both full and empty, both at once, always. Find the sun, and life shall be a full moon of love and honey. Fear. It is the basis upon which all edifices are built. The impetus at the basis of all civilization. Scarcity, the guarantee of crops, the fear of failure. Death. Humanity was once spontaneous, but we have forgotten who we are. We have succumbed to the human condition, when it is God that lives within our hearts. We are children of the divine-condition, but in taking refuge under the mind and no longer the spirit, we became human. This was the fall, when our actions began to be calculated, up to our whims and not those of the greater whole.

Our light, the Sun of the Spirit, became a waxing, waning Moon, a flickering dance of time that plays across the mind. Hearken, o Fire, and help me know the light of both at once. The perfect stillness of an eclipse, that the Spirit and the Mind can align perfectly into a veil between worlds.

Let us all recognize this reality we live in and understand it, integrate ourselves in it, live with it, not just inside of it quivering with fear, for only then shall we be human beings. Only then shall we be divine. Intellectual humanoids, rational bipeds, logistical homuncles, my teacher calls us all. This transformation begins with facing the fears we harbor towards our very own

*Mother, the black Lady whose face is the
night sky, the millions of eyes looking
up into that dark crystal, and she shall
devour us in death, back into the Love,
accept Her as our true home...for it is
the light of your own soul. You eat a
fruit, she has given it to you. She has
eaten. The times when we feel free and
fulfilled are the times when we look at
Her with eyes of beauty, accepting Her
with the effortless praise of the hesrt,
and thus accepting ourselves. My
friends, this is only the beginning.
Throw away the deck of cards and come
live in your real home.*

The muse kissed his brow, and the Romantic closed his
notebook upon the torn pages, as if a misplaced bookmark in the
flow of his mind. He took the Gardenia from his lapel and lay it
atop its leather-bound cover. "Divine Mother, destroy this e...I'm
heartbroken and I don't know why." He made his way into the
bedroom where Angelica had just opened her eyes, glossy and
alive, and they fell across each other onto the white sheets, turning
valleys into mountains with a kiss that sparked a flame so pure
that it could burn through anything under the three eyes of God.
In the midst of the emerging trance, Pallas Athene brandished her
spear and broke through the Karma, and the pages were ashes in
the morning.

But the night was far from over, for
far across Miami was the reality of this war.

~*~

What would one think if they were driving down *la Flag-
errr* at about ten o'clock on a weeknight and saw an older woman

in a *bata*, *chancletas* and a Spanish bun railing down the sidewalks, a bundle under her arm and a cigarette trailing ashen sparks out the side of her mouth? "Bitch is *on one*, Jules, you see that shit? 305 alive and kickin, *where da Swisher at* – " The people drove by, but most didn't pay much attention to her. Frankly, she didn't give a damn. Silvia was on a mission, and *La Sawesera* was still in the foggy and humid night, it was thick, balmy, sickly-sweet smoke crusted over by amber streetlights and headlights minding to their own tasks. She had been running for what seemed like hours, her heart was going to *explode*, taking the surroundings in on sheer instinct, wildly, an animal trying not to be eaten. She knew what needed to happen, but how to do it she had no idea. "Get it off of me, and it'll drink it's fill somewhere else," she repeated to herself. She had seen it, in the glare of the lamp. Clear as day, she had heard it. *"This belongs to all of us."* She darted around corners, crossing streets in shifty huddles and creeping through parking lots with wide eyes, laughing nervously at the pedestrians who watched her pass – *"Que Yeye se le ha bajao a esta vieja, eso'ta de pinga,"* said one.

"You don't see none o' that at the church,"said another, "'cept when they start the professin'."

On she ran into the night, through the amber glow of streetlights past L.E.D. white men and orange hands blinking at the crosswalks. She was horrifying, roused by sacred fires, riddled with the auras of spirits black and white. Blocks, miles away from her home in the torrid humidity of night, Silvia began to feel the forces pull at her left and right, catching up with her as she grew more and more tired. She was going nowhere, no time, no time to think, the rush had her on the edge of time, and her every step was guided in the moment, she felt the pulls like eagles flying by her side in great, swooping arcs of their wings. She smashed her toes into cracks in the sidewalks – *"Ay pinga!"* – and could feel her foot slipping around in hot, sticky blood between the rubber soles of her *chancleta*, but it mattered not. Nothing could stop her now, the vision had been that intense. *Thirty years, thirty years she saw.* Bushes stirred as she ran by and dark possums growled at her, her feet crushing cockroaches and dirt, candy wrappers and thousands upon thousands of spiders and vile worms that threw themselves before her with her every step. The end of evil was about her like a shroud, the demons threw themselves at her, only to be freed. Rats emerged from the gutters and scurried across her path, and nightbirds screeched into the stars that hovered silently above her. It was torrential, never had such light come in the midst of darkness, setting so many souls free.

"*Vete pal Carajo!*" she screamed, over and over again, stomping rats and swatting at raccoons, feeling the sickly silk of spiderwebs stick across her face as she ran through them. "*I see you! I see you, you bitch!*" She scratched at her face and tugged at her sweater, itchy and swollen and prickly all over her skin, and it only made her squeeze that forsaken bundle even more, that ungodly child she clutched to her breast, lest it slip from her hands and *into those of another.* It was the burden of burdens, *a cursed child, nobody deserved its blackened influence* — "*pal carajo, you'll see, you're going down, I'm gonna send you to hell!*" She kicked at all of the sickening things around her, casting oceans of evil beings into a wake of death and light, until she stopped at a crosswalk and dozens, dozens — *dozens* — of sick, slimy grey rats poured out of a gaping gutter that yawned desolately across the end of the sidewalk and swarmed up at her, biting at her feet and clawing at her clothes as she jumped up and down in fear, anger, a sanctimonious rage that poured about her like giant threads of kelp in the currents of life, *once-mil Virgenes* lashing everywhere around her with scourges of fire.

"*Again, She dances,*" the old man said, staring at his tablet with squinting eyes. "*Your play is relentless, Eshu-Bara!*" She stomped upon them, brandishing the blade and the blanket in her two hands swirling about, and through her *chancletas* she felt

323

everything, their bones cracking under the weight of her feet, their black blood coagulating between their compressed bodies, a carpet of mangy, oily fur. Her ankles cracked with the slaps of her feet onto the bare pavement over and over again. Skulls popped like walnuts and viscera gushed out of their swollen eyes and pink anuses as she stomped at them ravenously — whipping tails, vicious shrieks, blood and squelching, too much cussing. No one else was around, it was her and the greatest legion Miami had ever missed. The light turned and she ran, freezing chills shooting through her body as if running through patches of mist, and the rats bit at her heels, crawling all over her body, hanging off of her skirt like the bells of some depraved whore in the depths of a horrible abyss. In the middle of a crosswalk she met the snarling grill of a truck screeching to a stop halfway around a centripetous hook-of-a-left-turn. Slamming her hands onto its rusted hood, she looked through the windshield into the darkness, wide-eyed and bewildered, *furious.* dripping with rats, an old cooking knife in her hands, her chest heaving in the objective glow of insect-covered lights. Casting the blanket aside she held the *machete* up into the air, letting it glimmer in the yellow glow of the headlights. She cursed and shouted at the stoic windshield behind the shining grill that breathed hot breaths onto Silvia's thighs, onto her womb, and rats nibbled up her dress, around her shoulders, as she stared into the void. They leapt onto the hood of the truck, and to the clicking of rats' claws along the hood of the truck Silvia slammed the blade into the hood of the car and brought it back across her shoulder, leaving two halves of a rat writhing in agony on the hot vibrating metal, on either side of a generous new dent. The poor bastard kicked it into reverse and went right back onto Flagler — there was no one else around. "*Candeeeeelaaaaaa!*" he screamed, from a half-descending window. She smiled, pointing the *machete* where the driver would have been.

"*Tell your mother you saw the Tempest with your own shining eyes,*" she yelled into the glare as he jammed the window up and kicked it into drive with screeching tires and a muffled, *"ni me pagan pa quedarme aqui"*. Covered in rats and wielding a black machete, killing every bird the driver would ever own with those piercing green eyes, Silvia would never know the fear she instilled in the soul of that poor Juan who had decided to run another red light that fateful evening in Miami. Rumor has it he opened up a traffic school six months later, and quit drinking too.

"Silvia, Silvia!" wailed throat-less voices all around her. Shrieks and insults that made no sense accosted her from all sides, words that weren't words, slashes and burns in her mind that threw her into fits of pain and pressure all throughout her being. Close, close, I'm getting close, don't stop now, the person will come walking out into their yard, I will feel it, I will know it, the light is with me, they know it better than I do. With that her mind was caught as if in a terrible vice, and horrible feelings of shame and guilt swept across the expanse of reality all around her like a swarm of locusts, bringing her to her knees where she clutched at her head in agony; the world dissolved as she closed her eyes. The locusts, the spiders, the raccoons and the rats, they swarmed around her, but none came near. She was far too bright, even on the ground, fallen like the first Angels. Her heart ached with every throbbing blast against her ribs, her lungs screeching with hoarse complaints, thousands of pounds of pressure coming down on her chest, suffocating her with the weight of all the night in the sky. Flashing images came across her mind, seated saints convulsing in contemplation, their sexes clenching as their world dissolves into itself from the bottom up in terminal electrocutions. Evil cowers at the light of awakening, a light that devours oil, soot, and smoke like lamps and sweetmeats placed before ancient, starved idols. Little Silvia swung her scythe at the stalks of sugarcane, her palms searing, Anaíli's palms covered in blood, clenching her teeth as she seized into wrenching arcs upon dirty bedsheets she gripped at with white knuckles, painting roses on virgin mantles, burning herself on spilling pots and pans in vain

attachment to senseless obligations she would leave behind at the gate of death, all disease be upon her as she held the foreheads of her sick children back, their vomit frothy bile under red, watering eyes. There, in the shadow of her peril, in the frothy trough of every wave, she finally saw the only thing that mattered, and she was able to let go of it. Dark, veiled love, hidden in the depths of the world, in her heart, in her every action and behind all of them everywhere, and it had never been hers. It is evil, it is cruel, it is effortless and blissful, the love and the hate all at once, it is the epitome of all experience, intangible beauty, light so bright it could not be seen. And it was on its last legs, how many lives does it take to get to the center of a witch?

"*Silis, levantate de ahi que te vas a ensuciar la bata.*"
It was Barbarita. *Bab-barita.*
"*Bab-barita!*" said Silvia, her mouth agape.
"*Mijita teikirisi, ya hace tiempo que andamos tu y yo.*" Fear not, my child, for we have been together for a long, long time already. She was clad in a bright orange-and-red robe and head-wrap, a large, wide bow falling over the left side of her head. She toked on her long cigarillo as she smiled to Silvia in the lingering shock of silence, but in her eyes was the darkness itself, complete and devoid, devouring the light around her like the black flame that was allowing her to reveal herself in the moment. Here was the shadow created in the wake of the light, here was the putrid fruit at the center of a love that frothed over into a horrible accident. Here was desperate clinging, shameless revenge and demonic satisfaction from the other side of the veils of life, and all around them there was stillness. It was the eye of the storm, the peace at the center of the hurricane. Flickering streetlights. Off. On. Off. Off. On. Off, into the distance. Silvia looked up into the perfection of it all, the timing, the cooking, the marriage, the jealousy, "*ya que al fin es mmmmioooooo...*", her death, their leaving, her cold, dark eyes. Piercing green eyes. Kills birds, I heard. "*Always so pissed, infeliz.*"

"*Mami,*" Silvia whispered, into the pavement. "*Mami,* I, I thought it was you, *Mami.*"

"I'm your *Mami,* Silis, I've been your Mami all these years, what are you talking about?" laughed Barbarita. "The day you married my son, the day you *took him away from me,* you became mine as well, I saw to that..." and she took a long, deep drag of her cigarillo. "I wouldn't stop until you died a death as lonely as my own," she smiled, "I began to burn on the wick of your heart *everyday* as I made love to him, more and more, until the well went dry." She took a deep breath and stared boldly into Silvia's wrenching eyes. "It was *your marriage* that *killed* me, that gave me life all the way to the tomb."

"You...made love...*what?*"

"You will die if you kill me, Silis. We are one, my son is yours, and you are both *mine.* It has been this way for far too long, Silis, I've got more *muertos* than the well of fucking Lourdes, and you're next on my list."

"*ComePINGA!*" yelled Silvia. "I have never been your daughter, and much less am I yours!" And she stood with a surging wave of light at her back, the breeze of the eagles tossing the hair that had fallen out of the Spanish bun. "If there is *one* thing I know, in all these years of *shit* you have brought upon us from your *black heart,* it is that *my* heart never *once* turned from *La Santisima Virgen de la Caridad!*" and with that Silvia suddenly became piercingly aware that she was holding the machete in her left hand. She bolted her eyes up at Barbarita.

"*Dale,*" she said, putting her cigarillo to her lips and setting her hands on her hips defiantly. "The well of fucking *Lourdes, mijita!*"

And with a mighty contortion of her face, the black flame all about her churned into a bulging black beehive that whirled about her like a cloud of seething electrons, dark matter come to light. Silvia's heart began to palpitate with the hum of a sub-woofer jetting up the sound register before a fatal drop, but in the midst of it all she saw the years of food she had prepared, the flavor and the memories as she stirred the *café* and pounded the *platanos*, the mystery that Chiche could never and would never figure out, it was the mystery of the living woman, the very face of beauty in this world, and this was the love that had no end, it was Chiche, forever blind to the nest of golden eggs at the top of Silvia's family tree. 'That was you, *Mami*,' she thought out loud, "that *is* you, that is your presence, she's telling me stories—" and her eyes lit up, to the surprise of Barbarita, who was watching it all with a growing disdain for the light coming off of Silvia's back,—"*it's what she did to the explosion that destroyed the tentacles she had spread from her family tree onto ours, this pain, this blade that was given to us by our ancestors six generations back at the top of the tree, to return justice to this little nook of the world, so dearly does God love us all, to the very hairs on our head.*" Silvia's eyes grew into slits closed over the sun itself, and with gritted teeth she raised the blade into the air—"She turned it into the same bullshit, tried to get me to *kill him and not banish her from the parasitic hold she took on our your household, mija*, she tried to steal the power of God for her own diabolical and pitiful schemes, and here it is before her, this liar! She's doing it now, *mija*, she LIES!" And with that, Silvia charged at the black flame, at *Bab-barita*, the cunning witch who had been the backdrop of the bullshit for thirty years, unnoticed as the darkest devil. And try as she could, she could not move, nor her body nor her mind, for up above her head, little Eleggua had taken hold of her like a full-nelson—"*Damn, this bitch right here can you believe this?!*"—and he smiled, his eye closed in the wince of holding a cigar.* Her eyes bolted open in alarm, and the darkness shriveled from them like a spider in the microwave, into the emptiness, the love, that had been there the whole time. For the heat of this moment, an unstoppable flow of Karma and grace, from behind Silvia and up into the very throne of Heaven, and back down with a tremendous blaze of righteousness heaved from the brilliant fingertips of Changó, King of Africa, into the eagles and blazes behind Silvia and out through her arm, into the *machete* that surged forward with the force of a thousand whirlwinds and straight into the solar plexus of the orange-and-red Afro-Cuban putrefaction of a limb across the family tree. And there was a sound louder than a crack of lightning that echoed out for what must have been more than thirty miles, and car alarms flashed into response for as many blocks as anybody could see.

A tremendous orb hovered at the end of the Machete, larger than Silvia, shining with the light of a hazy aquarium. Inside, the phantasm, the holographic flashing of Barbarita moved in terribly slow motion, her eyes changing between alarm, pity, begging, the most sincere apologies, the lies, alarm, and the orb began to coalesce, slowly, closer and closer to the blade that it was set upon, like a great cotton candy. And Silvia watched, bathed in the iridescent blue of the ritual, as the orb caved into itself, as the witch grew smaller and smaller, as the machete drank the light like a nursing child. It vibrated with more and more force in Silvia's iron grip until it drank every last drop of the orb, of Barbarita's soul and her every captured and enslaved Spirit, and the light disappeared and all was normal again. Silvia blinked in the darkness and threw the machete onto the ground.

"*Su PINGA!*" she said, with enough juice coursing through her to run a marathon, and with that she burst out into the best laugh she had ever enjoyed in all her life. It was as if she had rediscovered her own body, her heart and soul. And though Silvia had seen none of it, laughing as she was, it had been her Mother Idelkys Guerra who performed the ritual, and who had thrown herself over Silvia when the darkness would have ripped her Spirit to shreds. And she sat back into the darkness behind Silvia's shoulders and kissed her heart with the innocent love of a newborn child.

The thought of the Virgin came into Silvia's mind — "*Ay, Virgensita!*" shouted Silvia at the top of her lungs, and she fell to her knees, where she suddenly realized that it had been the Virgin, and not her who had performed this sacred task. Her heart swarmed with emotion, and as all the chaos and grace up to now hadn't been enough, it was only then that the *utter reality* of La Virgen's presence finally clicked somewhere within Silvia's being, and she saw how insignificant she was, and yet how unique, how personally loved in the most perfect way she was, and the greatness of such a love was overwhelming. There was nothing to do but surrender to the heat rising all about her like a shroud, and in the tremendous release she died unto herself, then and there, and the entire world beheld it, speechless. That was it. She had hit the bedrock-bottom of shameless reality, and the entire universe showed itself for exactly what it was, and everything was but a flutter in the veils about Her womb.

"Look into the sky, mija. There is your answer, there is your prayer."

And the night sky tore itself in two, opening unto a cascade of stars that tumbled down, enmeshing themselves with spiderwebs and the biting dew of morning's languid approach to the eternal promise of dawn.

It was the ascent of the Sun from the peak of an icy mountain, blinding brilliance, the Blessed Virgin, regally crowned with a diadem of eleven stars.

Holding the hems of Her black, intricately laced veil were softly crooning blackbirds, tiny and forlorn, their gazes held away from the glory of Her soft, radiant, moon-like countenance.

The brilliance of a billion stars shone from the night sky that she wore about her secret, her complete and utter perfection. Feet too pure to touch the ground, their song is heard in the patter of falling ashes, the white remains of a billowing, smoky sigh.

Her eyes were sallow stars gazing emptily upon roses dried and tinted with the blood shed by tortured souls, questioning Her as they kissed the hem of a veil they finally touched at the moment of death.

Her finger graced upon a thorn beneath a crumbling blossom, piercing uncertainty, releasing the mystery of life. A drop of Her blood fell to the Earth and hardened, life within death, and from this bead emerged the hardness of denying an act of charity.

Every heart in every moment hails to Her between every fleeting beat, an instant's sweet return to Her. We are dead just as often as we are alive, this is the song of the Lady's joyful servant, at her feet is freedom found in death, Thy will be done, Thy Kingdom come. My *Queen*.

"ECCE MATER TUA", read the strip of parchment at her feet.

A glimmer of Her nocturne tresses slipped from under her veil, and therein was the hope shining in all the worlds of children as they went to sleep. Though you have never seen Her, Beloved, know She is there.

A child gazed distantly with soft, giant cowrie eyes, gushing in the embrace of Her sweet breast, his body swathed in robes of regal cobalt blue. His lips smiled with solemnly-held secrets, and Her hands cradled him softly, like stars clinging to the fingertips that have crafted them, one by one. Every constellation is but a pattern in the frills of Her lace.

She fills the mystery in every shadow, the morbid face of her own great burden set upon herself in sixty-million different ways, that you too might give it all up and fall into the sweetness of her embrace, inspired words wrought in the most beautiful lace.

Here, under Her garments, in the scent of roses and dried orange blossoms, every tear might hold its share of sugar and salt, every heaving sigh a moment of relief, the death of an enemy, the curse of an lover.

The sting of impulse is the flesh of Her lips, quietly smiling, modest, the Queen, washed over with Her very own tears. She births all things, only to take them back into Her black veil and thrive in their merciless demise, and She cries for you, for she is your Mother, and she is your Death as well.

Between the two is an unconquerable love.

"Forget me not, mi Reina, my joy, my dream, my fear and my hope, we have nothing to hold on to but you. You know our pains better than we do, for from you they have come, and to the light do they bring us all." She raised her face, in the sudden light of a smile. *"I was with your child!"* she laughed, *"and we saw Obi with his shining eyes."* The Virgin smiled, moving slowly, immaculately, and kissing the child on the brow as she dissolved into the darkness from where she had come. Silvia could have swallowed the moon, so open was her heart.

"She said nothing to me," she laughed, falling onto all-fours. "Nothing." She felt a faint slap across her face, just like her Mother used to do when she was disrespectful as a lit—*"Mami!"* she laughed. "Oh my God, it's all so real, it's been you this whole time, this, this right here, the memories, the love, the sighs of relief...who needs to hear the Virgin when one can always speak to her, in the language of the heart?"

And then she heard in her Mother Idelkys' voice, clear as a Cuban morning:

"If you could hear La Virgen talking to you, I'd fancy you a witch." Eyes went wide. Her gaze snapped down to the *machete.*

"Vaya..." said Silvia, *"that bitch is in there."* But there was no response. Everything, everything was perfect. And she picked up the machete and threw it over her shoulder as she lit the best cigarette of her life, and made her way back home as if nothing else mattered in the whole entire world. It was bliss to Silvia, but it was simply that for the first time, she was clear of everything she had created throughout her whole life, everything that had

been thrown upon her by life and society and rotten branches of the family tree, and she was finally seeing the universe for exactly what it was, feeling it in exactly the way it should be, a direct and clear reflection, and this was bliss, this was how things should be for everyone, she felt like she was on top of the world. And the entire world basked in the waves of love that emanated from her in the middle of the night, there in the hot, empty streets of Miami—

"Yo Jules, aint that that — *SHAKEDOWN, BITCH!"* And before she realized what had happened, she was looking into the bright green eyes of a misled youth who turned her around and emptied her pockets of the nothing that they had in them, keys, cigarettes, and the capricorn lighter, and he let her go and she listened to him shuffle back to the car door, which slammed shut as they drove off and left Silvia with nothing on her save for the cigarette half-smoked in her lip and the *bata* she was wearing, thanks be to God. She turned, staring fixedly at the license plate of the car, which read: 'E8UL4R0Y3' — far more characters than Silvia had ever seen before — but when she squinted her eyes and took a drag of her smoke, the license plate came into focus and simply read '3XU84R4'.

"They took it," she said to herself, "*You* took it," and that was it.

"*Poncho Pilate.*" Silva smoked the rest of her cigarette as she walked off, slowly — "Stole my Goddamn smokes..." Flurries of relief poured behind her as she slinked back the way she had come, her neck sparkling in the moonlight, her hips swaying lightly with every graceful step. She could have been balancing a jug of water on her head — she was Fifteen, sweet *Quinceañera* all over again, and it would never go away. It was her heart, finally on her sleeve, finally free for the world to see, and it was beautiful, such complexity veiled in those piercing green eyes. And she arrived at her house, where everything was still absolutely ravaged by Silvia's mythical bitch-fit, but she didn't care, she went back into to her bedroom, where she lay down next to Chiche's cold and undead body, just as she left him, and there, huddled tight to the man she hated, the man she loved, whispered into his ear:

"Te quiero tanto que te podria matar." I love you so much I could kill you.

He would come back after three days, back from the dead like his own *San Lazaro*, like *Jesucrísto*, like so many slaves who died fighting for the same thing we all fight for in this life, Jesus included: freedom. In this freedom is the end of suffering, and it is the suffering that guides us to the freedom, the liberation is learning how to dance with the world. This is the power of that blade we all bear within, that machete, that spear, that axe, that sword, that *unstoppable power of the human spirit*. The evils that life itself doth bid us conquer and prevail. She rested her head on his chest, for she new there would always be another day, *Otro Dia*, and it would always bring light to the memory of storms we have suffered. It will set us all free.

"Santa Maria, Madre, de Dios" she prayed into the darkness, *"ruega por nosotros que tenemos el yo pecador, ahora y en la hora de nuestra muerte...Amen."* And the light of ten-thousand Suns sparkled through dark windows.

~*~

FIN

Epílogo: Aquellos Ojos Verdes

"And where is your charming son?" asked Andalucía, twirling the ice in her drink with her finger.

"*No se,*" said Silvia, smoking a cigarette softly in her chair. "He said he would come after lunchtime, and as far as I'm concerned, it's after lunch," she said, "though I haven't eaten a *thing* yet at this party..." She pursed her lips—'*bueee!*'—casting a quick glance at Margarita, hostess of the party and wife of the man everyone called *El Pitirre*. His name was Julian, but people named him after a quirky little bird in Cuba who seemed to match his personality. Keenly aware of his surroundings, *Pitirre's* eyes constantly darted around under serious brows, in a way that betrayed his fear of some impending danger that, all things considered, probably didn't exist. As if sensing the gossip churning around her name, Margarita scurried into the house, emerging from the shade behind her screen door with a platter of cheese cubes, salami and Spanish olives, placing it on the table by the circle of ladies.

"*Bueeeno,*" said Silvia with a sultry smile. "I spoke too soon." She bit her tongue in jest. Zoila, the woman next to her, rolled her eyes with a slight smile, reaching for an olive. Silvia took a quick drag of her cigarette, since the smoke wasn't quite ready to be tossed yet, *almost* at the butt, and flicking the ash once more, she set it into the crystal ashtray Margarita had set out for them. It was an intricate piece that she herself had never used. One could imagine the way she cringed on the inside every time the ladies snuffed their cigarette butts into its flowering center; it had remained untouched in the living room for the last twenty years. Silvia set the butt in the ashtray, letting the smoke continue to rise slowly from it like a cone of incense—cigarette incense—and the scent curled delicately in the still, hot air, like a charmed serpent, graceful, eerily languid. And she crossed her legs, her beautiful calves blossoming into the bright light of the after-lunch sun.

Most, if not all of the older wives in attendance sat in somewhat of a circle, and chatting amongst each other they looked like a bed of plush, exotic flowers. The younger women were here and there, tending to their children, speaking like *comadres* whenever they addressed their litters. *"Oswaldito, caaaarajo! Que te vea brincar por ahi otravez! De dejo cojo, cabron!"* Margarita was busy keeping everyone happy, and the men were scattered about in twos or threes, some smoking cigars in their flowery *guayaberas*, others talking politics and history (which often overlapped when speaking about Cuba, which is what they were actually talking about) with their drinks in their hands, and others still sat with their women, laughing, while the older few sat in folding chairs around the fragile card-table that was being used to play game after game of *domino*. The table rocked and creaked with every move, every *slap* of the ivory *fichas* that the men brought down to the table with laughter, and sometimes, well-hidden anger. "Nice move, nice move," from under a focused scowl. Eye contact? "Fuck you, this is getting serious. Get me another drink, I'm pissed."

"Waaaahahahahahahahhaaa..." Raul tallied points, game after game, in red-faced silence. They drank to every move, the bad ones, the good ones, and the grudges were always extinguished in the icy draughts of *mojitos* and *Cuba Libres* that they took happily over and over again, passing the time.

Over in the corner, Eduardo and Jacínto, the old *Santero* with cotton-ball hair who had been a high priest of Orúla as well as an active Freemason back in Cuba, both swayed forward and back in their chairs, laughing at the *Guajiro* verses they improvised on their guitars in an even exchange. Though they had turned out to be the impromptu entertainment for the party, the two of them were having a party of their own passing verses back and forth from guitar to guitar, rhyme by rhyme, and they hardly noticed when the people came up and started watching them play, sipping their drinks with nodding heads and smiles of nostalgia. You can't find this on a Friday night in Miami.

"...*Yo soy un viejo Santero!*" sang Jacínto, "*De donde canta el Gorrión, y junto hacia'l malecón, yo sigo con mi bolero, un ritmo rrrrrrrico y salsero, soy el Padrino'el danzóooooon,*" and he swooshed his head over toward Eduardo, who sang along in the chorus and took to a verse of his own:

> "*Guantanamera! Guajira Guantanamera!*
> *Guantanameeeeeeeeera, Guajira Guantamanera....*"

> "*Y por alla en Cienfuegos,*
> *Siempre se agita'l ambiente,*
> *Baila Casino la gente,*
> *Gozando Rrrumba! hasta el ciego,*
> *Yo que le canto a mi geeeente,*
> *Con el dulce Son Matanzeeeeeroooo...*"

> "*Guantanamera! Guajira Guantanamera!*
> *Guantanameeeeeeeeera, Guajira Guantamanera....*"

> "*Yo fui un día al Bembé – Ay Yeye!*
> *Porque Madrina me manda,*
> *Y rechazando esperanza,*
> *Una Morena enganché,*
> *Y aunque gozo el potaaaaje!*
> *Salio negrito el neneeeee...*"

> "*Guantanamera! Guajira Guantanamera!*
> *Guantanameeeeeeeeera, Guajira Guantamanera....*"

> "*Con cada verso que tiro,*
> *Medio borracho y capado,*

Como Marti fue soldado!!!
En tierra de su desfilo,"

And together they both joined in,
for a magically improvised final chorus line:

Gozando aqui buenos tieeeeeeempos,
Con la Margarita y el Pitiiiiirrreeeee..."

Silvia, her legs crossed, ran her hand over her smooth,
well-shaped calves, taking a deep breath and sighing with a long
gaze into the sky. Compared to the other ladies, she was vibrant
and beautiful, though they all looked the same age— *don't* ask,
the answer's hardly a day over 20. Not a greeting went by where
the ladies didn't ask about what product she had finally found,
you look so great, *mira* it made your *patas de gallo* disappear, it
looks like this is the one, does it change once you wash your face
though, I hate those, I saw this one on that informercial, they
really did send me two, did they charge you for shipping? It
doesn't make you look like the girl in the commercial, though, I
still can't fit into those Yoga pants...it's just like all the rest of
them.

"*Mmmmmmmm,*" grimaces, smirks, and sips of the drinks.
"I knew it was bullshit." Square one, again, and again, and again.
Such is the art of idle chatter. Hot as ever, the party would not
have been pleasant at all if they weren't under the thick, meshy
awning that *El Pitirre* prided himself in showing all the men who
he mixed drinks for. "Put it up myself," he told them, shaking the
lime and *Havana Club* in a steel mixing-cup to get the manhood
mixed into the *mojitos* right. "My friend Pepito's cousin Osvaldito
took it off overstock at the store he works at, didn't pay a cent for
it. *That's* why *I* like it. Shade's good too, it still lets you tan if you
want, something about the size of the holes. Ain't these inventors
something else..." He poured the drink into a tall glass and held
it, waiting.

"Oh, yeah, yeah, it's nice, Goddamn right," the man next

to him stammered, to *El Pitirre's* delight. "Look how the *hembras* are enjoying the shade...yeah." *Pitirre* gave the man his drink, slapping him on the back.

"I'm glad you like it, go pull up a chair, enjoy yourself."*

Over in the corner near the fence was the pig-box. Since the night before, preparations were made. An entire pig, about fifty-five-sixty pounds for this party, was slaughtered and brought to *El Pitirre's* house, where Margarita mixed up a batch of her grandmother's famous *adobo*, made with *Sazón Oya* and *vino seco*, cumin and bay leaf, garlic, salt and various other spices that kept the recipe a deliciously-kept secret, and basted the pig with it. Armed with the bowl of *adobo*, which left the blender stinking for months despite wash after wash and a silver *machete* that gleamed hazily in the dim light of energy-saving bulbs, she had stabbed the pig in all the tender cuts and poured tap after tap of *adobo* into the soon-to-be *lechon asado*, whose pink corpse smiled drunkenly all the while, splayed out in the box with its ribs and spine held together firmly under opaque strings of connective tissue. '*Que cosa la vida...*' it seemed to mutter. The box itself, however, was something worth mention. It was a Cuban invention, *meng* – of course it was, would I lie to you? *Dale*.

Unlike the spit-roasts of the *guajiros*, the pig-box, or *caja china*, was an urban innovation (though 'Chinese' was in it's name, because Chinese remedies are infallibly crafty, and so too are their inventors) that any partying householder had – or more, had *built*. *That's* a man, Goddammit, fetch me a *drink!* Layers of metal and wood hugged a framework of insulation and chicken-wire, which cradled a layer of steel inside of which was placed an iron grill, thick and sturdy, which was more for keeping the roast off the bottom of the box than anything, and on top of this went the mesh-wire grill with long, wiry handles with which the pig could be lifted into and out of the box itself. Another grill, much like the one on the bottom, was placed on top of the pig, for turning it over. Covered with a heavy sheet of iron, the box was heated by a blanket of coals that was placed on top of it and heated the pig from *above*, assuring that the heat that rose naturally wouldn't cook the pig unevenly and instead used the transferred heat into the box itself to roast the pig evenly on all sides at once. Because of this, the pig couldn't touch the bottom of the box, and it all took about six hours, during which copious amounts of rum had to be consumed. This was especially entertaining if the pig was a lunch item — the crew of men who cooked it would have to assemble at 4 AM to get the box going and have the pig ready by noon. Drinkin' at 4? It must be Christmas Eve. One can thus see the inspiring implications of having *lechon asado* for lunch, it's a breakfast party unlike any other: gossip, booze, *croquetas* and *pastelitos* and *café*, and perhaps some profitable conversation, for all Cuban men were businessmen despite their profession, and deals struck over a roasting pig took on a significance of mythical proportions, so long as at least one end of the deal remembered it the next day. *"Oye! Dejen el jaleo y entren, que ya los huevos estan fritos."*

"Ñoooo, hasta el desayuno aqui, no se olviden que la fiesta es despues, caaarajo!"

Today's pig had been put to the heat at eleven in the morning, making it likely that, carving included, the people would be serving themselves at 7:30, a most appropriate time for a Cuban dinner (because this means people will be eating at 8:00 *y un piquito porque donde pinga puse las tenazas*). Cuban time, it's both Latino and Island at once. *Squared.* They hadn't wanted to do a lunch. The reason: no one would've gotten there on time, making it a dinner anyway, and *El Pitirre* would have felt bad drinking all by himself at four in the morning. He didn't have many friends...they made him *nervous*. That, and he didn't want to wake his wife so early just to lift a pig into a box. She had plenty of work ahead of her, *la pobre*: *congrí, arroz blanco*, thousands of *mariquitas y tostones y maduros amelchochaitos, yuca, fricasé de pavo,* appetizers (we can see how that went), and as a specialty, *tostones rellenos de camarones,* stuffed bowl-shaped *tostones* that held a saucy concoction involving shrimp and spicy *sofrito,* or whatever else your creative mind could imagine. Don't get too creative, we're still among the old-timers... At eleven o'clock, then, *El Pitirre* had lowered the pig into the box with Margarita on the other end of it and proceeded to pour himself a drink, waiting for the guests to show up as he watched the cars go by the gate.

La caja china sat in the corner, ashy embers covering it and making the fence squiggle with waves of heat that rose from the blanket of coals. A couple of kids played around close to the box, for the thrill of defiance perhaps, and they must have leapt back three feet when they heard a deep *thump* come from somewhere inside the box. A man nearby, in a long-sleeved white *guayabera,* laughed and told the kids that the pig had kicked, *shoulda listened to me ten minutes ago, you see? That's why I have a drink in my hand and you don't.* That sound of released pressure has filled the eyes of Cuban children with awe to this very day. The man looked at his gold-rimmed watch. "*Pitirre!*" he yelled, without moving a muscle. "Bout time we turned this *marrano* over, ah *peliculero?*" *El Pitirre* looked at his watch, tapping the ash off the tip of his cigar, and stood up...*slowly.*
"*Peliculero?*"
"*Si, pero por pelo en el culo, beng paca coño!*"
"*Bueno,*" he said, "grab the handles," he laughed to himself with a groan. "*Por pelo en el culo.*" The man hunched over, groaning as he grabbed the pieces of copper piping used as guards against the hot iron of the box, and he tapped a tinking *clave* with a smile as *El Pitirre* grabbed the other two: *tak-tak-tak, tak-tak.* They slid them over the rods that stuck out of the cover, and on the count of three they lifted the sheet of coals off of the box and a searing flurry of steam rose swiftly up, and over itself into a mushroom that continued on high into the sky. The people cheered, raising their drinks to the pillar of steam: "*Ñoooo, que caché.*" They set the cover down on the ground and with old rags

grabbed the handles of the grills and lifted the pig out of the box, counting to three again —

On three, or on three-go? On
three, one two three and then we go.
    Wait no no you said one two and
        go on three —
    *SON OF AAAaaaa*and *flipping it over* — *"Wwwwwaaaah!"*
and setting it on the ground. Stinkeyes from Pitirre's silent brow.
Siiiiiiiiiiiiip. Half of the men at the party approached the pig,
toasted and crunchy, but still grinning. The men, the men, not the
pig.

"*Si hombre,* it was ready to be turned, look at that," said
one, from a healthy distance.

"*Bueno,* I'd say it was ready to be turned about an hour
ago," said another. "*Pero* my family likes it cooked more, so the
grease cooks out." El Pitirre looked up to him and said nothing.
'*So the grease cooks out...*' he mouthed to himself.

"*Pitirre,*" the man in white said, "it's looking fine, *mira,*"
and he grabbed the *machete* off the side of the fence. He tapped
the crunchy skin of the pig, satisfied with the coarse slap of steel
against blackened bubbles of *pellejo,* and he proceeded to lift its leg
and prod it in what would have been the inside of its thigh. Clear
adobo ran from the white flesh, moist and juicy, but deep inside it
betrayed hints of pink.

"Yeah, lookin' good, ah?"
            "*Mmhmm.*"
    "Okay."
    "*Bueno, dale.*"
                "*Pues si.*"
        "*Bueno.*"
                        "*Dale.*"
    "*Bueeeeno.*"
                    "*...Bue.*"
"You sure you wanna turn it over now? It's only two."
"*Si,* just put it back in that way, it's alright."

"It'll be ready at six?"

"Hope so." A moment of silence. Drinks sipped.

Eyes darting.

"*Zoraida!*"

A woman stood from the flowerbed of ladies and made her way over to the group. With her veiny hands clad in gold, tipped with freshly painted nails, she stuck a finger into the thigh, wiggling it around and prying the incision open further with the edge of the *machete*.

"*Mmhmm,*" she said, sucking her finger and returning to the flowerbed.

"Okay."

"*Ah-ha. Si, claro.*"

"*Bueno.*" They put the pig back in, face down this time *pa que se tuehte'l cuero pa'los chicharrones* and lifted the bed of coals again, the chorus of commentators wavering forward and back with their drinks in their hands, ready to help if needed. The man in the long-sleeved *Guayabera* ticked another meter of *clave* with his pipes and set them down again, groaning, to which he lit a smoke, picked up his drink and walked off, winking at *El Pitirre*, who was already toking his cigar out of the side of his mouth. A raw smile, billowing smoke, sealed the deal. The pig was turned.

"Jesus Christ, I need another drink."

"*Pues vamos.*"

"*Parajitos, paja...del ala la'ajena...*

ño, paggg-carajo, ando cud-da, si, vamos."

"*Bueno, Pitirre,*" said the man in the long-sleeved *Guayabera*, "now that we got through that, lemme tell you a joke I thought about the other day.

"*Dale,*" said *El Pitirre*, "*que lo que estamos aqui es para reirnos.*"

"*Si claro,* so these two *Gallegos* walk into a bathroom, and each of them post at the urinals on either side of this big, big black guy, ah? *Un Don-Negro, ah?* and by sheer chance, one of them goes to wipe his nose as he's doin' his business and happens a glance at the fockeen beas-t that has it's head hidden in the bowl of the urinal—to this day, he couldn't tell if the guy was peeing, or *drinking water*, you know what I'm sayin?"

"*HhhhhhhhhhhhhhhhhhhAAAAA!*"

"*Na, na, na, oyeme,* so he just can't help but clear his throat and admit to his *falta de pudor y vergüenza,* his poor etiquette, saying '*Señor,* I couldn't help but notice the, ah, gargantuan proportions of your...ah, member, you know?' To which el Don Negro laughed, and the other *Gallego* coughed and sputtered in the shock of hearing his friend speak such words to a man who could have probably beaten both of them to death with his...*ya tu sabes.*"

"*Ñoooo, esto esta...peligroso,*" said one of the guys as he sipped his drink.

"The man, however," the other guy continued, "didn't seem to take offense to it, because, you know, it was indeed something to be proud of, this...*insssstrrrrumento* of his. He was probably happy to have people know about it. The *Gallego* continues and asks, 'Is there a secret to it? You *gotta* tell me, how did it get so damn big?' The black man tells the *Gallego,* 'well, when I was just a baby, my Mama would tie a brick to it and let it stretch out little by little, for years, adding weight onto it until well,' and he shook it off, stuffing it back into his pants with considerable effort, walking off with a smile. The *Gallegos* were left holding their Volkswagen Beetles with grins—"*Joder!* We'll do it, *madre de las tres putas amplias!*" and then two weeks passed by. The one *Gallego* called his friend and asked, '*Oye,* Manolo, what did you make of that guy in the bathroom a few weeks ago? Did you really do it?'

'*Pues claro que si, hombre,* of course I tried it, but I took that salty whore off my instrument after five minutes, you know? Thought it was gonna give me a hernia.' There was silence.

'What about you, Venancio? Did you do it?'

'*Bueno*, I have to say, I did, I left it on for the whole two weeks, and *longer it did not grow, but it sure as hell turned black! Waaaaaaaaaaaaaaaaaaaaaaaa!!!!!"*

"HhhhhhhhhhhhhhAAAAAAAAhahahahahahahahaha!"

"HhhhhhhhhhhAAAAAAAAAAAAhahahaha!"

"Ah-ah-ah-ah-ah-"

"Ehhhhhhehehehehehehehehehe"

"Su puta Madre, vayaaaaaahahahahahahahahahahahaha...."

And the man in the long-sleeved *guayabera* took
a sip of his drink, to victory.
"To the *Gods*."

Who should walk into the scene then but Jennifer, her tight jeans strangling her Cuban thighs and her hair moussed back, bangs glued, lips lined with sharpie and her earrings big, *big* golden hoops. She paused in the middle of the yard — *can't handle dis, bichesss* — singing *"Mami, mi corazon de melocoton!"* and ran over to the flowerbed where the ladies welcomed her with glee that was so real it couldn't be fake, some with genuine smiles, others with silent, tight-lipped nods of the head. Eyes that cannot lie. Silvia put out her cigarette.

"Ven aqui y darle un beso a tu madre, carajo!" she said, her smile the realest of them all. Jenny leaned over and kissed her mother on the cheek, and Silvia kissed her back, and then Yennifer proceeded to make her way around the circle, going through the motions over and over again, kiss, turn, cringe, shuffle, kiss, turn, cringe, shuffle, kiss, turn, cringe...she wafted in and out of about thirteen different perfumes and emerged from the whole ordeal battered with lipstick and practically buzzed off inhalants. Blinked — '*Ñoh,*' she thought to herself. It was the secret joy of being an old lady, to do this to the kids. It wasn't a kiss, it was a squelchy bite of the milky white youth: *witches*, every last one of them!

Jennifer pulled up a chair and sat in the flowerbed —
"*Guarda esa cajita de mierda!*" shouted Silvia, catching her daughter
with her hand halfway out of her pocket.

"Damn nigga she *on* one!" she said, slouching into her
chair. In one swipe of the hand she had stolen Silvia's drink and
swigged half of it. This, perhaps, was the only thing faster than
chismes: mischief.

"So, Yennifer," said one of the women, known by the other
women as '*esa chismosa de mierda*', and considering how much
everyone gossiped anyway, this said a lot. "Tell me what you've
been up to lately, it's been *ages* since I've seen you." She smiled,
pleased with her trap.

Jenny, keenly aware of what was going on, answered
accordingly. "*Bueno, Doña Juarez*, I've been in and out of school,
doing my thing, and in the fall I'll apply to college, you know, get
a degree, since that's what you need these days to keep up in this
world, and after that I'll probably look into starting a family,
since, *ya tu sabes*," and she shot a glance at her mother, who stifled
her laughs behind the end of a cigarette, "that's what really
matters, you know? *Si, si*, things are going well." She sighed,
throwing her arm around her mother. "*Y que*, what's up with
you? Holding up well?"

"Ay, Yennifer," Silvia said inside of her own head, "that's
how you *do* it!"

"Of course," the woman said, putting her finger to her eye
to remove a lash that had sprung out of her thickly-applied
makeup. "We've been doing well, *Yonny* is working, and Maria is
thinking of going to London to find work there," she said, her eye
rolled into her cocked head as she picked at the lash. She got it,
lifting her drink to her lips casually. "*Si*, and Roberto is doing fine
as well, he recovered from his surgery and is probably going to be
working next week, *si Dios quiere*." Jennifer smiled at her brightly.

"*Que bueno*," she said. Both women knew that the truth

had been told, elegantly dipped in white lies like ladyfingers hovering in a thick Tiramisu. *Tiramesamentirita.* The taste of the twisted words lingered on their tongues like the espresso that passed by every hour or so...such were the ways of the flowerbed.

An overweight woman, Gladys, who looked rather like a motherly hen, leaned in and asked, "*Y Juana,* what did Roberto go into surgery for? You hadn't told me anything about that." *La chismosa de mierda* raised an eyebrow — 'of course I wouldn't tell you *my* own *chismes, vieja cagalitrosa con sus diapers de enferma, tu crees que no te veo el bulto ahi con ese vestidito de tres chiquitrines puesto'* — "He went in," and she paused, debating for a second between the truth and the 'truth', "for his knee...he hurt it at work, you know? As you can see, however, he is already fine, it was just a little procedure." The ladies all looked over at Roberto, who was rubbing his aching back, still recovering from surgery, thst had accomplished nothing *'except wasting three grand, Juana!'* and he frowned, confused at the idea of so many old ladies looking at him at once. '*Chismosas,*' he thought to himself, and he raised his glass to them with a smile. If only she was alone with him, Juana thought to herself, she would have *smacked* him for rubbing his back when she was gossiping about his knee. His *knee, Roberto! Get it straight!* She scoffed, drawing a pattern in the fog on the side of her glass. "*Si,* working so hard is getting us old quicker than we would like to...*pero asi es la traicionera, la vida que no para pa nadie.*"

"*Ay Juana,*" said Silvia, "don't worry about it. I have come to learn something that I feel all of us *viejas* should think about, and tell our grandkids so they can tell theirs." She put her cigarette out in the crystal ashtray. "*Cuando el diablo te manda limones,*" she said, with an air of grace, "*se hace una limonada del carajo.*" She put emphasis on the last word. When the devil sends you lemons, you make one *hell* of a lemonade. She ladies sipped their drinks in silent acknowledgement. Things had gone oddly deep for a party. There must be Angels among us.

"Did you hear about the story the other day on '*He Dicho?*'" another woman asked. "It was a good one," she said. "Dr. Ana-Margarita Colón, that *beacon* of a woman, had to settle a case between these five sketchy-looking *Palero, brujo*-looking assholes, where the younger one, who looked better than the rest, had tried to kill them all with this *machete* he got at the Flea Market across town, he said." Silvia choked on her drink. "But someone called the cops at all the screaming, and the officers had Dr. Ana-Margarita Colón sort it out, because they knew it would make some *damn* good TV. *Damn* she's good." The ladies said nothing, waiting for more. This was their moment, the stuff of their relationships, the drama. "And you know," the lady continued, "they got theirs, because the guy said he threatened to kill his brothers only because he was sick of their shit, they were charging people lots of money, I mean *lots* of money, to *kill* people with their black magic, you know, from a distance—no evidence, no nothing, and the guy brought pictures of all this freaky shit to prove it, slaughtered pigs and big black cauldrons all full of freaky shit, skulls and feathers and you know, and pictures of people upside down and all burned and shit—you know, the pictures— *Dios mio!* I would have changed the channel if it wasn't so *fockeen interesting.*" The ladies laughed, and she went on.

"This guy even brought the *machete* in, to prove that he didn't kill anyone with it, '*que solo estaba amenazannndo,*' and the security guard with the little *mojonsitos* on his head, you know, you know which one I'm talking about, he takes it with the white little gloves he has to wear and they analyze it over the commercial break and *guess what.*" The woman took a sip of her drink, smiling at the flowerbed in her regal seat of gossiping-power.

"*Dammit*, what!" screamed Silvia. The women cheered at the breaking of the tension. The woman smiled.

"They found DNA on there from thirty thousand people. Thirty thousand!"

"Nah, thats a lie, they always lie on TV," said one woman, her mouth contorted with skepticism. "Trust me, my nephew works for channel 23."

"*Oye*, I'm just telling you what I saw, *okay?* That's where it gets good. *They bring in a Babalawo, ok?* A big-ass *negro* with the white robes and everything, right? He even had the little hat. And you know what he did?" She paused again.

"*Ay dale*," said the same woman again, "my tits have fallen a half-an-inch since you began this story, *vieja, coño!*"

"KWAAAAAAAA*kwakwakwakwakwakwakwakwakwakwakwak wa!*"

"*Ya, ya, ok!*" insisted the woman. "The big black *Babalawo* comes into the studio, sees the knife and *runs the hell out of there! Like that!*" and she snapped her fingers. "You know, though, that show's as scripted as Lidia's thank you cards."

"*KWAAAAAAAAAkwakwakwakwakwakwakwakwakwakwakw a!*" Lidia pursed her lips and took a sip of her drink.

"Yeah, so they jailed those bastards, and that was it. It was over too quick. In two minutes some *chusma* in Tweety-bird sandals was fighting about the little dog she had left at her ex-boyfriend's house. Some of these Cubans, I swear..." Silvia looked to the sky, smiling to herself as the conversation moved on. '*Bueno*,' she thought. 'It's making its rounds...*que Dios los bendiga a todos.*' God bless them all. She sipped to *la Virgen*, her heart glowing.

"*Ay Chiche*," she said.

Over on the other side of the party, Chiche sat with his legs open on a couch that had been brought out from the living room for seating purposes, and he thought to himself, drink in hand, 'How do I feel? *Tranquiiiiiiiilo.*' He laughed out loud, a deep, heart-felt laugh that tickled his insides and made his belly jiggle under his favorite dress-shirt, which he wore every time he needed to dress up. It made sense, no? *Si, tranquilo.* Next to him was another man, a little fatter, a little younger, but with a thick, bushy moustache and gold-rimmed glasses who did some sort of business no one knew about and seemed to do well with it. He turned his head and said, "*Dime*, Orestes, which one of these ladies is your wife again?" Chiche looked over to the flowerbed and smiled, yelling "*Negra!*" without moving a muscle. Silvia turned around with a smile, nodding her head and said "*Que quieres, manganzón?*" His smile grew and he nodded *what?* as if it were Silvia who had called *his* attention. She shook her head with a laugh and turned back to the ladies, muttering '*Negro de mierda,*' under her breath.

"Ah, Silvia, *no?*" the man said. Chiche nodded his head to the rhythm of the music playing. "*Si, si, si hombre,*" he said, and he picked a speck of lint from the couch off of his knee. Leaned forward with a grunt, he grabbed a handful of chips, the cheesy tortilla chips that always made their way to Cuban parties. *Tortillitas* and mild salsa; *that* was a Cuban appetizer. No guacamole or *chile*, though Chiche enjoyed Guacamole—only when Silvia made it, of course. So it was with many ethnic foods; Cubans didn't go out of their way to eat them, or to enjoy them, but when the *wife* of the family made them, they were the best in the world.

"You like fried rice?" Chiche asked the man randomly, wanting to tell him about Silvia's. The man puckered his lips, thinking for a bit before shaking his head and said, "*Na.* I ate at that one place downtown a couple of times, but it was never that good." He smiled. "But my *wife's* fried rice? *Coño*, I swear the woman was Chinese last time around, you know?"

"Oh, you believe in that shit, ah, what is it? *Reencarnacion?*"

"*Nah meng, Católico hasta la muerte!* I believe in *La Virgen*, in *Jesucrísto*, in *los Santos*, all that—see?" He pulled his chains out of his shirt and showed Chiche his wonderfully crafted *San Lazaro*, *Virgen de la Caridad, Santa Barbara, San Judas Tadeo.* He had 'em all.

"*Bueno, mi estimado amigo, La Virgen* does not look down

upon those who investigate the matters of the universe," said a pleasant voice coming out of the back door. Angelica's hair shimmered in the light breeze of the sunny afternoon, and by her side Tico's two-toned shoes clacked on the soft, painted concrete of the back yard. His Gardenia shone whiter even than his clean, clean suit.

"Ah, Tico, it's been a long time," the man said. "I always love seeing that Gardenia you wear, it reminds me of the good music you don't hear anymore."

"*Si hombre*, but it's a secret I only share with my good friends like you, José-Ernesto, that it's not truly a flower." He smiled. "I wear my *heart* on my lapel, so it can be that much closer to the people I love. To the world." He leaned over and kissed his father on the cheek. "*Que paso, Caballo Viejo!*" He leaned out further and said, "It's nice to see you, José-Ernesto." He gave José-Ernesto a hug, shaking his hand in the process, like good men. Tico sounded hollow as José-Ernesto brought his burly hand, decorated with a thick golden bracelet, over and over again on his back in between laughs. Tico stood up and took a deep breath. "Do you smell that wafting fragrance?" he said. "If I'm not mistaken, I believe Zoraida is here, I've always taken to her perfume quite well." The men said nothing. "But it might just be the mixture of all those other perfumes over there in that circle of *viejas, ah?*" They all laughed, and Tico, sighing on the inside, made for the flowerbed. "I've got to go bid my *saludos* to everyone. I'll be back, yes?" He pointed to José-Ernesto, who nodded and threw his arm around Chiche.

"You've got a good son, Chiche," he said. "The kid knows the good things in life, aint afraid to be himself. I can only *imagine* his ass on South Beach."

"Good things, like *reencarnacion*? *Vaya...*"

"*Bueno,*" he laughed. "He's a thinker—and *that's* what counts, *me entiendes?*" They nodded, raising their drinks to Tico and his pretty girl over by the flowerbed saying hello to the ladies.

They watched the couple lean in at each hairdo, over and over again, and Tico looked awkward, trying not to get any lipstick on his white suit. The women seemed pleased to meet Angelica, who presented herself very well.

"So, like I was saying," José-Ernesto continued, "that fried rice, it's gotta be one of my favorite things to eat, you know? And that's compared to the Cuban food we've all been raised on, you know? I'm telling you Chiche, maybe I'll have you guys over sometime to taste Gladys' *arroz frito*," which he pronounced '*arrofrito*'. Chiche thought about it for a second and smiled. 'He stole my damn conversation...*pinga*.'

"That would be nice, José-Ernesto. I don't think I've been over to your place yet."

"No? *Coño meng*, I got it set up nice. You know, I set up a room for the guys, for the *chulos*, you know what I'm sayin?" He laughed, nudging Chiche on the shoulder, and Chiche simply nodded his head, visibly pleased at the prospect of going over to someone else's house to visit. "*Si hombre*, got a pool table, some old pictures of Havana, a little stereo system Rafaelito set up for me, you know, all that good stuff. For the *boys*." He laughed out loud, slapping his knee. "And the good stuff, I almost forgot." He traced a big box with his hands. "Got a *big* fridge full of *cervecitas* and whatever the hell else, you know," he shrugged, "*Pecksi, Sebena'*, you know, for the kids. And the bar, yeah, I got a bar goin', with some *siete añejo*, some *Bock-ka* (which was the Cuban way of saying 'Vodka'), even Tequila, 'cuz I got into it when we went on that cruise to Mexico." Chiche feigned interest. He looked around at the other people, seeking the solace of eye contact.

"*Si, hombre*, it was good. Stopped at Puerto Vallarta, Cabo San Lucas, Puntacana, all the good spots." He paused. "*No, no*, Puntacana was a different cruise—" he nudged Chiche again— "*Pshhhhhh*, I was at this bar, and they were playin' that Reggaeton stuff that all the kids grind their nuts to, and my wife had had a little *too much to drink, ah?*" He bobbed his eyebrows. "So I'm there, had a little too much to drink myself, and we're dancing this Reggaeton music, her ass all up on me and I'm like 'what the hell is this?' I wouldn't let my *daughter* do this, you know? Let's just say my engines got revved up after a long time of watching it happen from 8-11 every weeknight." He sat back and sighed a long, relaxed sigh. "*Si, si,* that was a good one," and they were quiet for a few seconds. 'Jesus Christ,' thought Chiche, pursing his lips. 'Haven't revved mine up in years.'

"So yeah, I got your number somewhere, I'll give you guys a call, ah?"

"*Si,* do that. We'll have some of that *Arrofrito* you've been talking about," Chiche laughed. "*Coño meng,* you made me hungry now," he said, popping another chip into his mouth. "When is the pig supposed to be ready?" he said, getting up and looking at the box.

"*Pitirre* said about six, six-thirty, but you know how it is, we'll probably be eating around seven, ah?" He slapped his knee again. "You better eat some more of those chips, and we could use some more drinks, no?" He stood up as well—'Ay, *Madre que me parió.*' "Come on, Orestes, let's go. We'll have a *Cuba Libre* this time around." Chiche followed him over to the bar, shaking his head, and *El Pitirre* was mixing drinks behind the bottles and ice like it was his job.

"*Dos Cuba Libres, Señor Bad-tennnder,*" said José-Ernesto playfully, treating the *asunto* like a business deal.

"*Estaria yo feliz con uno solo,*" said *El Pitirre* with a wink. 'I'd be happy with just one.' *Cuba Libre:* 'Free Cuba.' Some people call the drink a *Mentirita:* a 'Little Lie'. *Pitirre* poured their drinks happily to *that.*

"*Cuba Libre,*" he said, raising the drinks into the air. José-Ernesto and Chiche made their way back to their couch, where they ate some more chips, sipping their drinks happily and welcoming anyone who happened to walk by the couch.

"*Y* Silvia," said Gladys, "I always see you at *La Ermita* on Sundays with your sister, what has she been up to?"

"*Bueno*," said Silvia, "she has been keeping up at her place, working, you know, just getting by." Silvia sighed. She hadn't called her in a while. Things had been a little crazy...she'd call her back at home.

"Will she *ever* find herself a man?" said another of the ladies, nudging the woman next to her, but this Silvia did not see.

"*Hmph*," said Silvia, "I've told her to get on one of those Cuban dating services, you know? I've heard of lots of women finding good men on those, but you know her, gentle as a dove, a little *palomita*. She'll marry the first guy who approaches *her*...and meets all of her ridiculous needs." She scoffed. "The simple ones are the most difficult."

"A good woman like her needs a man who can get her out of her head...and into the *bed*," said Gladys. "*Tu sabes,* a good *sacudón* or two, she'll be frying *platanos* in three days."

"*KWAAAAAAAAAAkwakwakwakwakwakwakwakwakwakwak wakwa!*"

"*Ay stop it, estupebish,*" Silvia giggled. For anyone listening, she called Gladys a 'stupid bitch,' but it's okay, *estupebish*, we're all drunk anyway.

"Bless her heart, she's so cute," Gladys said obliviously, sipping her drink. "Isn't it funny how it's the bad ones who have no trouble finding men?"

"*Bueno, mijita*, its up to us to put the *quesíto* on the *dulce de guayaba, me entiendes?*" said the other lady, who sipped her drink happily to the laughter of all the others.

"*Si, si*, you have to give it to 'em on a Cuban cracker, let them taste, you know?"

"But then you take it away after their eyes go wide, *no?*"

"*Pal carajo!* If I had known that, I'd still have some *guayaba* left to give to *my* man, *sabes?*" The flowerbed erupted with laughter.

"*No, no,*" said Silvia, "we Cuban women *never* run out of *Guayaba.* That's the difference between these white *refinadas* and us. They are little *pastelitos,* all cute *y* proper, tasty for a little bit but then what?" She lit a cigarette. "A real woman is the *mata de Guayaba,* solid and standing tall, with new fruits growing all the time, and *we* decide when the fruits fall from the tree!" The women cheered, and she flicked the ash off her smoke triumphantly. "We can start out with *pastelitos,* but then we can give 'em *dulce,* we can give 'em *casquitos,* even *melcochito, me entiendes?*" She took a drag. "A true *Cubana* never runs out of the good stuff." She put her cigarette out, half-smoked, and looked up at the women slyly. "I mean, but that's just us *Guajiras,* you know?"

"*KWAAAAAAAkwakwakwakwakwakwa!*" sounded the laughs from the flowerbed. All the men looked over to their women, nodding, smiling, blowing kisses and raising their drinks, and their faces seemed pleased, but more confused than anything. They knew what these women were up to...no, no they didn't.

We all know that the man 'runs the show',
But the woman's the one who lets him do it.
His 'ley of the land' is the flower that falls from her hand,
It's a sacred tension, this alchemy of chiral manipulation.
Some call it lying, I call it teamwork. Love,
Where everyone gets to have their cake and share it, too.
Is this home-made? Of course it is, right sweetie?*
White lies, they make us all friends, they make us all lovers.

"Those women don't know what the hell they're talking about," said José-Ernesto happily. "I'm just glad they can come here and entertain themselves, ah? They can leave us *hombres* to our business, ah, Chiche? Ah?" He nudged him on the shoulder, over and over again.

Chiche smiled wide, straight from his heart, not moving a

muscle. "*Si hombre. Tranquiiiiiilo.*"

"*Tranquiiiiiilo,*" laughed Roberto. In a moment of grace, a light breeze blew by, and everyone was silent for that ephemeral second. *El Pitirre* looked around just then, and felt so pleased. The pig was in the box, silent — *callado.* The people were talking amongst themselves, seated — *sentados.* There was no one in line for drinks, the bar was empty — *vacido.* Even Margarita was over by the ladies, near the flowerbed but with another woman whose kids scurried around the pig-box. Either way, she was sitting, for once — *sentada, la pobre.* The only real movement in the party was that *Bohemio* in the white with his Colombian blonde, who fluttered from group to group like Hermes from throne to throne in the heavens of Greece — *chismeando.* But there was peace, and this feeling of doing nothing together was one of the most sacred things, so subtle that it could not be created, only entertained. The times were good. For once, *El Pitirre* could go out into the clusters and enjoy his own party — *andando, gozando, tranquiiiiiilo!* The only thing that would set things off would be — *ay, caramba.*

"*Mira!* It's José-Ernesto's boy, Reniel!" said Zoraida above all the voices.

"*Oye, oye,* he's mine too, ah?" chimed Gladys. "That kid spent nine months in *this* right here, okay?" She pointed at her paunch, tight under a yellow dress. "Got the stretch-marks to prove it, too." Half the women grinned, looking at each other. "Anyway, he's *my son* — José just pays for his shit."

"*KWAAAAAAAAAAAAAAAAAAAAAAAAAAAwakwakwakwakw akwakwa!*"

"*Que paso, Mami?*" The one Zoraida had called Reniel leaned in and gave his mother a kiss. He looked up and nodded at the rest of the ladies In the flowerbed.

"*Oye niño,* what the hell was that? '*Que paso, Mami...ah?*" She scoffed drunkenly. "What ever happened to '*Buenas tardes,*' or '*Hola, mi Madre querida, Madre que me parió?*'" The ladies laughed softly, shaking their heads. "Come on, *mijo*, go on and say hello. All that nodding is for your *chulo* friends," and she frowned, puckering her lips and *'wussupin'* the flowerbed. The ladies erupted into laughter, commenting on today's youth as Reniel began to make his way around. He sighed, unable to escape the brunt of those rough-edged jokes from the old women that found their way into every Cuban family.

"*Buenas tardes* *muah*, *Buenas tardes* *muah*, *Buenas tardes* *muah*, *Buenas tardes* *muah*,*" repeated Reniel, his head bobbing up and down like one of those birds with the glass of water that…what the hell did those birds do anyway?

"*Buenas—*" Reniel paused, his eyes taking on a sudden light. Jenny ran her fingers across her glued bangs, laughing a little. Passed a napkin across her chip-chewing lips. "*Buenas Tardes,*" he said, grinning sheepishly into his nervous smile.

"*Ay, I feel it from here,*" whispered one of the flowers.

"*Yennifer!*" nudged Silvia. "*Darle la mano, coño!*" She lifted her hand, laughing nervously, and Reniel took it in his, laying a soft kiss on the crease between her index and middle fingers. It tickled her neck. The flowerbed was silent—sipping, smiling, smoking, but saying nothing. With their mouths, at least.

"*Yennifer,*" she said to him, holding his gaze.

"*Reniel,*" said Reniel. Zoraida leaned over to Gladys' ear and said with a sloppy whisper, "*Casados.*" Married. They began to comment on what the kids would look like, chittering happily. And it was only later that Jenny realized she could finally throw away that glass of honey in her closet, with those other things sitting inside of it. Oh the things she would tell Ofelia on Wednesday at 10.*

"*Vaya,*" those women don't know what the hell they're talking about," said *El Pitirre* to Roberto across the yard. "They're all sloshed by now anyway." He looked around, toking his cigar quietly in the ambience, and said, "This is where the party's at, *sabes?*" They tinked glasses. *"Claro que si."* He smiled around his cigar. *"Waaahaha."*

"I'm so glad you know how to smoke a cigar, *Pitirre,*" said Roberto. "I swear, I *enjoy* watching you smoke. Half of these guys who didn't grow up like *Guajiros* in the hills think they can be Cuban with their smuggled *Puros* and their Salsa music, but you can tell who's really Cuban by the way they smoke a cigar." He held his hands out, as if he were holding a pair of heaving breasts; they made him grimace. "You know? You get these guys, think they got it goin' on, yeah, I'm *Cubano,* city guy, *'de la 'Bana',* but then they light their *Cohibas* and look like they're sucking some *negro's —*"

"Oyyyyeme!" He stopped, taking a sip of his drink. *"Bueno,* you know, there are kids around, but...*ya tu sabes."* He slapped *Pitirre* on the back happily, who merely smiled into the sky with his skinny face all in leathery folds, cigar puckered between his lips, and his shoulders bobbed softly with laughter that didn't make any noise. It was both a celebration and a scolding of crude commentary at once.

He pulled the cigar from his mouth, looking at the bib of spit that had saturated the tip. "Tastes good, though," he said, savoring the smoke like one savors a *buchito* of *Café.* "He *must* be Cuban."

"HHHHHHHHHHHHhhhhhhhhhhhhhhhhhhhhhaaaaaaaaaaaaa!"

Jenny and Reniel had already moved to a quiet corner of the party, drinking sodas and talking about 'everything, like o-m-f-g for serious'. In how many ways could one dress their practically-threatening desires into innocent comments? Perhaps they would find out. Jenny smiled, giddy with childish gratitude. Silvia, watching them silently, looked up at a sudden shadow that overcame her, and she saw Chiche's thick head above her, obscured by the sunlight. He watched his daughter with contemptuous lips, as if watching the Discovery Channel, and

Silvia pulled him down by the collar, kissing him on the lips for what seemed like the first time. It tickled, all through both of their bodies. She said nothing, leaving him wandering, wondering, into her own newly innocent eyes, *aquellos ojos verdes,* and everything was perfect, for that is all there can be, *Ma,* full of grace. Perfection. Light so bright it can't be seen, until the night passes and the Sun makes the shadows of our past dance in the light of dawn.

~*~

What is good, and
What is evil, Ma?
Does it matter when
I look into your eyes?

Its so amazing

To gaze upon the mirror
Of my own faults,
My shortcomings,
My virtue, my meaning,
My husband, my wife,
My struggles, my life,
And to come back to you

Yet another day *alive,*

Hoping that I can
Better cater to you,
Breathe my every breath
For you,
My lover, My partner, My worship,
For just another day,
Ay, mi Virgen, por
Otro Dia.

~*~

Lorenzo Ramos is a first-generation Cuban-American. He resides
in the East San Francsico Bay Area and has devoted his life to the
Work. This is his first great (in length and effort) literary work.
He has a spiritual music practice as well, and is studying to bring
true and authentic spirituality to the common person. His current
Work is the creation of a Consort Yoga manual for Spiritual
Relationships. Though many readers so far have mentioned it, in
no way is Tico Campos a direct reflection of the author, though
both share some superficial similarities. Indeed, Tico represents
the farce of taking Western Esoteric practice too seriously — if
anything, he is like all of the characters, a reflection of Lorenzo's
past.

~*~